MW00779949

FROM
Grace
TO
Glory

A Present Day Journey
Through John Bunyan's
Pilgrim's Progress

Carolyn Staley

Solid Ground Christian Books
Port St Lucie, Florida USA

FROM GRACE TO GLORY

A Present-Day Journey Through
John Bunyan's *Pilgrim's Progress*

by Carolyn Staley

First Edition—May 2019
ISBN: 978-159925-3992

© Ron & Carolyn Staley, May 2019.
ALL RIGHTS RESERVED.

SOLID GROUND CHRISTIAN BOOKS
1682 SW Pancoast Street
Port St Lucie FL 34987
(205) 587-4480
mike.sgcb@gmail.com
http://www.solid-ground-books.com

Cover and Layout Design by
Borgo Publishing, Tuscaloosa, Alabama

Printed in the USA

TABLE OF CONTENTS

PREFACE

My journey to the Celestial City began at the age of nineteen when the Lord opened my heart, brought me to the Lord Jesus Christ, and saved me by his grace. In those early days as a young Christian, my tendency toward morbid introspection caused great mental anguish concerning the assurance of my salvation. During that dark period, I first became acquainted with John Bunyan when I was given two of his books, *Grace Abounding to the Chief of Sinners* and *The Pilgrim's Progress*. At first I was actually afraid to read them, afraid that they would confirm my worst fears.

However, as I began to read and ponder these works written so long ago, a glimmer of hope began to arise in my mind. I was not alone after all! John Bunyan suffered the very same things and wrote of them. At last I could give a name to the spiritual turmoil I had so often experienced. It was the murky Slough of Despond. The tormenting fear that so often held my heart and mind captive also had a name, Doubting Castle, baronial estate of Giant Despair. Thus I felt an immediate affinity with the humble tinker of Bedford that greatly encouraged me in those first days of my own pilgrimage.

Many years later when I was asked to teach *The Pilgrim's Progress* to our teenagers in Sunday school, I gladly accepted the challenge and began an in-depth study of that great work. Using those early lessons as a foundation, I later expanded and revised them into a series of thirty meditational studies that were published in *Adam's Rib*, a monthly periodical especially designed for Christian women. These meditations provided the framework for an even more comprehensive study that resulted in the writing of this book.

I truly believe that we write best of what we have learned from personal experience. At this point in my own journey, I have covered much of the ground that John Bunyan's pilgrim did and met the same characters he encountered along the way. As a result, I am well acquainted with the places Christian visited, as well as the trials, temptations, and difficulties he faced. An added benefit from the Lord is the privilege of being married to a godly pastor who faithfully expounds and teaches the Word of God. For the past forty-five years, I have served by my husband's side as his helper and co-laborer. The experience I have gained through the years and the spiritual lessons learned have been of invaluable assistance in giving me a more thorough understanding of *The Pilgrim's Progress.*

This best known work by John Bunyan is a captivating story told in a highly dramatic setting; but for those with eyes to see, it is much more than that. The truths of which he wrote are just as relevant to the people of God today as when he penned them in the 17th century. Therefore, every true child of God will find that he is on familiar ground when reading of Christian and his journey to the Celestial City.

In writing *From Grace to Glory,* I have taken John Bunyan's metaphors, his characters and places in particular, and considered them at length from the perspective of a 21st century Christian. Throughout the whole, I have endeavored to faithfully interpret *The Pilgrim's Progress* in light of clear Scripture truth, as John Bunyan evidently did when he wrote it. Moreover, in elaborating upon his metaphors and their meanings, I have taken care to stay well within the bounds of biblical truth.

As you read this book, I urge you to read *The Pilgrim's Progress* in conjunction with it. The more familiar you are with John Bunyan's great work, the more you will glean from my interpretation and contemplation of it. I also suggest that you take the time to read and ponder the Scripture references I have included throughout it. Doing so should prove highly beneficial in helping you understand both the spiritual principles upon which it is based, and their practical application.

Above all, it is my earnest desire that the Lord Jesus Christ receive all the honor and glory for anything that might be accomplished through this book. Without his constant help, my best endeavors would prove vain indeed.

Carolyn Staley

INTRODUCTION

If we are to properly understand *The Pilgrim's Progress*, we must keep its allegorical nature ever in heart and mind. While a strictly literal interpretation may give us a general understanding of it, this approach will rob us of the greater part of its true meaning and spiritual depth. John Bunyan possessed the rare combination of keen spiritual insight and the brilliant use of metaphor. So if we would rightly understand his precious allegory, we must endeavor to delve into his thought processes and see it through his eyes.

The Pilgrim's Progress may rightly be thought of as a tale of two spiritual cities and the rival kingdoms they represent. Within this framework, we find the story of one man's journey and the ongoing battle for his soul, beginning with his deliverance from the City of Destruction and ending with his entrance into the Celestial City. Thus in the course of his travels from the one city to the other, we find the sum and substance of the Christian's life in this world.

In order to discover the spiritual meaning of John Bunyan's metaphors, we must look beneath the surface of the apparent. Each character Christian meets, each place he visits, each situation he encounters and each trial he faces is pertinent to the whole story. Even seemingly minor details should be weighed carefully in relation to the general context. When factored in, these little things often add significantly to a more comprehensive understanding of the entire work.

My dear brother or sister in Christ, *The Pilgrim's Progress* is very like a mine containing rare jewels of exceptional quality. There is high doctrine for us to learn, godly principles to put into practice, and ageless truths to keep our feet on solid ground. If you and I are willing to invest the time and effort to search for them, we will discover priceless treasure that will encourage our hearts as we, also, make our journey toward the heavenly Zion.

Although we all share a great deal in common, each believer in Christ is a unique individual. All of us walk the same path that leads to a single destination (Proverbs 4:18), but each of us will have a one-of-a-kind experience along the way. As to the circumstances that make our journey like none other, our infinitely wise heavenly Father knows what is best. Therefore, he designs the particular course that will best purify and strengthen our faith, purge away the dross, and nurture the development of a Christ-like character.

Toward the accomplishment of this end, God uses certain instrumental means, and in his masterful way, John Bunyan personifies them in many of his characters and places. Evangelist, Help, and the Shepherds of the Delectable Mountains depict faithful ministers of the Gospel and their invaluable service. The Palace Beautiful illustrates the character, function, and essential nature of the local church. The Interpreter's House pictures the ministry of the Holy Spirit as he enlightens our understanding of the Word of God, teaches us more of our Lord Jesus Christ, and guides us in the way we should go.

Certain characters denote those voices from without, or promptings from within that affect our growth in grace. Some of these are things designed to strengthen us in the faith and help us to live a more godly life, but many of them represent sinful tendencies that must be conquered. Still other characters and places depict those experiences that all believers have in common. For instance, were not we all first delivered from the City of Destruction? Has not each of us entered the way of life through the Wicket Gate? Have we not all been required to ascend the hill Difficulty at some point along the way? Does anyone follow Christ without having to pass through the Valley of Humiliation and the Valley of the Shadow of Death? Does not our pathway take each of us through Vanity Fair and across Enchanted Ground? Must not every child of God cross the Dark River before entering into his everlasting habitation, the Celestial City?

Yes, every true child of God will quickly discover that he or she is on familiar ground when reading The Pilgrim's Progress. However, the Christian who is a serious student of God's Word will have a distinct advantage in understanding John Bunyan's timeless classic. For throughout its entirety, The Pilgrim's Progress is saturated with biblical truth and Scripture allusion.

Our journey to the heavenly Zion, which is taking place within us day by day, is a miracle of God's sovereign grace. From the first stirrings of his Spirit within, all the way to our final overcoming, this secret work of God will make its presence known in every aspect of our lives. Along with our deliverance from the City of Destruction, there comes an immediate change of heart and allegiance. Before, we were children of disobedience, proud citizens of the kingdom of darkness, and completely under the dominion of the god of this world. Having been born again by the Spirit of God, we are now strangers in this world, passing through but not belonging to it. Like Abraham of old, we live as exiles who look *for a city which hath foundations, whose Builder and Maker is God.* In common with the great heroes of faith who desired this better, heavenly country, we also have the same assurance that God *hath prepared for* (us) *a city.* (Hebrews 11:16)

In this world we have no solid foundation, no continuing city, and nothing in which our souls may safely rest and trust. (Hebrews 13:14) The Lord Jesus Christ is our rock, our firm foundation and chief cornerstone. In him we have a sure and steadfast hope, an anchor of the soul, an eternal goal toward which we press. Under his kingly rule, we bow as willing subjects who gladly assume the status of pilgrims in this life.

Our earthly life is a time of needful preparation in which trials and difficulties figure prominently, but all of them are designed to more perfectly mold us into the image of Christ. When we finally reach the golden city, and see the Lamb of God upon his throne, it will have been worth it all. Realizing at last how much we owe to his grace, we will give all glory to him for loving us, giving himself for us, and bringing us safely there. In that day, we shall stand dressed in his righteousness and perfectly conformed to his beautiful likeness. (Romans 8:28-30) Paradise lost will be Paradise restored forever! As fellow pilgrims, this is our glorious destiny, and we are nearer to it now than when we first believed.

Concerning the sum total of Christian's journey and its relevance to us today, I have chosen five scriptural metaphors and woven them throughout this book. There is a pathway we must walk, one that is leading us ever forward and always upward. There is an ongoing battle we must fight, one in which we must prevail and win the day.

There is a race we must run, all the way across the finish line. There is a life we must live, in which we overcome the world through patient and obedient faith. There is an eternal kingdom we must enter, by God's grace and for his glory. Entrance into this kingdom is not an easy matter, however. Since the way that leads to eternal life can only be entered through a strait gate by faith, relatively few people find it. Most by-pass the Wicket Gate and opt for one of the many alternatives forming the broad way that leads to destruction.

The Pilgrim's Progress is a narrative of those who *do* enter this narrow way and walk it by faith. Far from minimizing the difficulties of the Christian life, John Bunyan deals with them openly and honestly. One clear message resounding throughout his entire work is the precious truth that our loving heavenly Father has ordained everything that comes our way. What's more, he presently oversees and governs all that concerns us for our eternal good. What a comfort it is to know that when the work of preparation is finally over, all who have followed the Lord Jesus Christ as pilgrims and strangers in this life will, without doubt, appear before him in Zion.

So dear reader, come share my contemplation of the man named Christian and his incredible journey. May you receive God's blessing in reading it as I have in the writing of it. If you do not yet know the Lord Jesus Christ, it is my earnest prayer that you would seek him with your whole heart, and in seeking, find the only way that leads to life eternal. If you are a fellow believer in Christ, I pray that the Lord will encourage, strengthen, and challenge you in your own pilgrimage as you press toward the mark for the prize of the high calling of God in Christ Jesus. (Philippians 3:14)

> *The path of the just is as the shining light,*
> *That shineth more and more unto the perfect day.*
> Proverbs 4:18

PROLOGUE

IT IS LONG PAST MIDNIGHT AND THE CITY LIES IN DARKNESS. WITH THE EXCEP-
TION of an occasional car or the distant siren of an emergency vehi-
cle, the streets are virtually deserted. At this hour all seems peaceful
and calm, and yet, an uncanny silence rules the night, giving a false
impression of the great City of Destruction. Within its borders, there
is no peace to be found at all, for a greater darkness than that of midnight reigns over it.

But wait! On this particular night, something is stirring in a
remote corner of the city. A light shines through a single window of
one of its more modest dwellings, revealing the shadow of a lone figure. It is a man unknown to us as yet, a troubled soul pacing back and
forth, murmuring to himself, and wringing his hands as if in despair.
His wife and children have been in bed for some time, but he is so
disturbed in his mind that, for him, sleep is well nigh impossible.

What has happened to this poor man to cause such extreme distress? He could scarcely explain it should you ask him. While his family slept soundly in another part of the house, he has had a wake-up
call that has shaken him to the very core of his being. With the awakening, came the stark realization of things unknown before, and the
certainty of it all has unnerved and terrified him.

For the poor sufferer, this night must seem endless; but soon now,
faint shades of grey will begin to lighten the horizon. Perhaps the
terrors that plague him so cruelly in the night will be banished by the
breaking of day.

Part One

THE JOURNEY COMMENCES

Jesus saith unto him, I am the way, the truth, and the life:
no man cometh unto the Father, but by me.
John 14:6

CHAPTER 1

The City of Destruction Complex:
Its Description, Nature, and Citizens

IN EARLY SPRING, THE VAST FIELDS OF GREEN SURROUNDING THE CITY OF Destruction seem to touch the heavens as they extend toward the horizon in every direction. Due to the extreme flatness of the land, one gets the impression that on a clear day you really can see forever. Farmhouses, barns, and other buildings dot the landscape here and there, while silos and grain elevators stand tall amid the fields of new grain. In some of these very same fields, you can hear the steady drone of drilling equipment as it extracts oil from beneath the surface of the rich farmland.

Yes, the countryside around the great city is filled with images of rural beauty and prosperity, but its serenity is interrupted here and there by an occasional town or village. These suburbs were founded long ago by those citizens who preferred a safer and less hectic environment in which to live and raise their families. There are a number of these places from which to choose, but those who settle in these outlying areas still live within the boundaries of the City of Destruction complex.

When surveying the great city from across the plain, you will find nothing unusual about it. As for its arrangement, it is quite similar to any other major city. The more affluent sections of town, with their beautiful homes and manicured lawns, are truly lovely to the eye. Some of these properties are magnificent estates belonging to the city's most distinguished residents. Surely, happy families must dwell behind those doors! The majority of the town's citizens live in modest, middle-class neighborhoods, which are pleasant enough in their own right.

It is true that there are several parts of town that are notoriously unsavory in character. Ironically, many of the city's oldest and most historic buildings are located in these areas. Now abandoned, these once-beautiful structures have fallen into ruin and bear the marks of the vandal's hand. If you drive through these sections of town by day, you will notice that the remaining businesses and occupied homes all have bars on their ground-floor windows. A not-so-subtle warning against venturing into these areas after dark!

In common with other large cities, the skyline of the City of Destruction is filled with impressive structures, each one vying to be the tallest and the most striking in appearance. All kinds of businesses and commercial enterprises are represented here in the heart of the city, and the intricate network of highways, tunnels, and bridges providing access to it can be difficult to navigate, especially during rush hour.

As we continue to look toward the city, the first rosy blush of dawn is tinting the eastern sky. Soon now, the inhabitants will be leaving their homes and heading toward their places of employment. Previously empty streets will be congested with vehicles of all kinds, as another business day begins. From our vantage point outside the city limits, it seems to be a thriving place, alive with people engaged in the normal pursuits of everyday life. When viewed in this way, the great city creates a favorable enough impression. But come with me if you will, and take a closer look at this place called the City of Destruction. A terrible secret lurks just beneath its pleasant exterior, and a quick glimpse of this morning's newspaper will tear away the mask and give us deeper insight into its true character.

Look at the front-page headline! A homegrown terrorist found guilty of mass murder was executed last evening by lethal injection, while opponents of the death penalty protested outside the federal prison where the execution took place. Up to the day of his death, the condemned man gave no indication of remorse for his heinous crime. On the contrary, his final statement, read just before the hour of his execution, revealed that pride, rebellion, and arrogance still ruled in his heart. This statement, which consisted of the reading of the poem "Invictus" [1] by William Ernest Henley, ended with the words, "It matters not how strait the gate, how charged with punishments the scroll, I am the master of my fate. I am the captain of my soul." In so doing, the condemned man's final act was to raise a defiant fist against heaven and the God that he would shortly face in judgment. This is the top story in today's edition, but there are better things to be found as well.

The area's newest medical center, Metropolitan General Hospital, will be dedicated this Friday afternoon at two o'clock. This extensive facility will provide the latest in state-of-the-art diagnostic and imaging equipment, as well as the finest Level 1 trauma center in the country. As a major community service, the hospital will also offer a comprehensive in-patient drug and alcohol rehabilitation program.

Another item of news concerns the construction of the state's newest and largest prison facility, which is scheduled for completion by the end of the year. This maximum security prison will help to alleviate the current overpopulation of the state's penal system.

On the national scene, world-renown scientists announced that additional funding will enable the space program to continue its quest to discover the origin of the universe, and thus, the beginning of life itself. Several exploratory missions have been planned over the next several years with this particular objective in view.

Other items of local interest such as the weather forecast, business news, sports section and classified ads are included in today's edition. However, most of the news stories indicate that there is something fundamentally wrong in the City of Destruction.

Then there is the obituary section in which we find the names of the latest residents of the city to depart this life. Their personal achievements are listed here in glowing terms, but the thoughtful reader cannot help but wonder what difference such things make now. Here is the end of their glory! These souls, whatever their particular situation in life happened to be, have all met the great leveler of mankind—Death, and eternity thereafter.

If we now lay our newspaper aside and walk through the streets of the city, you will notice something ironic in light of today's news.

This is obviously a very religious place, with churches, synagogues, mosques and modern worship centers to be found everywhere. However, this does not seem to have made much difference. In fact, if we could enter the homes and catch a glimpse into the private lives of the worshipers, we would find examples of every kind of human suffering imaginable. Although Henry David Thoreau was not known to be a godly man, he accurately assessed the human condition when he said, "Most men lead lives of quiet desperation and go to the grave with the song still in them." [2] So in spite of the city's religious veneer and pleasant appearance, it is a stronghold of human misery. Quite aptly it is named the City of Destruction.

Dear reader, you have undoubtedly realized that the great city is no literal place. It has no actual geographic location, even though it is worldwide in scope. This fair city with its well-kept secrets is a picture of sinful mankind, his condition by nature, and his life in this world apart from the Lord Jesus Christ. As we continue our study of *The Pilgrim's Progress*, we will discover that the city is really a huge complex incorporating all of its surrounding towns and villages. These places and their residents portray various aspects of man's sinful nature, for even though all men are equally depraved, all do not manifest it in the same way. Some are grossly immoral, while others are outwardly respectable. Some are atheists and skeptics, but most are religious. Many are outright scoundrels, while some are great philanthropists. All, however, are natural-born citizens of the great metropolis known as the City of Destruction. Each one may trace his ancestry to a single man, Adam.

Therefore, the City of Destruction is not a new thing. It originated in the Garden of Eden. Like the metaphorical city I have described, man's outward appearance is not necessarily an accurate reflection of his heart. His real problem lies deep within, for he is dead in trespasses and sins. By nature, he hates the truth, loves sin, and is a rebel against God. Content to reside in the City of Destruction, he has neither the will nor the power to leave it. If he is to escape the eternal destruction that awaits the inhabitants of this place, another must deliver him. A divine visitor must knock at his door.

The Word of God is explicit in its description of fallen mankind, and the picture is not a pretty one. Very early in man's history we find the divine indictment against him, as recorded in these words:

And GOD saw that the wickedness of man was great in the earth, and that every imagination of the thoughts of his heart was only evil continually. And it repented the LORD that he had made man on the earth, and it grieved him at his heart. And the LORD said, I will destroy man whom I have created from the face of the earth; both man, and beast, and the creeping thing, and the fowls of the air; for it repenteth me that I have made them. (Genesis 6:5-7)

From Scripture, we know that the Great Flood reduced the earth's population to eight living souls. The human race was given a fresh start, as it were. But far from being remedied by the deluge, man's condition was only confirmed afterward. (Genesis 8:20-22)

How is it possible that otherwise intelligent human beings are content to dwell in the City of Destruction? Are they really so unmindful of the danger to which it exposes them? Can they not see the precariousness of their existence and the folly of seeking their security there? No, they cannot.

By nature, man is an earth dweller. His heart and mind are set upon the things of this world. He lacks the capacity to know the one true God, and also the heart to live according to his commandments. Yet man is innately religious. In attempting to fill his spiritual void, he devises and worships gods fashioned after his own imagination. Then after false hope has lulled his conscience to sleep, he thinks himself secure, even in the City of Destruction. Aspiring to nothing higher, he is content to seek his treasure there, little suspecting the terrible consequences. The irony of it all is that when his name finally appears in the obituary section of his city's newspaper, he will leave behind all that he held dear, and all that he labored so diligently to accomplish.

The Lord Jesus Christ warned his hearers of the dangers of man's insensibility and spiritual ignorance in light of divine judgment. Citing the days of Noah and of Lot, he illustrated man's complacency in the face of imminent judgment. (Matthew 24:37-41; Luke 17:26-37) They knew not that divine wrath was hanging over their heads; therefore, they could go about their everyday lives as if there was no God, and no judgment to come. This is ever the case with all who live, move, and have their being in the City of Destruction.

Thus in the outlying towns and villages, as well as in the great city, self-interest reigns supreme. Men labor to build their figurative towers of Babel. By their own efforts, and sparing no expense, they seek to make a name for themselves upon the earth. In common with those first builders, their goal is to ascend to the heavens, to control their own destiny, and to be their own god. (Genesis 11:1-4) They labor diligently, but self-exaltation is the motive behind their effort. Like the fool in Psalm 14:1, natural man says in his heart, *There is no God*. First he gave heed to the lie of the serpent. Now he believes the lies of his own deceived heart.

What does God say concerning the residents of the City of Destruction? In Romans 3:10-19, he explicitly describes the extent of man's depravity:

As it is written, there is none righteous, no, not one: There is none that understandeth, there is none that seeketh after God. They are all gone out of the way, they are together become unprofitable; there is none that doeth good, no, not one. Their throat is an open sepulchre; with their tongues they have used deceit; the poison of asps is under their lips: Whose mouth is full of cursing and bitterness: Their feet are swift to shed blood: Destruction and misery are in their ways: And the way of peace have they not known: There is no fear of God before their eyes. Now we know that what things soever the law saith, it saith to them who are under the law: that every mouth may be stopped, and all the world may become guilty before God.

In light of this testimony, men are commanded to be silent and confess their guilt before a holy God. Yet they do not, because they are blind to their true condition. Therefore, they remain content to pursue vain, empty things. Being alienated from the life of God, they walk in darkness and spiritual ignorance, and from this unclean fountain, all sorts of evil deeds spring forth. (Ephesians 4:17-19)

We do not overstate the case by saying that unsaved men are dead men walking. God declares this very fact in Ephesians 2:1-5. In light of this truth, what hope is there for anyone to be delivered from the City of Destruction? Apart from the mercy of God, there is no hope at all. It is solely through divine intervention that one who was as a sheep going astray ever returns unto the great shepherd and bishop of his soul. (1 Peter 2:25)

* * * *

What a terrible mental image the City of Destruction evokes now that we understand the meaning of its name! Yet there is hope for those who dwell there, in spite of their seemingly hopeless situation. Although they are incapable of ascending to heaven, the Lord Jesus Christ came down to them from out of the ivory palaces (Psalm 45:8) and walked among them. In obedience to his Father's will, the Son of God became a man, but without the least taint of sin. As the perfect, sinless Son of God and Son of man, he suffered the death of the cross and rose from the dead in order to justify and secure the salvation of his people. (Matthew 1:21) Shortly before he ascended to his Father's right hand, the Lord Jesus commissioned his disciples to preach the Gospel unto the ends of the earth. As a beacon of truth, the good news of salvation was to go forth into the darkest corners of the City of Destruction, wherever men are found. (Acts 1:8)

On the Day of Pentecost, the Lord Jesus Christ sent his Spirit to empower the Church to fulfill her great mission. (Matthew 28:16-20) From that day until now, the Word of God has been proclaimed throughout the world, and through the same power that brought all things into existence, many have been quickened to spiritual life.

Study Questions

1. What sort of place is the City of Destruction, and who are they who reside there?

2. What can we learn about the city and its residents by reading its local newspaper?

3. How are the surrounding towns and villages related to the great city?

4. How would you summarize the figurative meaning of the City of Destruction and the spiritual condition of its citizens?

5. Is there any hope for those who dwell in the City of Destruction?

CHAPTER 2

Escape from the City!

THE OPENING SCENE OF *THE PILGRIM'S PROGRESS* FOCUSES UPON A solitary figure, a man who is nameless to us as yet, but known and loved of God. Not long ago, he was part of the vast multitude living contentedly in the great City of Destruction. In observing him now, however, we find him dressed in rags, holding a book in his hand, and standing with his face turned away from his own house.

The poor man's appearance is a reflection of his great inner turmoil. Note the burden he carries on his back. Hear his anguished cry, "What shall I do?" Clearly, he knows that he is in deep trouble, but has no idea what to do about it. Although he little suspects it yet, he is about to embark upon a life-long journey that will begin with his deliverance from the City of Destruction. Moreover, his escape from the city will have a ripple effect there, even though we have no hint that he is more than an ordinary man.

His ragged clothing deserves our careful attention, for it denotes his condition before God. Previously, he was unaware of it; but his eyes are finally open to see himself as he actually is, sinful and spiritually destitute. Self-righteousness, which seemed more than adequate before, is now accounted as nothing. The pillars of self-reliance and spiritual indifference have collapsed beneath him, leaving a sense of overwhelming helplessness in their place. Before, he slumbered happily enough in the City of Destruction, but something has shaken him from that deadly sleep.

One dominant characteristic of all men by nature is that there is no fear of God before their eyes. (Romans 3:18) Therefore, they can live as they please, while deluding themselves into thinking that all is well with them. When the Spirit of God begins his work of conviction, spiritual lethargy is overturned, as was the case with the solitary man. The result was the terrible fear that has now gripped his heart.

The burden he carries on his back is highly significant, for it represents the sin and guilt that now felt like an unbearable weight. The substance of his burden was there all the time, but the man was not aware of it. Now he can scarcely move because of it. How he longed for deliverance! As his guilty conscience cried out against him, the man was filled with a desire to flee. Before, he had given little thought of judgment to come, but now he is desperate to find a place to hide from it.

What has happened to this man to reduce him to such a state of mental anguish? The answer is found within the pages of the book he carries, the Word of God, God's revelation of himself to us. Up to this point, he had no eyes to see the truth, no ears to hear it, and no heart to understand and obey it. But when the two-edged sword of God's Word pierced his soul, he could finally see, hear, and understand. (Hebrews 4:12) Although his initial knowledge was rudimentary, he understood enough of the Gospel message to realize his sinful condition before a thrice-holy God. Like the legendary sword of Damocles, divine judgment hung over his head by a slender thread. But what was he to do about it?

A common misconception of one who has been brought to this point is the feeling that he must *do* something. He mistakenly thinks that he must prepare himself in some way before coming to Christ. The guilty sinner will often try to change his ways and clean up his life. Yet he is poor and needy, helpless and defiled. What can he possibly do to make himself acceptable in God's sight?

As the Word of God continued its soul-searching work, the man eventually became convinced that his efforts to make himself better were futile. At the same time, a holy resolve was taking form within him. The thing he needed most was not to be found in the City of

Destruction. Where then should he go? He struggled with this question for quite some time, having no idea what to do, but fully persuaded that he could not remain as he was. All evidence indicated that a genuine work of God's grace had begun in his soul, one that would not diminish with the passing of time. On the contrary, his distress increased in spite of all efforts to ease it.

Such is not always the case. Far too often, men become disturbed when hearing the Gospel, but forget the impression quickly enough once they are away from its influence. Conviction, saving faith, and the new birth are works of the Holy Spirit. When this work is truly begun, the sinner will not be able to rest until he rests, by faith, in Christ alone.

Happy is the one who is brought to the end of himself, only to discover that Christ has done all for him! It is not until he is convinced of his spiritual poverty that he will see Christ as the all-sufficient Savior. Everything needful for life and godliness is found in him. By faith, the sinner reaches out with empty hands and receives all from him, and with this happy change of condition comes an immediate change of citizenship. He who was a resident of the City of Destruction is now a citizen of Zion, a child of Zion's King.

However, as the man in our story could attest, deliverance from the city is never accomplished without opposition. While he struggled under his burden, a great battle was raging within him. As fear overtook his heart and mind, human reason tried hard to quieten his conscience. In addition to this inward turmoil, he experienced opposition from family and friends. There were many ties that bound him to his former life of sin and ungodliness. Their power over him had to be broken before he could make his escape from the city.

It is highly significant that the man's face was turned away from his own house. His family home denoted his settled condition in the City of Destruction. It represented the former ease, contentment, and security with which he had lived there. With his conviction came the realization that he could not continue as before. He would perish if he did. In fact, he had no desire to remain as he was.

It was a terrible thing to have to suffer alone, but this was the poor man's situation for the time being. Those who were closest to him, his own family included, were at a loss to understand what was happening to him. Therefore, he was isolated in his misery, and yet, he continued to pray, read the Scriptures, and try his best to understand their meaning.

In spite of the man's mental anguish, his thoughts and concerns were not for himself alone. He also feared for the spiritual welfare of his family, but all attempts to convince them of their own danger fell upon deaf ears. At first, they considered his state of mind to be a temporary mental delusion and tried to be sympathetic. When his distress continued, however, their early concern quickly turned to indifference and finally to outright contempt.

The experience of John Bunyan's pilgrim underscores the fact that deliverance from the City of Destruction is, of necessity, an individual matter between the soul and God. As the man continued to struggle alone, his new resolve was urging him to wait no longer. Up to this point, he had spent his time and energy laboring for the vain things to be gained in the City of Destruction. Now he saw them for what they really are. At last, he understood that the most desirable things this world affords are temporary at best, and can be lost in an instant. More importantly, life itself is as fragile and fleeting as a cloud of vapor in the air.

Our Lord explicitly warned his would-be disciples, *No man can serve two masters*. If we would follow him, we must do so with single-ness of heart. Flight from the City of Destruction entails setting our hearts on an eternal goal and seeking treasure that is incorruptible. So as the man prepared to flee, he refused to be hindered any longer by the protests of his family. Competing loves must give place and every tie that binds to the City of Destruction must be broken. (Luke 14:26-33)

* * * *

The sinner's greatest need is a hiding place from the wrath of God. Although the poor man had this desire in earnest, his lack of direction caused him to waver with uncertainty. But having brought him this far, the Lord would not leave him to flounder in spiritual confusion. Behind his seemingly angry countenance, God has the kindest of intentions toward those whom he saves. He wounds in order to heal, and afflicts that he might deliver and relieve. He breaks those whom he intends to make whole, and empties those whom he intends to fill with the knowledge of his love and grace.

Every true child of God experiences this work in his soul, although in varying measure. Some endure the agony of conviction for a longer period of time, and to a greater extent than others. However, all who are made alive by God's Spirit will eventually be led to the only remedy for sin. For it is not enough to flee from the City of Destruction. We must flee unto something, or rather someone!

Although the awakened sinner does not realize it at first, he seeks the Lord because the Lord is seeking and drawing him. The Good Shepherd, who gave his life for his sheep, will seek, find, call and bring every one of them into his fold. To assist in this great work, he calls and ordains under shepherds as the instruments through whom his purpose is brought to pass.

Thus in the hour of the burdened man's deepest need, one named Evangelist was sent to him with a message of life and hope. He received it with deep gratitude, like a drowning man grasping a lifeline. The prophet Isaiah said: *How beautiful upon the mountains are the feet of him that bringeth good tidings, that publisheth peace; that bringeth good tidings of good, that publisheth salvation; that saith unto Zion, Thy God reigneth*! (Isaiah 52:7)

Evangelist was one such bearer of good news. From the Word of God, he both warned the man to flee from the wrath to come and instructed him where to flee. He neither attempted to prematurely relieve the man's distress nor offer him a quick fix for his burden. There is only one place of safety to which a guilty sinner may flee, and Evangelist pointed the man toward it. The Wicket Gate signifies this hiding place. All who would enter the Celestial gate must first enter by this one, for it alone stands at the entrance to the way of life. (John 14:6)

Although the man was not yet able to see the Wicket Gate, he could faintly discern the light that radiated from it. As long as he kept his eyes fixed upon that beacon, he would reach the gate safely. So with his ears stopped against the pleas of his family, and not so much as a single look backward, he ran away from the city, crying "Life!

Life! Eternal Life!" In so doing, the man took an irrevocable step. The die had now been cast, and he knew in his heart that there was no turning back.

> Hail, Sovereign love that first began, the scheme to rescue fallen man;
> Hail matchless free eternal grace, that gave my soul a hiding place;
> Against the God who rules the sky, I fought with hand uplifted high,
> Despised the mention of His grace, too proud to seek a hiding place.

> Enwrapped in thick Egyptian night, and fond of darkness more than light;
> Madly I ran the sinful race, secure without a hiding place.
> But thus th' eternal counsel ran, "Almighty love arrest that man!"
> I felt the arrows of distress, and found I had no hiding place! [1]

Study Questions

1. The solitary man in this chapter is obviously in deep distress. What does his ragged clothing tell us about his anguished state of mind?

2. What is the spiritual meaning of the burden he carries on his back?

3. By what means did the man become alarmed and convinced that he must flee from the City of Destruction?

4. How would you describe the battle taking place within the troubled man?

5. Who does Evangelist represent, and how did he help the desperate man in the hour of his greatest need?

CHAPTER 3

Trouble at the Outset

THE MELODRAMATIC SCENE IN WHICH THE SOLITARY MAN FLED FROM THE City of Destruction, and the vehemence with which he closed his ears to the pleas of his family, further emphasize the allegorical nature of *The Pilgrim's Progress*. If taken strictly at face value, we would conclude that he abandoned his family and his responsibility to them. However, the man did not actually leave his home and desert his family. Such a thing would be directly contrary to Scripture teaching. His flight took place within his inner being. The city he left behind represented his former life of rebellion, unbelief, and ungodliness. The house from which he turned away denoted his former contentment with his life in this world, and his delight in the vain things it offered.

The man's actual circumstances had not changed, but he had! Up to now, he dwelled securely enough in the City of Destruction, but not anymore. Although he did not yet grasp the full significance of what was taking place within him, he had abandoned his former life and embraced a new one. The idols that had formerly captured his heart were laid aside, and another love took their place. A wondrous transformation was occurring within him, a total life-change that will lead him in a completely new direction. (2 Corinthians 5:17) Satan's power over him had been broken, and he now fled toward the place of refuge from the wrath to come.

However, his pilgrimage has just begun. His heart is firmly resolved to reach the Wicket Gate, and his eye steadfastly fixed upon the light that showed the way. Little did he suspect that forces were already at work that would try their utmost to sabotage his journey, from the outset. Even as he fled from the city, two such enemies were right on his heels. Moreover, from their aggressive manner, it appeared that the strength of his resolve was about to be put to the test.

Several of the man's former neighbors had personally witnessed his flight from the city. A few had mocked him, while others cried after him to return. However, the two that actually chased after him were determined to bring him back to the city, by force if necessary. Why did they care whether he escaped or not? What was really behind their joint effort to oppose him?

Although it may sound strange, the answer lies within the man himself, for he was more intimately acquainted with these neighbors than he cared to be. Although he had no desire for their company, he was hard pressed to resist their forceful arguments. So Obstinate and Pliable, for such were their names, hounded the poor man for all they were worth.

When one is born again, a godly principle is planted within. The Spirit of God takes up residence in his heart and leads him in a radically new direction, in the paths of righteousness, in the footsteps of the Lord Jesus Christ. However, a life-long struggle also begins, one in which the flesh wars against the Spirit of God and strives for dominance over the believer's heart and mind. The man's flight from the city while being actively pursued by his two former neighbors signified the beginning of this conflict. Although he was determined to reach the Wicket Gate, he felt himself being pulled in two directions at once.

My friend in Christ, is it not just the same with us? Strong tendencies dwell within us that would have prevented our fleeing to Christ, if possible, and even now would turn us from following him if they could. They would succeed if a greater power did not reside within us. Obstinate and Pliable represent two such inclinations, and even though they were seeming opposites by nature, they were united in their purpose to undermine the man's resolve.

The persistent opposition of these two neighbors reminds me of an important truth. Even though we receive a new heart in regeneration, our flesh is not eradicated, and neither are the scars of a sinful past. Old habits and sinful propensities may no longer dominate, but they will continue to afflict, trouble, and vex our souls. Each of us has sins with which we struggle and particular weaknesses to which we are prone. Two major changes occur with conversion, however. We come to hate what we once loved, and to love what we once scorned and rejected. Moreover, the Spirit of God is our powerful ally who helps and enables us to eventually overcome the flesh.

Our conflicts would be few indeed if the principle of godliness within us was unopposed. The world would hold little charm, and Satan's flaming arrows would fall wide of their mark, if not for our flesh. But even though we wish it otherwise, we must contend with this internal traitor as we journey to Zion. Just when we think ourselves victorious in one area, something unsuspected arises to vex us, and cause us to cry with the apostle Paul: *O wretched man that I am!*

From our human perspective, it would seem to be much better if we had no opposing tendencies with which to do battle. Yet in his infinite wisdom, God has ordained this life-long struggle. The journey to Zion was never intended to be easy. It is our time of preparation for eternity with Christ, and a crucial part of it involves the mortification of indwelling sin. Another necessary part is the trial, purging, and purifying of our faith. Both of these things are accomplished as we face opposition, learn to endure hardness, and are enabled by the power of God to overcome every obstacle along the way.

We do well to remember that God is more glorified as we overcome opposition and difficulty than he would be if we walked the path of life unopposed. The power to overcome, to persevere, and finish the race comes from him alone. Our struggles and trials will result in ultimate victory, but the power is of God and all glory for it belongs to him alone.

What about the specific assault launched against John Bunyan's brand new pilgrim? Who were the two enemies that pursued him out of the city, disguised as two of his former friends? Obstinate and Pliable are sinful tendencies that are deeply rooted in all men by nature, and the City of Destruction is the place to which they naturally belong.

Since unregenerate man possesses a stubborn will that is determined to have its own way, the sin of obstinacy is easily detected in even the youngest residents of the city. Is not the word "no" one of the first things that children learn to say? Even before an infant is able to articulate the word, he learns to shake his head "no." We often smile at this gesture and think it cute, but it is one early indication of a way-ward heart. Careful parental discipline may teach the child to control his obstinate tendencies, and self-interest may urge him to suppress them. However, a stubborn will eventually asserts itself and becomes more firmly fixed as he gets older. Only the power of God can subdue and change an errant, obstinate heart.

Man's willful nature is rooted in another of his innate character-istics, the sin of pride. Like twin pillars, pride and obstinacy support each other, and are two chief ways in which man's rebellious heart manifests itself. Self-will makes him ungovernable, while pride fuels his headstrong nature. Scripture succinctly describes the natural man's stubborn will by stating that he is stiff-necked and uncircum-cised in heart. It is not a very flattering picture, is it?

One tragic consequence of obstinacy is that it goes hand in hand with ignorance. A stubborn nature causes one to resist instruction because he is wise in his own conceit. Arrogance and pride of opin-ion tend to render one inflexible, unteachable and, therefore, doomed to remain ignorant. Sadly, those who are the most spiritually igno-rant also tend to be highly opinionated and vocal in expressing their views. This tendency is one chief characteristic of the religious hyp-ocrite. Misdirected zeal drives his religion, rather than love of the truth. Intolerance and bigotry fuel his actions, not love for Christ. Self-interest rules in his heart, not the grace of God. Thus he is like a tree without fruit and a plant without root, a soul destined to be plucked up and cast away.

When we consider the man named Obstinate, and the sins of pride, rebellion, and spiritual ignorance that he represents, we have no difficulty viewing his action against the new pilgrim as a highly significant matter. He embodies not only the early assertion of a strong, opposing tendency, but also the beginning of victory over it. As the more overbearing of the two neighbors, he refused to leave the city, and was determined to prevent the fleeing man from doing so. Attacking in the form of the distressed man's own human reasoning, Obstinate charged him with folly for leaving the city.

As you might expect, Obstinate argued his case boldly and logi-cally. He was unwilling to leave his friends and comforts behind, and strongly urged the fleeing man to change his mind. However, the friends and comforts he valued so highly were those very things that make the City of Destruction what it is. Using his most compelling arguments, Obstinate tried to detain the man, going so far as to imply that he was mentally deranged. Yet even in the face of such adamant persuasion, the man refused to turn back. His resolve was based upon something far more substantial than an emotional response to the Gospel, for he had heard the call of God's Spirit. Therefore, it was with a holy resolve that he faced and rebuked the voice of human reason in his own mind. Furthermore, as the sincerity of his resolve stood the test, a momentous thing occurred. The previously unidentified man is at last given a name, "Christian"!

Some might ask, "What is so important about that?" The great Elizabethan playwright William Shakespeare posed a similar question when he wrote, "What's in a name?"[1] A thoughtful response would be that one's name implies much more than the words on his or her birth certificate. Name denotes character, reputation, and the kind of person he is known to be. (Proverbs 22:1) One's name, then, signifies a great deal.

Before his awakening, Christian's name was Graceless. It is a name that all unregenerate people share in common, and a fact that he will reveal later in his story. He had been like every other resident of the City of Destruction until the mercy of God made him to differ. (1 Corinthians 4:7) His new name was first made known when he firmly stated his resolve. To Obstinate's insistence that he return to the city, Christian boldly replied, "That can by no means be." Human obstinacy met holy resolve head on and tried its best to quench it. By the power of God, however, holy resolve overcame every argument that human reason raised against it.

Christian's new name indicated both his change of character and condition. His action was no mere flight of fancy or impetuosity, and neither was it an act of his human will. Such things are tenuous at best, changeable and subject to time and circumstance.

Even though Christian heard the arguments of obstinate unbelief and human reason in his own mind, he pressed onward, toward the Wicket Gate. In saying "I have laid my hand to the plough," he stated the holy intention of every true pilgrim. So his was a promising beginning.

* * * *

Please bear in mind that Obstinate, an unmistakable enemy, represented only one of the neighbors who pursued Christian as he ran from the city. What of the other one, the man named Pliable? Was he not the very opposite in character to Obstinate? On the surface it would appear so. After all, Obstinate withstood all of Christian's arguments and returned to the city while, with very little persuasion, Pliable agreed to accompany him on his journey. However, even though he posed as a friend, Pliable would also do his best to overturn Christian's resolve.

Why was this seemingly amiable man really no friend at all? In fact, do we go too far by openly declaring him to be an enemy? Not at all! Pliability may seem to be a desirable thing until we weigh its spiritual implications. If allowed to have control, it will weaken the steadfastness of character that is crucial in order to successfully navigate and finish the Christian race.

Yes, Obstinate and Pliable were opposites by nature, yet neither of them would enter the Wicket Gate. Likewise, the character traits of obstinacy and pliability are opposite inclinations, but are equally strong in trying to hinder one's entrance into the kingdom of God. Both are tendencies that relate to individual human volition, to man's fallen will. They are close neighbors indeed! As natural-born residents of the City of Destruction, they belong strictly to the realm of the earthly and the fleshly. Considered together, they hold a powerful sway over the hearts and minds of men, causing many to scorn the way of life, and others to turn from it after seemingly making a start.

As followers of the Lord Jesus Christ, we must struggle with and overcome both of these sinful tendencies. Yielded submission to Christ and the fixed purpose to follow him must replace both a stubborn will and an easily moved resolve. For in the race to eternal glory, many leave the starting gate, but relatively few cross the finish line.

Predictably, neither Obstinate nor Pliable was motivated by anything higher or nobler than self-interest. The former was satisfied with his portion in this life and was not about to leave it behind. He never even considered leaving the city. The latter actually left with Christian, but only because it seemed in his best interest to do so. As he listened to Christian talk of the Celestial City, Pliable only heard of the pilgrim's happy final condition. What Christian sought seemed to be a better deal than what Pliable currently enjoyed. He little thought to count the cost. In fact, it did not even occur to him that there was a cost, self-denial and a cross. (Luke 14:26-33)

So even though Pliable set out on the journey with Christian, his pilgrimage was doomed from the start. Godly fear was not the motivating factor in his decision. The absence of a burden on his back betrayed the fact that he had no real sense of sin or guilt before God. He was a prime example of a double-minded man who is unstable in all his ways. It had taken very little to convince him to join Christian. What will it take to make him abandon the whole idea?

Study Questions

1. Although several of the man's neighbors witnessed his flight from the city, two of them actually chased after him. Who were they, and what did they hope to accomplish?

2. In what sense were these two men his neighbors?

3. Although seemingly opposite in nature, Obstinate and Pliable chased the fleeing man with a united purpose. Write a brief character sketch of these two men and explain the thing they had in common that made them both the man's enemies.

4. In this chapter the fleeing man is finally given a name. What is it? What brought about his change of name, and why is it so significant?

5. Against all arguments, the man fled out of the City of Destruction. What about his neighbors? What happened to Obstinate and Pliable?

CHAPTER 4

Unexpected Fall into the Slough of Despond

As Christian trudged onward, still weighed down by his heavy burden, little did he suspect that he had entered the field of a holy war. In addition to his inner conflict, dark enemy forces had noted his escape from the City of Destruction, and they were already plotting his downfall. Can he withstand such an onslaught as this one is likely to be? Will he be able to continue in the face of that kind of opposition? Yes, by God's grace he can! The seed of truth has been planted in his soul, and its dynamic power was already altering his thought processes. However, as he struggled toward the Wicket Gate, Christian still had Pliable in tow.

You may remember that the broad plain surrounding the City of Destruction is broken here and there by the occasional neighboring town or village. Each of these suburbs has direct access to and from the great metropolis via a network of well-traveled roads. The way in which Evangelist directed Christian to go avoided every one of these busy highways. He was to follow the road less traveled, for it alone led to the Wicket Gate.

As the two men walked along together, Christian spoke freely and enthusiastically of the beautiful city that was his destination. While all that he said was true, he knew little, as yet, of the pathway to the city. Even though he had the heart of a true pilgrim, he was not prepared for the difficulties that were sure to come. Therefore, Christian's heart was so filled with the glories of the Celestial City, and his attention so distracted by their conversation, that he failed to notice a subtle change in the landscape.

In the very midst of the plain directly in their path was a very dangerous parcel of ground, a miry slough fed continuously by numerous underground springs. Although it extends over several acres, this dismal swamp is mostly concealed within a densely-wooded area of Cypress trees draped with Spanish moss. Furthermore, the tall marsh grass growing out of the shallow water, and the lush vegetation floating on its surface, give the false appearance of solid ground. An unpleasant, reeking mist hovers over this particular wetland more or less continuously, and no distinct border marks its edges. To make the area even more hazardous, its mossy boundary is level with the surrounding ground, causing many an unsuspecting traveler to stumble right into it.

Those who are familiar with the lay of the land are aware of its hidden dangers, and also know the location of stepping stones by which the slough can be safely crossed. But strangers to the area are generally at a loss to tell just where the solid ground ends and the treacherous slough begins. Unlike the gently rounded edges of a pond or lake, its perimeter is jagged and irregular, piercing randomly into the solid ground. Therefore, the hapless traveler often does not suspect trouble until the firm ground under his feet suddenly gives way.

Although the murky water of the slough is actually shallow, its bottom is covered with a deep layer of dead leaves and other kinds of decaying organic material. This muddy layer conceals the slough's underlying depth, and gives no hint of the dangerous pockets of quicksand that are hidden there.

For all of its shallow appearance, the slough's miry bottom is quite deep, and well able to swallow a grown man without a trace.

One who happens to fall into the slough will quickly lose his sense of direction, and the numerous trees with their low-hanging foliage disorient him all the more. As he struggles to free himself, his desperate thrashing only stirs up the muddy bottom and causes him to sink more deeply. Unless someone realizes his predicament and comes to his rescue, he could well perish there.

This particular bog has a rather unusual name. It is known throughout the region as the Slough of Despond. As Christian and

Pliable hastened across the middle of the plain, they were heading directly toward it. Since they were deep in conversation, neither man happened to notice the impending danger. They were speaking of the nature and glories of the Celestial City at the end of the pilgrim's journey. Or rather, Pliable listened as Christian talked of these things.

While it is true that Pliable resisted the arguments of his friend Obstinate, and joined Christian in leaving the city, he had in fact been persuaded a bit too easily. His obvious lack of understanding indicated that he was ignorant of God's Word. Worse still, the eagerness with which he followed Christian concealed an ulterior motive.

As for Christian, he was convinced that the Word of God is true and its author faithful and infallible. Now that he understood his condition before God, the terrors of sin, guilt, and judgment weighed heavily upon him. From the Scriptures, however, he also found a reason to hope in the Lord for mercy and salvation.

Pliable relied solely upon Christian's testimony, having no personal experience of these things. So it should come as no surprise that Pliable's hearing was seriously flawed. He accepted Christian's word without question because it sounded good. But at best, his was a second-hand faith. His attention was so captivated by the joys and delights at the end of the journey that he failed to consider the journey itself. His heart readily embraced the glories of the Celestial City, but missed all mention of the sufferings that would precede that eternal joy. He failed to consider the tears that would be wiped away at the journey's end. Self-interest motivated him to begin the journey, and therefore, his eagerness to reach their destination made him desirous to quicken their pace. For unlike Christian, he traveled without the encumbrance of a burden.

Thus it happened that neither man noticed they were fast approaching the slough named Despond. Their failure to watch their step soon proved a costly one, however, for John Bunyan tells us that "they being heedless did both fall suddenly into the bog." They were equally unprepared for this unexpected difficulty, and yet, how very dissimilar was their reaction to it.

In what way were they heedless? They failed to consider the true nature of the Christian life. Many a person professes faith in Christ with the mistaken idea that his troubles are essentially behind him.

This notion is the result of either ignorance, or failure to heed the Scripture truth that it is with great difficulty that we strive to enter the path of life and walk therein. So in looking for blessing, Christian and Pliable were caught totally off-guard by this sudden trouble. Nevertheless, the trial of the slough brought many important things to light.

Pliable's true character and fickle heart were not made known until after he fell into the slough. His interest in becoming a Christian had been shallow and self-seeking from the start; therefore, it was not equal to such disillusionment. Since he had expected only happiness, prosperity, and an easier time of it, this abrupt reversal in circumstances changed his amiable manner into one of derision, anger, and offence. Little wonder that he promptly abandoned his decision to accompany Christian!

It is significant that Pliable was not trapped in the slough to the same extent that Christian was. After all, he knew nothing of the conviction of the Holy Spirit, and therefore, he was not troubled by any genuine sense of guilt, remorse, or despondency. As he struggled to free himself from the slough, he managed to escape on the side nearest to his house, a point of exit that happened to be furthest away from the Wicket Gate. Thus he returned to the City of Destruction, where his heart had really been all the time.

Why did Pliable fall into the slough at all? It was probably due to Christian's influence. In the strictest sense of his name, Pliable denotes an impulsive soul who is easily swayed by what he hears at any given moment. The Lord Jesus Christ told of such characters in the Parable of the Sower. (Matthew 13:18-23) Like the stony ground hearer, Pliable was an unregenerate man who was temporarily moved while under the influence of truth, but his heart remained unchanged.

When the Spirit of God begins to work in the heart, he persists until the sinner is brought to faith in Christ alone. However, Pliable was of the sort who eventually draws back into overt unbelief. (Hebrews 11:38-39) His conscience was finally soothed to the point that he was able to free himself from the slough, which is the typical experience of one who is enlightened by the Gospel, but not to the point of regeneration.

After Pliable returned home, his condition was far worse for having begun the journey and then forsaking it. Exposure to the truth made him more accountable before God. Moreover, in light of his fickle behavior, who even among his friends could really respect him? It is true that some who hated the way of life congratulated him and called him wise for returning. But for the most part, he was mocked and despised for his cowardice. (Luke 14:26-33)

What about poor Christian, who had also fallen into the slough? How did he fare in its dark, murky waters? At first, he lost all sense of direction. Worse still, the more he struggled, the more deeply he sank into the miry bottom. The thought must have occurred to him that this was the end. Perhaps he would simply vanish, leaving his family to wonder what became of him! Yet even in this extremity, he did not consider turning back. The fear of God still drove him toward the Wicket Gate. Why then has he suddenly been stopped dead in his tracks? What is this terrible place called the Slough of Despond?

The slough represents a virtually hopeless state of mind into which an awakened sinner can sink without warning. As long as one remains indifferent to Christ, the enemy does all in his power to keep him that way. He brings nothing to mind that would alarm the sinner concerning his spiritual condition, but does all in his diabolical power to keep him in darkness and spiritual insensibility.

However, when one begins to see his spiritual danger, the enemy launches an all-out offensive against him. Satan will do anything he can to prevent one from fleeing to Christ. Furthermore, the awakened sinner's own mind and conscience provide fertile ground where this battle can be waged. The slough represents one such attack, the debilitating struggle with fear and mistrust resulting in depression, despair, and hopelessness. Those who fall therein find themselves in a desperate state of mental anguish, much like helpless captives in a dark, dismal place. (Lamentations 3:55) So the Slough of Despond is a formidable barrier that must be breached if the convicted sinner is to reach the Wicket Gate.

Christian's experience in the slough was that of an awakened soul trapped by a sense of his inward corruption, and the outcries of his guilty conscience. (Psalm 130:1-2) His knowledge of the way of salvation was sketchy at this point, and he was not yet fully resting in Christ as his only hope. Therefore, he was highly susceptible to the tormenting doubts and fears for which the Slough of Despond is notorious. Its polluted water is cluttered with many such hindrances, all of which are designed to keep the sinner from trusting himself completely to Christ and resting in his finished redemption. A fall therein might well be called the revival of sin, as the awareness of guilt before God suddenly overwhelms the mind and heart, bringing great fear and alarm. (Romans 7:9)

While a proper fear of God draws the seeking soul unto Christ, unbelieving fear makes him hesitant to approach. The power of the slough lies in its ability to keep the awakened sinner's eyes fixed upon himself instead of looking to Christ. A deep sense of sin and unworthiness triggers morbid introspection, and this, in turn, fuels fear and despondency. The more we struggle with such dark, despairing thoughts, the deeper we sink into its cruel vicious cycle.

This terrible struggle is not an uncommon one among the people of God. Many of them can testify of a frightful ordeal in the Slough of Despond. John Bunyan was one of them. So am I. But God does not will that his people be held as perpetual captives to doubt and fear. Help is available for those who find themselves trapped in this slough. God's providence may allow some of his children to fall therein, but his mercy will deliver them from it in due time.

Without question, unbelieving fear is the primary stronghold of the slough, and it finds a powerful ally in the troubled conscience. Unbelief acts as a kind of mental quicksand that traps the soul and would destroy it if it could. However, laying hold upon the promises of God by faith will set the captive free.

The trial represented by the Slough of Despond is made all the more painful by its solitary nature. Even though it is not unusual among God's people, this battle with fear, mistrust, and overwhelming despair is a very lonely one. Human aid or sympathy is not enough to pull one from its terrible clutches. When unbelieving fear casts one headlong into the slough, God-given faith alone can release him from its grasp, but not without a terrible struggle. Christian's burden was so heavy that it nearly pulled him under the dark waters of the slough, but it also provided a strong incentive for him to reach the Wicket Gate.

Even though he put up a valiant fight, Christian was unable to free himself from the slough's strong grasp. His faith was still weak and his knowledge small, but he knew which way he must go. So even while he tried to keep from drowning, he struggled to reach the side of the slough that was furthest from the City of Destruction.

Christian's situation appeared hopeless until one named Help came along and extended a hand, pulling him out of the slough and onto solid ground. Who could he be, and how did he happen to be close by at just the right time? The man named Help was an officer of the King, a minister of the Gospel who has been called and commissioned by Christ to assist, counsel, instruct and shepherd the people of God. He and his fellow officers are placed wherever God's people are found, ready to assist them whenever the need arises.

The nature of his help is worthy of particular note, for it consisted of pointing the struggling man to Christ alone. Christian had been overwhelmed by fear and despair because his eyes were on the wrong things. However, the preaching of Christ in clarity and power is well able to break the slough's lethal grasp. Sound biblical instruction applied to the heart and mind by the Spirit of God has pulled many a desperate soul from the Slough of Despond. Moreover, looking unto Jesus places our feet squarely onto the solid ground that leads to the Wicket Gate. It is only as we have a right knowledge of Christ and his love that we will flee to him for refuge. When we do, we can say with a thankful heart: *He brought me up also out of an horrible pit, out of the miry clay, and set my feet upon a rock, and established my goings.* (Psalm 40:2)

The stone steps providing safe passage through the slough represent this right understanding of Christ and his Gospel. In particular, they signify the promises of God to those who truly believe in Christ, promises of forgiveness, cleansing, and acceptance by God. Although the steps were strategically placed where they were easy enough to find, doubting souls tend to miss them. Such was the case with poor Christian. Heedlessness caused him to miss the steps and fall into the slough, but giving attention to sound instruction set him right once again. Thus Gospel instruction serves to help some pilgrims avoid the Slough of Despond, while for others, it is the means whereby they are delivered from it.

Although many attempts have been made to drain the Slough of Despond, it remains the same dangerous parcel of ground today as when Christian passed that way and fell in. Why have all attempts to improve it been unsuccessful? The King's laborers are continually busy with the ministry of God's Word, but in spite of their diligence and excellent instruction, it seems the slough is something that most Christians will experience to one degree or another. Apparently, few find the steps that enable them to cross safely over it. The more common experience while under conviction is to endure a time of fear, doubt, and despair.

As hard as this trial is sure to be, when God begins a work of grace in the soul, he brings it to ultimate fruition. When his little ones flounder helplessly in the depths of the slough, he is well aware of their distress. Moreover, he will send help and eventual deliverance at the appointed time.

* * * *

There is another aspect of the Slough of Despond that is too important for us to overlook. It can prove an impassable barrier for certain would-be pilgrims. There are some who seem content, and even think it pious, to continually wallow in misery there. Others are never able to see past themselves, their works, or their efforts to improve themselves. Still others, like Pliable, are so offended by the difficulties of the pilgrim way that they quickly abandon the whole idea and turn back to their former life. All of these have one tragic thing in common. They never make it to the Wicket Gate; that is, they never truly come to Christ by faith alone.

My fellow pilgrim, pliability of character will not stand the test of the slough, or any other significant difficulty, in the long run. Furthermore, like Christian's traveling companion, it is probably closer to us than we think. Therefore, this tendency must be purged from us, and yet, we must never suppose that personal strengths or weaknesses determine whether we persevere in grace or not. The holy resolve that enables us to continue in faith is the work of God's Spirit. As he forms this resolve in us, those things that oppose it will be gradually diminished and overcome.

Since the man named Pliable was never truly converted, he was easily moved by circumstances. He failed to count the cost, and built without laying a proper foundation. (Matthew 7:24-27) Is it any wonder that his so-called faith was overthrown at the first sign of trouble?

A clear lesson here is that the inclination to be easily influenced is not conducive to the life of faith. As Christians, we must demonstrate submissiveness to Christ and compliance with his will and guidance, even while standing firm in the face of every kind of opposition that would turn us from following him. Those who lack these things will be easily plucked up. However, the one in whom Christ dwells will be like a tree planted by a river of living water, deeply rooted and continually nourished by his Spirit through his Word.

Christian had experienced this inward operation of grace, while Pliable had not. Thus the two men came to a parting of the ways at the Slough of Despond. Although the loss of his traveling companion must have been a bitter disappointment to Christian, it did not alter his purpose. In fact, as he hastened toward the Wicket Gate alone, his heart and mind were more resolute than ever.

Study Questions

1. As Christian and Pliable headed toward the Wicket Gate, they were unaware of the Slough of Despond lying directly in their path. In what way were they heedless? How did their inattention cause them to fall into the slough?

2. This unexpected difficulty brought Pliable's true character to light. What did it reveal about him? How did he react when he found himself in the slough?

3. What does the Slough of Despond represent? Describe Christian's experience when trapped therein.

4. Unlike Pliable, Christian was unable to free himself from the slough. Who was the man named Help? What was the nature of the help by which he pulled Christian from the slough's strong grasp?

5. What do the stone steps through the Slough of Despond represent? Why do so many people miss them?

Part Two

ENCOUNTER WITH A STRANGER

For the preaching of the cross is to them that perish, foolishness;
but unto us which are saved, it is the power of God. For it is written,
I will destroy the wisdom of the wise, and will bring to nothing the
understanding of the prudent.

1 Corinthians 1:18-19

CHAPTER 5

Sidetracked by Dangerous Counsel

WITHOUT A DOUBT, THE GIFT OF HUMAN INTELLECT AND RATIONAL THOUGHT IS a tremendous blessing from the Lord. It is a gift that only man enjoys, for he alone was created in the image of God. When sin entered the scene, the gift of rational thought became a channel of rebellion against God. As a result, man's will is far from being free; it is in bondage to sin, and his heart firmly set in him to do evil.

When we are born again, we receive a renewing of our minds. A new principle is placed within that alters our thought processes and leads us in the right ways of the Lord. However, the old principle of sin will continue to assert itself and oppose the principle of godliness in every way it can. Thus we find ourselves caught in the midst of a fierce battle with human reason. Striking hard at our resolve to walk by faith, this inner voice will invariably tempt us to lean to our own understanding. But yielding to it can lead us into big trouble.

As Christian struggled to reach the Wicket Gate while still carrying his heavy burden, we find him drawn into this very battle. Common logic argued that without his burden, he could travel faster and reach his goal sooner. This rationale makes perfect sense, until we remember that the laws of human wisdom rarely agree with the way of faith. There is a divine paradox operating within our Christian experience that often runs contrary to human logic. Its purpose is to correct the natural tendency to rely upon our own understanding, which can make for many a frustrating situation. So even though the good and perfect work begun in us by the Holy Spirit will be brought to eventual completion, its joyful end is usually attained through great tribulation. (Revelation 7:13-17)

Therefore, adversity proves to be our friend, although it scarcely seems so when we are in its grasp. Trouble may perplex and cloud our judgment for a time, but it cannot overturn genuine faith. Opposition will strengthen, rather than daunt, the true pilgrim's resolve. Tribulation will advance, rather than hinder, our growth in grace. Thus the divine paradox confounds the best counsel of human wisdom, and justifies the ways of an all-wise heavenly Father in the eyes of his dear children.

We see this spiritual paradox hard at work in Christian, as he pressed onward in spite of rigorous opposition. By now weariness was beginning to set in, for he had carried his burden a long time and it was not getting any lighter. His resolution to reach the Wicket Gate was as strong as ever, but it was still nowhere in sight.

Observing him more closely, we notice that his garments are stained from his recent fall into the slough. This is a significant fact, given the figurative meaning of that terrible place. Although he had been delivered from it, he was still suffering mental anguish about his spiritual condition. So the very same frame of mind that caused him to fall into the Slough of Despond now brought him into the vicinity of a place known as Carnal Policy.

Until now, Christian's distress of mind kept him from noticing the large town that was visible on the distant horizon. Situated just across the river from the City of Destruction, it was actually an integral part of that great complex. Had Christian been more observant, he would have noticed that one of its citizens was rapidly coming his way. Very soon now, their paths are going to cross. Before they do, it would be well for us to consider the place from which the man, Mr. Worldly Wiseman, hailed.

Of all the towns and villages comprising the City of Destruction complex, Carnal Policy is undoubtedly the most outstanding. Luxurious mansions with immaculate lawns and gardens grace the town's most scenic avenues. These exclusive neighborhoods are further adorned by rows of ancient oak trees and ornamental gas lighting. Throughout the town, tastefully designed parks add a touch of rural character to its otherwise urban flair. In a number of these parks, great monuments have been placed in honor of the town's most illustrious citizens.

Altogether, Carnal Policy seems the very essence of all that is charming and elegant. It exerts a subtle aura as well, a distinctive blend of human philosophy and sophistication of which Worldly Wiseman is the essence. First-time visitors often say that the town has a magnetic effect upon their hearts and minds that is not easily forgotten.

As to the kinds of people who make this place their home, most of them are former residents of the City of Destruction. When the smaller town was founded long ago, it quickly became a haven for those who appreciate the finer things of life. As more and more of the great city's intelligentsia moved there, it soon acquired its reputation as a community of highly enlightened individuals.

Thus, very early in its history, Carnal Policy gained prominence for its outstanding institutions of higher education. These prestigious colleges and universities, with their massive Norman towers and gothic architecture, lend a charming, old-world atmosphere of which the town residents are understandably proud. Little wonder that the brightest minds to be found in the City of Destruction compete ruthlessly for admission to these ivy-shrouded institutions.

Carnal Policy, the birthplace of human reason, also deserves its reputation as a great cultural center. World famous art galleries, museums, theatres and elaborate centers for the performing arts all reflect the refined tastes of its residents. Something is offered here for even the most discriminating person.

Shortly after the town was incorporated, the ruling council of the City of Destruction decided to make it their official seat of government. After all, did not the wisest and brightest minds live there? Were they not the ones best qualified to make laws and determine public policy? Who could better manage affairs of state and of society than the worldly wise? Did they not all embrace the same humanistic philosophy upon which the town was originally founded? Thus the matter was settled and their intricate legal code written, but it was based upon what is practical and expedient, rather than what is right and true. Moreover, without the standard of any moral absolutes, their judicial system takes a liberal approach that permits wide latitude when interpreting the law. All of this squares perfectly well with the ruling powers in the City of Destruction.

In order to accommodate the affairs of state, the town of Carnal Policy approved and commissioned an extensive government complex to be constructed near the heart of town, one that would be worthy of its existing grandeur. The resultant city of marble consists of magnificent Greco-Roman buildings patterned after those built by ancient civilizations in honor of their gods. Before long, this city within a city became a place of renown, both for its architectural splendor and collective wisdom. However, the more thoughtful viewer, when gazing upon all of its outward magnificence, will perhaps remember the end of the "splendor that was Greece and the glory that was Rome."

One final structure crowning the central government complex is its vast library. Scholars from around the world visit this multi-domed, elaborate facility containing the largest collection of human wisdom in existence. One massive wing is dedicated solely to rare manuscripts and authorized texts of famous classical writers. Information on just about any subject can be found within the walls of this literary treasure house, which some have likened to the great library of the ancient world in Alexandria, Egypt.

Adjacent to this massive government complex, you will find the great archives of the City of Destruction. This building contains all of the official records and public documents since the city was established. Proudly displayed within its central rotunda, you will find the original charter of the great city. In order to protect this irreplaceable document from the elements, it has been placed in a pneumatically sealed glass case. Long lines of visitors form daily to view this ancient document, but many of them are mystified by its strange opening statement, the first words of which are *Hath God said…?* Few, however, connect these enigmatic words to the town's most famous landmark.

Located squarely in the middle of a large circular green, this imposing structure was built as a tribute to man, his superior intellect, wisdom and worldly achievements. As a historic landmark it is truly without equal, rising to a towering height before tapering into the shape of a pyramid. It should be noted that even though the granite memorial points heavenward, its foundation is rooted deeply in the town's bedrock. All of this is by design, because the massive structure marks the exact center of Carnal Policy and has captured the very essence of its town spirit.

If you stand near the foot of this splendid monument and study it carefully, you will perhaps notice that it bears a striking resemblance to a shrine. Dear reader, this is not your imagination. The town landmark is the visible symbol of man's opinion of himself, and his inclination to worship and serve the creature more than the Creator. (Romans 1:25) In this, we discover a decidedly religious aspect to the town spirit, one in which there is no conflict with human wisdom.

As you put these thoughts together, you might recall the golden image built by King Nebuchadnezzar on the plain of Dura long ago. (Daniel 3:1) It makes one wonder whether the town of Carnal Policy is all that it appears to be. Could its lavish beauty and outward splendor conceal a sinister character? What sort of place is it really, and why does it lie so close to the pilgrim's path? Moreover, why is one of its most prominent citizens coming toward Christian with such perfect timing as to make the crossing of their paths inevitable? Before we can answer these questions, we need to explore the meaning behind the metaphors.

We have already identified the allegorical town as the birthplace of human reason. As for Worldly Wiseman, he represents the voice of human reason, a voice that opposes and exalts itself against the wisdom and knowledge of God. Linked together, Carnal Policy and Wiseman represent one of the strongholds spoken of by the apostle Paul in 2 Corinthians 10:3-6. Thus they denote strongholds that must be broken down by the hammer of God's Word. (Jeremiah 23:29) Even though he comes in the guise of a friend, this man is a deadly enemy who will attempt to turn Christian from the right path.

Take a good look at him, my friend. He may appear to be a fine, upstanding gentleman, even a pillar of society. But note the self-assurance with which he initiates a conversation with poor Christian, even going so far as to offer unsolicited advice concerning his burden. Does not his bold, patronizing manner suggest that he thought very highly of himself? He clearly considered himself an authority on subjects of any importance, and competent enough to advise others. To sum it up, he viewed himself as better educated, more intelligent, and wiser than the average mortal.

These character flaws might have been little more than a nuisance if he not been so quick to offer ready answers to some of life's most perplexing questions, even those pertaining to matters of eternal consequence. So even though his counsel might sound reasonable, we do well to consider its source.

Who then is this man, and why did he dare confront a stranger as he did Christian? He clearly had some inkling of Christian's trouble; therefore, he was able to strike in his most vulnerable area, that of his burden of sin and guilt. With the skill of an expert marksman, he inquired about Christian's family, and in so doing, he hit upon those earthly things that were dearest to the afflicted man's heart.

After observing that Christian's distress of mind was ruining his legitimate enjoyment of his family, and discovering that he was traveling toward the Wicket Gate for relief, Worldly Wiseman offered another solution. There was an easier way for Christian to be rid of his burden, a way that would avoid the dangers and troubles that Christian had only begun to experience if he maintained his present course. So spoke the voice of human reason. However, the character of any counsel can best be known by the direction in which it leads.

Man's most ambitious goal is to be in control of his own life and happiness. His most presumptuous thought is that he can be the master of his destiny, the captain of his soul. In the rather complex character of the Wiseman, we find both of these things at work. He depicts the voice of human reason in the mind of one who is under conviction of sin, but has not yet fully rested in Christ. As such, he will argue loudly against the way of faith in Christ alone. He also personifies the flesh's desire for ease, its tendency to focus on the difficulties that attend the life of faith, and its inclination to resist the will and ways of God. In brief, he signifies man's attempt to bypass God's prescribed remedy for sin, and substitute one of his own making.

What does all of this have to do with Christian, who was no longer a resident of the City of Destruction? Why has his journey brought him to a place where he would rather not be? Has he not fled from his old life of sin, unbelief, and rebellion against God? Yes, he has. Christian is done with those former things. To his chagrin, however, he is finding out that they are not done with him. With all his heart, he desired to reach the Wicket Gate as soon as possible, but acute mental anguish landed him squarely within the jurisdiction of Carnal Policy.

If taken at face value, Mr. Wiseman's initial words could be misconstrued as good counsel. He seemed to have Christian's best interest in mind when claiming to have a solution for his burden that would enable him to be settled in his mind and enjoy the blessings of God. Christian's desperation made him open to suggestion, and vulnerable to any offer of help. The poor man stood in need of good counsel to be sure, but he lacked the discernment to judge the value of this offered help. By failing to recognize its source, Christian gave the fine looking gentleman a hearing. After all, by the man's own admission, he was older and wiser.

What sort of counsel did he give? Was it godly advice that could be safely followed, or should it be viewed with suspicion and rejected? Its true nature came quickly to light when Worldly Wiseman began to speak against the way of salvation in Christ alone, and tried to deter Christian from following that course. He spoke contemptuously of both the Word of God and the ministers of Christ, even daring to suggest that only ignorant, weak-minded people sought the way of Christ and his cross. The citizens of Carnal Policy were not so easily duped! As one of the more enlightened ones, he knew better than to expose himself to such unnecessary risk! There was a better remedy at hand for troubled souls, one that promised safety, friendship, and contentment.

His counsel contained a serious flaw, however. By casting doubt upon the Word of God, it produced immediate confusion in Christian's mind. Wiseman's policy, the rule by which he lived, was based entirely upon the creed of human reason. Therefore, it was earthly, sensual, and devilish. (James 3:15) In rejecting God's way of salvation, his counsel echoed the mindset of unregenerate men. Even though it was the best advice that human reason could give, it was the wisdom of the spiritually ignorant. Thus his supposedly good advice would do nothing to remedy Christian's trouble.

In the beginning, the heavy burden Christian carried had prompted him to follow the godly counsel of Evangelist. Now it moved him to hear what Mr. Worldly had to say. With the unexpected intrusion of another voice giving contrary advice, the poor man came to a standstill. What should he do? He possessed the heart of a true penitent, so why did he now waver between two opinions?

His pressing dilemma underscores the danger of giving heed to opposing voices, including those within our own hearts and minds. Godly counsel had pointed Christian in the right direction, but when the way seemed long and the burden increasingly heavy, he yielded to the thought that there was another solution. Human reason offered him a quick fix, an easier way to be rid of his burden. However, in bypassing the cross, it missed the heart of the matter entirely.

The great arrogance of Wiseman lay in setting aside God's way, and presuming to offer one of his own. His boasted wisdom was based primarily on that which was practical and convenient, rather than the higher, nobler principles of truth and right. In common with most of his kind, he was not overly burdened by a guilty conscience, but he had a ready solution for those who were. What solution does human reason have to offer for the problem of a guilty conscience? What remedy can it recommend that would enable one to enjoy the blessings of life again? Carnal Policy's answer consists of directing the sinner's attention to things physical, rational, and temporal – things relevant to time and sense. Moreover, it casts a further stumbling block in his way by allowing plenty of scope for him to be religious.

This was the essence of Worldly Wiseman's counsel to Christian. It was a hybrid of humanistic philosophy and man-centered religion. Although it was the best advice that carnal wisdom could give, it completely ignored Christian's truest need of peace with God. In this, we discover its fatal flaw!

Of what then did his counsel actually consist? He advised Christian to go to the nearby village of Morality and consult with Mr. Legality, who claimed to be skillful in the removal of burdens like the one that Christian carried. Legality, with the assistance of his son, Civility, could help him find the peace of mind he needed in order to begin enjoying life once again. Christian need not return to his former life in the City of Destruction; in fact, he did not recommend it. But neither should he continue his dangerous journey toward the Wicket Gate. He and his family could settle in the little hamlet of Morality, where living conditions were highly favorable and the necessities of life were cheap. Many houses stood empty, and Christian could have his choice of any of them. Among the inhabitants of Morality he could dwell securely, live respectably, and be happy. Or so he was led to believe!

* * * *

O, my brother or sister in Christ, how careful we should be in what we desire! The figurative town of Carnal Policy and the character of Worldly Wiseman represent a way of thinking that is characteristic of all unsaved men. However, this worldly mindset can find its way into our thoughts as well. The temptation to lean to our own understanding will doubtless prove a life-long battle, just as it will for Christian.

We are never more susceptible to the voice of human reason than when we nurture a discontented spirit against the providence of God. Instead of seeking instant solutions to our problems, we do well to wait upon the Lord, while trusting him and following his revealed way. When we fail to do so, alternate ways will often open before us, but they usually lead us in the wrong direction. Blatant error is easy enough to discern and reject, but subtle alteration of the truth is much harder to detect. There is no counsel more deceptive than that which mixes truth with error. Moreover, there is no by-path more treacherous than one that leads away from the Lord Jesus Christ and his cross.

Christian's particular dilemma when accosted by the Wiseman was typical of an awakened sinner seeking relief for his distress. However, when an easier way presented itself, Christian intuitively hesitated before inquiring further about the village of Morality. Why did he vacillate? He had heard the call of God's Spirit through the preaching of the Gospel and believed it. But as another voice argued against what he knew in his heart to be true, he was tempted to rethink the matter. Two ways now lay before him, and in the weakness of the moment, he yielded to the inner voice of human reason. Had not a mightier hand than his own been guiding his steps that day, Christian's pilgrimage would have come to an abrupt halt on the outskirts of Carnal Policy.

Study Questions

1. What sort of place was the town of Carnal Policy? What was its connection with the City of Destruction?

2. Who is Mr. Worldly Wiseman and what does he represent? What is significant about his deliberate encounter with Christian?

3. Why was Christian willing to receive unsolicited advice from a perfect stranger, especially when it contradicted what Evangelist had told him?

4. What was the substance of the counsel given by Mr. Worldly Wiseman? Could it be safely followed, or did it contain a fatal flaw?

5. After listening to the Wiseman from Carnal Policy, two ways now lay before Christian. Why did he hesitate before heading toward the village of Morality?

CHAPTER 6

By-Path to the Village of Morality

SINCE HUMANISTIC PHILOSOPHY RARELY ENDORSES OUTRIGHT WICKED-ness, few people recognize it as the spiritual enemy it really is. In practical matters, it endorses a code of moral behavior as being in the best interest of all concerned. Moreover, it often sanctions a form of godliness that can be achieved through human effort. As we are about to see, Legality, Civility, and the village of Morality are products of this way of thinking. Worldly Wiseman represents the philosophy itself, which is why his supposedly good counsel will only make matters worse for Christian.

It bears repeating that the character of any counsel is best known by the direction in which it leads. Proverbs 14:12 explicitly warns: *There is a way which seemeth right unto a man, but the end thereof are the ways of death.* Human reason is one such way, and by giving heed to it, Christian was heading straight toward the edge of a dangerous precipice. The outcries of his guilty conscience and the concern for his eternal welfare were pressing him so heavily that he could think of little else. Until this vital issue was settled, even as he spoke of his beloved family, he described himself as being like one of "those who had none."

Hence, the tyranny of the urgent brought him to a place where two ways meet. Should he follow the way in which Evangelist had directed him? Should he take the seemingly easier route endorsed by Mr. Wiseman? Which way should he go? Sadly, the thought of a quick remedy for his trouble was a greater temptation than he could resist.

The road that Christian now followed was a little country lane meandering gently downhill before reaching the scenic village. Although Morality lacks the grandeur of Carnal Policy, many people prefer its small-town charm. As a rule, its residents are hardworking individuals known for their decency and respectability. Therefore, a wholesome atmosphere pervades the area.

The village is nestled in the midst of rolling hills dotted here and there with beautiful farmsteads. Various kinds of livestock graze the rich pastureland for which the area is noted. Broad fields and orchards are filled with healthy crops that will soon be ready for harvest. Bright red barns and other neatly kept outbuildings complete the pleasant rural setting.

Away from the bright lights and incessant clamor of its larger neighbor, Morality is a peaceful community where its people live together in seeming harmony. They find the proximity to Carnal Policy convenient, however, since a natural affinity exists between the two places.

Like the surrounding countryside, the town is known and admired for its wholesome appearance. Most every building and private home is kept in immaculate condition. The same holds true for those houses that stand vacant, and for some strange reason, there are quite a number of these. Yards are beautifully maintained and fences kept freshly painted and in excellent repair. In like manner, every street and public area is neat, clean, and attractive.

The village's pleasant exterior can also be observed in its residents. Insofar as outward appearance can tell, they are morally upright and considered to be persons of good repute. Locked doors and security systems are a rarity because crime is virtually nonexistent here. In fact, the residents are noted for their benevolence toward others as well as their personal integrity.

While Carnal Policy allows scope for the lusts of the flesh, that is not the case in Morality. Its local ordinances are designed to keep any sort of lewd conduct outside its borders. Since establishments that encourage moral vice are forbidden, the somewhat decadent spirit of the adjacent town is not felt in its smaller neighbor. No effort is spared to protect the villagers from contamination by outside influences. By working hard, doing good deeds, living moral lives and abstaining from outward vices, most of the residents manage to keep up appearances.

If judged solely by the outward, this little town would seem the ideal place to live and raise a family. Why then are so many of its houses vacant, given that the cost of living is so low? Could it be that the town's exterior fails to tell the whole story? Is it really the Utopia it appears to be, or like its near neighbor, does Morality also harbor a terrible secret? Are the private homes as clean and nice inside as their exteriors indicate? For that matter, what about the village residents? Are they really what they seem to be, or does something quite different lie hidden beneath their outward demeanor?

The answers to these questions are found in the persons of Mr. Legality and his son, Civility. To quote John Bunyan, these two specialize in helping those who are "crazed in their wits" by such burdens as Christian carried. In other words, they claim to have a remedy for those who are suffering from a guilty conscience and the fear of God's judgment. Many troubled souls have already consulted them for help, and those who followed their advice now populate the village. By listening to the forceful words and false promises of Mr. Worldly Wiseman, Christian was now headed in the very same direction. However, little did he suspect the grave danger to which it would expose him.

The supposedly good counsel that pointed Christian toward the house of Legality was really deadly error. If followed, it would lead him away from Christ alone for salvation and into the way of self-righteousness. Like Cain, it is in the nature of fallen man to think that he can make himself good enough to be acceptable in God's sight. (Genesis 3:3-5; 1 John 3:12; Jude 11) Yet every such attempt is done in ignorance of God's perfect righteousness and what his justice requires.

One day, those who go this route will discover that their very best was not good enough. All thought of merit must be repudiated! There is enough sin in our very best works to condemn us before God, to say nothing of our secret thoughts. Carnal reason whispered to Christian that safety, fellowship, and contentment could be had on easy terms in the village of Morality. But it was all a lie!

Since there is no true virtue apart from godliness, the quality of being morally good must never be mistaken for a Christ-like character. While godly people are indeed moral, those who are outwardly decent are not necessarily godly. Human goodness at its highest will always fall short of the divine standard of perfect righteousness. However, the village's abundant population is proof that many believe doing their best is good enough to obtain God's favor. This explains why the picturesque little town has become the haven of many a deluded soul.

A godly character is the result of a living union with Christ through regeneration. Therefore, godliness goes far deeper than the exterior. Those who possess this quality have received both cleansing (purification) from sin, and the imputation of the perfect righteousness of Christ. When this godly principle dwells within, it produces the fruit of a Christ-like character.

Those who settle in the village of Morality are content with the mere appearance that all is well with their souls. They may deceive themselves and others, but they cannot deceive God. Religious pretense is a poor substitute for true piety, a cheap counterfeit for the work of God's Spirit in the hearts of his children. (Titus 3:5) This thought brings to mind the many houses that stand vacant in the town. Does not this suggest that many who choose the route of self-righteousness eventually abandon it and return to their former condition, or worse? (Matthew 12:43-45) In all likelihood, it does.

* * * *

As the village founder, Legality embodies the spirit of Morality. He represents man's attempt to establish his own righteousness by keeping God's law to an acceptable degree. (Romans 3:19-26) Civility, the offspring of self-righteousness, portrays the outward behavior of the residents, which can be summed up as a moral exterior coupled with a courteous way of dealing with others.

Therefore, father and son make a good team as they govern the town. Although the two of them manifest it in a more subtle form, they possess the same spirit as Mr. Wiseman. Moreover, their close relationship with him labels their religion as the brainchild of carnal reason. My friend, it is a three-fold cord of deception that is not easily broken.

Study Questions

1. Does the immaculate exterior of the little village accurately reflect its character? Or does Morality harbor a terrible secret?

2. Why are there so many empty houses in the village of Morality? Could it be that the town's residents are not at all what they appear to be?

3. How does the theology of Mr. Legality keep the town spirit of hypocrisy and self-righteousness alive and well?

CHAPTER 7

The Secret Place of Thunder

I AM HAPPY TO TELL YOU THAT CHRISTIAN NEVER REACHED THE VILLAGE of Morality that day. A terrifying obstacle stood in his way, a high, smoking hill with violent thunder and lightning bolts issuing from its summit. At the sight, Christian was nearly paralyzed with fear, and his burden seemed an unbearable weight. He dared not approach any nearer, for the mountain seemed ready to fall upon him. Thus Christian was providentially hindered from ever reaching Legality's house. Mt. Sinai prevented him from making that fatal mistake.

Worldly Wiseman's scheme had utterly failed, but it was hardly due to Christian's superior discernment. He had made a grievous error by yielding to the voice of carnal reason. Yet we have cause to believe that those better things that accompany salvation were at work within him, even though he had been sidetracked for the present. (Hebrews 6:9)

Why did the sudden appearance of Sinai cause Christian to stop dead in his tracks and rue the day he listened to Wiseman? The justice of God and his holy law form an impassable barrier between the quickened sinner and any thought of making himself righteous. From the *secret place of thunder*, Christian heard the message clearly. (Psalm 81:7) This mountain was no hiding place where he could flee from the wrath of God, and neither was the village of Morality. In this, we perceive the gracious design of God's law.

Within his law, God's holy character and the demands of his justice are plainly made known. As Christian looked more closely into the mirror of God's Word, he realized that the quality of being morally good could never make him acceptable in God's sight. In addition, this clearer understanding increased his sense of guilt and his awareness of impending judgment. Therefore, he shuddered with fear at the base of the mountain, unaware that divine mercy was in close pursuit of his soul.

For those who are content with a form of godliness, fiery Sinai is no barrier at all. Being ignorant of having broken God's holy law, they pass by it easily and settle comfortably in the little village beyond it. Although they dwell beneath its very shadow, they are satisfied with doing their best and presuming that God will accept it as well. With hearts that are deceived and consciences that have been lulled to sleep, they rest securely upon a false hope.

However, this is not the case with one who knows he has broken God's law and stands condemned by it. Along with the knowledge that he can never be justified by the works of the law, there comes the understanding that the law can do nothing to remove his guilt. At best, it can only bring him to a guilty silence. (Romans 3:19)

Now more strongly than ever, Christian knew he needed a hiding place from the wrath to come. Given that he had turned out of the proper path, the thought occurred to him that perhaps all hope was lost. Yet even as he trembled in fear and uncertainty, he saw his faithful friend, Evangelist, coming toward him. Here was one who could offer genuine help, but poor Christian was ashamed to face him.

Since Evangelist genuinely loved Christian, he did not hesitate to rebuke him sharply. Unlike Mr. Wiseman, he did not placate Christian or offer an immediate solution to his problem. As a faithful man of God, he instructed Christian more perfectly concerning Christ as the only hope of sinful men. A major part of his teaching centered upon the dangers to which Christian had exposed himself.

As he listened attentively to Evangelist, Christian better understood the nature of his recent mistake. By giving heed to carnal reason, he had turned out of the right way and rejected the counsel of God. Although not deliberately done, he had committed a grave error. The easier solution to Christian's burden amounted to putting on the guise of a hypocrite, which was something the Lord Jesus Christ harshly condemned in Matthew 23:25-28. True righteousness is the gift of God's free grace through the merits of Christ and his redemption alone. There is no acceptable substitute for it. The legalistic hypocrite may claim to be a Christian, but in lacking the perfect righteousness of Christ, he is like the man who was found not wearing the required wedding garment. (Matthew 7:21-23; Matthew 22:10-13)

By the mercy and power of God, Christian was delivered from this deadly snare. He now saw the town of Morality in its true character; it was a haven for religious hypocrites. There was nothing for him there, no peace, no relief, and certainly no safety. With this deeper understanding, he also saw the Wiseman in a clearer light. In spite of his arrogant manner and boasted wisdom, he was spiritually ignorant and very likely to remain that way. (Proverbs 26:12) Worse still, his perverted view of Christ and his cross showed him to be a fool of the worst sort. How could he possibly offer good counsel to Christian or any other person on the way to the Celestial City? In fact, do we not detect the subtle hiss of the serpent behind his smooth, persuasive words? (Genesis 3:1-5)

Thus the wisdom of this world is characterized by both folly and spiritual ignorance. Therefore, it stands in sharp contrast to true logic and flies in the face of divine wisdom. (Proverbs 9:10; John 1:1-5) Paradoxically, it is through the cross of Christ that the wisdom of God is most highly exalted and man's wisdom set at naught. (1 Corinthians 1:18-25) Yet worldly wisdom remains a stronghold that is deeply rooted in the human mind. Earthly weapons cannot conquer it. The casting down of carnal reason only takes place as the thought processes are brought into subjection to Christ through his Spirit. (2 Corinthians 10:3-6) When through the power of the Gospel, the stronghold of worldly wisdom is dethroned in the mind, spiritual ignorance and folly are routed as well.

Although those who visit Legality for help are unaware of it, his house is strategically placed near this field of battle in order to deceive the gullible. Since John Bunyan tells us that the village founder is the son of the bondwoman, we might well ask how he could help others to be rid of their burdens. (Galatians 4:21-25) It is a good question! His area of expertise was actually in deceiving men and leading them to perdition, while carefully hiding the fact. In this task he was joined by his son, Civility. Together they accomplish their purpose through subtle alteration of the truth.

The purity of the Gospel is tainted whenever anything is added to or taken from it. The ministers of Christ are commissioned to hold fast to the one true Gospel and proclaim it faithfully. (1 Corinthians 2:1-5) They willingly accept this charge and fulfill it to the best of their ability, but others are not so scrupulous. Disguised as wolves in sheep's clothing, they raise their voices in subtle opposition to the truth. Legality and Civility were of this sort, striking at the very heart of the Gospel by perverting the truth of justification by faith in Christ alone. There is no deadlier error than that of adding man's works to the grace of God. Like oil and water, God's grace in Christ will not adhere to even the best of man's works. The attempted synthesis does not merely form a useless mixture. It produces a lethal one. (Galatians 2:16-21)

Note the horror and consternation in the apostle Paul's words as he rebuked those who had yielded to this very same error:

O foolish Galatians, who hath bewitched you, that ye should not obey the truth, before whose eyes Jesus Christ hath been evidently set forth, crucified among you? This only would I learn of you, Received ye the Spirit by the works of the law, or by the hearing of faith? Are ye so foolish? Having begun in the Spirit, are ye now made perfect by the flesh? (Galatians 3:1-3)

This severe correction underscores the danger of listening to such false voices. They can beguile and seduce us away from Christ if we listen to them. Therefore, we must reject them soundly and hold tenaciously to the truth. (Galatians 3:10-14)

What about those who have traveled far down the path to Zion and acquired a fair measure of wisdom and spiritual discernment? Are we safe from the danger of false voices because we have known the Lord for a long time? No! We could quite possibly be more susceptible, if we should fall into the trap of over-confidence. Paul gave a solemn warning that we should keep continually in heart and mind when he said: *Wherefore let him that thinketh he standeth take heed lest he fall.* (1 Corinthians 10:12) We will never advance so far in grace that we are immune to such a fall, and never attain sufficient wisdom and knowledge so as not to need more. In order to remain steadfast in the path of life, we must continually grow in the grace and knowledge of our Lord and Savior Jesus Christ. (2 Peter 3:17-18)

Was Worldly Wiseman an actual person, or the promptings of Christian's own human reason? The answer is really beside the point, although most believers in Christ would probably incline toward the latter view. Can we honestly say that we have never encountered him or felt the influence of Carnal Policy's humanistic spirit? Have we ever been tempted to seek help from Mr. Legality and Civility in the village of Morality? Do we dare say that we have never listened to these voices, and by the grace of God, been saved from ourselves? Sadly, we cannot! When faced with difficulty, our flesh will always seek the easier route of human reason, if allowed to have its way.

Although Christian desired immediate relief from his heavy burden, his greater need was peace with God. (Ephesians 2:11-17) Jesus Christ is the sinner's only hiding place, the city of refuge for our guilty souls. Our burden of sin can only be taken away through his cross. Then peace with God will yield the fruit of the peace of God ruling in our hearts.

Wiseman was right about one thing, however. The pilgrim's way is filled with many dangers, difficulties, and trials. The Lord Jesus Christ never deceived his would-be followers on this point. On the contrary, he explicitly warned them to count the cost before placing their hands on the Gospel plow. (Luke 9:62) Once our hand is placed upon it, there must be no looking back.

The way of Christ will never be the easy path, but it alone leads to the heavenly Zion. Hymn writer Katharina von Schlegel expressed this well when she wrote:

> Be still, my soul: the Lord is on thy side;
> bear patiently the cross of grief and pain;
> Leave to thy God to order and provide;
> in every change he faithful will remain.
> Be still, my soul: thy best, thy heavenly friend,
> through thorny ways leads to a joyful end. [1]

It was toward this joyful end that Christian aspired. By God's grace, he had received the heart of a true pilgrim, and this was evident by his penitent spirit when he came to understand his sin. (Ezekiel 36:26-28) Although the providence of God had allowed him to stumble, provision for his recovery had been right at hand. The timely appearance of Evangelist illustrates the primary way in which God keeps his people safe in the path of life. In an instrumental sense, he is saving us through the faithful ministry of men whom he has called for this purpose. Thus the apostle Paul admonishes young pastor Timothy:

Let no man despise thy youth; but be thou an example of the believers, in word, in conversation, in charity, in spirit, in faith, in purity. Till I come, give attendance to reading, to exhortation, to doctrine. Neglect not the gift that is in thee, which was given thee by prophecy, with the laying on of the hands of the presbytery. Meditate upon these things; give thyself wholly to them; that thy profiting may appear to all. Take heed unto thyself, and unto the doctrine; continue in them: for in doing this thou shalt both save thyself, and them that hear thee. (I Timothy 4:12-16)

What a comfort it is to know that God does not save us and then leave us drifting on a sea of spiritual confusion! His Word is the chart and compass by which our journey to the Celestial City is safely made, and his ministers are faithful watchmen who show us the way. Two related exhortations concerning the vital nature of their ministry are given in the book of Hebrews. In chapter 13:7-9, we are admonished to follow the example of the godly minister's faith and manner of life. In verse 17 of the same chapter, we are commanded to submit to their spiritual oversight; we are to hear, receive, and obey the Word of God as they proclaim it.

To the ministers of Christ, the preaching of the Gospel is central, and the things concerning his kingdom are of paramount importance. So they labor to know him more perfectly, to understand his Word, and to faithfully proclaim it. Evangelist was such a man. From the fact that he intervened at once, we can infer that he cared deeply for Christian and was close at hand in case he was needed.

Primarily, his rebuke consisted of exposing Wiseman, Legality, and Civility for the enemies they really are. We cannot know all that Evangelist said to Christian, but we can safely assume that his correction was given from the Word of God. Perhaps he began by quoting the apostle Paul's indignant rebuke, as recorded in Galatians 1:6-9:

I marvel that ye are so soon removed from him that called you into the grace of Christ unto another gospel: Which is not another; but there be some that trouble you, and would pervert the gospel of Christ. But though we, or an angel from heaven, preach any other gospel unto you than that which we have preached unto you, let him be accursed. As we said before, so say I now again, if any man preach any other gospel unto you than that ye have received, let him be accursed.

As Evangelist continued his reproof, he may well have repeated the scriptural warning given in Colossians 2:8: *Beware lest any man spoil you through philosophy and vain deceit, after the tradition of men, after the rudiments of the world, and not after Christ.* Then he may have expressed his deep love and concern for Christian by saying, again with the apostle Paul:

Would to God ye could bear with me a little in my folly: and indeed bear with me. For I am jealous over you with godly jealousy: for I have espoused you to one husband, that I may present you as a chaste virgin to Christ. But I fear, lest by any means, as the serpent beguiled Eve through his subtilty, so your minds should be corrupted from the simplicity that is in Christ. (2 Corinthians 11:1-3)

It is highly significant that Christian's recent misstep was due to poor spiritual judgment rather than willful disobedience. Moreover, his reaction to the severe rebuke says more about him than the fact that reproof was necessary. Rather than becoming defensive and resentful toward the man of God, Christian received his correction with a humble, repentant spirit and a grateful heart. In so doing, he manifested an important characteristic of Zion's true children. (Proverbs 9:9)

Christian's greatest concern at this point was whether, after such a false step, he could still pursue the way that leads to life. Had God abandoned him because of his sin? Was all hope now lost? No, he could proceed to the Wicket Gate once again, but he had better not listen to any other false voices and wander out of the way of truth again. (Psalm 2:12)

With a final word of exhortation, Evangelist directed Christian toward the same path as before. Thus the poor burdened man resumed his journey, drawn more strongly than ever toward the light that leads to the Wicket Gate.

* * * *

My friend in Christ, if you and I are to remain in the right path, we also must firmly reject the counsel of Worldly Wiseman and his kind. Human wisdom always adds something of man's doing to God's salvation, but like the stone altar commanded in Exodus 20:25, anything of man's contribution defiles it. Some try to make the Gospel more acceptable to natural men by altering it in some way, but to do so is equivalent to raising a carving tool to the stones of the altar. Anything that man adds to the finished redemption of Christ perverts it into another gospel.

Charles H. Spurgeon expressed this truth perfectly when he said, "The Lord alone must be exalted in the work of atonement, and not a single mark of man's chisel or hammer will be endured. There is an inherent blasphemy in seeking to add to what Christ Jesus in his dying moments declared to be finished." [2]

Mount Sinai, the secret place of thunder, was never meant to be a hiding place for souls who are weary and heavy laden. No rest or relief is to be found at that smoking, fiery hill. If we would be free from our burden of guilt and sin, we must come to the hill of Mount Calvary. We must come to none other than the Lord Jesus Christ. (Galatians 2:16)

Indignant justice stood in view, to Sinai's fiery mount I flew;
But Justice cried with frowning face, "This mountain is no hiding place!"
Ere long a heavenly voice I heard, and mercy's angel form appeared;
Who led me on with gentle pace, to Jesus Christ my hiding place. [3]

Study Questions

1. Why did Christian never make it to the village of Morality that day? How did the sudden appearance of Mount Sinai bring him to a standstill?

2. Once again Evangelist appeared on the scene, this time to rebuke and correct Christian. List some of the things Christian learned from his instruction.

3. In what sense were Mr. Legality and his son wolves in sheep's clothing? Why is it so dangerous to listen to such voices?

4. Although Christian desired deliverance from his heavy burden, what was his greater need?

5. The timely intervention of Evangelist illustrates the primary way that God keeps his people in the path of life. How do the ministers of Christ fulfill this great task?

Part Three

WITH THE FORCE OF A LODESTONE

Then spake Jesus again unto them, saying,
I am the light of the world: he that followeth me shall not
walk in darkness, but shall have the light of life.

John 8:12

CHAPTER 8

The Light that Leads to the Wicket Gate

I LOVE LIGHTHOUSES! SILENT WATCHMEN OF THE NIGHT! BEACONS OF hope to those in peril on the sea! Whether shrouded in mystery, or the subject of local legend, each lighthouse has its own unique story and special place in maritime history.

Although lighthouses have long held a particular fascination for me, it is perhaps not for the same reasons that most people are drawn to them. In common with others, I love to contemplate their invaluable service to those traveling by sea, especially in times past. My imagination is stirred as I think of the days before electric lights, when the coastlines were hidden in darkness each night. What a welcome sight the beam from the lighthouse must have been in those days!

One well-beloved beacon is located on Hatteras Island in the tiny village of Buxton, North Carolina. It stands guard over a notoriously hazardous cape where the warm waters of the Gulf Stream merge with the frigid Labrador Current. In addition, miles of submerged and shifting sandbars (shoals) lie hidden just below the surface, creating an extremely dangerous stretch of ocean. Numerous ships with their entire crews lie silent beneath these turbulent waters, which have justly earned the nickname "The Graveyard of the Atlantic."

The Cape Hatteras Light, also known as America's Lighthouse, has another interesting claim to fame. In 1999, it was moved one-half of a mile from its original site to protect it from the eroding shoreline. Its familiar day mark, a bold black and white spiral pattern, adorns the coastal landscape by day. However, its service does not really begin until the evening.

This quiet hour is my favorite time to visit another Outer Banks lighthouse, Bodie Island, my personal favorite. My husband and I love to go there after sunset and sit on the back porch of the light-keeper's house, waiting for the first beam of light from her powerful first-order Fresnel lens. Under the cover of twilight, we have watched as white-tailed deer venture from the forest and enter the clearing around the base of the tower. On several occasions, we heard the distinctive hoot of a Great-Horned Owl keeping vigil from one of the recessed windows of the lighthouse.

As evening progresses into night, an almost palpable darkness covers the land. Away from the artificial lights of distant coastal villages, one is dazzled as he looks toward heaven and sees the Milky Way in its splendor, a magnificent sight declaring the transcendent power and glory of its Creator. It is in the stillness of this hour that I can best meditate upon the lighthouse and her metaphorical significance.

No doubt, the day will come when the function of the lighthouse is obsolete, yet multitudes will continue to visit them. Why are they a source of such compelling interest? In some cases, I suspect it is because of the legends and aura of mystery that often surrounds them. After all, lighthouses are frequently associated with tragic events, and some of them are thought to be haunted. Their greater appeal is probably due to what they represent, both a warning against the treachery of the sea and timely guidance into a safe harbor. It is easy enough to imagine the terror and despair of a mariner lost amidst a raging sea. One can almost feel his thankful heart when he catches sight of the familiar beacon shining through the stormy night and knows that he is almost home.

Dear friend in Christ, the lighthouse also speaks to us of something infinitely more precious, does it not? It reminds us of our Lord Jesus Christ and his gracious words: *I am the light of the world: he that followeth me shall not walk in darkness, but shall have the light of life.* (John 8:12) In the nightly watch of the lighthouse beacon, I think of the Gospel as it goes forth into a world darkened by sin. Most will ignore the warning and go on their way to their doom, but others will hear the effectual call of God's Spirit. They will behold the light and gladly come to it. (John 6:44-47)

Therefore, when I see a lighthouse beacon shining in the night, I think of the light that leads Zion's pilgrims to the Wicket Gate. I can almost see Christian running from the City of Destruction, unable to see the gate and barely able to discern the light that radiated from it. Yet with eyes fixed upon its faint beam, and in spite of stiff opposition, he struggles hard to reach it.

I can well remember being in the same spiritual condition. Once I was also like a ship drifting upon a raging sea, with no safe harbor in sight. I was lost, helpless, without an anchor and floundering without direction until I saw that same beacon of light that Christian saw. Then being drawn with the bands of everlasting love, I fled for refuge to the hope set before me. I came to Christ, the sinner's only hiding place. (Hebrews 6:17-20) Since that day, the knowledge of what the Lord has done for my soul is never far from my thoughts. My heart is overwhelmed with gratitude as I remember the mercy and love with which he drew me unto himself and rescued me from certain destruction.

A terrible thing happened when Adam sinned against his Creator. The light of the glory of God within him was not merely dimmed, it was permanently extinguished. As a result of his sin, the entire human race became plunged into spiritual darkness. Man has need of a light to arise and shine in his soul. He needs someone to recover the glory of God's image in him, which was lost because of sin. However, he must first come to see his true condition before God.

Scripture likens salvation to a call out of darkness unto light and life in the Lord Jesus Christ. It is a radical event requiring nothing less than a spiritual resurrection, and deliverance from the power of darkness. (Ephesians 2:1-5; Colossians 1:13) By nature, man's understanding is darkened and his eyes are blind to the truth. (John 3:1-7) He neither desires nor seeks the Lord Jesus Christ. The light of his presence and power is something to be dreaded and avoided because it exposes the evil that is hidden within. (John 3:19-21) So unregenerate man shuns the light, and follows a path of his own choosing.

Ironically, this inward departure from God can be hidden beneath a religious veneer, causing men to think themselves enlightened when, in fact, they are blind. When the Lord Jesus healed the blind man in John 9, he exposed the spiritual ignorance and hypocrisy of the religious leaders of his day. They considered themselves to be the enlightened ones, and were revered as the spiritual guides and teachers of the Jewish people. Tragically, the light that was in them was really darkness, and by rejecting the one who is the light of the world, they were confirmed in that darkness.

As God's covenant people, the nation Israel historically enjoyed great spiritual advantages. It was to them alone that God made known his ways and displayed his wondrous works. (Psalm 103:7) Jehovah set his love upon this single nation and committed his oracles to their trust. (Deuteronomy 7:6-8) His law was a light to them, and so was the testimony of his prophets. John the Baptist, the last and greatest of the Old Testament prophets, was a burning and a shining light. Still greater, the Lord Jesus Christ was a light that far excelled all of these. (John 5:31-40) As we learn in John 1:4-5: *In him was life; and the life was the light of men. And the light shineth in darkness; and the darkness comprehended it not.* The eyes of men could not behold his light because their hearts and minds were hardened to the truth he spoke.

Thus he was despised and rejected, even by most of the religious leaders among the nation. Those who walked in darkness responded to his words of truth with open skepticism and derision. So even though he was the friend of sinners, even though he came to seek and to save the lost, they would have none of him. Few among them had eyes to see and behold the Lamb of God, which takes away the sin of the world. (John 1:29)

Look around you dear reader, for it is just the same today. Natural men are still content to dwell in darkness and live out their lives in the City of Destruction, seeking happiness and fulfillment in vain, perishing things. Yet there is hope, even for those who dwell in darkness. Like a lighthouse beacon shining in the night, the Gospel of Jesus Christ penetrates the darkness of a sinful world. However, unlike the welcome beam of a lighthouse, the Gospel light invades enemy territory. Satan, the god of this world and the prince of the kingdom of darkness, blinds the minds of men so that they neither understand nor desire its truth. (2 Corinthians 4:3-6) It is little wonder that the Gospel message is viewed as an unwelcome intrusion, or that it meets with such fierce opposition.

When the light of the knowledge and glory of Jesus Christ enters the soul, nature's night is vanquished. As the thoughts and intents of the sinner's heart are revealed, he sees himself, in measure, as God sees him. Self-righteousness is accounted as a garment of shame and condemnation. Self-sufficiency collapses in the realization of actual soul poverty. Carnal security evaporates as quickly as a castle in the clouds. Thus every barrier is broken down as the enlightened sinner is brought to the end of himself.

As the Spirit of God reveals the Lord Jesus Christ through his Word, he who had been blind is able to see. (Psalm 19:8; Isaiah 42:6-7) He who was deaf to the truth suddenly hears the joyful sound of the Gospel, and in hearing, he lives. (Isaiah 35:5; Isaiah 55:3) Blessed is the one who has experienced this miracle of God's amazing grace! He alone can say with the psalmist: *With thee is the fountain of life: in thy light shall we see light.* (Psalm 36:9)

The lighthouse beacon gives both warning and direction to those who travel by sea. A wise mariner will note its location and plot his course accordingly. Those who are foolish enough to disregard its light do so at their own risk. The same holds true concerning those who hear the Gospel of Christ but refuse to obey it. In supposing that they can steer their own course, they reject its light and do what is right in their own eyes.

Many parallels could be drawn between a lighthouse beacon and the light that leads to the Wicket Gate, but a notable difference exists between them as well. The sole function of the lighthouse is to warn and guide those who navigate by sea. It has no actual power to deliver anyone from danger. However, the Gospel of Jesus Christ is not a passive entity to be either heeded or disregarded at will. No one who comes under its powerful influence is left untouched. Those who refuse its light do so at the peril of their souls.

When the Gospel message is accompanied by the call of God's Spirit, it is the dynamic power of God unto salvation. (Romans 1:16) Far more than a mere warning or invitation, the Gospel carries within it the authority of divine command. (1 Peter 4:17) The duty of the lighthouse caretaker to keep the beacon burning brightly is an excellent depiction of the Gospel minister and his responsibility. He is charged with holding tenaciously to the one true Gospel, and proclaiming it plainly and faithfully to men. In making clear that salvation is in Christ alone, he discharges his duty by pointing men unto him. As the Spirit of God causes the good tidings to illuminate the heart and soul of a hearer, he does so with resurrection power, bringing the penitent sinner to Christ by faith. (John 5:21-27)

Therefore, coming to Christ is equivalent to entering the path of life through the Wicket Gate, and the Gospel is the light that shows us the way. When we hear and obey its gracious call, it is because the Sun of Righteousness has arisen in our souls with healing in his wings. (Malachi 4:2)

* * * *

This miracle of grace has already begun in the character named Christian, and sound Gospel instruction pointed him in the right direction. Godly fear, the prelude to spiritual healing, drove him toward the Wicket Gate in the knowledge of his deep need. He felt like one who has been diagnosed with an incurable disease, but it was his soul that was in jeopardy. Even though he still trembled with fear, a precious hope has been set before him. There was a balm in Gilead, even for him! So with the desperation of a drowning man grasping for a lifeline, he ran toward the only one who could help him, the Lord Jesus Christ, the Great Physician.

His entire focus was now set upon reaching the Wicket Gate. Like the irresistible force of a lodestone (a rock with magnetic properties), he was drawn toward its radiance with little thought for anything else. Although he still carried his heavy burden, deliverance was near at hand. Through the Gospel, a new day had dawned in his soul as the day star arose in his heart. (1 Peter 1:19)

O Christian, *Seek ye the LORD while he may be found, call ye upon him while he is near*! (Isaiah 55:6) Hear the words of Isaiah the prophet crying: *Arise, shine; for thy light is come, and the glory of the LORD is risen upon thee.* (Isaiah 60:1) Flee to the light while it beckons to you, and let nothing make you linger! The Lord Jesus Christ said: *Come unto me, all ye that labor and are heavy laden, and I will give you rest.* (Matthew 11:28) Make haste and run to him without further delay!

Study Questions

1. In what way does a lighthouse remind us of the Lord Jesus Christ? Give a Scripture reference to support your answer.

2. If the Gospel of Christ is the light that leads to the Wicket Gate, how is a lighthouse beacon a picture of it?

3. Why do unsaved people reject the light of the Gospel and refuse to believe it?

4. Explain how salvation is a call out of darkness and into light and life.

5. When the Spirit of God reveals Christ to the sinner's heart, what are the effects of it? What evidence do we have that this miracle of grace had taken place in Christian?

CHAPTER 9

Beatitude of Sovereign Grace

Human ingenuity has devised many ways in which men think to obtain peace with God and gain the hope of eternal life. However, man's highest efforts in this regard will never succeed in altering or expanding what God has strictly defined. All such efforts merge to form the broad way that leads to destruction. Therefore, in seeking to be the master of his own destiny, man seals his doom as a rebel against God.

True Christianity stands apart from all humanistic religions for many reasons, the foremost of these being that it alone has a living, reigning Lord and a cross. (Luke 14:26-33) It centers in the person of the Lord Jesus Christ, and the essence of its narrow way lies in self-denial and following him wherever he leads. Those who know the grace of God in salvation love this narrow way, but human wisdom despises the way of the cross, and man's pride is offended by its implications. In its most devious form, humanistic religion perverts the Gospel of Christ while giving lip service to it. Worldly Wiseman and his cronies are among those who heartily endorse this brand of Christianity.

There is but one way that leads to the heavenly Zion, and it lies beyond the figurative Wicket Gate. Scripture calls it the path of the just, and compares it to the shining light that shines more and more unto the perfect day. (Proverbs 4:18) Most people never see this light; consequently, they miss both the Wicket Gate and the narrow pathway beyond it. However, those who do behold its quickening rays will flee to the Lord Jesus Christ for refuge.

In this, we understand that saving faith is more than intellectual persuasion or mental consent to the propositions of the Gospel. While these things are essential, true faith is the revelation of Jesus Christ to the soul. When the Spirit of God shines into our hearts and imparts saving faith, we behold the Lamb of God, and in beholding, we live.

From the very outset of our journey, our eyes are fixed upon our eternal home. Having tasted that the Lord is gracious, we find that the former things once valued so highly have lost their appeal. Our hearts are now set upon things higher and more excellent, for we serve a new master. Earthly cares may still press heavily upon us, and we could yet be sidetracked upon occasion. Our hearts will undoubtedly be troubled now and then, and our minds subject to doubt and confusion. Yet nothing will disrupt or overthrow God's purpose for his children. Through the power of his Spirit and the light of his Word, he keeps our eyes fixed upon the Lord Jesus Christ, and guides our steps onward and upward.

An incorruptible inheritance awaits all of those who complete the journey that begins with their entrance through the Wicket Gate. In that day, no one will boast of his merits or claim credit for success-fully finishing his course. The universal cry of the redeemed will be: *Worthy is the Lamb that was slain to receive power, and riches, and wisdom, and strength, and honour, and glory, and blessing.* (Revelation 5:12)

As we have witnessed in the man named Christian, a radical upheaval must take place within before one will seek the Lord Jesus Christ. This violent shaking is the necessary prelude to our entrance through the Wicket Gate. Thus entry therein is attended with great difficulty, which is figuratively comparable to the agony of natural childbirth. We observed this spiritual travail taking place in Christian even before he fled from the City of Destruc-tion. Prior to that time, he had been happy enough with his life there, until the Spirit of God shook him to the very core. Under this terrible conviction, he was persuaded that the City of Destruc-tion could not provide the things he now craved the most, such as peace with God and a conscience free from condemnation. In order to find them, Christian had to forsake the place of his birth, his natural heritage in Adam.

From the very beginning of his journey, trouble seemed to dog his steps. While some of it came from outside sources, most of it resided within Christian himself. When he yielded to the voice of human reason, he committed a serious offence that could have proved his undoing. He learned a valuable lesson from the experience, however, as should we. Even though his error was unintentional, he now realized just how easily his own heart could deceive him and lead him astray. Therefore, Christian's narrow escape outside the village of Morality left an impression that he was not likely to forget.

When he finally neared the Wicket Gate, its beacon was shining so brightly that he could see something in the road just ahead. At first there appeared to be a solid wall across the path, but a closer look revealed the outline of a very small door. It was the Wicket Gate! He had reached it at last! Now he could see that the tiny door was actually built into a massive wall that blocked the path. It was, in fact, the only way to reach the narrow pathway located on the other side of the wall.

The small size of the gate is worthy of our attention, for it indicates a strictly limited point of access. Since it was barely large enough to admit one person at a time, travelers could carry nothing with them as they passed through. Another peculiar thing about the Wicket Gate was that there was no mechanism by which to open it from the outside. How was Christian to get through? Should it not be standing wide open so that poor, weary souls could enter in? What was he to do now? Had he come all this way for nothing?

Upon closer inspection, he saw something that had escaped his notice before. Over the lintel of the tiny door was an inscription that said: *Knock, and it shall be opened unto you.* How his heart leaped for joy as he read those words! There was a welcome for sin-burdened pilgrims here after all! The Wicket Gate offers a gracious reception to all who come to it. Even though the traveler cannot open the door himself, an unseen gatekeeper waits on the other side, ready to receive those who knock for admission. (Matthew 7:7-8 John 6:37)

Dear fellow believer, once again it is time to remind ourselves that we are in the realm of the allegorical. The Wicket Gate is a picture of the strait gate and narrow way of which the Lord Jesus Christ spoke in Matthew 7:13-14. As such, it represents the very essence of the Christian experience, the focal point upon which the destiny of the soul rests. Any deviation from it places one into the mainstream of those who are on the broad way to destruction. No matter how zealous or sincere one may be, there is no alternative to the Wicket Gate. All who would enter the Celestial City must first enter here.

Just as deliverance from the City of Destruction is a solitary event between an individual and Christ, so is entrance into the Wicket Gate. Christian was alone when he finally arrived there, but this does not suggest that he had abandoned his family. He was still with them, loving and providing for them just as before. However, a great gulf now existed between him and his loved ones.

Likewise, entrance into the Wicket Gate is not a physical act. It takes place in the soul, and is by faith in Christ alone. The ever-increasing light that shows us the way denotes a clearer understanding of the Gospel of Christ, and the narrow size of the gate signifies that we must enter empty-handed. There is no room to carry the trappings of our former life. No efforts, works, talents or credentials will avail to secure our admission. Leaving all thought of worthiness behind, we must come to the Lord Jesus Christ as poor and needy sinners.

Many times, a deeply troubled conscience will cause one to hesitate in coming to Christ when it should compel him all the sooner. While an attitude of self-righteousness or entitlement will certainly exclude one from the Wicket Gate, the knowledge of one's sinful condition never will. So those who think themselves worthy need not apply, but those who know their need of Christ may freely come to him and buy wine and milk without money and without price. (Isaiah 55:1)

The hymn writer Joseph Hart, expressed the love of the Savior toward heavy-laden sinners when he wrote these precious, encouraging words:

Come, ye sinners, poor and needy, weak and wounded, sick and sore;
Jesus ready stands to save you, full of pity, love and power.
Come, ye thirsty, come, and welcome, God's free bounty glorify;
True belief and true repentance, every grace that brings you nigh.
Let not conscience make you linger, nor of fitness fondly dream;
All the fitness he requireth is to feel your need of him.
Come, ye weary, heavy laden, lost and ruined by the fall;
If you tarry till you're better, you will never come at all. [1]

The response of new-born faith causes the quickened sinner to cry with a grateful heart:

> I will arise and go to Jesus, he will embrace me in his arms;
> In the arms of my dear Savior, O, there are ten thousand charms.[2]

* * * *

How the power and glory of God are displayed every time a ransomed soul is delivered from destruction! When commenting upon Psalm 110:3, Charles H. Spurgeon wrote, "None are saved unwillingly, but the will is made sweetly to yield itself. What a wondrous power is this, which never violates the will, and yet rules it! God does not break the lock, but he opens it by a master key which he alone can handle." [3]

In poetic language that is really a beatitude of sovereign grace, Psalm 65:4 expresses the return of a soul to God, and the eternal implications of that return. Writing under divine inspiration, King David wrote: *Blessed is the man whom thou choosest, and causest to approach unto thee, that he may dwell in thy courts: we shall be satisfied with the goodness of thy house, even of thy holy temple.*

Blessed indeed are those who are the recipients of God's mercy and the happy objects of his gracious choice! Having been brought nigh unto him through the precious blood of Christ, we are destined to appear before him in Zion, and live in his presence forevermore. The figurative Wicket Gate portrays this new and living way in which sinners may come to God through the Lord Jesus Christ. (Hebrews 10:19-22)

As Christian stood before the fast-closed gate, he knew that he must not only enter therein, but also walk the narrow path beyond it. Moreover, in common with all who have gone before him, he must enter by faith, not knowing what lies ahead. Since entrance through the Wicket Gate is strictly one-way, spiritually speaking it is the point of no return. Yet a much clearer understanding of Christ and his redemptive work lies beyond it. There are things to learn that are most excellent and rare, and precious treasure to encourage his heart along the way. So with a trembling frame and a palpitating heart, the burdened man raised his hand to the tiny door and resolutely knocked.

Study Questions

1. In what way does true Christianity stand apart from all humanistic religions?

2. How does saving faith differ from mere intellectual persuasion?

3. What did Christian see when he finally reached the Wicket Gate?

4. The allegorical Wicket Gate is the strait gate and narrow way spoken of by the Lord Jesus Christ. As such, what does it represent?

5. What does it mean to enter the Wicket Gate?

CHAPTER 10

Through the Wicket Gate!

THE SOVEREIGNTY OF GOD IN SALVATION IS A TRULY WONDROUS THING, and so is the uniqueness with which he has created each one of us. Although these grand truths stretch the limits of our human comprehension, we can understand that our heavenly Father designed our course in this life with an infinitely wise purpose in mind. Moreover, the various means and circumstances he uses in order to bring it about are as individual as we are.

There is one vital thing that all of God's children share in common, however. Through the working of his secret providence, every one of them hears the joyful sound of the Gospel and comes to Christ as a guilty sinner with nothing to bring and no merit to plead. They come to the Wicket Gate as humble petitioners and enter it by faith. Does this mean that they are better than those who refuse to come? No, it does not! The grace of God alone makes one to differ from those who harden their hearts against the truth. (1Corinthians 4:7)

As the vigorous cry of a newborn infant means that he is alive and well, so the earnest prayer of a soul at the Wicket Gate denotes that he has received spiritual life. By nature, no one desires or wills to come to Christ. Those who seek him do so because they have been drawn by everlasting love. (Jeremiah 31:3; John 6:44-45)

The Savior's mission, the work that the Father gave him to do, was to seek and to save that which was lost. (Luke 19:10) Having come into the world to redeem them with his own precious blood, he now seeks his sheep and brings them into his fold. (John 10:9-18) In this, he fulfills the express will of the Father. (John 6:37-40)

Therefore, no sinner need fear that mercy's door will be barred against him. The good shepherd who gave his life for the sheep will never abandon them in their distress and leave them desolate, outside the gate. Any seeming delay in answering their cry is only a waiting that he may be gracious. (Isaiah 30:18) Is it possible for a thirsty soul to be denied the water of life? Never! Many fears will trouble the hearts and minds of those who tremble at the Wicket Gate, but fear of rejection should not be one of them. (Revelation 22:17)

As noted before, knocking at the gate is equivalent to coming to Christ by faith and calling upon him for mercy. Like Christian as he stood at its threshold, we have no idea what lies ahead when we seek admission there. Not only must we enter in by faith, we must walk the path beyond it in exactly the same way. Moreover, our Lord would have us clearly understand that once we enter this narrow gate, we take an irrevocable step.

With all of his attention focused upon the tiny door, Christian failed to notice that there was a castle situated nearby, just a little distance from the path. It was an ancient fortress, with something evil and forbidding about it. The absence of windows indicated that it must be very dark inside. However, there were numerous slits in its walls, which were just large enough to permit archers to fire their arrows at unsuspecting travelers who passed by.

Although this castle is very old, it remains incredibly strong and virtually impregnable. Its gigantic portcullis is rarely opened and the adjacent gatehouse and outer wall are heavily guarded at all times. The massive towers and ramparts of the citadel provide ample battle stations from which to launch a full-scale attack against those who happen to come within range. Altogether, this stronghold is a fearsome-looking place, suggesting the power and dominion of a dark, evil lord.

This is indeed the case! While such castles were primarily designed to offer sanctuary and protection from hostile invasion, this one was built for the express purpose of waging offensive warfare. Its huge central tower, the castle's keep, is stocked with an arsenal of highly effective weapons and legions of soldiers who are skillful in their use.

The prince who rules over this dark fortress had a particularly evil design in mind when placing it so close to the Wicket Gate. From that convenient position, he can lie in wait and quickly muster his forces whenever he sees a burdened soul struggling toward the tiny door. What's worse, the element of surprise is all on his side. Unsuspecting travelers are far too preoccupied to notice the danger lurking nearby.

A casual bystander watching Christian come within range of the enemy's castle would surely wonder what chance he had of making it through the Wicket Gate. Does not the very presence of the evil fortress suggest the reality of great power and an enemy kingdom? Indeed it does, and yet, a mightier hand than that of the dark lord was guiding Christian, a mightier sovereign who rules on the throne of an unshakable kingdom. No evil weapon, however strong or skillfully aimed, can thwart his will. No enemy power, however determined, can overthrow his purpose of grace.

Although we are given no time frame between Christian's deliverance from the City of Destruction and his arrival at the Wicket Gate, it must have seemed very long to him. Considering the perils he has already faced, it is little wonder that his heart was faint as he stood outside the gate and knocked for admission. Looking upon the closed door, apprehension contended with hope. But rather than deterring him, it fueled Christian's resolve to knock repeatedly when his first knock was not answered at once. Why did he do so in the absence of any immediate encouragement? He knew full well that reaching the gate was not enough. He must actually enter therein.

Eventually, a man with a solemn countenance opened the small door. His name was Goodwill, the keeper of the Wicket Gate. Before permitting Christian to come inside, the man asked who he was, where he came from, and what he wanted. After hearing Christian's heartbroken confession, the account of his spiritual troubles, and his plea for admission, the gatekeeper then startled him by pulling him quickly through the gate. As Goodwill explained his action, Christian looked toward the castle for the first time as he learned of Beelzebub, captain of the great fortress. He and his evil allies stalk those who seek admission to the Wicket Gate, hoping to destroy them before they can enter through it. The faithful watchman had pulled Christian to safety before the arrows could harm him.

What is this metaphorical castle from which invisible, yet deadly, arrows are fired? Who is the covert enemy with such a mighty army at his beck and call? What is the meaning of the sniper-like assaults upon helpless pilgrims who are no threat to anyone?

The fortress near the Wicket Gate and its dark lord are spiritual entities that we dare not underestimate just because we cannot see them. Beelzebub denotes Satan, the sum of all evil, the archenemy of the Lord Jesus Christ and men. His castle represents his kingdom of darkness, the seat of his power as the god of this world. (2 Corinthians 4:3-4; Ephesians 2:2) Envy and deep-seated hatred for the human race drive him to use extreme measures against them, and the deadly weapons of his army denote the power at his disposal. Those who fall victim to them are taken captive and imprisoned in his bleak stronghold. That is, they remain under his power and dominion.

Given that the arrows of the enemy are fired with the specific intention of keeping sinners from fleeing to Christ, a solemn thought comes to mind. This must explain why many would-be pilgrims turn back before ever reaching the Wicket Gate. Like Pliable, they travel along for a while, but when they run into trouble or come under enemy fire, they quickly give up the whole idea. It is a different matter with those who have heard the call of the Holy Spirit. They not only reach the gate, they enter it.

Here is cause for great rejoicing, my friend. In spite of all of his strength and furious warfare, Satan and his kingdom will not prevail in the end. He may be a strong man, but a stronger one has defeated and bound him. (Matthew 12:25-30; Mark 3:23-27; Luke 11:17-22) Our great adversary is bound in the sense that he cannot prevent the going forth of the Gospel, the salvation of souls, or the expansion of God's kingdom. His flaming arrows cannot prevent God's children from entering the Wicket Gate, but he never ceases to try.

As already noted, Beelzebub's castle implies the existence of another kingdom that is its polar opposite, a throne of transcendent power that rules over all. (Psalm 103:19) It is, of course, the kingdom of God under the sovereign rule of the Lord Jesus Christ. He is Lord of creation and Lord over the realm of salvation. All things, seen or invisible, are under the dominion of his golden scepter. Thus in spite of the enemy's rage and fury, the gates of hell cannot prevail against God's will and purpose. His kingdom is infinite and eternal, but not so the stronghold of Satan. One day it will utterly fall, and its dark lord with it. For now, however, God permits the enemy's castle to remain intact and his flaming arrows to fly, but all is according to his infinitely wise design.

Figuratively speaking, we could say that a battle line between these two opposing kingdoms has been drawn near the Wicket Gate, and the souls of men are caught in the crossfire. All who knock for admission can expect a measure of opposition, and some will endure a greater trial of passage than others. While many are admitted immediately, others must knock repeatedly. Like Christian, these appear to strive with the Lord as if he were hesitant to receive them. But it is the sinner's resolve that is really on trial here. How earnestly does he desire to enter the path of life? Is Christ truly the longing of his heart?

The awakened sinner's hunger and thirst for the Lord Jesus Christ is only increased by a seeming delay at the Wicket Gate. Furthermore, it is only a seeming delay. Those who come to him and call upon him by faith are the very ones for whom he died. He welcomes us freely, with open arms! It is our doubts and fears that make it seem as if mercy's door is shut against us, or a grudging entrance allowed. Any struggle that we experience here will only render our Lord more precious to us, and in time, it will help us to better understand the vastness of his love.

The allegorical Wicket Gate is the focal point upon which the destiny of the soul rests. It speaks to our hearts of Christ as our only source of hope and relief. He is the only way to God, the sinner's only hiding place. Even though no one enters this gate unopposed, the awakened soul will not turn back because of any difficulty encountered here. God's purpose of salvation will firmly stand. Moreover, Satan is the unwitting servant of God's providence. His flaming arrows help prepare us for a life-long battle. Take heart then, my brother or sister in Christ. We serve a reigning, victorious Lord! Satan is a defeated foe, even though it scarcely seems like it now. His mighty weapons cannot inflict eternal harm if we truly belong to the Lord Jesus Christ. (John 10:27-30)

In Ephesians 6:12 we are forewarned that *we wrestle not against flesh and blood, but against principalities, against powers, against the rulers of the darkness of this world, against spiritual wickedness in high places.* In the face of such formidable enemies, we must remember that the battle is the Lord's. He will ultimately win the day. Yet unless we are armed for conflict, how will we be able to stand firm in the evil day? (Ephesians 6:13) The Christian life is not for the spiritually timid or faint of heart. Every single step forward, every inch of spiritual ground gained, is done so in the face of stiff opposition.

* * * *

In common with every other true pilgrim, Christian safely reached the Wicket Gate and entered it in spite of the diabolical suggestions of Beelzebub. If we think about it, this conflict was not really new to him. Has he not already met with and overcome similar attacks that tried to turn him from the path of life?

Yes, Christian battled with many an enemy before ever reaching the gate. However, he had now come to a critical point in his pilgrimage. To enter here is to enter the path of life. To be delivered from the kingdom of darkness is to be translated into the kingdom of God. Herein we find the reason behind our great conflict with the powers of darkness. Satan never relinquishes any of his captives without a fight. He would rather destroy his own subjects than have them become the servants of the Lord Jesus Christ. So from this time forward, he will not cease to war against Christian, dog his steps, and plot his downfall.

Since Christian has already been so deeply embroiled in this conflict, he was all the more grateful to be safely inside the gate. With true humility of heart, he acknowledged his unworthiness and freely confessed that God's love and mercy alone had brought him there. He now had a much clearer understanding of our Lord's words in Matthew 7:13-14:

Enter ye in at the strait gate: for wide is the gate, and broad is the way, that leadeth to destruction, and many there be which go in thereat: Because strait is the gate, and narrow is the way, which leadeth unto life, and few there be that find it.

Study Questions

1. Briefly describe the sinister-looking castle near the Wicket Gate. How does it differ from the usual medieval fortress, and why is it located where it is?

2. When the gatekeeper finally answered Christian's knock, why did he quickly pull him safely inside?

3. Who is the dark lord of the evil fortress? What is the nature of his kingdom and warfare against God's people?

4. Why does God permit the enemy's castle to remain intact and his flaming arrows to fly?

5. Can Satan and his kingdom prevail in the end?

Part Four

THE JOURNEY CONTEMPLATED

*But the God of all grace, who hath called us unto his eternal glory
by Christ Jesus, after that ye have suffered a while, make you perfect,
stablish, strengthen, settle you. To him be glory and dominion for
ever and ever. Amen.*
1 Peter 5:10-11

CHAPTER 11

Our Race to Eternal Glory

IF THE GREAT CLOUD OF WITNESSES WHO HAVE ALREADY FINISHED THEIR EARTHLY course could send a message to those of us who are still running the race, what would it be? They would most likely remind us that it is not enough to begin the race, or to run it well for a time. If we would join our brethren who have already entered into their eternal rest, we must finish our course while looking unto Jesus, the author and finisher of our faith. (Hebrews 12:1-2)

This exhortation strongly implies that there are no passive travelers along the path of life, at least not any who complete the journey. No aspect of it is to be taken lightly or complacently because our way is filled with dangers, snares, and temptations that often materialize without warning. When we least expect it, our course may suddenly veer through a dark, lonely valley or bring us face-to-face with a seemingly insurmountable obstacle. In the providence of God, a measure of such trials is appointed to each of his children. Moreover, since our path also leads us through enemy territory, we face even stiffer opposition of another kind.

Confronting us in a wide variety of forms and disguises, the world is an ever-present medium by which the god of this world hopes to recapture our hearts and minds. In addition, seemingly innocent by-paths emerge here and there, offering tempting alternatives to the narrow way. All of these are clever tactics by which the adversary tries to confuse our spiritual direction and lead us off course. They can baffle the mind of even the most watchful Christian for a time, but are particularly dangerous to those who are less vigilant. It is also rumored that giants lurk in the shadows near these byways, ready to seize any who happen to stray from the right path.

In addition to the providential difficulties we face and the diabolical powers that continually plot our downfall, we harbor a traitor within. Our own flesh, the old man, will oppose, deceive, and betray us if not continually mortified and kept in check. (Romans 6:12-14) Thus we can ill afford to let down our spiritual guard at any time.

Although the pathway we travel will ultimately lead us into the full possession of our inheritance in Christ, we are not there until we are there! Nor will we enter the heavenly city by being "carried to the skies on flowery beds of ease." [1] There is a race to eternal glory, and every true follower of Jesus Christ is fully engaged in it. Even though we cannot complete it in our own strength, this race will require the very best we have to give. Eternal glory waits at the end of our journey, but the victor's crown is only for those who go the distance.

By placing the Wicket Gate at the head of the path of life, John Bunyan brilliantly illustrates the truth that salvation is in Christ alone. In Matthew 7:13-14, our Lord warns that relatively few find this narrow way, while the masses of mankind choose the broad way to eternal destruction. This very fact of two ways indicates a necessary struggle in order to enter the strait gate. Sincerity and earnest intentions are not enough; neither are zeal and diligent effort, in and of themselves. Those who strive to enter in must do so at the right gate.

In Luke 13:24-27, the Lord Jesus Christ gives another aspect of the strait gate. This passage centers upon the two-fold danger of knocking after it is too late and claiming knowledge of Christ that is not according to truth. False presumption is the culprit in both of these fatal mistakes. The danger of knocking too late signifies undue delay, which presumes upon tomorrow. (Proverbs 27:1) The Scriptures give no latitude for procrastination; therefore, we must strive now to enter the strait gate. (Isaiah 55:6-7) The day of grace is always the present time. Mercy's door may be forever shut tomorrow, for we may not live to see tomorrow. Therefore, salvation is a matter of the utmost urgency.

Likewise, they also labor under an equally strong delusion who claim knowledge of Christ that has no basis in fact. These may have a cursory understanding of God's Word, but Christ does not live in their hearts by faith. Therefore, instead of striving to enter through the narrow gate, they endeavor to climb over another way through their own efforts. Tragically, false presumption keeps them squarely in the broad way. So those who would enter in at the strait gate must avoid this two-fold error.

Moreover, having entered therein, we must take care not to view our striving as a one-time event or an end unto itself. It is actually the beginning of a life-long struggle. Like the graces of genuine faith and repentance, this striving is an exercise of soul that is to characterize our entire Christian experience. Entering the narrow gate must progress to the struggle required in order to walk the narrow way beyond it. Yet every step forward takes us a little closer to our heavenly goal, that glorious city whose builder and maker is God. (Hebrews 11:10)

We do not travel far down the path of life before we discover that we must also struggle against our own natural inclinations. As we develop a more accurate self-knowledge, we become increasingly more aware that sin is mixed with everything we think, say, or do. Our very best efforts are still tainted with imperfection. Our highest and most noble deeds are not as free from questionable motives as we would have them to be. Moreover, our strongest intentions are still subject to discouragement. Do not these things make us tremble because of our seeming lack of spiritual growth? Is it not our deepest fear that we will miss the mark and fail to reach our eternal goal?

Although such thoughts will disturb our peace, they serve us well by rooting out a complacent spirit. It is not God's will that we be held captive by a spirit of doubt and fear. (2 Timothy 1:7) Such a frame of mind will prove a hindrance to our spiritual progress. But neither is it his will that we become spiritually lethargic and indifferent. Salvation is never a static thing. Watchfulness, vigilance and continual effort are vital as we march to Zion! (1 Timothy 6:12) Those who are accounted worthy to enter that city are they who are covered with the perfect righteousness of Christ. Being *justified freely by his grace through the redemption that is in Christ Jesus*, they are *accepted in the Beloved*. Yet Scripture repeatedly calls them overcomers. (Revelation 2:7, 11, 17, 26; Revelation 3:5, 12, 21; Revelation 7:9-17; Revelation 12:11)

If we are to run the race all the way to its finish, nothing must be allowed to divert us from our goal. Perseverance therein requires us to press forward with our hearts fixed upon the Lord Jesus Christ and things that are eternal. When this is truly our case, every earthly concern will be subservient to Christ and his kingdom.

Moreover, in our race to eternal glory we must resist the temptation to look backward. The past is irrevocably gone, and revisiting it will prove worse than useless. Therefore, until we reach our eternal destination, we must press ever onward and always upward. When the race is won and we see the King in his beauty, it will have been worth it all. Bowing before his sovereign majesty, the Lamb upon his throne, we will give all glory to him alone.

Looking forward to that blessed day, we must never forget that our reception into his kingdom of glory has nothing whatever to do with our striving or personal worthiness. It is secured by the merits of Christ alone and his redemptive work on our behalf. Since our very best efforts come short of God's glory, we should bemoan rather than boast of them. Nevertheless, if we are in Christ, we are to be diligent laborers in his vineyard, not sluggards!

Like an Olympic athlete training for the big race, we must be prepared, disciplined, and focused on our heavenly goal. But unlike those who contend for worldly glory and place all their hopes and aspirations on their one moment in time, we race toward an eternal prize. (1 Corinthians 9:24-27) Is it not heartening to know that our race is not just for the swift? All who persevere in it and cross the finish line will receive the victor's crown. (Hebrews 12:1-2)

I love the hymn written by John S.B. Monsell, in which he beautifully expresses the nature of our path and its glorious end, saying:

Fight the good fight with all thy might;
Christ is thy Strength, and Christ thy Right:
Lay hold on life, and it shall be thy joy and crown eternally.

Run the straight race through God's good grace,
lift up thine eyes, and seek his face;
Life with its way before us lies, Christ is the Path, and Christ the Prize.

Cast care aside; upon thy Guide lean, and his mercy will provide;
Lean, and the trusting soul shall prove Christ is its Life,
and Christ its Love.

Faint not, nor fear, His arms are near; He changeth not, and thou art dear;
Only believe, and thou shalt see that Christ is all in all to thee. [2]

Although Christian would undoubtedly have disagreed, he has begun his race well. In spite of a few serious missteps, he had reached a crucial juncture in his pilgrimage. At last he stood before the keeper of the Wicket Gate and readily confessed that he deserved no credit for his safe arrival. God's providence and tender mercy had overshadowed him each step of the way and brought him there.

Since the gatekeeper customarily interviewed each one whom he admitted through the gate, he asked Christian several pertinent questions about his journey so far. However, his purpose went far beyond obtaining information. His comments suggest a thorough acquaintance with all of the places Christian had been and the people he had encountered along the way. Moreover, I suspect that he knew full well who Christian was and why he had come. Why then was it necessary? It was conducted entirely for Christian's benefit. As he was forced to face himself in order to answer the gatekeeper's inquiry, some highly significant things came to light.

As Christian answered Goodwill's initial questions before entering the gate, his testimony was both honest and forthright, omitting none of his errors and failures. He told of the deep distress that had compelled him to flee from the City of Destruction, and the godly counsel that had directed him where to flee. Thus he came as a poor, needy sinner, and as such, was granted immediate entrance.

The gatekeeper's second line of questioning had to do with why Christian traveled alone, and this took Christian back to the earliest days of his journey. It was a painful reminder of how he alone had come to understand his grave danger and to flee from the wrath to come. Although he had done his best to persuade his family that they were also in danger, his arguments fell upon deaf ears. Not only had they refused to accompany him, they chided him for his fears. In fact, they finally concluded that he was delusional and mentally unbalanced. Therefore, he set out on his journey by himself, which had been an especially painful thing to bear.

His solitary journey indicated something else that gave it added credibility. Christian was apparently not under pressure from an outside influence or following someone else when he set out on his journey. Neither was his action the result of a momentary whim. He had been convinced from the Word of God that he must flee from the City of Destruction, even if he had to do so alone.

The final series of questions pertained to the nature and strength of Christian's resolve. What conflicts, if any, had he faced so far? Had anyone tried to persuade him to turn back? What effect did their opposition have upon him? As he was questioned concerning the testing of his resolve, Christian did not have to think too hard in order to answer. The vehement protests of his family were still fresh in his heart and mind, but they had failed to alter his resolve. Moreover, he had gained a significant victory against the arguments of unbelief, as signified by his neighbor Obstinate. The fact that Pliable joined company with him was a bit more troubling though, especially when we remember what Pliable represented. Considering the fixed purpose that Zion's pilgrims must maintain, Pliable was not the best traveling companion for Christian.

It is true that the two men came to a parting of the ways at the Slough of Despond. While Christian's resolve stood the test when trapped in that awful place, Pliable beat a hasty retreat to the City of Destruction. However, as we have already seen, Christian was not totally rid of him.

Goodwill's comment concerning Pliable brought forth an interesting response from Christian. He could have fancied himself better than Pliable for being the stronger of the two. Who knows? Perhaps back then he did glory a bit until his own resolve nearly gave way in the matter of Worldly Wiseman and his dangerous counsel. Christian now viewed Pliable's failure in a different light after nearly doing the same thing himself. After much soul-searching, Christian judged himself to be no better than Pliable. The valuable lesson he learned at the secret place of thunder was permanently etched in his memory.

Christian's interview with the gatekeeper gave him an excellent opportunity to reflect upon his journey so far. It was a time to remember how the Lord had led him, delivered him from every peril, and faithfully kept him in the way. A proper sense of his unworthiness attributed it all to God's mercy and gave all glory to him. So as he related his recent danger, and his recovery through the timely intervention of Evangelist, Christian's heart overflowed with gratitude as he said:

"It was God's mercy, that he came to me again, for else I had never come hither. But now I am come, such a one as I am, more fit indeed for death by that mountain, than thus to stand talking with my Lord: but O! What a favour is this to me, that yet I am admitted entrance here?"

* * * *

Dear reader, what about the man named Goodwill, the keeper of the Wicket Gate? Who is he? We understand that the Wicket Gate portrays a spiritual reality rather than an actual tiny door through which we must squeeze in order to enter the path of life. Who then is its keeper?

His grave manner and solemn responsibility could mean that he was another man of God such as Evangelist or Help. At the conclusion of the interview, he instructed Christian more particularly concerning the path that he must follow. This instruction is certainly consistent with the Gospel minister's charge to be a faithful watchman over the souls of men. The spiritual discernment and knowledge with which he interviewed and then advised Christian are what one would reasonably expect a seasoned minister to have. Perhaps his grave countenance was due to his burden for those under his pastoral care, especially as he entered into their spiritual struggles, trials, and afflictions. On the other hand, there are compelling reasons to suspect that he is more than a man.

Does not his very name suggest that Goodwill was no mere man? (Luke 2:10-14) We could ask the same concerning his authority as the gatekeeper. His willingness to open the gate was matched by his ability to do so, and his power to deliver the petitioners from danger. Is this not indicative of divine omnipotence and sovereignty? (Revelation 3:7-8) His love for the souls of men, his insight into the enemy and his tactics, his rescue of Christian from the arrows of Beelzebub and the keen insight with which he questioned Christian all make a compelling case that he is far more than a man. In fact, they strongly suggest that he represents the man Christ Jesus.

Like the allegorical gatekeeper in *The Pilgrim's Progress*, the Lord Jesus Christ has the City of Destruction and its ever-present cloud of pollution ever in his sight. He well knows the desperate condition of men by nature and the tragic consequences of it. With a heart full of pity, he beholds the devastating effects of sin in his creation. But his omniscient eye is particularly fixed upon those who were given to him by his Father before the foundation of the world. (John 17:6) They are his peculiar treasure and he loves them so much that he gave his life for them.

At the appointed time, he seeks them out from among the vast multitudes in the City of Destruction. He is near at hand when enemies accost them and try to sabotage their escape. He observes their struggles should they fall into the Slough of Despond, and he knows the intent of their hearts as they strive toward the Wicket Gate in spite of it. His watchful eye is always upon them and his ear is open to their cries. By the power of his Spirit, he draws them unto himself, and as they make their laborious way to the Wicket Gate, he stands with open arms to receive them. (John 6:37)

Who then is the gracious keeper of the Wicket Gate, the one who opens the door to sin-burdened pilgrims? Is he one of God's faithful servants who direct men into the way of eternal life, or is he the one who said: *I am the way, the truth, and the life: no man cometh unto the Father, but by me*? Christian was struck by the gravity of the gatekeeper's countenance. Was this because the nature of his calling entailed beholding so much grief and sorrow, as he bore the burdens of those under his charge? Or was his countenance grave because he was a man of sorrows and acquainted with grief?

We cannot say for sure whom John Bunyan meant to represent in the person of the gatekeeper. He could very well be one of the King's commissioned officers. However, I am personally inclined to believe that he is the King himself.

Study Questions

1. In Luke 13:24-27, the Lord Jesus Christ gives another aspect of the strait gate (Wicket Gate) and entrance therein. What two-fold danger does he warn against in this passage?

2. In what way does the Christian's struggle against sinful tendencies help to guard against a complacent spirit?

3. If we are to persevere in the race to eternal glory and finish it, what are some of the things that we must do?

4. Why did the gatekeeper interview each one whom he admitted through the Wicket Gate? How was this time of soul-searching beneficial to Christian?

5. Although John Bunyan does not reveal the identity of Goodwill, he seems to hint at two options. Who do you think the gracious keeper of the Wicket Gate is, and why?

CHAPTER 12

Onward to Zion by the Road Less Traveled

IN CONCLUDING HIS WELL-KNOWN POEM "THE ROAD NOT TAKEN," ROBert Frost wrote, "Two roads diverged in a wood, and I, I took the one less traveled by. And that has made all the difference." [1] His intent was to show that the easiest or most widely accepted choices in life are rarely the best ones. When faced with crucial decisions, those important crossroads in our path, the choices we make can have a profound and lasting effect upon our lives. In some cases there is no going back. Our course is altered permanently, for good or for ill.

The well-beaten path taken by the vast majority is generally the path of mediocrity. Those who desire something higher and nobler must seek it in another direction. As a rule, that which is more excellent requires extraordinary effort in order to achieve it. Since few are willing to make the necessary sacrifices, the more excellent way becomes the road less traveled.

Two ways also lie before men in a spiritual sense. Natural birth places all men squarely on the broad way to destruction, and if left to themselves, they will neither desire nor seek anything higher. On the surface of it, this path would appear to be the easier choice; after all, it is the way of least resistance. Those who walk it may comfortably go with the flow of prevailing thought and popular opinion. They see no need to rock the boat like narrow-minded fanatics who are opposed to everything. Such is the general consensus of those who travel the broad way. However, they fail to consider where that path is leading them.

The path of the just is placed in sharp contrast to this reputedly easier way. Even though it is the highest and most excellent way there is, no one who understands its true nature would ever call it easy. In general, it leads through places that are difficult and dangerous, and those who follow it are often despised and misunderstood. So the path of life remains the spiritual road less traveled, even though it alone leads to a joyful end.

Although every child of God is resolved to walk this path, even they may have some misconceptions about its true nature. An important part of the gatekeeper's duty was to address and clarify these issues. Therefore, after he instructed Christian in this regard, the gatekeeper pointed him forward and set him on the road less traveled.

This path is aptly called the King's Highway, since it alone leads to the city of the great King. (Psalm 48:1-3) In order to travel this royal road, we must follow the Lamb wherever he leads, and the true sheep of the Lord Jesus Christ do just that. (Revelation 14:4; John 10:27-30) His way is the way of faith and obedience, which is a road desired and sought by few.

But travelers beware! Danger lurks close at hand, even here! Alien voices will call to you from crooked by-ways, promising an easier, more pleasant journey. The child of God has the inward discernment to reject these false voices, but the unwary soul who gives heed to them may lose his way and never find it again. (Proverbs 2:10-20) Tragically, this is the fate of many who begin the journey.

Although they are relatively few in number when compared to the multitudes on the broad way, new travelers are constantly entering the King's Highway. Even though it takes them through a dry and desolate wilderness, their souls will prosper under the continual influence of the Gospel. (Isaiah 35:1-2) According to the Word of God, the King's Highway is the way of holiness in which the redeemed of the Lord walk. For now, it is often dampened with their tears; but in due time, they shall come to Zion with songs and everlasting joy upon their heads. (Isaiah 35:8-10)

The path to Zion may be filled with danger, yet there is none that is as safe. The eyes of the Lord are ever upon us, guarding and guiding each step we take. We need not fear when enemy forces appear to have us surrounded, for the Lord is our rock, our shelter, and our strong tower from the enemy. (Psalm 61:2-3) How often he has proved himself a friend that is closer than a brother when our hearts were overwhelmed with sorrow! (Proverbs 18:24) How often he has lightened our way so that we did not stumble and fall when we walked through dark, lonely places!

Although we need to understand the nature of the way we take, brooding upon its difficulties serves no useful purpose. Even though we need preparation and instruction concerning the path of life, we will not find it profitable to dwell upon its negative aspects. After all, the way to Zion is the path to eternal joy, peace, and rest.

The more deeply we consider the nature of our path, the more we will find in which to rejoice. For one thing, a careful reading of Scripture assures us that the King's Highway is a path of abundant provision. The spiritual nourishment of God's people was prefigured in various Old Testament types and shadows, most notably the miraculous provision of manna and water from the smitten rock. However, these figures fade in comparison to their New Testament fulfillment in our blessed Lord. (John 6:48-51; 1 Corinthians 10:1-4)

As the all-sufficient Savior who gave his life for his sheep, the Lord Jesus Christ has personally undertaken our care. He perfectly knows the path we take and all that we will encounter along the way. Moreover, he has promised to supply everything that is needful to serve him and persevere in our journey. (Psalm 34:8-10; Psalm 132:13-16) This sustenance consists of the choice blessings of his love and grace, all of which flow to us from his cross. (John 6:53-58)

Psalm 107:9 gives us the blessed assurance that *he satisfieth the longing soul and filleth the hungry soul with goodness.* They who hunger and thirst after righteousness will know the bountiful outpouring of these graces. (Matthew 5:6) Since all of his people hunger in this way, each of them finds that Christ is the essence of their sustenance. He is our life! He alone can satisfy our longing souls.

A further illustration of his tender care is seen is Isaiah 40:11: *He shall feed his flock like a shepherd: he shall gather the lambs with his arm, and carry them in his bosom, and shall gently lead those that are with young.* What a precious picture is this! Our Lord takes care of us according to his intimate knowledge of our individual needs and circumstances. He leads every one of us, but is particularly careful of his little ones, his lambs who are weak and helpless. He holds these most fragile ones close to his heart and carries them in his arms when their strength fails. Dear reader, is this not often the case with you? I know that it is so with me.

If we truly belong to the Lord Jesus Christ, we may confidently say with David: *The LORD is my shepherd; I shall not want. He maketh me to lie down in green pastures: he leadeth me beside the still waters. He restoreth my soul: he leadeth me in the paths of righteousness for his name's sake.* (Psalm 23:1-3) As the bread of life, he sustains and gives us strength to walk in the way that he leads. His Spirit is a fountain of living water, an endless supply that refreshes and revives us. (John 4:10-14; John 7:37-39) Like a glorious river, he restores our souls and gladdens our hearts, providing strength and stability when all around us is chaos and confusion. (Psalm 46:1-5)

How often we stand in need of these life-giving waters that flow to us from the throne of our loving Lord, because the path to the Celestial City invariably leads us through the Valley of Baca (the "vale of weeping")! Times and seasons of spiritual grief and heaviness will come to every true Christian. During these times our path is often watered with our tears, but not one of them escapes the notice of our loving Lord. With fatherly pity and compassion, he provides pools along the way, pools filled with healing waters from which we may drink deeply and be strengthened. Through seasons of darkness, when our souls seem withered and dry, he furnishes a table in the wilderness and streams in the desert. Then we may encourage ourselves in the Lord and say with the psalmist: *Why art thou cast down, O my soul? And why art thou disquieted within me? Hope thou in God: for I shall yet praise him, who is the health of my countenance, and my God.* (Psalm 42:11)

O yes, great blessedness attends our way, even though we must pass through the valley of tears. There is no actual cause for fear or alarm because our Shepherd-King has us ever in his sight. With his strong arm he keeps us from falling, carries us when need be, and upholds us every step of the way. So lift up your head, weary pilgrim! Your heart may be heavily burdened for now, but ponder these encouraging words in Psalm 84:5-7:

Blessed is the man whose strength is in thee; in whose heart are the ways of them. Who passing through the valley of Baca make it a well; the rain also filleth the pools. They go from strength to strength, every one of them in Zion appeareth before God.

The path of the just is not only a well-provisioned way, but a carefully chosen one as well. Its blueprint was designed by the infinite wisdom of God, and his sovereignty and providential care permeate the whole. (Psalm 32:8; Proverbs 3:5-6) In the course of our earthly journey, much will happen that is baffling and mysterious to our human understanding. However, our way is perfectly known to God, and all is working according to his eternal purpose. When in the midst of great sorrow and perplexity, godly Job eventually realized this truth and found comfort in it, saying:

Behold, I go forward, but he is not there; and backward, but I cannot perceive him: On the left hand, where he doth work, but I cannot behold him: he hideth himself on the right hand, that I cannot see him: But he knoweth the way that I take: when he hath tried me, I shall come forth as gold. (Job 23:8-10)

Even though we walk it imperfectly, the path of the just is a perfect way. Our Shepherd-King leads us in the paths of righteousness for his name's sake. Moreover, even though we do not follow a visible road, our path is clearly marked for those with eyes to see. (Proverbs 2:6-9)

In many respects, our earthly pilgrimage is comparable to Israel's wilderness experience. God had mercifully delivered them from Egyptian bondage, but they had not yet reached the Promised Land. Likewise, the people of God, who have been redeemed from the bondage of sin, must sojourn through the wilderness of this world as pilgrims and strangers before we reach the heavenly Canaan.

The Hebrew people had no designated path to follow as they wandered through the wilderness of Sinai for forty years. They also had no means of sustaining themselves in that desolate land. However, in spite of their continual murmuring and complaining, God was faithful to supply their every need, as Moses reminded them in Deuteronomy 2:7: *For the LORD thy God hath blessed thee in all the works of thy hand: he knoweth thy walking through this great wilderness: these forty years the LORD thy God hath been with thee; thou hast lacked nothing.*

Through the giving of his law on Mount Sinai, God made his will known to them. By means of a pillar of cloud by day and a pillar of fire by night, he led them throughout their entire wilderness journey.

We are blessed with something far better than even these visible representations of God's presence. In his Word, he has given us the chart and compass by which to discern and safely navigate the path of life. (Proverbs 4:10-13) Moreover, by means of his Spirit, the Lord Jesus Christ speaks to our hearts through his Word and leads us in the way everlasting. So even though our way may sometimes be lonely, we never walk alone. Our heavenly guide goes before us, lighting our path and making the way plain. In Isaiah 30:21, we have the promise of his gracious leading: *Thine ears shall hear a word behind thee, saying, This is the way, walk ye in it, when ye turn to the right hand, and when ye turn to the left.*

Earlier in their history, when the Hebrew people had settled in the land of Egypt, they quickly discovered that it was a place of spiritual darkness. It is interesting to note that a palpable darkness was one of the plagues sent by God before the Exodus, as a judgment upon that land. This darkness covered the furthest extent of Pharaoh's domain, except the land of Goshen where the Hebrew people lived. In the midst of darkness so terrible that it threatened to drive the Egyptians mad, God's people had light in their dwellings. (Exodus 10:21-23)

As welcome as it must have been, the light enjoyed by the Hebrews long ago was far inferior to the radiance that illuminates our path. For those who know and love the truth, God's Word is a lamp unto our feet, and a light unto our path, our guiding principle of life and godliness. Its precepts are perfect and complete; therefore it is our sole authority.

Thus the Word of God is the infallible standard that defines the path we take and lightens our steps along that path. When darkness closes in and threatens to engulf us, we may confidently say with David: *The LORD is my light and my salvation; whom shall I fear? The LORD is the strength of my life; of whom shall I be afraid?*

The pathway of the believer is also a well-protected way, a carefully guarded path. How blessed we are that this is so! Although dangers and temptations lurk at every bend in the road, the Lord Jesus Christ is our refuge and fortress. When fears alarm and troubles threaten to defeat us, we may take great comfort from the promise given in Proverbs 18:10: *The name of the LORD is a strong tower: the righteous runneth into it, and is safe.* Under his shadow, which never varies, there is peace and safety for all who trust in him. (Psalm 91:1-4) When our hearts are overwhelmed and it seems as if he is far away, we may rest assured that he is near, hearing our faintest cry and sending timely help when we have reached our wit's end. (Psalm 61:1-4)

Our Lord's tender care over us does not mean he will remove the troubles and sorrow that come our way. A measure of such things is appointed to each of us. However, it does mean that nothing will pluck us out of his hands. Our safe passage to Zion is a charge that he has willingly taken upon himself; our eternal safekeeping is in his hands. Therefore, in our weakness and insufficiency we may boldly say: *Behold, God is my salvation; I will trust, and not be afraid: for the LORD JEHOVAH is my strength and my song; he also is become my salvation.* (Isaiah 12:2)

Another protective aspect of the path to the heavenly Zion is that it is enclosed, walled, and fortressed all around. The prophet Isaiah spoke of this security and the great assurance that it gives to the people of God in Isaiah 26:1-4:

In that day shall this song be sung in the land of Judah; we have a strong city; salvation will God appoint for walls and bulwarks. Open ye the gates, that the righteous nation which keepeth the truth may enter in. Thou wilt keep him in perfect peace, whose mind is stayed on thee: because he trusteth in thee. Trust ye in the LORD for ever: for in the LORD JEHOVAH is everlasting strength.

The military posture of this defense denotes the strength and invincible security that surrounds and protects those who belong to Christ. In a more intimate sense, his protection is also likened to an enclosed garden in Song of Solomon 4:12-16. What a precious reality is found in this incomparable Song of Songs! What a tender portrait of the Lord Jesus Christ surrounding his bride with his love, nurturing and protecting her, dwelling with her and enjoying sweet fellowship with her! How privileged we are to be part of the garden of Christ, to be trees planted by his own hand!

* * * *

Turning our thoughts back to Christian and the solitary journey that lies before him, one final thing comes to my mind concerning the nature of our path to eternal glory. Although it is the spiritual road less taken, it is still a well-traveled way. Many pilgrims have walked it before us, and if the Lord tarries, many more will come after. In finality, the redeemed will comprise an innumerable multitude when gathered together before the throne of God and of the Lamb. (Revelation 7:9-17)

So the path of the just is indelibly marked with the footprints of countless pilgrims. (Hebrews 11) It resounds, not with the reverberation of audible footsteps, but with the example and testimony of the saints of all the ages. In walking the path of life, we walk in their steps and follow the same commander, the Lord Jesus Christ, the captain of our salvation. As part of his church militant we face a daunting battle, just as our brethren who came before us. Yet, with the joyous anticipation of dwelling in his presence forevermore, we gladly march forward under his royal standard, the banner of the cross.

Thy saints, in all this glorious war, shall conquer, though they die;
They view the triumph from afar, and seize it with their eye.[2]

Study Questions

1. Why is the path of the just the spiritual road less traveled?

2. The King's Highway is a way of abundant provision for those who travel it. Give some ways in which the Lord provides and cares for his people.

3. Name some ways in which the Christian's earthly pilgrimage is comparable to Israel's wandering in the wilderness.

4. What is the infallible standard that defines the direction we take?

5. The pathway of the believer is a well-protected way. Does this mean that the Lord will remove our troubles and sorrows? Explain your answer.

Part Five

A VAST TREASURE HOUSE

Howbeit when he, the Spirit of truth, is come, he will guide you into all truth: for he shall not speak of himself; but whatsoever he shall hear, that shall he speak: and he will show you things to come. He shall glorify me: for he shall receive of mine, and shall show it unto you.
John16:13-14

CHAPTER 13

Portrait in the Entrance Hall

A<small>LTHOUGH</small> C<small>HRISTIAN</small> <small>LISTENED ATTENTIVELY TO THE GATEKEEPER'S</small> parting counsel, his eyes were already fixed on the road ahead of him. While impatient to be on his way, he was still greatly troubled by the burden that remained on his back. Expecting to be delivered of it when he entered the Wicket Gate, he was surely disappointed to learn that he must carry it a little longer. The place of deliverance was near at hand, however. When Christian reached it, the gatekeeper assured him that his burden would fall off by itself.

After traveling some distance past the gate, he came upon what appeared to be a large private residence. It was a house of ancient stone constructed right by the wayside, but due to the high wall surrounding it, passers-by could hardly guess its immense size. Christian, however, decided to stop and have a closer look. As he gazed through the wrought iron bars of the front gate and studied the beautiful features of the house, he noted that it had all the warmth and charm of an English manor house. But there was a palatial air about it as well. Several wings extended from the central portion of the house, giving it added dimension and linear perspective. Its steeply pitched roof formed decorative gables over the ends of these wings, and large turret rooms placed at every corner in the upper story provided further architectural interest.

Four matching chimneys crafted from ornamental masonry towered above the lofty slate roof, with gentle streams of smoke coming from each of them. The family coat of arms, engraved in gold, was prominently displayed over the main entrance of the home. But beyond all doubt, the most notable feature of this grand dwelling was its windows.

A large octagonal window was the focal point over the main entryway at the front of the home, and a pair of matching oval windows framed the massive oak door. These three windows, all of which were leaded stained glass, added significantly to the beauty and elegance of the structure. The rest of the home's abundant windows were of mullioned glass and varied from one another in size and shape. Every one of them was sparkling clean, but the thing that struck Christian the most was the soft, glowing light that radiated from them all.

This figurative house of light was the place spoken of by the gatekeeper, the place in which Christian would be shown excellent things to help him on his way. Everything about it seemed to invite him to come inside and partake of its hospitality, for unlike the Wicket Gate, this one had a simple latch that was easy to open. So he entered the gate, crossed the flagstone walkway, and knocked at the front door.

For those who know it well, the House of the Interpreter is no ordinary dwelling. The home's exterior gives little indication of its actual measure, and its outward grandeur hints but slightly of the vast treasure hidden inside. Its location beyond the Wicket Gate is worthy of particular note, for this house was specially designed for those who have entered through that narrow door. The rare jewels of wisdom and knowledge found within its walls belong to Zion's children, for they alone have the capacity to receive them. (1 Corinthians 2:11-16)

Thus we discover what we strongly suspected before. The Spirit of God is the divine Interpreter and master of this domain, and a visit to his house signifies his unique ministry to those who are in Christ. There are precious truths concerning Christ and his salvation that we cannot know, understand, or apply without his help. Within the walls of his house, we will find all that we need in order to serve and follow our Lord Jesus Christ, but not such walls as are composed of brick and mortar. The walls of the Interpreter's House denote the new heart that has been sprinkled and made clean by the saving grace and redemptive power of the Lord Jesus Christ. (Ezekiel 36:25-27)

In Scripture, we learn the astounding truth that the believer's body is the temple of the Holy Spirit. (1 Corinthians 6:19-20) As the redeemed of the Lord Jesus Christ, we are set apart unto him, wholly consecrated to his service, and our bodies are his dwelling place through his Spirit. (1 Corinthians 3:16-17) The Holy Spirit is a precious gift of love, sent to us from God the Father and our Lord Jesus Christ. Living inside the hearts that he has sanctified, he is pleased to teach us more of our precious Lord. (John 15:26)

As our resident teacher, he enlightens our minds with an ever-increasing knowledge of his Word. (John 14:26) As our constant guide, he applies its truth to our hearts and teaches us to walk more perfectly in its precepts. (Romans 8:1-14) As our divine comforter, he ministers the help and strength we need to persevere in the way of faith and obedience. (John 14:15-21) As our heavenly friend, he is gradually forming the image of Christ in us so that we may more perfectly reflect his light in a world of spiritual darkness. (Philippians 2:12-16)

The vast treasury found within the Interpreter's House is filled with the unsearchable riches of Christ. It is accessible to all who visit there, but like gold hidden in the deep places of the earth, this spiritual treasure must be sought and mined. The fact that Christian had to knock repeatedly before the door was opened in no way suggests hesitation on the Interpreter's part. Rather, it emphasizes our duty to ask, seek, and knock diligently. (Luke 11:9-13)

The opening of the door by the master of the house denotes the divine authority of the Spirit of God and his equality with the Father and the Son. His welcoming invitation to "Come in" expresses the delight with which he enlightens our minds to the things of Christ. Take careful note of the candle in his hand, for it is the source of the light that fills this house and shines from its many windows. It is not the kind of light that can be kindled through natural understanding. The Spirit of God must ignite the flame within our hearts and illuminate our minds if we are to receive and understand spiritual truth.

As you have undoubtedly guessed by now, the Lord Jesus Christ is the sum and substance of the Interpreter's House. In him are hidden all the treasures of wisdom and knowledge, for in him dwells all the fullness of the Godhead bodily. The endless chambers in this great house illustrate the immensity and infinity of his unsearchable riches. However, our weakness and frailty hinder our ability to comprehend the vast benefits that are ours in Christ. We are vessels of limited capacity and leaky vessels at that. Therefore, our Lord communicates a measure of his truth to us through his Spirit, as we are able to receive it.

Dear reader, as the Interpreter conducts Christian through his wonderful house, we will witness our Lord's tender regard for our individual limitations. Although the new pilgrim will only be shown some of its rooms, they are choice ones, with each chamber containing a profitable lesson for him to learn, reflect upon, and lay to heart. So while the gracious host of this great house ushers Christian into his inner sanctum, let us also follow on, listen carefully, and learn.

One man among a thousand

As the Interpreter leads the way into the first private room, notice that it contains a single item, a portrait hanging on the wall. Although it is not a great masterpiece or the work of a famous artist, study it carefully, my friend. Who is the solemn person depicted there, and why is his portrait displayed so prominently in the Interpreter's House?

Although the Holy Spirit lives in every child of God as his or her resident teacher and guide, we have need of instrumental help if we are to safely navigate the path of life. God graciously provides this help by calling and gifting men to be his watchmen, the guardians of his flock. Upon the Gospel battleground, these men form the vanguard and bear the brunt of the conflict. At the same time they must guard the flank lest the enemy break through, for part of their calling entails protecting the flock against the intrusion of deadly error. The man of God does this by his uncompromising declaration of the truth and by maintaining a vigilant watch over those who have been placed under his pastoral care.

The godly minister is a rare and precious gift. Like Great-heart in *The Pilgrim's Progress: the Second Part*, he is the conductor and spiritual guide of those entrusted to his charge. His faithful ministry is highly instrumental in their conversion, spiritual growth, and perseverance in faith. Therefore, he occupies a vital place in the kingdom of God even though he usually lives and labors in relative obscurity. This is the man in the portrait, one man among a thousand.

However, all who claim to preach the Gospel are not the true servants of Jesus Christ. Many assume the name and claim the office when they are really wolves in sheep's clothing. These imposters are driven by ulterior motives, not genuine love or concern for the flock of Christ. Through clever words intended to deceive, they pervert the Gospel and create havoc in the churches. (Acts 20:28-30)

How are we to distinguish between the true minister of Christ and the false pretender? By what criteria are we to make this vitally important judgment? Take a close look at the man in the portrait. Ponder his expression and note well his features, for in them we shall find the answer.

Studying the characteristics of the imposter will do little to help us identify a minister of Jesus Christ. He is only known by a careful consideration of the true. The portrait hanging in the great entrance hall of the Interpreter's House is placed there for just this reason. It is a composite of the genuine under shepherd of Christ, both as to his godly character and the exercise of his divine gift. Its distinguishing features show the high standards required for this highest and most noble calling. So as we carefully ponder each feature of the man in the portrait, what do we see?

First, we must understand that he is a man, not an angel or a super-human being. He would be the first to say that he is fallible, limited in wisdom and knowledge, and fully aware that his strength is not equal to his great task. Yet he is a very special man, described by John Bunyan as "one of a thousand." He is what he is by the grace of God, a chosen vessel filled with the Spirit of Christ and set apart for special service in the kingdom of God.

The sober mind and Christ-like character of the man of God can be traced in the deeply etched lines of his face. There is no hint of frivolity there, for the heavy responsibility and serious nature of his labor is ever in his thoughts. The sorrows and burdens that are unique to his calling give his face its rather care-worn appearance, yet there is a beauty in his features as well, the beauty of one who is selflessly devoted to the service of his Lord. (1 Timothy 6:11-12)

His eyes are worthy of particular attention, for they reveal both the nature of his calling and the orientation of his heart. Rather than looking straight ahead, his eyes are lifted upward, and even though you cannot see it, so is his heart. This precious servant of Christ has answered a heavenly call. Thus he labors tirelessly for both time and eternity, not out of mere duty or for earthly honor or reward, but out of love for his Lord and the souls of men. The power to faithfully perform his commission comes from the Spirit of God, who called him and placed him in the ministry. (2 Timothy 2:1-4)

Although he is a man of spiritual strength, he is keenly aware of his utter dependence upon the Lord. Therefore, he spends much time in prayer, seeking help and strength from the one whom he serves and to whom he belongs. Then coming out of his prayer chamber, he goes forth as a mighty man of valor, prepared for spiritual battle with the whole armor of God.

After duly noting the man's uplifted eyes, our attention is next drawn to the book in his hand. This book, which is continually in his heart and mind, is the Word of God. As his sole authority, it constitutes both the rule of his life and the message of his lips. Shunning the commandments and doctrines of men, including his own personal opinions, he diligently labors to learn and rightly interpret the Scriptures. In so doing, he is equipped for the task of properly expounding it to others. (2 Timothy 3:14-17)

Even though the minister of Jesus Christ is a leader of men, he is a leader led by his heavenly master. He is well aware that he can only accomplish his great task if the Spirit of God is the source of his knowledge, wisdom, and unction. Therefore, the man of God is no stranger to the house of the Interpreter. In fact, like Pastor Greatheart, he is a frequent resident there. Within the refuge of its walls he communes with his Lord, receives instruction in the truth, and seeks guidance as to its proper application. In this way, he becomes an able minister of Jesus Christ, skillful in the Word of God and apt in the ready defense of the Gospel. Then being filled and led by the Spirit of Truth, he is a proper guide for other pilgrims on their way to Zion. (1 Timothy 4:12-16)

The next feature of the man, the "law of truth written upon his lips," is not visible to the natural eye. It is a characteristic that has to do with the godly example of the minister of Christ. (1 Timothy 4:12-13) Truth flows from his lips because it is a living reality in his heart. Since his life is consistent with his message, the man of God is a worthy example to his flock. (1 Timothy 4:6-8; Hebrews 13:7)

We might presume that a man of such exemplary character would be loved and appreciated by all who know him, but this is not the case. Since he labors for the approval of God and not men, and since he buys the truth and sells it not, he is often misunderstood, slandered, and despised. (2 Timothy 2:1-15) He expects no better treatment from men of the world, but ironically, a significant part of this kind of suffering comes from those who claim to be brethren in the Lord. However, the truly spiritual person will love and respect him for his courageous defense of the truth.

After studying the various features of this very rare portrait, the perceptive viewer will observe that the world is placed behind the man's back. He serves a heavenly master, a risen, reigning Lord; therefore, his heart is firmly set on things above. The world and its vanities hold no charms for him. Whatever earthly position or honors he could have attained, or temporal goals he might have achieved by pursuing a lesser calling, are gladly sacrificed to his Lord. Knowing full well that no man can serve two masters, he follows his Lord with singleness of heart and mind. Moreover, he does so joyfully, out of love for the one who saved him and placed him in the ministry. (2 Timothy 2:1-4)

Gazing still more closely upon the countenance of the man in the portrait, we observe that he "seemed to plead with men." In this, we may infer much concerning both his ministry and his heart of love for the souls of men. The imposter has no genuine care for men. He possesses nothing of the true shepherd's heart, but ever seeks his own selfish purposes. Therefore, when the tide turns and trouble or persecution comes, he is the first one to flee.

Unlike the false pretender, the man of God loves people enough to tell them the truth, even when he must do so at great personal cost. As an ambassador of Jesus Christ to whom the ministry of reconciliation has been committed, he faithfully declares the good news that through Christ, men are reconciled to God and made the righteousness of God in him. (2 Corinthians 5:17-21) Since this precious truth is neither universally loved nor accepted, suffering is an inevitable part of his bold defense of it. Yet he does not shun the pain that often attends his valiant stand for the truth, but can honestly say with the apostle Paul: *Therefore I endure all things for the elect's sake, that they may also obtain the salvation which is in Christ Jesus with eternal glory.*

Then there is the parental aspect of his calling, which is evident in his concern for the spiritual growth and welfare of those placed under his care. As they strive to follow the Lord and be more like him, as the image of Christ is gradually being formed in them, their pastor suffers spiritual birth pains right along with them. (Galatians 4:19) He can truthfully say with the apostle John: *I have no greater joy than to hear that my children walk in truth.* (3 John 4) On the other hand, he knows no greater anguish than seeing those whom he loves reject the truth and depart from it.

What possible reward could be due such a man as is represented by the portrait? It would certainly be nothing that this world has to offer. But he does not seek earthly recognition, esteem, or reward. The "crown of gold hung over his head" signifies that a heavenly reward awaits him. (2 Timothy 4:7-8) When earthly honors and corruptible crowns have all been left behind, something far higher is reserved for the faithful under shepherd of Jesus Christ, a crown of glory that will not fade away. (1 Peter 5:1-4)

* * * *

Dear brother or sister in Christ, there is perhaps another reason why this portrait is given such a prominent place in the Interpreter's House. Although the Spirit of God is the only infallible Interpreter, every Gospel minister also bears the name in that he is taught by the Holy Spirit in order to rightly teach others. Moreover, in a very real sense, every gathered assembly of saints is an Interpreter's House, part of the household of God, the habitation of God through the Spirit. (Ephesians 2:22) Those who have the divine Interpreter living within will discern the gift of God and hear the voice of Christ through his appointed under shepherds. (Ephesians 4:7-16)

So before we leave the antechamber, join me in taking one last look at the portrait hanging there, for it is actually a study in contrasts.

By rightly interpreting its features, we should be well able to distinguish the true minister of Christ from those who merely claim to be. Moreover, the way in which we regard and treat the man of God says much about our spiritual condition. (Matthew 25:34-45) Therefore, let us give him diligent heed and follow his authority, remembering that he is commissioned by the King of kings to guide us safely through the difficulties we will encounter in this life. (Hebrews 13:17) Many false voices will clamor for our attention along the way, but armed with the increased knowledge gained in the Interpreter's House, we should be much less likely to fall for the lies of the false pretender. (1 John 2:18-27)

Study Questions

1. Who is the Interpreter and what does his house represent? What kind of treasure is hidden there?

2. Who is the man in the portrait, and why is he called one man among a thousand?

3. How are we to distinguish between the true minister of Christ and the imposter?

4. Study the man in the portrait, then list his features and the character traits they signify.

5. What valuable lessons are to be learned from studying the man in the portrait?

CHAPTER 14

Invaluable Instruction by the Master Teacher

WITH THE ADMONITION TO ALWAYS REMEMBER THE PORTRAIT IN THE entrance hall, the Interpreter took Christian by the hand and led him into a large, dusty parlor. After giving him a little time to reflect upon the scene, the Interpreter called for a man to sweep the filthy room. Christian nearly choked as he was forced to breathe the dust-laden air! Then the Interpreter called for a lady to bring water, sprinkle the room and sweep it again. After the room was swept clean, the Interpreter revealed the meaning and significance of it all.

The dusty parlor is a picture of man's sinful heart apart from saving grace, a heart that is full of corruption and completely defiled. The man who first tried to clean the room signifies the law of God. In spite of the man's best efforts, his vigorous sweeping could not get rid of the dust, but only made matters worse. In this, we see the operation of God's holy law as it stirs up the deadened conscience and brings an increased knowledge of guilt and condemnation. (Romans 7:5-12)

When one experiences this inward revival of sin, his first thought is often to try to do something about it. However, in attempting to better himself, he is no more successful than one trying to get rid of a thick layer of dust with a dry broom. He may stir up the dirt and move it around but he cannot get rid of it. Eventually, it will settle right back into the same old resting place. Man's best efforts prove the futility of self-reformation. They can do nothing to remove his guilt before a thrice-holy God. Christian had learned this fundamental truth well, when trembling beneath the fiery Mount Sinai. The law condemns men but is powerless to cancel guilt. It can neither justify nor sanctify the soul.

The Spirit of God, not the deeds of the law, must cleanse the heart of man. (Ezekiel 36:25-27; Titus 3:4-7) Moreover, his work of salvation is consummated in the very same way, and it all flows to us through the merits of Christ and his cross. (Psalm 51:1-10; Hebrews 10:22) This is Gospel cleansing! The ability to savingly believe on Christ, overcome the flesh, and walk in righteousness comes from the gracious influence of the Spirit of God, through the power of the Gospel. (Romans 8:1-4) This is the only way that the power of sin is vanquished and the heart is sanctified and made a fit habitation of God. (Ephesians 5:25-27)

As the Interpreter opened the door to the next chamber, Christian saw what appeared to be a typical schoolroom setting in which two minor children were working at their desks. Their father had arranged for them to be educated under the guidance and discipline of a highly qualified tutor. But even though the boys were brothers, they were exact opposites in character and temperament.

Passion, the elder brother, rebelled against the authority of his father's house. Driven by a restless spirit and covetous heart, he was eager to cast off the restraints placed upon him by his teacher. Like the prodigal son in Luke 15, he demanded his inheritance immediately, spurning the wise counsel of his tutor that it would be in his best interest to wait. When his desire was granted, Passion gloated over his brother and flaunted his freedom, but he possessed neither the prudence nor the self-control to manage his inheritance wisely. Thus he yielded to his fleshly desires in the attempt to satisfy them and obtain a measure of contentment and happiness. Not surprisingly, his folly outlasted his inheritance, and in time, he was reduced to abject poverty. Unlike the prodigal son, however, Passion gave no indication of remorse or the desire to return to his father's house.

Patience, the younger brother, displayed a completely different orientation of heart. He possessed a quiet spirit that was submissive to his father's will. Therefore, he followed the counsel of his tutor and was willing to wait for his inheritance until the time appointed by his father.

If taken strictly at face value, the scenario of two brothers teaches a highly practical object lesson, and it certainly has merit in that respect alone. However, if we consider these two young men as allegorical figures, we will discover the primary meaning behind the schoolroom drama and glean an important spiritual principle from it. The two boys represent two kinds of people: those who are saved by God's grace (Patience) and those who are not (Passion). Thus every member of the human race must identify with one or the other of them.

Passion was a natural-born son of Adam. Therefore, his heart was unrestrained by grace and he was ruled by the intensity of his own selfish desires. Being incapable of sound, spiritual judgment, he lived for the moment, hoping to satisfy his inmost needs with temporal pleasures. In common with the rich fool in Luke 12:16-21, he cared for nothing more than a comfortable existence in this world. So even if he had attained a good measure of worldly success, the elder brother would still have been spiritually bankrupt. (Ecclesiastes 2:9-11) His situation is particularly tragic because he wasted his substance on things that can never really satisfy, while refusing to buy what he could freely have and keep forever. (Isaiah 55:1-2) In living for this present world he ended up losing everything, including his own soul. (Mark 8:34-37)

Although Patience was related to Passion by natural birth, he was a child of God by new birth. In contrast to the stony heart of his brother, his heart had been prepared by the Spirit of God to receive the good seed of the Word. As the grace and knowledge of Christ increased in his soul, the desires and inclinations of his flesh were gradually being subdued and conquered. Thus he was content to follow his tutor, the Spirit of God, and patiently wait upon his heavenly Father's will and good pleasure.

Unlike those who seek their portion in this life, the child of God lives for the world to come. Because his treasure is in heaven, his heart is fixed on things above. All of his earthly labors and responsibilities are performed with regard to God's kingdom and righteousness. Therefore, he diligently strives to glorify God in all that he does, even when it places him at a worldly disadvantage.

Why are God's people willing to endure this? Unlike the unregenerate person, we understand that the best things are yet to be. Therefore, we realize that our race to eternal glory must be run and completed with patience. (Hebrews 12:1-2) Moreover, we understand that patience is one of the virtues of a Christ-like character. (2 Peter 1:2-11) Finally, we know that genuine faith does not exist in the absence of the spiritual fruit of patience. (Hebrews 6:11-12)

So Passion may ridicule his brother and account him a fool if he likes, but Patience is really the wise one. He waits for an inheritance that is sure, incorruptible, and eternal. (1 Peter 1:3-4) Passion will share the doom of the rich man in Luke 16:19-31, while Patience can confidently say of his Lord:

Thou shalt guide me with thy counsel, and afterward receive me to glory. Whom have I in heaven but thee? And there is none upon earth that I desire beside thee. My flesh and my heart faileth: but God is the strength of my heart, and my portion for ever. (Psalm 73:24-26)

A passing strange sight was in store for Christian when he entered the third chamber. He saw a fire burning against one of the walls even though a man stood nearby, pouring water continually upon it. However, the harder the man tried to extinguish the flames, the stronger and brighter the fire burned. An unquenchable fire? How could that be? More to the point, what does it mean? This unquenchable fire speaks of something that brings immense comfort and assurance to our hearts as God's children.

The key to this great mystery was hidden on the other side of the wall, where another man continually fed the fire by pouring oil upon it. As the Interpreter took Christian behind the scene to behold this secret work, a precious truth began to dawn upon his understanding. This extraordinary sight illustrated the reason why believers in Christ are able to persevere in faith.

The Spirit of God ignites a fire in the heart of every child of God, the unquenchable flame of faith and love for the Savior that nothing on earth or in hell can extinguish. Various kinds of water will come in like a flood and try to put out the fire. Moreover, we lack the power to prevent these destructive forces from doing their worst. Yet in spite of Satan's strongest efforts to quench the flame, it burns steadily on. The Lord Jesus Christ secretly maintains the work he has begun through the continual flow of the oil of his Spirit. (Philippians 1:6)

When we find ourselves in the midst of great adversity, it is hard to perceive this gracious work taking place in us. Because it is hidden from our view, we may feel sure that we are going to be conquered by our trouble. However, if our hearts are aflame with love for the Lord Jesus Christ, the promise is certain that *many waters cannot quench love, neither can the floods drown it.* (Song of Solomon 8:7a) What's more, the opposition of Satan, by which he intends to defeat and destroy our faith, actually has the reverse effect. In the providence of God, it is used toward our greater spiritual good. Instead of the flame being extinguished, God's grace causes it to burn even stronger and brighter. In his infinite wisdom, God designs our trials in order to purge and purify our faith. Therefore, under his careful regulation, our faith will never be extinguished, though at times it seems to burn as dimly as smoking flax. If we truly lay it to heart, this knowledge will bring great peace and comfort to our souls when we find ourselves in the depths of affliction.

Next, the Interpreter led Christian to a place where a highly dramatic event was in progress. The setting was a beautiful palace, the very sight of which evoked feelings of delight in Christian's heart, feelings that perhaps he could not have easily put into words. He saw a number of persons dressed in shining garments walking along the palace ramparts, interested to see the outcome of the action below. Another large group had gathered just outside the palace door, desiring to enter but not daring to try. The reason for their hesitation was all too clear, for the entrance was blocked by heavily armed guards placed there to stop any who attempted to break through.

This scene would appear to be that of a typical battle for possession of a strategic fortress if not for one rather extraordinary detail. Close by the castle entrance, a man sat at a table ready to record the names of those who did dare to enter therein. However, these were few and far between. Finally, a single man of determined countenance approached the palace, gave his name to the recorder, drew his sword, put on his helmet and rushed toward the door. He was one man among many, and one man against many! Although the armed men threatened him with deadly force and actually wounded him, the valiant man refused to retreat. He eventually fought his way through the enemy lines, pressed through the door, and entered the palace. As he did so, he heard the welcoming voices of those who witnessed the conflict from the castle walls crying, "Come in, Come in; Eternal Glory thou shalt win."

As Christian silently thought upon this remarkable drama and its happy outcome, it struck a familiar chord, causing him to smile and say to the Interpreter, "I think verily I know the meaning of this!" He understood its significance because he had experienced pretty much the same thing. What about you, dear reader? Can you also identify with the man who stormed the beautiful palace?

We who are God's people are presently the citizens of his heavenly kingdom and living under the dominion of his sovereign rule. The stately palace denotes this kingdom and the glory toward which we look forward, an abundant entrance into the everlasting kingdom of our Lord and Savior Jesus Christ. (2 Peter 1:11) The observers walking on the battlements must depict those who have already finished the race, won the battle, and entered into glory. The multitude that desired to enter the palace but dared not try could well represent those who have a nominal interest in following the Lord, but are unprepared and unwilling to face the difficulties that attend the Christian life.

What about the man recording the names of those who do resolve to enter? He reminds me of an especially precious truth. Those who successfully storm this palace are not generally numbered among the world's elite. They are not usually recorded among the great ones of earth, the mighty, the noble or the wise. (1 Corinthians 1:26-29) However, they are known by name in the palace of the King of kings! In the court of heaven, they are the children of the King. Obscure in this world they may be, but their names are written in the Lamb's book of life! (Luke 10:20; John 10:3, 14; Philippians 4:3; Revelation 3:5, 13:8 and 21:27)

The stiff opposition encountered outside the palace door is no trivial matter. It comes from the forces of a rival kingdom, the same ones who inhabit Beelzebub's castle. Their chief aim is to oppose and prevent those who would enter the palace from actually doing so. Those with only a nominal or fleeting interest will not endure the conflict for long. But there are some who refuse to flee in the face of the enemy. Although relatively few in number, they have hearts that have been cleansed and sanctified by the Spirit of God, and the kind of patient, obedient faith that will stand firm under fire. These, my friend, bear the hallmark of Zion's true pilgrims!

Like the fiercely determined man, we must understand that the kingdom of God is not entered without a struggle. Salvation is all of grace, and yet, taking possession of the kingdom engages us in a fierce conflict that requires both a forceful resolve and aggressive action. (Matthew 11:11-12; Luke 9:62; Luke 16:16) We must never suppose that we can fight this battle unarmed, because we wrestle *not against flesh and blood, but against principalities, against powers, against the rulers of the darkness of this world, against spiritual wickedness in high places.* (Ephesians 6:12) Therefore, we must be protected by the helmet of salvation and armed with the sword of the Spirit if we are to win the day. (Ephesians 6:17)

Then by faith, we may take our place among the blessed, *who through faith subdued kingdoms, wrought righteousness, obtained promises, stopped the mouths of lions, quenched the violence of fire, escaped the edge of the sword, out of weakness were made strong, waxed valiant in fight, turned to flight the armies of the aliens.* (Hebrews 11:33-34)

From its beginning, all the way to its joyful end, this battle can only be fought and won by faith. The watchers viewing the conflict from the safety of the palace ramparts remind us that many saints have already attained the glory toward which we now strive. Dear friend in Christ, does not that knowledge encourage your heart as we, also, travel toward the same eternal goal?

A fearful possibility

So far, every room shown to Christian by the Interpreter had contained something to strengthen and encourage him in the faith. However, the next chamber revealed a scene of an entirely different sort, one that was designed to be highly disturbing. Its immediate effect upon Christian was sobering, but when pondered afterward, he would find it to be both profitable and instructive.

Upon entering this gloomy chamber, Christian was shocked to find a man imprisoned in an iron cage. Although the room was quite dark, he could tell that the man "seemed very sad," for his eyes were downcast, and he sighed deeply within himself. Abject misery was clearly written on his face, which formed a striking contrast to the valiant man who stormed the stately palace.

What could possibly have happened to bring him to such a condition? As Christian talked with the man, he learned that he had once professed faith in Jesus Christ and claimed to be his follower. Since an outward change had accompanied his profession of faith, those who knew him had no reason to doubt his sincerity. He apparently joined an assembly where the Word of God was preached, since his conversation with Christian revealed a fair amount of Bible knowledge. But his heart was deceived, and therefore, his hope was ill-founded from the beginning.

In the process of time, his true character began to assert itself. His outward reformation, which had passed as an evidence of conversion, was the result of his own efforts rather than the fruit of Christ living within. Therefore, his so-called faith, like Pliable's, was doomed to be temporary. (Luke 8:12-13) Although he managed to suppress his fleshly lusts for a time, eventually they would not be denied. Since the Spirit of Christ did not live in his heart, there was nothing to restrain the power of sin. Thus it increased in strength until the man was once again enslaved to his own base desires. (2 Peter 2:20-22) As a result, he was in a worse condition than before he professed to be a Christian.

While the man's frightful state of being never characterizes the true Christian, it is common among nominal professors. (Romans 6:12-18) Apart from the new birth, exposure to the truth will only have a superficial and temporary effect. (James 1:21-25) In order for the Word of God to take permanent root and become fruitful unto life, the Spirit of God must apply it to the heart. The man in the iron cage had never experienced this work of God's grace. As a consequence, he eventually proved to be a tree without fruit, a spiritual derelict. While it is true that he was bowed down with sorrow, his sorrow was not of the godly sort that leads to repentance. (2 Corinthians 7:10) He may well have desired the benefits of salvation, but he loved sin more.

When one turns from following Christ, when truth and righteousness are forsaken and a false hope is finally shattered, nothing remains except despair. The allegorical iron cage denotes the utter hopelessness from which the man could not escape. Moreover, the fact that there was no one else to blame for his wretched condition must have added significantly to his torment. Alone, with overwhelming misery as his sole companion, the man was forced to face himself. He had lived a lie while enjoying the pleasures of sin for a season; but now, the day of reckoning had come. (Hebrews 11:25)

What could be more horrible than to have no hope? The man in the iron cage could not escape this agonizing thought, as he faced the certainty of God's justice and eternal retribution. His deep despair reminds me of the inscription placed over the portal of Dante's fictional *Inferno*, which reads, "Abandon All Hope Ye Who Enter Here." [1] These words, which were designed to strike terror into the hearts of the condemned, now formed the substance of the imprisoned man's thoughts.

Since this fearful scene took place within the inner chambers of the Interpreter's House, we might infer that the man's true condition was not obvious to others. He had enough knowledge of Scripture to understand the character of a true Christian, so perhaps he still maintained a form of godliness. In his inmost being, however, he knew full well that he was weighed in the balances and found wanting. (Daniel 5:27) Even if he was still able to deceive others, he could not escape the omniscient eye of God Like many before him, he may have worn the tattered rags of self-righteousness, but he utterly lacked the wedding garment of the redeemed, the perfect righteousness of the Lord Jesus Christ. (Matthew 22:11-13)

Why do you think this study in contrasts was included in Christian's visit to the Interpreter's House? Why did he need to witness the terrible sight of a man imprisoned by despair? What instruction did it contain for him? Would he ever face a similar situation? I suspect that the purpose was two-fold: to serve as both a warning and encouragement to the new pilgrim. It was essential for him to remember that neglect, complacency, and indulgence in willful sin are dangerous tendencies that must be given no place. To trifle with the grace of God is both a perilous and foolish thing. More often than not, it results in dire consequences. (Hebrews 2:1-3; 2 Peter 3:17-18; James 1:12-16)

On the other hand, God's gift of salvation is never rescinded once it has been bestowed. Its recipients are kept by the power of God and will never be lost. (John 10:27-29) Yet every one of them must persevere in faith and be counted as overcomers at the last. (1 John 5:4-5) The patient faith that withstands and endures every adversity it encounters is beyond our ability to produce. Our heavenly Father works this grace in each one of his children, through the intercession of his beloved Son. (John 17:11-12)

The Lord Jesus Christ reigns in the hearts of his people, and his grace within is a highly effective teacher. (Titus 2:11-14) By his Spirit, he applies the Word to our hearts and causes us to walk therein, and yet, we need the instruction, discipline, and correction that also come from his grace. Therefore, with fatherly pity and particular regard to our individual needs, he chastens and corrects us so that we will walk more perfectly before him. (2 Peter 1:1-4)

Since the process of chastening is difficult and painful, we are tempted to view it in a strictly negative light. But when we consider its beneficial effects and our great need of it, we will be more likely to account it a blessed thing. Every believer in Christ brings forth fruit to his glory, although not all to the same degree. Each one of us has a race to run. Whatever our Lord has chosen for us to do, his discipline and training are an integral part of it. All is designed to fit us for even greater service in his kingdom. (John 15:2)

Another precious thing about God's chastening is that it carries with it the assurance of our sonship. (Hebrews 12:5-8) How then do we dare complain when under the stroke of his fatherly correction? Should we not rather kiss the rod, especially when we remember the man in the iron cage, who was allowed to go his own way uncorrected? (Proverbs 3:11-12)

After his disturbing conversation with the wretched man, Christian was more than a little inclined to depart and continue his journey. I can well imagine how his tendency to doubt his own salvation must have made a strong resurgence here. Nevertheless, there was one more thing that he must see before leaving the Interpreter's House.

This last room contained a solitary man who was rising out of bed and trembling as he dressed himself because he dreamed that the Day of Judgment had come and he was not ready. Visions of the night, and the terrors they evoked, had shaken him to the very core and caused this rude awakening. Clearly, this was no mere nightmare, since its horrible images did not diminish with the light of day, and neither was it the phantom of an overactive imagination. The man's dream, and his waking from it, signaled a momentous event that would transform him forever.

His slumber denoted the man's former condition and the indifference with which he had regarded spiritual realities. A darkened understanding caused him to readily dismiss all concern for his soul and the certainty of judgment, whenever they came to mind. So he slumbered and slept, oblivious of any real danger to himself, until his terrible dream!

Since we know from Scripture that God no longer speaks to us through dreams and visions, we may safely infer that the man's dream was metaphorical rather than prophetic in nature. (Hebrews 1:1-2) Its content suggests that he had some Bible knowledge, at least concerning the Day of the Lord and the certainty of final judgment. However, knowledge alone was not enough to shake him from his insensibility.

The man's dream and the terror that resulted from it, denotes another crucial office of the Spirit of God, that of quickening the soul from spiritual death. (Ephesians 2:1-5) Unlike the man in the iron cage, the awakened sleeper had every reason to hope, even though his heart was presently filled with fear. Although he dreamed that the Day of Judgment was come, it had not! The day of grace was not yet over; therefore, there was still hope for him. (Isaiah 55:6-7)

In this poor man's situation, we have an illustration of how the Spirit of God works in the heart of a sinner. Before he whispers peace and comfort to the soul, he first causes one to see his grave danger. In due course, the anguish of conviction will bring him to the light and life of new birth. Then the sorrow of spiritual travail is turned to incomparable joy! How perfectly our dear brother, John Newton, expressed this very truth when he wrote:

> Amazing grace, how sweet the sound that saved a wretch like me!
> I once was lost, but now am found, was blind, but now I see.
>
> 'Twas grace that taught my heart to fear, and grace my fears relieved;
> How precious did that grace appear, the hour I first believed! [2]

Even though there is still hope for those who slumber in spiritual darkness, the terror of the awakened sleeper reminds us that one day his dream will come true. (Matthew 25:1-13) In that day sinners will fear and tremble before God, but it will be too late. When least expected, mercy's door will be shut forever, bringing to mind the awful words of the prophet Jeremiah: *The harvest is past, the summer is ended, and we are not saved.* (Jeremiah 8:20)

For the people of God, the promised appearing of our Lord will be a day of joy and final deliverance, but it will signal the beginning of eternal woe for those who know not Christ and have not obeyed his Gospel. (2 Thessalonians 1:7-10) How unspeakable will be their horror in that day, when all hope is truly gone and nothing remains except the agony of regret! (Revelation 6:12-17)

Unlike the awakened sleeper, God's children do not anticipate the return of our Lord with fear and dread. The promise of his appearing is our blessed hope, our confident expectation and hope of eternal life. (Titus 2:13; Titus 3:7) It is our hope of glory, an immovable, steadfast hope that is to us an anchor of the soul. (Colossians 1:27; Hebrews 6:19)

In light of the believer's glorious future, why did Christian need to see the awakened sleeper and hear the account of his frightful dream? Does it contain an application and timely warning to true believers? If so, what scriptural message is concealed within the figure of the sleeper?

Although we are advancing toward the blessed hope of our Lord's return, we are not given to know when it will be. Therefore, we are to live in watchful expectation of his appearing and to pass the time of our sojourn here in fear. (1 Peter 1:17) Not the fear and dread of the unbeliever, but the reverential fear of a child who desires above all to obey and please our heavenly Father.

Does not the prospect of seeing our Lord face to face provide the strongest of incentives for walking uprightly before him now? Should not the promise of his return be a living reality in our lives, prompting us to yield our bodies to him as living sacrifices? (Romans 12:1-2) Should it not cause us to have our minds sharply focused upon eternal realities, while persevering in faith and hope? Yes indeed, it should! (1 Peter 1:13-16)

As the people of God, we are the children of light, and the children of the day (1 Thessalonians 5:5); therefore, we are to walk as befits our high calling. Maintaining a diligent self-watch is a crucial part of this walk, since we are more easily overtaken by temptation or led astray than we think. To aid us in this vital duty, the Word of God gives us explicit instruction concerning how we are to live as we await the return of our Lord.

While others are deceived and lulled into spiritual slumber, we are to be alert, watchful, and sober-minded. (1 Thessalonians 5:1-10) While others indulge in all manner of lusts and yield to the uncleanness of the flesh, we are to guard our hearts and minds while practicing godliness. (2 Peter 3:10-18; Titus 2:11-14) While others stumble out of the way in blind unbelief, we are to walk by faith and continue in steadfast hope. (John 8:31-32; Colossians 1:21-23; Hebrews 10:38-39) While multitudes do that which is right in their own eyes, we are to abide in Christ as his obedient children so that we may be found faithful at his appearing. (1 John 2:28-29)

We cannot accomplish this in our own strength, to be sure! The grace of God, which produces persevering hope in us, also supplies the means to live in light of it. What a vast benefit is this, flowing to us from Christ and his cross! Through his Spirit, our Lord Jesus Christ both ignites and maintains the flame within. The strength and grace to overcome every adversity is evidence of this secret work that is preparing us for the consummation of our salvation. (Romans 13:11-14)

As we wait for the return of our Lord, we also look for a wondrous metamorphosis, a mysterious change that we can now but faintly imagine. For in that day, the glorious day of his appearing, our mortal bodies will either be resurrected from the grave or instantly transformed, if we are yet living. Until then we watch and wait, anticipating the time when the last enemy, Death, is finally destroyed and we are clothed with immortality. (1 Corinthians 15:50-58)

* * * *

What wondrous things Christian has seen in the Interpreter's House! When he first entered the door, his spiritual understanding had been small and his discernment weak. Within its vast storehouse, he has viewed some of the rarest jewels of wisdom and knowledge that the house contains. Moreover, the instruction he received was of the most practical sort, valuable truths to hide in his heart and keep always in remembrance. Through the guidance of the master teacher, he came to see things that would nurture both hope and a proper godly fear within his heart. Precious truths to guide his steps, encourage his heart, and stabilize his soul! Excellent things! Rare and profitable things that will sustain him in the days ahead, when his way becomes dark and difficult!

Even though Christian had enjoyed the unique hospitality of the Interpreter's House, he was now eager to be on his way. While he had seen many wonderful things, he had only experienced a very small measure of the riches therein. Why then, was he so impatient to depart when there was so much more to be learned here?

The answer probably lies in the fact that he was a new pilgrim. Far too often, those who are young in the Lord tend to overestimate their spiritual perception and maturity. They have yet to learn what leaky vessels they are. Early zeal, even when driven by genuine love and faith, is often more self-confident than prudent and well informed. Therefore, to be up, running, and busy seems the best plan. Quiet solitude in the presence of God, and the exercise of soul that it entails, is not yet valued as much as it will later be. Moreover, in Christian's case, he did still carry his burden.

Whatever the reasons for Christian's hurry, he will eventually learn that time spent abiding in the house of the Interpreter is time well invested, and that for eternity. Thus dear brother or sister in Christ, abiding therein should be a top priority of our lives as well. When we tarry there, even though it may seem to delay our journey, we will find that it actually speeds us on our way.

With the Interpreter's parting words, "The Comforter be always with thee," we are once again reminded that we are in the realm of the allegorical. Christian's visit to this special house of light was not a single event in his life. It signifies the unsearchable riches that are ours in Christ, and to which we have continual access through his Spirit. What a comfort it is to know that the Holy Spirit is not merely an occasional host to whom we may go for help. He dwells within us and ministers to us continually as our teacher, comforter, and guide all the way until we enter the Celestial City.

O divine Interpreter, give us the wisdom
to quietly and contentedly abide in thy house.
Take the things of Christ and reveal them more clearly to our hearts.
Fill us with thy heavenly light until
the beauty of Christ shines in and through us!
Amen

Study Questions

1. What vital truth can we learn from the scene in the dusty parlor and the man's futile attempt to cleanse it?

2. Contrast the characters of the two brothers, Passion and Patience, and show the two kinds of people they represent.

3. What spiritual truth is taught from the view of the unquenchable fire in the third chamber?

4. Who does the man who stormed the heavily-guarded palace represent, and what is the spiritual meaning of his action?

5. Why did Christian need to witness the frightening sight of the man in the iron cage? How does the hopeless prisoner of despair differ from the awakened sleeper in the final chamber of the Interpreter's house?

Part Six

DELIVERANCE AND RELEASE

Jesus said unto her, I am the resurrection, and the life: he that belie-
veth in me, though he were dead, yet shall he live: and whosoever
liveth and believeth in me shall never die. Believest thou this?

John 11:25-26

CHAPTER 15

Gateway to the City

THE GIFT OF FAITH, SO FREELY BESTOWED BY THE GRACE OF GOD, WAS never meant to lie dormant in the souls of those who possess it. It is given as a crucial life principle that must be put to good use in order to strengthen and grow. Even though saving faith is the genuine article, it must be proven before it can shine forth as gold to the glory of the one who gave it. Therefore, if we are to be fruitful in the service of the Lord Jesus Christ, our faith must be purged and purified. (Isaiah 48:10; 1 Peter 1:6-7)

This is one reason why God does not exempt his children from difficulty. The more we ponder this fundamental truth, the better we will understand why our way seems to become more difficult the further we go. Truly, the path we follow as Christians is an ever ascending one in which we will face trials of many different kinds. However, there is an infinitely wise design behind every impediment in our path. So we who are God's people may rest assured that our Lord is neither a passive nor an indifferent observer as we journey through this life. As our preserver, protector and defender, he keeps us ever in his sight and governs all that concerns us. (Psalm 121:3-5; Psalm 125:1-2)

Although it is not visible to those who travel this path, the enemy has a garden situated close by, just as he has a great castle. The trees growing there bear no resemblance to any earthly variety, however, for they are perpetually laden with luscious, yet deadly, fruit. As John

Bunyan describes in his sequel to *Pilgrim's Progress*, the branches of these trees extend right over the wall that encloses the King's Highway, tempting unsuspecting travelers to taste of their forbidden fruit.

Why has the enemy been allowed to plant this garden right beside the path of life? What is the significance of the mutant trees bearing lavish fruit that is pleasant to the eyes, but has the effect of deadly poison? What does it all mean for those who pass by on the path of the just?

These figurative things serve to remind and warn us that spiritual danger is all around us, and will appear in many deceptive forms. As we travel to Zion, we must be on our guard, lest we fall victim to the wiles of the enemy. However, the walls named salvation and the watchmen placed thereon also remind us that we are ever in God's care. He has made every provision for our safe passage. (Psalm 33:18-20) The enemy who owns both the garden and the castle is under God's absolute control and can go no further in his evil designs against us than God permits.

Therefore we may take heart, even when our way is dark and difficult. Our blessed Lord is ever close at hand, leading us by his providence, sustaining us by his grace, and furnishing every means for our perseverance. By his powerful hand, he will keep us in that very same narrow, enclosed path that Christian took after he left the House of the Interpreter.

As Christian rushed forward along the road that lay straight before him, he did so with much clearer insight. The rare and excellent things he has just seen now filled his vision, reviving his spirit with renewed hope and urging him onward as quickly as his burden would permit. Since his path had now taken a decidedly upward direction, he found that he was a little short of breath. But as he gazed into the distance, he could see a cross placed at the top of the hill. When he reached the summit, Christian knew intuitively that he had reached the place of deliverance at last.

O, how precious is faith's first view of the cross! It is a sight that never grows old! What a marvelous display of God's love, mercy, and grace we see there! My brother or sister in Christ, does it not fill your soul with wonder and make your heart rejoice? Taste of it anew with me as we watch Christian standing there, gazing in awe upon the scene while a great light dawned within him and assurance filled his soul. The effect upon him was immediate and dramatic, for the burden he carried on his back suddenly loosened, fell from him, and tumbled down the hill into an empty tomb, never to be seen again. Deliverance had come at last, just as the keeper of the Wicket Gate promised.

Perhaps more than anywhere else in *The Pilgrim's Progress,* the scene at the cross reminds us that we are in the realm of the allegorical. In order to rightly interpret this momentous event in Christian's journey, we must do so in light of its figurative nature. There are many who regard the cross as a religious symbol having supernatural power or an icon to be worshiped. In my opinion, this is superstitious idolatry of the worst sort.

In his great allegory, John Bunyan does not portray the cross and sepulcher as religious relics or visible representations that Christian actually saw and visited. He depicts them as spiritual realities concerning salvation that only a renewed heart can receive. Christian's close-up view of the cross denoted his clearer understanding of the redemption that is in Christ Jesus. In Scripture, to see the Son of God and come to him are equivalent to believing on him. (John 6:37-40, 44-47) To behold the Lamb of God by faith is to hear and believe his Word. (John 12:44-45; Romans 10:17) The only ones who see the Son are those who have received the gift of spiritual life. When interpreted in this light, Christian's view of the cross marked a major turning point in his pilgrimage.

Until now, he has been tormented by doubt and fear concerning his spiritual condition. (1 John 4:18) Even his entrance through the Wicket Gate failed to give him the assurance he so longed for. In the House of the Interpreter, however, he was given to see the precious truths concerning Christ and his so-great salvation with a much clearer understanding. (Romans 8:15-16; 2 Timothy 1:7) The Spirit of God, who is ever the revealer of Christ, applied these truths to Christian's understanding and directed him toward the only source of rest and refuge for the troubled soul. Thus Christian was enabled to *Behold the Lamb of God, which taketh away the sin of the world* (John 1:29), and by faith, to embrace the implications to his own soul.

What does the eye of faith see when it surveys the cross of Christ and the empty tomb? It understands and claims as its very own the testimony of God's Word concerning the person of Christ, his death, and resurrection. It beholds the highest manifestation of God's eternal love, a wondrous love beyond all human comprehension. (John 15:13) It receives the blessing of salvation, which is without doubt God's greatest gift to sinful mankind. (John 3:16; 1 John 4:9-10)

The sufferings of Christ and his resurrection from the dead took place exactly as God foreordained. (Acts 2:22-24) However, in order to accomplish the redemption of his people, Christ had to be manifested in the flesh. He must come to earth, a child born and a son given in order to die, since there was no other way for sin to be removed. (Mark 8:31; Acts 4:10-12) He was born to die, yet destined to reign forever. (Isaiah 9:6-7; Acts 2:29-32)

Therefore, in God's appointed time, the Lord of glory became a partaker of our humanity. (Matthew 1:18-25) As the unique Son of God and virgin-born Son of man, he was *holy, harmless, undefiled, separate from sinners, and made higher than the heavens.* (Hebrews 7:26) What condescension that he would deign to walk among men as Emmanuel, God with us! Mysteriously alluding to his express mission on earth, he said: *Verily, verily, I say unto you, except a corn of wheat fall into the ground and die, it abideth alone: but if it die, it bringeth forth much fruit.* (John 12:24) He stated his purpose more explicitly to his disciples when he said: *Behold, we go up to Jerusalem, and all things that are written by the prophets concerning the Son of man shall be accomplished. For he shall be delivered unto the Gentiles, and shall be mocked, and spitefully entreated, and spitted on: And they shall scourge him, and put him to death: and the third day he shall rise again.* (Luke 18:31-33)

So when his hour came in which God's eternal purpose of salvation would be fulfilled, he yielded completely to the good pleasure of his Father's will. (Matthew 26:36-46; John 12:27) In bearing our sins on the cross, the Lord Jesus Christ bore the heaviest burden of time and eternity. In taking upon himself our sins, he felt the weight of every one of them as no other ever could. (Isaiah 53:4; Matthew 27:46) By offering himself as a sacrifice for sin, he tasted death for his people and secured our redemption once for all. (Hebrews 2:9-10; Hebrews 5:5-10)

Though he was rich, yet for our sakes, he became poor. Yet what a wealth of benefits flows to us from his poverty and the travail of his soul! What unsearchable riches of his grace! It was the remembrance of God's goodness and tender mercies that impelled David to bless the Lord with all of his ransomed being. (Psalm 103) In this divinely inspired doxology, he offers to God the spiritual sacrifice of a grateful heart. It is the beautiful song of a soul set free from guilt and condemnation.

These same benefits, which David viewed by faith in the coming redeemer, belong to all who are in Christ. Forgiveness! Spiritual healing! Redemption from the path of destruction! Crowning with loving-kindness and tender mercies! Abundant provision to serve him! Renewed strength to stay the course! (Psalm 103:1-5) Vast benefits! Covenant mercies all flowing to us freely from the cross and the sepulcher of our risen, reigning Lord! Surely our feet stand on holy ground as we contemplate the rich blessings of salvation that are ours in Christ!

God's wondrous grace in Christ is never more precious than when we remember the hopeless condition in which he found us, and from which he rescued us. Sin forms an impassible barrier between God and man. By nature, man lives under the curse and bondage of sin; he is alienated from the life of God and unable to do anything about it. If the great chasm between men and their creator was to be spanned, God alone must initiate and complete it.

Man also had need of an advocate, a sinless mediator who could plead his case in the court of heaven before the judgment bar of a holy God. None among the children of Adam would do, but in the person of his only begotten Son, God provided the perfect mediator between himself and man. What God's justice demanded, his grace and mercy abundantly supplied. In Christ, he provided the legal basis by which men could be reconciled to God, justified freely in his sight, and delivered from sin's penalty and power.

Unseen by mortal eyes, the great exchange that secured our redemption took place at the cross. (2 Corinthians 5:17-21; 1 Peter 3:18; Romans 5:6-10; Hebrews 9:11-12) By his death, our Lord forever satisfied the demands of God's holy law and paid the debt we owed to divine justice. (Romans 3:19-26; Romans 5:1-2) Through the cross, God vindicated his holiness so that he might be just, and the justifier of those who believe in the Lord Jesus. Moreover, by the resurrection of

Christ, God demonstrated his complete satisfaction with his redemptive work on the cross. (Acts 2:22-36)

Thus it is at the cross and the empty tomb that we find the answer to the age-old question of how a man may be just before God. (Job 9:2; Romans 5:17-21) There the enmity between God and man was removed and reconciliation made. (Colossians 1:20-22) At the cross, the great chasm separating man from God was done away, and now, sinners are brought nigh to God. (Ephesians 2:13-18; Colossians 2:13-15)

In Romans 15:13, the apostle Paul pronounces a benediction upon his readers saying: *Now the God of hope fill you with all joy and peace in believing, that ye may abound in hope, through the power of the Holy Ghost.* Peace! What a precious gift it is! As the children of God, we may confidently rest in our Lord and his redemptive work in our behalf because he is our peace. Through his merit, we are granted the right to boldly approach the throne of our heavenly Father with the assurance that he remembers our sins no more. (Hebrews 10:16-22)

This wondrous truth gives rise to a seriously flawed conclusion in certain quarters. The apostle Paul faced it in his day and answered it by asking the rhetorical question: *Shall we continue in sin, that grace may abound?* He then immediately puts the sword to this false notion by exclaiming: *God forbid. How shall we, that are dead to sin, live any longer therein?* (Romans 6:1-2) A proper consideration of these questions will bring to mind another virtue that is bestowed upon the people of God through the cross – the virtue of spiritual healing.

When the sun of righteousness arises in the soul, he does so with healing in his wings, spiritual healing that only comes through the merits of Christ and his cross. (Isaiah 53:5; John 3:14-18) He alone is the balm in Gilead, the Great Physician who administers the remedy for all of our spiritual woes. (Jeremiah 8:22)

The spiritual healing secured at the cross creates a new principle within all who are born again. It is a transformative process by which those who were the servants of sin now delight in living unto righteousness. As a result, they no more desire to live in sin than they would wish the recurrence of a terrible disease. This principle of godliness does not mean that we will no longer struggle with sin. However, it does signify that we will no longer live under its dominion and mastery. (Romans 6:6-16)

The virtue of spiritual healing also has another greatly liberating influence. It purges the conscience from its burden of guilt and shame. (Hebrews 9:13-14) One of the most harmful effects of sin upon the human constitution is its bondage of the mind. Through the liberating power of the cross of Christ, we are released from this terrible captivity and freed to walk in paths of righteousness and obedience. (John 8:34-36)

With all of these precious truths in mind, we have a more comprehensive understanding of what Christian saw when he stood before the cross and the empty tomb. It is there that we behold the Lamb of God in the hour of his greatest humiliation as well as his highest triumph and exaltation. (Philippians 2:8-11) There we hear the Savior's victorious cry, *It is finished,* as he bowed his head and died and *the veil of the temple was rent in twain from the top to the bottom.* (Mark 15:37-38) What assurance and peace this whispers to the believing heart!

The basis of our confidence is not only that Christ died, but that he also lives and reigns as Lord of all. Listen to the words of comfort he spoke to the apostle John, who saw him in glorious vision and was stricken at the sight: *Fear not; I am the first and the last: I am he that liveth, and was dead; and, behold, I am alive for evermore, amen; and have the keys of hell and of death.* (Revelation 1:17b-18)

Our Lord lives and holds us safely in his hand. What power is able to breach that security? He is our great high priest, and because he lives, his priesthood is unchangeable. With this assurance in our hearts, we may come boldly and without fear before our heavenly Father's throne. Does not our surety sit at his right hand? Then we may rest in the knowledge that *He is able also to save them to the uttermost that come unto God by him, seeing he ever liveth to make intercession for them.* (Hebrews 7:24-25)

Because the Lord Jesus Christ lives and is the mediator of the everlasting covenant, he has secured all that is needful for our ultimate perfection and safe arrival home. (Hebrews 13:20-21) Our sure hope of eternal life rests securely in the knowledge that he not only died, but he lives. (1 Corinthians 15:17-20) Because he lives, we who are in him will also live forever. This certain hope emboldened the apostle Paul to actually taunt death by proclaiming: *O death, where is thy sting? O grave, where is thy victory? The sting of death is sin; and the strength of sin is the law. But thanks be to God, which giveth us the victory through our Lord Jesus Christ.* (1 Corinthians 15:55-57)

For Christian, the year of jubilee had come at last! Had he persisted in following the counsel of the Worldly Wiseman, he might never have seen the wondrous sight of the cross and sepulcher. By God's mercy, however, he has been recovered from that snare and freed from the burden he had carried for so long. Why was it not until now?

It was not until he better understood the meaning of the cross that the terrible image of Mount Sinai was finally eclipsed in his mind. Through a more perfect understanding of God's Word, which was the work of the divine Interpreter, he came to realize that his burden of sin and guilt had been borne by his sinless substitute. He was free, delivered and cleansed, because the Savior had endured the wrath of God in his stead.

Previously, he understood many things concerning Christ and his redemption, but it was not until he viewed the cross in this clearer light that assurance of salvation filled his soul. His guilty conscience was finally purged through the knowledge of sins forgiven. A sure hope had been set before him and he gladly seized it by faith. At last, he comprehended that through the cross, his Lord had provided the only sure foundation for his settled peace. (Romans 8:31-39)

Thus dear reader, it was at the cross and the empty tomb that Christian finally understood his standing in Christ. It is little wonder that he experienced a lightness that was previously unknown, or that tears of joy flowed unimpeded from his eyes.

In the ministry of the three shining ones and the things they gave Christian, we discern the gifts of the triune God that accompany salvation. Through the Gospel, the Spirit of God whispers glad tidings of peace to the believing heart. (Isaiah 52:7) This priceless gift was purchased by our Savior and is foundational to the three specific articles given to Christian by these figurative beings. (John 14:29) Without the assurance of peace, we would be hard pressed to recognize the presence of these three gifts.

The change of garments given to Christian denoted the consciousness of his complete change of condition before God. Clothed no longer in the filthy rags he wore by nature, he now understood that, in

God's sight, he was covered with a spotless, white garment, the perfect righteousness of Christ. Adorned in this beautiful apparel, he knew that he was justified, declared righteous in the sight of a thrice-holy God. (Romans 5)

The mark placed on Christian's forehead was highly significant. It denoted the seal of the Holy Spirit, which marked Christian as one of God's own. (Revelation 14:1) By right of redemption, Christian belonged to his Lord, and the seal, which was visible only to God, was the earnest of his eternal inheritance. (Ephesians 1:13-14)

The sealed roll given to Christian is not explicitly mentioned in Scripture, but it depicts that which is closely connected to the gift of saving faith. This special scroll, which he was to guard carefully and make use of as he traveled to the city, apparently represented the assurance of his salvation through Christ alone. Since it was to be kept in possession until he entered the heavenly Zion, the sealed roll must correspond to the living hope that characterizes each true believer in Christ. (1 Peter 1:3-5) When Christian reaches the Celestial City, his hope will be fully realized, and faith will reach its culmination when he sees his Lord face to face. (1Corinthians 13:12-13) But until then, he must persevere in faith and hope.

* * * *

Salvation, that wondrous and mysterious revelation of Christ to the soul, is entirely the work of the divine Interpreter. (John 16:13-14) When the Holy Spirit opens our hearts, we see that the mercy of God and the grand display of his righteous character meet in the person of the Lord Jesus Christ. At his cross alone can it be truly said that *mercy and truth are met together; righteousness and peace have kissed each other.* (Psalm 85:10) Only in him can the righteous God bestow his mercy upon unworthy sinners without the slightest violation of his justice. (Romans 3:19-26)

Nothing so inspires our hearts to true worship and sincere praise than the remembrance of God's great mercy in Christ. The prophetic anticipation of it caused David to sing: *Blessed is he whose transgression is forgiven, whose sin is covered. Blessed is the man unto whom the LORD imputeth not iniquity, and in whose spirit there is no guile.* (Psalm 32:1-2)

Like David, we who are the grateful recipients of God's saving mercy will also keep it ever in heart and mind as we make our way toward Zion. Even when we must pass through the Valley of Baca, the remembrance of God's past mercy gives us every reason to trust in him and hope in his mercy as we face the fearful unknown.

Dear friend in Christ, the more we "survey the wondrous cross on which the Prince of Glory died," [1] the better we will understand the great debt of love we owe to our blessed Lord. Our only proper response is to yield ourselves to him as living sacrifices; for as we contemplate the cross and the empty tomb we learn that we, too, must die and live unto him. (Romans 12:1-2)

The full realization of how much we owe to our Lord and his grace must wait until we see him face to face. Eternity will not even begin to diminish the wonder of it. Therefore, as we stand with Christian and view the cross and the empty tomb with the eyes of faith, let us ponder anew God's great love and mercy demonstrated to us there. Moreover, let us resolve to carry the remembrance of it with us for the remainder of our earthly pilgrimage. When this passing life is over and we appear before our Lord in glory, faith will consummate in sight and we will see him as he is. Then we will know how much we owe, and love him as we ought.

> By the cross of Jesus standing, love our straitened souls expanding,
> taste we now the peace and grace!
> Health from yonder tree is flowing, heavenly light is on it glowing,
> from the blessed sufferer's face.
>
> Here is pardon's pledge and token, guilt's strong chain forever broken,
> righteous peace securely made;
> Brightens now the brow once shaded, freshens now the face once faded,
> peace with God now makes us glad.
>
> All the love of God is yonder, love above all thought and wonder,
> perfect love that casts out fear!
> Strength, like dew, is here distilling, glorious life our souls is filling,
> life eternal, only here!

Here the living water welleth; here, the rock, now smitten,
telleth of salvation freely given:
This the fount of love and pity, this the pathway to the city,
this the very gate of heaven. [2]

Study Questions

1. Since *Pilgrim's Progress* is an allegory, we know that Christian did not see a literal cross and empty tomb. What then does his close-up view of the cross actually mean?

2. What did the loss of Christian's burden signify? Why did he not lose it until now?

3. To survey the cross of Christ by faith is to believe the testimony of God's Word. (John 5:39) Name some of the great truths concerning the person of Christ and his work of salvation that we learn from his Word.

4. The resurrection of Christ was absolutely vital in order to secure our salvation. What great assurance do we have in knowing that our Savior lives?

5. After the loss of his burden at the cross, Christian received three gifts from three shining ones. What were these gifts and what did they represent?

CHAPTER 16

A Troubling Question

COULD IT BE POSSIBLE THAT, IN SPITE OF HIS DEEP SPIRITUAL INSIGHT, JOHN Bunyan misplaced the cross in his great allegory? Some have suggested that maybe he did, giving rise to speculation as to exactly where he should have placed it. Should he have put it adjacent to the Wicket Gate, or just beyond it, perhaps? Why was the cross situated well beyond that crucial milestone that marked the entrance to the path of life? I must admit that I had somewhat of a struggle with this question myself.

In striving to properly understand and interpret *The Pilgrim's Progress*, I have endeavored to keep three relevant facts uppermost in mind. First, the work is allegorical as to its literary form, giving the author a fair measure of poetic license with his figures, and allowing us a certain degree of latitude when interpreting them. Second, although laden throughout with Scripture truth and allusion, the work neither has nor makes any claim to divine inspiration. Even though its author had an exceptionally brilliant spiritual mind, he was not exempt from error. Finally, the Word of God is infallibly and unalterably true in its entirety, and in every part. Therefore, it is the cornerstone of proper interpretation, and any view that is not consistent with the Scriptures must be summarily rejected.

Since it is my fervent desire to interpret *The Pilgrim's Progress* as accurately as possible, and well within the parameters of clear Scripture truth, I have taken a deliberately cautious approach in the use of conjecture. In this regard, I am grateful to my pastor/husband for his example. He diligently strives to give a proper exegesis when preaching the Word of God, and does so by using sound hermeneutical principles when interpreting Scripture. Moreover, he has taught his congregation to do the same.

One vital principle he often stresses is that the allegorical, symbolic, and parabolic portions of Scripture must always be understood in light of its clear doctrinal teaching. Otherwise, it is possible to not only miss the mark of a right interpretation, but go wildly astray from it. This is a spiritually dangerous course along which many have erred.

I have endeavored to understand *The Pilgrim's Progress* by applying these same principles, with the Word of God as my constant reference and sole authority. Therefore, I have attempted to interpret its allegorical figures in light of sound doctrinal truth and to defer any personal speculations to Scripture revelation. So in considering the placement of the cross, I asked myself whether it was consistent with the Word of God. Did John Bunyan have scripturally valid reasons for placing the cross and the sepulcher exactly where he did, or does a spiritual quandary exist in his great work?

I understand full well that John Bunyan was not infallible in either his comprehension of the Scriptures or his written work. However, it would be strange indeed for a man of his spiritual stature, wisdom, and knowledge to make such a serious error as to misplace the cross. That kind of mistake would surely cast doubt upon the credibility of his entire work. But after careful consideration, I am personally convinced that he did not. Although I cannot possibly know his mind on this subject, I believe he sheds further light upon it in the parallel passage of his sequel, *The Pilgrim's Progress: the Second Part*. Listen to what he has to say after recounting the admission of Christiana, her boys, and Mercy to the Wicket Gate:

"Now I saw in my dream, that he (the gatekeeper) spake many good words unto them, whereby they were greatly gladdened. He also had them up to the top of the gate, and shewed them by what deed they were saved; and told them withal, that that sight they would have again as they went along in the way, to their comfort."

Although no specific mention is made of it, Christian must also have viewed the cross from the perspective of the Wicket Gate. After all, we are told that Christiana and her company followed where he had already been. Furthermore, we recall that he had received excellent instruction from the gatekeeper while there. Yet even though he may have seen the cross in the distance, from the vantage point of the Wicket Gate, Christian did not understand its full significance at that time. It was not until after his visit to the House of the Interpreter that he gained a much clearer insight into the implications of the cross and the empty tomb. Through instruction in the Word of God, and the application of it to his heart by the Spirit of God, Christian finally understood the way in which his pardon was forever secured. He could then say with the prophet Isaiah: *Behold, for peace I had great bitterness: but thou hast in love to my soul delivered it from the pit of corruption: for thou hast cast all my sins behind thy back.* (Isaiah 38:17) This more perfect knowledge of Christ and him crucified brought a settled peace and assurance to his soul that he had never known before. (Isaiah 32:17-18)

If we keep the allegorical nature of *The Pilgrim's Progress* always in mind, we should have no difficulty understanding that the story is neither strictly chronological as to the timing of events, nor sequential as to the order of events. In this same context, we must not forget that Christian's journey was an odyssey of the soul, a work of God's grace within him, just as it is with us. From its beginning and throughout its entirety, his journey took place as he lived and labored among his family and friends.

Once we understand that Christian did not follow a tangible pathway, we have no problem seeing that there was no actual geographical distance between the Wicket Gate and the cross and sepulcher. The narrow gate standing at the head of the path of life, and the cross, the gateway to eternal glory, are spiritual entities that are inseparably linked. They express the same foundational truth that there is but one way to eternal life, and the Lord Jesus Christ is that way. To find him is to find and to have life eternal. (Matthew 7:13-14; John 14:6 1; John 5:12; Proverbs 8:34-35)

The beacon of light that led Christian to the Wicket Gate is the Gospel, the good news that salvation is in the Lord Jesus Christ alone. It did not cease to shine once he had entered therein. On the contrary, that very same light will continue to illuminate his path and shine with increasing brilliancy as he advances toward the perfect day. At times, he will find his way to be very bright. At other times, the light will shine but dimly. However, this fluctuation is never due to any deficiency or variation in the light itself. The problem always lies with the beholder.

Therefore, any perceived gap between the Wicket Gate and the cross existed entirely within Christian's limited understanding. The problem was not that he lacked genuine faith until he reached the cross. Other factors lay at the heart of his lack of assurance.

There are many who wrongly suppose that the possession of salvation and the full assurance of it are one and the same thing. This presumption, which is sometimes taught as fact, gives rise to increased mental anguish in those who already struggle with doubts about their salvation. It is one thing to be in Christ and quite another to always feel like it. Those who were in the ark with Noah during the great flood may well have been terrified by the sound and fury of the cataclysmic destruction taking place outside. Yet there was no valid reason for them to be afraid, because the ark was kept afloat by the power and providence of God. Their safety in no way depended upon their feelings. In spite of any anxiety and doubt on their part, they were quite safe and secure in the ark.

To enter through the Wicket Gate is to come to Christ, and to come to Christ is to savingly believe on him. However, full assurance of salvation does not always immediately follow. Insufficient knowledge can produce a fragile assurance that is easily shaken, but so can an overly introspective nature. There are many dear children of God who suffer great mental anguish because of their tendency to doubt and fear. The problem is made even worse by the malicious taunts of Satan. Those who have experienced this agony of soul will testify that it is a terrible thing with which to struggle.

When lack of assurance comes from an insufficient understanding of the Scriptures, clearer instruction concerning Christ and his cross will prove to be highly beneficial to one's resting in Christ. For the brooding, introspective soul, however, lack of assurance is a much more complex problem. Often, this one will try to find peace by looking for it within, but spiritual peace will never be achieved that way. Seeking relief through a deeper, more thorough self-examination will only make matters worse. Rather than obtaining peace and rest in

Christ, this inward focus generally results in greater mental torment by finding new reasons to doubt and fear.

John Bunyan knew what it was to have a deeply introspective mind that tended to spiritual depression. Since he personally endured a terrible ordeal with the lack of assurance of salvation, it makes sense that he would create the same inclination in his main character. If so, Christian's burden probably contained a significant weight of doubt, fear, and troubling questions about the eternal welfare of his soul. But whether we view his burden as being composed of his original sin and guilt, or of doubt and fear, the remedy is exactly the same.

The soul that is burdened with sin and guilt can only find relief by looking to the Lord Jesus Christ, believing in him, and resting in his vicarious work of redemption. He dares not look for assurance within himself, for he will find none there. But in beholding the suffering Lamb of God, who is also the risen Lord Jesus Christ, he may say with Charles Wesley:

> Arise, my soul, arise, shake off thy guilty fears:
> The bleeding sacrifice in my behalf appears:
> Before the throne my surety stands, before the throne my surety stands,
> My name is written on his hands.
>
> Five bleeding wounds he bears, received on Calvary;
> They pour effectual prayers, they strongly plead for me;
> Forgive him, O forgive, they cry, forgive him, O forgive, they cry,
> Nor let that ransomed sinner die!
>
> My God is reconciled; his pardoning voice I hear;
> He owns me for his child, I can no longer fear;
> With confidence I now draw nigh, with confidence I now draw nigh,
> And "Father, Abba, Father" cry! [1]

* * * *

Dear reader, are you laboring under a heavy burden of doubt and fear? Gaze by faith upon the same blessed sight. Both the bestowal of salvation and the assurance of it flow from the same source, Christ and his cross. Those who are looking for peace must seek it here, for is it only to be found by looking away from self and unto Christ and his finished redemption. Hear the words of the prophet Isaiah saying: *And the work of righteousness shall be peace; and the effect of righteousness quietness and assurance for ever.* (Isaiah 32:17)

You might ask, "Can I really have true peace, quietness of soul, and assurance forever?" Yes, my friend, these can be yours, but only as you look to the Lord by faith, for the work of righteousness and peace with God is his work. Quietness and assurance forever are the effects of it. In believing the testimony of God's Word concerning our Lord Jesus Christ, we will find it to be the only solid foundation for both our faith and the full assurance of hope.

Peace with God, which was secured at the cross, can never be interrupted or lost, but our peace of mind certainly can. Peace and assurance are only maintained within as our hearts are fixed upon the Lord. Again the prophet Isaiah gives a precious promise concerning our peace saying: *Thou wilt keep him in perfect peace, whose mind is stayed on thee: because he trusteth in thee. Trust ye in the LORD for ever: for in the LORD JEHOVAH is everlasting strength.* (Isaiah 26:3-4)

Those who suffer from a lack of assurance, and the spiritual despondency that accompanies it, will probably find the tendency to be recurrent. It may lie dormant for a while but resurface unexpectedly, bringing a resurgence of doubt and fear. However, these episodes of mental and spiritual turmoil do tend to diminish in severity and frequency as we grow in the grace and knowledge of the Lord Jesus Christ. He is the remedy for every spiritual woe to which we, as the children of God, are subject, including this one. Nothing so quickly casts out doubt and fear as the remembrance of the great love wherewith he loves us. (John 15:13; 1 John 4:7-10; Ephesians 2:4-10) The wonder of it all will be the everlasting theme, the new song, of the saints in glory.

Study Questions

1. Did John Bunyan have scripturally valid reasons for placing the cross where he did? What light does the parallel passage in his sequel to *Pilgrim's Progress* shed upon the subject?

2. Can one truly possess salvation and yet lack the full assurance of it? Explain your answer.

3. What is the scriptural remedy for lack of assurance?

Part Seven

WAYFARING STRANGERS BUT NOT TRUE PILGRIMS

Wherefore the rather, brethren, give diligence to make your calling and election sure: for if ye do these things, ye shall never fall: for so an entrance shall be ministered unto you abundantly into the everlasting kingdom of our Lord and Savior Jesus Christ.
2 Peter 1:10-11

CHAPTER 17

The Ever-Present Danger of Carnal Security:
Simple, Sloth, and Presumption

DEAR READER, WE HAVE NOT VIEWED THE CROSS OF CHRIST ARIGHT unless we are radically changed by the sight. The virtue that flows to us from his finished work of redemption secured our sanctification as well as our justification. (1 Thessalonians 5:23-24) Therefore, we dare not claim to be partakers of God's wondrous grace in Christ unless his salvation is an evident reality in our lives. (Galatians 2:20; Philippians 2:12-13; 2 Peter 1:4-11) There are many, however, who eagerly embrace the promise of full and free salvation, but not the life of submission and self-denial that is an integral part of it. These have never viewed Christ and his cross aright.

The new heart given in regeneration is the heart of a trusting, obedient child. It is a heart overflowing with love for the Lord Jesus Christ, and the fervent desire to honor and please him in all things. As we quickly discover, however, the power to serve him acceptably must come from him alone. (Philippians 1:6) So as we run the race that is set before us and follow the pathway to the Celestial City, our eyes must remain fixed upon our crucified, risen, reigning Lord. (Hebrews 12:1-3)

Scripture describes the Christian life in no uncertain terms by using such action verbs as labor, fight, run, strive, stand, resist, flee and contend. Moreover, the graces of saving faith and repentance must be put to continual use, for it is only as they are exercised that they become strengthened and increased. Sadly, this is not the case with all who claim to be on the way to Zion. There are many who seemingly enter the Wicket Gate, but do not make it much farther. Like Pliable and his kind, these would-be pilgrims desire to have the assurance of heaven, but fail to consider either the cost or the implications of true discipleship. (Matthew 16:24-26; Luke 14:26-33)

To struggle with the lack of assurance of salvation is a terrible thing to endure, but what about those who flaunt their blessed assurance when there is not a shred of evidence to support their claim? What greater personal tragedy could there be than to lose one's soul? Moreover, how much more tragic the loss if it should take place near the cross? Is such a thing within the realm of possibility? Yes, my friend. It is quite possible for one to perish while being part of a sound ministry where the Gospel of Christ is faithfully preached. The very richest of spiritual blessings are attended by unforeseen danger, if we are so foolish as to take them for granted. To the wise in heart, this fact alone is sufficient reason to remain alert and watchful during their entire journey. However, if we should fail to do so and allow ourselves to be at ease in Zion, we unwittingly place ourselves in harm's way. (Amos 6:1)

Christian came face to face with this dangerous possibility right after losing his burden at the cross, when he looked down the hill and saw three men lying there. They were not dead, as he may have first supposed, but fast asleep and with heavy iron chains on their feet. Their location was highly significant, for they lay just "a little out of the way," and so were their names, which happened to be Simple, Sloth and Presumption.

Apparently, they did not realize that to slumber along the King's Highway was to be fair game for a terrible adversary. (I Peter 5:8-9) Or else they did not care! At the shocking sight of the men chained and fast asleep, Christian's heart was filled with concern and an alarm sounded in his memory. Perhaps they reminded him of the man in the iron cage. But whatever his thoughts may have been, he was more disturbed for them than they were for themselves. Therefore, in spite of his best efforts to rouse them from their stupor, Christian met with no success. On the contrary, they responded to his expression of concern and offer to help free them from their chains by mumbling lame excuses and going back to sleep.

Regarding this unexpected encounter with Simple, Sloth, and Presumption, we might well ask why Christian found them where he did. It would not have been surprising to find them slumbering in the City of Destruction, or somewhere between the city and the Wicket Gate. But why were they lying on the upward side of the Interpreter's House near the cross? These three sleepers represent the danger of carnal security to those who profess to know the Lord Jesus Christ.

Carnal security, or resting in a false hope, tends to manifest itself in one of two major ways. In its more passive form, it is characterized by an attitude of spiritual indifference and complacency. It can also hide behind a screen of outward activity and religious zeal. Those who profess to know Christ but are deceived as to their true spiritual condition will exhibit either one or the other of these tendencies. However, they pose a distinct threat to the children of God as well.

Although Simple, Sloth, and Presumption are pictured here as three separate individuals, they actually represent the sin of carnal security in its more passive form. Considered together, their names describe the chief characteristics of carnal security, and their lethargic behavior, chained feet, and utter indifference show the devastating effects of it in those who do not truly know the Lord. Moreover, their names also denote the chains that bind, deceive, and keep them oblivious to their great danger.

Although his name might suggest one who is dull-witted or mentally deficient, the sleeper known as Simple was not merely simple-minded. Neither could he claim the excuse of inexperience or childlike naïveté, even though these things do expose one to the danger of being more easily swayed than those who are wiser and more discerning. The simplicity denoted by his name is much more sinister in nature, for it represents spiritual ignorance of God and his ways.

It is not uncommon to find this state of being in those who are otherwise well educated, articulate and worldly wise. More surprising, perhaps, is that it can also lie hidden behind a fair measure of Bible knowledge. Spiritual ignorance is a pernicious thing, however; its presence means that one is void of the fear and knowledge of God, even though the fact might not be obvious to others. (Proverbs 1:7) As a character trait, it stems from the refusal to hear, heed, receive and apply the instruction of God's Word. (Proverbs 1:22-25) This explains why Simple saw no danger. He was content with being a nominal Christian, while living pretty much as he pleased. Therefore, he could easily harden his heart against the truth and shut out anything that threatened to shake him out of his comfort zone.

Since he was void of spiritual understanding, Simple was also a foolish man. He was self-deluded and incapable of judging properly between good and evil; therefore, the choices he made were both spiritually and morally detrimental. (Proverbs 7:7; Proverbs 14:18) But ironically, he was wise in his own conceit, and his proud, unteachable spirit kept him bound in chains of spiritual ignorance. (Proverbs 1:29-32; Proverbs 26:12) So even though he was apparently in a place where he heard the truth, he was in no condition to benefit from it. (Romans 3:11, 18)

Sloth, the second sleeper, may have had a better head than Simple, but he made no better use of it! Bound by chains of spiritual complacency, he willfully neglected the things of God and the means of grace provided for his spiritual growth and well-being. Therefore, in response to Christian's earnest appeal, he lazily mumbled, "Yet a little more sleep." Although he was probably diligent enough in other respects, he was careless and indifferent to those things that were of paramount importance.

Such negligence rarely occurs suddenly. More often than not, it begins by gradually relegating the things of God to a place of lesser importance. The seeking first of God's kingdom and righteousness is far from being the overruling priority of life. Little by little, as spiritual complacency overtakes the heart and mind, the cares and concerns of this life choke out matters of eternal import.

As with spiritual ignorance, the sin of pride also lies at the root of spiritual sloth and complacency. (Proverbs 26:16) Those who are in bondage to it can render many a reason why they neglect spiritual duties and privileges, but they protest too much! Their very arguments bear witness against them and cast serious doubts about the credibility of their Christian profession.

The third sleeper, whose name happened to be Presumption, may have lacked many things, but self-confidence was not one of them. In fact, his over-inflated ego provided an ample foundation upon which all three of the sleepers could recline with ease. His excuse for his inaction, which was that "every tub shall stand upon its own bottom," is quite revealing. As I pondered the spiritual implications of his words, the prophecy given in Zechariah 5:11 came to mind. It contains a highly disturbing thought for those such as Presumption. In this verse, to be set upon one's own base denotes the determination to follow the way of establishing one's own righteousness while rejecting God's prescribed way. It was the course taken by the majority of the nation Israel. (Romans 10:1-3)

In applying this truth to the man named Presumption and his thoughtless words, it becomes clear that he represents the danger of spiritual deception. His heart and mind were blinded and chained by it; therefore, he wrongly supposed that all was well with his soul. Moreover, in presuming that he was sufficiently capable of directing his own life, he failed to consider the end of such a plan. (Proverbs 14:12) Like the other two men sleeping soundly near the cross, his deceived heart was concealed behind a religious exterior, and a haughty one at that.

Is it not amazing how spiritual delusion can so easily breed an attitude of self-assurance? How often a presumptive spirit wears a mask of over-confidence, even an air of superiority, no matter how ill founded it may be! (Proverbs 16:18) As for the man named Presumption, his tub actually had no bottom upon which to stand. However, this fact had completely escaped his notice. Although he foolishly presumed upon the grace of God, and convinced himself that all was well with him in God's sight, there was no evidence to support him. The source of his hope, the false premise upon which he rested and trusted, had no scriptural basis whatsoever.

When taken together, this trio of sleepers portrays the fearful condition of one who is religious but unsaved. We do not travel far down the road to Zion before we begin to meet such people, and the encounter is always disturbing to the true child of God. It prompts us to examine ourselves to see if we are real. Sometimes it seems that for every true believer, there are many more who simply claim to be. Often, these will relate a religious experience that happened years ago and trust in it as evidence of salvation. Even if their present manner of life calls their so-called conversion experience into serious question, they cling to it tenaciously.

Like Simple, Sloth and Presumption, the person who is religious but lost is a little out of the way. He is close to the path, yet not quite in it. Whatever may have prompted him to profess faith in Christ, his heart remains unchanged, and yet, his condition is worse than it was before, because he now clings to a false hope. With the insensibility like that of a drunken man, he is unconscious of his danger, and deliberately blocks out anything that threatens to disturb his confidence. (Proverbs 23:29-35) Therefore, like Simple, he refuses to hear the truth. In common with Sloth, he is content to remain as he is. Presumption forms the basis of every such false hope, with willing ignorance and spiritual neglect being its fruits. Folly and religious pride are the common bonds that link all three together.

Like the foolish virgins in Matthew 25, Simple, Sloth and Presumption had no oil in their vessels. Their spiritual stupor is the direct opposite of what the true Christian is supposed to be. However, these dangerous tendencies lurk in our flesh as well, ready to do us harm if given the opportunity. As you may remember in Matthew 25, the wise virgins slumbered and slept along with the foolish ones. So perhaps Christian's encounter with the sleepers was an instance of what is called preventative grace. Dear brother or sister in Christ, we are wise to be on the lookout for such tendencies as well, and to make use of the antidote that will prevent them from overtaking us.

Godly wisdom, which is spiritual knowledge rightly applied, is the only remedy for spiritual ignorance, but we cannot attain it through natural means. Wisdom is placed in the soul at regeneration, when the Spirit of God takes up residence there and the seed of God's Word takes permanent root. (2 Timothy 3:14-15) With divine truth as a guiding principle, the fear and knowledge of God begin to operate within, leading us to follow God's will and ways. (Psalm 19:7-11) Every believer in Christ, no matter how mature in the Lord, stands in need of more of these necessary graces. Therefore, our heavenly Father has made abundant provision for our increase in wisdom and spiritual understanding.

Even though God gives these graces in the new birth, their increase is not automatic, nor is it passively attained. We must actively pursue wisdom and knowledge through the means that God has ordained by seeking our Lord diligently in prayer, reading and meditating in his Word, and attending a local assembly where Christ is faithfully preached and honored. (James 1:5; 1 Peter 2:1-3; 2 Peter 3:17-18; Hebrews 10:23-25) But we should take care that we do these things for the right reasons.

If pursued as an end in itself, knowledge can foster pride and actually hinder our spiritual growth. The only proper motive for seeking more Bible knowledge, wisdom, and understanding is that we might walk more perfectly in its light. (Psalm 119:18, 33-35, 97-100) When we diligently strive to walk in wisdom's ways, prideful tendencies will be gradually checked and the grace of humility will begin to grow in proportion. (Proverbs 4:7-13; Jeremiah 10:23; James 4:10; 1 Peter 5:5-7)

So it is not enough to simply know the truth. We must walk in its precepts and put it into daily practice. (James 1:22-25) In Proverbs 19:15 we are warned: *Slothfulness casteth into a deep sleep; and an idle soul shall suffer hunger.* Since this principle is certainly true concerning earthly matters, how much more does it pertain to our spiritual life? Clearly, diligence in spiritual matters is the antidote to spiritual complacency, but we can no more achieve it through natural means than we can attain godly wisdom in that way. We must have a spiritual mind, a renewed mind, in order to rightly receive and retain the Word of God. (Proverbs 2:1-5) When Christ, the Wisdom of God, dwells in our hearts by faith, we will diligently seek to walk the path uprightly before him. (Ecclesiastes 10:10)

Yet even true believers are not immune to the dangers of spiritual neglect. Nothing will lead more quickly to the lowering of our guard and laying aside of our spiritual armor than the neglect of spiritual duties and privileges. When this is our case, we will prove an easy mark for an enemy, who never relaxes his vigilance. Whether he comes with the outward boldness of a roaring lion or the subtle whisper of a serpent, our great enemy seeks prey continually. Therefore, we cannot afford to indulge an indolent spirit. (1 Peter 5:8-9)

Those of us who are born again will quickly discover that we are engaged in an active warfare that is both difficult and often perplexing. For this reason, it is not enough for us to simply maintain our spiritual status quo. (Ephesians 6:10-13) In fact, this is not possible to do because, at best, we are forgetful hearers and leaky vessels. Even the richest store of wisdom and spiritual knowledge will begin to diminish if it is not continually replenished and put to use. True faith motivates us to diligent action and conquers our natural inclination to sloth, but none of this takes place without a struggle.

Although we long for it, God's people are painfully aware that we have not yet attained perfection, either in godly wisdom and understanding or in manifesting a Christ-like character. Their increase requires our active pursuit of godliness and truth and our diligent attendance to spiritual duty. The antidote to spiritual lethargy is principally found in these Godward pursuits. (Philippians 2:12-13; Hebrews 13:20-21)

* * * *

In Psalm 19:12-13 David prayed: *Who can understand his errors? Cleanse thou me from secret faults. Keep back thy servant also from presumptuous sins; let them not have dominion over me: then shall I be upright, and I shall be innocent from the great transgression.* His prayer is the earnest cry of every soul who truly fears God and dares not presume upon his grace.

The only antidote to false presumption, or spiritual deception, is the presence of godly fear in the soul, a filial reverence that is an inseparable part of genuine faith. Whereas the natural man is void of the fear of God, every born again soul possesses it. Through the Spirit of God, truth dwells in his inward parts, and so does godly wisdom. (Psalm 51:6; Proverbs 9:10) While the fear of man brings a snare, godly fear is a powerful teacher and infallible guide that keeps our feet solidly in the path of life. (Psalm 34:8-11; Proverbs 14:26-27)

When the grace of God dwells within, it teaches us to pass the time of our earthly sojourn in fear. (Hebrews 12:28-29; 1 Peter 1:17) Moreover, a proper fear of God and genuine faith are always found together. Those who truly fear God also trust in him and walk by faith. Child-like faith that causes us to distrust ourselves and look to our Lord for spiritual direction! Vital, active faith that desires above all to please the Lord and walk in his ways! (Psalm 86:11) Patient and obedient faith that casts down pride and self-reliance, and bows to God's wisdom and providence!

Thus godly fear and its fruit will check the tendency toward spiritual sloth and prompt us to make our calling and election sure. Even though the fear of God co-exists with true peace and assurance, it gives no leeway for presuming upon the grace of God. The true Christian loves and reveres his heavenly Father, and dreads doing anything that would displease him. Therefore, he often prays with David: *Search me, O God, and know my heart: try me, and know my thoughts: and see if there be any wicked way in me, and lead me in the way everlasting.* (Psalm 139:23-24)

The comprehensive remedy to the three-fold danger of carnal security is only found in the Word of God, and the Spirit of God is the one who must apply the cure. A synopsis of this antidote is contained in what is surely some of the wisest counsel found in Scripture: *Trust in the LORD with all thine heart; and lean not unto thine own understanding. In all thy ways acknowledge him, and he shall direct thy paths. Be not wise in thine own eyes: fear the LORD, and depart from evil. It shall be health to thy navel, and marrow to thy bones."* (Proverbs 3:5-8)

Within these four verses, we find the summation of our Godward duty as believers in Christ. Our Lord never intended that the way to Zion be an easy one, but neither does he command his people to do anything beyond what he enables them to do. Therefore, the commands contained in Proverbs 3:5-8 are not harsh and burdensome, but are given for our spiritual benefit. Moreover, their corresponding promises contain the secret to Christian contentment and soul prosperity.

Our safe arrival to the heavenly Zion is never contingent upon our own efforts. Our final salvation as God's people is by his grace in Christ alone. However, the way he leads us to our eternal home is always by the path of faith and obedience. As it brings us ever closer to the perfect day, we increasingly realize that it is wisdom's way, and therefore, the only way of true peace and spiritual joy. (Isaiah 26:2-4)

Study Questions

1. Christian came face to face with a dangerous possibility when he saw three men in chains and fast asleep near the cross. Who were they, and what kind of danger did they represent?

2. Briefly describe each of the three sleepers and give the chain that bound each man.

3. When considered together, how do the three men portray one who is religious but lost – Christian in name only?

4. Since the sins of spiritual neglect and complacency pose a danger to the true Christian as well, how are we to guard against them?

5. The comprehensive remedy to the danger of carnal security is found in the Word of God. A synopsis of it is given in the book of Proverbs. Where?

CHAPTER 18

The Ever-Present Danger of Carnal Security:
Formalist and Hypocrisy

To trust in Christ and rest in him for salvation is a far cry from slumbering near his cross. In Simple, Sloth, and Presumption we have a prime illustration of carnal security in its more passive form. They characterize one who is content to profess faith in Christ and then trust in that profession for his assurance of salvation. Should you ask about his hope of eternal life, he will gladly relate his past experience when he settled the matter with the Lord. As to the nature of true discipleship, however, he gives little thought and even less concern. If you should press him further by pointing out that his life fails to measure up to what is expected of a true follower of Jesus Christ, he will make excuse and dismiss your objection at once. Therefore, as Christian discovered, you will find it next to impossible to shake him from his vain hope.

While it was pretty obvious that Simple, Sloth, and Presumption were in deep trouble, carnal security also exists in another, more sinister form. Christian encountered it suddenly while still mulling over the three slumbering men, when two other men jumped over the wall and joined him. From all appearances they were the exact opposite of the three sleepers, for they were wide awake and busily engaged in the Lord's service. At least they claimed to be.

While Simple, Sloth, and Presumption rested contentedly "a little out of the way," these two were actually in the way. However, their point of entry into the path was highly disturbing, as was their bold manner and confident air. So even though they took Christian completely by surprise, he instinctively knew that something about them was not quite right.

There was just cause for him to be suspicious because these men bore the marks of those who claim to be Christians but are actually living a lie. Like their more passive counterparts, their faith rested upon an unstable foundation, but it made perfect sense when you consider their birthplace. Formalist and Hypocrisy came from the land of Vain-Glory, and to quote them directly, they were "going for praise to Mount Zion." Instead of entering the path by way of the Wicket Gate, however, they scaled the wall some distance beyond it. My friend, this alone was enough to cast grave doubts upon their credibility as true pilgrims.

Christian's immediate alarm for these two men equaled the distress he had felt for the three sleepers. Of chief concern was the fact that they had deliberately bypassed the cross by not entering the King's Highway through the Wicket Gate. According to Scripture, this was sufficient in itself to mark them as thieves and robbers. (John 10:1-10) When Christian tried to convince them that their mode of entry violated the Lord's clear command, they remained adamant in the belief that their way was just as good. In fact, they argued that it was better because it was shorter and easier.

Although Formalist and Hypocrisy were walking at liberty and fully alert, Christian had no more success in persuading them of their jeopardy than if they, too, had been chained and fast asleep. Like Simple, they saw no danger. In common with Sloth, they had no inclination to alter their present course. Akin to Presumption, they assumed that their condition was just the same as Christian's, even though he had entered the path via the narrow gate that stood at its head. They clearly walked according to their own reasoning instead of God's prescribed commandment, and were convinced that they had valid reasons for doing so. Yet in defending their action in by-passing the Wicket Gate, they proved their identity as native-born sons of Vain-Glory beyond a reasonable doubt.

Using the arguments of long-standing tradition as well as the example and testimony of countless others, Formalist and Hypocrisy tried their best to justify their conduct to Christian. If need be, they could cite precedent that would support their behavior in the eyes of any judge. It would hold up in court! What more proof could be needed? So they summed up their argument saying: "Besides, if we get into the way, what's matter which way we get in? If we are in, we are in. Thou art but in the way, who, as we perceive, came in at the gate; and we are also in the way, that came tumbling over the wall. Wherein now is thy condition better than ours?" Brilliant deduction, is it not!

Their argument that the end justifies the means is an age-old one. Dear fellow believer, what will we do if we are confronted with a similar situation? Or perhaps I should say when, because we will surely encounter the likes of Formalist and Hypocrisy at some point along the way. Therefore, it is imperative that we, like Christian, be able to give a reason for our hope, with meekness and fear. (1 Peter 3:15-16) Moreover, we had better have a scriptural rebuke for the politically correct, but totally erroneous notion that what one believes does not really matter as long as he is sincere.

Since their pompous speech so closely mirrored the opinions and counsel given by Mr. Worldly Wiseman, Christian cut to the chase with these two. He rightly discerned that they had no valid hope of being received into the Celestial City. Their inability to distinguish between his condition and their own, in addition to their failure to understand the significance of his garment, the mark on his forehead, and his sealed roll, numbered them among the spiritually ignorant. In fact, they represent two primary characteristics of those who are religious but lost. However, in citing legal precedent, these two deluded souls were right about one thing. Many have followed their pernicious ways!

When considered together, Formalist and Hypocrisy represent those who trust in their own righteousness and suppose that God will accept them because of it. Clinging to this false hope, they conformed outwardly to certain laws and ordinances, and relied upon the commandments and traditions of men for their authority. (Galatians 2:16) Although they claimed to be going to Zion, they lacked the covering of the righteousness of Christ and gave no evidence of genuine faith. Everything about them indicated that they were imposters, but the fact that they deliberately by-passed the Wicket Gate, and thus the cross, decided their case beyond a doubt. (Romans 10:1-4)

The man named Formalist denotes one major characteristic of those who are merely religious. Living up to his name, he focused his attention upon the outward show of religion. Active service, zealous performance of religious duties, and strict observance of religious rites and ceremonies were all done with meticulous care. He may even have been faithful in observing the biblically-commanded ordinances, but did so out of a sense of duty, or in trying to earn favor with God. He knew nothing of spiritual sacrifices offered from a heart of love for the Savior. (Romans 12:1-2; Philippians 4:18; Hebrews 6:10; Hebrews 13:15-16; 1 Peter 2:5)

For his authority, Formalist cited religious customs and traditions rather than the Word of God. But since these things are usually in conflict with divinely-revealed truth, his observance of them was vain. (Mark 7:5-13) Nevertheless, scrupulous attention to outward form and custom was of utmost importance to him. The more ostentatious the ceremony or the duty to be performed, the better he liked it and the more comfort he derived from it. To the casual observer he might seem to be genuine, but he was really a poor imitator of what he claimed to be.

Thus Formalist portrays an unsaved man who tries to conceal his unregenerate heart behind a pious exterior. Although he was diligent in the performance of good works, he entirely lacked the hallmark of genuine faith and a Christ-like character. The path he followed was one of his own choosing; therefore, his worship was vain and his service completely unacceptable in God's sight. (Matthew 15:7-9)

What about the man named Hypocrisy who walked in company with Formalist? These two are inseparable companions, two sides of the same coin, so to speak. Religious fervor that is void of true substance goes hand-in-hand with hypocrisy. Moreover, its shallow view of God's Word and his righteous commands creates the perfect environment for a self-righteous spirit to grow and flourish.

So Formalist and Hypocrisy displayed the very same characteristics as the scribes and Pharisees who opposed and rejected the Lord Jesus Christ. (Matthew 23:25-28) They had the same self-righteous spirit that thinks oneself a keeper of God's law and assumes that God is as pleased with him as he is with himself. Many said of

Formalist and Hypocrisy that they looked like Christians. Yet as is often the case, appearances were deceiving. Behind their pious exterior lurked hearts of rebellion and unbelief. Rather than resting and trusting in Christ and his finished redemption, they trusted in their own righteousness. Sad to say, they can be found in even the soundest of churches, playing their part quite well and walking among us unawares. However, the ability to distinguish between the hypocrite and the sincere Christian is not the primary lesson to be learned from their example. We who are God's children need to examine ourselves to see if anything of their spirit lurks in our hearts.

Salvation is not a commodity to be purchased by good works or religious deeds, no matter how well done or sincerely performed. It is the gift of God, freely bestowed in his beloved Son. (John 3:16-18) Christian's encounter with Formalist and Hypocrisy is a stark reminder that the way to eternal life can never be entered by human effort or personal merit. (John 3:3-7)

Due to the strictly limited nature of the path of life, the Lord Jesus Christ warned his hearers that relatively few would find it. Most, like Formalist and Hypocrisy, seek it in the wrong places. In looking for an easier way, they choose an alternate route that is better suited to their liking and more palatable to their desires. Rejecting the true Gospel, they devise a salvation that allows them to pursue their own course while enjoying the esteem of men and the pleasures of this life. They embrace a salvation that carries no stigma with it, and promises, no matter how falsely, both a comfortable existence in this world and a certain acceptance in the next. In short, most seek a way to eternal life that has no cross.

All such alternate routes broaden what God has narrowly defined, but each one of them originates and ultimately terminates in the City of Destruction. (John 14:6) Since Formalist and Hypocrisy were following one of these by-paths, it is little wonder that Christian's rebuke fell upon deaf ears. In vain he tried to convince them that shunning the Wicket Gate was a grievous error. The significance of his garment, the imputed righteousness of Christ, totally escaped them. The mark in his forehead and the sealed roll he carried were accounted as nothing. Both men lacked these vital things, which distinguish God's people from all others.

* * * *

It is crucial for us to remember that not all faith is saving faith. In spite of what they claimed, Formalist and Hypocrisy were not true followers of Jesus Christ. They lacked the renewed heart and transformed mind that enables God's children to worship him in spirit and in truth. (John 4:21-24) To their way of thinking, a form of godliness was enough. A contrite heart, a desire for God, and a hunger and thirst for righteousness were all alien concepts. They refused to believe that form without substance and religious pretense without new birth produce an equally vain hope. (Job 8:13-15; Job 27:8)

To make matters worse for Formalist and Hypocrisy, they despised Christian and laughed him to scorn, even though they had no answer to his objections. Yet what else could we expect from those who were "going for praise to Mount Zion"? By their own admission, their chief desire was for the praise and honor of men, not the glory of God. (Matthew 6:1-4, 5-6, 16-18) Therefore, a proud spirit was the impetus behind their religious zeal and good works, making them confident that their good deeds would not only be approved, but generously rewarded.

In this they remind me of King Saul, who played the part of the hypocrite when he acted according to his own will rather than obeying God's clear command. He even went so far as to excuse his incomplete obedience by making it seem a pious act. (1 Samuel 15) In rebuking King Saul, the prophet Samuel said: *Behold, to obey is better than sacrifice, and to hearken than the fat of rams.* What God requires of his people is heart obedience rather than outward form. Thus there was a preponderance of evidence that Formalist and Hypocrisy had missed the mark. All pointed to the fact that they were as sure to miss the heavenly Zion as they had missed the Wicket Gate. None but Zion's children will safely reach the City of God and appear before their Lord, glorified at last. As they stand with him on Mount Zion, their only desire will be for him to receive all the glory for loving them, giving himself for them, and faithfully guiding them there.

The lesson of the cross is a clear and simple one. God will accept nothing less than a perfect righteousness, the righteousness of his own son, Jesus Christ. Only those who are clothed with this spotless garment have the hope and assurance of eternal life. As for Formalist and Hypocrisy, and all others who suppose that they can gain acceptance with God by their own works and merit, they will share the same fate as the deluded souls in Matthew 7:21-23. Instead of a joyous reception into the Celestial City at their journey's end, all such imposters will hear the Lord's awful words of final condemnation: *I never knew you: depart from me, ye that work iniquity.* Dear reader, my earnest prayer is that you will never have to hear that awful sentence!

Study Questions

1. When Formalist and Hypocrisy jumped over the wall and joined company with Christian, how did he know at once that something about them was not quite right? What was his primary concern about them?

2. What did these two men have in common with Simple, Sloth, and Presumption?

3. How did the man Formalist live up to his name?

4. What sort of man was Hypocrisy, and in what sense was he the inseparable companion of Formalist?

5. How do Formalist and Hypocrisy serve as a warning to God's people?

Part Eight

WHEN TROUBLES SEEM
LIKE MOUNTAINS

Hear my cry, O God; attend unto my prayer. From the end of the
earth will I cry unto thee, when my heart is overwhelmed;
lead me to the rock that is higher than I.
Psalm 61:1-2

CHAPTER 19

An Unexpected Impediment!

MY FELLOW PILGRIM, A GLORIOUS DESTINY AWAITS US AT THE END OF OUR earthly pilgrimage, and it is one for which our entire Christian experience will have prepared us. Just how this wondrous transformation takes place is not given us to see. It is hidden within the secret counsel of God and brought to pass through the mysterious workings of his providence. But Scripture does reveal its end result.

The zenith of our high calling in Jesus Christ is to be conformed unto his beautiful image and likeness. (Romans 8:28-29) This call to eternal glory is not a thing easily attained, however, nor is it at all within our ability to achieve by our own efforts. It is only wrought through the infinite skill and patient, yet persistent handiwork of our heavenly Father. (Job 23:10; 1 Peter 5:10)

A very peculiar sort of refining process is necessary in order to accomplish this metamorphosis, one that involves many painful elements. Therefore, as concerns our condition in this world, we are not called to a life of ease and complacency. Neither are we to live in pursuit of pleasure, self-interest or vainglory. Since we are destined to partake of the glory of our Lord, we must also expect to enter into the fellowship of his sufferings. (Philippians 3:10-11; 1 Peter 4:12-13)

Even though the Lord Jesus Christ was forthright concerning the cost of being his disciple, few of his followers have an accurate conception of what it really entails, at least in their earliest days as believers. Christian was no exception. While he had experienced significant opposition prior to entering the Wicket Gate, his deliverance at the cross filled him with such joy and lightness of spirit that he may well have concluded the worst to be behind him. In spite of the admonitions given him by Evangelist, Goodwill, and the Interpreter, Christian had but a dim notion of what lay ahead. Likewise, he was largely unaware of what still resided in his flesh. He had been scandalized by the careless indifference of Simple, Sloth, and Presumption, but how would he respond if faced with the same fleshly tendency?

The unexpected encounter with Formalist and Hypocrisy, who now lagged some distance behind him, had given Christian something new to think about as he journeyed on alone. As he made his way forward, he experienced a season of relief and comfort in his solitude, although it was mixed now and then with feelings of inexplicable heaviness. (1 Peter 1:6) However, in spite of these conflicting emotions, he was learning to use his precious scroll and finding it to be the only source of true spiritual strength. (John 6:63; John 8:31-32; 1 Peter 2:1-3) The more he thought upon the precious truths and promises of God's Word, the more he learned of the Lord Jesus Christ, who is the bread of life and the foundation of all his hope. (Psalm 34:8-10; Luke 24:25-27; John 5:39; John 6:35; Hebrews 10:4-7) Through diligent use of this means, Christian was laying in store things that would be of invaluable help to him when the going was rough.

As Christian thought upon the Scriptures and reflected upon God's faithfulness to him in his journey so far, he paused occasionally to study the landscape around him. Therefore, he probably noticed the single mountain far in the distance. It seemed a lonely mountain, standing there by itself, and it was evidently of great height, because its summit was completely hidden above the clouds.

On a relatively clear day, an aerial view of this mountain will reveal much more of its character. Large portions of it are covered by dense woods, but other parts are composed mainly of massive boulders and sheer rock face with treacherously steep cliffs. Under certain conditions, the heavy fog hovering near the peak will creep down the hill and settle into its lower elevations. However, in spite of the generally overcast sky above the mountain, occasional rays of sunlight and small patches of blue break through the clouds here and there. From Christian's distant vantage point, the solitary mountain had a bleak and somewhat menacing appearance, but it was too far away to give him any real cause for concern. Yet the road he traveled was leading him directly toward it.

Although there was no marker to warn the traveler, the name of this lofty, imposing hill was called Difficulty. Due to the peculiar nature of the surrounding landscape, Christian had no idea that he was approaching it until he reached its base. Only then did it dawn upon him that his way lay straight up the hill! If he was to remain in the narrow path, he had no choice but to make the ascent.

While gazing upward and pondering the strenuous climb ahead of him, Christian heard the splash of a nearby waterfall. Looking toward the sound, he saw a large rock out of which water gushed forth and cascaded down the mountainside. At the foot of the hill the ice-cold water formed a large natural pool, which became a stream at its lower end and flowed away from the base of the hill. The hidden source of this water was a spring located high up the mountain. Plunging down from its granite fountain, the water glistened in the sunlight with iridescent color. As it flowed away from the pool at the foot of the hill, it looked like a typical mountain brook. Yet those who trace its course say that its banks gradually widen until the small stream becomes a mighty, resplendent river. (Ezekiel 47:1-9)

As Christian stood near the pool listening to the rhythmic sound of the waterfall, its crystalline water had a strange drawing effect upon him. What a pleasant place this was, with its soft blanket of moss and several varieties of ferns growing in the shade there. How welcome the sight must have been to Christian as he knelt there, suddenly aware of how thirsty he was. As he drank deeply, not only was his thirst quenched, but he also felt restored in spirit and invigorated for the arduous climb he must soon make.

Another feature of the hill Difficulty worthy of particular note is the crossroad located near its foot. This intersection, where three ways meet, poses quite a dilemma for certain travelers who happen to have made it this far along the King's Highway. Although the path to the Celestial City goes directly up the hill, two additional roads offer seemingly easier alternatives on level ground. Therefore, this crossroad has proved a major turning point for many who pass that way.

You will recall that up to this point, Formalist and Hypocrisy had been following Christian at a discrete distance. However, when they reached the base of the mountain and took one upward look, they quickly decided to take the easier routes instead of attempting the climb. Moreover, neither man drank from the nearby spring. Perhaps they did not see it. But I am inclined to believe that they deliberately by-passed it because they were not thirsty, and felt no need of it. (Matthew 5:6)

How the two of them must have congratulated themselves for their superior wisdom, and pitied poor Christian for his folly! After all, was it not feasible that they could circle the base of the mountain and reach the other side long before Christian made his laborious way over it? They could achieve the same result while avoiding the difficulty, could they not? Was not Christian a glutton for punishment? So the two men might have reasoned between themselves as they turned from the proper path, one to the right, the other to the left.

Unfortunately there was a serious flaw in their reasoning, for in taking the two by-ways they left the path of life. The road that turned to the left was called Danger, although there was no signpost to warn of this fact. The man who chose that way discovered, too late, that it led into a deep, dark forest. Once he entered therein, he quickly lost his way and was never heard from again.

His companion decided to take the path to the right, which was a seemingly better choice, for it led into a broad meadow. This first impression was deceptive, however, because the unmarked path called Destruction eventually took him into a land filled with dark mountains. Almost as soon as he entered that evil place, the poor misguided soul stumbled and fell to rise no more.

So it was at the foot of the hill Difficulty that Christian, Formalist, and Hypocrisy parted company for good. The event was predictable, really. Few things in life divide the false professor from the true child of God more quickly than adversity. Like Formalist and Hypocrisy, those who lack genuine faith will always choose the easier route of sight and sense. But in taking the two alternate paths, both men came to a bad end. Having previously heard the truth and rejected it, they were already walking in darkness. (John 11:9-10) Now by willfully leaving the path of life, they wandered into far greater darkness from which there is no recovery. (Matthew 15:13-14; John 12:46-48)

While those who are merely religious may be permitted to seek their portion in this life, we who belong to the Lord Jesus Christ are called to follow an infinitely higher path. The ways in which God leads us are those best designed to promote soul prosperity rather than earthly comfort and ease. Therefore, he will not permit us to walk by sight. We must follow the path of life by faith, even in times when the way before us is uncertain and the going proves hard.

Christian was beginning to understand this fundamental truth more clearly as he gazed upon the lofty mountain. Therefore, his heart was drawn upward, in spite of its considerable height. It was not that he relished the climb itself, but he would much rather face it than turn aside from the right path. However, since it was obvious that the ascent would require uncommon exertion, Christian knew that his strength was unequal to the task. Thus he drank deeply from the pool of water located at its foot before beginning the long, upward climb. (Isaiah 12:2-3)

Since no two climbers have exactly the same experience, each one who ascends this steep hill gives a different account of it. For one thing, weather conditions are highly unpredictable and subject to sudden change. Then there is the terrain itself. As noted before, parts of the mountain are densely wooded, while other areas are rocky and exposed. Much of its surface is covered by deep shade, but there are a few places where sunlight manages to break through. Although the path slopes gently here and there, it is mostly steep and treacherous, making it hard for climbers to maintain their footing.

So even though Christian began the ascent at a fairly good pace, he soon found the going considerably slower. In the worst places, the path was so steep that he could scarcely see more than a few feet ahead of him. At those times he was forced to grope for a hand or foothold in order to pull himself upward. Moreover, the rocks and dirt were so loose that he frequently lost his traction and slipped backward, making it seem that he was getting nowhere fast.

At no point during his arduous climb was Christian able to see the mountain's summit. He had to press forward, not knowing how far he was from the top. This particular feature of the hill Difficulty, as well as everything else about it, is by divine design. Those who ascend it must do so by faith, one step at a time.

* * * *

Dear brother or sister in Christ, I have little doubt but that you have also encountered this same imposing mountain and been compelled to scale its heights. If so, you know full well that, like every other place in *The Pilgrim's Progress*, the hill Difficulty has no literal geographical location. It depicts a state of being in which we, as believers in Christ, often find ourselves. It is one that goes beyond the earthly afflictions that are common to all mankind.

As a result of sin, trouble and sorrow form a common thread that runs throughout man's allotted time on earth. (Job 5:6-7; Job 14:1) Thus of man's earthly existence apart from the grace of God in salvation, it may truly be said that all is vanity and vexation of spirit. (Ecclesiastes 1:13-14) As concerns the child of God, the sorrows and afflictions that come our way are designed for our eternal good, and often serve as a means of preventative grace. (Psalm 55:22) Therefore, the hill Difficulty is a thing apart from the ordinary troubles to which all mankind is generally subject. It is reserved for God's providential dealings with his children and pertains to his eternal purpose of grace for them.

The fact that the way to Zion goes directly up this allegorical hill is too significant to be overlooked. It reminds us that we must expect to ascend it, not just once but many times during the course of our earthly pilgrimage. (John 16:33; 1 Thessalonians 3:1-4) While the crucible of affliction tends to harden the heart of the natural man, it serves as a refining process for the people of God. (Malachi 3:3; Romans 5:1-5) We are not required to understand exactly how the sorrows and afflictions allotted to us are working toward our ultimate spiritual good. Our duty is to submit to God's wise providence and trust in him, as concerns the outcome.

So Christian's encounter with the hill Difficulty denoted a particularly grueling ordeal that was appointed by God for him, personally. Whatever its specific nature, it materialized in his path without warning and the steep ascent indicated the strenuous trying of his faith. (1 Peter 1:6-7) Since he possessed no more inherent courage than any other man, the prospect before him was daunting. Yet by the grace of God, he faced it with uncommon valor. Moreover, during the course of the climb, he will discover that while genuine faith does not diminish the hardship encountered, it does instill the spiritual fortitude to conquer the mountain, in spite of personal frailty. So by faith he ventured ahead, even though the way before him seemed very like an unfamiliar mountain path shrouded by impenetrable fog.

Like the hill itself, the invigorating water at its foot also represents a precious spiritual truth. While the hill signifies a period of great trial and affliction, the flowing spring depicts God's gracious provision for his people when they call unto him for help in such times. (Isaiah 41: 17-18) Its life-giving water is readily available to all who know the Lord Jesus Christ and are joined to him in an eternal union. (Romans 8:35-39) Since it is the secret to our conquering of the hill Difficulty, we feel the need to drink of it continually. (Isaiah 58:11) But no one else takes note of it or desires it.

What a comfort it is to know that God will never require more of us than his grace abundantly supplies! This water flows from the very throne of God and of the Lamb, the Lord Jesus Christ. (Revelation 22:1) Therefore, it is living water for thirsty souls, and healing water that restores, strengthens, and sustains us from within. The Lord Jesus Christ is the giver of this living water, and the source of our light and life. (Psalm 36:8-9; John 4:10, 13-14; John 7:37-39) Through his Spirit, he ministers to us and provides all that we need in order to walk in the light and persevere in the path of life, even in our darkest hours. Through his Word, and the application of it to our hearts, he is faithful to nourish and maintain the life that he gave. Moreover, he does so freely, abundantly, and according to his intimate knowledge of our individual needs. (Psalm 23:2-3; Isaiah 35:6-8; Isaiah 49:10; Revelation 21:6)

So my fellow pilgrim, are you in the midst of a trial that is overwhelming? Does it seem much like a high mountain you must climb, even though you lack the strength to do so? Look to this restorative fountain, for you will find it ever close at hand. The healing properties of its water, which flows from a smitten rock, will supply all the grace you need to endure the trial and triumph by faith. Although Fanny Crosby was physically blind, she clearly saw the spring at the foot of the hill Difficulty and wrote of it, saying:

All the way my Saviour leads me, cheers each winding path I tread,
Gives me grace for every trial, feeds me with the living bread.
Though my weary steps may falter, and my soul athirst may be,
Gushing from the rock before me, lo, a spring of joy I see![1]

Study Questions

1. What were Christian's thoughts and frame of mind as he approached the hill Difficulty?

2. How did Christian respond when realizing that the pathway to the City led straight up and over the mountain?

3. How did Formalist and Hypocrisy react when faced with the same obstacle? What was the result of their decision there?

4. What does the allegorical hill Difficulty represent' How does it relate to God's purpose of grace for his people?

5. What is the spiritual significance of the pool located near the foot of the hill? How would drinking of it help Christian to make the difficult climb?

CHAPTER 20

Incident in the Arbor

ABOUT MIDWAY IN HIS DIFFICULT CLIMB, CHRISTIAN CAME UPON AN UNEX-pected blessing, a pleasant arbor that was a beautiful and obviously well tended place. It was a quiet, secluded spot that opened right onto the path. The ground there was covered with lush, green grass, and the abundant trees and plants growing in the alcove made it a fruit-ful, vibrant place. Altogether, the pleasant combination of cool shade and dappled sunlight, as well as the peaceful character of this secret place, provided a haven of rest for weary travelers who make use of it.

Like the spring of pure water at the foot of the hill, this peaceful retreat was designed by the Lord of the hill to be instructional as well as provisional. Its location is also by divine design, to emphasize the place of our true rest and how we are to access it. Before we can prop-erly grasp the meaning of the arbor, we must first remember that each trial we face is ordained of God, and so are the means by which he sustains and keeps us through such times. It is a provision of which our Lord Jesus Christ is himself the essence. He is our true resting place when our path leads us to heights, or depths, of overwhelm-ing affliction. (Psalm 61:1-2; Matthew 11:28-30) To withdraw into this quiet place, to rest in the arbor, is to flee to our Lord for help when trouble is near.

In this context, to rest is figurative language meaning to trust. So to rest in Christ is to trust in him and cast our burdens upon him, to commit our way unto him and leave the outcome to him. (Psalm

55:22; Psalm 37:5) To rest in him is to seek him as the source of our help and strength in trouble, to await his good pleasure, and hope in his mercy. (Psalm 37:39; Psalm 33:18-20) In this we find that to rest in Christ is a wakeful, conscious thing requiring our submission to God and the exercise of faith. (1 Peter 5:6-9) The arbor on the hill Difficulty was never meant to encourage or promote fleshly ease or sloth. Time spent there is a time to watch and pray, meditate upon God's Word, and remember his promises. (Matthew 26:41; 1 Thessalonians 5:6) It affords a prime opportunity to reflect upon his past goodness and unfailing mercy, to seek him fervently in prayer for wisdom and guidance, and enjoy the fellowship of his presence.

To rest in the Lord also has the sense of being quiet and submissive before him. (Psalm 46:11) To be quiet before the Lord in the midst of great difficulty is to demonstrate child-like faith in our all-wise heavenly Father. (Psalm 131) The essence of it is to submit to his will and providence rather than complaining and contending against our difficult circumstances. Although this heart attitude is never an easy thing to attain, and harder still to maintain, it is the secret to the perfect peace that passes all understanding. (Isaiah 26:3-4; Philippians 4:6-7)

Thus withdrawal into this secret arbor denotes our seeking Christ in our difficulty, not looking for relief apart from him. (Psalm 91:1-2) When we do so, our faith will be strengthened and we will know the sufficiency of God's sustaining grace. (Matthew 11:28-30) In his presence, we learn that Christ is our only true rest in life's darkest hours. (Psalm 46:1-5) As we seek him in our weakness and perplexity, we find him to be a never-failing refuge, a tower of strength for our weary, troubled souls. (Psalm 18:1-2; Psalm 31:1-3, 7-8; Proverbs 18:10)

Dear brother or sister in Christ, is it not comforting to know that the Lord Jesus Christ is Lord of all, including the hill Difficulty? He it is who appoints our trials and places them in our path, as he deems best. Can we not trust his infinite wisdom in such times? Surely it is our wisdom to do so! As our great high priest and partaker of our humanity, he perfectly understands our frailty and has compassion upon us in our weakness. (Hebrews 4:14-16) Moreover, as our hiding place in the midst of deepest trouble, he is faithful to supply the grace to not only endure it, but also profit from it. (Psalm 32:7)

In a very real sense, our entire Christian life is characterized by difficulty, even though we are not always under severe trial. After all, the pathway to Zion does wind through the vale of weeping, which serves as a perpetual reminder that this world is not our rest. So we are foolish indeed to seek a comfortable existence and be content to settle here. Should we do so, we will find that our Lord loves us too much to permit it.

As to this, the solitude of the peaceful arbor and the spiritual rest it provides are not just to be sought when we are in trouble. We should learn to withdraw there often and make use of it continually, for if we do not seek God's presence and commune with him day by day, we are not likely to do so when adversity comes.

When Christian first entered the quiet sanctuary, he immediately sat down to rest. Under the sweet influence of that tranquil resting place, he began to read from his scroll and ponder its contents. The precious words were a balm to his weary soul, ministering much-needed comfort and peace within. Then he thought upon the spotless garment that had been given him at the cross. Very good! These were excellent things upon which to contemplate! Before long, however, an inexplicable lethargy began to creep over him, which he was unable to resist.

While Christian slumbered, oblivious to his surroundings, two critical things occurred. The afternoon was quickly waning and the soft, golden hues of sunset were already beginning to tint the mountain. Of much greater significance, his cherished roll fell from his flaccid hand as he slept.

Perhaps you are wondering why the incident in the arbor was of such significance. Was it so wrong for Christian to sleep in that peaceful place, which was obviously designed for rest? There was certainly nothing wrong with the arbor itself. The solitude offered there was divinely appointed, and therefore, it posed no inherent danger whatsoever. So the arbor was not to blame. The problem lay in Christian's inadvertent misuse of it.

Quite often, God uses trials and afflictions to instruct, correct, and discipline his children. The hill Difficulty figures prominently in this process of child training, for it is frequently upon its heights that God draws us apart in order to deal with us as sons. (Hebrews

12:5-11) Due to the frailty of our human nature, we may grow weary under his rebuke and correction. This particular kind of weariness is equivalent to what Scripture calls fainting, and the implication is too clear for us to miss. Should we grow weary under divine chastening, we could easily yield to spiritual lethargy. (Proverbs 3:11-12; Proverbs 24:10; Hebrews 12:3-5)

Although this fatigue is not the same thing as bodily exhaustion, it does tend to drain us of both physical and mental strength, leaving us generally weak and vulnerable. Christian fell prey to this very thing while under heavy trial; therefore, he slumbered in the arbor when he should have remained alert and watchful. Since we are also prone to the same kind of lethargy, it would perhaps be well to consider the deeper implications of Christian's sleep.

If to rest in the arbor means to trust in Christ when under heavy trial, what does it mean when we sleep there? To sleep in the arbor is to become so discouraged that we cry like David in Psalm 55:6: *Oh that I had wings like a dove! for then would I fly away, and be at rest.* It is the language of one who has yielded to fear and mistrust.

To sleep in the arbor on the hill Difficulty is tantamount to growing weary under God's providential dealings. When under the stress of prolonged trial and affliction, there is the temptation to give in to spiritual battle fatigue. Instead of trusting in the Lord and waiting patiently for him, we become negligent in spiritual matters and lax in using the means of grace. However, in neglecting God's Word, we will become forgetful of what we have already learned and may also be guilty of misinterpreting the promises of God. Moreover, our failure to seek God diligently in prayer results in both the loss of his conscious presence and the strength that is imparted through fervent prayer. When we succumb to spiritual indolence in this way, we are inclined to take a rest from duty rather than resting in the hope of God's mercy while diligently performing our duty.

As a general rule, spiritual weariness does not manifest itself by outward sin. It works deep within, dulling our spiritual senses into complacency. When we yield to its dangerous influence, we are much more likely to try to flee from difficulty rather than seeking the Lord all the more diligently in it. Following this natural inclination solves nothing, however. On the contrary, it will only make matters worse.

The Lord Jesus Christ is our only source of true peace and rest. (Psalm 119:114) When we seek him in adversity, he refreshes and restores our souls in the midst of it. But if we seek diversion from trouble by looking in other directions for relief, our fellowship with the Lord will be interrupted, our spiritual focus distorted, and our faith subtly undermined. Vigilance and acute spiritual discernment are compromised at the very time when we need them the most.

Thankfully, our heavenly Father will not allow his children to slumber in this way for very long. He is faithful to recover and provoke us to duty and renewed watchfulness, even while allowing us to suffer the consequences of our lapse. We see this gracious recovery at work in Christian as he is finally awakened by a divine rebuke, which was perhaps akin to the words of Proverbs 6:9-11: *How long wilt thou sleep, O sluggard? When wilt thou arise out of thy sleep? Yet a little sleep, a little slumber, a little folding of the hands to sleep: So shall thy poverty come as one that travelleth, and thy want as an armed man.*

It must have been a fearful awakening, especially when Christian called to mind the three men slumbering near the cross. To his consternation, he realized that the same tendency also dwelt in his flesh. By nature, he was no better than they, and yet, they had been allowed to slumber undisturbed, while he had not. There was clearly no room for vainglory here, only deep penitence and gratitude to the one who did not let him get by with it.

Once he was fully awake, Christian left the secluded arbor and resumed his climb, undoubtedly pleased to find that the ascent was now a bit easier. This circumstance may have led him to conclude that he was none the worse for his temporary nap, but even though he did not yet suspect it, he had suffered a spiritual declension while he slept. The loss of his scroll denoted the loss of something very precious: the encouragement, strength, and assurance he had received from the Word of God. In becoming a forgetful hearer, some of what he had previously laid to heart had slipped from his memory. But of this he was also yet unaware.

Like his sleep in the arbor, the loss of his treasured scroll was a highly significant event for Christian. In fact, the latter was a direct consequence of the former. His scroll represented the infallible promises of God's Word, especially as concerned his standing in Christ. It was the very testimony of God concerning his eternal inheritance in Christ, and thus, the only basis upon which the assurance of faith can truly rest. (Ephesians 1:3-12; 1 Peter 1:3-5) Although its loss did not signify the loss of Christian's salvation, it would temporarily rob him of his peace and assurance.

The great and precious promises of which the scroll was a figure, give strength and encouragement when all around us seems dark and difficult. Without their constant help, we would be hard pressed to run the race to eternal glory, much less finish it. (John 3:14-18; John 6:37-40; John 10:27-30; Romans 5; Romans 8:33-39; Hebrews 6:17-20) On the other hand, a one-sided view of these promises can foster a careless attitude and lead to the neglect of personal responsibility that is not only inappropriate, but also dangerous. (Philippians 2:12-13; 2 Peter 1:1-11) Dear friend in Christ, we must never suppose that we are above this danger. Like Christian, we are capable of misusing the divinely-appointed means for our spiritual relief and comfort. We, too, may take the promises of God for granted and neglect his gracious provision for our spiritual help. However, we will suffer substantial loss if we do, one that will leave us highly vulnerable to the taunts and accusations of a terrible adversary.

In a very short while, Christian met this enemy head-on in the form of two men running toward him. Running, then, the wrong way! Their names were Timorous and Mistrust and, as you may guess, they were the bearers of bad news. Since they had been traveling to Zion, they assured Christian first-hand that the way ahead would only become more difficult and dangerous. What's more, they had heard a rumor that there were lions somewhere in the path ahead. For them, the mere report of lions on the prowl was the proverbial straw that broke the camel's back. So with no further investigation to determine whether the report was true or not, they decided to turn back. Moreover, they strongly urged Christian to do the same.

It is highly significant that Christian's encounter with Timorous and Mistrust did not occur until after his sleep in the arbor and the loss of his scroll. These two men represent the arguments of unbelieving fear assaulting his mind when he was already in a weakened spiritual condition. His earlier neglect had been more costly than he suspected at the time. It robbed him of vital spiritual strength and made God seem far away. Also, much of the comfort he had previously received from the Word of God now seemed just beyond his grasp. In such a condition, Christian was ripe for attack by despondent thoughts, and when they came, his former peace was badly shaken. To make matters worse, he now noticed that the sun was just about to set. At that point, any remaining assurance failed him utterly, plunging him into a vicious cycle of doubt and fear – a slough in the mind!

As twilight deepened, Christian's imagination ran wild as he thought upon the terror that might lie in his path ahead. Even so, he did not seriously consider turning back. Temporary ease and safety could be had that way, perhaps, but also death and the ultimate loss of his soul. Nothing but the City of Destruction lay behind him. The path to everlasting life was straight ahead. So for Christian the die was cast, as it had been long ago. Unbelieving fear urged him to turn back, but faith, even though it wavered for a time, now caused him to say "I will yet go forward."

Every true venture of faith, every inch of spiritual ground gained, is accomplished in the face of risk and uncertainty. Moreover, I suspect that all such endeavors are accompanied by a measure of anxiety and fear. Still, genuine faith sells all for Christ and gladly ventures all for him. (Matthew 13:45-46) When weighed against the promise of eternal life, any risk attached to it seems small indeed.

Therefore, Christian refused to follow the example of Timorous and Mistrust, but their discouraging words still lingered in his mind. Then he remembered the scroll and knew that he would find comfort and help therein, as he always had before. So he reached for it, but his treasured scroll was not where it was supposed to be.

Asleep! Awakened! Alarmed! In the midst of sudden panic and mental confusion, Christian finally connected his sinful sleep in the arbor to the loss of his scroll. He must have dropped it there! Even though he sincerely repented and asked God for forgiveness, Christian knew that he must return to the place of his slumber in order to search for his lost treasure. How could he have been so careless and negligent! The scroll had never been more precious to him than in that moment when he realized it was gone.

His experience surely corresponds to the incident recorded in Song of Solomon 5:1-8. In this passage, the bride did not immediately arise from her bed of ease and open the door to her beloved when he knocked. When she finally did open the door, she discovered, too late, that he had withdrawn himself and was gone. It took the loss of his presence to awaken her from lethargy and prompt her to diligently seek until she found him once again.

We can only speculate as to how Christian must have reproached himself while retracing his steps. After all, his present dilemma was due to his own neglect of God's gracious provision. So with a heavy heart, he reflected that he was entirely to blame for his predicament.

* * * *

Dear friend in Christ, what about you and I? How do we react when sudden difficulty appears in our path and enemies are near at hand to taunt and tempt us? Do we stand, or snooze? Do we watch and pray, or become negligent and forgetful? Do we seek God's face for help and strength to bear the hard thing that his providence has sent? Or do we look to other things for respite? Do we turn to our Lord for comfort, rest, and relief, or do we neglect his gracious provision and trust in our own resources? Trials are a proving time for us, in many respects. Not only do they purge and purify our faith, but they also give us valuable insight that nothing else can do. In addition, afflictions tend to have a humbling effect upon us, teaching us many things about ourselves that we would not otherwise see. Yet what slow learners we are!

How thankful we should be that our Lord is faithful even when we are not. He keeps us in the proper path, often in spite of our folly. Similar thoughts must have occurred to Christian as he was returning to the arbor. Revisiting it would bring increased sorrow because of his sin there, but also give him clearer insight into the arbor's meaning. He now understood that instead of availing himself of its intended purpose, he had failed the test. As he cried, "How many steps have I taken in vain!" he remembered Israel and their forty years' wandering in the wilderness because of the sin of unbelief. Their tragic example is a solemn warning for us as well. (Hebrews 3:12-19)

Since he was forced to retrace his steps, Christian lost ground spiritually, or so it would seem. However, he learned some invaluable lessons from the experience. So even though he grieved over the time lost, he would profit from it in the end. Moreover, by God's mercy, his renewed watchfulness would be duly rewarded.

When Christian finally reached the arbor and carefully searched it, he found his scroll lying exactly where he had dropped it. He would now treasure it all the more for having temporarily lost it. As he considered how easily it had slipped from his hand without his even suspecting it, he determined to guard it with much greater care. (Hebrews 2:1-3; Psalm 119:11,71; Proverbs 3:1-4)

Although the incident in the arbor and its aftermath had been a grueling experience for poor Christian, he gave thanks to God for his goodness and mercy. With his priceless scroll now safely tucked in place once again, he resumed his journey with renewed joy in his heart. As he did so, the evil report of Timorous and Mistrust finally began to fade in his memory. When, at last, he stood on the summit of the hill Difficulty, it was with a distinct sense of euphoria. At that moment, at least, his troubles seemed far behind him.

Study Questions

1. What is the figurative meaning of the peaceful arbor on the hill? Who designed it and for what purpose was it placed there?

2. If to rest in the arbor is to make proper use of it, what does it mean to sleep there? What deeper implications can we draw from Christian's sleep while there?

3. What happened to Christian while he slumbered in the arbor? In what way was God gracious to him even though he had sinned?

4. What consequences did Christian suffer because of the loss of his scroll?

5. In what way was Christian's sleep in the arbor and loss of his scroll related to his encounter with Timorous and Mistrust?

CHAPTER 21

Alone in the Dark!

Several years ago, my husband and I visited Mammoth Cave National Park. Prior to our arrival, we made reservations for one of the guided tours available there. The particular tour that we selected was a two-hour, moderately strenuous one that showcased several unique rock formations and huge domed chambers. Upon first entering the cave, our path sloped immediately downward and continued so for a good while before finally becoming level. Once we were fairly deep inside the cave, we reached a huge tower of steps, which we descended easily. The return trip requiring us to climb the same tower was another story!

After reaching the bottom of the steps, the guide led us into a massive underground chamber in which no natural light could penetrate. Gathering our group close together, he explained how utterly dark that place was without artificial light, and since a picture is worth a thousand words, he proceeded to demonstrate his point. So after warning us to be prepared, he turned off the lights, leaving us in darkness so complete that we could not see our hands in front of our faces.

As I stood still, afraid to move a step in any direction, our guide then asked us to imagine being lost there, as some have actually been. Standing in darkness that could almost be felt, I had a sense of absolute helplessness, even though I knew other people were close by and I could hear the guide's reassuring voice. But what horror, what utter despair, one must feel if lost in that dark place all alone! Our guide informed us that a person trapped in such a situation would not retain his sanity for long. When he turned the lights back on, our group seemed to breathe a collective sigh of relief to have that part of the cave tour behind us.

Those brief moments in the depths of Mammoth Cave reminded me that few things in life are more daunting than finding oneself alone in the dark. How much more terrifying to be lost at night, all alone and in unfamiliar surroundings? All sorts of hidden dangers could be lurking close by. A vivid imagination would quickly supply reasons to fear that might or might not have a basis in fact. There are few people who would not dread being overtaken by darkness, when they were all alone. Likewise, who in his right mind would want to be stranded by himself on an isolated mountain path at night?

Dear reader, try to imagine yourself in such a predicament. Under the best of circumstances, your situation could be dangerous. Even on a clear night, your field of vision would be significantly reduced and your sense of direction unreliable at best. Without the ability to properly determine your location, you could easily take a wrong turn and lose your way. Unforeseen obstacles and hazards might cause you to stumble, fall, and be seriously injured. Fear of the unknown would doubtless play havoc with your mind, whether in the form of wild animals, dangerous terrain, or evil men hiding in the shadows. Terror might well get the better of you and overtake you more quickly than the darkness had done. Such a frame of mind would tend to impair your judgment all the more.

Christian found himself in this very circumstance shortly after reaching the summit of the hill Difficulty. Twilight at the top of this particular mountain is a very fleeting thing. Once the sun has set, nightfall is swift and deep. The poor man never imagined that he would be caught that way. But then he considered that had he not slept in the arbor, lost his scroll, and been forced to retrace his steps, he would have been well beyond the summit while it was still daylight.

With the encroaching gloom came a revival of Christian's earlier doubt and fear. The dire warning of Timorous and Mistrust echoed loudly in his mind once again, especially their report of lions in the way ahead. Was that a low, menacing growl he heard? Quite naturally, he dreaded the thought of running into such vicious, fearless hunters.

Christian realized that darkness would not hinder them in the least. Perhaps even now they were stalking him, silent and unseen.

Standing alone in the deepening shadows of evening, Christian's imagination quickly took flight. Although he had no intention of turning back, he could not help but wonder what would happen if he should encounter the lions. They would probably attack before he even saw them! What on earth would he do then? Perish on the spot, he supposed! He would certainly be powerless against their superior strength. How could he ever hope to evade their stealth and cunning? Was his journey to end in such an appalling way? Such fearful thoughts must have raced through his mind, and yet, he cautiously made his way forward in spite of them

If we are to keep Christian's experience in its proper perspective, we must never lose sight of the fact that his journey is allegorical in nature. The ascent of the hill Difficulty represents a time of unspecified trouble and the way in which he reacted to it. The laborious nature of his climb pictures his great inner conflict when his faith came under heavy fire. To make matters worse, it was a battle that his unbelieving family was at a loss to understand. Thus he felt all alone in his suffering.

Christian's sleep in the arbor portrays the weariness to which he succumbed under the heavy trial, and his unexpected encounter with Timorous and Mistrust was the direct outcome of it. The two men with their evil news represent a breach in his assurance that rekindled his inclination to doubt and fear. Yet even though unbelieving fear strongly urged him to turn back, Christian refused to retreat.

So what about the lions? The report of their presence ahead was no mere rumor. It was all too true! In fact, Timorous and Mistrust were their forerunners. Moreover, Christian would be attacked by them, but not in the way that he supposed. These particular lions were not literal beasts of prey, although they bear a striking resemblance to their earthly counterparts. The lions in Christian's path depict a much more sinister enemy, the lion-like adversary of the souls of men. Christian has already come into contact with him at least once, if you remember, near the Wicket Gate.

Satan is a tenacious and determined foe whom we do well not to underestimate. Even though he could not prevent our coming to

Christ for salvation, he will never cease trying to reclaim us for his dark kingdom. With great power and predatory skill, he stalks us with stealth and cunning. Being far too clever to spring prematurely, he bides his time until the moment is right. Thus it is crucial for us to be aware of his tactics because we, also, are his intended prey.

How the mighty roar of a lion strikes terror into the heart of its victim so as to distract his attention and prevent his escape! Our lion-like adversary employs similar tactics against us when he assaults our minds with discouraging and oppressive thoughts. Should he gain an advantage over us he presses it hard, determined to take us down. Literal flaming arrows could scarcely do more damage.

His primary objective is to devour us, to overthrow our faith and claim us as a spoil. To this end, he directs the full weight of his malice and diabolical craftiness. When failing in that, he continues to dog our steps by endeavoring to snatch the Word of God from our minds, shake our confidence in the Lord, undermine our faith and thwart our hope. If, in our weakness, he succeeds in diverting our eyes from the Lord for a time, he gains a significant victory, and we lose ground spiritually, just as Christian did when he slept in the arbor.

By his very nature, Satan is a creature of the night, who *as a roaring lion, walketh about, seeking whom he may devour.* (1 Peter 5:8) Lurking nearby in our times of darkness, he hopes to catch us when our defenses are down. He can lie in wait at any point along our path, hoping to catch us off guard. But I think that he must have a strong preference for the hill Difficulty, viewing it as a prime opportunity to carry out his evil design.

Without a doubt, Satan is a powerful enemy with a full arsenal of weapons at his command. In our own strength we are no match for his wit, much less his craft and power. Although his flaming arrows are potentially lethal ones, they could do little harm if they did not strike something flammable in us, some weakness upon which to kindle. Far too often we lend an ear to his disheartening suggestions, especially when we are already depressed in spirit. We lower the shield of faith and his arrows hit their mark. However, this does not need to be the case because we serve the one who has utterly defeated our terrible adversary, and has made ample provision for our defense. (Ephesians 6:10-13)

Although Satan is still permitted to roam at large, he is bound by the power and providence of God through the cross of Jesus Christ. He may roar at us and disturb our minds, but he cannot destroy or reclaim any who truly belong to the Lord Jesus Christ. Even though we have no natural defense against Satan's wiles, we can stand when he engages us in battle if we trust our Lord and obey his commands. (Psalm 108:12-13) Our first responsibility, which is crucial to our victory, is to humble ourselves under the mighty hand of God. Then we must be sober and vigilant, we must be on guard and maintain a careful watch, because only then will we be able to resist our enemy steadfastly in the faith. (1 Peter 5:6-9)

Whether his attacks come boldly by day or stealthily in the night, Satan is a fiercely determined foe. Moreover, if we try to take him on in our own strength, our striving would be losing. How blessed we are to have the Lord Jesus Christ on our side, for he alone must win the battle! As our shield and defender, he will not permit our feet to be moved. It matters not at all to him whether the attack comes by night or by day, because his eyes are always upon us and his omnipotent hand is strong to preserve and deliver us. (Psalm 121) With the Lord as our refuge and our fortress, no weapon in the hand of the enemy will ultimately prosper against us. (Isaiah 54:17)

Rise, my soul, to watch and pray, from thy sleep awaken;
Be not by the evil day unawares o'ertaken,
For the foe, well we know, oft his harvest reapeth
While the Christian sleepeth.

Watch against the devil's snares lest asleep he find thee;
For indeed no pains he spares to deceive and blind thee.
Satan's prey oft are they who secure are sleeping
And no watch are keeping.

Watch! Let not the wicked world with its power defeat thee;
Watch lest with her pomp unfurled she betray and cheat thee.
Watch and see lest there be faithless friends to charm thee,
Who but seek to harm thee.

Watch against thyself, my soul, lest with grace thou trifle;
Let not self thy thoughts control nor God's mercy stifle.
Pride and sin lurk within all thy hopes to scatter;
Heed not when they flatter.

But while watching, also pray to the Lord unceasing.
He will free thee, be thy stay, strength and faith increasing.
O Lord bless in distress and let nothing swerve me
From the will to serve thee. [1]

The deep, dark night of the soul

Have you ever noticed how that trouble always seems to be worse at night, no matter what sort it is? If you have an infectious disease, your fever will almost invariably spike at night. Pain is often more severe and acute illness tends to reach its crisis point in the long, weary hours before dawn. Likewise, doubts, fears, worries and perplexities all seem to loom larger and be more overwhelming in the dark of night. When morning breaks, things often seem better even when nothing has really changed. The light of day somehow alters our perspective concerning the things that tormented us so cruelly in the midnight hours.

This principle holds equally true in a spiritual sense. When our souls are filled with the light of the knowledge of Christ, peace reigns within no matter what our outward circumstances happen to be. However, when darkness overtakes our mind, that peace is shattered and mental anguish takes its place. This truth reminds us that since the lions roaming near the summit of the hill Difficulty were figurative, so must also the darkness be that descended upon Christian there.

That particular darkness was indeed of an uncommon kind that had nothing to do with the actual time of day. It was indicative of Christian's state of mind after he had succumbed to spiritual weariness when under affliction. The fall of this unearthly darkness signaled the onset of spiritual depression, which some have termed the deep, dark night of the soul. Its rapid descent had an isolating effect upon Christian. Moreover, it weakened him substantially and exposed him to direct attack by the rumored lions.

You may recall that the incident on the mountaintop was not Christian's first experience with spiritual depression. He was previously held captive by it in the Slough of Despond, and will undoubtedly face it again before reaching his heavenly destination. So will many other dear children of God as they follow the same pathway.

Spiritual depression does not usually come upon us when we are strong. It is far more likely to take us captive when we are already in a weakened condition, perhaps due to severe or prolonged difficulty. Once it descends upon our minds, all seems dark and former hope shines dimly, if at all. We are cast down as into a deep, dark pit from which we cannot seem to free ourselves. Anxious, mistrustful thoughts bombard our minds as our faith comes under intense attack and our spiritual strength is sapped. Bitterness and self-pity rise to the forefront, but instead of giving relief, they only serve to aggravate the trial. Therefore, considering the harmful nature of spiritual depression, it is easy to see what a powerful deterrent it can be.

Like the allegorical darkness that obscured Christian's way on the mountain path, spiritual depression will dim our perspective and alter our sense of spiritual direction. By diverting our focus inwardly, it also renders us more vulnerable to diabolical suggestions. Irrational thoughts and fears clutter and perplex our minds, seriously impairing the ability to make sound, spiritual judgments. The lowering of our guard, which usually accompanies this state of mind, makes us more susceptible to temptations of all kinds and can even compromise our physical health. It usually descends without warning and feeds itself by means of despondent thoughts and feelings of misery and despair. However, it need not be a permanent condition.

The divine remedy for spiritual depression is found in Psalm 42:11: *Why art thou cast down, O my soul? And why art thou disquieted within me? Hope thou in God: for I shall yet praise him, who is the health of my countenance, and my God.* Our Lord Jesus Christ is sovereign over all things, including our most difficult and painful circumstances. The refreshing spring and peaceful arbor on the hill Difficulty depict the provision of his sustaining grace and are readily available for our use. As our very present help in trouble, he is with us in every trial.

Moreover, he who neither slumbers nor sleeps has fatherly pity upon us when we do. (Psalm 103:13-14)

Christian will shortly discover how true this is. He was trapped in the darkness of spiritual depression for the moment, but it will not consume him. Even though Christian could not sense his presence, the Lord was near at hand, and his ears were open to the needy man's faintest cry of distress. Christian was downcast, but light will arise in his soul again. His night of weeping would end before long; joy would come in the morning. (Psalm 30:5) The flaming arrows of the enemy were flying thick and fast for now, but they will not succeed in destroying him. On the contrary, his faith will be strengthened and purged as a result of the conflict. Therefore, instead of retreating in the face of the enemy, Christian could confidently say with the prophet: *Rejoice not against me, O mine enemy: when I fall, I shall arise; when I sit in darkness, the LORD shall be a light unto me.* (Micah 7:8)

* * * *

Dear friend in Christ, although we might wish that we could glimpse into the future, it is of God's mercy that we are not permitted to know what lies ahead. If we could see the sum total of every heartache, trial, and affliction that awaits us, would not such knowledge eclipse every joy and fill us with dread? It would undoubtedly prove an unbearable burden that would crush our spirits, consume our thoughts, and render us unfit to face the day at hand. How thankful we should be to our loving, infinitely wise heavenly Father for his compassion upon us in this regard. He withholds from us the knowledge of what we will face tomorrow so that we may walk in his strength and serve him without distraction today. Thus through the abundance of his grace, we are able to walk the path of life one day at a time.

Like Christian's allegorical pilgrimage to the Celestial City, our earthly life is an odyssey of faith in which trials figure prominently. So before we judge Christian too harshly because of his harrowing ordeal on the hill Difficulty, perhaps we should step back and take a good look at ourselves. How closely does his experience there mirror our own? Can we honestly claim never to have been guilty of a similar lapse? We will surely recognize something of our own history in Christian's, especially when we remember the many spiritual lessons that we, too, have had to learn the hard way.

Since we have embarked on the same spiritual journey, there are many practical applications to be drawn from Christian's story that should prove beneficial to us. Like the allegorical road to the Celestial City, our path also leads us through unknown territory in which we cannot see too far ahead. Although we understand that various trials and afflictions will surely meet us along the way, we rarely see them coming. Adversity usually meets us unexpectedly, sometimes appearing in the form of seemingly insurmountable obstacles that threaten to stop us in our tracks. Passage through these severe trials is difficult, even when we understand that God's providence led us there.

Like Christian, we will get into trouble if we look to other things when tried and afflicted, instead of the means that God has appointed for our relief. The Lord Jesus Christ is our only source of true help in such times. When we hope in his mercy rather than succumbing to unbelieving fear, he will minister healing to our weary souls. The spring at the foot of the hill Difficulty and the arbor located at its halfway point represent the abundant help and relief available to us when we look to him in trial.

Just as it is not given us to anticipate our trials, neither are we permitted to know ahead of time the course that any particular trial will take. Since we cannot see the end of the thing until it comes, we must learn to endure it by faith, just as Christian scaled the steep, treacherous hill. However, not with such a faith that stoically resigns itself to its fate. A child-like faith is required, one that humbly submits to the wisdom and providence of God for the outcome. When this is truly our case, we will find that a distinct blessing attends our way, even when we are called to brave the heights of the hill Difficulty. Moreover, if we should attain the spiritual insight to perceive its good and gracious design, we will be better able to count our time there all joy. (James 1:2-4)

Christian's successful ascent of the mountain, in spite of all that happened to him there, should give us great cause for encouragement and hope. God will also be faithful to keep us from falling, when his will leads us up that same rocky path. We cannot face such a thing in our own strength, but through the sufficiency of his grace, we may climb every mountain and pass through every dark valley. (2 Corinthians 12:9; Philippians 4:13)

When facing deep adversity, we may as well expect unbelieving fear to attack our minds and argue against faith. As in the case of Timorous and Mistrust, and ten of the Hebrew men who were sent to spy out the land of Canaan, unbelief always gives a discouraging report. (Numbers 13) Such is the power of unbelieving fear that it cannot see beyond the lions in the way or the giants who inhabit the land.

Like Caleb and Joshua, let us resolve instead to venture forward by faith, even when human reason argues vehemently against it. (Numbers 13:30) As we contemplate our journey to this point, and consider that the providence of God has brought us safely this far, we may confidently trust in him to lead us all the way home.

Therefore, dear brother or sister in Christ, when the hill Difficulty materializes unexpectedly in your path, remember that you will not have to brave its rocky heights alone. God's omniscient eye will be upon you there, and his loving hand will guide your every step. If sudden darkness should overtake you there, listen as he whispers to you this precious promise from his Word:

Thus saith the LORD that created thee, O Jacob, and he that formed thee, O Israel, Fear not: for I have redeemed thee, I have called thee by thy name; thou art mine. When thou passest through the waters, I will be with thee; and through the rivers, they shall not overflow thee: when thou walkest through the fire, thou shalt not be burned; neither shall the flame kindle upon thee. (Isaiah 43:1-2)

Study Questions

1. Why was Christian overtaken by darkness on the summit of the hill when he should have been well beyond it by now? What effect did the sudden darkness have upon his imagination?

2. Since the lions were not literal beasts of prey, what sort of enemy did they represent? Describe the nature of the enemy attack and the evil intention behind it.

3. The kind of darkness that overtook Christian had nothing to do with the actual time of day. What did it represent? What sort of effect does it have upon one who is entrapped by it?

4. What is the scriptural remedy for spiritual depression?

5. What practical applications can be drawn from Christian's experience that would be beneficial to a present-day Christian?

Part Nine

A TABLE IN THE WILDERNESS

He brought me to the banqueting house,
and his banner over me was love.
Song of Solomon 2:4

CHAPTER 22

Haven by the Wayside

WHAT WOULD IT TAKE TO TURN YOU OUT OF THE PATH OF LIFE? A soul-searching question is it not, dear reader? Would it require a major impediment or upheaval, or could something relatively minor be enough to turn your steps out of the narrow way? Would it take lions in your path, or simply the rumor of them? If you are truly a child of God, nothing will succeed in diverting you from the path of life in finality. However, since many things will war against you and try to overthrow your faith, perhaps it would be more profitable to consider what it takes to keep you in the narrow way. (Proverbs 4:7-13)

Like John Bunyan's character, Christian, every true believer in Christ will encounter lions of some sort during the course of his or her earthly sojourn. They may take on various forms and pose many differing kinds of threats, but all of them seek to hinder our walk with the Lord. Sometimes they assume the disguise of political or religious persecution, as was the case in John Bunyan's day. (Matthew 10:16-18) Or perhaps their vicious roar is confined to the more intimate circle of family and close connections. (Matthew 10:34-38) The reproach that comes from bearing the name of Christ before a world at enmity with God is probably one of the most common ways in which they appear. (1 Timothy 4:10; 1 Peter 4:12-16) However, these lions can also appear as things that tempt rather than terrify or discourage, such as the desire for ease, material gain, vainglory or worldly success. The ways in which they confront us are numerous;

but whatever form they happen to take, their single intention is to turn us from following the Lord Jesus Christ.

God's protective care of his people is a wondrous thing to contemplate, especially in those times when lions appear unexpectedly in our path. By his unseen hand of providence, He forms a garrison around us by which he guards and keeps us in all our ways. (Psalm 34:7; Psalm 121) This divine protection overshadowed Christian while he struggled in the darkness on the heights of the hill Difficulty. It kept him securely in the right path, even when frailty caused his steps to falter. (Psalm 37:23-24) Moreover, it was leading him toward an unexpected refuge where he would find the help he so desperately needed for his weary spirit and depressed state of mind.

Just when Christian felt that he could not go much further without proper rest and refreshment, he noticed a very stately palace right by the wayside ahead. It offered the promise of a much-needed respite, a shelter from the darkness and danger that lurked on the mountain. Here was a vital means of grace whereby the people of God are kept in the way of life. After his narrow escape on the mountain, Christian felt all the more drawn to the magnificent palace and anxious to see if he could obtain a lodging there. His first impression was an accurate one, for those who by-pass this palace will miss a major source of spiritual benefit and blessing.

As Christian studied the approach to the palace, he quickly noted that the narrow path became even more constricted as it led to the porter's lodge. Then to his great consternation, he saw the dreaded lions! To have heard of them was one thing, but there they were right in his path! So as Christian scrutinized the narrow passageway, he faced a terrible dilemma. Turning back at that point was certainly one option. However, if he would enter the stately palace, he must first pass by the lions. He must confront his great fear, even though it seemed to promise certain death.

Who would build a magnificent palace in such an unlikely location? To the casual observer it must seem strange indeed, but this palace was placed there with careful forethought, as a haven of rest for those who have scaled the great hill. Like Christian, we who travel through this life as strangers and pilgrims quickly find that the world offers no legitimate sanctuary. However, the palace standing near the summit of the hill Difficulty provides just such a safe haven for us.

Although we are destined for eternal glory, we are appointed to adversity and affliction while on earth. (Isaiah 48:10) Therefore, the stately palace is located near at hand, right in our path, and is designed by our Lord to help us stay the course. Within the security of its walls we are nourished, strengthened, and armed to face the rigors of a pilgrim's life. Moreover, this palace represents God's witness, his voice on earth. From its beautiful gates, the Gospel of Jesus Christ goes forth into a lost, sinful world. Is it any wonder that vicious lions are ready to threaten any who would enter therein?

While Christian stood trembling at the prospect of a close encounter with the lions, his little courage would perhaps have failed utterly had it not been for the keeper of the gatehouse, a valiant man named Watchful. Standing guard there by divine calling, he was constantly on the lookout for pilgrims in distress. Since he was a highly perceptive man, he was quick to observe Christian's reluctance, but also understood the reason behind his fear and uncertainty. So even though he rebuked Christian for his little strength, he urged him onward by assuring him that the lions were chained.

Who is this one named Watchful laboring so diligently by the palace gate? He represents a true minister of Jesus Christ serving as a watchman over this beautiful house. (Isaiah 62:6; Ezekiel 33:7; Hebrews 13:17) Thus he is a very special kind of watchman in that he stands guard over and cares for the souls of men. After informing Christian that the lions were chained, Watchful admonished him to "Keep in the midst of the path, and no hurt shall come unto thee." Then he explained the express purpose of the lions. They represent a trial of faith for those who possess it and a means of disclosing its lack in those who do not.

In a highly astute observation concerning these particular lions, Charles H. Spurgeon wrote: "Unbelief generally has a good eye for the lions, but a blind eye for the chains that hold them back." [1] On the other hand, genuine faith enables us to view them in a proper light, and to understand that all such lions are chained by God's providence. Therefore, saving faith will neither retreat nor turn back because of them.

An immovable resolve distinguishes those who have genuine faith from those who do not, even though their courage may at times be shaken. The only safe course lies, not in the avoidance of danger, but by watchful continuance in the straight and narrow way in spite of it. God-given faith does just that. Therefore, after taking careful heed to the porter's instruction, Christian began to approach the palace gate by way of the long, narrow passageway. Although he trembled as he did so, Christian's desire to enter the stately house overcame his natural fear of the lions. As he drew nearer, the mighty beasts did not touch him, although they roared viciously. Passing by them in the midst of the path he was safely out of their reach, just as the porter had said.

Having passed this preliminary trial of his faith, Christian probably expected a hearty welcome into the palace, but the porter wished to know more about him first. Their initial conversation brought some interesting things to light concerning both the nature of the palace and the desire of Christian's heart. When Christian inquired about lodging for the night, he learned that the palace was much more than an ordinary inn. Like the spring and the arbor on the hill Difficulty, it was another gracious provision made by the Lord of the hill. Then the porter conducted a query of his own, asking three pertinent questions of Christian that would help determine his suitability for admission to the palace.

The chief responsibility of a minister of Jesus Christ is to protect and guard the spiritual interests of those given into his charge. (Hebrews 13:17) One way in which he performs this duty is by carefully considering all who wish to join his flock, thereby protecting the church from impostors insofar as it is possible. Another way in which he guards their spiritual well-being is by impressing upon each believer the necessity of a diligent self-watch (Proverbs 4:23) and an appropriate self-examination. (2 Peter 1:1-11) The man of God knows well that an attitude of spiritual watchfulness is the friend of true assurance and peace. It promotes the exercise and growth of genuine faith. On the other hand, it effectively puts the sword to false presumption and carnal security.

When the porter asked where he came from and where he was going, Christian replied that he was born in the City of Destruction, but was now on the way to Mount Zion. In response to the question concerning his name, he answered without hesitation, "Christian, but my name at the first was Graceless." What a marvelous thing to be able to honestly say! "Graceless" before, but not anymore! Now he bore the name of the one who loved him and died for him, the one to whom Christian now unreservedly belonged.

In response to the porter's desire to know why he sought shelter so late in the day, Christian recounted the incident in the arbor and its aftermath. Even though he was weary and desirous of the palace's hospitality, he did not attempt to conceal the truth of what had happened to him on the hill Difficulty, or to minimize his sinful actions there. Perhaps he anxiously wondered whether the porter would be scandalized by his confession and send him on his way. But not the porter of this palace!

Before admitting Christian into the intimate family circle, Watchful called for one of the virgins of the palace to interview him further, a "grave and beautiful damsel" named Discretion. Although she was reserved by nature and her demeanor said as much, this lady asked some candid questions pertaining to the validity of his Christian profession. Each question revealed evidence of her keen insight and sound spiritual judgment. In particular, she was interested to know how Christian had entered the path, his experience along the way, and again, what his name was. Far from being offended by the personal nature of her inquiry, he answered her questions honestly and without hesitation.

The more he talked with her, the more earnestly Christian desired to join fellowship with the palace residents. In fact, his longing increased even more when he discovered that his Lord was the builder of this special house. His heart-felt confession of this desire brought a quiet smile to Discretion's lips and tears to her eyes.

How is it that Christian's words evoked such an emotional response in this gentle, dignified lady whose very countenance spoke of self-control and quiet serenity? Perhaps because she discerned that the wayfaring stranger at the palace gate was a true brother in Christ, with whom she felt an immediate affinity of heart and mind. This was not the case with all who applied for admission there. After conversing with him a while longer, her studied impression was that he was another who loved what she loved. Moreover, she discerned in Christian a striking resemblance to the rest of the family and a character that was consistent with his name. So after calling for more family members to join her in talking with him further, Christian was warmly welcomed into the palace. Once inside, he was received as a brother in the Lord and invited to partake of the unique hospitality of this very special dwelling place, the Palace Beautiful.

In the palace of the King

What kind of place is this house that offers refuge to pilgrims and strangers? Its name brings to mind a splendid mansion richly adorned and lavishly furnished, a place of great beauty and grandeur. So how was it that poor, weary Christian dared to make inquiry and seek admission there? Do not palaces belong to the great and mighty ones of earth? Do they not house those who are of noble or royal birth? To knock at its door and ask for lodging would seem the height of audacity, except that this dwelling bore no resemblance to a literal earthly palace. It is noted for something of a far more enduring quality than outward beauty and splendor. Those who abide within its walls know, love, and honor the Lord Jesus Christ. They openly confess him as Lord and worship him in spirit and in truth.

The Palace Beautiful is an earthly depiction of the heavenly Zion, the Church, the mystical body of Jesus Christ. (Ephesians 5:23-27) As to its situation near the summit of the hill Difficulty, this stately residence portrays a local assembly of God's people who have been joined together for their mutual edification and spiritual benefit. Even though they live as strangers and pilgrims in the world, the true and faithful believers gathered there are part of the family of God, a holy temple in the Lord. (Ephesians 2:19-22; Ephesians 3:14-21) As citizens of the heavenly Jerusalem and part of the bride of Christ, they are a people destined for greatness. (Philippians 3:20-21; Hebrews 12:22-24; Revelation 21:1-4, 9ff) However, their glorious destiny is more often than not concealed behind the relative obscurity of their earthly circumstances. For this reason, few truly perceive the palace's beauty.

Yet for those with eyes to see, she is beautiful, a glorious bride glowing with inner beauty that her Lord alone can see! (Song of

Solomon 2:14 and 4:7) Her beauty will never diminish or fade away because it is not hers inherently, but a gift of divine grace. (Psalm 45:10-11) Her inward beauty is splendid because it is the righteousness of Christ, her heavenly bridegroom. (Isaiah 61:10; Psalm 45:13-15) It manifests itself as she reflects her Lord's glory, as she bears his image and character. Her beauty, then, proceeds entirely from him, for *"Out of Zion, the perfection of beauty, God hath shined."* (Psalm 50:2)

The situation of the palace is not only beautiful, but royal as well. Even though not noted for outward magnificence, it is the royal dwelling place of the great King. (Psalm 48:1-3) The Lord Jesus Christ reigns over her as sovereign head, and even though those who are not a part of the palace find it strange, the cross is the golden scepter by which he rules over this unique house. His people, those who are joined to him by faith, make their abode there as part of his body. (Colossians 1:16-19) They are his grateful subjects, his peculiar treasure, the jewels in his royal diadem. (Isaiah 62:1-4; Malachi 3:16-18) Within the safety of the palace walls, they are sheltered, protected, and nurtured into spiritual maturity.

Therefore, the residents of the Palace Beautiful constitute a royal household that extends to every nation, tribe, and people on earth. They are the children of God by new birth and his legal heirs by adoption. (1 John 5:1; Ephesians 1:3-6) Moreover, those who are part of this very special family, which is a household of faith, are the spiritual descendants of Abraham and heirs to the promise made to him by God. (Genesis 17:1-8; Galatians 6:10; Romans 4; Galatians 3:26-29)

Since it is built and inhabited by the Lord Jesus Christ, the Palace Beautiful is a great house, but not one that is made with hands. It is a spiritual temple, with Jesus Christ as the chief cornerstone. Moreover, it is a living temple composed of living stones built upon a foundation laid in Zion. (1 Peter 2:4-6)

Those who inhabit this spiritual house, this beautiful, royal palace, also constitute a holy priesthood that offers up spiritual sacrifices, acceptable to God by Jesus Christ. (1 Peter 2:5) It is then, truly, a house of worship. Those who are part of it have received a glorious change of estate. (1 Peter 2:9-10) Nevertheless, even though their condition is regal, they are the humble and willing servants of their Lord and King. (Romans 4:10-11; Revelation 5:8-10; Revelation 7:9-17)

With Jesus Christ as both the foundation and builder of this marvelous structure, the Palace Beautiful is notable for her strength, security, and permanence. Yet those who know her history the best will tell you that it is a record of continual warfare. From ages past until the present time, enemies have attacked her from without, and false brethren have attempted to subvert and destroy her from within. However, none of these powerful foes will ever succeed in breaking down her walls or removing her towers. To this day they stand firmly intact, but not by her might and power.

The Lord Jesus Christ is the everlasting strength of his people, his church. Therefore, those who are part of her have a song of victory even when sorely afflicted and tried. Her stability, and thus her security, rests entirely in his hands. Her ramparts are the eternal truths that she has received from him and upon which she firmly stands, the faith for which she earnestly contends. (Jude 1-3) As long as her Lord reigns over her, the walls and towers of the Palace Beautiful will remain in place and her impregnable bulwarks shall enclose her securely. Just walk about her and see! (Psalm 48:12-14)

It was to this royal household, this palace so aptly named Beautiful, that Christian now came. While part of God's everlasting kingdom, his mystical body, it also represents an assembly of his dear children on earth. The fervent desire of Christian's heart was to become one of these faithful followers of the Lord Jesus Christ. However, before he was invited to share a meal with them, several other family members expressed the desire to talk further with him in order to learn more about him. Significantly, their names happened to be Piety, Prudence, and Charity.

The questions they posed to Christian concerned things of which they obviously had first-hand knowledge, and the spiritual insight with which they spoke revealed a depth of understanding and experience that far exceeded his own. Yet their inquiries brought many things vividly to Christian's remembrance, while his honest answers reflected an appropriate measure of spiritual growth.

Piety was the first of the three ladies to speak. Her primary concern, and the most essential one, had to do with what first prompted Christian to seek a pilgrim's life. After all, the beginning of his pilgrimage was the most crucial part, for it was foundational to the validity of his profession of faith in the Lord Jesus Christ. Piety knew well that just as the journey to Zion has an ultimate end, it also has a definite beginning. One cannot become a child of God through spiritual osmosis. Saving faith cannot be conferred upon one person by another, and neither can it be acquired through natural under-standing of Bible truth. Saving faith comes through an inward work of God's grace.

Likewise, eternal life is never transferred through the privilege of having Christian parents or growing up in a church that faithfully declares the truth. It is the result of Christ living within. Faith that is merely intellectual or second-hand is not enough, and neither is the kind of faith of those who claim that they have always believed. Always is a bit too long!

As we saw with Formalist and Hypocrisy, no one is truly on the pathway to the Celestial City who has bypassed the Wicket Gate, no matter what he may have done instead. Christ is the only way to that glorious city. The way of the cross is the only way that leads home.

So as Christian gave an account of his journey so far, Piety listened with rapt attention. He related how great fear had come upon him while in the City of Destruction, and how Evangelist had instructed him and directed him toward the Wicket Gate. As he shared the wonderful things he had seen in the Interpreter's House, Piety took note that Christian had not merely received the truth outwardly. The Holy Spirit had obviously given him the capacity to understand and receive the things of Christ.

Then Christian told of his marvelous deliverance at the cross, when he finally understood the fuller implications of what Christ had done for him. It was only in beholding the cross and the empty tomb that his soul was released from its terrible burden of doubt and fear.

As Piety inquired of him further, Christian told of his disturb-ing encounter with Simple, Sloth and Presumption, and of his con-frontation with Formalist and Hypocrisy shortly thereafter. Then he summed up the chronology of his journey with his ascent of the hill Difficulty. Instead of excusing his untoward fear of the lions, he freely admitted that he might have turned back rather than having to face them had it not been for the timely help of Watchful, the palace porter.

Since many are verbally fluent enough to give an impressive testimony of their past experience, Piety's query then took another direction that was designed to reveal the present orientation of Christian's heart. When asked if he still thought of the country from whence he came, Christian replied without hesitation that he remembered it, but with shame instead of regret. He nurtured no longing whatsoever to return to that awful place because his heart's desire was set upon another country, and to that heavenly country he was now traveling. In this, Piety discerned the heart of a true pilgrim.

At the conclusion of this initial dialogue, the lady named Prudence stepped forward to continue the inquiry. Her questions focused upon matters that pertained to Christian's inner struggles. Once again, he answered her in a truthful manner, confessing that he was not rid of all fleshly desires but contended against them. Things that had formerly been his delight now caused him grief and vexation of soul. His chief desire was to be free of them, but he had to admit that they continued to torment and war against him. (Romans 7) At times the pull of his flesh could be strong, but when he thought upon the Lord Jesus and all that he had in him, the power of his flesh was significantly weakened.

Prudence then asked Christian why he so longed to go to Mount Zion. It was a pointed question, and a vital one as well, one to which many ambiguous answers have been given. Christian's forthright reply showed that he had a living hope within, a firm and confident expectation. The desire of his heart was to see the one who died for him and was alive forevermore. (Revelation 1:18)

When Prudence was satisfied with the responses she had received, Charity took up the interview by introducing the painful and very personal subject of Christian's family. The shadow of a deep, abiding sorrow was immediately evident in his countenance as he replied, "I have a wife and four small children." His brief response, so full of grief and regret, was not that he had a family, but because they had refused to come with him. Many believers can identify with Christian as he described his home situation with an unbelieving wife and children. It was unquestionably one of his most bitter trials. Moreover, joining the fellowship of the Palace Beautiful without them caused him acute pain and suffering. He must have grappled long and hard with the fear that he was somehow to blame for their obstinate unbelief and hardness of heart.

However, as he reflected upon that particular part of his history, Christian related how he had shared the Word of God with his family and done everything in his power to lovingly persuade them to accompany him. Although he made no pretense of being perfect, he had endeavored to live a life before them that was consistent with his verbal witness. So even though he was painfully aware of his many shortcomings, Christian's conscience was clear that he had not been a stumbling block to them because of a hypocritical spirit. The truth of the matter was that God's Word was offensive to them. Moreover, they were unwilling to forsake the world and its ungodly ways. Christian's salvation brought a breach in his household, and even though he would continue to be a witness to them and pray for them, his painful family situation could prove a long-term trial.

* * * *

Undoubtedly, there are some who would be highly insulted, even outraged, by the intense scrutiny and deeply personal interrogation to which Christian was subjected before being admitted into the inner circle of the Palace Beautiful. However, as we have already noted, his face bore not the slightest hint of offense. On the contrary, he perceived a strong spiritual bond with the palace residents that became even more evident the more he talked with them. It transcended even the relationship that he enjoyed with his earthly family. Up to this point in his journey he has traveled essentially alone. Now he fervently desired to join company with these precious people and become a part of them. Although he could not have easily expressed it in words, the peculiar union of heart and mind that he experienced with them made him feel as if he had come home.

Study Questions

1. Who was the man named Watchful? What did he say to Christian that put his fear to rest about the lions that were beside the narrow passageway to the palace?

2. Before admitting Christian to the palace, Watchful questioned him very carefully. What were the three particular things he wanted to know?

3. The porter then called a family member named Discretion to talk further with Christian. What kind of questions did she ask him? What was her impression of Christian after talking with him at length?

4. What kind of place is the Palace Beautiful? What does it belong to, and who are those who reside there?

5. After being admitted to the palace, Christian was questioned even further by three more family members: Piety, Prudence, and Charity. Their questions all concerned the validity of his profession of faith in Christ, and in answering them, Christian gave an honest account of his journey so far. Why do you think that this was necessary before he was invited into the family's inner circle?

CHAPTER 23

Family Life in the Palace Beautiful

SITUATED AS IT IS, JUST BEYOND THE WEATHERED SUMMIT OF THE HILL Difficulty, the Palace Beautiful has welcomed many a travel-weary pilgrim through the years. In its most comprehensive sense, it depicts the mystical Church of Jesus Christ, his beloved bride whom he purchased with his own blood. (Ephesians 5:25; 1 Peter 1:18-19) However, the palace also represents a microcosm of the bride of Christ, a local body of those who truly know and love the Lord Jesus Christ. It is for their mutual comfort and spiritual benefit that God joins his people together in places where he is known and his truth is proclaimed. (Song of Solomon 1:7-8)

Quite often, as was the case with Christian, they have known the pain and sorrow of earthly relationships strained or even severed because of their faith in Christ. What a blessing it is when God places the solitary traveler in company with others of like precious faith! (Psalm 68:6; 2 Peter 1:1) Christian's arrival at the Palace Beautiful and admission there illustrates this very thing. Up to this time, his pathway has taken him through some bleak, lonely places, but now God's hand has guided him here. During the course of his stay, he will be initiated into the various aspects of palace life, and we will gain deeper insight into the proper order and function of a scriptural New Testament church.

Uniting with an assembly of like-minded Christians is not an incidental matter for the new believer. (Matthew 28:19-20) Like the covenant of marriage, it should never be entered into lightly or ill-advisedly. On the contrary, this major milestone is a time for sober reflection and self-examination. Nevertheless, many professing Christians join a church with the same casual attitude with which they become members of a civic organization. In fact, they often do so with far less loyalty, eventually forsaking the church just as impulsively as they joined it.

Being part of an assembly where Christ is honored and his Word faithfully proclaimed is a high privilege that should never be taken lightly or viewed as optional. On the contrary, it entails a solemn commitment that should form a chief priority in the believer's life. Vast spiritual benefits are in store for those who take this important step; therefore, those who are saved by God's grace should not be negligent in this matter.

What a blessed thing it is to gather together and worship the Lord in a spirit of unity and brotherly love! Outwardly, the meeting place may be far from palatial, but within its humble walls, the Lord Jesus Christ is pleased to meet with his people. As a body, they receive spiritual nourishment from his Word and enjoy the mutual edification of those who are part of the same household, the family of God. It is little wonder that faithful attendance here is so invaluable to our spiritual growth and perseverance in grace. Neither is it difficult to understand that the deliberate neglect of it is sure to have serious consequences.

In spite of the importance of the local church, some professing Christians refuse to become part of one because they view the church as unnecessary. Worse still, others are of the opinion that no assembly is good enough for them. In my experience as a pastor's wife, those who have this mindset are usually driven by a haughty, proud spirit. Preferring to be freelance Christians, they are generally unteachable and wise in their own conceit. (Proverbs 15:31-33; Proverbs 26:12) Through the years, we have had our share of such individuals to join our assembly and attend for a while. In time, however, they all followed a similar pattern by leaving us without a word of explanation, but not before stirring up trouble among us.

Of such people William Jay made the following comment: "To such union, they prefer rambling, or at least detachment. They fix nowhere, or at least commune nowhere. No church is wide enough or strict enough, or pure enough, or sound enough for them: no one is completely modified to their taste. Constantine said to such a self-conceited Christian, 'Take a ladder, and climb to heaven by thyself.' If all were like-minded with some, there would be no such thing as a Church on earth." [1] Viewed in this light, perhaps it is just as well that these individuals stay away from the local church, seeing that they specialize in disturbing the peace and the spiritual unity that is so pleasing to the Lord Jesus Christ. (Psalm 133; Ephesians 4:1-3)

On the other hand, receiving new members into a local congregation should never be done heedlessly either. Great care is called for and spiritual discernment as well, because the desire for numerical growth is a risky venture carrying with it the temptation to compromise. In the watchful attitude of the porter who guarded the palace entrance, and the careful scrutiny of those who applied for admission there, we see the duty of a local church to maintain a regenerate membership, insofar as it is possible.

However, a word of caution is perhaps needful here. Although great care should be taken and due consideration given before receiving new members, the church is not to be exclusive or to have an elitist attitude. The desire for numerical growth is right and proper as long as the higher concern is that the planting of new members be of the Lord.

A local church is only as strong as the individual members that comprise it. An assembly that has a faithful watchman as pastor is blessed indeed, but it is also imperative that both pastor and people strive to maintain the spiritual purity of the body. Ideally, its membership should consist only of those who are truly born again, but even the most discerning churches are limited in this respect. God alone can search and know the human heart. When one presents himself for church membership, we often must take him at face value. He may be able to give a credible testimony, but whether he is real or not will only become evident with the passing of time.

Nothing so weakens a true assembly as the presence of nominal professors in its midst. Moreover, this happens more frequently than you might suppose. A little relaxing of scriptural standards is all that it takes, but once a church lowers the bar by receiving those who give little or no evidence of regeneration, it inadvertently sows the seeds of apostasy. Thinking to strengthen itself by increasing in number, it chips away at its very foundation, which may once have been sound. Once the seeds of apostasy take root and begin to grow, recovery of the church's former condition is rare.

Both pastor and the inhabitants of the Palace Beautiful were well aware of this danger, which explains why they questioned Christian as they did. However, when his answers indicated the heart of a true pilgrim, and he was recognized as bearing the family likeness, they received him with a hearty spirit of brotherly love.

Now that we have clearer insight into why Christian had to undergo such intense scrutiny before being admitted to the Palace, our thoughts turn to the four virgins who interviewed him. Are they actual persons? If so, who are they? If not, who or what do they represent? Are they, like many other characters in *The Pilgrim's Progress*, largely symbolic in nature? I am strongly inclined to believe so.

While Scripture generally refers to individual believers in the masculine, as sons of God, the Church as a corporate body is presented in the feminine gender. So the four palace virgins appear to represent the family of God as a composite of the bride of Christ in her virgin character. (2 Corinthians 11:2; Ephesians 5:25-27)

Although not perfect in themselves, the palace virgins depict that which is of a true and enduring substance. Their names denote inward graces that flow from the sanctifying work of the Holy Spirit, graces that are the fruit of wisdom, godly fear, and the true knowledge of God in the soul. (Proverbs 2:1-12; Proverbs 9:1-10) Thus Discretion, Prudence, Piety and Charity are present wherever God's people gather together.

This explains why the beautiful palace is such a resplendent place. The glory of God dwells therein, but not as it did in the tabernacle and temple of old. (Exodus 40:34-35; 1 Kings 8:10-11) The glory of his presence no longer appears in visible form, like the cloud overshadowing the Mercy Seat on the Ark of the Covenant. His glory now resides within his people and is made known as they reflect his holy character. (2 Corinthians 3:18; 4:6; Revelation 21:9-11) Thus every true child of God bears a measure of this spiritual fruit. (John 15:1-8; Galatians 5:22-23)

While an individual believer may increase in Bible knowledge apart from the church, the development of a Christ-like character and the manifestation of it is another matter entirely. The godly virtues portrayed by the four virgins are not easily attained, and neither are they acquired through mere human effort. In a rather mysterious and inexplicable way, we need the fellowship of other believers for these graces to properly develop and grow.

Therefore, an assembly like the Palace Beautiful proves an excellent environment for the gifts and graces of the Holy Spirit to operate. Such a body forms a spiritual garden where those who are planted by the Lord grow and mature in Christ together. (Ephesians 4:11-16) In the fertile soil of this well-tended garden, the righteous will flourish like the palm tree and grow like a cedar in Lebanon. (Psalm 92:12) The presence of the Lord Jesus Christ is the secret to their spiritual vitality. He provides all that we need to grow strong in him and bear fruit for his glory.

Before we conclude our thoughts upon the four virgins, there is another thing about them that is worthy of note. The graces they signify must operate together in order to accurately portray the godly character of the palace inhabitants. Each of them is necessary in order to truly reflect the image of the Lord Jesus Christ.

For example, the virgin named Discretion suggests a strongly developed spiritual discernment that enabled her to reflect deeply on a matter and form sound judgments concerning it. This rare quality was evident in both her conduct and her speech. However, in order to maintain a proper spiritual balance, a wise, discerning mind must be tempered with the virtue of Christian love (Charity). Likewise, a frame of mind that enables one to conduct himself wisely and discreetly (Prudence) must be joined with genuine faith, reverence for God, and dependence upon him (Piety).

One may be wise and prudent in earthly matters, while entirely lacking genuine faith and devotion to Christ. Prudence without piety is little more than worldly wisdom. Moreover, discretion without brotherly love tends to promote a critical spirit and intellectual pride rather than the meek and humble spirit that is to characterize the servants of the Lord.

Since the glory of the Palace Beautiful is the presence of Christ in his people, there is absolutely no room for vainglory on our part. In fact, the extent to which we show forth his lovely character is directly proportionate to our humility of spirit. (Philippians 2:5-8) Therefore, the glory for it all belongs to God alone. All is designed *to show that the LORD is upright.* (Psalm 92:15)

At the table of the King

As rare and precious ointment releases a sweet fragrance when it is poured forth, so the savor of Christ permeates every part of his Palace, just as it had the Interpreter's House. (Song of Solomon 1:3) He is both its founder and builder; he is the head and unseen host of this very special abode. As Christian joined the family around the table, surely his heart cried with the bride in Song of Solomon 2:4: *He brought me to the banqueting house, and his banner over me was love.*

Perhaps the beloved hymn writer, Isaac Watts, had the Palace Beautiful in mind when he wrote, "How sweet and awful is the place with Christ within the doors, while everlasting love displays the choicest of her stores." [2] The meal of which Christian was invited to partake that night was no ordinary one. It was the celebration of a memorial feast, the observance of the Lord's Table. (1 Corinthians 11:23-26) It was an especially precious occasion for Christian since it was the first time that he had been a participant in this New Covenant ordinance. (Matthew 26:26-28)

To his delight, Christian found that everything in the Palace spoke to his heart of the Lord Jesus Christ. All that was said and done centered upon him as the suffering, dying Lamb of God, the only Savior of sinners. Therefore, their observance of the Lord's Table was no mere ritual. It was a precious time of remembrance, worship, and spiritual fellowship. As the family communed together around his table, a glorious display of God's everlasting love was set before them:

- The incomparable Christ: his wondrous love, and the riches of his grace. (John 3:14-17)
- His magnanimous sacrifice and redemption, and how that through his cross he defeated the one that had the power of death. (Hebrews 2:14-15; Revelation 1:12-18)

- How that as the mighty conqueror he arose from the dead, and through his resurrection he now reigns forever as Zion's King. However, he will not dwell on Mount Zion alone. As the captain of our salvation, he is bringing many sons to glory. (Hebrews 2:9-13; Revelation 7:9-17; Revelation 14:1-5)
- The reason why he built the Palace Beautiful. (Ephesians 2:19-22 ; Peter 2:5-6)
- How that in humbling himself, he was not only highly exalted but has secured a glorious change of condition for all of those who belong to him. (1 Peter 2:9-10)

All of this had a striking effect upon Christian, causing him to love his Lord even more fervently than he had before. As he thought upon his present condition and what it had been before, perhaps his heart cried with Isaac Watts, "Why was I made to hear thy voice, and enter while there's room, when thousands make a wretched choice, and rather starve than come?" ³ How the grace of God was magnified in his soul that night!

Like Christian, those who enter the Palace Beautiful will quickly find that the Word of God is the sole authority and basis of the fellowship there. Its inhabitants hunger and thirst for the Word and love to hear their minister preach and teach it. As he does so, the sweet savor of Christ fills the house, ministering life and spiritual health to each heart prepared to receive it. Under the gracious influence of his Holy Spirit, there is an abundant supply of all that is needful to satisfy their hungry souls. (Psalm 107:8-9)

Sad to say, this is not always the case with those who claim to believe the Word of God. No one will truly appreciate and benefit from this Gospel feast except those who have been born again by the Word of truth and tasted that the Lord is gracious. (James 1:18; 1 Peter 1:23; 1 Peter 2:2-3) Having once tasted of the living bread, however, they will be satisfied with nothing else. (Psalm 34:8-10; Matthew 5:6; John 6:51-58)

Dear reader, does it surprise you to learn that an assembly like the Palace Beautiful is a relatively rare thing? Probably not! The City of Destruction, you may remember, is filled with religious institutions of every kind. So is 21st century America, with multitudes of mega-churches claiming to be Christian when they are really so in name only. Thinking to do church in novel ways that will have a broader appeal, they lower the bar of truth and come up with a plan that gives people what pleases them the most. Thus they draw in the crowds by offering programs and activities to suit the tastes of their members and appeal to the unchurched in the community. Just name it and you will find it somewhere in the City of Destruction's version of Christianity. Likewise in Post-Christian America!

Since this is hardly the case in the Palace Beautiful, the world views it as living in the past and completely out of sync with what modern worshipers expect. However, they fail to see the marvelous transformation taking place among those who gather there. As the truth of Christ is preached in power, the character of the Lord Jesus Christ is being more fully developed in his people as they strive together to follow his example. What a rare privilege to be part of it!

When the Spirit of God is so evidently working in the midst of his people, he will also inflame their hearts with love for those who are lost. Therefore, as they leave the Palace Beautiful and go about their daily responsibilities, they take the Gospel message with them and share it with others. Furthermore, they strive to be living examples that are consistent with their faith in the Lord Jesus Christ.

Had it been pleasing in God's sight, he would have designed for us to serve him best as solitary travelers along the path of life. Instead, he purposed that we serve him together as part of a community of kindred minds. We are most likely to be fruitful and attain optimal spiritual maturity when joined in company with those who are of like precious faith. This explains the supernatural union that binds our hearts together as brothers and sisters in Christ.

The strongest of human ties will eventually be severed by death, but in Christ we are part of an eternal union that transcends every earthly barrier. Each redeemed soul is part of this body, this glorious Church of the firstborn. (Hebrews 12:22-24) We are a family related by new birth, a spiritual temple composed of brethren from every nation, tribe, kindred and tongue upon earth. The fellowship we now enjoy is but a foretaste of heaven when the entire family of God is gathered together forever.

However, it is not my intention to portray the Palace Beautiful in overly idealistic terms. Although it is a fellowship of kindred minds, its members are not in perfect agreement concerning every minor point of doctrine. Neither is this assembly free from personality conflicts, differences of opinion, and other possible areas of irritation and discord. After all, it is a body of redeemed souls who are still residing in bodies of flesh. We are destined for perfection, but not there yet! Even so, the Palace Beautiful does represent a body of believers who hold steadfastly to the doctrine of the apostles, pray together, worship their Lord in spirit and in truth and keep the commanded ordinances. They mutually edify, strengthen and encourage one another in the faith, and by love, they serve one another.

This brotherly love is a major distinguishing mark of God's people. In fact, it is the tie that binds our hearts together. (John 13:34-35; 1 John 4: 7-12) Moreover, it is a thing stronger than death, for it is the love of Christ shed abroad in our hearts by his Spirit. (Romans 5:5) Likewise, our unity in Christ gives us a common purpose that is leading us in a single, upward direction. As spiritual brethren and fellow travelers along the road to Zion, we look forward to the same glorious destiny.

Outside the palace stronghold, a very different situation exists. Beyond its fortified walls, the masses of mankind struggle in order to maintain an uneasy existence. Whatever their earthly circumstances happen to be, they all seek for that elusive thing called peace. The mighty ones of earth think to acquire it through power and influence, while the wealthy are willing to spend a fortune in quest of it. The highly intelligent suppose that it can be found through superior wisdom and knowledge. As for the average person, he merely hopes to find it somewhere, perhaps in one religion or another. Yet true peace remains just beyond the reach of them all.

No peace! What a terrible state of being! Many claim to have found it, but they cry *Peace, peace; when there is no peace.* (Jeremiah 6:14) Since man by nature is estranged from God, he is blind to his true need, and therefore, ignorant as to the source where true peace may be found. So the masses of humanity continue as they have always been, trapped by an undercurrent of restless desperation from which they cannot escape. (Isaiah 57:20-21)

Far from the hustle and bustle of a tempestuous world, there is a quiet resting place. Away from the inward fear, turmoil, and strife that rules in the human heart by nature, there is a peaceful habitation where one may rest in perfect safety and freedom from alarm. However, only those who have peace with God have access to it.

When the palace family was ready to retire for the evening, Christian was taken to a large upper chamber in which to rest for the night. Its single window faced due east toward the rising of the sun; therefore, in the morning, he would be able to witness the dawning of a new day. The name of this quiet chamber was Peace, and Christian was all the more thankful for it because he well remembered when he, too, had no peace.

What is this secluded chamber where Christian withdrew for the night? How is it that he, who had been so disturbed and depressed in his spirit before, now slept soundly and peacefully, and awoke with a song in his heart? The chamber named Peace signifies the effect upon Christian of his time spent in the Palace Beautiful. As the family heard the Word of God together, the Spirit of God ministered to each heart, applying the Word of truth. Christian's withdrawal into the chamber for the evening depicts this gracious work of spiritual healing and renewal of which he stood so greatly in need. Moreover, for him it was also a time of self-examination, self-judgment, repentance and confession before God. The effect of it all was a cleansed conscience, quietness of soul, and solitude in which to pray and meditate upon the things he had heard.

Those who are intimately acquainted with the Palace Beautiful know quite well why it is so conducive to their peace and tranquility of soul. The presence of Christ and the comfort he gives through his Word are as the balm in Gilead, especially in times of great trial. He alone can calm the troubled soul and grant the peace that passes all understanding to hearts and minds made anxious by many things. (Philippians 4:6-7)

* * * *

Blessed indeed are those who know the Prince of peace! (Isaiah 9:6) He is the substance, the only true source of our rest. He alone can minister it to our needy souls, for it is only through our Lord Jesus Christ that we have peace with God and healing of the soul. (Isaiah 53:4-5; Isaiah 57:19; Ephesians 2:13-17) This wondrous peace, which was proclaimed by angels on the night that he was born, now goes forth as tidings of peace wherever his Gospel is proclaimed. (Luke 2:8-14; Isaiah 52:7)

To all who believe the good news of the Gospel and receive him by faith, the Lord Jesus Christ gave a legacy of eternal peace. (John 14:27) It becomes a living reality as our hearts and minds are fixed upon him. (Isaiah 26:3-4) The securing of this everlasting peace and covenant mercy cost him dearly, but because it is derived from his works and not our own, we need never fear its removal. (Psalm 103:17; Isaiah 26:12; Isaiah 54:10-13) This very same peace is one chief characteristic of his kingdom, and the effects of it in those who learn to rest and trust in him in the midst of life's storms are glorious indeed. (Isaiah 11:10; Isaiah 32:15-18; Romans 14:17)

The Palace Beautiful is the perfect environment for the fruit of spiritual peace to prosper and grow. Through his Word and the gracious influence of his Spirit, our Lord makes us to lie down in green pastures and leads us beside still waters. (Psalm 23:2) By his grace he has made of Zion a peaceful habitation, a quiet dwelling place for us in the midst of a world that has no peace. (Isaiah 33:20-21) Since it is founded solely upon the righteousness of Christ and his redemptive work on our behalf, nothing can cause a breach in it. Even though many things will threaten to disturb our peace, it abides as an immovable stronghold, a secret place where our souls may abide in perfect safety.

Inner turmoil will quickly overtake our minds if we seek our rest in other things, or look for it within. When in the midst of stormy circumstances we will only know true peace by looking to our Lord and trusting in him, for he alone can calm the tempest. Then we may confidently say with the psalmist: *My soul, wait thou only upon God; for my expectation is from him. He only is my rock and my salvation: he is my defence; I shall not be moved.* (Psalm 62:5-6)

Resting in the Lord is as vital to our spiritual well-being as a proper amount of sleep is to our physical health. Christian's time of quiet repose denotes this very thing, the inner peace, assurance, and child-like trust that had been strengthened by his stay in the Palace Beautiful. It was exactly what he needed in order to fit him for the day at hand.

Dear brother or sister in Christ, are not our hearts as easily troubled and subject to anxiety as Christian's was? Then let us also commit ourselves to the Lord Jesus in the confidence that he who keeps us will neither slumber nor sleep. Because he gives his beloved sleep, we may lean upon his breast without fear, for he is our confidence by day or by night, in good times and in bad. Therefore, we may say with David: *I will both lay me down in peace and sleep: for thou, LORD, only makest me dwell in safety.* (Psalm 4:8)

This sweet rest that is free from anxious fear is ours in the Lord Jesus Christ. Remember the words of comfort he spoke to his disciples, saying: *Come unto me, all ye that labour and are heavy laden, and I will give you rest. Take my yoke upon you, and learn of me; for I am meek and lowly in heart: and ye shall find rest unto your souls. For my yoke is easy, and my burden is light.* (Matthew 11:28-30) Such rest of soul can only exist in the knowledge of complete forgiveness of sin through the blood of Jesus Christ. There is no peace equal to this, as spoken by our Lord in Isaiah 40:1-2: *Comfort ye, comfort ye my people, saith your God. Speak ye comfortably to Jerusalem, and cry unto her, that her warfare is accomplished, that her iniquity is pardoned.* This heightened understanding, and the quietness of conscience that attended it, was the essence of Christian's peaceful sleep that first night in the Palace Beautiful.

When he awoke the next morning, the wondrous things he had seen and heard the evening before were still fresh in his mind. Standing by the chamber's solitary window, he watched as the new day began to dawn. With the rising of the sun came the vivid remembrance of the time when the sun of righteousness arose in his soul with healing in his wings. (Malachi 4:2) In that moment, he realized more strongly than ever before that Christ was the only source of his peace and rest.

Although Christian had awakened from his restful sleep refreshed in mind and spirit, he knew that he must not rely upon the blessings of yesterday. A new day was before him. Therefore, as he left his bedchamber and rejoined the palace family, he did so with the eager anticipation of receiving more.

Study Questions

1. Why is it important for a church to exercise caution and discernment when receiving new members? How does the presence of nominal Christians weaken a congregation?

2. Who are the four palace virgins who interviewed Christian? Were they actual persons? If so, who were they? If not, who or what did they represent?

3. What kind of feast did the family partake of at the table of the King? What was the center and substance of their conversation as they communed around the table? What is the sole authority and basis of their fellowship?

4. What is one major distinguishing mark of God's people? Include a Scripture reference with your answer.

5. Christian was taken to a chamber called Peace to rest for the night. What does this chamber represent? What were the effects of Christian's time there?

CHAPTER 24

The Palace Framework and Remarkable History

ALTHOUGH IT MAY SEEM STRANGE TO PRESENT DAY TRAVELERS ALONG THE path of life, the Palace Beautiful is a structure of great antiquity. In fact, its blueprint originated in the eternal counsel and purpose of God before the foundation of the world. (Ephesians 1:3-6) The palace founder and master builder is the ancient of days, the one who is eternal in his generation, whose goings forth have been from of old, from everlasting. (Daniel 7:9-14; Revelation 1:13-18; Micah 5:2)

This unique person, the divine-human one, is Lord of the Palace Beautiful. Its family is his family, his beloved children whom he redeemed with his own blood. His history as the incarnate Son of God is inextricably linked to theirs, which in an earthly sense can be traced to the dawn of creation. (See genealogy in Luke 3:23-38, verse 38 in particular) Therefore, a vast store of rare and precious things has been committed to the Palace Beautiful for safekeeping. Although many of them date back to ancient times, these priceless treasures are not mere relics of the past. They are timelessly relevant to Christians of every age. (Proverbs 3:13-18)

The family members who were well versed in palace history were eager to share it with their new brother in Christ. So after a good night's rest, they took him into the palace study in order to instruct him more thoroughly regarding his spiritual heritage. This study was a very special room in which the wonderful works of God could be viewed and pondered. As Christian listened attentively to the expo-

222

sition of God's Word, which furnished all of the reference material used, he was able to more clearly understand truths that had somewhat mystified him before. In this, dear reader, we perceive one of the most vital functions of the local church.

In his charge to young pastor Timothy, the apostle Paul spoke of the *house of God, which is the church of the living God* as the *pillar and ground of the truth*. (1 Timothy 3:15) God has entrusted the rare and excellent treasure of his Word to his Church. Thus his eternal, unchangeable Word forms both the foundation upon which she is built and the pillars that support and uphold her. Since there are many enemies who seek to undermine, pervert, and destroy her framework, the Church must faithfully keep this trust by teaching the Scriptures without compromise. To this end, the Palace Beautiful places the highest emphasis upon sound doctrine and vital, life-altering truth. (Luke 1:1-4)

What is truth? asked Pontius Pilate, even as he sinned against the light of his own conscience. (John 18:38-19:6) Men still grapple with this question today, and each one has his own opinion as to the definition of truth. Many claim to believe the Word of God, but few among them have a scriptural conception of what truth really is.

The truth that is believed and faithfully proclaimed in the Palace centers in a person, the Lord Jesus Christ. (John 5:39-40) He is the only one who could rightly say, *I am the Truth*. Therefore, while Christian was in the study, he received more particular instruction about his Lord's unique character as the Son of God and Son of man, his essential deity, eternal generation, and divine attributes. Moreover, after being well-grounded concerning the person of Christ, Christian was instructed more perfectly concerning the works of the Lord Jesus, his willingness to forgive even those who had sinned grievously against him, and the blessed estate that he has secured for his people. This comprehensive theological instruction served to both reinforce and expand upon what he had previously learned.

Then Christian was further initiated into the Palace history, most notably things concerning family members in the past who had faithfully served their Lord and followed him, some even to a martyr's death. These were not super-heroes, as might seem the case. They were ordinary men and women who served an incomparable Lord who is ever faithful and true. (Revelation 19:11) One who kept his promise never to leave or forsake them! (Hebrews 13:5-6) One in whom all power and authority in heaven and earth are vested! (Matthew 28:18-20)

Palace history certifies that many of these ordinary believers performed extraordinary feats, but not in their own strength. Through personal weakness they prevailed and were made strong so that, by faith, they could perform mighty deeds of valor in the face of incredible odds. The only way they did so was by considering him that endured such contradiction of sinners against himself. (Hebrews 12:3) Through faith they saw beyond this life to a better one to come. Like Abraham of old, they looked for a city which has foundations, whose builder and maker is God. (Hebrews 11:10) Therefore, they have their place among the ranks of those who *through faith subdued kingdoms, wrought righteousness, obtained promises, stopped the mouths of lions, quenched the violence of fire, escaped the edge of the sword, out of weakness were made strong, waxed valiant in fight, turned to flight the armies of the aliens.* (Hebrews 11:33-34)

Before Christian left the palace study, he was given an insider's look into something else that would prove to be of great encouragement in his journey, if he kept it in a proper perspective. This part of his instruction concerned the final outcome of all things, especially the ultimate victory of God's people and the eventual destruction of every enemy that opposes them. Once again, the Word of God was the source of his tuition. As the prophetic Scriptures were opened and expounded to him, Christian began to understand that God's wondrous plan of redemption not only spanned human history, but eternity as well. As he listened attentively, Christian could see God's marvelous plan unfolding with the coming Redeemer first veiled in Old Testament types and shadows, and then appearing at the appointed time, as the prophets foretold. (Galatians 4:4-5; 1 Peter 1:10-12)

He rejoiced greatly in the knowledge that the Lord Jesus Christ was not defeated at the cross, as many have supposed. That dark hour was the hour of triumph, the moment for which the world itself was created. His cry *It is finished* was a resounding proclamation of victory. With his resurrection and ascension to the throne of David, the long-awaited salvation of his people was secured forever. (2 Samuel 7:12-13; Acts 2:29-36)

With the realization that he was part of God's eternal plan of redemption, Christian was able to view even his greatest difficulties in a different light. All things were even now moving toward the final consummation when Christ would come in power and great glory and put everything right. In that day, when God's purpose of salvation is fulfilled, his people's warfare will be over and the eternal day will dawn at last. (2 Corinthians 4:17-18; 2 Peter 3:7-14)

The palace armory

The Church of Jesus Christ is a mighty army marching steadily throughout human history. Her ranks are constantly changing, as some soldiers depart the earthly scene and enter into the presence of their Lord, while others become part of her through new birth. All the while, and in spite of constant warfare, she is advancing toward her glorious eternal destiny. (Revelation 21) Every inch of spiritual ground is dearly won, however, for she is hated, afflicted, and persecuted by strong enemies who continually seek her annihilation. Still she moves onward and upward, even though she must brave the very gates of hell to do so.

How is it that the Church is able to stand in the face of the enemy and put to flight the armies of the wicked one? According to outward circumstances she appears to be surrounded, outnumbered, and defenseless. The secret of her successful warfare and final victory over her enemies lies within the next room shown to Christian, the palace armory.

Could there really be an armory in the Palace Beautiful? What purpose do weapons of warfare have in this house of brotherly love, spiritual fellowship, and peace? Surely an armory would be out of place here! So it would seem, until we remember the armed forces of Beelzebub and the reality of the Church's great warfare.

The Church on earth is the church militant, an army marching under the royal standard of the cross of Christ. This fact alone sets her at odds against an unbelieving world. Her mission is not to conquer nations, change the world, or reform society. She is to boldly proclaim the Gospel and be a beacon of truth and light in a world of spiritual darkness. (Matthew 5:14-16) Her goal is to advance the kingdom of God and the kingly rule of the Lord Jesus Christ in the hearts of men. In order to fulfill her great mission, she must uphold and defend his Gospel, but her strength is not equal to her task. Like Israel of old, who faced mighty armies and chariots of iron, the Church of Jesus Christ encounters enemies much stronger than she is, humanly speaking. So the armory is not only an appropriate part of the Palace Beautiful; it is essential to her very existence.

When Christian first entered the armory, he probably had a preconceived notion of what he would find there. After all, had he not already learned of the uncommon courage with which many of God's people in the past had performed mighty deeds of valor? His curiosity was aroused and he was eager to see the lethal weapons with which they had won the day.

Imagine his surprise when, one by one, these engines of war were pointed out to him! The rod by which Moses parted the Red Sea! (Exodus 14:13-16) The hammer and nail used by Jael to slay the wicked Sisera! (Judges 4) The lamps, pitchers, and trumpets by which Gideon and his little band confused and put to flight the armies of the Midianites! (Judges 7) The ox-goad with which Shamgar killed six hundred men! (Judges 3:31) The jawbone that proved such an effective weapon in the hands of Sampson! (Judges 15:15-16) The slingshot by which a young shepherd boy named David brought down the mighty giant, Goliath! (1 Samuel 17)

Without a doubt, these were unlikely instruments of war, and yet, each had proven to be highly effective when put to the test. How could it be? They were all wielded by faith, for the honor and glory of God. Still, these particular weapons were but moldering reminders of battles fought and won long ago, and of warriors long gone to their eternal rest. Of what use were they to Christian, and how are they relevant to the people of God today? They remind us that the path we walk is not one of earthly comfort and ease. We are part of the same church militant and fellow soldiers with our faithful brethren who have gone before. If, like them, we are to be useful servants in the kingdom of God, we must be armed and ready for battle.

This sobering thought calls to mind, once again, the metaphorical nature of the Palace Beautiful. Everything therein depicts a spiritual truth concerning the Church of Jesus Christ, and the armory is no exception. The ancient weapons shown to Christian were not religious relics of battles long past, things that could easily become objects of idolatry. In fact, they were not on actual display at all. Christian viewed them as he was instructed from the historical passages of Scripture. From the Word of God, he learned of these unlikely weapons and the heroes of faith who performed extraordinary deeds of bravery with them. In the time of crisis they used what they had on hand, and God gave them the victory! As Christian pondered these things in his heart, he quickly realized that the palace armory would not be stocked with conventional weapons ready for issue. It would be filled with that which was perfectly suited to arm God's people for fierce, spiritual combat.

The Word of God gives us fair warning that the warfare we face is unlike anything else on earth, and so are the weapons with which we fight. In 2 Corinthians 10:3-5 the apostle Paul tells us: *Though we walk in the flesh, we do not war after the flesh: (For the weapons of our warfare are not carnal, but mighty through God to the pulling down of strong holds;) Casting down imaginations, and every high thing that exalteth itself against the knowledge of God, and bringing into captivity every thought to the obedience of Christ.*

As God's people, we find ourselves engaged in a conflict that we cannot win through natural means such as sheer determination, innate courage, physical strength or human wisdom. Faith, not military prowess, is the means by which we triumph in this battle. (1 John 5:4-5) Like the ancient heroes honored in Hebrews 11, we must bear the hallmark of overcoming faith.

Therefore, my brother or sister in Christ, we also must be prepared for this life-long battle. Although church history is filled with the record of past victories, each generation of believers must bear its part in the conflict. Moreover, in this army there are no exemptions from service granted. Every soldier is called to active duty. So if we are to stand in the heat of battle, we must be equipped from the very special armory provided by our Lord.

Humanly speaking, we face overwhelming odds on the field of this mighty conflict. Through his cross, however, the captain of our salvation has already secured the high ground for us and won the day. (Hebrews 2:10-11; Revelation 14:1-5) From his own royal arsenal, he provides every needful weapon, as well as all the protective armor required to fully equip his children. Moreover, when we are called to face the battle, he marches in the vanguard with his regal standard lifted high, in plain view of the enemy's forces.

In Ephesians 6:10-13, the apostle Paul issues a clear call to arms to every follower of Jesus Christ, saying: *Finally, my brethren, be strong in the Lord, and in the power of his might. Put on the whole armour of God, that ye may be able to stand against the wiles of the devil. For we wrestle not against flesh and blood, but against principalities, against powers, against the rulers of the darkness of this world, against spiritual wickedness in high places. Wherefore take unto you the whole armour of God, that ye may be able to withstand in the evil day, and having done all, to stand.*

Herein is the secret to our victory, fellow pilgrim. We dare not face the powers of darkness unless we are clothed in full battle array. It is only as we are covered with the protective armor of God and skillful in its use that we will be able to endure the fierce attacks that are sure to come. (Ephesians 6:14-18) Therefore, we must be girded about with truth and covered with the breastplate of righteousness. Our feet must be prepared to carry the Gospel of peace to a world abiding in darkness. Moreover, in order to thwart the enemy's flaming arrows, we must keep the shield of faith firmly in place and have the sword of the Spirit, the Word of God, well in hand. All the while we must maintain an attitude of watchfulness and persevering prayer, without which the rest of the armor would be of little use.

In Romans 13:14, the apostle Paul leaves no doubt as to the substance of our spiritual armor, saying: *Put ye on the Lord Jesus Christ, and make not provision for the flesh, to fulfil the lusts thereof.* As all things in the Palace Beautiful center around Christ, so he is also the essence of its armory. To put on the armor of God is to put on the Lord Jesus Christ. He alone is our armor of light. (Romans 13:12) To walk in him is to walk in the light. (Ephesians 5:8-10; 1 John 1:7) He alone is our armor of righteousness. (2 Corinthians 6:7) Only as we are covered with his righteousness are we able to be holy in our manner of life and conduct. (1 Peter 1:15)

As the Word of God is highly instrumental in the development of a Christ-like character, so it is crucial in arming us for spiritual battle. One great purpose of the Gospel ministry in the local church is to equip us for spiritual warfare. Even though the gathered assembly is a place of relative safety from the stress and clamor of the battlefield, within its walls we are to be continually armed to go forth and face the rigors of combat once again. Those who will perform the greatest feats of courage and faith will be those who most closely follow their Lord.

Although the prospect of spiritual warfare is intimidating, great promises attend our way when we must face it. The captain of our souls is continually with us and has willingly undertaken our defense. The stronghold of Zion, the Church of Jesus Christ, will remain valiant for truth as long as he is on the field of battle with her. (Psalm 46:1-5; Psalm 60:11-12) Even if she is called upon to storm the very gates of hell, they shall not prevail against her. (Matthew 16:18) Thus we need never fear as long as we march under his royal standard.

Therefore, my fellow pilgrim, let us embrace the glorious promise of Isaiah 54:17 and claim it in the face of every enemy: *No weapon that is formed against thee shall prosper; and every tongue that shall rise against thee in judgment thou shalt condemn. This is the heritage of the servants of the LORD, and their righteousness is of me, saith the LORD.*

Soldiers of Christ, arise, and put your armor on,
Strong in the strength which God supplies through his eternal Son;
Strong in the Lord of hosts, and in his mighty power,
Who in the strength of Jesus trusts is more than conqueror.

Stand then in his great might, with all his strength endued,
And take, to arm you for the fight, the panoply of God;
From strength to strength go on, wrestle and fight and pray;
Tread all the powers of darkness down, and win the well-fought day.

Leave no unguarded place, no weakness of the soul;
Take every virtue, every grace, and fortify the whole.
That having all things done, and all your conflicts past,
Ye may o'ercome through Christ alone, and stand complete at last. [1]

* * * *

Eventually, the time came for Christian to leave the security of the Palace Beautiful, but we must not suppose his visit there to have been a single event. For the rest of his earthly days he will be a faithful member there. For now, however, he must go forth and put into practice the things he has learned.

Just prior to his departure, he was taken to the pinnacle of the palace in order to survey the countryside round about. The brethren who had greater knowledge of the way ahead pointed out some of its notable features. In particular, they directed his attention toward the Delectable Mountains far in the distance. Located deep in the heart of Emmanuel's Land, it was a beautiful scene with gentle rolling hills, secluded woodlands, fruitful vineyards and gardens. Like the Palace Beautiful, the Delectable Mountains were especially designed for the benefit of travelers on their way to Zion. However, they were a very great distance from where Christian now stood; therefore, he had to be content with viewing them from afar.

When Christian finally emerged from the palace gate he did so in full protective gear, armed and ready for whatever lay ahead. While bidding farewell to his good friend the porter, he was glad to learn that another pilgrim had recently passed that way, a man named Faithful. At the mention of his name, Christian exclaimed that he knew the man, for they had been close neighbors back in the City of Destruction. What a blessing to know that a fellow townsman had also escaped from the great city and was now traveling the same road! Perhaps they would soon meet and make their journey together, this time as brothers in Christ.

His dear friends Discretion, Piety, Charity and Prudence accompanied him as far as they could down the other side of the hill. Then, after giving him some final words of exhortation and provisions for his journey, they said farewell and returned to the palace. Thus finding himself alone once again, Christian began the slow descent into the valley far below him.

Study Guide

1. The next morning, Christian was taken to the palace study. What does this study represent? What kind of instruction did Christian receive while there?

2. What were some of the things Christian learned about the palace's history?

3. How can the Church of Jesus Christ be compared to an army? What is the nature of her warfare?

4. What were some of the ancient weapons that Christian learned about in the palace armory? Why were these unlikely instruments of war so highly effective in battle?

5. As Christians we face a warfare that is like nothing on earth, and we face it against incredible odds. What provision has our Lord made for us to not only stand in battle, but win the day?

Part Ten

OUT OF THE DEPTHS

*Therefore I will look unto the LORD; I will wait
for the God of my salvation: my God will hear me.
Rejoice not against me, O mine enemy: when I fall, I shall arise;
when I sit in darkness, the LORD shall be a light unto me.
Micah 7:7-8*

CHAPTER 25

Descent into the Valley of Humiliation

BY REASON OF ITS ALTITUDE NEAR THE SUMMIT OF THE HILL DIFFICULTY, the Palace Beautiful offers a spectacular view of the valley far below. Many a traveler standing at its gateway ready for departure is relieved to see that the way forward is downward. Presumably, the descending path will be easier going than the upward climb on the opposite side of the hill. Yet contrary to expectation, this is rarely the case.

Since Prudence had forewarned Christian by saying, "It is a hard matter for a man to go down into the Valley of Humiliation," he proceeded with caution. Nevertheless, he quickly found that descending the hill was every bit as difficult as climbing it had been. In fact, the downhill grade was so steep and slippery that he could barely maintain his footing. Therefore, as he made his way toward the valley he stumbled now and then; but with the blessings he had received in the Palace still fresh in his memory, he felt ready to take on this new challenge.

Concerning its unusual location, the Valley of Humiliation has long been the object of speculation. While most people do not give a second thought to the valley's proximity to the palace high above it, others wonder about a possible relationship between the two. These might well ask why the pathway from the palace to the valley floor is so treacherous and steep. Have there been any attempts to reroute or improve it? What is so significant about a fall or two on that slippery slope? Do all who descend that well-trodden path find it equally dangerous, or was Christian's experience the exception rather than the rule?

Was his mishap on the downhill slope somehow his fault? Could it be in some way related to the time he had spent in the Palace Beautiful? Surely it had nothing to do with the sweet fellowship he had enjoyed with his brethren while there. But what about the wonderful things he had seen and heard? Was there a possible link between those spiritual blessings and his present circumstances? If so, what could it be?

As already noted, Christian left the palace with a much clearer understanding of God's Word. However, such an increase in knowledge can cause one to think too highly of himself. (1 Corinthians 8:1-2) This could have been the case with Christian. Or perhaps the battle armor with which he had been outfitted gave rise to an attitude of overconfidence. Having successfully scaled the hill Difficulty and enjoyed the benefits of the Palace Beautiful, perhaps he felt equal to anything. Who can say what was really in Christian's heart and mind that day? Yet it is certain that although he had learned much, he still had much to learn.

There are lessons that we cannot master within the safe confines of the local church, or in the company of fellow believers. True wisdom, learning to walk in the fear and knowledge of God, is only attained through personal experience as we are alone with the Lord and taught of him. (Proverbs 2; Proverbs 4:7-13) Thus the acquisition of godly wisdom requires a proportionate growth in grace. (Proverbs 3:5-7; Proverbs 9:10; Proverbs 15:33) Herein is the link between the Palace Beautiful and the Valley of Humiliation. So whatever the secondary causes may have been, Christian's pathway was leading him directly into that, as yet, unfamiliar place.

Contrary to the mental imagery that its name might suggest, the Valley of Humiliation is actually a lovely place. Once the traveler has completed the slippery descent to the wide valley floor, he is pleasantly surprised to find that the path levels out and is much less strenuous. Gazing across the broad upland meadows around him, he notes that the valley is outlined high above on either side by a range of majestic mountains. From the depths of the valley floor, however, he cannot see their lofty peaks.

At its lowest point, the valley is divided by a gentle, winding river, and the traveler's footpath goes right beside it. By reason of its rich alluvial soil and temperate climate, this particular river valley is uncommonly fertile. While some forms of plant life may thrive in spite of the harsh weather conditions at the higher elevations, there is no comparison to this verdant lowland. It is in the cool, sheltered recesses of the valley that an abundance of luscious fruit and beautiful flowers can be found.

So there is nothing inherently wrong with the Valley of Humiliation. It is a wholesome, beneficial place, and yet, most travelers who pass through it find the going much more difficult than they expected. Why should this be? We will discover the answer by considering the valley's unusual name, and thus, its significance and purpose.

God's gracious design in bringing us low

As its name implies, the Valley of Humiliation is a place where we can expect to be reduced in rank. It is designed for the express purpose of bringing the sin of pride to our attention and forcing us to face it. Pride, the tendency to think of ourselves more highly than we ought to think, is deeply ingrained in our human constitution. It may manifest itself blatantly, through an air of superiority or a boastful tongue. However, pride can also lie hidden in our hearts until provoked. Thus it is easy enough to overlook in ourselves while having little problem detecting it in others.

Given its power to harm and destroy, there is nothing about pride to recommend it. A proud spirit not only prompts us to exalt ourselves at the expense of others, but also causes us to act contrary to our own best interest. Many years ago, I knew a lady who often boasted that she had no pride. Although she claimed to be a Christian, her subsequent history proved that her profession of faith was just as false as her show of humility. When, due to her own actions, she was finally exposed as a hypocrite, it became clear that she had pride enough to spare. What she lacked was self-respect. There is, I think, a critical difference.

The sad case of my former acquaintance is in no way characteristic of a true child of God. But since our flesh is not eradicated in regeneration, neither is our tendency to pride. While the new birth marks the beginning of a sanctifying process that will gradually subdue and overcome it, the work can be frustratingly slow. Just when we think that pride has been conquered in one area of our lives, it pops up in an unexpected quarter.

Although there are countless situations that can provoke a proud spirit to assert itself, for the sake of brevity I will name just a few. Perhaps we feel that our intelligence has been insulted or our judgment questioned. Quite a blow to the ego, is it not? Our hackles are immediately raised and sarcastic retorts come to mind. Or maybe we feel that we have been misunderstood, unfairly criticized, or unjustly judged. Surely it cannot be wrong to set the record straight! Maybe we were expecting some sort of honor or recognition and had to stand by while it was given to another. It was not fair, was it? Or perhaps we, or our children, have been unfavorably compared to those who have superior ability, greater gifts, or are more successful. How do we react? Do we let it pass and forget it? Or do we seethe with envy while calling it righteous indignation?

Our reaction to such things is a fairly accurate gauge of our pride-to-humility ratio. This fact alone should bring us low! Far too often we respond with offended pride, do we not? Worse still, pride is a highly destructive thing, even when others are unaware of our sinful response. It fosters a bitter spirit within us that is sure to infect others. Therefore, in our struggles with the sin of pride, we are often reminded of the famous quote, "We have met the enemy and it is us!"

Although pride can assume any number of different forms, spiritual pride must surely be the worst. As we suspect may have been the case with Christian, having a good measure of Bible knowledge can tempt us to overestimate our spiritual growth and secretly glory in it. Consequently, in the absence of an equal measure of growth in grace, intellectual understanding can actually prove a hindrance. For those who are studious by nature, acquiring Bible knowledge is relatively easy. Walking according to the truth received is, by far, the more difficult part. (James 1:18-25) When our knowledge outpaces our growth in grace, we will tend to think ourselves more mature in the faith than we really are. Pride rears its ugly head and we become puffed up without even realizing it. (1 Corinthians 8:1)

An overinflated ego is a shameful thing in anyone, but is especially so when found in those who bear the name of the Lord Jesus Christ. How unseemly the sin of pride is in his followers. How unlike the poverty of spirit that is to mark the citizens of his kingdom! What an affront to his holy character, to the incomparable humility and self-sacrifice that characterized his entire time on earth! (Philippians 2:5-8) Yet every child of God struggles with the sin of pride, to one extent or another. One thing is sure, however. God will not permit us to bring reproach upon his name by walking in pride, and neither will he permit it to rule in our hearts. Therefore, in order to check and correct this terrible character flaw, he brings us down into the Valley of Humiliation.

In James 4:10, we are admonished to humble ourselves in the sight of the Lord, and he will lift us up. Is it possible, then, to humble ourselves sufficiently and avoid the Valley of Humiliation altogether? Personally, I doubt it. If we did manage to do so, would we not secretly gloat over it? To wonder where that would land us is a classic no brainer! Therefore, I am convinced that the Valley of Humiliation is an inescapable reality for the Christian. There are lessons we must learn that can only be mastered in that lowly place, and spiritual fruit that can only bud and develop into maturity there.

Now that we have a general idea of the valley's meaning, there is no mistaking it as a literal place. It rather denotes a spiritual proving ground, a time of severe testing in which the mind of Christ is being more perfectly formed in us. Many latent inclinations dwell within us of which we are largely unaware, pride in particular. However, it will quickly rise to the surface under the right provocation. Conditions in this valley are such that they bring the sin of pride to our full attention and force us to do battle with it.

Prudence spoke from personal experience when she warned Christian that he would find it a hard thing to go down into the Valley of Humiliation. Although she was given a place of honor in the Palace Beautiful, her promotion came as a result of an intimate acquaintance with the valley. (Proverbs 15:33) Therefore, she knew first-hand that it was a good and beneficial place, but she also knew that the descent into that lowly place is a hard thing for the flesh to bear.

As there are many different situations that can stir up pride in the heart of a Christian, so there are various circumstances that can bring him low and lead his steps down into the valley. Perhaps he has suffered a serious financial setback due to circumstances beyond his control. He is ashamed that he may not be able to pay his debts and adequately provide for his family. Furthermore, his situation exposes him to criticism and the possible contempt of others. Or maybe the honor and recognition he felt he deserved was given to another, making him feel belittled and unappreciated. It could be that personal failure has plunged him into the valley, or a struggle with a particular sin. In either case, he may be tempted to lose heart and admit defeat.

Sometimes the trial comes in the form of physical affliction or disability of some sort, making him feel useless and a burden to others. Or perhaps he has been the innocent victim of vicious, lying tongues. The dishonoring of one's good name through false accusation is a particularly hard thing to bear, tempting the innocent victim to take matters into his own hands and avenge the injustice. Then there are fiery trials of an intensely personal and painful nature. Many godly parents have had their hearts broken and been led deeply into the valley by the conduct of their children.

Whatever the circumstances that bring it about, the refining work that takes place in the Valley of Humiliation is carefully and lovingly wrought by God's sovereign hand. We would never willingly choose it, so our heavenly Father orders both the time of our passage and every detail of our experience while there. So when our way takes us down into the valley, there is no choice but to follow.

One interesting feature of this particular lowland is that each one of us will have a unique experience while there, one that is mostly of our own making. Passing through it brings us face to face with ourselves, and the revelation is sure to be a painful one. Thomas Boston expressed this well when he said, "The crook in the lot is the great engine of Providence for making men appear in their true colours, discovering both their ill and their good: and if the grace of God be in them, it will bring it out, and cause it to display itself. It so puts the Christian to his shifts, that however it makes him stagger for awhile, yet it will at length evidence both the reality and the strength of grace in him." [1]

Since our time in the valley is designed to accomplish God's will and purpose for us as individuals, it is a trial of a deeply personal nature. Like the character named Mercy in *The Pilgrim's Progress: the Second Part*, the rare Christian who possesses a truly humble spirit will thrive while there. In its shady depths he or she will know the presence and sweet communion of the Lord Jesus Christ, fairest lily of the valleys. (Song of Solomon 2:1) However, those who lose their footing on the downhill slope are probably in for a rough passage. So how did Christian fare after he completed the descent?

Challenged to mortal combat

He barely reached the valley floor when he spied a hideous creature coming swiftly toward him from across one of the broad highlands. At first glance, the monster may have seemed a figment of Christian's imagination, but he was all too real and obviously up to no good. As the stunned man watched the creature's bold approach, his earlier confidence was shattered and terror seized control of his mind. Since the monster was almost upon him, there was little time to decide what to do. At best, his options were severely limited; he could either turn back and run for his life, or remain where he was and attempt to stand his ground. However, when he remembered that his armor provided no covering for his back, the choice was clear. Therefore, Christian resolved to venture forward, even though it meant a close encounter with the horrible being named Apollyon (destroyer). Had Christian been able to see it, an equally perverse nature was concealed behind his grotesque form. In brief, he was the sum of all that is evil, and his name left no doubt as to his true identity. (Revelation 9:11)

Thus it was a formidable enemy that assaulted Christian in the Valley of Humiliation with the intention of taking him down. His most conspicuous feature was his covering of scales, which formed a kind of armor. John Bunyan tells us that these "scales were his pride," a quote taken from Job 41:15 and referring to the creature called leviathan. (Job 41:1) From the detailed description given in Job 41:13-34, leviathan sounds very much like a fire-breathing dragon. By drawing this parallel, John Bunyan implies that Apollyon possessed a spirit so incorrigibly proud that it covered him completely and was as impenetrable as a coat of chain mail. If there was any doubt before, this fact alone is enough to link him to the prince of darkness, whose pride was the cause of his terrible ruin. (Isaiah 14:12-15) Once he was a creature of great beauty, but the sin of pride reduced him to a hideous monster. (Ezekiel 28:11-19)

In addition to his covering of pride, he had wings like a dragon. This speaks of his swift, destructive power, the evil intention with which he opposes the will and purpose of God, and the spiritual desolation he seeks to inflict upon God's people. (Revelation 12:3-4) His feet are also worthy of note, for they resembled those of a bear, a fiercely tenacious beast with powerful paws and lethal claws. As further proof of his hellish origin, fire and smoke issued forth from his mouth. Apollyon was a creature of darkness, and his language was that of the bottomless pit. With the boldness of a roaring lion, and also with the stealth and cunning of that mighty predator, he roams along the King's Highway searching for unsuspecting prey. (1 Peter 5:8-9) But perhaps the most repulsive thing about him was his proud, disdainful countenance.

Not surprisingly, Apollyon was well equipped for battle and ready to use every weapon at his disposal against Christian. His evil intention became clear the moment he spoke, boldly asserting that Christian belonged to him. As a doomed creature himself, his chief desire is to bring about the eternal ruin of the human race. Those who remain in the City of Destruction and its environs are already under his dominion and sway. Not content with these, however, he is fiercely determined to recover all who have been delivered from his power.

Since Christian's natural descent could be traced to the City of Destruction, Apollyon not only claimed him as a subject, but also demanded allegiance and service from him. To this declaration Christian replied that he had found Apollyon's conditions of service to be intolerable and his wages that upon which a man could not possibly live. (Proverbs 13:15; Romans 6:23)

When his claim to prior ownership failed, the fiendish creature resorted to bribery in order to win Christian back into his service. Since he had no intention of losing another one of his subjects, he was willing to negotiate more profitable terms of service if Christian would agree. However, Christian soundly rejected the offer of more favorable earthly circumstances and boldly pledged his allegiance to another king, the Lord Jesus Christ.

Since bribery had also failed to work, Apollyon switched to an entirely different tactic. He attempted to discourage Christian by mocking his faith, belittling the strength of his resolve, and implying that they were no more than the result of a temporary delusion. To add weight to this argument, he cited the case of many who had once professed faith in Christ, but now followed him no more. Sad to say, this statement is all too true.

Assuming that in this he had gained an advantage, and hoping to close the deal, Apollyon offered what he considered to be generous terms of amnesty. If Christian would only return to his service, all would be forgotten. But his pretended mercy concealed lying words, and Christian immediately saw through it. Therefore, he replied with added vehemence that not only did he serve his Lord willingly, but was well satisfied in his service. He had received nothing but good from the hands of his gracious, loving Lord.

When Christian refused to be swayed by this latest argument, the creature could barely contain his fury. However, since he thought it wise not to vent it just yet, he sought to frighten Christian with dire predictions of what could lie ahead for him if he continued in his present course. So he reminded Christian that God's people often suffer grievously while on earth, and their Lord does not intervene on their behalf. By this subtle argument, he implied that he was the more benevolent master because he rewards those who faithfully serve him.

In spite of Apollyon's deceitful words, Christian saw through them with no difficulty. He understood that God does indeed allow his children to be sorely tried, but he also knew that an infinitely wise and good purpose is behind it. (Romans 8:28) Although we must often be afflicted in this life, it is to purge and prepare us for eternal glory in that land where pain and sorrow shall be no more. On the other hand, Apollyon failed to mention the fearful end of those who die in his service!

When every other tactic failed, the accuser of the brethren brought forth his weapon of choice, with which he is especially skillful. (Revelation 12:10) He boldly charged Christian with being unfaithful to his Lord, and thus inflicted a masterful stroke! In painful detail, he reminded Christian of his many failures and shortcomings, laying stress upon every misstep and sin. Moreover, he exposed the desire for vainglory that secretly lurked in Christian's heart.

What a highly effective weapon this flaming arrow is, one that never fails to find its mark! To these harsh accusations Christian could only groan inwardly and agree, because his conscience bore witness against him. He was guilty as charged, and of much more besides. The mere remembrance of these things caused him untold grief and torment of soul. Yet for all of his past failures, he looked to the mercy of the Lord Jesus Christ, who stands ready to forgive and cleanse his repentant children as they walk the path of life. (1 John 1:7-9; Hebrews 4:15-16)

At this point, Apollyon could no longer suppress his wrath. Dropping all pretense of civility, he openly declared, "I am an enemy to the Prince; I hate his person, his laws, and people: I am come out on purpose to withstand thee." To this bold assertion Christian replied, "Apollyon, beware what you do; for I am in the King's highway, the way of holiness; therefore take heed to yourself."

Given his present state of mind, Christian's reaction to this violent threat may come as somewhat of a surprise. Why did he answer the creature in such a way? Did he really expect him to draw back when thus rebuked? We cannot say for sure, but whatever his motive, Christian's words brought the situation to a head. The battle lines were clearly drawn when the enemy straddled the path, blocked the way, and warned Christian to prepare to die. Previously, in the form of Beelzebub, he had aimed his arrows at Christian as he was approaching the Wicket Gate. That earlier attack had been more covert in nature, and he had been largely unaware of it. Now, in the Valley of Humiliation, he faced him again as Apollyon the Destroyer.

The ensuing fight was a dreadful thing to witness. As the flaming arrows came at him thick and fast, Christian soon discovered that he was no match for the monster. Although he managed to avert many of the darts by the skillful use of his shield (faith), he eventually received several critical wounds. Moreover, with each hit he grew substantially weaker.

We recall that during his visit to the palace armory, Christian had been equipped for just such a time as this. So as the battle continued to rage, he unsheathed his sword and pressed forward valiantly, in spite of his injuries. Just when the tide seemed to be turning in his favor, he lost his footing, dropped his sword, and fell to the ground. With the powerful weapon now out of his reach, it seemed fairly certain that Apollyon would make good his threat. Lying helpless in the dust, Christian nearly despaired of life as he awaited the final stroke. When the enemy seized his advantage and moved in for the kill, Christian's hand found the golden hilt of his sword once again. With his last remaining strength, he regained his footing and managed one forward thrust with his sword saying, as he had before on the summit of the hill Difficulty: *Rejoice not against me, O mine enemy! When I fall I shall arise; when I sit in darkness, the LORD shall be a light unto me.* (Micah 7:8)

At this critical point, the battle shifted decidedly in Christian's favor. Having discovered anew what a powerful weapon he held in his hand, he put his sword to good use again saying, *Nay, in all these things we are more than conquerors, through him that loved us.* (Romans 8:37) Upon hearing these words, the wounded adversary spread his dragon's wings and fled swiftly away out of Christian's sight, for the present.

* * * *

Dear reader, by now I'm sure you understand that the battle between Christian and Apollyon in the Valley of Humiliation was a figurative event. The hideous roar of the monster and the heartfelt sighs and groans uttered by Christian were real indeed; moreover, the stakes of the battle could not have been higher. In the adversary's fierce attempt to reclaim him for the kingdom of darkness, we understand that Christian's faith had come under heavy fire. Thus he found himself engaged in fierce spiritual combat, but his mind was the battleground upon which it took place.

As we have already learned, the weapons with which Christian fought were of a singular kind. Like the battle itself, they were spiritual in nature. Although Christian withstood the attack with uncommon courage, Apollyon managed to inflict significant damage by wounding him in his head, hand, and foot. According to John Bunyan this meant his understanding, faith, and conduct (manner of living). Since these were all vital areas to Christian's spiritual well-being, any mortal wound suffered there would have been his undoing. However, an unseen ally fought by his side in the mêlée, one that helped him not only to stand, but win the day. (Ephesians 6:13)

So what really happened that day in the Valley of Humiliation? Human pride met diabolical pride and the clash between the two was a terrible thing. There would have been no doubt as to the outcome, had not a wise and good purpose been behind it. By God's grace, however, the battle proved highly beneficial to Christian because it taught him how little strength he really had. It is a painful, yet essential lesson we all must learn. The knowledge he gained in the Palace Beautiful was put to the test in the valley. Furthermore, pride took a needful hit as Christian was brought low through a deeper understanding of himself.

When Christian realized that he had wounded his adversary, he lifted his face toward heaven and smiled, giving thanks to the one who had delivered him from the might of the enemy. With a grateful heart he acknowledged that all glory for the victory belonged to God alone. Yet as we closely observe his countenance, we wonder if perhaps he secretly gave himself a slight pat on the back for Apollyon's defeat. We cannot know for sure, but each one of us who struggles with the sin of pride will admit the possibility, knowing that the flesh will give itself credit whenever it can.

As for the wounds Christian received in battle, an unseen hand ministered to him by applying some leaves from the Tree of Life to his injuries. The result was immediate healing and restoration of soul that enabled him to resume his journey without further delay. Accordingly, after refreshing himself with the provisions given him by the palace virgins, he was ready to continue his passage through the valley.

Christian's overestimation of his spiritual strength is a sin of which any child of God can be guilty; but it is more common among those who are less acquainted with the Valley of Humiliation. Only after being brought low, perhaps many times, do we begin to see ourselves in a more accurate light. Therefore, Christian will undoubtedly pass this way again. For now he made his way forward, sword in hand. After all, who knew what other enemies might be lurking nearby? He had been caught off guard once because he was not nearly as ready for battle as he thought. From now on he determined to be much more watchful; but as he passed through the rest of the valley, he did so without further incident.

Study Questions

1. For what purpose was the Valley of Humiliation designed? List some of the things that can cause a proud spirit to assert itself.

2. Why is the sin of pride a particularly shameful thing in a Christian?

3. What are some of the trying circumstances that can bring a Christian low and cast him down into the Valley of Humiliation?

4. Who was the horrible creature that attacked Christian as soon as he reached the valley floor? What tactics did he use against the poor man?

5. What was the outcome of this terrible battle? What were some of the things Christian learned from it?

CHAPTER 26

The Valley of Humiliation Contemplated

WHEN PASSING THROUGH THE VALLEY OF HUMILIATION FOR THE FIRST time, many a weary traveler has gazed with longing toward the mountains bordering it to the right and left. His heart cries, "O to be delivered from this lowly place and stand once more on those majestic heights!" Is he doomed to live perpetually in low places while others dwell on the mountaintops, seemingly happy and free from care? In his heart, he fears that it might be so.

However, those who are better acquainted with this valley know that it is much more than a place of severe trial. Since we usually learn more from our struggles and failures than from our successes, it is also a place of great blessing and rare opportunity. Moreover, our usefulness as the servants of Christ is more likely to increase in its secluded depths rather than at the higher elevations above it? Therefore, my fellow pilgrim, our pathway must lead us through this figurative river valley.

As certain varieties of fruit and flowers require the cool, shady lowlands in order to thrive at their optimum, so do the godly qualities that make up a Christ-like character. The Valley of Humiliation, with its rich soil generously watered by the Spirit of God, provides the perfect conditions for spiritual fruit to blossom and grow. (Galatians 5:22-23) Moreover, our Lord Jesus Christ, fairest lily of the valleys, dwells and communes with his children there. So when our pathway leads us down into that secluded vale, we may rest assured that he is there.

Herein is the greatest blessing of the Valley of Humiliation. Our gracious Savior is Lord of the valley as well as Lord of the hill. However, our full enjoyment of his presence requires the mortification of our flesh and a truly humble mind. Those who resemble him most closely will have the sweetest fellowship with him there.

The Lord Jesus Christ, the beautiful rose of Sharon, is our highest example of humility and submission to God in suffering. (Luke 22:42; Philippians 2:5-8; 1 Peter 4:1-2) Even though he was the holy, sinless Son of God, he willingly humbled himself and became a servant for our sakes. Yet how hard it is for us to do the same! Therefore, one major purpose of the valley is to accomplish this work for us by reducing us in rank. Although it is a very painful thing to be brought low, we will know the peace and comfort of our Lord's presence and help when we submit to his wise purpose for us in it. (Isaiah 57:15)

Since passing through the Valley of Humiliation denotes a time of severe trial and affliction, it is a deeply personal experience that no else one can fully understand. Because it is strictly a matter between us and our heavenly Father, it can seem a dark and lonely thing. Whatever the particular circumstances that bring us low, all are designed to cast down our inclination to pride and vainglory and bring forth the fruit of godly humility. However, many who have been there will testify that it is quite possible to be humiliated without being humble.

Although the valley is designed entirely for our spiritual profit, we can expect a rough passage if we strive against God's purpose for us there. Yet far too often, we unintentionally do just that. When our will has been crossed in some way or our best-laid plans overturned, what is our first reaction? When our desires are thwarted or our dearest hopes dashed, do we submit to God's will and commit it all to him? Or do we complain bitterly, wallow in self-pity, and give in to despair?

Our proper response is to humble ourselves under God's mighty hand and confess the sins that made our descent into the valley necessary. However, our first response is often to deny the real problem by convincing ourselves that our will is also God's will. In so doing, we quickly find that our failure to submit to his will and providence causes us many a slip on the downhill slope. Moreover, it brings us directly within range of enemy fire.

Like the figurative monster that accosted Christian in the Valley of Humiliation, our spiritual archenemy is far cleverer than we are. He attacks with great subtlety, often posing as an angel of light. (2 Corinthians 11:14) Although he will confront us in a number of ways, his character is consistent and so is his diabolical purpose. In order to accomplish this purpose he uses many artful devices, and we cannot afford to be ignorant of them. (2 Corinthians 2:11) No matter the disguise he wears, he is Apollyon still, the ruthless destroyer who hates God and wars against his will and purpose. Since he is also the enemy of God's people, he is fiercely determined to overthrow our faith and reclaim us for his evil kingdom.

Far from being humbled by his terrible fall, Satan remains the same proud creature. Pride continues to master him, even after he was cast out of heaven and confined to his dark domain. Although John Milton's words do not carry the weight of divine inspiration and are not always doctrinally correct, I believe he captured something of the perverted mind of fallen Lucifer when he wrote him as saying:

> Infernal world, and thou profoundest hell
> Receive thy new possessor: one who brings
> A mind not to be changed by place or time.
> The mind is its own place, and in itself
> Can make a heaven of hell, a hell of heaven.
> What matter where, if I be still the same,
> And what I should be, all but less than he
> Whom thunder hath made greater? Here at least
> We shall be free; the Almighty hath not built
> Here for his envy, will not drive us hence:
> Here we may reign secure, and in my choice
> To reign is worth ambition, though in hell:
> Better to reign in Hell than serve in Heaven. [1]

As concerns this terrible creature of darkness, we are no match for either his craft or his power. Therefore, we are as vulnerable to his diabolical schemes as poor Christian was. Even though he does not confront us in visible form, he is capable of inflicting great injury nonetheless. In his battle for the Christian's mind, Satan employs those very things with which we have our greatest struggles, and he well knows what they are. For this reason he has a strong preference for the Valley of Humiliation, and makes full use of those times when circumstances have brought us low. Hoping to inflict maximum damage, he presses his advantage by aiming his weapons at our most vulnerable points.

At times, he will attempt to capture our hearts by setting the allurements of the world before us in contrast to our reduced circumstances. Should he succeed in distracting us from single-hearted devotion to Christ, he scores a great victory. He will also try to warp our spiritual perspective by bombarding our minds with arguments against the life of faith. On still other occasions, his fiery arrows come in the form of such severe discouragement that, like the prophet Jeremiah, we are tempted to admit defeat and call it quits. (Jeremiah 20:7-9) Although his missiles can assume any number of forms, he always fires them with a destructive goal in mind. Far too often they find their mark, leaving us weak and wounded. However, this need not be the case.

Our Lord has provided all that we need in order to stand in this great conflict – battle armor that is exactly suited to the kind of warfare we face. (Ephesians 6:10-18; 2 Corinthians 10:3-6) Without the covering of the whole armor of God, we would be helpless against the powers of darkness. Therefore, it is important to know of what this very special armor consists.

We have a girdle of truth that surrounds our souls and guards us from being led astray by deadly error. Our Lord has provided a breastplate of righteousness, the righteousness of Christ, whereby we are accepted in God's sight and kept in the way of holiness. We have been fitted with specially prepared footwear, by which we are made ready to carry the good tidings of the Gospel to others. The shield of faith protects our inner man against the enemy's potentially lethal darts. In addition, the helmet of salvation guards our minds, protects our thought processes, and preserves our hope of salvation. (1 Thessalonians 5:8) The sword of the Spirit, the Word of God, is our offensive weapon. This mighty sword exposes our great enemy as a liar and puts him to flight, even while it encourages and strengthens us in the faith. Moreover, it is the light that shines into our inmost being and sharpens our spiritual vision. (Hebrews 4:12) Last, but certainly not least, there is prayer, our vital lifeline. Without the defensive weapon of fervent, persevering prayer, the other armor would be of little use.

As mentioned before in our consideration of the palace armory, the Lord Jesus Christ is the essence of the armor. Since our strength is unequal to our task, it is only by being in union with him that we are able to prevail in battle. (Zechariah 4:6) Therefore, as we saw with Christian, there is no problem with the armor itself. It is perfect and complete. The difficulty lies in our failure to use it aright. For instance, the sword can also be knocked out of our hands, leaving us defenseless. What is the spiritual import when this happens?

The dexterity with which Apollyon knocked the sword out of Christian's hand denotes the skill whereby Satan can turn our offensive weapon against us. His most effective tactic is deception, and as a master in that art, he takes delight in misquoting and perverting the Word of God. In addition, he will either use the Scriptures to accuse us or cause them to slip from our memory. Then having discovered a weak spot in our armor, he attacks with even more fervor when we stumble and fall.

Considering these things alone might lead us to conclude that he has an overwhelming advantage, and truly the outcome would be dire indeed, if the Lord of Hosts did not personally undertake our defense. (Psalm 108:13) The great reformer, Martin Luther, expressed this exceptionally well when he wrote:

Did we in our own strength confide, our striving would be losing;
Were not the right man on our side, the man of God's own choosing.

> Dost ask who that may be? Christ Jesus, it is he,
> Lord Sabaoth his name, from age to age the same,
> And he must win the battle. [2]

Valley trials and their invaluable lessons

Although the Valley of Humiliation is specifically designed for God's people, the trials and difficulties we experience there are common to all mankind. The great difference lies in their effect. While the unregenerate person tends to become cynical and hardened due to life's trials and sorrows, the Spirit of God uses these very same things to produce the peaceable fruit of righteousness in us. Therefore, if only we had eyes to see it, the valley is a good and beneficial place. It is both a vale of tears and of blessing. A better acquaintance with it will convince us that our nights of weeping are just as necessary as our mornings of joy.

According to the writer of Psalm 119, affliction is a most effectual and powerful teacher. In verse 67 he wrote, *Before I was afflicted I went astray: but now have I kept thy word.* Dear Christian friend, this truth will encourage our hearts when we consider it rightly. Our bitterest trials often yield the sweetest fruit, although it can take us a while to recognize God's hand in them. Once we do, however, we are ready to profit from the valuable lessons taught in the valley. So when God leads us into that lowly place, we do well to pray, "Lord, what is it that you would have me learn?"

One thing we learn firsthand when under enemy fire in the valley is that the battle is the Lord's. We cannot fight it, much less be victorious, in our own strength. It is only as our honor is thrown down into the dust that we learn how weak we really are, how very poor and needy. (Psalm 70:5) The only way to effectively resist Apollyon is by humble submission to God in whatever situation he has placed us. (James 4:6-7)

Then there is the matter of learning to wait on the Lord, which is another fundamental lesson best taught in the valley. For most of us, this is probably one of the hardest things to master. How difficult it is to wait when our every impulse is to do something, to take matters into our own hands and find a solution to our problem. No, my friend, waiting on the Lord does not come naturally, nor is it easily learned. We generally will not do so until we must.

What then do we do in those times when our cloudy pillar stands still, but we are anxious to move forward? Do we forge ahead in spite of the lack of clear direction? Or do we wait on the Lord and trust in him until he makes the way plain? At such times, fretful restlessness will urge us to make rash decisions and take imprudent action, but yielding to it will cause us many a bitter struggle in the valley. We will have little peace until fretful restlessness gives way to child-like faith, and our hearts and minds become quiet before the Lord, even as a weaned child. (Psalm 131:2) It takes the courage of faith, patient and obedient faith, to wait on the Lord when we find ourselves in desperate circumstances. However, when we do, we place ourselves in the realm of divine promise. (Psalm 27:14; Psalm 31:24; Psalm 37:39-40; Psalm 40:1-3; Isaiah 30:18)

In learning to wait on the Lord, we also come to more fully understand how utterly dependent upon him we are for everything. It is only by struggling with our own insufficiency that we truly come to realize that he is the source of all our help and strength. Moreover, we discover anew how faithful he is even when we stumble and fall. We cannot walk the path of life aright unless we walk it in his strength. Upon this very subject, Charles H. Spurgeon wisely observed: "It is better for us to have God's strength than our own; for if we were a thousand times as strong as we are, it would amount to nothing in the face of the enemy; and if we could be weaker than we are, which is scarcely possible, yet we could do all things through Christ." [3]

Another valley lesson best learned under trial is that God's Word is essential to our very existence. It is the beacon of truth that guides our steps through this life and will bring us safely to the holy hill of Zion. (Psalm 43:3) Therefore, we must learn it, lay it to heart, and walk in its precepts. (Proverbs 7:1-3) It was the means by which we were born again, and it is also the means by which our new life in Christ is nurtured and sustained. (James 1:18; 1 Peter 2:1-3) It is the golden sword with which we do spiritual battle, but we must wield it by faith. Should our faith take a significant hit, we can drop this mighty weapon for a time. However, the remembrance of God's Word with its great and precious promises will cause faith to burn brightly once again. As with Christian, it is not our skill with the sword, but the power of the Word itself that puts the enemy to flight.

In close conjunction with the Word of God is the importance of a disciplined prayer life. Every lesson taught in the Valley of Humiliation underscores our need of this vital lifeline to our dear Savior, and yet, negligence in this regard often causes a weak spot in our armor. There are few things that drive us to our knees more quickly than finding ourselves under heavy trial. Feelings of helplessness and the sense of our great need prompt us to *come boldly unto the throne of grace, that we may obtain mercy, and find grace to help in time of need.* (Hebrews 4:16) A penitent spirit urges us to confess our sins and seek our Lord for mercy and forgiveness. Overwhelming sorrow bids us to cast our care upon him and bring our requests before him.

Therefore, in the valley we learn to pray as we never did before; but we should take care to make fervent prayer a top priority at other times as well. As properly oxygenated blood is crucial to our bodily health, heart-felt communion with our Lord in prayer is crucial to our spiritual well-being. Nothing can make up for the lack of it.

In a somewhat mysterious way, the lessons we learn in the Valley of Humiliation sort out our priorities on a very basic level. Our thoughts may have been consumed by many things before, but suddenly, life becomes simpler. We have a clearer understanding of what is really important; thus, our hearts and minds are fixed upon eternal realities more firmly than ever. Moreover, we view the things of earth in a different light. So in the valley, our thought processes and the desires of our heart undergo needful correction until they are more aligned with what they ought to be.

Since valley lessons are seldom learned apart from trial and affliction, we rarely come through them without bearing wounds of some kind. What a comfort it is to know that even though God may allow us to be wounded in the battle, he will never abandon us to the malice of the enemy. As the great physician, our Lord Jesus Christ ministers to us and heals any spiritual injury we may have sustained. He is the Tree of Life whose leaves have the power to restore our wounded spirits to vibrant health again. (Revelation 22:1-2) Moreover, if we should be permanently weakened by the ordeal, it is so that God's strength might be made perfect in our weakness.

Valley trials yield valley fruit

For those of us who are in Christ, spiritual growth is not an option; it is a commanded duty. (1 Peter 2:1-3; 2 Peter 3:18) However, it is also a task beyond our ability to accomplish through our own efforts. Therefore, our heavenly Father undertakes it on our behalf, most often in the Valley of Humiliation. Since trial and affliction accomplish a work in us that earthly comfort and ease could never do, spiritual growth generally takes place after we have been brought low and are the least aware of it. It is the direct result of valley lessons well learned. Moreover, it yields an abundant harvest of rare and precious fruit.

Hebrews 12:11 assures us that divine chastening has the beneficial effect of producing the peaceable fruit of righteousness in those who endure it. The mortification of sin, the subduing of the sin principle that still resides in our flesh, is an exceedingly painful process, and yet what precious valley fruit it brings forth. (1 Peter 1:13-16; 4:1-2)

Closely akin to the peaceable fruit of righteousness is faith that has been purged and purified through affliction. Genuine faith will prevail when it comes under enemy fire, but whether we have this kind of faith or not will only be made known as we are put to the test. When all is going well and our mountain seems strong, we presume that our faith is strong as well. (Psalm 30:6-7) However, we are probably wrong. Faith's strength, or its weakness, is only made known when it meets resistance. As it faces an unscalable height or unfathomable depth, faith's true character comes to light. Yet even when it proves to be genuine, its deficiencies will be brought to our full attention.

Faith's fiery trial clears our spiritual vision like nothing else can do. In the fire we are forced to take a good look at ourselves, and the reality check is sure to be disturbing. However, it is in these times that we find out what or whom it is that we trust. Through it all, our Lord teaches us the patience of faith as we learn to wait on him and hope in his mercy. One day, faith tried by fire will shine as brightly as gold, and valley fruit will be brought forth to the praise of his glorious grace.

Although the cup given us to drink may seem bitter, conditions in the lower regions of the valley are favorable for the development of a truly grateful heart. Even though we know that our heavenly Father is the giver of every good gift, we may still be guilty of taking his blessings for granted until we are threatened with their loss. What about the gift of affliction? Do we see God's hand of mercy when suffering in the valley? It is evidence of rare valley fruit when we are able to honestly say with the psalmist: *It is good for me that I have been afflicted; that I might learn thy statutes.* (Psalm 119:71)

Another evidence of valley fruit is a worshipful heart: a heart full of reverence, godly fear, and humble submission to God. A heart of sincere gratitude to him and praise to his name! Like David, we must worship God in spirit and in truth, and not only when life is good and our circumstances are favorable. David sought the Lord with his whole heart and worshiped him in sincerity even when walking in the midst of trouble. (Psalm 138:2,7) Therefore, he could bow to God's will and commit himself to God's mercy unreservedly.

So did Job. In spite of overwhelming sorrow and bitter anguish, Job worshiped God and blessed his name. (Job 1: 20-21) He endured severe affliction with exemplary patience and faith because, like David, he saw its end purpose. Thus he could say with conviction:

Behold, I go forward, but he is not there; and backward, but I cannot perceive him: on the left hand, where he doth work, but I cannot behold him, he hideth himself on the right hand, that I cannot see him: but he knoweth the way that I take: when he hath tried me, I shall come forth as gold. (Job 23:8-10)

My friend in Christ, the truest kind of worship is that which comes forth from a chastened, grateful heart – worship that is poured forth in the beauty of holiness. O, that you and I might demonstrate this valley fruit as well!

The spiritual benefits gained from our valley trials are not meant for us alone. There is something about suffering that softens our hearts and increases our care and compassion for others. Moreover, it will enlarge both our capacity and opportunity to minister to our brothers and sisters in Christ when they are walking through the valley. (Revelation 1:9) Like Prudence, the sweetest Christians are those who have spent the most time in the Valley of Humiliation.

The last of the valley fruit that we will consider is the quality of godly humility, which is undoubtedly the most fundamental of them all. First, however, we need to take a look at the problem of pride. Since we are poor judges of our own spiritual maturity, it is a great mistake to try to assess our progress in grace, or anyone else's for that matter. Pride is the chief culprit in every failure here, for it is sure to distort our judgment. Like an enemy lurking in the shadows, pride waits for an opportune time to rear its ugly head, and the problem is not limited to those with superior knowledge or exceptional gifts. Pride is common to us all, and in most cases, it takes little enough to provoke it. But even when we manage to hide it from others, a proud spirit always denotes a weak Christian character.

Unlike Apollyon's scaly covering of pride, God's people are to be clothed with humility. (Matthew 5:3-5; 1 Peter 5:5) Therefore, when pride rules in our hearts, our heavenly Father reduces us in rank by bringing things into our lives that will lower us in our own opinion, and perhaps in the opinion of others. But he brings us low in order to eliminate the things in us that are spiritually detrimental. (Psalm 66:10; Proverbs 22:4)

This abasing of pride requires having any distorted self-image shattered. It is humiliating to see ourselves as we really are, rather than as we like to imagine. This clearer insight brings great inner conflict, and often sets us at odds with other people as well. In commenting upon Matthew 7:2, Oswald Chambers made the incisive observation: "The things we criticize in others we are guilty of ourselves." [4] Therefore, if we find the proud spirit of another to be offensive, perhaps we should take a good look at ourselves, my friend. As we contend against pride in another, the Lord will use that very situation to show us some disturbing things in us. Thus the very people we view as adversaries are really friends in disguise, if our conflict with them results in bringing down our pride.

To grow in grace and knowledge of the Lord Jesus Christ is to become increasingly more like him, be of the same mind, and follow in his steps. This slow but sure work of dying to self and living unto Christ spans our entire lives as believers. Moreover, nothing so manifests the character of our Lord as a truly humble mind – a fact that our great enemy knows well.

Since pride was Satan's downfall, he desires that it be ours as well. Therefore, he scores a great victory when we display a proud spirit. As we seek to walk with the Lord, we quickly learn that we must do battle with our own flesh. (Romans 6:11-14; Romans 8:12-14; Galatians 5:16) When this battle plunges us down into the Valley of Humiliation, as it invariably does, our flesh often kicks against the pricks. To make matters worse, Satan will take the side of our flesh and play to its strength.

While pride is indicative of a weak Christian character, godly humility is an excellent indicator of spiritual health and prosperity of soul. In this, John the Baptist was a shining example. It was with a sincerely humble heart that he said, speaking of the Lord Jesus: *He must increase, but I must decrease.* (John 3:28-30). If we would be true followers of our Lord, we must be of the same mind; but we dare not claim to have the mind of Christ until we can honestly say, "Not my will but thine be done."

How good it would be if we learned from our past failures and mistakes! For most of us, however, godly humility is a hard lesson requiring repeated passages through the Valley of Humiliation. Thomas Boston expressed this well when he said: "Many a stroke must be given at the root of the tree of the natural pride of the heart ere it fall; ofttimes it seems to be fallen, and yet it arises again. And even when the root stroke is given in believers, the rod of pride buds again, so that there is still occasion for new humbling work." [5]

Far too often when under this humbling work, our first reaction is to murmur and complain, to question God's providence as if he owed us an explanation. Such a reaction will in no way alter God's purpose. It will only succeed in causing us greater trouble. Quiet submission in the midst of difficulty is never an easy thing. It develops gradually as faith grows in proportion. Faith that sees God's hand in everything and is learning not to second guess his wisdom or blame secondary causes! God brings us low as need be, so that he may exalt us in due time. (1 Peter 5:6) When will that be? Not until we are able to bear it with the dignity and grace of a truly humble mind.

* * * *

Dear fellow pilgrim, perhaps you are now enjoying a season of blessing and relative freedom from trial, and tempted to think that it will always be that way. But even as you walk in bright sunshine, the night of affliction could lie just beyond the next bend in the road. Therefore, when you stand on the high ground, it is well to remember that the way forward is downward. While it is right and proper to enjoy our seasons of rest, they should be times of serious contemplation. The very mountaintop upon which we presently stand could very well look down upon the Valley of Humiliation. It is no accident that the royal road to Zion takes us through both the heights of joy and the depths of sorrow. A measure of each is necessary in order to prepare us for an eternity in which trial and sorrow will figure no more.

Therefore, when the voice of the great shepherd calls to you from the valley below, do not fear to follow the call. His purpose in bringing us low is to fit us for more useful service in his kingdom. If we should meet the enemy face to face in that lowly place, our Lord will stand right by our side. By his grace and for his glory, he will enable us to stand in the evil day.

Christian was not the same after his sojourn through the valley, and neither will we be. Have we reached the point in our journey where we can sincerely thank God for our valley experiences? (James 1:2-4) If so, we will be better able to understand their wholesome purpose. It is only in the refinery called the Valley of Humiliation that pride and other fleshly hindrances are purged from us so that the beauty of Christ may shine forth more brightly.

So there is every reason to be encouraged, even when you find yourself under heavy trial yet again. Look up, dear brother or sister in Christ! When in the valley there is no other place to set your sights. Look upward, but not to the hills that outline the valley high above. Lift your eyes to the Lord Jesus Christ, for our help comes from him alone. (Psalm 121:1-2; Jeremiah 3:23) Eventually, you will reach the end of the valley, once God's purpose for you has been accomplished. Then you will know yourself a little better than before, and you will also have more intimate knowledge of the one who walked by your side and guided you safely through.

Study Questions

1. Apollyon is still attacking Christians today. What are some of the ways he seeks to harm and defeat us?

2. What provision has the Lord made for us in order that we might endure this battle?

3. Give some of the valuable lessons the Christian learns from his or her valley trials.

4. What is some of the spiritual fruit that is brought forth as a result of our valley trials?

CHAPTER 27

Into the Valley of the Shadow of Death

IF WE WOULD TRULY BE OUR LORD'S DISCIPLES, WE MUST ALSO HAVE HIS mind of humility, obedience, and suffering. (Philippians 2:5-8) We must be as silver refined, living day by day under the gracious influence of his Spirit. One of the primary lessons of the Valley of Humiliation is that we can neither produce this godly mind in ourselves, nor serve the Lord in our own strength. If we would be vessels fit for our master's use, we must first be brought low, emptied of self-will, and filled with his Spirit. For it is only in dying to self that we learn to live by his grace and for his glory.

What then should we expect when we finally reach the end of the valley? Is it not reasonable to hope for an end to the conflict, or at least a little time to recover from battle fatigue? What are we to think when we encounter another valley immediately thereafter, the Valley of the Shadow of Death? Does not its very name dash our hopes and put us on notice that our troubles are far from over?

The two valleys running end to end remind us that when trouble comes, it often comes in multiples. The apostle Peter addressed this issue when he spoke of the many temptations that come our way to try our faith, and of the heaviness that is a necessary part of it. Poor Christian is just about to experience this truth first-hand. As he knelt before the Lord with a heart filled with gratitude for his recent deliverance, little did he know that the end of the Valley of Humiliation marked the beginning of another, even worse one. However, when standing at the border of the second valley, he feared that his ordeal there would be even more harrowing than his awful battle with Apollyon.

His first impression was not incorrect! For one thing, a quick survey of the new valley gives advance warning that the way through it will probably be substantially more difficult. Unlike the first valley with its broad upland meadows, refreshing stream, and mountains far in the distance, this one more closely resembles a narrow, rocky gorge. Steep, rugged cliffs border each side of the path and nearly touch one another high above, virtually excluding all sunlight from the lower regions of the valley. Huge boulders perching high overhead threaten to fall at any moment and crush those who pass below. Here and there, deep fissures break the surface of the cliff walls; but the traveler who leaves the path in hopes of finding a shortcut will quickly lose his way. Therefore, the prudent traveler will take care to avoid these dangerous by-paths.

Altogether, the Valley of the Shadow of Death is a solitary and desolate place. Since rainfall is negligible, and no life-giving river flows through it, drought conditions are the norm. Consequently, little vegetation of any kind is found there. By most accounts, it is a desolate wilderness that has justly earned its name, so most people regard it as impassable and avoid it altogether. God's children do not shun its bleak and lonely depths, however, for their path goes directly through it.

The obvious hazards of the path itself are not the only things that make passage here so difficult. There are even worse things with which we must contend while here. As we make our way deeper into the dark, narrow canyon, we will find it to be a place where eerie voices of unknown origin echo from its rocky walls. Voices in the valley! This particular aspect of the gorge plays havoc with the mind by filling it with nameless terrors.

Before Christian had time to even wonder what might lie ahead for him here, he came face to face with trouble at the very border. Just when he could have used an encouraging word, disheartenment attacked him in the form of two men running toward him, bearing news of great danger ahead. They claimed to have first-hand knowledge about the terrors of the valley, and yet their report indicated that they knew nothing of its spiritual significance or the purpose of God in it.

These two heralds and their discouraging news bear a striking resemblance to the ten Hebrew spies who reported to Moses after surveying the land of Canaan. (Numbers 13:25-29, 31-33) Their assessment of the Promised Land came from hearts of unbelief, and was diametrically opposed to the favorable report and testimony of faith given by Caleb and Joshua. (Numbers 13:30; Numbers 14:6-9)

So in spite of what they claimed, the credibility of these two men was open to serious question. Their report was based on mere hearsay, since neither of them had actually entered the valley. The very sight of it had convinced them to cut their losses and turn back. Moreover, they advised Christian to do likewise, if he valued his life and peace of mind.

What had they seen or heard that caused such a drastic reaction? How did they perceive the valley, and how accurate was their assessment likely to be? We must admit that their gruesome account was enough to unnerve even a valiant-hearted pilgrim, and Christian was not the bravest soul to pass that way. Fearful images began to take form in his mind as they spoke of the palpable darkness and the horrible beings inhabiting the valley. Their graphic description was of a place haunted by the moans and screams of souls in torment, miserable beings imprisoned in chains of great affliction and despair. (Psalm 107:10-14) In their opinion, this valley was a place that savored of death and promised nothing good. Even more disturbing, they were convinced that it had an intangible point of no return, beyond which all who dared to venture would surely perish.

This was a shocking report, for sure, but even though their vivid description had a basis in fact, it did not begin to tell the whole story. More to the point, it entirely missed the true character and beneficial purpose of the valley. In spite of their terrifying account, the two men could not convince Christian to turn back. Neither could they persuade him that he had somehow gotten out of the right path just because there was trouble ahead. By now, he had enough discernment to believe that the way to the Celestial City went through this terrible valley just as surely as it led him into green pastures and beside still waters.

Christian's response to the two men and their discouraging news brings a thought-provoking question to mind. Were they actual persons, or figurative of something else? I personally believe they represent one of the voices heard so often in this valley. Christian heard it once before when he met Timorous and Mistrust near the summit of the hill Difficulty. Now he is bombarded by it again at the onset of this new trial. Anticipating what he might have to face, his imagination began to run wild as the inner voice of unbelieving fear quickly furnished the details, undoubtedly a worst case scenario.

Whatever his thoughts may have been, Christian's faith came under strong attack here, and his courage was badly shaken by the fear of the unknown. Nevertheless, his resolution remained firm even though he now had good reason to expect an assault of some kind. Thus he cautiously ventured forward, armed and ready to use his sword if need be.

Between a rock and a hard place

Dear friend in Christ, it is just the same with us. From beginning to end, our pathway to Zion requires careful attention if we are to stay safely therein. In some places, however, the way is so treacherous that there is very little margin for the smallest misstep. The first portion of the Valley of the Shadow of Death is one such place. As far as the eye can see, the path is not only extremely narrow, but also bordered by steep chasms on either side, making safe passage seem virtually impossible. Utmost caution is required in order to avoid a terrible fall here. Tragically, all who pass this way are not so careful. Therefore, many a promising pilgrimage has come to an abrupt end along this particular stretch of the King's Highway.

Valley trials are a spiritual proving ground in which our faith comes under heavy fire to try what sort it is. For most of us, this is a painful revelation in which we are made to see ourselves, in measure, as God sees us. As a result, pride takes a needful hit and self-reliance bites the dust, causing us to shed many a tear. So even though this dark valley is figurative, it is nonetheless a real and accurate picture of the people of God under bitter trial. Trace out its physical characteristics and you will find that they closely mirror our inward condition at such times. To make matters worse, we will face multiple dangers in this valley at a time when we are already low in spirit, weak, and weary. Moreover, we will be bombarded by nameless terrors just when we think ourselves unable to bear any more.

The drop-offs to the right and left of the path denote two specific hazards that we are likely to encounter early on when in this valley. As Christian assessed the situation, he realized that the slightest misstep in either direction could prove his downfall. His perilous situation denotes another danger for the Christian under severe trial, the voice of temptation. Although it may assault us at any time, we are never more vulnerable to this voice than when under great difficulty.

Just beyond the right edge of the pathway, the cliff plunges down into a very deep crevasse named Error. This chasm represents an assault upon our faith with the intent to subvert it. Multitudes of souls who once claimed to be pilgrims have fallen into this ditch and perished there. (Hebrews 3:8-14) Although they convinced themselves that they were bound for the Celestial City, these deluded souls grew weary of sound doctrine, and as a result, sought out false teachers who were more to their liking. (2 Timothy 4:2-4) Since the god of this world blinded their minds, they could neither hear nor receive the Word of God rightly. (2 Corinthians 4:3-4) Therefore, they proved an easy prey for the dangerous pitfall called Error.

This blindness is of a very peculiar sort. It denotes spiritual ignorance of the most vital things, especially the truths concerning salvation, and the ready embracing of deadly error. Those afflicted with it have the light of natural understanding, but not the light of truth and true righteousness. They may glory in their knowledge, but it is according to nature's light, which is really nature's night. It prevents them from coming to Christ, the true light. Thus they abide in spiritual darkness, and are content to have it so.

The Lord Jesus Christ warned against the hazardous ditch called Error, in which the blind lead the blind to mutual destruction. (Matthew 15:13-14) This particular kind of blindness is the result of a hard, impenitent heart, and it characterizes those who lack genuine faith. Because they do not understand the true nature of sin, they view it in external things rather than a matter of the heart. (Matthew 15:15-20) Spiritual blindness also prevents one from understanding the true nature of righteousness, viewing it as good works rather than an inward principle of life and godliness. In this respect, it parallels the legalistic hypocrisy of the Pharisees. (Matthew 23:23-28)

The effects of this blindness are striking in a number of ways. Those afflicted with it can clearly see wrong in others, but are oblivious to their own sin. (Luke 6:39-45) They are also quick to judge and condemn, but highly resistant to reproof and instruction. (2 Timothy 4:1-4) This is one of the most dangerous things about spiritual blindness. It tends to foster a proud, unteachable spirit, which keeps one ignorant of the truth even while boasting a superior knowledge of it. (Proverbs 1:7; Proverbs 26:12; John 9:39-41)

The pitfall called Error is a masterful creation of our archenemy, who is himself a hater of truth and righteousness. As the father of lies, Satan deceives the unwary by perverting the Word of God so as to make it more acceptable to the flesh. Those who are not saved are under his dominion, and since they would rather believe a lie than the truth, they are drawn toward this ditch as by a lodestone.

As the children of God, we have been called out of darkness. Having received the gift of spiritual life, the knowledge of Christ now fills our souls. Once we wandered in the realm of spiritual darkness, but now we walk in the light. (Isaiah 9:2) However, severe trial can bring even a true believer perilously close to the edge of this precipice. In such times, we may grow so weary that we are tempted by that which promises something better, yet is false and deadly. So as we pass through this land of darkness and shadow, we must have our battle armor securely in place. Be forewarned, dear friend in Christ. Our faith will come under severe attack here! If we are to avoid that which is false, we had better be girded with truth. Then the Word of God will lighten our path and guide our steps, even though we walk in dark places. (Psalm 119:105)

Those who pass through the Valley of the Shadow of Death must also take great care not to venture too close to the left side of the path. An extremely dangerous quagmire lies hidden in the shadows there, an abyss composed of hopelessness and despair. This marsh depicts another kind of assault against our faith, this time with the intent to bring about our moral downfall. Multitudes of careless souls, like the man in the iron cage, have been ensnared by sin and fallen into its depths. So travelers beware! This miry pit is not a thing with which to trifle. We are wise to avoid it at all costs.

Sin is a cruel, merciless taskmaster and the unregenerate person is held captive by it; but we who are saved by God's grace have been delivered from sin's power and dominion. It no longer rules us as it did before because we are dead to sin and *alive unto God through Jesus Christ our Lord*. (Romans 6:11-14) Therefore, we do not live according to the dictates of the flesh, but are the servants of righteousness. (Romans 6:16-18) Deliberate sin is both foreign and highly offensive to our new nature. We now delight in God's Word and earnestly desire to do his will.

However, even though sin's power over us is broken, it does not cease to be a problem. As long as we walk in bodies of flesh, we will struggle against sinful tendencies. (Romans 7:21-25) This inner conflict tends to rage more fiercely when we are in a weakened spiritual condition, when we are in the valley. The temptations of the flesh press hard and the particular weaknesses to which we are prone can overtake us, for a time. In the course of this inward battle between the old and the new man, we are often shocked to discover how many sinful attitudes and propensities still reside in us. Moreover, we are humbled to realize how much purging is yet to be done.

Although every child of God must contend with his own flesh, all do not fall into the swamp on the left side of the path. There are some who argue that a godly person cannot fall into this horrible pit, but they have forgotten the shameful example of King David. Even though he was a man after God's own heart, idleness and dereliction of duty gave occasion for his great fall. Instead of riding in the vanguard when his army went to war, he tarried in Jerusalem where he succumbed to temptation, committed adultery, and ordered the murder of an innocent man in the attempt to cover his sin. As a consequence, overwhelming guilt plunged him into an abyss of nearly hopeless despair.

Although David's crimes were heinous, God forgave his broken-hearted, repentant servant and delivered him from the horrible pit into which he had fallen. (Psalm 40:2; Psalm 51) However, his terrible sin was at great cost to David, his family, and his kingdom. (2 Samuel 12:7-12)

As Christians, we must never suppose that we cannot do likewise. Consider the apostle Paul's warning in 1 Corinthians 10:12: *Wherefore let him that thinketh he standeth take heed lest he fall,* and the Lord's admonition in Matthew 6:13 to pray: *Lead us not into temptation, but deliver us from evil.* Scripture is quite clear concerning the ever-present danger represented by this miry pit. (Romans 6:12-23; Romans 8:12-13) Therefore, all who pass through this dark valley should greatly fear falling into the quagmire. Even though some are rescued from its miry grasp, there is no guarantee of recovery. Dear fellow believer, it is not worth the risk! Countless lives of would-be pilgrims have been lost here!

Near the mouth of hell

Those who walk through the Valley of the Shadow of Death must walk a fine line, for in John Bunyan's own words, "The way to heaven lies by the gates of hell." A terrifying thought, is it not? False presumption and deliberate sin are our deadly enemies. They lie in wait, ready to claim the careless soul who wanders out of the path. If we are to steadfastly adhere to the narrow way without veering either to the right or the left, we must hold tenaciously to the truth and diligently maintain a godly, circumspect walk. (Proverbs 4:20-27)

At the time when Christian passed between the deep pit and the quagmire, the way was so dark that he could scarcely see where to place his feet. His precarious situation reminds me of the mythical voyage of Odysseus and his men as they sailed through the narrow passageway between the monster Scylla and the vortex Charybdis. In like manner, Christian was determined to avoid both dangers if possible; therefore, he advanced forward with extreme caution. In so doing, he was able to avoid both the steep precipice and the miry pit. However, it was a narrow escape in which his conflict of soul and heaviness of spirit were evident to anyone who happened to witness it.

Beloved friend in Christ, have you ever been so heavily burdened that you felt sure you could bear no more, only to have your situation become even worse? I have, and more than once. Moreover, I am convinced that it is a common experience among the people of God. Christian reached just such a crisis when he was about midway through the valley. By faith he had ventured deeper into that dark, lonely place, even though common sense urged him to turn back. Mocking thoughts assailed his mind and charged him with utmost folly, yet he refused to be sidetracked. However, when we trust God and his Word when all seems to be against it, we may as well expect to come under increased enemy fire.

Somewhere near the alleged point of no return, it seemed to Christian that his path practically touched the mouth of hell. He could sense its closeness, almost feel the heat of its raging flames, and see its blackened smoke. He even fancied that he could hear the pitiful cries of souls imprisoned in the regions of the damned.

Undoubtedly, there are some who would be highly skeptical of this account and call it the delusions of a seriously disturbed mind. However, the child of God who has walked through the Valley of the Shadow of Death knows better. He understands that a shadow means the presence of a reality, in this case, the close proximity of the kingdom of darkness. The unregenerate person abides in this shadow although he is not aware of it. But even though the child of God has been delivered from its power, his way sometimes leads him perilously close to it.

When we come into conflict with the powers of darkness, the ensuing clash is never a minor thing. Remember Christian's battle with Apollyon? These attacks generally come when our defenses are already down and our resistance is low. We can expect them somewhere near the middle of the valley, at the point when we are afraid to advance forward, yet not daring to turn back! At such times we are likely to hear another voice in the valley, the voice of hopelessness and despair.

Many dear saints of the Lord have yielded to this terrible voice when the candle of faith burns low. As a result, unbelieving fear comes strongly into play, inflicting mental anguish so severe that it defies description. God seems far away, as if he is withholding his help. In our distress, we are tempted to doubt his love and care, and just when we feel least prepared to deal with it, evil looms near.

At such times, we can become so confused that we are unable to properly consider God's Word, draw the needed strength from it, and rest upon its promises. We are bombarded with arguments to which we have no ready answer. This dejected state of mind can trigger thoughts of hopelessness and despair, even in those who are not normally given to depression. You will recall Christian's fall into the Slough of Despond, and also the strange darkness that overtook him on the summit of the hill Difficulty. In the valley it assaulted him once again, more strongly than ever.

Facing the very mouth of hell, as it seemed, Christian raised his sword; but contrary to his expectation, the frightful images that now filled his mind did not yield to it as readily as Apollyon did. Had the sword lost some of its power, or did his present state of mind prevent him from using it effectively? The latter, for sure! In times of deep inner conflict, our hearts can be so overwhelmed that the Word of God seems just beyond our reach. However, there is another choice weapon that is always close at hand, even if we should drop our sword. We can cry out to our heavenly Father and come boldly to his throne of grace for help in our time of need. (Psalm 70) Even though Christian was almost in the depths of despair, he made immediate use of it.

Deliverance did not come immediately, however. In fact, it now seemed that he was about to be destroyed by the evil that hovered so near. He imagined a company of fiends standing by, ready to claim his soul, and as a result, he was almost paralyzed by dismay. The thought of turning back occurred to him, but was quickly rejected as he remembered the many dangers through which he had already passed. Moreover, he considered that perhaps he was through the worst part of the valley.

What about you, dear brother or sister in Christ? Have you ever prayed earnestly for God's help, and instead of relief and deliverance, more trouble came upon you? If you have been a child of God for very long, you undoubtedly have had that experience, and have also probably grappled with the reason why. The answer may lie partially in our tendency to self-reliance, that is, to overestimate our strength and presume our faith to be stronger than it actually is.

The Lord Jesus Christ is the object of our faith; he is the only true anchor of our souls. He is our confidence and his infallible Word of truth the firm foundation upon which we can securely rest. However, saving faith is never a static thing; it must be strengthened through use. So in order for faith to grow strong, it must be put to the test. It must operate and prevail in the face of stiff opposition, which is a thing primarily accomplished in our valley experiences.

Faith's assessment of a difficult situation will always be radically different from the conclusion reached by carnal reason. It was genuine faith that finally enabled Christian to see beyond his present adversity and consider how far God had already brought him. Therefore, he was not about to turn back now. Yet even as he resolved to continue forward, the evil beings seemed to draw even nearer. His heart was fearful, but he pressed onward crying, "I will walk in the strength of the Lord God." At these words, the enemy forces retreated and let him pass.

Like a diamond showcased against a background of black velvet, faith shines brightest when all seems to be against it. Therefore, we must learn to commit our way to God even when we cannot see the path before us. We must continue to press forward even when it is against all odds. Our loving heavenly Father does not require that we understand the reason for our trials or his particular purpose for us in them. However, he does command us to trust him even when all around us seems dark and hopeless. Moreover, we will have little peace until we do. (Lamentations 3:17-24)

So dear afflicted soul, look upward and take heart. Our God reigns! From his eternal throne he oversees all that concerns us, and his heart toward us is one of fatherly compassion. (Psalm 103:13-14, 19) What a comfort it is to know that everything he brings our way is for an infinitely wise and good purpose! Therefore, with firm assurance we can pray with David, *What time I am afraid, I will trust in thee.* (Psalm 56:3)

As Christian made his way still further into the valley, there came a point at which he experienced a thing so terrible that it threatened to undo him altogether. The surrounding darkness combined with the certain knowledge that evil creatures were close by led to such spiritual perplexity that he had trouble discerning his own voice. Taking advantage of his weakness, one of the demonic creatures whispered blasphemous suggestions to his already troubled mind. The thing was so cleverly done and his consternation of mind so complete that Christian feared the horrible blasphemies had come from his own heart and mind. The thought that he had treated his Lord in such a shameful way caused him inward agony unlike anything he had ever known.

These satanic taunts and threats denote another voice heard in this valley, the voice of our great enemy, the ruthless accuser of God's people. His malicious accusations are cleverly designed to destroy our peace and torment our minds concerning our spiritual condition. It is one of his worst weapons, and therefore, one in which he takes great delight in using. When we give heed to his voice, Satan scores a great victory, and we suffer a stunning blow.

Christian was mostly unaware of the source of this attack, and neither did he stop to think that his horrified reaction to the blasphemous thoughts proved that they did not originate in his own heart and mind. On the contrary, his great vexation of soul was evidence of a heart of love for the Savior. Thus it gave the lie to the enemy's false accusations.

Although this latest assault was by far the worst one yet, Christian made use of the powerful weapon All-Prayer once again, saying: *The sorrows of death compassed me, and the pains of hell gat hold upon me: I found trouble and sorrow. Then called I upon the name of the LORD; O LORD, I beseech thee, deliver my soul.* (Psalm 116:3-4) Although the answer to such a cry for help may not come immediately, or in a way that we expect, the prayer of faith will never go unanswered.

* * * *

Even though the Valley of the Shadow of Death is not a literal canyon filled with darkness, danger, and the reverberation of horrific screams, that which it represents is very real. Passing through it denotes a time of great trouble and affliction that can come upon us without warning. It is an inner battle, a season of trial so deeply personal in nature that we seem to be all alone in it. Whatever the outward circumstances that bring it on, the worst part is the mental anguish that attends it, a thing too difficult to express in words, and often too painful or humiliating to share with others. In this particular valley, our hearts and minds are often so consumed by our trouble that we can scarcely think straight.

As John Bunyan makes quite clear using word pictures, the powers of darkness figure prominently in our valley trials. Satan's relentless purpose is to take us down and harm the cause of Christ in doing so. Therefore, he is the author of the voices that tormented Christian so cruelly in the valley. His evil design, his power to deceive, his clever tactics and mighty weapons all seem to give him an overwhelming advantage. But what an encouraging thought it is to know that all of this is according to God's perfect will.

For quite some time, Christian remained in a despondent frame of mind until he heard a voice some distance ahead of him saying: *Yea, though I walk through the valley of the shadow of death, I will fear no evil: for thou art with me; thy rod and thy staff they comfort me.* (Psalm 23:4) Now this was music to his ears! Upon hearing it, Christian took heart and was glad because he knew that he was not alone after all. Another who feared and trusted God was in the same valley, and the knowledge was like good news from a far country. (Proverbs 25:25) If God was with the unseen traveler, as his prayer clearly indicated, then he was with Christian also, in spite of the voices in the valley. Therefore, with renewed hope in his heart Christian picked up his pace, eager to meet the other pilgrim and enjoy his company for the rest of the way through the valley.

Eventually, the day dawned and the darkness passed, as it always does. In the new light of morning Christian looked behind him, anxious to have a better view of the dangers that had pressed so near in the night. It was an appalling sight! The ditch and the quagmire were both clearly visible now, and so was the extremely narrow pathway between them. Christian was still vaguely aware of the evil creatures that had vexed his soul during his long night of despair, but they kept their distance now that morning had broken.

Once again the Lord had delivered Christian from a far greater danger than he imagined. (Job 12:22) Moreover, it may surprise you to learn that the remainder of the valley was even more dangerous than the first half had been. The key difference was that Christian could now see where he was going. Countless snares, pitfalls, and hazards of all sorts waited at every turn of the winding path. However, the Word of God shed such light upon his way that he was able to evade those subtle dangers that have been the downfall of many. (Psalm 119:133)

What an encouragement for us as well! In our darkest hours, we may confidently trust that our Lord will turn the shadow of death into morning. (Amos 5:8) We need not fear when our path leads into the valley because we have the precious promise: *The LORD is good, a strong hold in the day of trouble; and he knoweth them that trust in him.* (Nahum 1:7)

Although we would avoid our valley trials if we could, they are crucial to our spiritual growth and well-being. One of the most important things we learn from them is that we cannot live the Christian life in our own strength. If we would run the race set before us all the way to the finish, we must do so in the strength of the Lord, our all-sufficient Savior. Through him, we are more than conquerors!

He is Lord of the valley as well as Lord of the hill. All that he designs for us is shaped in mercy and working together for our highest good. Therefore, we may rest assured that he will never lead us where his grace cannot keep us. Even though he takes us through times of great trouble and darkness, our shepherd-king is guiding us ever onward to higher ground, to a tableland of spiritual blessings in Christ Jesus that we have never known before.

Study Questions

1. Who are the two men who met Christian at the very border of the valley, bringing disastrous news? How did they describe the valley, and how credible was their testimony? What voice in the valley do they represent?

2. Soon after entering the valley, Christian encountered two specific dangers in the form of steep drop-offs on each side of the narrow path. What are these drop-offs called, and what kind of danger do they represent? Taken together, these hazards denote another voice that is often heard in this valley. What is it called?

3. What do you think John Bunyan meant when he said, "The way to heaven lies by the gates of hell"? How does he illustrate this in Christian's experience as he neared the midway point in the valley? What voice did Christian hear during that dark time?

4. In what way was Christian attacked so terribly that it brought him near the brink of despair? What voice played the major role in causing him such mental anguish? How did Christian respond when pressed hard by the enemy?

5. What did Christian hear in the distance ahead of him that encouraged his heart with renewed hope? How did the dawning of day help him navigate the rest of the valley in spite of its danger?

CHAPTER 28

Journey out of Darkness

I HAVE PASSED THROUGH THIS VALLEY AND WALKED IN ITS SHADOW, MY FRIEND. Since my initial experience in the Valley of the Shadow of Death so closely parallels that of John Bunyan's character, Christian, I remember it most notably as a journey out of darkness. As I write these words many years later, the recollection is a bittersweet memory that is almost surreal. In vain I tried to figure out the specific time or event that marked the beginning of the valley. Today I am still at a loss to know exactly how the darkness came upon me, or why. In retrospect, I realize that it came on gradually before I knew what was happening, much like the silent descent of fog.

Fog is a natural phenomenon that, although treacherous, is somewhat predictable and can be guarded against. Even the most impenetrable fog is temporary. The atmospheric conditions that produce it have a definite beginning, and end. Just as surely as it covers the landscape, the thickest fog will dissipate and the sun will shine brightly once again.

What about the darkness of spiritual depression? I have heard some deny that it can overtake the mind of a child of God. Is it possible for one who is a child of light to sink into this dark place, walk in its shadow, and hear the tempter whisper that he might as well give up and die? Can this really happen to one who is hidden in Christ, making him feel alone, forsaken, and as weak and helpless as a wounded lamb? Yes it is possible, as many dear saints of God can testify from personal experience. William Jay wisely observed that, "Religion does not preclude the evil day; but it prepares us for it; and shews itself to most advantage, when all other resources must fail." [1]

The fact that spiritual depression can be a problem for one who belongs to Christ raises another troublesome question. Why does God allow it to happen? He who is the sovereign ruler over heaven and earth could certainly ordain that his children walk in perpetual sunshine. Then why must so many of them experience this deep, dark night of the soul? Why does our loving heavenly Father permit seasons of darkness into our lives?

Although it is our natural tendency to question why God deals with us as he does, the reasons are not given us to know. We might as well try to measure the universe or fathom the depths of the ocean as to probe the mind of the one who framed the physical creation and set it into motion. (Job 38:1-6; Psalm 33:6-9; Romans 11:33-34) God's ways are mysterious indeed, and inscrutable to our finite comprehension. Such knowledge is too high for us; therefore, we waste precious time and energy when we try to figure out the why.

A proper response to God's providence is to trust him when we cannot see, to bow to his good purpose even though we do not understand it, and to continue in the way in which he leads. Speaking upon this very subject, Oswald Chambers said, "Faith is not intelligent understanding, faith is deliberate commitment to a Person where I see no way." [2] Well said, Brother Chambers! Trust and obey! It is simple, is it not?

Why then, must we spend our strength and reach our wit's end before committing our case to God and his wisdom? I suspect it is because faith often falters in the valley, and self-reliance rises to the forefront. In the hour of crisis, our first thought is to devise a way out of our difficulty instead of seeking God's face and yielding to his will in it. We lean to our own understanding, even though Scripture expressly warns against it, and as a result, the shadow around us deepens. (Proverbs 3:5-7)

One who is truly wise will seek God early rather than as a last resort; but this godly wisdom is usually acquired the hard way. Our valley trials will only be prolonged if we contend against God's purpose for us in them. Moreover, in so doing, we struggle with a mighty adversary, like Jacob did. Dear fellow believer, it is a battle we will not win! Our failure to submit to his will and providence can only end one way, in our utter exhaustion when our strength is finally spent. Then, with no choice but to cling to the one who afflicted us, we begin to learn the secret of true strength. It consists of child-like faith and submission. Our struggles in the valley may leave us weakened, but it is only as the flesh is withered and mortified that we will learn to walk in the strength of the Lord. (Genesis 32:24-32)

I am persuaded that Christian character is more fully developed and faith more perfectly refined as we struggle in the deep places of this valley. Spiritual ground is gained, even though we are at a loss to see it. For this reason, I have little doubt but that every heaven-born soul must experience, at least in measure, the Valley of the Shadow of Death. However, I am equally convinced that no true believer in Christ will ever be lost in its dark depths.

If God chastened us for every shortcoming and failure of which we are guilty, we would be crushed under the weight of it. Since his design is always corrective rather than punitive, he carefully measures our trials so that we are able not only to bear them, but also profit from them. Each affliction is designed to teach us some necessary thing, and to increasingly produce in us the character of our Lord. However, since all is done with tender regard for our frailty, each trial is carefully regulated so that the smoking flax is never extinguished and the bruised reed never broken. (Matthew 12:20)

In our darkest hours, we may be tempted to despair and fear that things will always be so with us, but our long night of affliction will eventually come to an end. The Lord Jesus Christ, the good shepherd who led us into the valley, will deliver us from it in his time. By his grace, the sun will shine once more, bringing light and renewed hope to our souls. Then we will be better able to perceive our heavenly Father's smiling face behind what seemed to be a frowning providence.

How long must we remain in the valley? We must endure it until the purpose of God for us has been accomplished. In my particular case it was approximately two years, and there were times when I feared that I would be swallowed up by the darkness. The fact that I was not is entirely due to God's mercy. Like Jacob of old, the whole experience weakened me in an inexplicable way; but after the fact, I could see more clearly because of it.

The thing for which I prayed so earnestly while in the valley was a right and proper thing. The wrong lay in insisting that the matter be settled in the way I thought best. Like the widow before the unjust judge, I fervently sought the Lord for the desire of my heart, and convinced myself that I was praying in faith. (Luke 18:1-7) In looking back, however, I must confess that unbelieving fear and an impatient spirit really lay behind those prayers. My will was unintentionally contending against God's will because, in my heart, I was afraid to commit the matter to him and leave it there.

In my distressed state of mind, I convinced myself that my way had to be best. After all, it felt so right! Therefore I argued my case before the Lord with every reason I could think of for him to grant my request, but the way of sight is never right! In vain I struggled against my divine opponent until all of my strength was finally gone; but unlike Jacob, I did not prevail. However, even during that dark and agonizing time, I was aware of God's mercy upholding and keeping me from the depths of utter despair. Deliverance did not come until I was finally able to commit to my heavenly Father the matter that caused me such mental anguish. At last, he enabled me to give up the struggle and honestly pray, "Not my will, but thine be done."

As I think back to that dark time, I am so thankful that my heavenly Father did not give me the desire of my heart. The thing I wanted so passionately would certainly have sent leanness to my soul, and to my loved ones as well, I fear. God's omniscient eye saw what I could not see back then; therefore, he withheld the thing for which I so vehemently asked him. Moreover, there was a quite inexplicable outcome from my initial valley experience. The inspiration for this book was born out of it.

Thus the Valley of the Shadow of Death will never destroy the true child of God. Its purpose is to purge away the sinful inclinations that oppose and hinder our progress in grace. Dark and difficult times are necessary in order to teach us that we cannot walk the path of life in our own strength. In the valley, when every prop in which we have trusted is removed and human help is of no avail, overconfidence takes a hard, yet needful, hit. Finding ourselves alone in the midst of severe difficulty, we are better able to understand the true source of our help. (Psalm 108:12-13) It is only as we are made weak that we learn to look upward, and find that truly the Lord is our confidence, our strength and shield, our very present help in trouble. (Psalm 46:1)

Therefore, like the sin of pride, undue self-reliance also has to go; but neither of these sinful inclinations will give way without a fight. We claim to believe that God is sovereign, but in the hour of crisis we find out whether we really do or not. Are we not far more inclined to take matters into our own hands and try to work out a favorable solution? The Lord will often allow us to struggle in this way until we learn that we are not in control of anything, and would ruin it if we were. Then rather than giving mere lip service to God's sovereignty, we will bow before it and be quiet enough in our souls that we can hear him say, *Be still, and know that I am God.* (Psalm 46:10a)

As God's children, we will have little peace until we give up this struggle and commit all into the hands of our loving Lord. A thing much easier said than done, admittedly! We will only do so as we look away from ourselves and walk by faith. (Habakkuk 2:4) When every source of human help is either withdrawn or proven vain, then we will learn to look to our all-sufficient Savior. Moreover, in so doing, we will find that he is truly the God of all comfort. (2 Corinthians 1:3-4)

Undue self-reliance is not the only sinful tendency with which we must struggle in the Valley of the Shadow of Death. Unbelieving fear is another thing we may expect to encounter there. Remember how Christian heard its terrible voice when at the very border of the valley? One particularly troublesome way in which it assaults the mind is with doubts about one's salvation. I can tell you from personal experience that this battle is a terrible and debilitating thing. Tormenting doubt can draw you into a vicious cycle in which you are so consumed with your own misery that you are able to think of little else. (1 John 4:17-18) Therefore, unbelieving fear is a major spiritual hindrance.

This natural inclination will also assault the mind by filling it with dark forebodings about the future. Our Lord specifically warned us not to worry about tomorrow. (Matthew 6:33-34) Our strength will be utterly wasted when we try to bear tomorrow's burdens today. Moreover, we will be unfit for duty as a result. God's promise of provision is sure: *As thy days, so shall thy strength be.* (Deuteronomy 33:25) If we would have peace of mind, even in the valley, we must trust our Lord to provide all that we need in order to serve him. (Philippians 4:6-7)

Since unbelieving fear is a major impediment to our spiritual well-being, its powerful hold over us must be broken. One major purpose of our valley trials is the casting down of this terrible enemy through the strengthening and purification of our faith. (1 Peter 1:5-7) Even though wounded in the battle, genuine faith will eventually conquer unbelieving fear.

So when we find ourselves in the midst of great conflict once again, let us take comfort in the words of Psalm 91:5-7: *Thou shalt not be afraid for the terror by night; nor for the arrow that flieth by day; nor for the pestilence that walketh in darkness; nor for the destruction that wasteth at noonday. A thousand shall fall at thy side, and ten thousand at thy right hand; but it shall not come nigh thee.* If Christ is truly our hiding place, if we dwell in the secret place of the most High and abide under the shadow of the Almighty, we may rest securely upon this great and precious promise.

Dear Christian friend, be assured that our Lord Jesus Christ will never abandon you to walk through the Valley of the Shadow of Death alone. Did he not say: *I am the light of the world: he that followeth me shall not walk in darkness, but shall have the light of life* (John 8:12)? When our way is so dark that we can scarcely see the path before us, he causes his candle to shine upon us. Then by his light we can walk in safety, even when we pass through dark places. (Job 29:2-3) As we grow in the grace and knowledge of the Lord Jesus Christ, we more fully realize how utterly dependent we are upon him for everything. Moreover, this knowledge has the highly beneficial effect of driving us to our knees.

In this regard, it is worthy of particular note that Christian made use of the weapon All-Prayer when unable to wield his sword. No matter how desperate our situation happens to be, or how dark the circumstances in which we find ourselves, we may flee to our Lord in prayer. When every source of human help is withdrawn and self-reliance fails, our powerful weapon All-Prayer is ready for immediate use. As we tarry long at the throne of grace, self-confidence takes a lower place and our confidence in the Lord becomes proportionately stronger. In committing ourselves and all that concerns us to him, we submit to the only one who can safely bring us through the darkest valley.

John Bunyan, who was well acquainted with both valleys, gave sage advice when he exhorts us to "Pray often, for prayer is a shield to the soul, a sacrifice to God, and a scourge for Satan." [3] So let us follow his counsel! Prevailing, importunate prayer is a highly effective weapon that we should master through constant use. (James 5:16-18) In the valley, we generally learn to pray as we never did before, and in the process, the nature of our prayers tends to change. At first, we may pray primarily for deliverance, which is a rather self-centered request. Eventually, however, we are brought to earnestly desire and pray, "Not my will, but thine be done."

* * * *

Dear brother or sister in Christ, there is a sense in which our entire Christian life consists of walking through the Valley of Humiliation and the Valley of the Shadow of Death. Although we will not experience continual fiery trial, neither will we be permitted to settle too comfortably in the world. Since a Christ-like character rarely develops under circumstances of earthly comfort and ease, the furnace of affliction is more or less our allotted portion. (Isaiah 48:10)

The godly qualities that shone to perfection in our Lord Jesus Christ must be gradually developed in us, but our wayward flesh resists the process at every turn. Since we naturally recoil from those things that are painful and difficult, the ultimate perfection to which we are predestined seems slow in coming, does it not? It is hard to imagine ourselves ever attaining it, and yet, we have our Lord's promise in Psalm 138:8: *The LORD will perfect that which concerneth me: thy mercy, O LORD, endureth for ever: forsake not the works of thine own hands.*

The lessons learned in the two valleys are diverse, but their purpose is the same. Therefore, the second valley is really an extension of the first. In the Valley of Humiliation, as pride is abased and the grace of humility gradually developed, we gain greater insight into who we are. (Psalm 138:6) In the Valley of the Shadow of Death, as self-reliance gives way to a sense of utter helplessness, we learn in greater measure who God is. (Psalm 138:7) Perhaps this explains why the sweetest and most spiritually-minded Christians are those who are most intimately acquainted with these valleys.

Speaking through the prophet Habakkuk, God gave a strong consolation to his people when they found themselves under great affliction. He wrote: *Although the fig tree shall not blossom, neither shall fruit be in the vines; the labour of the olive shall fail, and the fields shall yield no meat; the flock shall be cut off from the fold, and there shall be no herd in the stalls: yet I will rejoice in the LORD, I will joy in the God of my salvation. The LORD God is my strength, and he will make my feet like hinds' feet, and he will make me to walk upon mine high places.* (Habakkuk 3:17-19)

This is an especially precious promise to think upon when our path takes us through dark and lonely places. Moreover, when we finally reach the end of the valley, there is no better time to reflect upon God's providence in ordering our circumstances, and his great faithfulness in keeping us every step of the way. (Psalm 37:23-24)

Therefore, let us be of good courage when confronted with a dark valley. By faith we know that the light of day will arise once more, no matter how bleak our circumstances at the time. If we truly belong to the Lord Jesus Christ, the valley of Achor ("trouble") will prove to be a door of hope. (Hosea 2:14-15) So instead of faltering at the border, let us take heart and press forward, saying with David: *The LORD is my light and my salvation; whom shall I fear? The LORD is the strength of my life; of whom shall I be afraid?* (Psalm 27:1)

Lord, my weak thought in vain would climb to search
the starry vault profound;
In vain would wing her flight sublime to find creation's utmost bound.

But weaker yet that thought must prove to search thy great eternal plan,
Thy sovereign counsels, born of love long ages ere the world began.

When my dim reason would demand why that, or this, thou dost ordain,
By some vast deep I seem to stand, whose secrets I must ask in vain.

When doubts disturb my troubled breast, and all is dark as night to me,
Here, as on solid rock, I rest – that so it seemeth good to thee.

Be this my joy, that evermore thou rulest all things at thy will;
Thy sovereign wisdom I adore, and calmly, sweetly, trust thee still. [4]

Study Questions

1. Is it possible for a true Christian to be overtaken by spiritual depression? What is our proper response when God permits seasons of darkness to come upon us?

2. Why must we reach our wit's end in times of trial before committing our situation to the Lord?

3. What is the purpose of the Valley of the Shadow of Death?

4. In addition to undue self-reliance, what is another sinful tendency with which we must struggle in the valley? Name some ways in which this inclination asserts itself and assaults our minds.

5. In what sense is the believer's entire life spent walking through the valley?

Part Eleven

CHANCE ENCOUNTERS ALONG THE WAY

Not every one that saith unto me, 'Lord, Lord,' shall enter into the kingdom of heaven; but he that doeth the will of my Father which is in heaven. Many will say to me in that day, 'Lord, Lord, have we not prophesied in thy name? and in thy name have cast out devils? and in thy name done many wonderful works?' And then will I profess unto them, 'I never knew you: depart from me, ye that work iniquity.'
Matthew 7:21-23

CHAPTER 29

The Cave of the Giants

THE SPIRITUAL JOURNEY UPON WHICH WE AS THE CHILDREN OF GOD HAVE embarked begins with the wondrous miracle of new birth. At that moment, we receive a new heart that is wholly resolved to faithfully follow the Lord Jesus Christ. From the very beginning, however, many things will come against us that try to weaken and overthrow this resolve. Our own sinful tendencies will contend against it and may even gain the upper hand from time to time. In addition, we are sure to encounter opposition from unsaved family and friends, the philosophical arguments of secular humanism, the subtle dangers of false religion and the contempt of unregenerate men. Under certain circumstances, we could also face outright persecution.

Men often represent the Christian life as one that promises worldly success, financial security, and good health. However, these know nothing of the nature of true Christianity. Although multitudes have embraced this lie, the Lord Jesus Christ exhorted his would-be disciples to count the cost before even beginning the journey. (Luke 14: 26-33) Why would he seem to discourage those who were eager to follow him? He did so as a solemn warning that only those who love him more than life itself will remain faithful to the end. They alone will prove true soldiers of the cross who esteem Christ as both the path and the prize. (Philippians 3:7-14)

Christian was one such man, a truehearted pilgrim who has already experienced, in measure, the cost of following his Lord. Most recently he has been delivered from a lengthy period of severe trial, and the impressions of it were still fresh in his memory. As to what he may have expected when he finally reached the end of the Valley of the Shadow of Death, we can only speculate. It is fairly certain, however, that he did not expect to find the ground littered with the mangled bodies of pilgrims who had passed that way before.

While Christian stood gazing at the gruesome sight and pondering the massacre that must have occurred there, he happened to notice a little cave situated not too far from his path. Long ago, this cave had been the common dwelling place of two fearsome beings, giants named Pope and Pagan. The desecrated remains lying unburied near the mouth of the cave represent their unfortunate victims. At the time when Christian passed by, John Bunyan tells us that Pagan had been dead for "many a day" and Pope, due to the infirmities of advanced age, could do no more than make threatening gestures towards pilgrims who passed the entrance to his cave.

What could this mean? Who are these bloodthirsty creatures, and what is behind their malice and cruelty? Moreover, considering their present condition, of what relevance were they to Christian, or to us, for that matter? Are they merely the relics of an age long past? If so, why do they have a place in *The Pilgrim's Progress* at all?

The good news that one of the giants is dead and the other is powerless strikes me as a bit premature. In fact, I strongly suspect that these two creatures have an uncanny way of recapturing both their life and vigor. If this should indeed be the case, we need to know who they are.

These formidable creatures denote two exceptionally strong enemies that have formed an alliance in order to oppose and try to eliminate the people of God. Their status as giants serves as fair warning not to underestimate them. It also indicates that according to outward appearance, they have all the advantages of strength and power on their side. But so it seemed with Goliath of Gath, as he flaunted his superior strength while proudly defying the army of Israel. Yet even as we remember the dramatic downfall of the mighty Philistine, we must not lightly dismiss Pope and Pagan. It is highly significant that the way to the Celestial City passes right by their cave. Through the ages these two giants have captured and devoured many of God's faithful servants.

Why do they harbor such obvious ill-will toward the people of God that they lie in wait to destroy as many of them as possible? Why is their cave allowed to remain so near the path of life? These are questions worthy of our serious attention.

I have often thought that if I could add a subtitle to *The Pilgrim's Progress,* it would be "A Tale of Two Spiritual Cities." John Bunyan brilliantly represents them as the City of Destruction and the Celestial City. The believer's journey consists of his deliverance from the one city and all that takes place until he arrives safely and enters the other. But unlike the cities of London and Paris that figure so prominently in Charles Dickens' famous classic, these two cities are like nothing on earth. They are spiritual entities of which the masses of mankind are largely unaware, although every human being belongs to one or the other of them. A careful study of Scripture confirms their actual existence and the two spiritual kingdoms they represent, which are rival kingdoms in every sense of the word. Thus they are engaged in continuous warfare, and the people of God are caught in the crossfire.

The impetus behind this long-standing conflict can be traced back to the father of all evil, Satan himself, and his rebellion against God and his sovereign rule. (Isaiah 14:12-15) The human race was swept into the mêlée in the Garden of Eden when Adam sinned. As a result of his transgression and fall, God put a deep-seated enmity into place, creating a sharp distinction between his people and the children of darkness. (Genesis 3:15) From that day, a state of war has existed between the seed of the woman – the Lord Jesus Christ and his people – and the seed of the serpent. (Galatians 3)

Scripture often portrays the kingdom of God in terms of a metaphorical city. (Psalm 46:4-5; Psalm 48:1-3; Isaiah 26:1-2; Isaiah 40:1-2, 9; Ezekiel 48:35) The ancient fortress of Zion was a common Old Testament figure used to depict the kingdom of God as his royal abode, the seat of his eternal throne, and the place from which his sovereign rule goes forth. (Psalm 76:1-2; Psalm 2:6; Psalm 99:1-2; Psalm 110:1-2) It also represents the spiritual birthplace and eternal habitation of his people. (Psalm 87:1-6; Revelation 21) The kingdom of God is a kingdom of light and righteousness, a peaceful habitation where truth and justice prevail. (Isaiah 33:20-22; Psalm 89:14-18) It is variously called Mount

Zion, the heavenly Jerusalem, the city of God and Jerusalem which is above. (Galatians 4:26; Hebrews 12:22)

The kingdom of darkness, Satan's evil empire, is also represented in Scripture as a city. It, too, has a name, Babylon the great, and bears the character of a spiritual harlot who is the sum and source of all evil. (Revelation 17:1-5) This monstrous city, this stronghold of every unclean thing, is a horrible entity that is crazed by insatiable blood-lust. (Revelation 17:6) Standing in direct opposition to the sovereign rule of God, she is adamantly committed to the overthrow of his will and purpose. To this end she has formed a confederation with the kings of the earth, an alliance of those who are natural enemies but share a common goal. (Revelation 17:1-3, 9-18) Yet for all of her evil designs and powerful allies, she is a city doomed to destruction. (Compare Jeremiah 51 with Revelation 18)

In fulfillment of the prophecy given in Genesis 3:15, the prince of the kingdom of darkness tried his best to destroy the Lord Jesus Christ and thwart God's purpose of salvation. (Matthew 26:55-56; Luke 22:52-53; Revelation 12:1-10) When he utterly failed to do so, Satan turned the full measure of his wrath against the people of God. (Acts 2:22-36 Revelation 12:13-17) The ensuing conflict rages through every age of human history and always assumes two primary forms: the scornful hatred of an ungodly world, and the fierce opposition spawned by false religion. (Matthew 10:16-22; 1 John 3:9-13) In this, we are able to firmly identify the two cave dwellers. Pope and Pagan embody both the source of the enmity and the relentless persecution of God's people that results from it.

Like Christian, the children of God do not venture far down the path of life before they begin to experience the effects of this enmity. However, a measure of spiritual maturity is required in order to more fully grasp the true nature of the warfare and the dark powers behind it. The cave of the giants so close to the pilgrim's path denotes both this ongoing conflict and its ever-present threat. Although the two crea-tures are not really friends, they often join forces in their opposition to God's people. When considered together, Pope and Pagan represent the kingdom of darkness in both its religious and political aspects.

The mangled bodies scattered on the ground near their cave were pilgrims who had made it safely through the Valleys of Humiliation and the Shadow of Death. They were faithful to their Lord in every adversity, only to be devoured by these hideous creatures. But do not suppose that they were the losers thereby. It was only their bodies that perished. While these giants are sometimes permitted to kill the Christian's body, they cannot touch his soul. (Matthew 10:22-28) In fact, by taking his physical life they merely promote him into the presence of his Lord.

In the strictest sense, the giants represent the two faces of ancient Rome. Pagan signifies the heathen aspect of the Roman Empire, with its pantheon of gods and goddesses, divine honors, and worship of the Caesars. God alone knows how many of his beloved people were cruelly martyred by this bloodthirsty giant! Imperial Rome eventually declined and fell; but another giant arose from the ashes of her destruction – Pope, the face of ecclesiastical Rome. The common cave of these two giants indicates their evil intent and unity of purpose against the people of God.

Thus the malignant intention of pagan Rome against Christians did not really die after all. It merely assumed a new, embryonic form that claimed to be the true church of Jesus Christ, even though it was an imposter of the worst sort. Through the ages, this spiritual harlot has used her political and religious power to try to extinguish true Christians from the face of the earth. So even though Pope did not seem to pose much of a threat at the time when Christian passed by his cave, do not be deceived by his feeble condition. Time and political changes may have altered the scope of his power and influence, but his intimidating gestures toward passing pilgrims reveal that his character is the same as it ever was. Given the opportunity, he will quickly rise again and exert his tyranny with renewed strength and vigor.

We make a grave mistake, however, if we limit our interpretation of Pope and Pagan to the Roman Empire and the ecclesiastical giant that was born out of it. In a more general sense, they personify despotic political powers and false religion in whatever form they happen to appear. There is never a time in history when these two giants are not actively at work, although the degree of persecution they incite may vary greatly. Many times the two have formed a coalition, the sword of human government joined with the burning malice of false religion. (Matthew 23:29-35; Hebrews 11:4; 1 John 3:11-13)

This powerful alliance of church and state then becomes a mighty instrument of oppression against the followers of Jesus Christ, and many saints have perished at its hands. Herein we perceive the age-old enmity between the two rival kingdoms. The forces of darkness are behind this monstrous beast, unseen demonic powers waging constant war against the saints. (Revelation 17)

It might seem logical that the church would fare better once this vicious beast is subdued. However, when outward persecution ceases, another danger takes its place. The church is gradually subverted by the influence of worldly philosophy and the influx of false professors bringing heretical doctrines. While outward persecution tends to purify and strengthen the church, this subtle danger weakens and corrupts her from within. Therefore, we need to beware of both Pope and Pagan in whatever form they happen to appear.

* * * *

It is an inescapable fact that the Christian life is one of armed conflict, from beginning to end. (2 Timothy 2:1-5; 1 Corinthians 9:24-27) The two giants are a terrifying reality to all who pass by their cave, that is, to all who come within the realm of their influence and power. (Galatians 1:3-4) Yet for all of their evil intentions, Pope and Pagan will never overthrow the purpose of God. In fact, they are instruments in God's hands to help fulfill it.

So fear not, dear brother or sister in Christ. When the battle is finally over, all for whom Christ died will appear with him on Mount Zion. (Revelation 14:1-5) Thus the work of God's grace, which began with a miracle, also ends with one. Each one in whom that work of God was truly begun will be accounted an overcomer in that day. (Philippians 1:3-7; Revelation 12:11)

> The path of sorrow, and that path alone,
> Leads to the land where sorrow is unknown.
> No traveler e'er reached that bless'd abode,
> Who found not thorns and briers in his road.
> The world may dance along the flowery plain,

Cheered as they go by many a sprightly strain—
Where nature has her mossy velvet spread,
With unshod feet they yet securely tread:
Admonish'd, scorn the caution and the friend;
Bent upon pleasure, heedless of its end.
But he who knew what human hearts would prove,
How slow to learn the dictates of his love;
That, hard by nature and of stubborn will,
A life of ease would make them harder still;
In pity to the sinners he design'd
To rescue from the ruins of mankind,
Call'd for a cloud to darken all their years,
And said, "Go, spend them in the vale of tears." [1]

Study Questions

1. What shocking sight was in store for Christian when he finally reached the end of the Valley of the Shadow of Death? What sort of massacre had taken place there, and who was responsible for it?

2. Who are the two bloodthirsty giants who share a common cave near the King's Highway? Why do they bear such obvious hatred for the people of God?

3. What is the origin of the great conflict between the kingdom of God and the kingdom of darkness?

4. This conflict has raged through every age of human history, including the present day. What are the two primary forms it assumes? How do the giants named Pope and Pagan figure into the conflict?

5. In the strictest sense, Pope and Pagan represent the two face of ancient Rome. What do they personify in a more general sense that has made them a threat to God's people through the ages?

CHAPTER 30

One Brother Meets Another

AFTER SAFELY PASSING THE CAVE OF THE GIANTS, CHRISTIAN CONTINUED on his way until he came to the top of a small hill. Pausing momentarily to survey the road ahead, he was delighted to see another traveler not too far in the distance. It was the man he heard in the valley, the one who had been his former acquaintance in the City of Destruction! Now he was a pilgrim named Faithful, and since Christian was eager for his company, he called for his friend to stop and wait for him. However, without so much as slowing his pace, Faithful replied: "No, I am upon my life, and the Avenger of Blood is behind me."

At this passing strange response, for there was no one else in sight, Christian was even more determined to catch up with him. Running toward him with all his might, he finally overtook and then ran past him. That Christian was pleased with himself was all too obvious, for John Bunyan tells us: "Then did Christian vaingloriously smile, because he had gotten the start of his brother." He congratulated himself a bit too soon, however, because in failing to watch his steps, he stumbled and fell. Moreover, he was unable to get up by himself and was forced to lie in the dust until Faithful caught up with him and helped him to his feet.

What is the meaning of this seemingly trivial incident, and why was Christian so proud of himself just because he outran his brother? Could it mean he thought himself the more spiritual of the two? If so, how did he draw that conclusion? Was it by comparing their present circumstances? At the time, Faithful was fleeing for his life from the Avenger of Blood, while Christian was enjoying a season of relative peace. (His earlier battle with Apollyon had apparently slipped his mind!). If he did judge his brother by outward appearance alone, Christian may well have thought that he was the stronger man, that is, until he ended up flat on the ground!

As followers of the Lord Jesus Christ, we are indeed engaged in a race, but not one in which we compete against one another. What's more, self-confidence and fleet feet actually place a stumbling block in our way. It is the godly qualities of faith, humility, and the fear of the Lord that speed us along as we run this particular race. With these virtues operative within, we will be able to run the race with patience, looking unto Jesus, the author and finisher of our faith. (Hebrews 12:1-2)

If we are honest, however, most of us will admit that our tendency to pride causes us many a difficult struggle and more than the occasional fall. We may be tempted to excuse it, since pride is such a universal failing, but it is a serious offence against God and our fellow man. Moreover, it sets us up for big trouble down the road.

One particularly ugly thing about a proud spirit is that it makes us feel superior to others and show a condescending attitude toward them. But as Christian just discovered, pride is a subtle snare that can cause a humiliating fall. For the moment he had forgotten the scriptural admonition: *Wherefore let him that thinketh he standeth take heed lest he fall.* (1 Corinthians 10:12) As a result, he found himself in urgent need of help from one whom he judged to be weaker.

As Christian should have known by now, pride always brings us to the dust, and yet, a good thing resulted from the whole experience. He quickly realized that he was not nearly as strong as he had presumed. Moreover, he knew that he had probably misjudged a dear brother in Christ.

In spite of Christian's sinful behavior and humiliating fall, there is no hint that Faithful gloated inwardly because he got what he deserved. On the contrary, Faithful's immediate offer of assistance, with no comment upon Christian's rude, patronizing behavior, demonstrated the rare quality of godly humility. Does it not make you wonder which of the two men was really the more spiritual?

Dear friend in Christ, this incident reminds me of our Lord's admonition to his disciples after they were arguing among themselves as to which of them would be the greatest in the kingdom. In Mark 9:35 he both rebuked and instructed them by saying: *If any man desire to be first, the same shall be last of all, and servant of all.* How often we forget this fundamental kingdom principle! (Matthew 5:3-5) So before we judge Christian too harshly, perhaps we should ask ourselves how many times we have stumbled and fallen because of sinful pride. Have we not also found ourselves in need of help from a brother or sister whom we regarded as weaker in the faith? Since we tend to be poor judges of our own spiritual growth and maturity, why would we think ourselves competent to judge our brethren in Christ?

George Whitefield wisely observed: "Self-righteousness is the last idol that is rooted out of the heart." [1] His keen insight is all too true, undoubtedly due to the strong link that exists between the sins of self-righteousness and pride. It is an easy matter to criticize those who struggle with temptation and sin, especially when their particular area of weakness does not happen to be ours. How quickly we can fall into the self-righteous mindset of lifting ourselves up as a standard by which to judge others! Moreover, we often apply a double standard by excusing our own failings while censuring the faults of others. (Matthew 7:1-5)

Can a child of God really be guilty of harboring a self-righteous, hypocritical spirit? Yes, we can! John Flavel observed, "Hypocrisy is a weed naturally springing in all ground. The best heart is not perfectly clear or free of it." [2] Even though hypocrisy can take root and grow anywhere, God will not permit it to flourish in the hearts of his children. Those who are guilty of it can expect to feel the sting of his chastening rod.

Like a hypocritical spirit, the sin of pride is a serious heart condition. It largely determines not only how we view others, but also the way in which we behave toward them. A proud heart will tend to stir up strife and contention, while godly humility promotes peace and unity. (James 3:13-18) Moreover, pride causes us to exalt ourselves at the expense of our brethren, but a truly humble mind honors others above self. (Romans 12:10)

The apostle Paul gave very specific instruction concerning how we are to treat our brethren in Christ when he said: *Let nothing be done through strife or vainglory; but in lowliness of mind let each esteem other better than themselves. Look not every man on his own things, but every man also on the things of others.* (Philippians 2:3-4) The way in which we obey this command says much about our spiritual maturity, or lack thereof. Therefore, great care should be taken in this matter of judging our brethren in Christ, lest we be guilty of hypocrisy. When our hearts are right before the Lord, we will first judge ourselves, and then be more inclined to think twice before judging others. (Galatians 6:1)

In spite of the less-than-ideal circumstances of their meeting, Christian and Faithful quickly found that they were kindred souls. The immediate bond between them was based upon something far deeper than similar backgrounds, compatible personalities, and mutual interests. It was a rare and special bond of love that spans every racial, cultural, and socio-economic barrier.

The Lord Jesus Christ is the source of this brotherly unity, so beautifully pictured in Psalm 133. It does not denote total agreement in all things, however, nor does it rule out personality conflicts and other points of dispute. What is does signify is the spiritual relationship and communion of those who are in agreement concerning the most essential things. (Amos 3:3) Far from being an all-inclusive unity, it is based upon the saving knowledge of Christ and fellowship in his Gospel. (Philippians 1:1-7; 1 John 1:1-3). Therefore, it is a bond only known by those who are of like faith.

Christian and Faithful were now eager to become better acquainted as brothers in Christ. In spite of any personal differences, they shared these most vital things in common. Did they not love and serve the same Lord, and desire to talk about him? Were they not walking the same path toward the same heavenly destination? Had they not experienced many of the same things along the way? Yes, to all! They quickly discovered that they were well-suited traveling companions, for the substance of their conversation centered upon spiritual things. But is not this ever the case when one brother or sister in Christ meets another?

Faithful's testimony

Although it is generally unwise for us to compare our Christian experience too closely with that of other believers, we will find it profitable to share the different ways in which the Lord has led us. Many a brother or sister in Christ has been encouraged and strengthened in the faith through the timely help of a fellow pilgrim. This will certainly prove to be the case with Christian and Faithful.

As the two men headed down the road together, Faithful related some of the particulars of his experience so far. In some respects, it had been quite different from Christian's. His journey began, as it does for each true child of God, with deliverance from the City of Destruction. Although he had heard the report of Christian's departure from the city, Faithful did not leave until a while afterward. His testimony suggests that he was casually acquainted with Christian back then, so perhaps he was directly affected by Christian's experience. However, he remained in the doomed city until, to quote him directly: "I could stay no longer." This could have been Christian's testimony as well.

We recall that Christian's flight from the City of Destruction did not take place in an obscure corner. For a while, it was the talk of the town. Many who witnessed his terrible struggle were moved by it, at least temporarily. One man, our old friend Pliable, went so far as to accompany Christian out of the city, that is, until they both fell headlong into the Slough of Despond. At that point, Pliable left both his resolve and his traveling companion in the slough, and hastened back to his former life. Since all of this took place before Faithful left the city, he was able to give Christian an update. According to his report, Pliable did not receive a hero's welcome upon his return. Quite the contrary, for he was reviled as a turncoat and a coward.

Although God's people are often mocked and hated by the world, they are also grudgingly respected. Moreover, in times of crisis, those who are offended by their Christian testimony and godly lives will often seek their counsel and help. But no one respects a traitor, and no one trusts him either! So Pliable's credibility was destroyed. Furthermore, his quick renunciation of the Christian faith made him an object of derision by the very same ones who had mocked and scorned Christian for his firm resolve. Interesting, is it not?

Poor Pliable! He found himself an outcast of sorts, despised even by former friends and associates. Therefore, as Faithful personally witnessed, he was ashamed to show his face in public, but this was far from being his worst problem. Spiritually speaking, his condition was much worse now than it had been before he followed Christian out of the City of Destruction. His judgment would be far worse for having heard the truth and then turning from it. (2 Peter 2:20-22) Christian's heart was saddened to hear this report, and any lingering hope for his former companion was now completely dashed.

As Faithful began to relate some of his experience after he left the City of Destruction, it is interesting to note the ways in which it differed from Christian's journey. For one thing, Faithful escaped the Slough of Despond without falling in, and reached the Wicket Gate without incident. As to his experience between the Wicket Gate and the hill Difficulty, he had very little to say, but one striking difference between his journey and Christian's came to light at this point. For reasons that are not made clear, Faithful did not visit the Palace Beautiful. Unlike Christian, who was overtaken by darkness on the hill Difficulty and sought refuge in the Palace, Faithful enjoyed full daylight when he passed that way. We can only speculate as to why John Bunyan had such an extraordinary child of God by-pass this important means of grace.

Faithful's uncommon spirituality in spite of the fact that he was not part of an organized assembly reminds us of some important truths, however. As vital as the ministry of the local church is to our spiritual growth and well-being, our salvation is in no way contingent upon church membership. Many trust that all is well with them simply because they have been baptized and joined a church. So in and of itself, church membership is a poor indicator of one's spiritual condition. Moreover, God is in no way limited. He nurtures and leads each of his children in ways that he deems best.

Even though Faithful had lived up to his name so far, he admitted to being accosted by one named Wanton, from whose subtle wiles he had barely escaped. From this disclosure we learn that Faithful struggled with sexual temptation, and desired to share it with his newfound companion.

Wanton's name speaks for itself. It denotes a woman who is lewd and unchaste in both character and conduct, a moral derelict who has cast off every restraint and delights in leading others down the same path. To this end, she attempts first to deceive and then ensnare heedless souls. (Proverbs 7:6-12) Although she is bold and shameless, this hunter of men is noted for her subtle wiles. Outward beauty and a flattering tongue are her most effective weapons. (Proverbs 6:23-25; Proverbs 7:4-5) However, her flattering words promise that which she can in no way deliver. (Proverbs 5:3-5; Proverbs 7:10-21)

Due to her hardness of heart and long-deadened conscience, she cares nothing about the pain and suffering she inflicts upon others. In addition to her willing captives, she has left countless broken hearts, devastated homes, and shattered lives in her wake. Even though she is well aware of the damage she has done, her attitude is one of callous indifference. (Proverbs 30:20)

This character named Wanton figures rather prominently in the book of Proverbs. Solomon describes her as a strange woman and strongly warns his hearers to avoid her at all costs. She is a strange woman because she is an alien to truth, having deliberately turned from God and his ways. (Proverbs 2:16-17) Her profane manner and adulterous character mark her as a stranger to virtue and righteousness, even though she may claim to be religious. (Proverbs 7:13-15) To her way of thinking, the idea that she is morally accountable for her behavior is a foreign concept. She cares nothing for her own soul, and gives even less thought to the welfare of her victims.

Scripture likens Wanton the seductress to a deep ditch and a narrow pit. (Proverbs 23:27-28) No one who falls into her trap escapes unharmed, and many have perished therein. (Proverbs 7:25-27) Yet no one can claim to be her innocent victim. He who yields to her charms is fully accountable to God for his actions, and the terrible consequences that result from them. (Proverbs 6:32-33)

The temptation to sexual sin has a powerful appeal to those who are prone to it, as Faithful must have been. However, he resisted it by shutting his eyes to Wanton's charms so that he "would not be bewitched with her looks." To turn from such a strong temptation was no easy matter for him. Although he escaped from the trap she set for him, he was sensible that it was a close call. His words "I know not whether I did wholly escape her or no" are highly illuminating. They reveal both his honest character and the near success of Wanton's attempted seduction. Moreover, Faithful knew himself well enough to suspect he would probably battle this temptation again.

Why had Wanton pursued a man like Faithful so relentlessly? It was partly because she loves a challenge. Like certain predatory creatures in the animal kingdom, she enjoys the hunt more than anything. Such is her profligate nature that once her prey is captured, it begins to lose its appeal. To successfully seduce a wicked man is not much of a triumph for the likes of Wanton. However, it would be a rare victory to cause the downfall of a godly man such as Faithful. Since the captives she prizes most highly are those who are hardest won, she will patiently and persistently hunt for the precious life. (Proverbs 6:26)

How did Faithful escape her clutches when many others have been caught in her net? He desired above all things to walk uprightly before the Lord. True wisdom, the fear and knowledge of God, had taken deep root in his soul. (Proverbs 2:10-16; Titus 2:11-14) It was this godly principle within that had delivered him from the tempter's power and kept him in the path of life. (Proverbs 14:27) Moreover, the Word of God was highly instrumental in keeping Faithful from defiling himself. He was evidently a diligent student of the Word and had committed much of it to memory. So when faced with strong temptation, the Spirit of God brought the Scriptures immediately to his mind. (Psalm 119:11) He could not deny that there is pleasure in sin, but he also understood that the contentment it promises is a lie. In his heart, Faithful knew well that the pleasures of sin last only for a season. (Hebrews 11:25) The tormenting guilt and shame, however, remain long after the brief pleasure is gone. (Proverbs 7:21-23)

It was by God's grace alone that Faithful maintained his integrity and escaped out of the hand of the seductress, just as young Joseph long ago. Yet since he refused to yield to her charms and the precious life escaped her net, Wanton scorned Faithful bitterly. Perhaps she even plotted revenge against him, as Potiphar's wife did to Joseph, by bringing false accusations against him. (Genesis 39:7-21) Who can say what such a woman is capable of, when scorned?

Although women can certainly be guilty of sexual sin, John Bunyan depicts here a temptation that is primarily aimed toward men. Wanton has been around for a very long time. She lives in every age and can be found in every civilization and culture. Many an otherwise sensible man has been utterly ruined because he could not resist her beauty, flattering words, and beguiling ways.

We tend to think of Wanton as living on the periphery of decent society, lurking in the shadows, and plying her trade under cover of darkness. In some cases, this is true. Yet in our modern enlightened day, she is found everywhere and has no scruples about flaunting herself openly. Her decadent influence has permeated just about every aspect of society. What's worse, she can enter the privacy of a home and corrupt the hearts and minds of even the very young, by means of the Internet and other forms of media. There can be little doubt that Wanton is harder to avoid today than when John Bunyan wrote of her. But godly Job gave sage advice when he wrote: *I made a covenant with mine eyes; why then should I think upon a maid?* (Job 31:1) If diligently followed, his wise counsel will help one to escape her snare, even in our present day.

Valiant struggle with Adam the first

After his narrow escape from Wanton, Faithful had very little respite before being assaulted again, this time at the foot of the hill Difficulty and in the form of a seemingly harmless old man. The man's name was Adam the first and he came from the town of Deceit, a densely populated suburb of the City of Destruction. The stranger approached Faithful with a confident air and a carefully worded proposal that if Faithful would follow him home, he would be rewarded with many delightful things.

Who is this seemingly fragile stranger? Why did he openly confront Faithful and attempt to lure him back to the town of Deceit? He is really no stranger at all, but depicts the sinful disposition we all received from the first Adam. (Romans 5:12-14; 1 Corinthians 15:21-22) He rightfully claims every son and daughter of earth as his natural progeny and rules in their hearts in spite of outward restraints. Not only do his children serve sin, they have neither the will nor the power to break free of its awful bonds. (John 8:34-36; Ephesians 2:1-3)

When we are saved by God's grace, the power of sin is broken and we are no longer the servants of sin. The old man is crucified with Christ. (Romans 6:6-7) Adam the first is dethroned and no longer reigns in our mortal body. (Romans 6:6-13) We serve a new master and walk an infinitely higher path. Yet even though the dominion of sin is broken, Adam the first does not cease to trouble us. Sinful tendencies still cause great grief and the shedding of many a tear. We earnestly desire to be rid of these fleshly hindrances so that we might walk with the Lord unopposed. But for reasons known only to God, he has purposed that we struggle with our imperfections even as we walk the perfect path.

Our greatest struggles are usually inward, are they not? Things of which those around us are largely unaware, unless we choose to share them. This was the case with Faithful and his conflict with Wanton and Adam the first. In opening his heart to Christian he ran the risk of being misunderstood, but Faithful's disclosure was no foreign concept to Christian. The circumstances of his particular conflict varied somewhat from Faithful's, but Christian understood well that Adam the first is a common problem with God's children. Every fleshly tendency or weakness with which we struggle can be traced directly to him.

As Faithful relates the details of his inner struggles, we will gain valuable insight into the relentless warfare of our own flesh, the old man, Adam the first. The place of his residence is enough to warn us that Adam the first is not to be trusted. It is his practice to mislead, delude, and cheat any who give him a hearing. He offers plenty of allurements, but all of them are designed to lead us out of the narrow way. He is clever also, tempting us with things that appeal to our particular susceptibilities and presenting them in such a way as to seem innocent and harmless.

It is little wonder that Faithful nearly fell for his line. Before he consented to follow the aged man, however, he paused to consider what the Scriptures had to say. In doing so, he remembered that believers are expressly commanded to put off the works of Adam the first. (Ephesians 4:17-24) He promotes the works of the flesh, which are directly opposed to the fruit of the Spirit. (Galatians 5:19-24) Because it is his nature to dominate, Adam the first must be given no place. He must be put off, as one would cast aside a soiled, tattered garment, which is a thing much easier said than done! According to the personal testimony of the apostle Paul, the mortification of Adam the first engages the Christian in a life-long battle. (Romans 7:18-25; 1 Corinthians 9:24-27; Galatians 5:16-17)

In trying to close the deal with Faithful, Adam the first made a strange proposal to him – the offer of all three of his daughters in marriage. Their names were The Lust of the Flesh, the Lust of the Eyes, and the Pride of Life. Together, they comprised the best things that Adam the first has to offer, but what would such a marriage mean to a godly man like Faithful? It would ensnare him in an unequal yoke of the very worst sort, one that is expressly forbidden to believers in Christ. (2 Corinthians 6:14-18; 1 John 2:15-17) If entered into, this marriage would capture his heart and bind him to the very things that caused man's original sin. (Genesis 3:6) Furthermore, it would entangle him in an unholy alliance that would jeopardize his very soul. (James 4:1-4)

When considered from a scriptural point of view, the seemingly generous offer made to Faithful is easily seen for what it really is. Adam the first will always try to draw our hearts away from Christ, but his most tempting allurements give no lasting satisfaction. They promise fair, but leave a spiritual void. At best they give temporary pleasure, but always strike a deathblow in the end. (Romans 6:20-23)

Although Faithful admitted to Christian that he was somewhat inclined to yield to Adam the first, he refused to do so. Once again the Spirit of God brought the Scriptures to his mind, exposing the enemy for what he really is. Like Wanton, Adam the first promises what he can never deliver. He deceives, allures, entraps and finally kills! (James 1:13-15)

Like his encounter with Wanton, Faithful did not escape from Adam the first uninjured. As he labored to climb the hill Difficulty, his flesh opposed each step forward. When he reached the midway point, somewhere near the arbor where Christian had slept, he was suddenly overtaken from behind, knocked down, and left for dead. Although Faithful begged for mercy, his unknown assailant, Moses, refused to show mercy because of his "secret inclining to Adam the First." Faithful's situation was desperate! He would surely have perished at the hands of this avenger of blood had not an advocate stepped forward to intervene on his behalf. Even in his dazed condition, Faithful recognized that his deliverer, who commanded the attack to cease, was none other than his Lord.

Poor Faithful was hounded, overtaken, and knocked down by Moses! He had been left for dead, yet was living still! Although hotly pursued by the avenger of blood, he was still fleeing for his life! But what is the meaning behind this Old Testament allusion to the ancient cities of refuge? Does that provision of so long ago apply to one who has already fled to Christ for refuge from the wrath to come? Yes, dear fellow pilgrim, it does.

The Mosaic Law clearly stipulated that deliberate murder was a capital crime for which no clemency was to be shown. However, it also contained a proviso in cases where there were extenuating circumstances. After the Hebrew people were settled in the land of Canaan, six Levitical cities throughout the land were designated as cities of refuge. These safe havens were not a man-made idea. They were divinely appointed and carefully chosen for their location and ease of accessibility. (Exodus 21:13; Deuteronomy 19:1-10) One who had committed involuntary manslaughter, and was fleeing from the avenger of blood, could run to the closest city of refuge and be granted sanctuary until the proper authorities could hear his case. (Joshua 20) If they judged the murder to have been accidental, the manslayer would be given permanent asylum there.

My fellow believer in Christ, do you not see the connection between the manslayer fleeing from the avenger of blood and our struggles with Adam the first? Some would have us believe that he is eradicated when we are born again; but if this were true, temptation would have no effect upon us. Although we desire to be free of sin and walk in ways that please the Lord, our flesh opposes us continually. Sometimes it gains the upper hand and we yield to it. In Faithful's conflict with Adam the first, John Bunyan has clearly depicted our ongoing struggle, but he also illustrates the love of righteousness and hatred of sin that marks God's people from all others. (1 John 3:7-10)

This being the case, nothing is more unbecoming in a professing Christian than a casual attitude toward sin. We are not freed from sin in order to do our own thing. On the contrary, we are freed in order to serve and follow our Lord Jesus Christ, to yield our members as servants to righteousness unto holiness. (Romans 6:14-19) Presumptuous sin characterizes man's fallen nature, but the practice of deliberate sin is foreign to the child of God. Commenting upon this subject, William Jay said: "Poison in a serpent never produces sickness, but it does in a man; it is natural to the one, but not to the other. Sin does not distress the sinner; but it offends beyond every thing else the renewed mind." [3]

Then what can we do when we stumble and fall while struggling to walk uprightly? Is there a safe haven where we can find sanctuary when the avenger of blood is right on our heels? Yes, there is such a haven when we are in distress. The Lord Jesus Christ is our city of refuge. He is a precious, divinely appointed shelter to whom we may flee when pressed hard by temptation. (1 John 1:5-10) By his blood, he cleanses us from all sin and restores us to fellowship with himself. However, this gracious provision is only for those who walk in the light, as he is in the light. Those who practice deliberate sin have no valid claim to it. However, for those who pursue holiness and follow after Christ, there is a fountain opened for all uncleanness, and the troubled conscience can find peace and rest there. (Zechariah 13:1) As his redeemed children, we have continual access to this fountain of perpetual grace. (Hebrews 10:19-22)

What about the avenger of blood who was in such hot pursuit of Faithful? Thinking once again about this Old Testament allusion, we recall that the avenger of blood had the right to kill the accused manslayer if he dared to venture outside the city of refuge. (Numbers 35:26-28) In its historical context, the avenger of blood was the slain victim's next of kin, but who is it that hounds the children of God as we walk the path of life?

The law of God, as signified by Moses, is the ultimate avenger of blood. Since it reflects God's righteous character, the law is perfect and holy; therefore, it demands exact justice for every breach in thought, word, or deed. It demands satisfaction for each transgression, whether great or small. The law judges and condemns the sinner, but can do nothing to deliver him from sin's penalty or power. Like an indignant avenger of blood, divine justice pursues every member of Adam's race. (Ezekiel 18:4; Matthew 10:28; Romans 3:19-20; Romans 6:23) For those who have no hiding place, it will overtake and slay them one day.

However, for all of its forbidding countenance toward the sinner, the law had a gracious design. Concealed within various types and shadows, it pointed toward one to come who would deliver men from its condemnation, the Lord Jesus Christ, the perfect, sinless Lamb of God. Through a life of perfect obedience and by the offering of himself as the propitiation for sin, he fulfilled the law and satisfied its every demand in the stead of his people. (Romans 3:21-28) In bearing our sins in his own body on the cross, he forever removed the sting of death and the curse of the law on our behalf. (1 Corinthians 15:55-57; Galatians 3:10-14) So for those of us who are in Christ, divine justice has been fully satisfied once for all.

Why then was Faithful knocked down and left for dead due to his secret inclination toward Adam the first? Sin defiles the mind and conscience, and our great adversary loves to taunt us with every shortcoming of which we are guilty. Sad to say, his accusations are all too true. As a result, our own conscience becomes an avenger of sorts, by self-accusation and condemnation. Figuratively speaking, feelings of guilt can throw us off our stride and leave us in the dust. Moreover, this avenger of blood will continue to hound us and strike again and again.

Nevertheless, take heart my fellow pilgrim. We have a hiding place to which we may flee when our hearts are overwhelmed with the sense of our failure and guilt. The Lord Jesus Christ is a tower of strength to whom we may run and be safe. (Proverbs 18:10) He is our shield and defender, no matter what accusations the avenger of blood may bring against us. As our great high priest, he makes intercession for us and restores us to fellowship when we have sinned and are repentant. So as long as he lives and reigns on his throne, divine justice has no legitimate claim upon us. (Hebrews 7:24-28)

The ancient cities of refuge offered no asylum for those guilty of deliberate murder. Likewise, the Lord Jesus Christ is no safe haven for those who practice willful, presumptuous sin. Far from being a license to sin, his gracious forgiveness is reserved for his penitent children who stumble while walking in the paths of righteousness. (Romans 6:1-2)

Faithful was well grounded in these precious truths. Therefore, he fled to the Lord Jesus Christ with every accusation brought against him by his own contrite heart and tender conscience. So must we! By means of God's Word and the power of his Spirit, we will find grace in times of weakness and strength to overcome. As for Faithful, his nemesis will continue to stalk him, and he will continue to flee. Yet in the process, Adam the first will gradually diminish in strength.

Most of us are not as forthright about our struggles as was Faithful. In general, we try to put our best foot forward, hoping to make a favorable impression. Since our worst battles are usually inward, we may succeed in hiding them from others, but our heavenly Father is not deceived for a moment. He sees us as we really are, but also sees what we shall one day become, by his grace.

Faithful's ordeal in the valley

In the character of Adam the first, John Bunyan gives a scriptural name to the flesh principle that causes us so much trouble as God's people. Its presence within poses a terrible dilemma, for we cannot rid ourselves of it, and yet, it must be put to death. Therefore, the Valley of Humiliation was on Faithful's travel itinerary just as it had been with Christian. His experience while there was different in several respects, however. The monster Apollyon did not attack him directly and engage him in hand-to-hand combat, but Faithful discovered that our great adversary wears many faces and assaults in numerous forms. So even though his approach was not the same, Apollyon was lying in wait for Faithful also, as soon as he entered the valley.

The initial attack came in the form of one named Discontent, who bombarded Faithful with thoughts that he found difficult to ignore. They were thoughts that called into question the goodness and purpose of God and protested vehemently against the life of faith. Since discontentment is driven by self-interest, it dogged Faithful's steps and opposed his passage all the way through the Valley of Humiliation. The substance of its argument was that the valley was entirely without honor, and Faithful's friends, Pride, Arrogancy, Self-Conceit and Worldly Glory, would have no part of it. Although Faithful was badly shaken by this argument, he had enough spiritual insight to recognize that his former friends were really deadly enemies. He must claim an affinity to them by nature, but he had soundly rejected them. To follow their counsel was a risk he was not willing to take.

Since discontentment is one major characteristic of the Adamic nature, it poses great risk to our spiritual health and well-being. Those who struggle with it say that it is a particularly difficult thing to be rid of. Likewise, true contentment, the inseparable companion of godliness, is a thing that is painstakingly slow to acquire. (Philippians 4:11; 1 Timothy 6:6; Hebrews 13:5-6) So even though Faithful dreaded walking through the Valley of Humiliation, he understood that there was great benefit to be gained there. (Proverbs 18:12)

Through the help of the Holy Spirit, Faithful won this battle with discontentment, but a little further into the valley, he met with another strong enemy named Shame. In relating this particular incident to Christian, Faithful observed that, in his opinion, Shame "bears the wrong name." He was right about that! This villain is very bold in his manner, and surprisingly aggressive in making his case.

Fellow believer, sooner or later we, too, will encounter this bold opponent who haunts the Valley of Humiliation. Perhaps you have done so already. According to Shame, Christianity is for wimps, and a tender conscience is a cowardly thing. He further argued that striving to be holy in speech and conduct places one out of step with those who are more sophisticated and enlightened in their views. This is true enough! Moreover, he pointed out that to be a follower of Jesus Christ is to be found in rather poor company. Shame reinforced his point by quoting recent statistics indicating that relatively few of the world's great ones are to be found in their ranks. Again, touché, according to 1 Corinthians 1:26-29!

To further strengthen his argument, Shame declared that those who venture all in order to follow the Lord Jesus Christ are accounted fools by the world. They are often reckoned to be ignorant and out of touch because of their biblical convictions and uncompromising standards. They are fools for esteeming Christ over their earthly comforts, and for seeking first his kingdom and righteousness above all else! They are fools because they live by faith rather than human ingenuity, and walk in God's right ways instead of conformity to the world! They are fools for confessing Christ openly before a hostile world and risking the consequences of that! Then Shame concluded his rant with a familiar insult, "Christians are religious fanatics who are a little strange in the head."

These are potent arguments, are they not? They strike a powerful blow because they contain an element of truth. Since the lives and testimonies of God's people make those around them uncomfortable, we will be mocked and despised. Because no one wants to be thought a fool or be shamed before others, there is the temptation to avoid the reproach that comes from open identification with Christ.

This was the essence of Faithful's great struggle with Shame, but as he considered the matter according to the Scriptures, he began to see things in a proper light. Therefore, he concluded *that which is highly esteemed among men is abomination in the sight of God.* (Luke 16:15) Reproach is part of the cost of following the Lord Jesus Christ. (Mark 8:34-38; Philippians 3:7-8)

Faithful's thinking had been skewed by giving Shame a hearing. Listening to the arguments of his flesh caused him major problems until he remembered that the fear of shame does not even consider God, his Word, and the certainty of judgment. In the final analysis, the thoughts and opinions of men, even the best and brightest of them, will count for nothing. God will judge according to his perfect righteousness, and mete out exact justice. So Faithful wisely concluded that God's Word should be heeded and obeyed, though all else should argue against it.

Shame is the result of the fear of man, an inordinate fear that must be displaced by the fear of God. (Isaiah 8:11-13) According to Proverbs 29:25: *The fear of man bringeth a snare: but whoso putteth his trust in the LORD shall be safe.* To be accounted a fool for the sake of Christ is to be truly wise! To belong to Christ, though it entails great loss, is to gain unsearchable riches! Moreover, as Christian reminded his brother: *The wise shall inherit glory: but shame shall be the promotion of fools.* (Proverbs 3:35) Therefore, recognizing Shame for the terrible enemy it is, Faithful commanded him to depart.

However, Shame is a bold, persistent adversary that continued to torment Faithful and try to shake his resolve, even though he refused to be swayed. Most willingly he remained in the company of those faithful souls who go outside the camp, bearing the reproach of the Lord Jesus Christ. (Hebrews 13:13)

* * * *

Once in a while you will meet a professing Christian who denies any such struggle as Faithful has just related. In fact, he might go to great lengths to paint an unrealistic picture of himself and have you think that all is well with him, spiritually and otherwise. To hear him tell it, the temptations of the world hold no charms for him. He harbors no secret longings of which he is ashamed, or sinful attitudes that vex his soul, or so he would have you believe.

The man who bore the spiritually compelling name of Faithful was of an entirely different character. He was a humble soul, and honest enough to admit his own frailties and shortcomings. Some might be afraid of how such an admission would make them appear to others, but this was not his chief concern. As his name indicates, his highest goal was to be a true and faithful servant of Jesus Christ. He was a man who was full of faith, and wholehearted in his love for the Lord. Moreover, he was unswerving in his allegiance to the cause of Christ, honorable in his dealings with men, and proven worthy of their confidence. Altogether, he was a man who possessed many sterling qualities.

Even though he struggled with Adam the first, Faithful fled from anything that might distract or move him from his steadfast devotion. As we ponder his journey so far, are you not struck by his spiritual insight into the nature of the Christian's warfare, and his practical application of this knowledge? In each temptation, he looked to the Scriptures for guidance and help. In addition, he interpreted each trial and circumstance in light of the Word of God, submitted to its counsel, and endeavored to walk according to its instruction. (Proverbs 4:5-13)

Although he would be the last to say so, Faithful lived up to his name. He had a heart that was valiant and true. Therefore, it is little wonder that enemy forces bombarded him so ruthlessly, or that he bravely resisted each attack. Even so, his experience in the Valley of Humiliation had been an extremely grueling thing. Perhaps he had nearly reached the limits of his endurance after the repeated assaults there, because after his encounter with Shame, Faithful was granted a temporary reprieve. For the rest of the way through the Valley of Humiliation, and entirely through the Valley of the Shadow of Death, Faithful enjoyed a quiet passage with blue skies and bright sunshine.

Dear brother or sister in Christ, although we are running a race that is not limited to the swift, it is imperative that we complete it and reach our goal. There are many others running this same race and we could easily become distracted by them, if we are not careful. Therefore, we can ill afford to focus our attention upon those who are ahead of us in the race, or worse still, gloat over those who lag behind. The only way to avoid such costly mistakes is to keep our eyes fixed upon our Lord alone.

Nevertheless, we need the help and encouragement of our brothers and sisters in Christ as we run the race to eternal glory. Beyond a doubt, Faithful's stirring testimony was of strong consolation to his newfound brother, Christian. It speaks to my heart as well, reminding me that our loving heavenly Father will never permit us to be tested and tried beyond our ability to endure. As we struggle against sin and temptation, his watchful eye is always upon us. Moreover, since he knows the limits of our endurance, he carefully measures each affliction so that even the most fragile among us is not crushed beneath its weight.

Study Questions

1. Briefly describe Faithful's departure from the City of Destruction, and his update concerning the man named Pliable. What are some of the ways in which Faithful's journey after leaving the city differed from Christian's?

2. Even though Faithful was a godly man, he struggled with temptation. Who is the character Wanton who pursued him so relentlessly, and what does she represent? What does the Word of God say about her? How did Faithful escape her snare?

3. Who is the man that attacked Faithful on the hill Difficulty, and what was the nature of his attack? What kind of proposal did he make to Faithful, and what would have been the result had Faithful agreed to the proposed union? By what means did Faithful escape this unholy alliance?

4. Like an indignant avenger of blood, divine justice pursues every member of Adam's race. For the unsaved, there is no escape from it. However, God has provided a hiding place for his people, a figurative city of refuge. Where we can flee and find refuge from the avenger of blood?

5. What were the two particular things with which Faithful struggled in the Valley of Humiliation? Write a brief account of his battle with them while there.

CHAPTER 31

Anatomy of a Hypocrite

THE SUBJECT OF THE TONGUE, ITS USE AND ABUSE, FIGURES SO PROMINENTLY in Scripture that we do well to think long and hard before using ours! Without a doubt, the faculty of speech is a great blessing from the Lord, but along with everything else that he created as inherently good, sinful men pervert this gift into an instrument of harm and destruction. In fact, they do so to such an extent that James warns against the unbridled tongue, calling it an unruly evil full of deadly poison. (James 3:5-10)

The human heart is the fountainhead from which this venom flows. In Proverbs 4:23, Solomon warns his hearers: *Keep thy heart with all diligence; for out of it are the issues of life.* His meaning is unmistakably clear that our hearts determine who and what we really are, and our mouth is the wellspring that reveals our true character. (Matthew 12:33-37) Therefore, if we desire to know what is in our hearts, we need only listen to our speech.

It has often been said that not everyone talking about heaven is going there. Many claim to be on the pathway to Zion who are not really pilgrims at all. By their outward manner and perhaps even their knowledge of Scripture, some of them play their role very well, but intellectual understanding has left their hearts untouched. Consequently, their religion is shallow and vain, although their bold, confident air goes a long way toward concealing the fact.

Christian and Faithful are just about to meet such a person. Since he could wax eloquent in the use of his tongue, he often made a favorable first impression. However, as they watched him approach, it struck them that he was "something more comely at a distance, than at hand." When John Bunyan further describes him as being a "tall" man, I suspect he had far more in mind than his physical stature. The man claimed to be traveling to Zion and seemed eager to join Christian and Faithful for the purpose of profitable conversation. Yet from the outset, there was something not quite right about him.

Since this stranger could speak with some knowledge upon spiritual themes, his words might pass muster if taken solely at face value. Whether his fine speech would bear up under closer scrutiny or not remains to be seen. Notwithstanding this concern, the man's knowledge and demonstrative manner often passed for true spirituality, upon first making his acquaintance.

Christian and Faithful were eager to discuss the things they loved best. However, as they began to talk with the man, they were surprised to discover that he could talk equally well about the things of God or the things of the world. A bona fide philosopher stood before them, and self-made at that! He loved knowledge for its own sake and loved to share what he knew with others. Nevertheless, Christian and Faithful quickly discovered that although he was lavish with his conversation, a little of it went a long way. All too soon they grew weary of his company, for he was clearly taken with himself. In short, he had an overinflated ego and was full of hot air.

As if this were not bad enough, it soon became evident that the man's theology was seriously flawed. Although he was adept at quoting Scripture, he frequently violated its true meaning in order to support his own opinions. Therefore, his erroneous views were particularly dangerous because they contained an element of truth.

Unlike this stranger, who had no preference for either godly company or conversation, true Christians strongly prefer the company of those who are of like mind. When they are together, they love to talk of things that are spiritually edifying. This was the express desire of both Christian and Faithful, and their new companion agreed to it readily enough. After all, he was sure that he could teach them a thing or two because he considered himself an authority on many different subjects. Therefore, he was willing to render an opinion on just about any issue they could name. It would be a good opinion, too, in his humble estimation, for he fancied himself an apt instructor of the ignorant.

It is worthy of note that Faithful, rather than Christian, took the initiative in conversing with the man. Furthermore, it is significant that the man raised no objection when Faithful wanted to talk about spiritual things. This seemed a promising sign until the man revealed his strong partiality for the supernatural and sensational, rather than sound doctrine. This is always a red flag, my friend!

This unexpected turn in the conversation caused Faithful to raise an eyebrow and give the man a quizzical look, but he quickly adjusted his comments and gauged them according to Faithful's reaction. So among his other talents, he was a chameleon, also! But then the man began to speak of things that suggested he was well versed in the Gospel. As he spoke of the necessity of the new birth, the insufficiency of good works, and the need of Christ's righteousness, Faithful was impressed in spite of his earlier misgivings.

Sensing that he had gained an advantage, the man said: "By this (that is, by knowledge) a man may learn what it is to repent, to believe, to pray, to suffer, or the like: by this also, a man may learn what are the great promises and consolations of the Gospel, to his own comfort. Farther, by this a man may learn to refute false opinions, to vindicate the truth, and also to instruct the ignorant."

On the surface of it, this line of reasoning might be accepted as true. Yet in spite of his skill with words, the man did not understand the difference between knowledge attained by human effort and saving knowledge, which is the gift of God. In his mind, the ability to talk about spiritual things was enough. Therefore, he wrongly supposed that spiritual ignorance could be corrected through verbal instruction alone. After all, that was the way he had accumulated his vast storehouse of knowledge. However, the knowledge of Christ is not attained, nor is it increased, by intellectual exertion alone. When Faithful tried to point this out, the stranger adjusted his speech once again, to bring it more in line with Faithful's concern.

So even though he could discuss the Scriptures well enough in some circles, he was ignorant of vital, fundamental truth and the application thereof. He clearly lacked spiritual discernment; therefore, his talk came across as empty prattle to those who knew better. Thus in spite of his fine speech, the substance of his conversation was that it really had no substance!

Although the man's skewed theology made Faithful wonder about him, the tenderhearted pilgrim was still willing to give him the benefit of the doubt. Perhaps the stranger had been the victim of poor instruction, but his heart was in the right place. Not willing to trust his own judgment in so important a matter, Faithful whispered aside to Christian that the man was surely a "brave companion" who would make "a very excellent pilgrim." In so saying, he indirectly asked for his brother's opinion.

With no prior knowledge upon which to base his judgment, Faithful had been duped by the stranger's flamboyant manner and religious affectation. Many others have made the same mistake. But Christian, who had been uncharacteristically silent during this whole conversation, was under no such illusion. He saw right through the man's religious veneer and pretense of virtue. So with a modest smile, he quietly warned Faithful that this particular man had a gift for beguiling those who do not know him. That is, those who see him at a distance only. This comment prompted Faithful to ask Christian if he knew the man, to which Christian replied, "Know him! Yes, better than he knows himself." A strange response, is it not? Did it stem from legitimate sarcasm, or was there a deeper insinuation behind Christian's remark?

As Christian began an exposé of the man's true character, a clearer picture began to take form in Faithful's mind. Like an actor playing his part on the stage, the man had assumed a role and was pretending to be something he was not. To the undiscerning, his affected manner was sometimes mistaken for true spirituality. However, it was a mask that he could easily put on or cast aside, depending upon whom he was with at the time.

Unmasking the hypocrite

After biding his time for a while, Christian finally revealed the man's identity to Faithful. His name was Talkative, the notorious son of one Say-well. The family resided in Prating Row, a fairly large and generally affluent subdivision located in the westernmost part of the City of Destruction. Therefore, he was known throughout the region as Talkative of Prating Row. It was a nickname known by many but envied by few!

Although his understanding was faulty and so were his opinions, Talkative had the natural gift of expressing himself well. Therefore, he was able to give a better account of himself than was actually warranted. But considering his family, is it any wonder? His proud spirit was a legacy handed down from generation to generation. Consequently, Talkative had acquired some rather obnoxious habits, one being that he talked entirely too much and with far too little purpose. Moreover, he found idle chatter entertaining and sought out those who enjoyed the same. Not surprisingly, then, he was tiresome to those who knew him best, as talkative people usually are.

While he could speak glibly enough of spiritual things on a cursory level, his understanding was based upon carnal reasoning rather than Scripture truth. Therefore, he was a deceived soul and the deceiver of others, and since his true nature was hard to conceal in close company, he was generally reputed to be a "sorry fellow."

So Faithful's first impression that Talkative was a "very pretty man" was not very accurate, was it? It reminds me of an observation made by Thomas Adams, who said: "Hypocrites are like pictures on canvas, they show fairest at farthest."[1] A perfect assessment of Talkative! Although he could present an acceptable outward appearance at a distance, his mask of hypocrisy slipped a bit upon better acquaintance. Yet of all this, the poor man remained blissfully unaware.

Like most of his kin, Talkative appreciated the sound of his own voice, but failed to really listen to himself. He would gladly talk about anything, and he was as indiscriminate in his choice of companions as in his topics for discussion. Therefore, he was as comfortable talking with Christian and Faithful as he was when in the company of profane men at the local tavern. Moreover, Talkative was a frequent patron there, where his free use of alcoholic beverages dulled his inhibitions and loosened his tongue even more.

Notwithstanding his sinful behavior, the man was very religious; but as Christian aptly observed, "Religion hath no place in his heart, or house, or conversation: all he hath lieth in his tongue, and his religion is to make a noise therewith." What a tragic commentary! His religion consisted of nothing more than meaningless drivel and outward show. (2 Corinthians 5:12)

External piety without regeneration makes one worse than he was before, since it tends to produce a self-righteous, judgmental spirit. Moreover, it often scoffs at the idea of self-denial and mortification of the flesh. In short, religion without Christ is all about self and self-interest; thus, it is void of any true substance. (Matthew 23:1-3; 1 Corinthians 4:20)

It is not always easy, however, to distinguish between genuine believers and those who can merely talk the talk. Like Faithful, we can be taken in by one who has significant knowledge of Scripture and an eloquent way of expression. Yet even when the religious hypocrite is accomplished in the art of deception, his life and character never quite measure up to his claim. (Matthew 7:21-27; Matthew 15:7-8) So first impressions aside, we must delve beneath the surface to see if there is any reality there.

Since Talkative could assume a form of godliness when it suited his purpose, he put on a fairly convincing act in public. However, once he crossed his own doorstep, he laid aside all semblance of piety and became a brutal man who was unreasonable and abusive with his wife and children. Therefore, by all accounts, he was a miserable excuse for a husband and father, and his family had just cause to fear him and dread his return home.

Talkative also left behind all desire to discuss spiritual things, once he entered the privacy of his own house. In fact, he would have none of it there. Since he had no concern for his own soul, it is little wonder that he cared nothing for the spiritual instruction of his family. Not only was he hard-hearted and cruel in his manner toward his children, he habitually chided them for any signs of a tender conscience. In this way, he unwittingly taught them to follow his wretched example, as he had followed his own father's long ago. Altogether, his house was a desolate place, and he was the greatest disturber of its peace. (Proverbs 11:29)

Such duplicity cannot generally be hidden for long, so in spite of Talkative's attempt to wear two faces, his true character was more widely known than he supposed. Behind his back, close acquaintances had hardly a good word to say about him and often referred to him as "a saint abroad, and a devil at home." Since he was also known to be dishonest, his word had no credibility and no one would do business with him. Decent men shunned his company and were ashamed to be identified with him. Talkative would have been shocked (speechless, do you think?) if he knew what people really thought of him.

Although it probably never entered his mind, Talkative was a stumbling block to others. By his inconsistent life and religious hypocrisy, he brought great reproach upon the name of Christ. What's more, his confident manner and eloquent speech persuaded a number of gullible souls to follow his shameful example.

Dear reader, how do you suppose Christian had such detailed knowledge of Talkative, even concerning things that took place in the privacy of the man's home? Was his explicit description a caricature, or perhaps the repetition of malicious gossip? No, John Bunyan makes it clear that Christian's character analysis was both accurate and unbiased. He did, in fact, have the man's number, but how could that be? Was he really that intimately acquainted with the man? Or did the encounter with Talkative remind Christian of what he had been like in former days, when his name was Graceless? While we cannot say for sure, his keen insight into the hypocrite's character and personal habits gives sufficient reason to admit the possibility.

For whatever reason, Christian understood these things much better than Faithful did at the time, and to Faithful's credit, he deferred to his brother's greater knowledge. Such was the humble, teachable spirit of the man who bore so noble a name. (Proverbs 1:5; Proverbs 9:9)

What a striking contrast to Talkative of Prating Row, who balked at the very idea of giving heed to those who were wiser than he! (Proverbs 10:8) However, I suppose we must give credit where credit is due. The man had his problems, but timidity and low self-esteem were not among them. Just name your subject and he will be ready to discuss it, but do not expect to get a word in edgewise! No doubt about it, Talkative had justly earned his reputation, but it was a poor claim to fame.

After listening carefully to Christian's character sketch of Talkative, Faithful clearly understood that "saying and doing are two things." From now on, he would be more mindful of this vital distinction. Then Christian reinforced his point with a profound truth when he said: "The Soul of Religion is the Practick (practical) part." The Word of God leaves no doubt that this is indeed the case. (James 1:27)

Although the character named Talkative borders on the ridiculous, his story contains valuable lessons that we should all lay to heart. In spite of his boasted knowledge, he had never received with meekness the engrafted word that alone is able to save the soul. (James 1:21) He made the fatal mistake of presuming that hearing and saying were enough to make him a fine Christian, and in this, he was utterly deceived. (James 1:22-25) It would have been his wisdom to place a seal on his lips. (Proverbs 10:19) Yet he failed to consider that by indulging in idle chatter, he brought more condemnation upon himself. (Matthew 12:36)

As the example of Talkative so clearly demonstrates, the ability to speak well does not necessarily indicate a work of God's grace. True faith will make its presence known by the bringing forth of spiritual fruit. (Matthew 7:15-20) Moreover, it places a governor on the tongue, teaching us to be swift to hear and slow to speak. (James 1:19, 26)

Concerning fruit, it is interesting that Scripture likens the end of the world to a harvest of souls. (Matthew 9:37-38; Matthew 13:30; Revelation 14:14-18) In the last day, men will be judged by their deeds (their fruit), not by their fine-sounding words. All of God's children are wholesome grain, faithful servants who bring forth spiritual fruit to his glory. (Ephesians 2:8-10) In that day when the hearts of men are exposed before God, those who have genuine faith will shine forth in sharp contrast to mere pretenders. (Matthew 7:21-27; James 2:14-20) Proverbs 18:21 gives a solemn warning when it says: *Death and life are in the power of the tongue: and they that love it shall eat the fruit thereof.* So in a very real sense, Talkative's prating words would be his downfall. (Proverbs 16:22; Proverbs 17:27-28; Proverbs 26:12)

The heart of the matter

Thinking back to Faithful, we recall that what he lacked in practical experience, he made up for by solid Bible knowledge. As he considered the things that Christian shared with him, Faithful remembered the instruction given by Moses concerning beasts that are clean or unclean. (Leviticus 11:1-8) At first it may seem a strange application to make, but the connection actually indicated an astute spiritual mind. In the character of Talkative, Faithful saw one who resembled an unclean beast because he cheweth the cud but divideth not the hoof. That is, he spoke the language of Zion but had not parted company with his sinful ways and evil companions. Therefore, he continued to walk in the *counsel of the ungodly,* to stand *in the way of sinners,* and sit *in the seat of the scornful.* (Psalm 1:1)

Christian was impressed! Thus he responded: "You have spoken, for ought I know, the true Gospel sense of those texts." (That is, of Leviticus 11:1-8 and Deuteronomy 14:6-8). Furthermore, he reminded Faithful of the apostle Paul's teaching in 1 Corinthians 14:7, which says that things without life can still give sound. What a soul-searching truth, my friend! Fair speech is not nearly enough to indicate spiritual life. Again, I quote Thomas Adams who said: "A hypocrite is like the Sicilian Etna, flaming at the mouth when it hath snow at the foot: their mouths talk hotly, but their feet walk coldly." [2] Without saving faith and the grace of the Holy Spirit, even the most eloquent tongue is of no more value than sounding brass or a tinkling cymbal. (1 Corinthians 13:1)

The two brothers were now in full agreement concerning the man from Prating Row. Christian had never cared for his company, and now Faithful has had quite enough of him. So he asked, "What shall we do to be rid of him?" Christian immediately suggested that he and Talkative discuss the "Power of Religion." When Talkative agreed to the subject, Faithful asked him, "How doth the Saving Grace of God discover itself, when it is in the Heart of man?" Without even pausing to think, Talkative answered, "Where the Grace of God is in the heart, it causeth a great outcry against Sin." When Faithful objected that it rather manifests itself by causing one to abhor his own sin, Talkative asked, "What difference is there between crying out against, and abhorring of Sin?"

There is a critical difference, as every true child of God knows well. Faithful tried his best to show the son of Say-well that one may protest loudly against sin in general even while nurturing it in his own heart. In and of itself, such a stern outcry does not denote true virtue within. It has often been done in blatant hypocrisy, even from some pulpits.

At this turn in the conversation, Talkative began to suspect that Faithful was laying a trap for him, and in a sense he was, but not out of any desire to harm the deluded man. When Faithful pressed him further on this subject, Talkative told him that "great knowledge of Gospel Mysteries" was the second evidence of grace in the heart. Once again, Faithful was obliged to correct him since Bible knowledge may be acquired apart from a work of God in the soul. Some people study the Scriptures just for the sake of debate. Others, who are captivated by the supernatural or sensational, love to delve into the more obscure passages in order to engage in vain speculation. Still others, like Talkative, are eager to impress men with their superior knowledge. All of these are highly questionable motives for studying the Word of God. The apostle Paul characterizes such persons as *ever learning, and never able to come to the knowledge of the truth.* (2 Timothy 3:7)

Saving knowledge is always accompanied by heart obedience, and herein lies the test of true discipleship. (John 14:21) The essence of grace in the soul consists of doing, not merely saying. (James 2:14-20) Those who possess it are far more concerned with inward purity than outward show. (1 John 3:2-3) They indeed desire to grow in Bible knowledge, but for the noble purpose of walking according to its precepts. (Psalm 119:33-40)

At this point in the conversation, Talkative had nothing further to say. It was a thing that did not happen very often! Therefore, Faithful seized the opportunity to explain how a work of God's grace is truly made known. The work begins with conviction of sin and the knowledge of one's defiled, lost condition. This kind of knowledge produces godly sorrow and repentance. The Holy Spirit brings the guilty sinner to the end of himself and then reveals Christ to him. He gives faith to come to Christ and receive the gift of salvation from his gracious hand. (Acts 4:12; Revelation 21:6)

Although others cannot see this inward work of grace, an outward witness always accompanies it. The Christian will openly confess his faith in the Lord Jesus Christ, but the matter does not end there. He will strive to live a holy, obedient life that is consistent with his verbal testimony, and not just when others can see him. Since he is deeply concerned for the spiritual welfare of his family, the true believer will desire above all to set a godly example in the privacy of his home.

Having laid this foundation, Faithful asked Talkative directly about his spiritual condition. In so doing, he appealed to the man's conscience before God. Did he live up to his fine speech, or would a close examination of his life expose him as a fraud? In the face of such a bold confrontation, his first reaction was to blush with shame. The unexpected question struck too close to home, and Talkative was caught off guard for the moment. However, offended pride soon overcame the brief outcry of conscience, causing him to indignantly ask: "I pray will you tell me why you ask me such question?"

Talkative asked for it, did he not, and Faithful took full advantage of the opportunity to point out his hypocrisy. The man's religious pretense and tarnished reputation brought reproach upon the true people of God. Those who knew him tended to judge all Christians according to his base conduct and speech. In spite of Talkative's intellectual airs and pious exterior, it was fairly common knowledge that his religion was merely talk. His shameful conduct was equally well known. Moreover, his hypocrisy tempted some to follow his ways and embrace the same false hope. How much better it would have been if he had laid aside his false piety altogether, for in stubbornly clinging to it, he gave occasion for the way of truth to be evil spoken of. (2 Peter 2:2)

Christian had been right once again. When Faithful insisted upon discussing the operation of grace in the soul, Talkative had had enough. Christian and Faithful were not the kind of jolly companions whose company he most enjoyed. They were entirely too narrow-minded to suit his taste, being of that tiresome sort who take their religion far too seriously! Moreover, they failed to appreciate what a fine fellow he really was, or to be in awe of his superior wisdom and knowledge! In this we probably find the chief point of offense that caused him to finally take his leave of Christian and Faithful.

Upon his departure, the two brothers could only heave a sigh of relief and add a hearty good riddance. They had known no true concord all the while he was with them, and yet they bore him no ill will. (Amos 3:3) The whole encounter with Talkative was a tragic thing, really, since it left him more deeply confirmed in his religious hypocrisy than he was before. It was Faithful's fervent hope that the deceived man would think about what he had heard. Perhaps the Lord would stir his heart with the truth and show him the error of his ways.

Some well-intentioned souls might accuse Faithful of dealing too harshly with Talkative. Yet in speaking so plainly to him, Faithful proved a truer friend than all of his merry companions put together. Such an open, honest confrontation is never easy, but it is sometimes necessary. Those who are Christian in name only may know enough to talk the talk, but have neither the will nor the power to live accordingly. Turning a blind eye to their hypocrisy is not an act of kindness.

The fact that nominal professors often feel comfortable with God's people should cause us to examine the reasons why. It reflects a disturbing trend toward more and more compromise due to the fear of causing offense. Those who are Christian in name only are not merely tolerated, but accepted as brethren. Yet consider the cost! As the distinctions between the true Christian and the false pretender become increasingly blurred, the church weakens from within. Moreover, her testimony before the world is blemished by legitimate charges of hypocrisy.

By presenting Talkative of Prating Row in such derogatory terms, I have no intention whatsoever of belittling the importance of Bible knowledge. We cannot be ignorant of the Scriptures and expect to grow in grace. (2 Peter 3:14-18) Laboring to learn the Word of God is our sacred duty as believers in Christ, since those who are well-grounded in the truth will not be easily moved from it. (Psalm 1:1-3) Therefore, a proper understanding of Scripture truth and sound doctrine is vital to our faith and spiritual well being. However, knowledge that is attained as an end in itself is another matter entirely. For the true Christian, this will most likely puff him up with pride and stifle his progress in grace; but where saving faith is lacking, it lays the foundation for a false hope.

The fear and knowledge of God has a profound effect upon our entire being, not just our intellect. It leads us in the paths of righteousness and causes us to bear spiritual fruit. Poor Talkative utterly lacked this principal part of true wisdom, even though he did his best to hide the fact. (Proverbs 1:7; Proverbs 9:10) Therefore, his religious prattle was of no profit, either to himself or those who heard him. In truth, he was the direct opposite of what a true Christian ought to be.

Our Lord gave a strong warning in Luke 12:1-3 when he told his disciples: *Beware ye of the leaven of the Pharisees, which is hypocrisy. For there is nothing covered, that shall not be revealed; neither hid, that shall not be known. Therefore whatsoever ye have spoken in darkness shall be heard in the light; and that which ye have spoken in the ear in closets shall be proclaimed upon the housetops.*

What do leaven and hypocrisy have in common? How are we to understand our Lord's warning given here? As leaven grows and expands, it completely permeates the dough into which it has been mixed. Although the leaven is hidden from view, its effect can be clearly seen as the entire lump rises evenly into a light, fragrant loaf ready for baking. In like manner, the leaven of hypocrisy silently infuses the entire being of one in whom it dwells. From within the heart it exerts a powerful influence, first altering his thought processes and then manifesting itself in his speech and conduct. All the while, it creates a false impression that will undoubtedly influence others.

Therefore, hypocrisy is not a thing to be taken lightly. The solemn words of the Lord Jesus Christ remind us that we must guard against any signs of it in ourselves. As much as we dislike admitting it, we are still quite capable of pretense, but this inclination must be confessed and forsaken. If we fail to do so, we may as well expect divine chastisement. Our heavenly Father will not allow his children to dishonor his name by playing the hypocrite.

The person who walks in blatant hypocrisy may seem to get by with it, even when, like Talkative, he does much harm to others. However, the fact that the hypocrite walks after his own lusts will eventually betray him, in spite of his great swelling words. (Jude 16) As our Lord warned, all will eventually be brought to light. (Job 27:8) Moreover, even in an earthly sense the hypocrite is usually found out, for he plays a part that is not easy to maintain.

* * * *

How easy it is to be impressed by eloquent speech, or to be taken in by enticing words of man's wisdom! (1 Corinthians 2:4) We need to be more discerning, especially concerning religious pretense that is all talk. Sad to say there is plenty of it around, Talkative being a prime example of it. To him, religion was like a garment to be put on or cast aside according to his whims. Of saving faith and imputed righteousness he knew nothing at all.

Admittedly, the man from Prating Row is an extreme case, and in a way, he provides an element of comic relief to a narrative that is sober and weighty. In a greater sense, however, he is a tragic figure that serves as a warning that talk is cheap, and those who are Christians in name only do great harm to themselves and the cause of Christ.

Therefore, we need to be careful that our talk does not outpace our walk. The world expects to see a difference in those of us who claim to be the followers of Jesus Christ, even if it mocks and despises us for it. We are called to be lights in the world, a thing that requires us to follow the example of our Lord. (Philippians 2:12-16) When we earnestly strive to do so, our walk will be consistent with our profession of faith, and our speech will bear witness of the same. (James 3:17-18)

In Psalm 19, as David meditated upon the glory of God revealed in creation and the Word, he responded with the sincere desire to walk uprightly before God. As he concluded this Psalm, it was with the prayer: *Let the words of my mouth, and the meditation of my heart, be acceptable in thy sight, O LORD, my strength, and my redeemer.* Dear friend in Christ, may this be our earnest prayer as well.

While considering the practical applications that can be drawn from Talkative and his all too familiar story, I thought of my home state of North Carolina. It came strongly to mind because of its official state motto, "Esse Quam Videri," which means "to be rather than to seem." It is a worthy state motto, is it not, and one that should especially resonate in the heart of the Christian.

As followers of the Lord Jesus Christ, our lives must bear up under close scrutiny if we are to be pleasing in his sight. This fact should cause us to take a good look at ourselves as well as our Christian profession. Is there true substance behind our speech, or does it come across as empty prattle? Are we, like Talkative, "more comely at a distance, than at hand"? Are we really what we claim to be, or are we merely role-playing? How genuine does our Christian testimony appear to those who know us best? We may put on a good face and deceive others, but those who are closest to us know whether we are real or not. If we do not show forth a Christ-like character in the privacy of our homes, we had better fear making a pretense of it when in public.

Unlike the hypocrite, who is quite satisfied with being less than he seems, the children of God are grieved by the sinful tendencies still lurking within. Moreover, we are not content to maintain a spiritual status quo. Therefore, our watchword, like the motto of New York State, should also be "Excelsior"! As we march to Zion, we press toward a goal that is leading us always higher and ever upward. To that noble end, we earnestly desire to be exactly what we profess to be, doers of the Word of God and not hearers only. As the sincere and truehearted followers of our Lord Jesus Christ, our delight is to live lives that are as free from hypocrisy as possible. For when we pass from this earthly scene and enter the realm of the heavenly, we will attain that which is infinitely higher still!

Study Questions

1. When Christian and Faithful met Talkative, they sensed at once that something about him was not quite right. What red flags did they notice that made them suspect he was not what he claimed to be?

2. Talkative of Prating Row managed to hide his true character from those who did not know him well. To those who were better acquainted with him, what are some of the things about him that strongly suggested hypocrisy?

3. Although Talkative could put on a form of godliness when it suited his purpose, what kind of man was he in the privacy of his home?

4. After speaking with Talkative at some length, Faithful began to address the heart of the matter by pointing out the man's hypocrisy. Faithful did this by showing the sharp distinction between hypocrisy and a true work of God's grace in the soul. How did Talkative react to this rebuke, and why did he react as he did?

5. Since hypocrisy is a sin of which a true Christian can also be guilty, how are we to guard ourselves against it? On this same note, how is Talkative a solemn warning to us?

CHAPTER 32

Profitable Encounter with a Beloved Friend

AS WE THINK UPON THE MOST RECENT EXPERIENCE OF CHRISTIAN AND Faithful, did you happen to notice that they met Talkative while in the way? It is another solemn reminder that false pretenders walk freely among us on the path of life, and can cause us difficulty in a number of ways. For one thing, those who are Christian in name only seem to have an easier time of it than genuine believers do. Since they are mainly concerned with keeping up appearances, they give little thought to their actual heart condition before God. While true Christians mourn inwardly over their sin and are often plagued by doubt and fear because of it, hypocrites have no such thoughts. So they can display a condescending attitude toward poor, struggling believers who do, which is an especially hard thing to bear.

Since those who have the least of which to boast often boast the loudest, nominal Christians trouble us in another sense as well. Their claim that all is well with them could provoke us to envy, especially when comparing their blessed condition with our own difficult lot in life. Like Asaph, we cannot help but wonder why such people prosper in spite of their false pretense and evil deeds. (Psalm 73:1-12) However, this line of reasoning places a stumbling block in our way until we consider the end of the matter.

What might that end be? As Asaph realized, it is a clearer view of things as they really are. The trials and afflictions we must endure in this life are preparing us for eternal glory, but the hypocrite knows nothing of this sanctifying work. Therefore, he is left alone to go his merry way for now, while little suspecting that he walks a slippery path. One day his foundation will crumble beneath him and every false hope will utterly perish. (Psalm 73:16-19)

After parting company with the irksome man from Prating Row, Christian and Faithful found themselves in a desolate area, which would have made for a grueling journey had it not been for one another's company. The fellowship they enjoyed and the spiritual conversation they shared helped them both to make it through this rough stretch of wilderness without significant incident. What's more, it comforted their hearts and made their burdens seem lighter, as shared burdens always are.

As the two men neared the end of the rugged backcountry, Faithful happened to glance behind him and spy a familiar face. It was their beloved friend, Evangelist, following at a discreet distance. What was he doing out here in the middle of nowhere? He was keeping a careful watch over those to whom he has ministered the Word of God.

Although the godly pastor rejoices over every soul who professes faith in Christ under his ministry, his joy is mixed with guarded optimism. Many years of labor in his master's service have taught him some bittersweet lessons. He has watched some believers get off to a rocky start, causing him to hold out little hope for them, only to have them blossom and flourish spiritually, later rather than sooner. This unexpected turn of events is always an encouragement to his heart.

On the other hand, he has watched others embrace the pilgrim life with great enthusiasm, only to forsake it somewhere down the road. So even though he rejoices over each sign of early promise in new converts, he knows that their spiritual journey has only begun. The proof of salvation lies in their perseverance under fire, not in how dramatic their conversion experience or how eloquent their testimony. Every true pastor knows the heartbreak of seeing a hopeful beginning come to a tragic end.

Evangelist is one such man. With a heart of loving concern for their souls, he has carefully followed the progress of both Christian and Faithful. As an astute and experienced pastor, he is under no illusions. He knows both men well, has witnessed their struggles, and is aware of their particular areas of weakness. Even so, he has high hopes for these two. Therefore, he rejoices whenever he perceives any growth in grace, but stands ready to intervene should he detect the telltale signs of danger. (Galatians 4:19-20; 3 John 4)

Such diligent pastoral care is not always appreciated. In 2 Corinthians 12:15, the apostle Paul wrote to the Corinthian believers: *I will very gladly spend and be spent for you; though the more abundantly I love you, the less I be loved.* What a heartbreaking thing is such ingratitude! What a wretched recompense for all of Paul's love for them and labor in their behalf! What callous indifference it shows toward all of the sufferings he has borne for the Gospel's sake! (2 Corinthians 1:5-6)

This was not the present case with Evangelist, however. Christian and Faithful sincerely loved and had the highest respect for him. So while many people shun the company of God's men, they welcomed him warmly. Both men were keenly aware of the debt they owed him for his faithfulness to them. Therefore, they deeply appreciated him and his care for their souls. (1 Thessalonians 5:12-13)

After their initial greeting, Evangelist came right to the point. He wanted to know what had happened to them since he last saw them. In particular, he was eager to learn how they had conducted themselves; but his questions were not an attempt at small talk, nor were they the result of idle curiosity. He was deeply interested in their spiritual progress, and since he has been keeping a watchful eye over them all the while, I suspect that he already knew the answers to his own questions. Nevertheless, drawing them out in this way gave him the opportunity to instruct and encourage them concerning what lay ahead. Like most of God's men, Evangelist was not in the habit of mincing his words. He spoke the truth to Christian and Faithful forthrightly as always, even though some of the things he had to say would be difficult to hear. Nevertheless, if heeded, his counsel would prove highly profitable to them in the days to come.

What value should we place upon the advice and counsel of a godly pastor? It is a question we probably do not consider as often as we should. While in company with Talkative of Prating Row, Christian and Faithful had been subjected to a seemingly endless flood of religious nonsense. Needless to say, that conversation had been both unprofitable and vexing. Little wonder that their encounter with Evangelist was such a welcome change. Since he was a man of uncommon wisdom and knowledge, he had many excellent things to share with them. To their credit, they were wise enough to recognize both his spiritual gifts and their need of his counsel and instruction.

Although the two travel-weary brethren were understandably glad and encouraged to see their mentor, they were an encouragement to him as well. After all, they were the fruit of his ministry. He had sowed the Word of God, watched it take root in them, and begin to grow. To behold their spiritual progress was a token that his labor had not been in vain. (Galatians 4:11; Philippians 2:15-16) Yet even though he rejoiced with them because they had been victorious through many trials, Evangelist felt duty bound to add an important word of warning.

The substance of his exhortation is something that every true child of God must keep in heart and mind. Our race is not over until we cross the finish line; therefore, we dare not rest upon past victories. In our race to eternal glory, the crown belongs to the overcomer and to him alone. (1 Corinthians 9:24-25; Revelation 3:10-11)

Up to the present time, Christian and Faithful have run well. They have faced many enemies and continued onward, in spite of stiff opposition. However, this was not the time to pause and congratulate one another. The path still lay before them, and so did many unknown dangers and snares. There was yet much further to go before they reached the Celestial City. Although they had done battle with spiritual powers and prevailed, more of the same would surely come. Satan and his henchmen were as determined as ever to ensnare them and overthrow their faith. Trouble would continue to press them on every hand. Fleshly temptations awaited beyond every turn in the road. Seeing that all these things were against them, what hope did they have of ever completing their journey?

In truth, they had a sure and steadfast hope, but they must hold to it tenaciously. (Hebrews 6:11-12) If they would be counted conquerors at their journey's end, they must persevere through every adversity. With the kingdom of God ever before them, their sights must be set on things unseen and their hearts fixed on the glory that excelleth. (2 Corinthians 3:10) Yet they could not begin to do this in their own strength. Therefore, how sweet the words of Evangelist must have been when he said: "You have all the power in Heaven and Earth on your side"!

My fellow pilgrim, this mighty power of God's Spirit belongs to us as well. It works effectually within us as we see *him who is invisible.* (Hebrews 11:27) By *looking unto Jesus* and considering *him that endured such contradiction of sinners against himself,* we will be able to run the race with patience. (Hebrews 12:1-3) We will continue to press still onward and ever upward toward a kingdom that will never be moved (Hebrews 12:28)

* * * *

In their zeal to win converts and build large congregations, some men who claim to be Gospel ministers paint an unrealistic picture of the Christian life. By minimizing its difficulties, however, they place a stumbling block in the way of those who would be the disciples of Jesus Christ. Evangelist shunned that kind of deceptive practice. He was careful to speak only the truth, which made him quite unpopular in most circles. As for Christian and Faithful, they regarded him highly and deemed him a prophet who "could tell them of things that might happen unto them, and also how they might resist and overcome them."

Was Evangelist really a prophet? Yes he was, but not in the usual sense of the word. He could not foretell the future, as the Old Testament prophets were gifted to do. Nevertheless, as a true minister of the Gospel, he could warn the two men of what they should expect as they continued their journey.

When our Lord walked upon the earth, he lived under the shadow of the cross. Can we expect to do otherwise? Did he not warn his disciples: *In the world ye shall have tribulation: but be of good cheer; I have overcome the world*? (John 16:33) Every one of his apostles learned the truth of his words from personal experience, and could attest that it was the Christian's expected course. (2 Timothy 3:10-13; 1 Peter 2:19-21, 3:14-16, 4:12-16)

Therefore, Evangelist's warning to Christian and Faithful was not a new revelation; it came directly from the Word of God. Although he could not know precisely what would happen to them further down the road, he did caution the two men not to expect the way to become any easier. In fact, he added another word of admonition that was more specific in nature. The solitary wilderness through which they were now passing was about to come to an end. Shortly after they left it, Christian and Faithful would reach a town that harbored many enemies and would prove a hostile place. This being the case, they would suffer greatly there, and at least one of them would pay the ultimate price for his Christian testimony.

How was it that Evangelist could be so sure? This particular town was familiar territory, both from his personal experience and by guiding others through it. At the present time, Christians who passed that way often faced contempt from its ordinary citizens as well as harassment from the authorities. In fact, it was not a rare thing for a believer to seal his testimony with his blood.

So perhaps Christian and Faithful were soon to part company. However, they were not to lose heart, even if circumstances led one or both of them down the path of martyrdom. A crown of life awaits those who are faithful unto death. (Revelation 2:10) Therefore, if one of them was called to shortly give his life for the cause of Christ, his lot would be far better than his brother's.

In spite of this daunting prospect, Christian and Faithful were not to fear the future. Evangelist exhorted them to conduct themselves like men, although not by relying upon their own strength. When the hour of trial came upon them, they were to commit their souls unto God for safekeeping. Then, if need be, they could walk through the valley of the shadow of death with hearts filled with a peace that passes all human understanding.

Study Questions

1. As Christian and Faithful traveled along, they were joined by their dear friend, Evangelist. Why had he been following them? In what way did this show his heart as a faithful minister of Jesus Christ?

2. For what purpose did Evangelist question Christian and Faithful as he did? How did they respond to his evident concern for their spiritual welfare? In what way were they an encouragement to him?

3. Before seeing them on their way again, Evangelist gave them a word of warning and exhortation. What was the substance of it? Of what specific danger did he warn them?

Part Twelve

"NO MAN CAN SERVE TWO MASTERS"

Lay not up for yourselves treasures upon earth, where moth and rust
doth corrupt, and where thieves break through and steal:
But lay up for yourselves treasures in heaven, where neither moth nor
rust doth corrupt, and where thieves do not break through nor steal:
For where your treasure is, there will your heart be also.
Matthew 6: 19-21

CHAPTER 33

Incident in the Town of Vanity

FIGURATIVELY SPEAKING, THE PATHWAY TO THE CELESTIAL CITY LEADS US through a desolate place that offers little in the way of true comfort or help in our journey. If we try to seek happiness and contentment in earthly things, we will find our quest doomed to failure. However, if we view the wilderness of this world in its proper perspective, we will have little desire to settle here. The longer we live, the stronger our conviction becomes that this world is not our rest. (Micah 2:10) Each trial and affliction bears witness to it, as do our earthly successes, which give but brief satisfaction. (Ecclesiastes 2:11) Moreover, the ever-present reality of death testifies that our earthly life is brief at best, a mere vapor in the eternal scheme of things. (James 4:13-15)

The concept of a wilderness through which we must pass is not a new one. After miraculously delivering the Hebrew people out of Egypt and through the Red Sea, God led them into the wilderness of Sinai where they faced a time of severe testing. His purpose was to humble them, prove them, show what was in their hearts and see whether they would walk in obedience to his commandments or not. (Deuteronomy 8:2-5) They failed the test miserably, by murmuring and complaining even though God provided for their every need. Again and again they provoked him to anger and sinned against his goodness. Consequently, they were made to wander aimlessly in that barren place for forty years until they were finally confirmed in the sin of unbelief. Thus with the exceptions of Caleb and Joshua, the generation that was delivered from Egyptian bondage was barred from entering the Promised Land. (Hebrews 3:7-11)

Dear friend in Christ, we dare not follow their shameful example. (Hebrews 3:12-19) Our passage through this life is also a wilderness journey, a proving time in which our spiritual mettle will be put to the test. Even though our heavenly Father provides all that we need in order to make the difficult passage, he requires that we walk by faith. (Habakkuk 2:4) When difficulty comes, unbelief will often tempt us to murmur against God's providence and question his love. It could even prompt us to ask: *Can God furnish a table in the wilderness?* (Psalm 78:19). O, that faith would rebuke all such thoughts and answer loudly in the affirmative: *The LORD is my shepherd; I shall not want!* (Psalm 23:1)

Like every other true pilgrim, Christian and Faithful had to pass through this hostile wilderness. The portion through which they were currently traveling was an especially rugged backcountry, but eventually the worst appeared to be behind them. The overgrown path suddenly widened, leveled out, and became much easier to walk. However, the wilderness had not really ended at all; it had merely taken on another form. Gazing a short distance ahead, Christian and Faithful saw why the road was better maintained here. They had reached the boundary of a large, prosperous town.

For reasons not generally known, an elite faction within the local government decided long ago that it was best that they not post the name of the town. Those passing through might get the wrong impression, and that could be bad for business. So the decision to withhold the town's name became a matter of unwritten public policy. After all, they reasoned, what difference did it make? Vanity had its own unique claim to fame, a year-round fair that was the key to its prosperity. With merchants traveling near and far in order to compete in its marketplace, the town of Vanity was a bustling center of commerce.

What does this have to do with Christian and Faithful, who were now fast approaching the town's outer limits? How will they fare in that seemingly prosperous place, seeing that Evangelist foresaw great trouble for them there? A bit of background information will help us to unravel the mystery of his strange prediction.

The allegorical town of Vanity with its ongoing fair evokes a rather pleasant image as long as we ignore its name. Picture if you will, a county fair in earlier times or a rural village on market day, when every street is lined with vendors' booths filled with all kinds of merchandise. Even when the place is congested with prospective buyers, the abundant merchandise makes for stiff competition. Watch the more experienced merchants and notice how they arrange their wares in order to capture the interest of those who pass by. Listen to the hawkers in full cry, doing their best to draw a crowd and ply their trade. These clever salesmen are so skillful in the art of persuasion that many a shopper has been convinced to spend more than he can afford for trifles he does not need.

Therefore, the unwritten law of such a marketplace is Caveat Emptor, "Let the buyer beware!" Still, this kind of event serves a useful purpose by giving a boost to the local economy, but what about the fair in the metaphorical town of Vanity? Although the mental image it presents is harmless enough, the reality behind the image could hardly be more sinister. Vanity Fair is another representation of the kingdom of darkness under the rule of the god of this world.

The term world as portrayed by Vanity Fair does not refer to the creation. The physical realm is the handiwork of God. He established its precise order and the immutable laws and principles by which it functions. (Proverbs 3:19-20; Jeremiah 51:15-16) As the sovereign ruler, he upholds and sustains it by his wisdom and power. (Hebrews 1:1-3) Thus the creation bears silent witness of his existence and universally declares his glory, eternal power, and Godhead. (Psalm 19:1-4; Romans 1:19-20)

From among the vast universe he created and set in motion, God prepared the earth as a fit habitation for man and the venue where his eternal purpose of salvation in his Son would be fulfilled. Therefore, the earth became the stage where the great drama of man's creation, fall, subsequent history and redemption would be performed. (John 1:9-10, 29; John 3:16) The cross of Christ is the focal point of both human history and God's redemptive purpose, the very reason why he made the heavens and the earth. (John 12:23-33; John 19:30; Galatians 4:4-5)

After Adam sinned against his Creator and lost the dominion that God gave him over the earth, Satan was quick to usurp that dominion and establish his own dark domain. (Genesis 1:27-28) In God's eternal plan, he permits the wicked one to instigate great chaos upon the earth, but only until his redemptive purpose is complete. In that day the last Adam, our Lord and Savior Jesus Christ, will forever restore all that was lost in Adam the first. (Romans 5:12-21; 2 Peter 3:9-13)

For now, however, Satan is the god of this world and rules in the unseen realm of spiritual powers. The apostle Paul described the nature of his kingdom as spiritual wickedness in high places. (Ephesians 6:12) Fallen men live, move, and have their being under his dark rule and unwittingly do his bidding. The term world, especially as used by the apostle John in both his Gospel and first Epistle, usually refers to this unseen realm under the dominion of the prince of the power of the air. (Ephesians 2:2-3) Its governmental policy is set in opposition to God's will and sovereignty. (John 14:30) Moreover, its philosophy is two-fold: to promote that which exalts man above his Creator, and to legislate that which promotes man's wickedness and rebellion against his Creator. (Romans 1:18-32)

Therefore, it is an understatement to say that Satan's kingdom is at cross-purposes with the kingdom of God. They are rivals in every sense of the word. The world-system under Satan's dark rule is represented in *The Pilgrim's Progress* as the allegorical City of Destruction, established upon the ruins of man's terrible fall. Since that time, the human race lives and moves within the boundaries of that great city. Although many have tried to escape its pollution, its tentacles extend to the uttermost regions of the earth. Its influence is not uniform, however, but takes three principal forms: the subtle aura of Carnal Policy, the compelling spirit of Vanity Fair, and the intoxicating allurement of the Enchanted Ground.

As we have already considered in chapter 5, the town of Carnal Policy denotes man's attempts to rise above his fallen condition, be his own god, and determine his own destiny. Although it strives to maintain an image of respectability, outwardly at least, its town spirit is the driving force at work in the children of disobedience. (Ephesians 2:2) Moreover, its secular humanist brand of Christianity by which so many are deceived, is really the spirit of antichrist. (1 John 2:18-22; 1 John 4:1-6)

So the town of Vanity and its perpetual fair are inseparably linked to Carnal Policy. They are two facets of the system of this world, with Vanity representing the more visible aspect. Its fair is an ancient structure almost as old as man himself, and Beelzebub the usurper rules as the chief lord of the fair. As an integral part of the City of Destruction, Vanity is its great center of commerce, the major hub of everyday human life and activity under the direct influence of Satan's evil empire. The fair that is held there all year long portrays the town spirit and realm of its influence, a spirit that consists of worshiping and serving the creature more than the Creator. Its name is highly significant, for it describes the highest condition that man can attain, in and of himself. (Psalm 39:5-6)

Vanity Fair under the rule of Beelzebub reminds me of the ancient city of Tyre and God's judgment upon it, as prophesied in Ezekiel 27. Like the allegorical town of Vanity, Tyre was a major center of world commerce in which every sort of merchandise could be found. The prince of Tyre, also called the king of Tyre, is compared to Satan himself and his downfall. (See Ezekiel 28) So the ancient city of Tyre could reasonably be considered a prototype of Vanity Fair.

The Enchanted Ground denotes the intoxicating influence and deceptive power of the world and its vanities. As its name suggests, it poses a significant danger to the people of God. However, we will reserve our consideration of this third aspect of the kingdom of darkness until Christian and his traveling companion arrive there.

The town of Vanity and its thriving marketplace

In common with Carnal Policy, Vanity was chartered and built upon the ruin that followed man's great fall. Its original design, to which it has strictly adhered for several millennia now, was to draw men away from God and the true worship of him, to capture their hearts, and keep their sights fixed upon earthly things. As master of this particular craft, Beelzebub is second to none. Therefore, he tailored Vanity Fair and its merchandise to suit man's insatiable desire for things that please his sinful nature. However, the commodities offered there are wretched substitutes for the lasting treasure and true joy that are only found in the Lord Jesus Christ.

Since the prince of the fair would just as soon have men remain ignorant of this fact, his underlying objective is to destroy the Gospel and those who live by it. To this end, he makes sure that there is a wide variety of merchandise readily available for purchase. Therefore, as long as Satan is the god of this world, Vanity Fair will remain a thriving enterprise. (2 Corinthians 4:3-4)

Dear reader, in order to rightly understand the spiritual significance of Vanity and its fair, we must look well beyond its local aspect. Like every other place in John Bunyan's great allegory, this one has no actual geographical boundaries. It exists wherever men are found, from earth's remotest regions to the great cities of the world. Its universal appeal goes all the way back to Satan's temptation of Eve. If you compare Genesis 3:6 with 1 John 2:15-16, you will notice a strong correlation between the tactics Satan used against Eve and the alluring power of the world and the things that are in the world. Eve yielded to the same line of reasoning that still ensnares people today. As a subtle, yet highly persuasive salesman, Satan makes a broad appeal to men. Scripture summarizes the vast array of merchandise he offers in three major divisions: *the lust of the flesh, and the lust of the eyes, and the pride of life.* (1 John 2:16) The three daughters of Adam the first, you may recall!

Before we form a wrong impression of Vanity Fair, we should take note that it has its respectable side as well as its seamier aspects. The lust of the flesh is a general heading for all kinds of self-indulgence. It denotes the pleasures of this life that appeal to man's natural desires, whether outwardly respectable or overtly wicked. Since hedonism is the watchword in Vanity Fair, there are indulgences to suit every taste, from the most cultured and refined to the coarsest and most wanton. However, all of them target man's desire for ease, diversion, and pleasure.

The next general category of merchandise, the lust of the eyes, is a little more abstract than the first one, but closely linked to it. The eyes may be thought of as the gateway to the soul. One sees, he desires, and then pursues his heart's desire. But since there are many different kinds of things that catch the eye and capture the heart, this category is a very broad one. Some of its offerings are strictly sensual in nature. We do not have to look very far to find merchandise of this sort. Risqué images are hard to avoid because they seem to be everywhere. Not only are they promoted in every form of media, they even confront us every time we go to the local mall. Furthermore, what a shameful commentary on our decadent society that addiction to pornography has become such a major problem, even among the very young!

As the people of God, we must resolve with the psalmist to set no wicked thing before our eyes. (Psalm 101:3) Even so, the lust of the eyes can take on any number of forms, many of which are quite respectable in Vanity Fair. One major manifestation of it is seen in man's personal ambitions and covetous nature. Some are so driven by the desire for earthly treasure that they labor tirelessly in order to accumulate great wealth and material possessions. Others are motivated by the thirst for power and worldly influence. These make their way up through the ranks, ruthlessly if necessary, and pity the one who stands in their way! Still others set out to distinguish themselves in a particular way. For them, no sacrifice is too great in order to reach their goal. Moreover, they give little thought to those who might be harmed in the process, and no thought at all for the honor and glory of God.

These are just a few of the directions in which man's ambitious nature might lead him. But no matter what particular course it may take, the lust of the eyes will always drive him to seek his treasure in this world. Tragically, this quest is one in which he will never find true satisfaction. (Proverbs 27:20)

Then there is the pride of life, the third major category of merchandise found in Vanity Fair. It specifically targets man's desire for vainglory, his natural tendency to exalt himself at the expense of others. When we think of man's desire for vainglory, we tend to limit it to the more affluent residents of the City of Destruction, those who are generally deemed role models because of their worldly success. Some of them attained prominence in the political realm, whether due to their personal charisma, political savvy, or friends in high places. Others seek to distinguish themselves in the business world, perhaps as the CEO of a major corporation. For others, their ruling passion is to be part of the financial gurus of Wall Street, where they hope to achieve wealth, power, and prestige.

Still others seek worldly glory in the field of athletics. A case in point would be the Olympic hopeful who disciplines himself and trains vigorously for years, staking all his hopes upon that one moment in time when the eyes of the world will be upon him. Then there is the professional athlete who sacrifices all that is most important in life, and sometimes his personal integrity, in order to be known as the greatest of the great, for a little while at least.

Finally, there is the broad field of academia, which encompasses man's relentless quest for wisdom and knowledge. There is ample scope to distinguish oneself here, and countless ways in which to do so. This search for enlightenment is not equivalent to a quest for truth, however. Primarily, secular humanism is the philosophy behind it, and man's intellectual accomplishments are objects of veneration. Moreover, agnosticism is the accepted religion of this broad-minded sphere in which just about anything is tolerated except the one true God and his Word. (2 Timothy 3:7)

Admittedly, these are just a few ways in which men seek to make a name for themselves, and there is no shortage of opportunities to do so in Vanity Fair. But is the desire for vainglory only a problem for the brightest and the best? Is it limited to those who have great potential and strive to live up to it, or to those who are successful in their endeavors? No, indeed! The pride of life dwells in the hearts of all men by nature and silently festers there, whether they achieve earthly honor and glory or not. No matter how it happens to manifest itself, man's exaltation of himself always leads him to deny God as the sovereign Lord over all. (Psalm 14:1; Romans 1:21-25)

This thought brings us to the great irony of Vanity Fair. In spite of man's practical atheism, he is innately religious. So in order to accommodate this need, the fair has a distinctively religious aspect. Its clever lord makes sure that there is also sufficient merchandise available to fill man's spiritual void.

At the time when John Bunyan wrote *The Pilgrim's Progress*, what he termed the "wares of Rome" held a monopoly in Vanity Fair. That is not so much the case at the present time. Throughout Vanity's lengthy existence, her merchandise has proved to be highly adaptable. It has acclimated itself to every sort of human religion and offers something to suit every spiritual whim. But the town is particularly proud of its brand of Christianity, with its gospel that dilutes the truth until the offense of the cross is removed. (Galatians 1:6-9; 1 Peter 2:6-8) Therefore, buyers beware! The merchants of the earth who conduct business in Vanity's fair serve the kingdom of Satan, the seat of the beast, where they barter ruthlessly for the souls of men. (Revelation 18:11-19)

The merchandise offered for sale in Vanity's open marketplace is only limited by the imagination, but all of it is tainted by association with the prince of darkness. The infrastructure of Satan's kingdom, called Babylon the great in Revelation 17 and 18, is that by which he lures, deceives, and captivates the hearts and minds of fallen men. All is geared toward that which is earthly, sensual, and devilish, even those things that do not directly appeal to man's baser inclinations. Thus even the harmless joys and legitimate things that constitute everyday life, such as family, community, education and career, fall loosely within the realm of Vanity Fair because they pertain strictly to this life. Although these things are not inherently wrong, they will become idols should they capture the heart. Thus the warning given to us in 1 John 5:21.

So Vanity Fair denotes the love of the world and the things that are in the world. It dwells in the hearts of all men by nature, and herein is the root of the matter. Therefore, the unsaved person seeks even the lawful things of life within the realm of the kingdom of darkness. As long as he remains in that condition, he will inevitably fail to achieve true happiness, fulfillment, and meaning in life. Consequently, he will be discontented with God's provision and will abuse his goodness by perverting even that which is lawful. (Ecclesiastes 5:10-12; Proverbs 21:4)

It bears repeating that man's problem lies squarely in his heart, not in external things. His sinful nature will always lead him away from God and drive him to seek his portion in this life, whether in the realm of fleshly pleasure, earthly treasure, or personal vainglory. Perhaps it will even be a quest for all three! (Ecclesiastes 2:10-11)

The vanity of man's existence apart from the fear and knowledge of God is the theme of the book of Ecclesiastes. This conclusion was the result of the author's reflection upon a lifetime of rare privilege and successful enterprises, not the bitter experience of a poor, disillusioned soul who was never able to get ahead in life. The deduction was King Solomon's: *the Preacher, the son of David, king of Jerusalem.* (Ecclesiastes 1:1) He was a man who had it all in an earthly sense, and was a giant among men as to his superior intellectual attainments. (2 Chronicles 9:1-8) Moreover, he was also a man of vast wealth and power, a man sought after for his unmatched wisdom and knowledge, and a man filled with godly wisdom as well. (2 Chronicles 1:8-12)

Since he learned the vanity of earthly pursuits from the perspective of great wealth and success, who could have a more objective opinion upon the subject than he? (See Ecclesiastes 2:3-11) But we also know from Scripture that Solomon sinned grievously against the great wisdom and knowledge given him by God. (1 Kings 11:1-8; Nehemiah 13:26) However, we dare not discount his writings just because he failed to live up to them. They are the inspired words of God. Moreover, the way in which Solomon reached his final conclusion was also in the purpose of God. (Ecclesiastes 12:1, 13-14)

The preacher was well acquainted with Vanity Fair. Too well, in fact! Yet after experiencing its delights to the fullest measure and growing disillusioned with them, he turned from vanity in the end and returned to the God of his youth. In a very real sense, he learned a higher wisdom from his own folly, and as a result, the wise man counsels others to be wiser than he had been. (Proverbs 3:13-15)

Without the Lord Jesus Christ, man leads an empty, futile existence. He attempts to fill his spiritual void with the things of this world, but finds nothing that can satisfy his deepest needs. (Ecclesiastes 6:7-9) What's more, the very things that capture his heart will eventually render him a servant to trifles that are his for just a little while. All too soon he must leave them to another. (Psalm 103:15-16) When viewed in this light, the glittering ornaments of Vanity Fair are not so appealing after all, are they? Not only do they lack enduring substance, the bargains obtained at a discount there will prove very costly in the end. (Matthew 16:26)

In his infinite wisdom, God does not see fit to immediately take his people into his presence when he saves them. His purpose is for us to be lights in a dark world, and live for his glory as godly examples in a place where wickedness and corruption are the accepted norms. (Matthew 5:13-16; Philippians 2:15-16) Therefore, in order to reach the

Celestial City, our pathway takes us through the metaphorical town of Vanity just as surely as it leads us past the cave of the giants. Yes, dear reader, there is a definite connection between the two.

As we face this daunting prospect, what a comfort it is to know that our Lord walked the path before us, was sorely tempted by the fair's dark lord, resisted his every effort and would have none of his merchandise. (Matthew 4:1-11; Luke 4:1-13) His delight was to do his Father's will and fulfill the mission for which he came to earth. So even though he was the friend of sinners, he passed through the world and faced its temptations while remaining *holy, harmless, unde-filed, separate from sinners, and made higher than the heavens.* (Hebrews 7:26) We would have no hope at all had this not been the case.

Like our Lord Jesus Christ, we are not part of the world-system as represented by Vanity Fair. Before we were born again, we were right at home there; but now, we pass through it as pilgrims and strangers. (Ephesians 2:2-3, 11-13; Hebrews 11:13-14; 1 Peter 2:11-12) Therefore, we can expect no better treatment than our Lord received when he walked this way. (John 15:18-21)

Our Lord passed through the town of Vanity without receiving the least blot upon his righteous character, but sadly, we cannot claim the same. Although our heart's desire is to face temptation without falling prey to it, we are susceptible to its power and influence. There-fore, if we would keep ourselves unspotted from the world, we must guard our hearts with all diligence. (Proverbs 4:23-27)

Thomas Manton wisely said, "Worldly desires, like nettles, breed of their own accord; but spiritual desires need a great deal of culti-vating." [1] How right he was! Although some might be so foolish as to deny it, Vanity Fair poses an ever-present danger for the true child of God. Since our flesh still has its roots there, it wages continual war-fare against our new man. (Romans 7:21-25) Remember Christian's fierce battle with Apollyon in the Valley of Humiliation, and Faith-ful's terrible struggle with Adam the first on the hill Difficulty? Van-ity Fair appears in many different forms, does it not?

Some think they can escape the pollution of Vanity Fair through self-isolation and the practice of a strict ascetic lifestyle. However, its noxious influence will find the religious hermit in the remotest cave in the wilderness. Just as easily, it seeps through the stone walls of the most carefully sequestered monastery, and so does the love of its merchandise.

For the child of God, the alluring power of the world is broken even though it is not removed. The apostle John gave the secret of overcoming its deadly influence when he wrote: *Love not the world, neither the things that are in the world. If any man love the world, the love of the Father is not in him.* (1 John 2:15) So the battle with Vanity Fair is either won or lost in the heart and mind.

To live in this world without being a part of it requires a delicate balance. Earthly blessings are not likely to harm us as long as we view them in contrast to the incomparable treasure that is ours in Christ. (1 Timothy 6:17-19; James 4:13-14) But they can quickly turn into a curse if we set our hearts upon them. (Psalm 39:6-7) Likewise, we should strive for excellence in all that we do, but not for personal glory or worldly acclaim. Our chief priority is to honor God in all that we do. The wrong comes when self-interest, worldly ambition, and the desire for vainglory come into play, which they often do

Therefore, in spite of our best intentions, Vanity Fair poses a problem for us. We need help in order to properly enjoy our earthly blessings without abusing them, and we have it in our Lord Jesus Christ, our great high priest. Since he walked the path before us, he is *touched with the feeling of our infirmities.* He understands and sympathizes with us in our constant struggles because he was *in all points tempted like as we are, yet without sin.* (Hebrews 4:15) Even though he does not take us out of the realm of temptation, he ever lives to make intercession for us. So beyond the shadow of a doubt, he who overcame every temptation that Satan could hurl at him is well able to guard and protect his children from the tempter's snare. (John 17:5-9, 14-16)

An unprovoked incident

As Christian and Faithful entered the bustling town of Vanity, the last thing they intended to do was to create a public disturbance. Yet even though they did nothing to draw attention to themselves, their very presence sparked immediate controversy among the locals and outright animosity in the hearts of some. What was it that made them stand out as strangers rather than natural-born citizens of Vanity?

They were conspicuously different in their character, speech, and conduct..

Their strange clothing was one major cause of offense. Although well suited to their heavenly calling, their dress was unlike that which is usually seen in the streets of Vanity. Many of the residents wore the garment of self-righteousness and religious hypocrisy, but next to these, Christian and Faithful presented a sharp contrast. As true followers of Jesus Christ, they were striving to live godly lives and be separate from the world. Their strange garments denoted both their godly character and determination to maintain their moral integrity in spite of the evil influences and temptations all around them. (Ephesians 4:17-24) Not surprisingly, the locals resented the implication.

Their peculiar speech was another thing that aroused suspicion among the natives. It sounded so strange, almost as if they spoke a foreign language, which in reality, they did. Christian and Faithful spoke the language of Zion, a dialect that is contrary to the world's carnal policy, vain philosophy, and false religion. In speaking of precious truths concerning Christ and his kingdom, they talked of things that the citizens of Vanity neither understood nor desired. The fact that their godly lives were consistent with their Gospel witness did nothing to lessen the hostility. (Psalm 94:11; Psalm 144:7-8; 2 Peter 2:18)

The thing that stirred the people to anger more than anything else was Christian and Hopeful's indifference to the merchandise offered for sale in the town's fair. When asked what they would purchase from among the wide variety of commodities offered there, they boldly stated that they would *Buy the truth and sell it not.* (Proverbs 23:23) This refusal to negotiate in Vanity's marketplace did not mean that they were immune to its temptation, but it did reveal the orientation of their hearts. They were compelled by the knowledge that no man can serve two masters; therefore, their primary objective was to seek God's kingdom and righteousness with their whole hearts. (Matthew 6:24-34)

Since we have witnessed some of their struggles with conflicting desires, we know that neither Christian nor Faithful was perfect in this regard. However, with hearts that were firmly set upon higher pursuits, they were resolved to maintain their spiritual integrity.

(Psalm 119:37; Colossians 3:1-3) Thus they were unlikely to win any popularity contests in Vanity Fair!

Dear brother or sister in Christ, please bear in mind that irreconcilable differences exist between the kingdom of God and the system of this world, portrayed here by Vanity Fair. As the people of God, we are caught in the crossfire of this ongoing battle, and often made to feel it keenly. However, this is not the case with humanistic religion. By its focus upon the outward and ostentatious, it fits quite nicely into the scheme of things in Vanity. Moreover, since its chief selling point is the promise that one may have the world and salvation, too, there is no shortage of takers, as you can imagine.

Herein is the crux of the matter. Although man-centered religion is heartily endorsed in Vanity Fair, there is no market for the truth there. To this day, it remains strictly under the rule of Satan, the father of lies. (John 8:44) He knows full well that the Gospel of Christ threatens the very existence of his kingdom. Therefore, he does everything in his power to keep men blinded to the truth and its incomparable worth. (2 Corinthians 4:3-4; Proverbs 3:13-15) As a result of his diabolical scheme, the truth is universally hated in Vanity Fair.

When the Lord Jesus Christ came into the world, he was hated without a cause. Men refused to believe him because he told them the truth. (John 8: 43-45) It is just the same today. Those who do not obey the truth still cannot endure the hearing of it. Therefore, as the followers of Christ, we should expect no better treatment than he received.

We have already observed that the mere presence of Christian and Faithful was enough to produce offense among the town's residents. This unprovoked opposition is the world's typical response to a true Christian. (1 John 3:1, 13; 1 John 4:6) The people vented their contempt for the two men by mocking, taunting, and threatening them simply because they did what was right! Furthermore, when the people saw that Christian and Faithful refused to compromise, they took their verbal abuse to the next level. The resulting commotion reminds me of the uproar of the silversmiths in Ephesus when the apostle Paul preached the Gospel there. (Acts 19:21-32) Before long, news of the mêlée came to the attention of the local authorities, and the friends of Beelzebub were sent to look into the matter.

When asked about their strange clothing, Christian and Faithful explained that they were foreigners traveling to their own country, the heavenly Jerusalem. Since they spoke of a kingdom that the world neither sees nor acknowledges, their words seemed as nonsense to their interrogators. (John 3:3; John 18:36; Hebrews 12:22-28) In spite of the brutal manner of their inquisitors, Christian and Faithful stood firmly by their convictions and testimony. Consequently, they were shamefully mistreated and abused, and to add insult to injury, they were maligned and labeled as madmen. An interesting charge, since the real madmen are those willing to sell their souls for the trinkets of Vanity Fair!

Such was the experience of Christian and Faithful in the town of Vanity, much as Evangelist had predicted. Instead of responding in kind, however, they endured the wrongful suffering with dignity and grace, *not rendering evil for evil, or railing for railing: but contrariwise blessing.* (1 Peter 3:9) It was this rare quality of returning good for evil that captured the attention of some of the people. Moreover, those who had any sense of justice were troubled by the behavior of their compatriots, knowing that the two men had done nothing to deserve such cruel treatment. These began to lay the blame where it really belonged, and a few of them even ventured so far as to intercede for the strangers.

Before long, contrary opinions caused the people to take sides, with all of them shouting at the same time and each side blaming the other for the uproar. The few who dared to defend Christian and Faithful shared a measure of their fate, for they were mocked and scorned as well. Eventually, the heated exchange erupted into a near riot, and law enforcement was called in to disperse the angry mob and restore order.

Since majority opinion eventually carried the day, the few souls who had the courage to speak on behalf of the two men were silenced at once. Christian and Faithful were arrested, taken before the local magistrates, and charged with creating pandemonium. Being denied any due process of law, they were severely beaten, bound with chains, and paraded up and down the streets of Vanity. This despicable act of cruelty was done primarily as a warning to any who might be tempted to join them.

Thus the lord of the fair did his utmost to destroy Christian and Faithful's credibility and suppress their Gospel witness. However, they reacted in a way that he could neither deny nor challenge. As the persecution against them intensified, so did the meekness and patience with which they bore it. In this, they followed the example of their Lord who *when he was reviled, reviled not again; when he suffered, he threatened not; but committed himself to him that judgeth righteously.* (1 Peter 2:23)

Therefore, something else happened as a result of that day's incident in the town of Vanity. In spite of every attempt to prevent it, a few of the townsmen were won by their verbal witness and patient endurance under fire. It was an outcome that enraged their persecutors all the more, and the town now faced quite a dilemma. What was to be done with the troublemakers? Order must be restored, and the town's reputation upheld. The more radical faction argued that the only permanent solution was to kill the two perpetrators. These apparently had no scruples about condemning the men before their guilt or innocence could be established. In the end, however, cooler heads prevailed. Christian and Faithful were remanded to prison until their case could be brought to trial.

Even though they were guilty of no wrongdoing, the two brothers were cast into prison and fastened there in chains, pending charges of treason and other high crimes against Vanity Fair and its prince. Their situation reminds me of Paul and Silas in jail at Philippi. (Acts 16:19-25) In like manner, Christian and Faithful did not waste time wallowing in self-pity because of what they had suffered, or might yet have to face. They put the time to much better use by reflecting upon God's Word and his purpose in their circumstances. As they did so, the words of their beloved friend, Evangelist, came strongly to heart and mind in the quietness of their solitary confinement. It was no strange thing that had happened to them. Suffering is the believer's expected lot in this world, and for those with the spiritual discernment to understand, it is cause for rejoicing. (1 Peter 4:12-16)

One particular benefit of this kind of suffering is that it weans the heart even more from the vanities of this world and fixes it more firmly on things above. (1 Peter 4:1-2) So as Christian and Faithful pondered their situation and its probable outcome, they also remembered Evangelist's prediction that at least one of them would die in that place. (1 Peter 4:19) Even though neither man relished the thought, each of them knew in his heart that the martyr would have the better part.

* * * *

My brother or sister in Christ, Vanity Fair is still alive and well in our day. Therefore, we need not go looking for trouble in this world because it will find us soon enough. (Philippians 1:27-29) Like Christian and Faithful, we are citizens of a heavenly kingdom; thus, we are in the world but not of it. (Philippians 3:20-21) Our full allegiance belongs to another prince, the Lord Jesus Christ, and our hearts are set upon goals that transcend this fleeting life. All that is necessary for us to invoke the world's anger is to be true to our Lord and bear his name openly before men. (2 Timothy 3:12)

Soon now, Christian and Faithful will have their day in court and stand before the bar of justice. As we enter the courtroom with them and observe the judicial proceedings, we will gain deeper insight into the nature of the town of Vanity. We will also come face-to-face with many of its most prominent citizens, one of whom will be the presiding judge. Moreover, as we observe the jury, we will marvel at those chosen to perform this solemn duty. Later in the trial we will hear several of the king's witnesses testify on behalf of the prosecution. But will a single voice dare to speak on behalf of the accused?

Study Questions

1. What great entity does the allegorical town of Vanity represent? How is Vanity with its year-round fair inseparably linked to the town of Carnal Policy? In what way is the town of Vanity an integral part of the City of Destruction?

2. What was the original design, or purpose, of Vanity and its thriving marketplace? Who is the ruler of Vanity Fair? Into what three major divisions does Scripture summarize the merchandise offered for sale in Vanity's fair? Briefly describe them.

3. What is the great irony of Vanity Fair? How does the lord of the fair adapt its merchandise to accommodate man's inherently religious nature?

4. The very presence of Christian and Faithful created a public disturbance among the town's residents. What three things made them stand out as radically different from the native-born citizens? Briefly describe these three things.

5. What single thing stirred the people to anger more than anything else? When verbal abuse against Christian and Faithful escalated to outright cruelty, how did a small number of the people react to it? What did the authorities finally do in order to restore order?

CHAPTER 34

Tried in the Court of Vanity Fair!

IN THE SCRIPTURES WE LEARN OF OUR CALLING AS A DISTINCT AND separate people, called out of the world and set apart unto God. However, it is in the course of our daily lives, as we face the contempt of a hostile world, that this truth becomes a settled reality in our hearts. The longer we travel the path of life, the more clearly we understand that this kind of suffering is actually a beneficial thing. It serves as a continual reminder not to put down deep roots and settle too comfortably in a place that is not our rest. Under certain conditions, the fact that we are in the world but not of it can capture the attention of those in high places and even expose us to outright persecution.

The current situation of Christian and Faithful is a case in point. Their arrest, brutal treatment, and imminent trial illustrate just how offensive the Christian is to this world, its standards, and its sphere of operation. Even though the two men had no intention of causing trouble, their godly lives and testimonies made peaceful coexistence with the inhabitants of Vanity Fair a virtual impossibility.

In 2 Corinthians 6:14-18, the apostle Paul explains why this is so. Irreconcilable differences exist between the children of God and those who are not – differences that require our separation from the world and its ways. What common ground of fellowship can possibly exist between righteousness and unrighteousness? What basis for communion is there between light and darkness? What concord, what harmony, is possible between Christ and false religion? What thing in common, what equality can unite a believer with infidels? What foundation of agreement is there between the temple of God and idols? None whatsoever! In each case there is a great gulf that we dare not cross.

The world has little tolerance for the true followers of Jesus Christ. Since darkness hates light, it will always seek to suppress and extinguish it. Therefore, the more distinct we are from this present evil world, the more we will feel its enmity. The pressure to conform can be quite forceful, and for those who refuse to compromise, the world's attitude is often: "Let's get rid of the troublemakers!"

Christian and Faithful have now come to this extremity. At last their day in court was set, and at the appointed time they will face their accusers. Before they do, however, let us consider the court before whose bar they must stand and answer the serious charges brought against them. They will be tried in the court of worldly opinion, and if found guilty, sentenced by those who are their sworn enemies. So there will be nothing fair or impartial about this trial, and the interests of justice will hardly be served. Its sole purpose is to condemn the two men and extinguish their testimony before it spreads any further.

The standard of any court will rise no higher than the character of its presiding judge. On the day when Christian and Faithful were brought to trial, the honorable Lord Hate-Good sat on the bench. His infamy was widely known, for this particular judge was numbered among the vilest of men. (2 Timothy 3:3) Therefore, his presence in the courtroom made an open mockery of the whole proceeding. To be falsely accused and placed on trial for your life would be terrible enough, even if you were reasonably confident that you would receive a fair trial. But what upholding of the law, what justice could be expected from one whose very name marked him as a hater of righteousness, and by inference, a lover of evil?

Since Judge Hate-Good bore the image and character of his spiritual father the devil, he hated Christian and Faithful on sight. After all, he who despises good hates without a cause. Moreover, his heart was that of a murderer and liar, for they who hate good also despise the truth. (John 8:37-45) In brief, he was the very essence of all that is worst in fallen human nature, and therefore, well qualified to preside over the court of his evil master.

Even in the courtroom of such a judge, an attempt was made to maintain at least a semblance of proper procedure. So the trial opened with reading the formal indictment of all charges against the defendants. Although those who brought the charges were not really friends with one another, they were united in their hatred for Christian and Faithful. As to their accusations, they were based upon personal grievances rather than actual violations of the law.

The indictment contained three specific allegations against the two men. They were charged with disrupting the town's trade, holding the prince of the fair in contempt, and winning others to their opinion. Yet in bringing these charges against Christian and Faithful, their accusers really incriminated themselves before a much higher court. (John 3:19-20; Isaiah 5:20)

Dear reader, from this point through the rest of the trial, Faithful will stand at the bar alone and answer the trumped-up charges of their accusers. He appears to be the primary defendant and Christian merely charged with being his accomplice. If so, perhaps he was the bolder and more outspoken of the two men.

Concerning the allegation that he was an enemy to the fair's trade, Faithful honestly declared that he was only opposed to that which was in opposition to the one he served, the Lord Jesus Christ. As to the accusation that he had disturbed the peace in the town of Vanity, he answered that he was entirely innocent. Following in the steps of his master, he endeavored with all his heart to be a peacemaker. The disturbance came entirely from the enemies' camp, when he and Christian refused to compromise their convictions.

The charge that he and Christian had won others to their cause was a very serious one, but they had not deliberately sown seeds of rebellion, as was alleged. The truth of their words, and the patience with which they endured wrongful suffering, spoke louder than any verbal testimony they could give. However, Faithful's declaration that those who were won had "turned from the worse to better" was not likely to aid his defense. Neither was his answer to the charge that he and Christian had defied the laws of the town's prince, for he boldly stated that the prince was the enemy of his Lord. Thus by declaring his allegiance to the Lord Jesus Christ and openly defying Vanity's prince, Faithful probably sealed his fate before the trial really began.

Witnesses for the prosecution

After Faithful had answered the charges of his accusers, the evidentiary phase of the trial began. Dispensing with the formality of an opening statement, the prosecution called for witnesses to offer state's evidence. Three men stepped forward to speak on behalf of lord Beelzebub, the offended party in this case. Their names were Envy, Superstition, and Pickthank, which were rather strange names to be entered into the court's official record. As choice servants of the father of lies, these three are ever willing to raise their voices against the people of God. Moreover, their testimony is sure to be clever and convincing. But how credible are they, and how likely to speak the whole truth? Everyone knows that their master has a long history of bribing witnesses in order to alter the outcome of trials just like this one. Would the prosecution's star witnesses be willing to commit perjury? Dear reader, listen to them carefully and you will discover for yourself.

Envy was the first to come forward with evidence of serious crimes against the ruler of Vanity Fair. After being duly sworn to tell the truth, he gave some highly incriminating testimony against the accused. However, this witness had a personal vendetta against Faithful because, in common with the judge, he was a despiser of those who are good. He hated Faithful and Christian for being what he was not! Since he was quite apt in twisting and perverting the truth, he used Faithful's own words against him by taking them entirely out of context. In this way, Envy slandered Faithful by depicting him as a vile sort of man, a rebel against civil authority, a troublemaker who disregarded the town's laws and customs and a vocal proponent of heretical beliefs.

As Envy strongly denounced Faithful for both his Christian testimony and godly example, he was well aware that he had the jury's rapt attention. After all, envy has ever been a powerful tool of Satan to stir up hatred against the people of God. Therefore, Envy gained a sympathetic hearing among the jurors, because Faithful's bold witness had also offended each one of them personally. To reinforce his case, Envy quoted Faithful as saying, "That Christianity and the Customs of our town of Vanity, were diametrically opposite, and could not be reconciled." In this he spoke truth, but Envy tried to turn Faithful's sword against him by painting him as one who was narrow-minded, judgmental, and quick to condemn all the "laudable doings" of Vanity Fair.

Since the jurors were already prejudiced against Faithful, they were more than willing to believe the worst about him, and the king's first witness knew it well. Being highly skilled in the art of reading faces, he knew he had scored a significant point for the prosecution, and thought it best to quit while he was ahead. So Envy slowly stepped aside, giving the jury a few moments to consider what he had said, but their countenances were already set against the prisoner at the bar. As a result of his damaging testimony, it is safe to presume that jeopardy had already attached.

Who is this one named Envy, who argued so convincingly on behalf of his king? He is a destroyer, the brainchild of Apollyon the ultimate destroyer. (Revelation 9:11) Envy is really Satan's master as well as his servant, for it was envy against God that led to his downfall. (Isaiah 14:12-15; Ezekiel 28:13-17) Afterward, envy filled his heart with such hatred for the human race that he plotted and succeeded in instigating man's fall also. Envy has been actively at work in the human race ever since, inflicting untold damage under the direction of its diabolical master.

Since envy dwells in the hearts of all men by nature, it is actively at work in Vanity Fair. (Romans 1:28-32) Very early in human history, this green-eyed monster drove Cain to kill his brother, Abel. (1 John 3:11-13) It festered in the hearts of Joseph's brothers until it finally drove them to plot the murder of the innocent boy. (Genesis 37:4-28) Envy poisoned the heart of King Saul against his faithful servant, David. (1 Samuel 18:5-14) It prompted certain Chaldeans to denounce Shadrach, Meshach, and Abednego for refusing to bow to Nebuchadnezzar's golden image. (Daniel 3:8-25) Envy moved presidents and princes to bring charges against godly Daniel before King Darius, hoping to destroy him and win the king's favor with a single blow. (Daniel 6) It was envy that drove men to testify against Stephen and incite the people against him because of his bold Gospel testimony before the Jewish Sanhedrin. (Acts 6:8-15)

Thus Envy has raised his ugly voice on behalf of his master many times before, but without a doubt, his most despicable act was committed against the holy, sinless Son of God. Knowing that the Lord

Jesus was innocent of any wrongdoing, Pilate allowed envy to have its way by delivering him into the hands of his enemies for the sake of political expediency. (Matthew 27:11-26; note verse 18) Thinking of nothing beyond the furthering of his own personal interests, the governor of Judea turned a blind eye to what was true and right in order to pacify the Jews. (Mark 15:9-15)

There has never been a time in human history when envy worked more furiously to have its way. It sought and found false witnesses who were willing to testify against the Lord Jesus by perverting his words of truth and using them against him. (Matthew 26:57-66; Luke 22:66-71) Yet envy could not secure even a single credible witness. Many came, but none were found! (Mark 14:55-56)

Like his evil master, Envy hates the truth and those who live by it. Since he is the avowed enemy of the Lord Jesus Christ and his people, his testimony against Faithful should have been ruled inadmissible. But even though his allegations were false and he deliberately perjured himself by distorting the truth, the judge kept silent and the jurors received his testimony as true.

After Envy had taken his seat, Superstition came forward with additional evidence against poor Faithful. Like the first witness, this one also had his own personal agenda; therefore, the facts of the case were of little importance to him. After swearing to speak only the truth, he admitted up front to having little knowledge of the accused, and yet, he accused Faithful of being a "very pestilent fellow" based upon a single conversation with him. What had Faithful done to invoke such malice in one who was a virtual stranger to him? He had dared to speak the truth.

The witness named Superstition was living proof that men will believe a lie more quickly than they do the truth. It seems that Faithful had highly offended him by declaring that the town's religion was vain, and no one could please God by the practice of it. Moreover, this second witness for the prosecution was not alone in resenting the implication. The town's rather large religious population was also up in arms at the mere suggestion that they worshiped in vain, were yet in their sins, and would be condemned in the end. So even though this brief testimony was all the evidence that Superstition could muster, he had plenty of support in the courtroom.

Superstition takes deep root and thrives best in an environment of spiritual ignorance. Therefore, it is an integral part of all pagan cultures, manifesting itself in every sort of perverse ritual, cruel practice, moral degradation and idol worship. Superstition also lies at the heart of the more civilized forms of false religion, in which idols of wood and stone give way to idols of the heart. Darkened understanding is replaced by so-called enlightened thought, which is nothing more than spiritual ignorance of a more sophisticated kind. However, it is just as false and deceptive as the primitive forms, and just as full of enmity against the truth. So yes, dear reader, superstition is alive and well in the modern town of Vanity.

Aided and abetted by false religion, the philosophy upon which Vanity Fair was built incorporates the worldviews of both Pope and Pagan – bloodthirsty giants who hate pilgrims, if you recall. Superstition, who happens to be good friends with both giants, is a pillar that helps support the whole. Thus it holds a powerful sway over the hearts and minds of unregenerate men. However, the hammer of truth is able to bring down the entire structure of darkness and deception, and therein lies its greatest threat. (Jeremiah 23:29)

The prince of darkness finds that false religion (Pope) suits his purpose every bit as well as secular humanism (Pagan). Therefore, he has no problem with those who are religious, as long as they worship gods that are fashioned according to their own vain imaginations. (Psalm 50:21; Acts 17:22-29) But he will brook no opposition!

It is a tragic flaw in unsaved men that they would rather believe a lie than be disturbed by the truth. Thus they will cling to a false hope no matter how unreasonable it is. So if Envy is a destroyer, Superstition is a deceiver. Its roots can always be traced to ignorance of the truth; therefore, it thrives in the realm of false religion.

Because Superstition blinds men to the truth and gives rise to irrational fears, it prompts them to give heed to *seducing spirits, and doctrines of devils.* (1 Timothy 4:1) By its very nature, it leads them to embrace fables and believe lies while rejecting the true fear and knowledge of God. Moreover, it leads men to trust in the idols of their hearts rather than the living God.

Since it stands in direct opposition to the truth, Superstition always takes sides against those who believe and obey the Gospel. In its more flagrant forms, it lures men to become involved in idol worship and occult practices, which are commonly found in most pagan cultures. But in common with Envy, Superstition inhabits the minds of all men by nature, even those who would not dare to dabble in outward idolatry or the occult. It directs their hearts and minds in the ways of the evil one, which are ways of spiritual darkness and deception. No matter the form it happens to take, Superstition leads men in a downward path. So like his fellow witness, Envy, he is also a destroyer of men. (1 Samuel 28).

The third and final witness to give state's evidence was a man named Pickthank. Although there are many like him all around us, his name is rarely heard anymore. It is an archaic word meaning, "one who curries favor with another, as by flattery, or especially, by talebearing." [1] Pickthank justly deserved his reputation as an underhanded man who desired personal fame and fortune above all else. Like most of his kind, he was skilled in the art of flattery, had no qualms whatsoever about stretching the truth, and customarily sided with those who could do the most for him. Therefore, his testimony was for sale to the highest bidder.

Like most people who lack personal integrity, Pickthank bitterly resented those who stood firmly for truth and right. In particular, he despised those who desired to please God rather than men. Those who were his exact opposite! Men like Faithful! His appearance in court reminds me of the time when the apostle Paul appeared before Felix, the governor of Caesarea, to answer charges brought against him by the Jewish leaders in Jerusalem. These men hired an orator named Tertullus to present their case against Paul and persuade Felix to condemn him. (Acts 24:1-9) In like manner, Pickthank sought to ingratiate himself before the court as soon as he took the witness stand. Sensing the direction that the trial was taking, he gave his enthusiastic endorsement to the previous testimony, and did not hesitate to perjure himself by slandering the innocent man.

As Pickthank began his testimony, it was obvious that he had little of which to actually accuse Faithful, even though he claimed to have known him for quite some time. His chief bone of contention was that Faithful had spoken against "our noble Prince Beelzebub," and that he had held in contempt the prince's honorable friends: "Lord Old-Man, the Lord Carnal-Delight, the Lord Luxurious, the Lord Desire of Vain-Glory, my old Lord Leachery, Sir Having Greedy, with all the rest of our nobility." Furthermore, he quoted Faithful as saying that if he had his way, none of these noblemen would have a place in the town.

Dear reader, these friends of Beelzebub are presumably choice servants of his, since they have a place among the town's nobility. Ponder their names carefully and you will see that they represent the various lusts that rule in Vanity Fair and figure prominently in its bustling trade. Moreover, they rule in the hearts of the town's residents. In this sense they are lords indeed, because they control all who live under their power. Thus they do much to further the interests of their dark prince.

Pickthank summed up his malicious testimony by accusing Faithful of speaking against the judge and defaming him publicly along with most of the town's elite. We could say that he saved the best argument until last, for Judge Hate-Good just happened to be one of Vanity's most prominent citizens. Everyone in the courtroom knew that he was on the payroll of lord Beelzebub and served as one of his most devoted servants.

Since Pickthank understood this better than most, he used the knowledge to his own advantage by playing up to the judge. Long experience had taught him that a flattering tongue and ingratiating manner would go far toward gaining him favor in high places. So even though he had to resort to outright lies, he gladly took the part of Faithful's enemy. In this, Pickthank played the part of the devil's advocate rather well, did he not? Faithful had little hope of justice before this witness took the stand, but now his future looked bleak indeed.

When viewed in a spiritual light, there is more to these three witnesses for the prosecution than meets the eye. As we unmask them and ponder their combined testimony, we will gain deeper insight into the reasons behind the world's enmity against God's people. All three of them cooperated together with the common goal of suppressing the truth and those who proclaim it and live by it. Envy depicts the natural man's hatred of the truth, Superstition denotes his blindness to the truth, and Pickthank illustrates man's willingness to sacrifice truth and right for the sake of self-interest.

Not surprisingly, the king's star witnesses made their case very well. Upon hearing Pickthank's final argument, Judge Hate-Good, who should have recused himself at that point, became livid with rage. At his best, the wicked man was incapable of making a right judgment, but he now dropped all pretense of objectivity. Throwing courtroom protocol aside, he addressed the prisoner directly, hurling epithets such as "renegade, heretic and traitor" against him. Moreover, he did so with no thought of how his scathing outburst would prejudice the jury.

Alone but not forsaken

At this point in the trial, Faithful spoke up and asked permission to speak in his own defense. Acting somewhat out of character, the judge decided to extend leniency and allow him to speak, but not before declaring that the prisoner was not fit to live any longer. After all, Hate-Good must have reasoned, what could Faithful possibly say that would alter the outcome now?

I am sure it has not escaped your notice that Faithful faced his enemies alone in the courtroom that day. For whatever reason, no lawyer stood by his side to advise him, guard his interests, and protect his civil rights. He was appointed no defense attorney to speak on his behalf and raise objections against the damaging testimony given by the king's witnesses, much of which was either hearsay or clearly untruthful. As a result, the perjurers were allowed to spew their venom freely, for there would be no cross-examination to expose the contradictions and outright lies in their testimony. Furthermore, not a single witness came forward to testify on Faithful's behalf.

It would be bad enough to be tried in the court of Vanity Fair, but how much worse to stand at its bar of justice alone? Many who faced that dreadful prospect have sold the truth and denied the Lord in order to avoid persecution or spare their lives. Many more have done so because they feared the displeasure and reproach of the world, or worse still, because they loved the praise of men more than the praise of God. (John 12:42-43) In all such cases, the fear of man proved a deadly snare to their souls. But this was not the case with the man named Faithful. Although by nature he was no more courageous than any other man, Faithful feared God more than he feared the wrath of his enemies. Moreover, his Lord was with him when on trial for his life, strengthening and giving him grace to endure such great suffering without recanting.

From the outset of the trial, Faithful had been keenly aware that more fundamental issues were at stake than his acquittal. Yet even though personal safety was not his main concern, he must have quaked inwardly as he prepared to address the court. Perhaps he quoted Proverbs 29:25 to himself: *The fear of man bringeth a snare: but whoso putteth his trust in the LORD shall be safe.* What a precious promise to God's people when they face such trying times! All would be well with his soul no matter the outcome of the trial, and even though he appeared to stand alone, an unseen advocate was right by his side. This advocate would uphold him through the ordeal and give him wisdom and grace to answer each accusation, the very same one who pled for him in the court of heaven.

Faithful's chief desire was to proclaim and defend the truth as staunchly in the hour of trial as he and Christian had done in the streets of Vanity. Perhaps this would be his last opportunity to *earnestly contend for the faith which was once delivered unto the saints.* (Jude 3) Therefore, he made good use of it by answering the various charges without compromising his godly principles in the least.

As for the king's witnesses, Faithful had listened to each of them closely and assessed both their characters and testimony carefully. To the one named Envy, Faithful repeated what he had actually said, but Envy perverted. Faithful had declared that whatever rules, laws, customs or people were against the Word of God were directly opposed to Christianity. The Word of God is the truth, the only standard for faith and practice, notwithstanding the customs and traditions of men. Even when on trial for his life, he stood by his statement. Moreover, he challenged Envy to refute it to his face if he dared, but Envy had nothing to say.

In answering Superstition's charge that Faithful said the town's religion was vain, Faithful took the opportunity to set the record straight. He told the court that the true worship of God requires genuine faith, and genuine faith is the result of the revelation of Christ to the soul, through the hearing of God's Word. Anything else is completely unacceptable in God's sight. There is a human faith that exists apart from divine revelation, and it operates freely within the realm of false religion. However, those who have this kind of faith have no legitimate claim to eternal life.

Faithful prefaced his response to Pickthank's testimony by saying that he was not in the habit of using epithets. Then, while carefully avoiding name-calling, he boldly stated that the town's prince, his followers and all the nobility whom Pickthank had named were more suited for hell than to walk the earth. In so saying, he but spoke the truth about this farcical trial and the diabolical powers behind it. Therefore, as he concluded his defense, it was with the conviction that he had probably signed his own death warrant. So rather than pleading for mercy before the court of Vanity Fair, he committed himself to the mercy of God.

After hearing testimony from the king's witnesses and Faithful's response to their accusations, the judge informed the jury that the matter was now in their hands. They must ascertain the guilt or innocence of the accused, and their decision would determine his fate. But first, he would instruct them in the law, the law according to Vanity Fair, that is. This instruction was the legal guideline that they must use in order to properly weigh the evidence and reach a verdict.

Judge Hate-Good began by citing legal precedent for condemning Faithful. It is interesting that he took this precedent from the Scriptures rather than case law; but then, our enemies often try to use the Word of God against us, do they not? Like his diabolical master, the judge was skilled in perverting the Scriptures and using them for his own evil purposes. Therefore, he would make a strong case for justifying the unrighteous decrees that had been issued against God's people in times past. Of these he claimed that he could name many, but in order not to overtax the jury he mentioned only three.

First, there was the edict of Pharaoh, king of ancient Egypt and servant of Beelzebub, who ordered all newborn male Hebrew infants to be cast into the Nile River. Since the Hebrew people worshiped the one true God, they posed somewhat of a threat to Egypt, at least in Pharaoh's mind. When they began to rapidly increase in number, Pharaoh feared them all the more. His solution was to murder the innocent, a heinous attempt at population control that was heartily endorsed by Hate-Good. Yet he failed to tell the jury of the terrible judgments that God brought upon the Egyptians because of their cruel treatment of his people.

Then there was King Nebuchadnezzar, another valuable servant of Beelzebub, who commanded the three Hebrew children to be cast into a fiery furnace because they refused to bow down and worship his golden image. But once again, the judge did not mention how the scheming of the Jews' enemies backfired, or the king's subsequent repentance and promotion of the three godly men.

The third case of legal precedent was that of King Darius, who was bound by law to cast Daniel into a den of lions for no greater crime than praying to his God instead of the king. Yet again, Judge Hate-Good did not dare mention the horrible fate of Daniel's accusers or the effect of his miraculous deliverance upon King Darius.

At this point, it is important for us to remember that even though worldly governments are under the rule and sway of the kingdom of darkness, God is the sovereign ruler. (Psalm 103:19; Proverbs 21:1) He who has *his way in the whirlwind and in the storm* rules over all things in the interest of his beloved children. (Nahum 1:3) His mercy oversees all that concerns us, and nothing happens to us outside of his will and purpose. Moreover, he will be glorified in his saints, either by delivering them from the hands of their enemies or giving them grace to be faithful even unto death.

Judge Hate-Good's quoting of historical precedent brings these precious truths to our remembrance. It also reminds us that his attitude was not a new one. Throughout human history, many of his predecessors have tried to destroy God's people while thinking they did God service..

As the judge was about to conclude his instruction to the jury, perhaps he feared that he had gone a bit too far. Some of those in the courtroom might possibly recoil at the thought of murdering newborn babies. So in order to mitigate his arguments, he pointed out that Pharaoh's action was preventative in nature. It was a necessary evil! But in Faithful's case, an actual crime had been committed. By opposing the religion of Vanity and refusing to withdraw his denunciation of it, Faithful had spoken against the very foundation upon which the town had been established. Moreover, he had violated the spirit of those earlier laws already cited as legal precedent in this case. Therefore, he was guilty of treason against the prince of darkness and worthy of death.

Apparently, no one bothered to remind the judge that justice is supposed to be impartial and objective, or that it is supposed to be administered according to the rule of law. If he had ever known these things, he abandoned them long ago. So rather than conducting himself in a proper manner, Hate-Good openly sided with Faithful's enemies, and vented his own malice against the innocent man. In so doing, he displayed open contempt for both the rule of law and the exercise of justice, and in the process, he impeached himself in both word and deed.

At the conclusion of the judge's final instruction, the jury withdrew from the courtroom to begin deliberations, but this was a mere formality since their verdict was a foregone conclusion. In this particular trial, the identity of the jurors was highly significant. Their names were Mr. Blind-man, Mr. No-good, Mr. Malice, Mr. Love-lust, Mr. Live-loose, Mr. Heady, Mr. High-mind, Mr. Enmity, Mr. Liar, Mr. Cruelty, Mr. Hate-light, and Mr. Implacable.

It was not exactly a jury of Faithful's peers, was it? Dear reader, you are probably thinking that the judicial system must have scraped the bottom of the barrel when putting this jury together. Without question, they formed a composite picture of man in his worst manifestations of depravity. Yet we know enough about Vanity Fair to understand all too well that they accurately represented the town, as to its true character. (2 Timothy 3:1-8)

Their first order of business was to choose a foreman, Mr. Blind-man. What could be more fitting than for the blind to lead the blind? Next, the foreman took an initial poll to see where each juror stood. After voting by secret ballot, they found that they were already of one mind concerning Faithful. Since his bold declaration of the truth had exposed them for what they really were, each man had reason to hate him. Faithful had disturbed the peace of Vanity Fair; therefore, his voice must be silenced. So without further deliberation, they reached a unanimous verdict of "guilty." Returning to the courtroom, they handed the verdict to the bailiff, who took it to the judge.

With the reading of the verdict and imposing of sentence, Faithful's trial was over at last. He had been tried, convicted and condemned, and since there is no appellate court in Vanity Fair, the verdict would stand. Yet according to the words of the Lord Jesus Christ, Faithful was numbered among the ranks of the blessed. (Matthew 5:10-12)

* * * *

What does the allegorical trial held in Vanity Fair really signify? It pictures the world's judgment of God's people and the reasons behind it. Faithful's only crime was that of speaking the truth to those who did not want to hear it. (John 15:18-21) Therefore, the wicked judge who presided over the court and the jurors who bore the image of every sort of human infamy were of one mind concerning him. As for the witnesses who gave such incriminating testimony against Faithful, they represent three powerful factors behind the world's hatred of God's people. Envy, superstition, and the desire for self-aggrandizement are directly opposite to the character of a true Christian. Thus the outcome of the trial could hardly have been other than it was.

For reasons that still remain unclear, Christian was not condemned with Faithful that day, but was remanded to prison after the trial. As for Faithful, his guilty verdict meant a mandatory death sentence, which was to be carried out immediately. Malice against him burned so furiously in the hearts of his enemies that they were not content to put him to death in a relatively humane manner. Their venomous hatred demanded his utmost suffering; therefore, they devised the cruelest death imaginable, and last of all, burned him at the stake. Thus Christian's beloved companion and fellow pilgrim came to his end, as far as this world is concerned. But even though he walked the path of martyrdom, he was true to his name. He was faithful unto death. How the townspeople must have rejoiced in the streets of Vanity once poor Faithful was dead! They had successfully dispatched the troublemaker, and now, life could go on as usual, or so they presumed.

As far as the citizens of Vanity were concerned, Faithful came to an ignominious end, but they could not have been more wrong. Their cruel hatred was the means by which Faithful had been delivered from the wilderness of this world and received into the presence of his Lord. Humanly speaking, he may have been taken out of this life in the midst of his days, but his earthly troubles were over forever. (Psalm 102:24) Adam the first would never torment him again. At last, he was safely out of reach of the enemy, and just as Evangelist had predicted, his lot was far better than that of his brother, Christian. (Philippians 1:21-23)

Those with eyes to see beyond the tragic circumstances of Faithful's martyrdom know that he had passed from the earthly scene into the heavenly realm where sorrow and death are unknown. He had finally entered the city toward which he had been traveling for so long, the heavenly Jerusalem inhabited by the spirits of just men made perfect. (Hebrews 12:22-23) Within the peace and safety of her walls, the noise and strife of Vanity Fair are heard no more at all.

Study Questions

1. Remembering that we are in the realm of the allegorical, what did the courtroom represent in which Christian and Faithful were tried for their lives? Who was the presiding judge, and what kind of man was he? What were the three specific charges brought against the two men?

2. What were the names of the three witnesses for the prosecution, and what did each of them signify? Briefly describe the testimony of each witness.

3. Since Faithful had no defense attorney to speak in his behalf, he faced the court alone and spoke in his own defense. What was the substance of his testimony as he addressed the court of Vanity Fair?

4. How did the judge's behavior throughout the trial violate every principle of truth, justice, and right?

5. Considering their names, what did the jury represent as a group? Why was their unanimous verdict of "guilty" a foregone conclusion?

CHAPTER 35

Beauty for Ashes

IN PONDERING THE RECENT TRIAL HELD IN VANITY FAIR, DID YOU WONDER why Christian was not condemned along with Faithful? Perhaps there was a protest over the unusually cruel execution, since Faithful and Christian had gained a measure of sympathy among some of the town's more fair-minded residents. Although they were afraid to admit it publicly, many of the people had been moved by their testimonies, temporarily at least. These may have expressed disapproval over such a gross miscarriage of justice. If so, perhaps Christian was spared as a small concession in order to placate the people and restore order. But why speculate as to secondary causes when we know the primary reason Christian's life was spared. For purposes far wiser than we can understand, God's will ordained both Faithful's death and Christian's eventual release from prison. One had run his race with patience and finished it with joy, but the other's journey was not yet over.

Neither is ours, my brother or sister in Christ. Moreover, we cannot expect to fare much better in the court of worldly opinion than Christian and Faithful did. While we may not suffer outright persecution, we will inevitably encounter opposition by living as children of light in a dark world. If we are to be faithful to our Lord, we must serve him with undivided loyalty, for otherwise, our resolve will surely weaken in the face of adversity. It serves us well to remember that a measure of suffering for Christ's sake is allotted to each of us. The way of the cross is the only pathway to the Celestial City.

Like the allegorical pilgrim named Faithful, many of God's people have sealed their testimonies with their blood. Yet the tyrant's sword merely hastens the martyr into the presence of his Lord, and quite often, it sparks a flame of an unintended kind. This thought brings to mind the dying words of Hugh Latimer, who paid the ultimate price for his faith on October 16, 1555. Even as his body was engulfed in the flames that would soon take his mortal life, Latimer encouraged Nicholas Ridley, his companion in suffering, by saying: "Play the man. We shall this day light such a candle, by God's grace, in England as I trust shall never be put out." [1]

What prophetic words our dear brother spoke that day! The enemies of Christ cannot destroy his church or his Gospel by killing his people. The harder they try, the more surely they seal their own fate. Likewise, in spite of all the false accusations brought against Christian and Faithful in Vanity Fair, the light of the Gospel had gone forth in that dark place. Time alone will tell what the effect of it would be.

For now, the kingdom of darkness seems to have the upper hand. The City of Destruction remains the same thriving metropolis, Carnal Policy continues to hold sway over the hearts and minds of men, and the marketplace of Vanity Fair is busier than ever. However, one day the entire City of Destruction complex will meet its doom, just as surely as God reigns on his throne. That notorious city, called Babylon the great in Scripture, will be nothing more than a smoking ruin. (Revelation 18)

When the cry finally goes forth that Babylon the great is fallen (Revelation 18:2), Satan's kingdom of darkness will pass out of existence. His power over the souls of men will be forever broken, and he will trouble us no more. The fall of Babylon, in both its secular and religious aspects (Pagan and Pope), will signal the end of the Christian's warfare. In that day, our Lord Jesus Christ will destroy every remaining enemy that has made war against his people. Through all the devastation that attends this great upheaval, the City of God will remain; for unlike the kingdoms of this world, his kingdom is forever. So take heart, my fellow pilgrim! The fall of Satan's empire will be the dawning of the eternal day when sin and darkness are forever banished and all will be perpetual light and life. (Revelation 21-22) For now, however, we must be content to patiently wait for it.

When the apostle John was exiled on the Isle of Patmos, he must have been discouraged by prevailing circumstances. Less than a century after the resurrection and ascension of the Lord Jesus Christ, the outlook for his followers appeared dark indeed. Evil had the upper hand and false religion was flourishing. The infant church was threatened as to her very existence, or so it seemed.

However, the apostle's viewpoint changed dramatically when he was called to *Come up hither* and see *things which must be hereafter.* (Revelation 4:1) What did he see? John saw the earthly scene from a heavenly perspective, and was given to understand the temporal in light of the eternal. The focal point of this heavenly vision was a throne encircled by an emerald rainbow, and before the throne was a sea that was as smooth and tranquil as clear crystal. (Revelation 4:2-6)

How this sight must have calmed the apostle's troubled soul! It will comfort us as well, if we can but grasp it by faith. The Lord God omnipotent reigns, no matter how bleak things appear to be. All is quiet before his sovereign majesty. No enemy power can disturb or prevent the fulfillment of his decree. Although his ways are inscrutable to our finite understanding, he is moving all things toward the consummation of his eternal purpose. With the downfall of Babylon, his purpose will be accomplished. In that day, the *kingdoms of this world* will *become the kingdoms of our Lord, and of his Christ; and he shall reign forever and ever.* (Revelation 11:15) Beloved friend in Christ, you and I are part of this glorious destiny!

The prophet Isaiah spoke of a divine appointment for all of those who mourn in Zion. To those who hear the joyful sound of the Gospel and embrace it by faith, God will *give unto them beauty for ashes, the oil of joy for mourning, the garment of praise for the spirit of heaviness; that they might be called trees of righteousness, the planting of the LORD, that he might be glorified.* (Isaiah 61:3)

Christian has been the grateful recipient of this comfort many times since his conversion, and in every instance, it strengthened him in the faith. From the day he fled from the City of Destruction and set out for the Celestial City, he encountered one difficulty after another. However, the brutal treatment he suffered in Vanity Fair and the anxiety he felt during his imprisonment there, was unlike anything he had experienced before. Moreover, the stress of the trial and Faithful's condemnation and murder may well have threatened to push him over the brink. Without question, his heart was broken over what had happened to his beloved friend. Christian felt his loss keenly, but through all of his grief and pain, the grace of God sustained him and gave him a song.

Under the circumstances, you might think it very strange that Christian was able to sing as he headed toward the outer limits of Vanity. Yet he was greatly comforted to know that Faithful was in a much better place. As for himself, he knew the Lord's presence with him, giving help and hope all along the way. So even though his eyes were filled with tears of sorrow, he had a song in his heart, a hymn of praise and thanksgiving to his Lord. It was a far different tune than his enemies were singing!

Like all the saints who have gone before, we unconsciously leave footprints along the pathway as we journey to Zion, indelible impressions for others to see and perhaps follow. Our lives are living epistles that are known and read of all men. It is a sobering fact that our character and conduct speaks more compellingly that any verbal testimony we could give. So even though our words may be remembered after we depart this life, the footprint that is more likely to bring forth precious fruit is a life that was lived consistently to the glory of God. Since this was the case with the two brethren in Vanity Fair, Christian did not leave alone as he made his escape from that dark place.

Of the relatively few inhabitants of Vanity who were stirred by the travesty of justice inflicted upon Christian and Faithful, we have no further history. Perhaps the indignation that was so intense at the time quietly faded away as life resumed its normal course. Even the mockery that passed for a trial and Faithful's subsequent martyrdom were not enough to work any permanent change in Vanity's residents. With one exception, that is.

Like Saul of Tarsus, who heard the bold testimony of Stephen and witnessed the grace with which he died for his faith, there was one resident of Vanity who would never be the same again. (Acts 7:54-60) Faithful had not died in vain! As a result of his testimony, saving faith was sown in the heart of one of its townsmen, and a steadfast hope that would sustain him for the rest of his earthly days.

Quite fittingly, the man's name was Hopeful, and he was as anxious to leave Vanity Fair as was Christian. Until recently, he had been as much at home there as anyone else, but God's grace sought, found, and delivered him out of the kingdom of darkness and into the kingdom of his dear Son. Even though Hopeful did not really know Christian personally, he was inexplicably drawn to the older pilgrim. As for Christian, he instinctively knew that this brand new believer would prove to be a beloved brother and fellow companion along the path of life.

What a precious result of Faithful's suffering and death was this! One brother had died for bearing testimony to the truth, but like the mythical phoenix, another had arisen out of his ashes. What an example of the truth that persecution, rather than diminishing the influence of the Gospel, is often the means whereby it prospers and grows!

* * * *

In his well-known "Meditation XVII" the English poet John Donne said, "No man is an island, entire of itself." [2] His astute statement takes our thoughts back to the dawn of creation when, after forming Adam from the dust of the ground, God said of the newly created human being: *It is not good that the man should be alone.* (Genesis 2:18) Adam, the very first of his kind, was not complete in himself even before he sinned. Above all, he needed the presence and communion of his Creator, but he also needed the companionship of his own kind.

We were not created to lead a solitary existence as lone islands surrounded by a vast ocean. Neither are we suited to live in perpetual isolation from our fellow human beings. There is a sense in which all men are bound to one another merely by reason of our humanity. We are interdependent beings, reliant upon the support and companionship of fellow humans. Those who deny this basic need and shy away from social contact are probably not in a sound state of mind.

Since it is true that all men need one another, how much more vital is the fellowship that we as believers in Christ share with one another? As Christians we are members of the family of God, and the bond of brotherly love that exists between us is stronger than any earthly tie. Although it is an intangible thing, this unique bond is evident whenever God's people meet together.

However, once in a while you meet a brother or sister in Christ who is especially dear. One whose spirit so closely mirrors your own that you are immediately joined in heart and mind. I am privileged to have such a dear sister as my trusted friend and confidante. I can share my inmost thoughts with her, knowing that she will pray for me and never betray my confidence. Many times, I have sought her wise counsel and learned to treasure it because it is always founded upon the Word of God.

My dear sister's lot in life has been an especially difficult one. She and her husband have known the depths of sorrow and affliction of many differing kinds. Yet I have never known her to murmur or complain, much less blame God when under heavy trial. In fact, the more she is tried, the more perfectly I see the character of the Lord Jesus Christ in her. I remember the time that she and her husband received a particularly devastating blow, and her humility of spirit and submission to God's will in response to it. With faltering tongue, I tried to say something to comfort and encourage her, but her response to my feeble attempt was, "Carolyn, isn't God good!" Thus my afflicted sister encouraged me, as she has done so many times before.

Although I do not wish to portray her in overly idealistic terms, my beloved sister in Christ is a true and faithful soldier of the cross. The dignity and grace with which she bears each trial that comes her way is a wonderful testimony of what God's grace can do. Her strong faith has often been a shining example to me when mine was weak and faltering. Moreover, her godly character is a continual challenge to my soul, both as a believer and fellow pastor's wife.

I am so grateful that the providence of God allowed our paths to cross in this life. In her, I find a composite of both Faithful and Hopeful, the two special brethren whose encouragement and fellowship meant so much to Christian during his journey to the Celestial City. So even though my dear sister and I are many miles apart, geographically speaking, I count myself blessed indeed to have her as a treasured friend and fellow traveler along the path of life.

Study Questions

1. Why can Christians living today not expect to fare much better in the court of worldly opinion than Christian and Faithful did?

2. What is often the unintended result of the world's persecution of God's people?

3. Although Christian was heartbroken over the loss of his dear brother, what unexpected blessing took place as the result of Faithful's testimony and suffering?

4. What did John Donne mean when he wrote, "No man is an island, entire of itself"? In particular, how does this apply to Christians and our need of fellowship with one another?

CHAPTER 36

The Subtle Snare of Covetousness:
By-ends of Fair-speech

ALTHOUGH THE ESSENTIAL NATURE OF VANITY FAIR NEVER CHANGES, prevailing conditions vary sharply there from generation to generation. True Christians will always find this present evil world an inhospitable place, but there are certain periods of history when open persecution rages hotly against them. During such times, those who are nominal Christians will quickly abandon their religious pretense and turn back to the world. This kind of upheaval actually proves beneficial to the church in two major ways. It weeds out false pretenders, while weaning the hearts of true believers increasingly away from the world and its ways. Thus persecution strengthens the true church from within even though it reduces her ranks numerically.

Her greater trial comes when open persecution ceases and a shallow form of Christianity comes into vogue. When the political climate changes and it becomes socially acceptable to be religious, multitudes will flock to churches of all kinds. In many cases, however, their motive is less than honorable; they hope to obtain some kind of benefit by calling themselves Christians.

In such times, false professors also tend to find their way into sound churches where the Word of God is believed and preached. As a rule, they are respectable people who are outwardly moral and able to give a fairly credible testimony. Thus they are accepted as members without question. But as the pews begin to fill with those who are Christians in name only, a church that was once sound in the faith gradually begins to weaken. Strange notions and false doctrine gradually filter in, and the distinction between truth and error becomes increasingly more blurred. Such a church will generally apostatize in little more than a generation, once it heads down this path.

After Christian and Hopeful left the town of Vanity, they naturally spoke of the recent events there. It is interesting that Hopeful told Christian of many more in the town that would take their time and follow after him. These were temporarily moved after hearing the Gospel, but it seems the love of the world was still uppermost in their hearts. Their delay reminds me of Felix, who trembled as Paul preached the Gospel to him, but said: *Go thy way for this time; when I have a convenient season, I will call for thee.* (Acts 24:24-25) For Felix, the more opportune season never came. Time alone will tell whether the same will hold true for Hopeful's former countrymen.

As Christian knew well by now, and Hopeful is about to discover, trials come our way in many different forms. However, it is our inward struggles that tend to cause us the most trouble. Such a trial was just ahead for the two of them, and the initial phase of it began shortly after they left the outskirts of Vanity. Their curiosity was immediately aroused when they noticed another man walking away from the town. Could this be one of the townsmen of whom Hopeful spoke, or was he one of the merchants who conducted business in Vanity's fair? Was he a fellow traveler along the path of life, or one who merely used the King's Highway for purposes of his own?

When Christian and Hopeful caught up with the lone gentleman, they were naturally eager to talk with him and learn more about him. But even though he told them he was from the town of Fair-speech, the man was reluctant to give his name. As to his destination, he stated without reservation that he was headed for the Celestial City, but let it be known that he cared little whether they joined him or not.

Could one who made the town of Fair-speech his home really be headed toward the Celestial City? A similar thought must have occurred to Christian. Even though he was not generally of a suspicious nature, he perceived that something was not quite right about this stranger. His intuition was quite correct, for John Bunyan identifies the man for us as one named By-ends. He tried to conceal his identity because he was ashamed of his name, and who could blame him? It labeled him as one whose desire for personal advancement lay behind everything he did and said. So even though he did his best to hide his true motives, he eventually earned quite a reputation for it. A glimpse into his secret life will help us unravel the mystery of how he became who he was.

The man behind the mask

The town of Fair-speech is an exceptionally prosperous place located along the shoreline of one of the world's largest natural harbors. Due to its prime location, it quickly became the busiest seaport within the City of Destruction complex. All sorts of ships lie at anchor along its waterfront, including cruise ships and pleasure craft of every description. However, most of the ships sailing in and out of the vast harbor are trans-oceanic cargo vessels.

Thus Fair-speech has long been a major hub of worldwide commerce, but its economic prosperity is directly linked to its nearest neighbor, the town of Vanity. To one degree or another, most of the citizens of Fair-speech are engaged in the commercial trade of Vanity's fair, and many of them have made their fortunes in that thriving marketplace. Living in his mansion overlooking the picturesque harbor, By-ends is numbered among these wealthy residents of Fair-speech. Few would deny that he lives the good life, but how did he achieve such extraordinary success? A brief look into his family history will shed light on the subject, and explain why he had an edge before he was even born.

By-ends' ancestry, of which he is quite proud, has earned him a place among the town's elite. Since he is in the direct lineage of several of its founders, his family tree boasts its share of blue blood. Moreover, he claims a degree of kinship with most of the town's residents. A few of them are actively involved in political affairs, most notably Lord Turn-about, my Lord Time-server, and my Lord Fair-speech, for whose ancestors the town was originally named.

As their names indicate, these three gentlemen are noted for their exceptional flexibility. To a man, they are adept at knowing when and how to alter their opinions and manners to best suit the times. Like Pickthank, they make it their business to know which way the wind is blowing, and are careful to take the side of popular opinion, whatever it happens to be at the time. Since they are remarkably eloquent in expressing their views, they have gained the attention of those in high places. In fact, many of the powers that be find them extremely useful and reward them generously for their service. By such means, these three relatives of By-ends have achieved great wealth and prominence.

As he continued to brag about his relatives to Christian and Hopeful, he mentioned four more by name. The first was Mr. Smooth-man, who was well known for his oratorical ability. He was also proficient in the art of diplomacy by flattering as need be, and carefully avoiding all offence in his dealings with others. Then there was Mr. Facing-both-ways. This gentleman had the uncanny knack of taking both sides of an issue, depending upon whom he was with at the time.

Mr. Any-thing, who also happened to be By-ends' pastor, was so broad-minded that he embraced everything in general and nothing in particular. Since he made a point of avoiding all controversial subjects and kept his opinions well within the mainstream of prevailing thought, he was highly regarded in the town of Fair Speech. Finally there was Mr. Two-tongues, By-ends' uncle on his mother's side. He was so clever at speaking out of both sides of his mouth that no one ever knew for sure where he really stood on any given issue. Predictably, like the double-minded man of James 1:8, he was unstable in all his ways.

With such a family heritage to his credit, it is no wonder that By-ends had acquired such an easygoing manner. Moreover, through the art of imitation, he had learned to converse with anyone on just about any subject, with ease and self-confidence.

As he continued to share his family history, By-ends described himself as a "Gentleman of good quality," even though his great-grandfather was a mere waterman (ferryman). This rather humble branch of the family tree had the peculiar ability to look one way while rowing in another direction. (A dangerous practice, it seems to me!) By-ends had inherited this unusual gift from his great-grandfather, Mr. Facing-both-ways, I presume, and admitted that he had prospered in the practice of it. So in spite of his less-than-exalted vocation, By-ends considered himself a fine gentleman. After all, just look at the rest of his ancestry!

Perhaps we should do just that. For the most part, his family was made up of rather unsavory characters who lacked any real principles or moral standards. Even so, they have been highly successful in securing lucrative positions in the world. From his early youth, By-ends determined to do the same. Since self-interest was always uppermost in his mind, it was behind every major decision he made. This was equally true in his personal life as well as his business ventures. Therefore, when the time came for him to marry, By-ends chose the daughter of Lady Feigning to be his lifetime partner. In his opinion, it was a brilliant match that would advance his worldly prospects even more.

As he told Christian and Hopeful about his wife, it was evident that he was very proud of her. She was born into a highly respected family whose members were noted for their refinement and sophistication. From the days of her early youth, she was taught to conduct herself with civility and decorum, whether in the company of great or humble men. Therefore, she possessed many credentials that the world values highly, things that her husband could certainly put to good use.

Although he made particular mention of it, her virtue was scarcely worthy of the name. While she was outwardly moral, she lacked any true integrity. Therefore, she easily adapted her moral code to suit any given situation, even though she always tried to do so with delicacy and good taste. Her reputation as a woman of honor and virtue was a mere illusion, for like her mother, she lived a lie behind her refined manner. So in many respects, By-ends had married his true equal.

This being the case, it is little wonder that he was as blind to her faults as he was to his own. In his opinion she was a real asset, and his marriage to her was a highly advantageous thing, but what really lies behind their union? The marriage of By-ends to Lady Feigning's daughter pictures the merger of worldly ambition with deception of the worst sort. Their union further expedited his ulterior motives by hiding them behind a mask of respectability. From the example of his wife, he acquired a certain finesse that he had lacked before, and became more skillful in the art of pretense and duplicity. Moreover, by giving him an inroad to high society, she provided additional opportunities to achieve his selfish ends. Most would say that he had married extremely well, but at what cost?

Dear reader, I strongly suspect that By-ends and Lady Feigning's daughter did not marry for love. More likely, their union was a marriage of convenience from which each of them expected to benefit. From the days of early youth, By-ends had been indoctrinated in the philosophy that the end justifies the means. Since this perspective suited his covetous nature, he adopted it as his rule of life, and up to this point, it had served him well. Yet we can only imagine the evil he has committed while excusing it all as being for the greater good.

Worst of all, his philosophy of life extended to spiritual matters as well. In common with many of his fellow townsmen he was a religious man, but his creed was exactly what you might expect. Like Talkative of Prating Row, By-ends was another who was Christian in name only. Rather than having strong principles and standing true to them, he compromised his beliefs whenever it suited his purpose. Both he and his wife embraced a perverted form of Christianity that squares well with popular opinion and is well tolerated in Vanity Fair.

In a few words, By-ends explained his belief and practice saying, "Tis true, we somewhat differ in Religion from those of the stricter sort, yet but in two small points: First, We never strive against Wind and Tide. Secondly, We are always most zealous when Religion goes in his Silver Slippers; we love much to walk with him in the street, if the Sun shines and the People applaud him." In so doing, he and his wife had attained great wealth and social prominence.

All the while that the man talked with Christian and Hopeful, he still avoided mentioning his name. But in listening to him, and especially after hearing his philosophy concerning his religion, Christian figured out who he was. So he confronted him directly, saying, "Sir, you talk as if you knew something more, than all the world doth; and, if I take not my mark amiss, I deem I have half a guess of you: Is not your name Mr. By-ends of Fair-speech?"

In response to this direct question, By-ends continued to deny his name by claiming it was one he did not deserve. It was an epithet given him by his enemies, and therefore, a reproach he must bear. However, Christian was not about to let him off so easily. Therefore, he asked By-ends bluntly whether he had ever given occasion for men to call him such an obnoxious name. At the mere suggestion, the man could no longer contain his righteous indignation. He bitterly resented the implication, and vehemently denied it! Those who called him By-ends did so out of jealousy! They were green with envy because of his success!

Yet even while By-ends staunchly defended himself before Christian and Hopeful, it seems to me that he protested too much. His explanation was further evidence of just how richly he deserved his name. From earliest boyhood, he had learned to strike while the iron is hot. Carpe Diem ("seize the day") was the family motto and he had put it to good use. His compelling desire for material gain was so strong that he overlooked no opportunity to increase his personal fortune. Neither was he overly scrupulous as to his methods. If there was any profit to be made, he was among the first to take advantage of it. So in the process of time, this tendency became such a fixed part of his character that it defined who and what he really was.

In spite of Christian's bold confrontation and rebuke, By-ends did not appear to be shaken by it. In fact, he was willing to join company with the two brethren since they were all going to the same place. Although By-ends was not likely to lay it to heart, Christian tried to set him straight concerning the true nature of things. If he joined company with them, he must be more than Christian in name only. He must be a true servant of the Lord Jesus Christ, whether it was the popular thing to be or not. In order to do so, he must deny himself and bear the reproach of the cross.

To no surprise, By-ends would have none of that. Such a thing would infringe upon his liberty and hamper his freedom to do as he wished. Like many of his kind, he completely misunderstood the meaning of our liberty in Christ. True Christian liberty is founded upon our deliverance from the bondage of sin. Its essence is the freedom to serve God by obeying him in things essential (things commanded in the Scriptures), and by following our renewed conscience in non-essential matters. The overruling principle of our liberty in Christ is to do all that we do for his honor and glory, and by love to serve one another. (Galatians 5:13-14)

True to character, By-ends would not hear of it; therefore, he was ready to part company with Christian and Hopeful. There was clearly little to be gained by casting in his lot with them! Moreover, it might cause him trouble down the road, and that was a risk he was not about to take! He had chosen his course in life, but it would never take him to the Celestial City.

By-ends held to that brand of Christianity that permits one to hold Christ with one hand and the world with the other. He was willing to serve the Lord, or rather to give the appearance of it, in order to gain the respect of others and advance his worldly prospects. In speaking of such people Thomas Manton said: "Many men owe their religion, not to grace, but to the favor of the times; they follow it because it is in fashion, and they can profess it at a cheap rate, because none contradict it. They do not build upon the rock, but set up a shed leaning to another man's house, which costs them nothing." [1] In commenting upon this astute observation, Charles Spurgeon said: "They love honesty because it proves to be the best policy, and piety because it serves as an introduction to trade with saints. Their religion is little more than courtesy to other men's opinions, civility to godliness." [2]

Should the tide of public opinion turn, we can be sure that By-ends would drop his religious disguise as easily as he had assumed it. Like his great-grandfather, he was constantly on the lookout for that which would be to his advantage. Therefore, his principles and religious beliefs were as whimsical as popular opinion. In his current situation, being religious was the respectable thing to be, and he had found it useful in a number of ways.

For one thing, it gained him an entrance into the best social circles. Due to the influence of his wife he was able to converse agreeably with just about anyone, so he felt right at home there. Civility coupled with false piety earned him a fair reputation among those who did not know his true character. Furthermore, it gave him a distinct financial edge by putting him in the way of business contacts who were of like mind.

Therefore, he plied his trade freely in Vanity Fair, quite safe from the persecution that Christian and Faithful suffered there. (John 15:19) To his own way of thinking, he had managed to achieve just the right balance in life. How he must have congratulated himself for the skill and diplomacy with which he held to the world with one hand and his Christian profession with the other! Undoubtedly, there were those who envied him, but in supposing he could have the best of both worlds, By-ends fell headlong into a subtle snare. (James 4:4)

Voices from the past

My brother or sister in Christ, since we belong to a kingdom that is not of this world, we often find ourselves at odds with the world and its ways. Like Christian and Faithful, we can get into trouble just by following the Lord and speaking the truth. (John 17:11-16) Therefore, we must be prepared to suffer for our faith, if need be. Moreover, in going forth unto Christ outside the camp of the world and its false religion, we often find that we must stand alone. (Hebrews 13:13)

This was not the case with By-ends of Fair Speech. Such men never seem to lack companions who are of the same mind. He had found the company of Christian and Hopeful to be irksome, probably because he had no answer to the objections Christian raised concerning his philosophy of life. But as he thought upon these things, three men suddenly joined him who would undoubtedly be more suitable traveling companions. They were voices from his past, childhood acquaintances educated in the same school of thought and well able to reinforce his views. By-ends was in need of their help, for even though he hid it well, he had been badly shaken by his conversation with Christian and Hopeful.

Mr. Hold-the-World would strengthen his resolve to cling tenaciously to his "old principles" by reminding him that his interests were fully invested in Vanity Fair. He had exchanged the truth long ago in order to gain its trifles. (Matthew 16:24-26; Mark 8:34-38)

Mr. Money-love would remind By-ends that his dearest goal was to secure his financial assets and increase them as much as possible. His covetous heart, denoted by the voice of Mr. Money-love, argued against any pangs of conscience he may have felt because of

Christian's rebuke. The love of money had taken deep root within him many years ago. Therefore, he was better able to brush aside the scriptural warning that it was an unlawful love, the very root of all evil. (1 Timothy 6:9-10)

Mr. Save-all was in full agreement with the other two. If By-ends wanted to achieve his goals, he had better remember to look out for number one because no one else would do it for him. He must do his utmost to accumulate as much as he could in this life. However, Save-all failed to mention that in keeping all for himself, he would lose it all in the end. (Luke 12:16-20)

These three men had so thoroughly imbibed the spirit of Vanity Fair that it was the motivating factor behind all they did. Because their hearts were filled with the love of the world and the things that are in the world, they cared for nothing higher. So their united voices confirmed By-ends in his belief that he could have the world and still be a good Christian. In this, their ungodly counsel will prove a three-fold cord that is not easily broken.

Pondering the mindset of By-ends and his three former companions reminds us that our earliest impressions are often the most lasting. The tender years of childhood provide a brief, yet optimal, window of opportunity to instill lifelong principles and lay the foundation for character development. Thus the things stressed during our formative years tend to be remembered throughout life. It is the Christian parent's dearest hope that early instruction in the fear and knowledge of God will be used of the Lord in the salvation of their children. When coupled with fervent prayer and a consistent godly example, this has often been the case. (Proverbs 22:6)

On the other hand, as these four men exemplify, the effect of evil instruction and influence upon young, impressionable minds is a thing not easily corrected. Moreover, such early training does not meet with the resistance that godly instruction encounters and must overcome. Therefore, it tends to take deep root and grow strong.

Such was the case history of By-ends and his childhood friends. They adopted their philosophy very young in life under the tutelage of a master teacher named Mr. Gripe-man, who held his school in the market town of Love-gain, in the county of Coveting. As these names suggest, the schoolmaster had become very wealthy through highly questionable means. Second only to accomplishing his own goals was the driving passion to share his knowledge with others. Therefore, he loved to instruct his students in the secret strategy by which he had achieved worldly prosperity. Although he probably recommended the use of violence as a last resort, he freely promoted the means of flattery, fraud, and deceit or the more respectable route of assuming a "guise of Religion."

John Bunyan tells us nothing further about this allegorical school-master, so we cannot know exactly who or what he represents. However, since By-ends came from a long line of ancestors who shared the same skewed code of ethics, this teacher and his schoolroom must represent the evil influence, philosophy of life, and covetous practices learned at home. By-ends mastered his lessons well enough to instruct others, which by example, he surely did.

What does all of this have to do with Christian and Hopeful? We might say that they occasioned this reunion of former schoolmates. Keep in mind that By-ends and his friends had adopted a religious veneer, as endorsed by their teacher. Furthermore, Christian had challenged By-ends so strongly on this point that he had withdrawn temporarily in order to clear his head. Before facing Christian and Hopeful again, he needed the reinforcement his three friends could provide. As we listen to their dialogue, we will witness the terrible battle between By-ends' covetous heart and his conscience.

Conscience under siege

Since Christian and Hopeful could still be seen on the road ahead, Mr. Money-love was curious to know who they were. By-ends described them as "a couple of far-country-men that after their mode are going on Pilgrimage." Upon hearing this, Mr. Money-love was all for joining company with them since, as he supposed, they were all headed to the same place.

In spite of overwhelming evidence to the contrary, By-ends and his friends were convinced that they were headed to the Celestial City. They saw no contradiction between their worldly mindset and Christian profession. However, they were attempting the impossible, for the Lord Jesus Christ warned his hearers: *No man can serve two masters: for either he will hate the one, and love the other; or else he will hold to the one, and despise the other. Ye cannot serve God and mammon.* (Matthew 6:24) By adopting the spirit of Vanity Fair, the four men had embraced an equally vain hope.

Nevertheless, they were proud of their broad-minded opinions, with one exception, that is. They had little tolerance for those who insisted on walking the narrow way. Like most of those who prospered in the town of Vanity, they took a jaundiced view of true Christians. Therefore, By-ends described Christian and Hopeful in disparaging terms, depicting them as being too rigid in their views, intolerant of the opinions of others, and shunning the company of those who were not in perfect agreement with them. Upon hearing this, Mr. Save-all, who had not even met Christian and Hopeful, accused them of being "righteous overmuch" and condemning all "but themselves." Sounds familiar, does it not?

When asked about his major points of disagreement with Christian and Hopeful, By-ends cited the thing he found most offensive. The two brethren were totally given up to the Lord Jesus Christ. They were resolved to be true to him whether it was socially acceptable or not, to stand by their godly principles no matter the cost, and to follow their Lord wherever he should lead them. Their firm and unreserved commitment to the Lord seemed to trouble his conscience more than By-ends was willing to admit; for in his heart, he knew they were right

Sensing his inward struggle, his three companions were quick to bolster his faulty thinking. As for Mr. Hold-the-World, he declared that Christian and Hopeful were fools for risking material loss just for the sake of their Christian principles. Therefore, he judged that they must be of unsound mind, saying, "For my part, I like that Religion best, that will stand with the security of God's good blessings unto us: For who can imagine, that is ruled by his Reason, since God has bestowed upon us the good things of this Life, but that he would have us keep them for his Sake." Then thinking to add scriptural support to his arguments, he cited the examples of Abraham, Solomon, and Job, rich men who were also true believers. But in the case of Hold-the-World's judgment, a little knowledge was indeed a dangerous thing.

Abraham was a man blessed by God with great riches, but material wealth was his servant, not his master. Godly Abraham walked by faith and obeyed God despite all human reason. His heart was firmly fixed on things above; therefore, he walked through the world as a pilgrim and stranger. (Hebrews 11:8-10) These were pertinent facts that Hold-the-World failed to mention.

The righteous Job was also a rich man whom Satan accused of serving God on the basis of quid pro quo, that is, because it was profitable for him to do so. Mr. Hold-the-World carefully omitted Job's reaction when he lost everything that was most precious to him. His true heart was revealed when he said: *Naked came I out of my mother's womb, and naked shall I return thither: the LORD gave, and the LORD hath taken away; blessed be the name of the LORD.* (Job 1:21)

As for Solomon, he had it all in an earthly sense, more that his heart could desire. God gave him a brilliant mind, wealth, honor and power, all this and godly wisdom, also. Sadly, he failed to live according to what he knew to be true and right, but in the end, godly wisdom prevailed. His assessment of all that he had under the sun was summed up in three words, *All is vanity.* (Ecclesiastes 1:1) But of Solomon's conclusion, Hold-the World was entirely mute.

After a lengthy consultation, By-ends and his companions found that they were in agreement concerning Christian and Hopeful. They were birds of a feather, for sure! Thus they despised the two brothers for their whole-hearted devotion to the Lord Jesus Christ and their willingness to risk everything for his sake. They hated Christian and Hopeful for being what they were not. Moreover, in perverting Scripture to support their views, they exposed the depth of their spiritual ignorance. It would have been far better had they left the Word of God out of their arguments. Declaring human reason to be on their side was one thing, but to claim that God's Word justified their covetousness shows to what extent the human heart can deceive itself. (Jeremiah 17:9)

Dear reader, we never know what will result from a chance encounter. When we least expect it, a word fitly spoken may just bear unforeseen fruit. Concerning By-ends, he was obviously quite shaken by his encounter with Christian and Hopeful. Up to that point in his life, he had been driven by greed and thought little of it. Worse yet, he had hidden his avarice behind a cloak of religious hypocrisy. However, when Christian challenged his beliefs and practices and pointed out their dangerous fallacy, he gave the man some serious food for thought. But instead of abandoning his long-held principles, By-ends sought to ease his troubled conscience.

If he was indeed shaken by the encounter with Christian, the three companions who joined him thereafter could represent three of his most deeply cherished beliefs. Assuming that this was the case, let us consider his friends as being the arguments of his own covetous heart rather than as separate individuals. In so doing, we will see him as a man desperately trying to pacify his conscience by justifying what he knows, deep down in his soul, to be wrong.

Since it is always easier to theorize rather than look at oneself, By-ends proposed to test his arguments to see how they would square with the hypothetical case of a "Minister, or a Tradesman." (I cannot help but wonder which one best described him.) In the case of a minister, By-ends wondered whether he could not alter his beliefs, or at least pretend to, if it seemed profitable to do so. If it would be to his advantage, could he not become zealous in things that he had avoided before and still remain a man of integrity? He cannot, of course, and yet his desire for riches (Mr. Money-love) argued that a minister should feel free to do so. His attempt to justify such an action is worthy of our careful note.

By-ends reasoned with himself that if the offer of greater wealth was set before a minister, he could presume it was of God and could seek it without inquiring too deeply as to what it might involve. If said opportunity required him to compromise his principles in order to please the people, he should not hesitate to do so. The adoption of new doctrines and beliefs would require a good deal of additional research and study on his part and the proclamation of them would make him a more zealous preacher. These were good things, were they not?

Furthermore, in complying with the wishes of the people by relinquishing some of his deeply held beliefs, he would demonstrate an attitude of self-denial. By adopting a more winning disposition and deferential manner toward other people, he could avoid ruffling any feathers. Surely that would be a great asset to his ministry! (He had apparently never read Paul's warning in 2 Timothy 4:1-5.)

By-ends concluded this line of reasoning with the assumption that the minister who makes these small sacrifices in order to secure a more profitable livelihood has done a good thing. He has gained the approval of men and enhanced his worldly prospects while still pursuing his calling. Therefore, none should accuse him of covetousness just because he took advantage of a prime opportunity when it presented itself.

Unfortunately, this rationale was faulty logic of the worst kind. It attempted to justify, and even make a virtue of unlawful ambition on the part of one who claims to be a minister of Jesus Christ. Such a view sees the minister as a tradesman of sorts, one who does business in Vanity Fair by exchanging personal integrity for material gain. Such a person is willing to sell the truth for trifles and encourage others to do the same, while failing to consider the awful cost involved. (2 Peter 2:1-3) Such a man is a hireling, a modern-day Balaam. He will spend much time and effort twisting the Scriptures until they appear to support his false doctrine. However, his character is the exact opposite of the man whose portrait hangs so prominently in the house of the Interpreter.

Certainly, the ministers of Christ are to be diligent students of God's Word. To learn it, discern its true meaning, and faithfully expound it is the essence of their labor. In most cases, they will not win any popularity contests for all of their self-sacrificial labor, but then, they do not seek it. Their heart's desire is to know the favor and approval of God. (2 Timothy 2:15)

So the reasoning of Mr. By-ends concerning the case of a minister was fatally flawed and its fallacy all too obvious, but what about one who is engaged in a secular occupation? Is his situation any different? Does another set of standards apply in his case?

Although the ministers of Jesus Christ are held to the highest moral and ethical standards, Christians who labor in secular vocations do not get a pass either. By-ends would beg to differ, however. To his way of thinking, a man who becomes religious, who professes faith in Christ in order to improve his lot in life, is to be highly commended. It could greatly enhance his prospects, perhaps even secure him a rich wife or more profitable business connections. In his mind, he saw only virtue in this action, for after all, it was exactly what he had done.

After much inner turmoil, By-ends had finally sorted out the matter and convinced himself that he was right after all. With the corroboration of his friends, he was confident that his arguments were now airtight. Therefore, he was ready to face Christian and Hopeful again, just as soon as he could catch up with them. Surely he could persuade them this time! However, he would make the attempt in much the same spirit as the scribes and Pharisees who sought to entrap the Lord Jesus by raising frivolous objections against his teaching.

In particular, By-ends was eager to ask Christian the same question that he had mulled over with his three friends. The gist of it was whether or not one may become religious in order to improve his worldly prospects and still retain his integrity as an honest man. Due to the heated exchange that had already taken place between Christian and By-ends, it was deemed best that Mr. Hold-the-World ask the question instead.

Who was better qualified to ask it? Mr. Hold-the-World has been around for a very long time, and has been the ruling passion in By-ends' heart for many years. But even though the issue had been well thought out and the question cleverly worded, Christian was quick to answer. His ready reply showed that he had spent much time studying the Word of God. Therefore, both his reasoning and his forthright answer were based upon Scripture.

Christian began by quoting the Lord's words in John 6:26-27, in which he rebuked those who followed him because he had fed them and performed miracles in their presence. They had a kind of faith, but it was not true saving faith. Their motive in following the Lord was one of self-interest only. Therefore, they justly deserved his stern rebuke and warning.

Christian hastened to connect the scriptural example to By-ends' argument and prove that he had made a "stalkinghorse" of religion. His faith was a mere pretense and his religious profession a sham, a mask of deceit that hid his true motives and intentions. Moreover, Christian labored his point by declaring that only "Heathens, Hypocrites, Devils and Witches" thought it right to do as By-ends had done. This was a pretty strong accusation, but one for which Christian had plenty of biblical support.

To prove that By-ends' philosophy was also the way of the heathen, Christian cited the case of Hamor and Shechem. In order to secure Jacob's daughter Dinah for his son Shechem, Hamor agreed that all the men of his city would submit to the Hebrew rite of circumcision. The men only agreed because it was presented to them as a lucrative prospect, an opportunity to gain not only the daughters of the Hebrew people, but their wealth as well. So the men consented to adopt the religion of Jacob, by outward compliance at least, but they did so from a motive of sheer covetousness. (Genesis 34:20-24)

In showing that By-ends' mindset was also the way of the hypocrite, Christian gave the example of the Pharisees. These leaders of the Jewish people were masters in the art of hypocrisy, and not merely to gain favor with the people. It is true that under the guise of false piety, they paraded themselves publicly in order to be seen and praised of men. But worse than that, they enriched themselves by robbing poor widows of their very livelihood. (Luke 20:46-47) For their legalistic hypocrisy, the Lord Jesus Christ censured them in the strongest of terms. (Matthew 23:27-33)

Judas the betrayer also followed the same way as By-ends. Although he was the son of perdition, Judas Iscariot was actually numbered among the Lord's twelve disciples. Yet inwardly, he had the heart of a thief and was ruled by covetousness. His infamy in betraying the Lord of Glory for thirty pieces of silver has made his name a by-word to this day. (Luke 22:1-6, 47-48)

Finally, there was the case of Simon the sorcerer, who was of like mind with By-ends and his kind. In the days when many people in Samaria were converted under the ministry of Philip the evangelist, Simon also professed to believe in Christ. Since his conversion seemed genuine, he was subsequently baptized and continued with Philip. However, when Simon witnessed the gift of the Holy Spirit bestowed by the laying on of the apostles' hands, his true character came to light. He, who had achieved fame and fortune by his sorcery in times past, now saw an opportunity to profit even more as a Christian. But when he offered Peter money for the apostolic gift, he was sternly rebuked for his covetousness and warned of its dire consequences. (Acts 8:5-24)

Christian concluded his answer by saying, "A man that takes up Religion for the world, will throw away Religion for the world." How right he was! Christian had proved his point very well, using the Word of God as his sole authority. Those who embrace the philosophy of By-ends and his kind do indeed follow the way of the heathen, the hypocrite, and the demon possessed. In each case, covetousness was the common denominator.

Not only had Christian answered By-ends exceptionally well, he dealt him a stunning blow. The poor man had no further arguments. His mouth was finally shut and his logic silenced. Therefore, he and his three friends gradually dropped behind Christian and Hopeful.

Hopeful had been a quiet observer during this entire interchange, even though he was in complete agreement with Christian. When the two brethren were out of earshot of the other men, Christian turned to Hopeful and said, "If these men cannot stand before the sentence of men, what will they do with the sentence of God? And if they are mute when dealt with by vessels of Clay, what will they do when they shall be rebuked by the flames of a devouring Fire?" These are solemn questions worthy of prayerful consideration.

* * * *

Like By-ends of Fair-speech, many suppose that they can serve Christ and have the world, also. However, no one can rightly claim the blessings of salvation without embracing the life of faith, obedience, and self-denial that goes with it. So the crime of By-ends was far worse than covetousness alone. While having no heart for the Lord, he professed his name for the sole purpose of furthering his worldly ambitions. He acknowledged God with his lips, but gave no thought to whether his actions pleased the Lord or not. To say that he was a hypocrite of the first order does not even begin to describe him. In essence, he lived as if there was no God, thus playing the part of a fool. (Psalm 14:1) Moreover, he betrayed and sold the Savior just as surely as did Judas Iscariot.

By-ends was ruled by covetousness and its hold upon him was easy enough for Christian to detect. However, covetousness is indeed a subtle snare. It can lurk in the heart, quietly hidden until something comes along to trigger it. The example of By-ends is, admittedly, an extreme one, but it should cause us to examine our hearts to see if something of his character lies within us. What is our motive for serving Christ? Is it as pure and selfless as it should be, or is something lacking between what we profess and what we really are?

Dear friend in Christ, while it is difficult enough to know our own hearts, we usually have little problem seeing the faults and shortcomings of others, do we? How quick we are to detect the mote in another's eye while remaining oblivious to the beam that is in our own! Moreover, is it not easy to prescribe a remedy for the failings of others while making excuses for our own? How careful we should be in our dealings with others that we not play the part of the hypocrite!

You may recall that Mr. Save-all accused Christian and those like him of being righteous overmuch – a charge that is frequently leveled against God's people in one form or another. We need to examine ourselves carefully to make sure that the charge is not justly deserved. In Ecclesiastes 7:16, Solomon issued the warning: *Be not righteous over much; neither make thyself over wise: why shouldest thou destroy thyself?* Does he mean that we can be too holy or live a life that is too godly? Obviously he does not, as many other passages of Scripture make clear. (Romans 12:1-2, for example)

Then what is the essence of this warning? It is an admonition against self-righteousness, or being righteous in our own eyes and exalting ourselves above others. (Matthew 5:20; Luke 14:11) It is also a warning against being wise in our own eyes, one that Solomon reiterates in the book of Proverbs. (Chapter 3:7; Chapter 26:12) Even though pride and self-righteousness have no part in true Christian character, they still lurk within and cause us a terrible struggle. Therefore, when we presume to rebuke another, like Christian did, we must take care that the same thing does not lie in our hearts. (Galatians 6:1)

We cannot know for sure just how Christian stood on the matter of covetousness. He certainly answered the objections of By-ends according to clear Scripture truth. Yet we have already witnessed his struggles with pride and self-righteousness, so perhaps he was bothered by the sin of covetousness as well. Whatever the case with him may be, the very convictions he has so firmly voiced before others will shortly be put to the test.

Study Questions

1. By-ends of Fair-speech was a man who tried to hide his true identity. Write a brief character sketch of him, showing how the man behind the mask became who and what he was.

2. What was the motivating factor behind all that By-ends did? How did his marriage with Lady Feigning's daughter help to further his worldly prospects?

3. Being covetous by nature, By-ends had persuaded himself that the end justifies the means. Therefore, he professed to be a Christian because it was the socially acceptable thing to do. What sort of Christian was he really? What advantages had he gained by his religious hypocrisy? How did he respond when Christian rebuked him for it?

4. Even though he hid it well, By-ends was shaken by Christian's rebuke and warning. In his lengthy conversation with voices from his past, we catch a glimpse into the struggle between his covetous heart and his conscience. How did he finally resolve the matter within himself? What was his response to Christian's final warning?

5. In what sense is covetousness a subtle snare? How does this serve as a warning to us? What about Christian and Hopeful? Could they fall into this subtle snare?

CHAPTER 37

The Subtle Snare of Covetousness:
A Man Named Demas

IN OUR DAILY STRUGGLE TO BALANCE BUSY SCHEDULES FILLED WITH pressing duties, it is easy to forget that Vanity Fair is everywhere. Its tentacles reach far and wide; therefore, as long as we are in this world, we cannot escape its influence. Should we fail to guard our hearts from its ever-present danger, we could become dazzled by its alluring prospects and empty promises. Thus we have difficulty hearing the voice of our dear Savior above the clamor and strife of daily life on planet earth. As we saw from the tragic example of By-ends, those who are Christian in name only have little resistance to the temptations of Vanity Fair. Therefore, they will end up selling the truth for things that have no enduring value, gladly exchanging durable riches for fool's gold.

What about Christian and Hopeful? Up to now, they have resisted the pressure of Vanity and its bustling marketplace, and taken a bold stand against every argument that By-ends brought against them. Yet even though they had passed beyond the borders of Vanity Township, they had not really left it behind. Its temptations were all around them, and not just in the more obvious places. By this time in their journey, they were understandably a little travel weary. After all, they have just passed through the initial phase of what will prove to be a protracted trial of their faith, and strange as it may sound, the next phase began when things took a turn for the better.

After leaving By-ends and his friends some distance behind, the two men eventually came to a "delicate plain called Ease." It was a very pleasant place with soft, cool grass making a comfortable pathway for their sore feet. Moreover, the general atmosphere of the plain was crisp and inviting, tempting them to slacken their pace. Christian and Hopeful would have been content to linger there for awhile, but all too soon, they reached the other side of the plain.

Dear friend in Christ, in this we have a poignant reminder that even though the Lord grants us seasons of respite and comfort from the heat of battle, we must take care how and where we seek rest. Although we naturally dread trials and shrink from difficulty, these things are designed to further our progress in grace. However, in times of relative ease when all seems to be going well for us, we unknowingly enter a danger zone. Watchfulness can easily give way to complacency, tempting us to settle down in a place that was never intended to be our rest. (Micah 2:10) Our Lord is well aware of our weakness in this regard. He understands that we are prone to spiritual lethargy if permitted to become too comfortable in this world. Moreover, he loves us far too much to allow our hearts to become enamored with its vain pursuits. Therefore, as a general rule, he ordains that our seasons of ease and freedom from trial be comparatively few and far between.

After Christian and Hopeful reached the far end of the plain called Ease, they came to a little hill named Lucre. As its name suggests, it represents the opportunity to acquire great riches and enjoy a life of pleasure and ease, but it also has an evil ring to it. Many years ago, prospectors discovered the mother lode of a rich vein of silver ore there. Since that time, the mine beneath the hill has been the ruin of many who once called themselves pilgrims.

Due to the enormous wealth hidden in its depths, some who pass by cannot resist the lure of easy riches. They turn out of the path to have a closer look, not knowing that the ground near the mine is unstable and treacherous. Moreover, its entrance is not a gentle downward incline, but a deep, dark pit. So those who venture too near risk a two-fold danger: they could either be swallowed up as the soft, fragile earth gives way beneath their feet, or they could plunge headlong into unknown depths.

O, the irresistible lure of a mine! Even knowing the terrible dangers involved, men will delve deeply into the earth in search of the gold, silver, or precious stones buried there. It is a risky venture even when every safety precaution is taken. The large open pits that provide access to the mine's lower levels are but one of many hazards faced by those who seek their fortune there. Due to the mine's intricate network of tunnels, one can easily become disoriented and hopelessly lost. Moreover, the tunnels themselves form a kind of honeycomb that causes the ground overhead to be fragile and subject to sudden collapse. So there is the constant danger of cave-in and instant death by being buried alive under tons of earth and rock. There is also the possibility of a slow, painful death by asphyxiation, as the trapped miner's oxygen supply is gradually depleted.

Still, many are willing to face all of these hazards for the prospect of great wealth, but the hill called Lucre contains danger that goes far beyond the obvious. Although many who approach its silver mine perish outright, others are merely maimed. To those who know no better, it might seem that the risk to these survivors was well worth it. However, those with clearer insight will tell you that even though the wounded continue to live, they are never really able to escape from the mine. Therefore, all who venture too close are consumed by it in one way or another.

Right by the silver mine and just a little way off the road, there stands a man who calls to all who pass by. As Christian and Hopeful drew near, they heard him cry, "Ho! Turn aside hither, and I will shew you a thing." Like By-ends, this man did not tell his name, but John Bunyan identifies him for us as one named Demas. His presence by the silver mine denotes his inextricable link to it.

Christian responded by saying, "What thing so deserving, as to turn us out of the Way?" It was a good question, for in order to satisfy their curiosity, Christian and Hopeful would have to leave their path. Demas assured them that there was much to be gained by stepping just a little out of the way, and then told them of the silver mine and the vast treasure it contained. Moreover, he told them that they would be richly rewarded if they would just take the time to search its depths. In a material sense, they would be set for life. But this whole scenario raises a pertinent question. What does a desire to view the mine signify? It indicates the orientation of one's heart. To view the mine is to covet the treasure buried there, and to actually approach it is to actively seek its riches.

Since Hopeful was younger in the Lord and less experienced than Christian, he was all for going to at least have a look. However, Christian warned against it, saying, "Not I…I have heard of this place before now." He then told of the hidden dangers of heeding Demas' voice. Many who have done so perished there, and many more have been permanently ensnared by what they found in the silver mine. At the least, it proves a spiritual hindrance to those who seek treasure there. (1 Timothy 6:9-10)

It was Christian's decided opinion that they should not venture even a single step from their designated path. Safety lay in avoiding the area of the mine altogether. So instead of heeding the voice of Demas, Christian pressed him to admit that the mine was a dangerous place. Demas responded by saying, "Not very dangerous, except to those that are careless." But in so saying, he at least had the decency to blush.

At that point Hopeful happened to think of By-ends, who still lagged somewhere behind them, and wondered aloud how he would likely respond to Demas' call. Hopeful assumed that By-ends would be eager to see the mine, and to this, Christian heartily agreed. After all, the silver mine with its promise of easy riches was right up his alley! So Christian was also of the opinion that By-ends might venture too close to the mine's entrance and perish there, swallowed up by his desire for earthly riches.

Before Christian and Hopeful passed out of hearing, Demas called to them a second time. Being of a rather persistent nature, he urged them again to just come and merely look at the mine. But Christian rebuked him soundly and accused him of being an enemy to the "right ways of the Lord." To prove his point, Christian declared that Demas had already been condemned by one of "his Majesties' Judges" (the apostle Paul) for doing the same thing he now urged Christian and Hopeful to do.

To his credit, Christian took a firm stand and did the right thing. Moreover, he influenced his brother to do the same, and yet had Christian not been tempted at all, this incident at the hill called Lucre would hardly have been worthy of mention. Personally, I am inclined to believe that Christian felt drawn to the silver mine. We already know that Hopeful did. If this was indeed the case, Christian's conversation with Demas could denote his inward struggle with the thing offered. Still, both he and Hopeful resisted the temptation because, above all, they desired to stand before the Lord with the boldness that only comes with doing what is right in his sight. The fear of God kept them from succumbing to what many have found irresistible. (Psalm 119:37-38; Proverbs 1:29-33) Moreover, it made them an example to all who would follow after them that faith is indeed *the victory that overcometh the world.* (1 John 5:4)

Demas the mine keeper

Upon hearing Christian's strong rebuke, Demas protested that he, also, was a fellow believer. In fact, if they would wait a bit, he would prove it by joining them in their journey. But how long and for what exactly should they wait? Who was this man Demas standing post at the hill Lucre? What was his connection to the silver mine, and the wealth that lay hidden deep within it? Moreover, considering all that he had said to Christian and Hopeful, how likely was he to ever leave the place where his treasure so obviously was?

These are all pertinent questions, and from his knowledge of Scripture, Christian had a good idea of the answers. Since he recognized who Demas was, Christian had undoubtedly read the scriptural account of his infamy. When confronted with these facts, Demas was forced to admit his name. He still evaded the issue, however, by calling himself "the son of Abraham."

As he had done in the case of By-ends, Christian quickly set the record straight concerning the man's true identity, and he did so from the Word of God. In a spiritual sense Judas was his father, not Abraham. (Matthew 26:14-15) Since he followed in the steps of Judas the betrayer, Demas could not expect to fare much better, in the final analysis, than he whom the Scriptures call the son of perdition. (John 17:12; Matthew 27:1-6)

Demas also had his Old Testament counterpart in one named Gehazi, the servant of Elisha, the man of God. (2 Kings 5:20) After the prophet Elisha healed Naaman the Syrian of leprosy, he refused any compensation for the service he rendered. But his covetous servant, Gehazi, saw a prime opportunity to enrich himself by taking advantage of Naaman's gratitude. (2 Kings 5:15-23) However, he did not enjoy his ill-gotten gain much longer than Judas did. (2 Kings 5:25-27)

Demas is mentioned in Scripture only three times; but from that brief account, it is obvious that he was the perfect choice to be custodian of the silver mine. Long ago, he had been Paul's companion and fellow-laborer in the Gospel ministry. (Philemon 24) Until the time of Paul's second Roman imprisonment, he obviously had confidence in Demas and considered him a brother in the Lord. (Colossians 4:14) But in his last epistle, which was written from his prison cell, Paul wrote to Pastor Timothy: *Do thy diligence to come shortly unto me: for Demas hath forsaken me, having loved this present world, and is departed unto Thessalonica.* (2 Timothy 4:9-10) This is Scripture's final word concerning the man named Demas.

The apostle's words, *Demas hath forsaken me, having loved this present world,* remind us that the treasure in the silver mine is not limited to precious metals and rare gemstones. It includes all the merchandise offered for sale in Vanity Fair, whatever it is that captures the heart and draws it away from the Lord Jesus Christ.

By-ends of Fair-speech had never been more than a fair weather Christian, but Demas once had a credible testimony as a follower of Jesus Christ. It was apparently not until his later years that he made the wretched choice to forsake not only Paul, but Christ and his cause as well. Unlike Moses, who esteemed *the reproach of Christ greater riches than the treasures in Egypt* Demas cast aside the name of Christ when the cost became too great. (Hebrews 11:26) Thus he turned traitor and returned to the world, where his heart was all along. (Matthew 6:21)

Shortly after Christian and Hopeful left the vicinity of the silver mine, By-ends and company arrived there. As expected, they turned aside at Demas' first beckon, but what happened to them next is a matter of pure conjecture. Perhaps they ventured too near the mouth of the pit and fell to their deaths. Or they may have safely descended into the depths of the earth only to be overcome by the poisonous gases that can accumulate in old mines. It is also possible that they found the treasure they desired so fervently. But one thing we know for sure. They were never seen again along the King's Highway.

Like Demas and By-ends, all who are worldly-minded will seek their treasure in this life, whether silver and gold or some other idol that has captured their hearts. In this quest, no risk is too great and no sacrifice too much. Yet even when the desired treasure is obtained, it is theirs to enjoy for such a little while, and in spite of expectations to the contrary, it will never make them truly happy.

On the other hand, there is a quest for treasure that leads to an eternally joyful end. Those who seek and find it will keep it forever because they also find eternal life. Moreover, this search is a highly profitable one, for it alone results in true blessedness. (Proverbs 8:32-35) I speak of the quest for true wisdom, the rare treasure that only wisdom's children seek, for they alone can discern its matchless worth. (Proverbs 3:13-18; Proverbs 8:17-21) But where is wisdom to be found?

The search for true wisdom begins and ends with the Lord Jesus Christ. He is the source, the fountain, the quintessence of wisdom in its fullness and perfection. (1 Corinthians 1:18-24; Colossians 2:1-3) In seeking him, we find godly wisdom and excellence of knowledge. (Philippians 3:8) This knowledge of the truth sets us free from the bondage of this present evil world. (John 8:31-32) Moreover, it keeps our feet safely in the path of life. (Proverbs 2:1-9)

To those who know him in salvation, the Lord Jesus Christ is indeed our priceless treasure. Of what value are silver, gold, and precious stones in comparison to the one whom Scripture calls the pearl of great price? He is the highest and best treasure, to be gained at whatever cost; for in him are durable riches and a heavenly inheritance that will never be diminished or taken away. (Matthew 13:44-46)

Yes, dear fellow pilgrim, the Lord Jesus Christ is our priceless treasure, and wonder of wonders, we are his! (1 Peter 2:6-10) We are precious jewels that are a crown of glory in his hand, a royal diadem for the King of kings and Lord of lords! (Isaiah 62:1-3) What an abundance of comfort there is in this knowledge! What assurance of our eternal safety! Not a single stone will be missing from his royal diadem, in that day when he makes up his jewels. Every one of them will be safely gathered unto him. (Malachi 3:16-18)

For now, however, we are being polished, shaped, and prepared to shine until we reflect his glory. As silver is refined and gold is tried, we are being made ready for the day when the righteous will shine forth as the sun in the kingdom of their Father. (Zechariah 13:9; Matthew 13:43; Titus 2:11-14) So Christian and Hopeful did well to avoid the hill Lucre and its dangerous mine, did they not? After all, what does it really have to offer? Nothing that is comparable to the unsearchable riches of Christ! At best, the treasure found there provides temporal ease and pleasure. But at worst, it carries with it a lifetime of misery and an eternity of loss.

Like Christian and Hopeful, every one of us who travels down the path of life must pass by the hill Lucre and hear the call of Demas. In one form or another, we all will face the temptation to seek our portion in this life. To even toy with the idea is a dangerous impulse with no assurance of recovery to those who succumb. Therefore, let us be mindful of the terrible risk involved and heed our Lord's solemn warning in Matthew 6:19-21: *Lay not up for yourselves treasures upon earth, where moth and rust doth corrupt, and where thieves break through and steal: but lay up for yourselves treasures in heaven, where neither moth nor rust doth corrupt, and where thieves do not break through nor steal: for where your treasure is, there will your heart be also.*

Remember Lot's wife

Shortly after leaving the plain called Ease, Christian and Hopeful came to a place in the road marked by an ancient monument. It was remarkably well preserved in spite of its age, but its form was passing strange. At first glance it looked like a single pillar, perhaps marking an historical event long forgotten. Upon closer inspection, however, the monument took on the distinct form of a woman.

At first, the two men were somewhat taken aback by this rather bizarre and unexpected sight. As they paused to consider its meaning, Hopeful noticed an inscription above the head of the statue, but was unable to decipher the words. After much thought, Christian decoded the ancient message containing just three words: *Remember Lot's Wife.* He interpreted its meaning through the use of God's Word, which contains both the monument's history and the Lord's startling reference to it in Luke 17:32. Long ago, the pillar had been a living, breathing woman identified only as Lot's wife.

From the biblical account in Genesis 19:15-17, we learn that God sent angelic messengers to deliver Lot, his wife, and two daughters from the judgment that would shortly come upon the cities of the plain. As they drew the refugees out of harm's way, the angels warned them not to look behind them. However, Lot's wife could not resist the urge to look back upon the utter desolation of all she had known and held dear. Although she fled from that wicked place, she left under compulsion. Clearly, her heart had remained behind.

Thus she perished where she stood, overcome by the sulfurous fumes that filled the air, and quickly encrusted with salt. Now she stands as a silent reminder to all whose hearts are inclined toward the world and its vanities. After their recent encounter with By-ends and the incident at the hill called Lucre, the memorial was an opportune sight for Christian and Hopeful. It reinforced what they had already learned and helped them to draw spiritual applications from it concerning their present circumstances.

The life-like monument and the remembrance of its tragic history had a striking effect upon Hopeful, in particular. With bitter regret, he realized that if he had heeded Demas' call, the fate of Lot's wife could have been his as well. However, in spite of his self-recrimination, he was not at all like Lot's wife, who was a daughter of Sodom at heart. He possessed the heart of a true pilgrim, and it now overflowed with sincere repentance for his recent weakness. He was also well aware that it was God's grace alone that kept him from falling into the subtle snare of covetousness. But what about Christian, who had taken a firm stand at the silver mine and rebuked Hopeful for his indiscretion there? Moreover, what about his harsh words to Demas, when he said: "Assure thyself that when we come to the King, we will do him word of this thy behavior"?

This was quite a bold statement, a threat really. Yet Christian's slightly disdainful attitude toward his brother in the Lord is even more disturbing. Perhaps he was inclined to be a little righteous overmuch, as Scripture warns us not to be. He certainly seemed to rub it in that Hopeful nearly succumbed to the mine's temptation while he, Christian, refused every offer to do the same. Was he a little proud of himself for being more spiritual than his brother? It appears he may have been. Apparently he had forgotten the lesson he learned the day he first met Faithful. So while Hopeful chided himself for his sinful inclinations, it seems that Christian congratulated himself that he had not done likewise. His vainglorious attitude would be short-lived, however, for this chicken would shortly come home to roost. (Galatians 6:1)

Why did John Bunyan place the ancient landmark that was once Lot's wife so close to Demas' mine? He did so as a monument to the folly of those who set their hearts on earthly treasure rather than the spiritual riches that are in Christ alone. Lot's wife escaped the destruction of Sodom only to fall victim to a more terrible judgment. To this day, her fate serves as both a warning and example to all who pass by on their way to Zion. But rather than a literal monument standing beside the King's Highway, her history is preserved in perpetuity in the eternal Word of God. (1 Corinthians 10:11-12)

In 1 Corinthians 10:13-14, we find both a precious promise and strong admonition: *There hath no temptation taken you but such as is common to man: but God is faithful, who will not suffer you to be tempted above that ye are able; but will with the temptation also make a way to escape, that ye may be able to bear it. Wherefore, my dearly beloved, flee from idolatry.*

The connection between these verses and our present subject is far too important to overlook. In essence, the subtle snare of covetousness is idolatry. (Colossians 3:5) Lot's wife looked back upon the desolation of Sodom because the idols of her heart were there. Our Lord's admonition to remember her gives fair warning to any who are tempted to do likewise, for such a regression is often permanent. The pathway to the city is the only one of its kind and it is specifically designed to be one-way. Once entered, our feet are not to stray from it. Therefore, neither must our hearts.

Perhaps because he had a close call at the silver mine, Hopeful heard the message of Lot's wife loudly and clearly. Moreover, he recalled the biblical account of Korah, Dathan, and Abiram, who rebelled against the Lord by rebelling against his servant, Moses. (Numbers 26:9-10) As Hopeful thought upon the horrible judgment that falls upon those who do not heed God's warning, he was amazed that Demas could be so self-assured. The ancient pillar stood in clear sight of the silver mine, yet it did not seem to bother Demas in the least. It is a fearful thing that Lot's wife was judged for merely looking back when she was warned not to. There is no suggestion that she took even a single step back toward Sodom, but we understand that looking back was tantamount to turning back.

How could Demas be oblivious to his great danger? He was so blinded by sin that he could not see what was plainly before him. Like the men of Sodom, he forgot that he was a sinner before the Lord. (Genesis 13:13; Proverbs 5:21; Proverbs 15:3) So it is with those whose hearts are deceived. The judgment of another neither dampens their zeal nor gives them pause to consider. Therefore, they rush down the same path with boldness and confidence. But like their predecessors, they rush headlong to their own destruction.

Dear reader, sin is a terrible taskmaster, is it not? When it has free reign in the heart, it prompts one to sin against God's goodness and against the light of his Word. Those know the truth and sin in spite of it will incur the most severe judgment. (Luke 12:47-48) This was undoubtedly the case with Demas. As for Hopeful, I doubt that he will ever forget the lessons learned at the hill Lucre. The more he thought about it, the more he marveled at God's great mercy to him. He, also, could have been a shameful example to others, had not God delivered him instead. As a result, three essential things had been reinforced within him: a thankful heart toward God, a proper fear of him, and the perpetual remembrance of Lot's wife.

In Luke 12:15, the Lord Jesus Christ gave warning against the sin of covetousness by saying: *Take heed, and beware of covetousness: for a man's life consisteth not in the abundance of the things which he possesseth.* Most ignore his warning because covetousness dwells in the hearts of all men by nature, and it often becomes the ruling passion of one's life, as with the rich fool in Luke 12:16-21. So the subtle snare of covetousness, which is a temptation to all, proves a deadly pitfall for many. According to the Parable of the Sower, the deceitfulness of riches is one major factor in the downfall of the thorny ground hearer. (Matthew 13:22)

Unlike those fleshly lusts that are difficult to hide from others, the sin of covetousness is not readily apparent. It is deeply embedded in the unregenerate heart, and from that polluted wellspring it defiles from within. (Mark 7:21-23) Sometimes a covetous heart lurks behind a religious veneer and tries to justify both its mindset and actions by supposing that gain is godliness. By-ends exemplifies this kind of person who, in spite of his religious pretense, is destitute of the truth. (1 Timothy 6:5)

A covetous disposition can also hide behind a manner that is benevolent, outwardly moral, and devout. The rich young ruler comes to mind as a prime example of this kind of person. Unlike the man called By-ends, the rich young ruler was no hypocrite. He was a sincere man whose heart was inclined toward the Lord so that he actually sought him and inquired about the way to eternal life. The young man obviously had some knowledge of the Lord Jesus, perhaps by hearing him teach the people. Moreover, he was disturbed enough to seek him out and ask: *Good Master, what good thing shall I do, that I may have eternal life?* (Matthew 19:16)

Those who knew this young man would have been hard pressed to understand his concern, for he was a devout Jew who knew the Law of Moses and endeavored to keep it. Yet he who searches and knows the human heart, answered, *If thou wilt enter into life, keep the commandments,* and then specifically named several of the Ten Commandments. (Matthew 19:17-19) The young man was so convinced he had obeyed the law that he answered: *All these things have I kept from my youth up: what lack I yet?*

Even though he was religious and morally upright, the man knew something was lacking, but had no idea what it was. However, the Lord Jesus saw the idol that reigned in the heart of the devoutly religious young man. The truth of the matter was brought to light by the Lord's pointed command: *If thou wilt be perfect, go and sell that thou hast, and give to the poor, and thou shalt have treasure in heaven: and come and follow me.* (Matthew 19:21) Even though he was inclined toward the Lord Jesus, his covetous heart caused him to turn away from the one who is the way, the truth, and the life. (Matthew 19:22; John 14:6)

After the young man's departure, the Lord Jesus used this opportunity to instruct his disciples concerning one particular danger that accompanies material wealth. The subtle snare of covetousness often leads one to trust in riches (Mark 10:23-26), and thus fall short of the kingdom of God. This warning astounded the disciples, who had left everything in order to follow him. Yet the Lord spoke no idle words, for even his most devoted followers need to beware of this deadly snare.

Although most of God's people are not rich in worldly possessions, covetousness is still a problem. Discontentment with God's providence is really just another form of it. We compare our life situation with that of those around us and always seem to be on the losing end. Others succeed and gain the pre-eminence while we struggle with feelings of frustration and envy.

My fellow pilgrim, there is a strong link between godliness and true contentment. Moreover, as the apostle Paul told Timothy: *Godliness with contentment is great gain.* (1 Timothy 6:6) Spiritually speaking, it is a highly profitable thing whatever our earthly circumstances happen to be. Covetousness is truly a subtle snare, but contentment with God's gracious provision is its antidote. (Hebrews 13:5) Even for those believers who have been blessed with earthly riches, the best things are yet to be!

Set against the tragic case of the rich young ruler is the example of the apostle Paul. For him, it was the knowledge that he was guilty of covetousness that convinced him of his sinful condition before God and was highly instrumental in his conversion. His credentials as a devout Jew were impeccable, for he described himself as a Hebrew of the Hebrews, and as touching the law, a Pharisee. (Philippians 3:5) Paul was a highly respected and deeply zealous leader of the people, a young man with exceptional promise and destined for great things. In Galatians 1:13-14, he described himself before his conversion saying: *Ye have heard of my conversation* [manner of life] *in time past in the Jews' religion, how that beyond measure I persecuted the church of God, and wasted it: and profited in the Jews' religion above many my equals in mine own nation, being more exceedingly zealous of the traditions of my fathers.* In Philippians 3:6, he elaborates upon his religious zeal and how it was perceived: *Concerning zeal, persecuting the church; touching the righteousness which is in the law, blameless.*

Like the rich young ruler, Saul of Tarsus was outwardly moral and devout. Others viewed him that way and he was content to do the same. As a Pharisee, he was thoroughly instructed in the Law of Moses and saw himself as a faithful keeper of it until the Spirit of God began to stir his heart and convict him of the sin of covetousness. The knowledge was a rude awakening; for then, he saw his legal righteousness for what is really was. The knowledge of sin within became a reality in his heart and mind, and as a keeper of the law, Saul died. (Romans 7:7-13) His clearer understanding of the law put the sword to any notion of self-righteousness. Thus Saul the blameless became Paul, the chief of sinners. (Philippians 3:6; 1 Timothy 1:15)

Unlike the rich young ruler, Saul of Tarsus was delivered from the subtle snare of covetousness by God's marvelous grace, and became Paul the servant of Jesus Christ. Speaking of the creed by which he now lived, Paul said: *But what things were gain to me, those I counted loss for Christ. Yea doubtless, and I count all things but loss for the excellency of the knowledge of Christ Jesus my Lord: for whom I have suffered the loss of all things, and do count them but dung, that I may win Christ, and be found in him, not having mine own righteousness, which is of the law, but that which is through the faith of Christ, the righteousness which is of God by faith."* (Philippians 3:7-9) Paul was never the same after his encounter with the Lord Jesus Christ on the Damascus road. From that day forward, he pressed toward the heavenly prize that had so completely captured his heart, and was faithful to his beloved Lord even unto death.

* * * *

Although it is a difficult thing to admit, we do ourselves a great disservice if we deny that we struggle with covetousness. Doing so could mean that we are as deceived as the rich young ruler. Rather, we should heed our Lord's warning lest we also fall prey to the deceitfulness of riches. But in what sense are riches deceitful? They promise what they cannot possibly deliver, things such as happiness, contentment, security and peace of mind. Moreover, since covetousness is an insatiable desire, it will become a driving force if given free rein in the heart. Worse still, it will turn the heart away from seeking those things that are of transcendent worth.

Therefore, it is imperative that we carefully guard our hearts against the sin of covetousness. (1 Timothy 6:9-11) To this end, we should regard the case of the rich young ruler as a solemn warning, and the example of the apostle Paul as a stirring challenge. Demas fell headlong into the subtle snare of covetousness even though he had the godly example of the apostle Paul continually before him. As a result, he wasted his substance for that which is not bread. (Isaiah 55:1-2) He bought the truth only to sell it in his later years. Worst of all, he bartered his soul and betrayed the Savior for a mere trifle.

Dear brother or sister in Christ, what about you? What do you seek as your highest goal in life? I have asked myself the same question. In Matthew 6:21 our Lord Jesus said: *Where your treasure is, there will your heart be also.* Since we will seek that which we love the most, do we dare cast our eyes in the direction of Demas' mine? Are we not subject to the same frailty as he? Yes, we are! How we need our Lord's warning to remember Lot's wife!

Her tragic case also reminds us that this world is under certain judgment. Vanity's days are numbered, and its end may come sooner than we think. So as we anticipate our Lord's return, let us carefully guard our hearts, lest they be captivated by the spirit of Vanity Fair. In that day when the Lord Jesus Christ comes to gather his own out of this present evil world, may he find us faithful. Therefore, let us heed his warning: *Be ye also ready: for in such an hour as ye think not the Son of man cometh.* (Matthew 24:44) As we march onward and upward to Zion, let us pray fervently for grace to refuse anything that would divert us from the path of the just. Moreover, let us pray for hearts that are thankful and contented with our lot in life, knowing that our infinitely wise heavenly Father planned it all.

In concluding this chapter, it would be remiss of me not to stress the truth that covetousness is a heart condition. It is not a sin to be wealthy, nor does great wealth necessarily denote a covetous nature. Sin lays squarely in the heart, in the love of money, not the possession of it. Discontentment with God's provision and the insatiable desire for more are sins of which poor and rich alike are guilty.

So if God has blessed you with earthly treasure, thank him for it and keep in mind that it really belongs to him. He has entrusted it to you for just a little while; therefore, while it is in your possession, seek to be a wise steward. View your prosperity as an opportunity to benefit the kingdom of God. As you are able, use it for the furtherance of the Gospel and the benefit of God's people. Covetousness is indeed a subtle snare, but the rich need not be caught in it.

In Psalm 119:36-37, we read the prayer of one whose heart was firmly set on things above. Thus he prayed: *Incline my heart unto thy testimonies, and not to covetousness. Turn away mine eyes from beholding vanity; and quicken thou me in thy way.* May this be our prayer as well, whatever our earthly circumstances. Our Lord Jesus Christ is the pearl of great price. He is our priceless treasure. What greater wealth could we have than to be partakers of his salvation? Yet as the apostle Paul reminds us: *We have this treasure in earthen vessels.* (2 Corinthians 4:7) We are weak vessels of clay in which there is still so much that needs to be purged away.

O, that we might remember this the next time our heavenly Father brings trial and affliction our way in order to further purify our faith! May we also keep in mind that it is only in the face of strong resistance that we make spiritual progress. In such times, we often feel as if we cannot stand the stress, but will be hopelessly crushed by it. May God grant us eyes to see that these times are necessary, in order that *the excellency of the power may be of God, and not of us.*

Study Questions

1. What terrible danger did the silver mine in the hill called Lucre represent? What did a desire to view the mine signify, and what would Christian and Hopeful have to do in order to see it? How did the two differ in their opinions concerning the mine?

2. Write a brief character sketch of Demas the mine keeper. What particular thing did By-ends and Demas have in common?

3. There is a quest that leads to an eternally joyful end. What is it? How is the Lord Jesus Christ our priceless treasure?

4. Why did John Bunyan place the ancient landmark that was once Lot's wife so close to Demas' silver mine? What profound effect did the sight of the monument have upon Hopeful? Why?

5. Since none of us is free from the sin of covetousness, how are we to guard our hearts against it?

Part Thirteen

BESIDE THE STILL WATERS

Behold, a king shall reign in righteousness, and princes shall rule in judgment. And a man shall be as an hiding place from the wind, and a covert from the tempest; as rivers of water in a dry place, as the shadow of a great rock in a weary land.
Isaiah 32:1-2

CHAPTER 38

A Season of Refreshing

WHEN WE FIRST COME TO KNOW THE LORD, WE ARE AS RAW ORE TAKEN from the heart of the earth. Although delivered from darkness and placed into his kingdom of light, we are far from being 24 carat gold. While accepted in the Beloved and new creatures in him, we face a long journey of preparation before we will shine forth in his image. Therefore, like precious metal in its raw state, our preparation for eternal glory requires the application of the refiner's fire. (Isaiah 48:10; Zechariah 13:9; 1 Peter 5:10)

The art of metallurgy is an exact science requiring the skill and precision of a master's touch. Before one undertakes the refining process, he must have extensive knowledge of the substance with which he plans to work. If he is to successfully unleash its hidden potential, he must thoroughly understand both its unique elemental properties and particular weaknesses and strengths. While an apprentice might cast the raw material aside as worthless, the true artisan views the ugly lump with an eye toward what he can make of it.

The refiner of silver knows that in order to achieve his purpose, he must avoid two costly mistakes. If he fails to complete the process, his effort will have been in vain. On the other hand, if he takes it too far by subjecting the alloy to a temperature that is too extreme or exposing it to the fire for too long a time, he will ruin the fragile metal. Since the precision required to complete his task allows little margin for error, the craftsman cannot afford to be distracted or inattentive. But at the end of the day, the thing of beauty he has produced is ample reward for all of his patience and care.

Our heavenly Father has an eternal purpose for us that requires a very similar process. (Job 23:10) If left alone, there are many natural tendencies within us that would make us poor representatives of our Lord Jesus Christ. However, God has willed that we reflect the beautiful character of his Son, grow strong in faith, and become increasingly more fruitful servants in his kingdom. It is to this end that he undertakes our transformation until we are as silver refined. (Malachi 3:1-3)

As the refiner of his people, our Lord tries our hearts much like an assayer tests a metallic compound in order to determine the quality of a particular metal. (Psalm 66:10; Proverbs 17:3; Jeremiah 20:13) This analogy brings to mind the solemn message King Belshazzar received from God, as recorded in Daniel 5:27: *Thou art weighed in the balances and art found wanting.* Expressed in metaphorical terms, the wicked king is here compared to base metal that has failed the assayer's test. He has been measured and come up short. In Belshazzar's case, God tried and proved him unto condemnation, but how very differently he deals with his own children!

When our loving heavenly Father tries our hearts and takes our measure, he does so in order to purify and perfect us, not condemn us with the world. (1 Corinthians 11:31-32; 1 Thessalonians 2:4) With careful regard to our human frailty, he mixes our wine cup in exactly the right proportions, tempering the bitterness of our trials with sweet seasons of refreshing so that we are not crushed by our troubles. So when we have reached the limits of our endurance, he speaks to our hearts saying: *Rise up, my love, my fair one, and come away. for, lo, the winter is past, the rain is over and gone; the flowers appear on the earth; the time of the singing of birds is come, and the voice of the turtle is heard in our land; the fig tree putteth forth her green figs, and the vines with the tender grape give a good smell. Arise, my love, my fair one, and come away.* (Song of Solomon 2:10-13) These times of spiritual refreshing, in which he lifts us above the shadow and fills our hearts with joy and gladness, are also a vital part of our refining process.

At this point in their journey, Christian and Hopeful were in great need of such a season of rest. From the hustle and bustle of Vanity

Fair to the relative obscurity of the hill called Lucre, they have been bombarded with the temptation to step slightly out of the narrow way in order to better their lot in life. They have also been advised to not take their religion quite so seriously and compromise a little here and there in order to have an easier time of it. They stood firm in spite of this continual assault. But even though John Bunyan does not expressly say so, he implies that the protracted trial was beginning to take its toll. The brief respite on the plain called Ease had really been no rest at all; it had rather been a subtle part of the same trial. Moreover, the disturbing image of Lot's wife haunted Christian and Hopeful long after they passed by her monument.

In addition to the fearful warnings of Scripture, there are equally sure promises of our eternal safety in Christ. There is no contradiction between the two; both of them are crucial truths. Without the strong warnings given in Scripture, we might tend to become spiritually complacent. On the other hand, we could never have the full assurance of faith that is so vital to our spiritual well-being apart from the great and precious promises found in God's Word. (2 Peter 1:4; Hebrews 10:19-22). The Lord's admonition to remember Lot's wife is a perpetual reminder that we must never trifle with the grace of God. Yet it is equally certain that salvation is of the Lord from beginning to end. (Jeremiah 3:23) Unless he keeps us by his grace, we will surely fall. (Psalm 127:1; Proverbs 2:6-8)

This realization of our utter dependence upon the Lord is actually a sign of spiritual strength. Furthermore, clinging to him in the consciousness of our weakness and need is indicative of faith that is strong and vital. It was exactly in this way that the patriarch Jacob prevailed with God in the place he called Penuel. (Genesis 32:24-31; Hosea 12:3-4)

Like Jacob, our hope is well placed when we trust in the living God and look to him for mercy. This hope will never cause us to stumble out of the right path, for it is sure and steadfast, an anchor of the soul. Since the stability of our hope depends entirely upon the one in whom we trust, how comforting it is to know that he is the same one of whom the psalmist wrote: *The steps of a good man are ordered by the LORD: and he delighteth in his way. Though he fall, he shall not be utterly cast down: for the LORD upholdeth him with his hand.* (Psalm 37:23-24)

Take heart then, my brother or sister in Christ. Our gracious Lord is both our Savior and keeper. Our enemies may devise many weapons against us, but none of them shall prosper in the final analysis. (Isaiah 54:17) These may wound and dismay us for a time, but they cannot bring about our ultimate downfall.

Of our Lord Jesus Christ, the prophet Isaiah wrote: *The pleasure of the LORD shall prosper in his hand.* (Isaiah 53:10) Because of his cross, nothing can sever us from his love or snatch us out of his powerful hand. (John 10:27-30) As our fortress and shield, he stands between us and the forces of darkness that would strike a lethal blow, if they could. (Psalm 48:11-14) By appointing salvation for walls and bulwarks, he surrounds and protects us from the spiritual powers that continually plot our overthrow. (Isaiah 26:1-2) When his providence leads us into the heat of battle and the enemy appears certain to win the day, our Lord enters the field as our mighty champion. (Isaiah 59:19) Since he has already won the victory through the cross, we may confidently say: *Behold, God is my salvation; I will trust, and not be afraid: for the LORD JEHOVAH is my strength and my song; he also is become my salvation.* (Isaiah 12:2)

What a sure hope we have in Christ Jesus our Lord! Although he does not remove every obstacle in our path, he will supply all that we need in order to overcomer in spite of them. (Philippians 1:6) The way in which the Holy Spirit accomplishes this work is a truly wondrous and mysterious thing. Even though we are the beneficiaries of his constant guidance and help, we would be hard pressed to explain it without the clear teaching of God's Word. Scripture abounds with figures of speech that help us to understand the secret providence by which we persevere in faith and are made more than conquerors through him that loved us. (Romans 8:37)

In describing the circumstances of Christian and Hopeful after they left the vicinity of Demas' mine, John Bunyan drew upon several of these metaphors. For example, he placed their footpath right along the banks of a pleasant river. What a welcome change it must have been! For those who have had the opportunity to experience it, a walking trail beside a river is an especially delightful thing. It is one of my favorite places to hike. The melodious sound of flowing water seems to temper the heat of the day, calm my restless mind, and energize my spirit. But as you already suspect, it was no ordinary river that cheered the hearts of Christian and Hopeful as they walked beside it that day.

A glorious river

The pleasant river flowing alongside the King's Highway is truly of an exceptional nature. I mentioned it briefly in Chapter 12, "Onward to Zion by the Road Less Traveled." This particular river corresponds to a divine provision made for every battle-weary traveler making his way to the Celestial City. Since it is a spiritual entity, it possesses certain remarkable attributes that set it apart from any kind of earthly waterway.

Ezekiel the prophet saw it flowing out from under the threshold of the temple, a symbolic structure that, like the river itself, has no literal earthly counterpart. (Ezekiel 47:1-2) Long afterward, the apostle John saw a vision of this very same river, which he described as *a pure river of water of life, clear as crystal, proceeding out of the throne of God and of the Lamb.* (Revelation 22:1)

It is interesting that John saw the river flowing *out of the throne of God and of the Lamb,* while Ezekiel beheld it as coming *from under the right side of the house* (the prophetic temple), *at the south side of the altar.* There is no contradiction between the two accounts, however. Both allude to the source of the river, and the implications of it are monumental. Ezekiel saw the brazen altar while John beheld the sacrifice. (John 1:29; Revelation 5:5-10) The fountainhead of this river originates with the Lord Jesus Christ and his cross. He is the smitten rock from which its pure water flows and carries the blessings of salvation wherever his Gospel is preached. As a result of the river's wholesome influence, places that were barren and desolate bloom into life and fruitfulness. (Isaiah 35:1-7)

Although the river's flow is constant and changeless, it ministers the joy of salvation to weary pilgrims in various forms. Often it appears as springs of water in the most unlikely places, just when such relief is desperately needed. As you may recall, it was a spring from this very same river that formed a pool of water near the base of the hill Difficulty. By drinking deeply from it, Christian was refreshed in his spirit and strengthened for the strenuous climb ahead of him. (Isaiah 41:17-18)

Scripture frequently depicts this river as living fountains of waters that have the power to satisfy those who hunger and thirst after righteousness, and minister comfort to those who mourn spiritually. (Matthew 5:4, 6; Revelation 7:17) Its cleansing properties are available to all who are sensible of their need. Thirsty sinners who come to this fountain find it to be the water of life, and having once been a partaker of it, they continually drink of its life-giving stream (John 7:37-38; Revelation 21:6; Revelation 22:17)

When the Lord Jesus spoke to the Samaritan woman who had come to draw water from Jacob's well, he used the occasion to tell her of a well of water that springs up into everlasting life. (John 4:10-14) The woman was naturally eager for this extraordinary water. Although she was slow to understand his meaning at first, the Lord made it clear that he was both the source of this living water and the giver of it. To come to him is to draw water out of the wells of salvation. (Isaiah 12:3)

This river of salvation has another characteristic that is worthy of note. It varies greatly as to its depth, or rather to the perception of its depth. (Ezekiel 47:3-5) Like the Christian life itself, this river was small in its beginning. Yet the longer it flows and the further it goes, the deeper, broader, and more expansive it becomes. From a tiny rivulet to a glorious river! With its increase the kingdom of God, which was like a grain of mustard seed in its beginning, will eventually encompass *a great multitude, which no man could number, of all nations, and kindreds, and people, and tongues.* (Mark 4:30-32; Revelation 7:9) By means of abundant outlets and streams, its vast benefits are readily accessible to all who are part of God's kingdom, wherever they happen to be. (Isaiah 44:1-5; Zechariah 14:8-9)

Dear reader, by now you have probably solved the mystery of this metaphorical river. It signifies the ministry of the Holy Spirit in the souls of the redeemed. He is the wellspring from which salvation is imparted to believing sinners. (John 3:5-8) He is the divine teacher, comforter, and guide of all in whom he dwells. Depicted in Scripture as a river flowing from the throne of God and of the Lamb, the Spirit of God is the gift of the Father's love and the bequest of our blessed

Savior. (John 15:26-27; John 16:7-15) The Lord Jesus likened his presence within to rivers of living water. (John 7:37-39) For all who come and drink of this fountain; to all who come to Christ by faith, the living water becomes in them a well of water springing up into everlasting life. (John 4:10, 13-14)

What a precious gift! The Holy Spirit is the earnest of our inheritance in Christ. (Ephesians 1:14) Furthermore, it is through his sanctifying work that we are *kept by the power of God through faith unto salvation ready to be revealed in the last time.* (1 Peter 1:5) This glorious river, then, also pictures the mysterious way in which God keeps his children safely in the path of life.

Far from the noise and strife of Vanity Fair with its waterways congested with worldly commerce, there is a quiet place where we may retreat for a season of refreshing. In this secret place, we discover that our glorious Lord is unto us a place of broad rivers and streams. (Isaiah 33:21) From the bountiful supply of his grace, he provides all that we need in order to stay the course. This river also contains healing properties for every spiritual disorder to which we are subject, by ministering to us freely the vast benefits that are ours in Christ. Without a doubt, the greatest of these is the redemption that is ours through the blood of Christ, and our cleansing from sin once for all, forever. (1 Corinthians 6:11; Titus 3:5-7; Hebrews 9:14; Revelation 1:5) Every other spiritual benefit flows forth from this one.

In spite of our best efforts, our feet will invariably become soiled as we walk the path of life. (John 13:5-10) Although we do not live under the dominion of sin, we have not yet achieved sinless perfection. Thus we need daily cleansing even as we walk in the light, and the Holy Spirit ministers this cleansing by means of God's Word. (1 John 1:7-9; John 15:3; Ephesians 5:25-27) As we confess our sins and seek his mercy, our Lord is faithful to forgive, cleanse, and restore our souls through the merits of his cross.

When we are low in spirit and discouragement threatens to stop us in our tracks, he ministers comfort to our troubled minds. When we are weary and faint of heart because our strength has utterly failed, he gives power to press onward by faith. (Psalm 27:13-14; Isaiah 40:28-31) Moreover, he gives grace to not only rise above every adversity, but soar with wings as eagles.

In times when fear and sorrow rush in like a flood and threaten to carry us away, *there is a river, the streams whereof shall make glad the city of God.* (Psalm 46:1-4) When we look away from our circumstances and unto our Lord, he imparts joy of which the world knows nothing. Through his Spirit, he is gracious to give *the oil of joy for mourning, the garment of praise for the spirit of heaviness.* (Isaiah 61:3)

Should all around us appear on the verge of imminent collapse, our Lord Jesus Christ is the rock of ages, providing stability that nothing can shake. (Psalm 27:5-6; Psalm 46:5-7) As we cast our cares upon him and rest in him by faith, he whispers peace to our troubled hearts and imparts the peace of God, which passes all understanding. (Philippians 4:6-7) Although he may not see fit to deliver us from the thing that troubles us the most, he is well able to give us grace and peace in spite of it. (Psalm 46:8-11; 2 Corinthians 12:7-10) Since he is the giver of this peace, nothing on earth can take it away. Furthermore, it carries with it the blessed assurance of safety, even when we find ourselves caught in the crossfire of a terrible battle. (Psalm 91:4-10) With God as our refuge and strength, our very present help in trouble, we may safely rest under the shadow of his tender care. (Psalm 46:1; Psalm 91:1-2)

My fellow pilgrim, it is an understatement to say that we live in a troubled world. The evidence is before us daily and serves to remind us that this world is not our home. Although we must pass through, we do not belong to it. How foolish, then, to seek our stability and security here. What a blessing to know that we have a better dwelling place, a *quiet habitation, a tabernacle that shall not be taken down*! (Isaiah 33:20) Although many will try, no enemy can successfully breach the security of our refuge and fortress. (Psalm 91:2) Neither earthly foes nor powers of darkness can destroy what God has established. (Psalm 125:1-2) However, the measure of our peace in times of trouble will largely depend upon our consciousness of his presence. (Hebrews 13:5-6; Psalm 46:10-11)

In spite of our feelings, which are changeable at best, our Lord is ever with us. He loves us with an everlasting love and lives in our hearts through his Spirit. This is the secret of our victory. May we know the joy of following him by faith and committing ourselves to his providential care! May we live in the knowledge of his continual presence with us, as we press onward to the City of God!

Glorious things of thee are spoken, Zion, city of our God;
He whose word cannot be broken formed thee for his own abode:
On the Rock of Ages founded, what can shake thy sure repose?
With salvation's walls surrounded, thou may'st smile at all thy foes.

See, the streams of living waters, springing from eternal love,
Well supply thy sons and daughters, and all fear of want remove:
Who can faint, while such a river ever flows their thirst t'assuage?
Grace which, like the Lord, the giver, never fails from age to age.

Round each habitation hov'ring, see the cloud and fire appear
For a glory and a cov'ring, showing that the Lord is near:
Thus deriving from their banner light by night and shade by day,
Safe they feed upon the manna which he gives them when they pray.

Saviour, if of Zion's city I, through grace, a member am,
Let the world deride or pity, I will glory in thy Name:
Fading is the worldling's pleasure, all his boasted pomp and show;
Solid joys and lasting treasure none but Zion's children know. [1]

Memories of Elim

Given the extraordinary nature of the unseen river flowing near our path, who can wonder that it has the power to cheer the heavy-hearted and strengthen the faint? After all, life springs forth wherever it goes. (Ezekiel 47:9) In order to better illustrate the river's life-giving properties, John Bunyan placed a verdant oasis on either side of it. In many respects, it reminds me of the desert oasis of Elim.

After their deliverance from Egypt and exhausting trek through the Red Sea, the Hebrew people pitched their tents in Elim, *where were twelve wells of water, and threescore and ten palm trees.* (Exodus 15:27) By the refreshing waters of Elim, they enjoyed a much needed time of rest and recovery from their harrowing ordeal.

John Bunyan's riverside oasis can be thought of as the spiritual counterpart of Elim. Due to its rich alluvial soil, numerous varieties of large shade trees grew by the river, providing a broad canopy overhead and a cool resting place below. Like many a weary traveler who passed that way before them, Christian and Hopeful gladly took shelter there.

In common with the river itself, the concept of an oasis is taken directly from Scripture. Both the prophet Ezekiel and John the apostle had similar visions of such an oasis and its beneficial effects. (Ezekiel 47:7-9; Revelation 22:1-2) In both instances, the spiritual meaning is consistent. The river is a lifeline providing continual nourishment to the trees growing beside it.

Ponder the scene in your mind, if you will. The interpretation is pretty clear, is it not? We have already established that the river signifies the work of the Holy Spirit in regeneration, and the secret providence by which he sustains the life he gives. The lush oasis pictures the effect of his work in the soul. The life of Christ within is the secret of all our spiritual growth and fruitfulness.

What about the trees growing so tall and stately along the river's edge? Their equal is not to be found among any of earth's botanical species. Not only are the leaves of these trees perpetually green, they are endowed with medicinal properties that can heal any spiritual disorder when ingested properly. In fact, when taken beforehand, they can prevent many problems and diseases to which the traveler might otherwise fall victim. (Romans 6:5-12; Romans 8:1-6; Galatians 5:16-23)

Another exceptional characteristic of these trees is the manner in which they bear fruit. Not a single one of them is barren. On the contrary, each one brings forth differing kinds of fruit that is uniformly fresh and wholesome. They are extraordinary trees, to be sure, but only by reason of their close proximity to the river. (Ezekiel 47:12)

In conjunction with the river itself, these trees depict one of the most precious truths found in Scripture. Like the river that caused them to put down deep roots, these trees are of divine origin. (Isaiah 41:17-20) They were set in place by God himself, *that they might be called trees of righteousness, the planting of the LORD, that he might be glorified.* (Isaiah 61:3)

My friend in Christ, we are these trees! Through the agency of his Spirit, our Lord Jesus Christ imparts all that we need in order to grow in grace and become firmly established in the faith. Moreover, any spiritual fruit we bring forth is due to his power alone. Thus we must drink of the river of life continually. As we do so, our vital union with Christ is nourished and maintained. He is the vine, the source of our life. He is the tree of life. We are merely branches, living and bearing fruit only because we are fully attached to him. (John 15:4-5) Moreover, since it is God's will that we glorify him by bearing much fruit, he purges us so that we will be more fruitful still. (John 15:1-2, 8)

What a blessed place to be, planted by rivers of living water where faith can prosper and grow! With this thought in mind, consider the sharp contrast found in Jeremiah 17:5-8: *Thus saith the LORD; cursed be the man that trusteth in man, and maketh flesh his arm, and whose heart departeth from the LORD. For he shall be like the heath in the desert, and shall not see when good cometh; but shall inhabit the parched places in the wilderness, in a salt land and not inhabited. Blessed is the man that trusteth in the LORD, and whose hope the LORD is. For he shall be as a tree planted by the waters, and that spreadeth out her roots by the river, and shall not see when heat cometh, but her leaf shall be green; and shall not be careful in the year of drought, neither shall cease from yielding fruit.*

Contemplating these verses brings Psalm 1 immediately to my mind. Therein we learn that the Word of God is another vital means to our stability and perseverance in grace. The work of God's Spirit in the soul is always in conjunction with his Word. (1 Peter 2:1-3) As we meditate in the Scriptures and find them to be the delight of our hearts, a wonderful thing takes place. We become the blessed man in Psalm 1, who is likened unto *a tree planted by the rivers of water, that bringeth forth his fruit in his season; his leaf also shall not wither; and whatsoever he doeth shall prosper.*

Therefore, consider the riverside oasis and its application to us as present-day travelers along the path of life. If we have been planted by this river of living water; that is, if Christ Jesus lives in us through his Spirit, we have great cause to rejoice and take heart. Herein is the secret to the successful completion of our journey. There exists no need that cannot be supplied here. Every Christian virtue, every godly quality, and every spiritual excellence springs from this fountainhead. There is strength to endure the hardships we face and to overcome every obstacle in our path. There is forgiveness and cleansing when we have missed the mark, and the fruit of obedience and righteousness by which we honor God in our lives. Here we find every grace to run the race with patience and finish it with joy. All these benefits are imparted to us through the gracious influence of God's Spirit and the dynamic power of his Word. This is the sum and substance of the metaphorical river flowing beside our path. This is the essence of the spiritual nourishment that revives our souls day by day.

This pleasant river with its lush oasis serves as a continual reminder that Christ is our life. Without his constant help, we would not make it very far down the road to the Celestial City. But he is ever faithful to supply all that we need to serve him in this life. Moreover, when the time comes for us to leave this earthly realm and exchange it for the heavenly, we will discover what we now experience but in part. This very same river, which sustained us while on earth, will continue to do so in the heavenly Jerusalem. Throughout the ages in his kingdom of glory, Christ will evermore be our tree of life. (Revelation 22:1-2)

Our times of spiritual refreshing must never be confused with earthly happiness or temporal joy, for they often come in the midst of trial and sorrow. Moreover, these times should be considered the norm for the Christian life, rather than the rare exception. They are not the fruit of neglect, however, or the result of mere attendance to duty. As a rule, the secret to our spiritual renewal lies in our private devotional life and daily walk with the Lord. As we seek him fervently and humble ourselves before him, he draws near to us, fills our vision, and speaks to our hearts of many things. (James 4:5-10; Psalm 42:1-2) Therefore, daily partaking of the bread of life and living water is the key to our prosperity of soul. (Joshua 1:8)

So rather than considering our quiet time with the Lord as a perfunctory duty before we begin our day, we should view it as our spiritual lifeline. It is the secret to our power and victory while living as pilgrims and exiles in this vain world. Time well spent with the Lord will set the pace for the rest of our day by drawing our hearts upward and our thoughts Godward as we go about our business. But how can we be strong in faith and able to resist temptation if we are content to remain at a distance from the river of life?

Using the pastoral imagery found in Psalm 23, John Bunyan expanded his riverside oasis to include a cool, inviting meadow through which the pleasant river flowed. It was a beautiful place where lilies grew in profusion and the grass was soft and green all year long. Under the watchful eye of the shepherd guarding it, those who seek refuge in this particular meadow can lie down and rest in perfect safety. Christian and Hopeful, who were overcome with weariness by this time, took full advantage of this welcome provision.

Dear brother or sister in Christ, you and I have access to this very same meadow. When we have reached the limits of our endurance, we may enjoy a season of quiet rest in these same green pastures. (Psalm 23:2) We can experience the tranquility of soul that comes from leaning upon our Beloved and trusting ourselves to his care. When we are troubled and tempted and our souls run dry, he leads us beside the still waters, which are surely an outlet of the very same river. (Psalm 23:2) Never fear that time spent lingering here is time wasted. This is the very way in which our Lord restores our souls and leads us in the paths of righteousness for his name's sake. (Psalm 23:3) Walking in his strength, we may face the wrath of our enemies with equanimity, for he will never forsake us in time of need. (Psalm 23:5) Moreover, when our path takes us through dark and dangerous places like the valley of the shadow of death, we have the calm assurance of his protection. (Psalm 23:4)

Therefore, why should we fear if we can honestly say: *The LORD is my shepherd; I shall not want?* (Psalm 23:1) Our times of spiritual refreshing are but the earnest of something far better that lies ahead for us. Until then, let us continue to press onward with the certain hope that: *Surely goodness and mercy shall follow me all the days of my life: and I will dwell in the house of the LORD for ever.* (Psalm 23:6)

* * * *

According to John Bunyan, Christian and Hopeful enjoyed the benefits of their season of refreshing for several days and nights. During that time, they repeatedly drank of the river's living water, ate of the abundant fruit growing on the trees, and made use of their medicinal leaves. In other words, they knew God's presence and power in their lives in a very special way. Undoubtedly, they spent much time in the Word of God and in prayer, and enjoyed close fellowship with the Lord and with one another. As a result of this time of spiritual rest and renewal, they were refreshed in body, mind, and soul. With this restoration of soul came a proportionate return of strength and vigor; therefore they were ready and eager to resume their journey. Even though the verdant oasis was like a foretaste of heaven, it did not mark the end of their journey. There was much farther to go and many more trials yet to face. For the present, however, their season of refreshing was highly instrumental in speeding them on their way.

As they hastened down the road, the beneficial effects of their time of rest were evident, for their footsteps were much lighter than before and they had a song in their hearts. Moreover, the din and cry of Vanity Fair had retreated far into the background. By-ends with his compelling arguments was but a dim memory, and the wealth of Demas' mine seemed as nothing in comparison to the riches of Christ and his salvation. Very recently, they had grappled with the subtle snare of covetousness and been somewhat tempted by it. But now, they saw the vanity of this world for what it really was, and understood more clearly than ever where their true treasure lay.

Study Questions

1. In Scripture, we find both fearful warnings and great and precious promises of eternal safety for those who are in Christ. Why are both of them vital to our spiritual health and well-being? How is the realization of our utter dependence upon the Lord actually a sign of spiritual strength?

2. The pleasant river flowing by the King's Highway depicts God's gracious provision for his children as they journey through this life. What is the source of this great river, and what effect does its pure water have upon the weary soul? In what other forms can this life-giving water minister to God's people? In what way does this living water also minister to thirsty sinners?

3. This glorious river signifies Christ living in his people through his Holy Spirit. To what does our Lord Jesus liken his presence within us? Show several ways in which he ministers to us by his Spirit. Going a little further, show how his presence with us protects us and keeps us safely in the path of life.

4. Describe the trees growing beside the river of life and tell what they represent. What is the secret to their exceptional fruitfulness? Who planted them where they are, and for what purpose were they planted? On this same note, how important is the Word of God to our spiritual stability and perseverance in grace?

5. The lush meadow through which the river flows draws our attention to Psalm 23. Read this great Psalm and briefly describe the tender care of our great Shepherd, and the abundant provision he makes for us until our journey is over.

Part Fourteen

BEWARE THE "WAY THAT SEEMETH RIGHT"

Gracious is the LORD, and righteous; yea, our God is merciful.
The LORD preserveth the simple: I was brought low, and he helped
me. Return unto thy rest, O my soul; for the LORD hath dealt boun-
tifully with thee. For thou hast delivered my soul from death,
mine eyes from tears, and my feet from falling.
I will walk before the LORD in the land of the living.
Psalm 116:5-9

CHAPTER 39

Remove Not the Ancient Landmark!

IF WE ARE TO HAVE A CORRECT UNDERSTANDING OF GOD'S SALVATION, WE must first acknowledge the relationship between divine sovereignty and human responsibility. Many well-intentioned souls err by taking an extreme view of either side of this issue, but Scripture does not leave us in the dark on the subject. The sovereignty of God in salvation is a fact beyond dispute; therefore, the pathway to Zion is a safe and protected way. (Isaiah 26:1-2; Philippians 1:6; Philippians 2:13) On the other hand, the scriptural admonition to *work out your own salvation with fear and trembling* implies that there is no path quite so dangerous. (Philippians 2:12)

In our contemplation of *The Pilgrim's Progress*, we have had ample opportunity to observe this dual aspect of our spiritual journey. While Christian has remained safely in the right path so far, he has encountered quite a few individuals who set out for the Celestial City, only to turn back somewhere along the way. A single message ringing loudly and clearly throughout each of their histories is that the sovereignty of God in no way negates human responsibility. Our Lord has secured the safe passage of every one of his people; therefore, not a single one of them will be lost. (John 10:27-29) Yet each of us must finish the race as we began it, by continuing in the faith of the Son of God. (Galatians 2:20; Hebrews 12:1-3)

The promises of God are sure and steadfast; we can utterly depend upon them, for they will never fail. They are not given without qualification, however, but only pertain to those who are faithful unto the end. (1 Corinthians 9:24-27; 2 Peter 1:10; Revelation 3:21) Equally certain are the warnings to travelers who are careless and spiritually indolent. (Hebrews 10:35-39) These have no legitimate claim to the assurance of safety. So we do not overstate the case in saying that the royal road to Zion is both safe and perilous.

As Christian discovered early on, he who strives to enter the strait gate must also give due diligence to walk the narrow path beyond it. Yet in order to do so, he must be able to discern that single path from every other way. Many a pilgrimage has come to a shameful end due to failure in this regard, which poses a vital question. Just how may the path of the just be distinguished from those ways that seem right, but lead to a tragic end? (Compare Proverbs 4:18 with Proverbs 14:12) The answer lies not so much in the path itself as within the hearts of those who claim to follow it.

In recalling the characters Christian has met along the way so far, you remember that some of them began the journey to Zion for reasons that were highly questionable. Moreover, they felt at full liberty to plot their own course while claiming to do God's will. Some of them made it further than others, but each one made the fatal mistake of avoiding the Wicket Gate.

This is not the case with those who are truly born again. My fellow believer, Christ lives in us through his Spirit and this makes all the difference. He alone is our hope of glory, the inner wellspring from which we receive every grace needed in order to live godly lives in this present evil world. (Colossians 1:27) He gives power to overcome temptation and strength to persevere when our faith comes under fire. Moreover, he gives wisdom to discern the truth from every false voice.

The indwelling of God's Spirit is the birthright of every true Christian. (Romans 8:9-17) Without his gracious influence to teach, correct, and guide us day by day, we could not possibly navigate the path of life. (Jeremiah 10:23) However, the way in which he leads is a thing often misunderstood and abused. As a result, many unspeakable deeds have been done, and grievous sins committed, by those who claimed they were led of God. Likewise, others have rejected the truth and made ruinous decisions while convinced they were following the will of God.

In all such cases, fallen human nature deserves full credit for doing the leading, not the Spirit of God! With self-interest, personal desire, and worldly ambition as motivating factors, it is not surprising that untold mischief and outright scandal are frequent consequences. But the Spirit of God is not the author of them!

Another common misconception about the work of the Holy Spirit is that it is made known through certain outward manifestations such as frenzied behavior, uncontrolled emotional outbursts, and ecstatic experiences. However, none of these things indicates either his presence or his power. With the surrender of rational thought, which nearly always accompanies this kind of behavior, there comes an equivalent lack of self-control that is contrary to the fruit of the Spirit.

Furthermore, even though the leading of the Holy Spirit is a mystical thing, it is not made known through mystical experiences such as dreams, visions, or others kinds of mental impressions. When one attempts to decipher God's will through such things, personal desire and natural inclination will invariably take the lead. One of the most painful aspects of the Gospel ministry lies in watching people refuse godly counsel and make spiritually detrimental choices while claiming to be led by God's Spirit. Moreover, there is the added heartbreak of witnessing their suffering as they reap the consequences of those choices.

Dear friend in Christ, you and I must never suppose that we are incapable of making the same mistake. Many false voices will try to lure us from the right path, and some of the strongest of them dwell within us. By simply following our own desires, we can easily convince ourselves that our will is also God's will. Yet there is a far more excellent way. (Proverbs 3:5-7)

The path of the just is an ancient one corresponding to the *old paths, where is the good way* spoken of by Jeremiah the prophet. (Jeremiah 6:16) Isaiah called it the way of holiness walked by the redeemed. It is along this single path that God leads his children to be with him forever. (Isaiah 35:8-10)

However, we should not think of the ancient path to the heavenly Zion as a straight line, the shortest distance between two points. It is a circuitous route meandering through dangerous country, and lying adjacent to various byways designed to confuse and distract the traveler. Yet even though the way can be highly perplexing at times, it is made known by certain landmarks established long ago by the patriarchs, Moses and the prophets, the apostles and our Lord most of all. Although they were set in place as permanent guideposts for those who would follow thereafter, many consider them mere relics of the past, obsolete and irrelevant to the 21st century traveler. But such is not the case.

These ancient markers, all of which pertain to our redemption in Christ, are as crucial to us today as to those who first set them in place. Often called the fundamentals of the faith, they form the foundation upon which our hope of eternal glory is based, the very same foundation upon which the Lord Jesus Christ is building his church. (Acts 4:10-12; 1 Corinthians 3:9-11) Established solely upon God's Word, each marker represents an eternal truth to guide his people along the right path. In this, they remind me of the strategically placed signposts pointing the way to the ancient cities of refuge.

Given the vital nature of these Gospel landmarks, each is to be prayerfully considered, diligently obeyed, and continually kept in heart and mind. The traveler who faithfully follows them will grow strong in the Lord and increasingly more established in his truth. Therefore, he will not be easily sidetracked, but many a heedless soul has wandered out of the way by simply disregarding them.

Solomon's explicit warning *Remove not the ancient landmark, which thy fathers have set* certainly applies to these fundamental truths of the Gospel. (Proverbs 22:28; Revelation 22:18-19) Yet even though it is forbidden to alter, remove, or in any other way tamper with them, there are those who have no scruples about doing so. These spiritual vandals are guilty of untold damage. Some of them attempt to tear down the sacred landmarks altogether, leaving each individual to do what seems right in his or her own eyes. (Judges 17:6) Others, who pride themselves upon their superior intellect and knowledge, pervert Scripture truth with humanist thought by adding the commandments and doctrines of men. Still others substitute guideposts that are more pleasing to fallen human nature. In essence, all of these are guilty of the same thing. They reject the old paths in order to follow a way of their own choosing. But in rejecting God's truth and his appointed way, they turn to fables and wander into ever-increasing darkness. (1 Timothy 4:1; 2 Timothy 4:3-4)

This solemn fact reminds me of the psalmist's concern in Psalm 11:3: *If the foundations be destroyed, what can the righteous do?* It is a highly relevant question today as well. Sometimes there is but a very fine line separating the path of life from alternate routes that appear before us here and there. In addition to the ancient landmarks that show us the right way, we will come upon false markers placed there by enemy hands. Some of these are quite deceptive in nature and appear so innocent that they easily mislead the unwary. Therefore, a finely tuned spiritual discernment is crucial if we are to shun the false and adhere strictly to the true. (Psalm 119:104; Hebrews 5:14)

Although we walk the path of the just by faith, we must make diligent use of Scripture in order to do so. Penned under divine inspiration by men who were willing to forfeit their lives rather than deny its truth, God's Word is the substance of the ancient landmarks that direct our steps. Its eternal, unchangeable truth sheds an infallible light upon our way that, if diligently followed, will guide us safely all the way to our heavenly home. (Psalm 119:105, 130)

In addition to the guiding light of God's Word, we have the inward illumination of his Spirit to teach and lead us in the way of righteousness and truth. Without the benefit of his continual help, we could never properly interpret the ancient landmarks or distinguish them from their subtle counterfeits. Therefore, we would be *tossed to and fro, and carried about with every wind of doctrine,* and prove an easy prey for those who *lie in wait to deceive.* (Ephesians 4:14)

We live in a day when seducing spirits and doctrines of devils confront us on every hand. As they clamor for our attention, many give them a hearing and eventually depart from the faith. (1 Timothy 4:1) How can we avoid this deadly snare? How are we to distinguish between the spirit of truth, and the spirit of error? (1 John 4:6) We can only do so by taking diligent heed to what we hear, and carefully judging it in light of God's infallible testimony. (Isaiah 8:20)

The Spirit of God always performs his work in conjunction with the Word of God. In spite of what many claim, he will never lead us in a way that is contrary to its truth. Therefore, since the leading of the Holy Spirit will always be in perfect accord with Scripture, their dual witness is really a single one. The Lord Jesus Christ, who is the truth, is both the sum and substance of their testimony.

The single grand theme of God's Word is like a scarlet-colored thread woven throughout its entirety. That theme is his wondrous redemption and the gradual unfolding of his eternal purpose. (John 5:39-40) Foreshadowed long ago in Old Testament types and figures, and foretold by prophets through the ages, all eventually fixes upon one central personage, the suffering Servant of Jehovah. (Isaiah 42:1-3; Isaiah 52:13-53:12) These ancient prophecies all have their perfect fulfillment in the incarnation of the holy Son of God. (Matthew 1:20-23; Matthew 5:17-18: compare Psalm 40:6-8 with Hebrews 10:4-9)

Likewise, the Spirit of God also testifies of the Lord Jesus Christ. His mission is not to speak of himself, but to draw our hearts and minds away from the vanities of this world and focus them upon Christ and him crucified. (John 16:13-15) Thus he keeps us ever looking to the Lord Jesus Christ as our highest example to imitate and follow, and leads us in paths that are pleasing in his sight.

Therefore, the double witness of the Holy Spirit and the Word of God points us in a single direction, the way of Christ and his cross. (Matthew 16:24-25; Luke 9:23-24). The Gospel mileposts all along the way serve as beacons of truth to lighten our path. As we walk this ancient path, looking unto Jesus the author and finisher of our faith, we follow in his footsteps, which is our sacred duty.

* * * *

Since God's appointed way is the only right path, it is of utmost importance that we be able to discern it from all others. How can we recognize it for sure? The ancient path to the Celestial City is only made known through his Word. The psalmist said: *Through thy precepts I get understanding: therefore I hate every false way.* (Psalm 119:104) When we seek God's guidance through his Word and prayer, with hearts that are set upon obeying him, he will grant us wisdom to distinguish the right path from every false way. (James 1:5)

Therefore, my fellow pilgrim, if you and I would remain steadfastly in the path of life, we must keep to the *old paths, where is the good way.* The essential truths that form its signposts have led countless others safely home; thus it is our wisdom to adhere to them tenaciously. I have known many who claimed to follow the Lord Jesus Christ, but due to negligence in this matter, eventually turned from the truth. As far as I know, not a single one of them ever found the ancient path again.

Perhaps someone near and dear to you has made the same terrible mistake and your heart is broken out of concern for his or her soul. Do not despair if such has been your experience. Continue to pray fervently for your loved one. Even though recovery after such a false step may be relatively rare, nothing is too hard for the Lord.

O send out thy light and thy truth: let them lead me;
Let them bring me unto thy holy hill, and to thy tabernacles.
Psalm 43:3

Study Questions

1. In what way is the royal road to Zion both perilous and safe?

2. How would you describe the path of the just? How can we distinguish this single right way from all others?

3. What kind of markers were set in place long ago to guide travelers along the path of the just? How are we to regard these Gospel landmarks? What is the consequence of ignoring them?

4. Many have deliberately tampered with or even removed some of these landmarks and set up false markers in their place. By what two specific means can we shun every false way and strictly follow the true one?

5. The Word of God and the Holy Spirit give a dual witness that is really a single one? What is the sum and substance of their united testimony? Briefly elaborate upon your answer.

CHAPTER 40

Stile into By-Path Meadow

DEAR BROTHER OR SISTER IN CHRIST, AS WE MAKE OUR JOURNEY THROUGH this life, there will be certain times in which we experience our Lord's presence in an exceptional way. These are much-needed interludes in which our Shepherd-King speaks to our hearts through his Word and prayer, causing faith to burn brightly and the cares and distractions of this life to seem far away. O, how we should cherish these times, for such will not always be our case. Due to the very nature of our path, we cannot expect to walk in perpetual sunshine or live on the mountaintop. Even though we will have periods of relative freedom from trouble, cloudy days and valley trials are more the norm for us as God's people. Therefore, our times of spiritual refreshing are prime opportunities to lay up a reserve of those things upon which to draw when the winds of adversity begin to blow once again. (Proverbs 2:1-9).

It was with joyful hearts and lively steps that Christian and Hopeful resumed their journey after their invigorating season of rest, and for some time thereafter, travel was easy. All too soon, however, the pleasant river with its verdant oasis diverged from their path. Furthermore, the road had now become so rugged that their feet quickly grew sore, and general weariness forced them to slacken their pace considerably.

There is great spiritual significance behind this sudden reversal of circumstances. As long as the river flowed close to their path,

Christian and Hopeful knew the Lord's presence in such measure that their earthly burdens seemed few and light in comparison. With its abrupt change of course, we are reminded that there will also be times when we feel as if the Lord has withdrawn his help when we need it the most. Like the psalmist, these seasons of distress and anguish drive us to the throne of grace, crying: *As the hart panteth after the water brooks, so panteth my soul after thee, O God. My soul thirsteth for God, for the living God: when shall I come and appear before God?* (Psalm 42:1-2) Moreover, to our dismay, we may find his help to be slow in coming. This will always prove a sore trial until we learn to trust our Lord and wait patiently for him. (Isaiah 30:18)

Although the departure of the river from their pathway denoted just such a time for Christian and Hopeful, it did not mean the divine provision was no longer there. Rather, it marked the onset of unspecified trouble and their reaction to it. No doubt about it, their brief respite was over! Once again, they found themselves *in heaviness through manifold temptations* to such an extent that it overshadowed the remembrance of their precious time with the Lord. (1 Peter 1:6) Temporary forgetfulness of God's goodness and mercy altered their perception of the river. In short, they lost sight of it by focusing upon their difficulty, and accordingly, their steps faltered as they began to lose heart.

Without question, the two men now found themselves in a situation that had taken a decided turn for the worse. Although we are not given the particulars of this new trial, their faith was under severe attack once again. During such times, it is especially important that truth believed become truth applied. Christian and Hopeful knew this, but instead of seeing God's hand in their present situation, they forgot the admonitions in his Word concerning chastening and its gracious design. (Hebrews 12:5-6, 10-11) For the time being, the promises of God slipped from their memory and they gave in to discouragement. (Hebrews 2:1) As a result, they were brought to the verge of a spiritual declension that, if allowed to run its natural course, would take them down with alarming swiftness.

Like partners in crime, discouragement is rarely content to dwell alone. It quickly gives rise to a spirit of discontentment, as with Christian and Hopeful when they began to murmur and complain about their situation. While discouragement causes us to wallow in self-pity, discontentment urges us to take matters into our own hands. Thus discontentment now provoked Christian and Hopeful to wish for an easier way, a way out of their trouble. The children of Israel committed a similar offense by murmuring against God and Moses when their journey through the wilderness grew increasingly more difficult. (Numbers 21:4-5) Present adversity wiped out the remembrance of their former bondage and God's great mercy in delivering them from it. So instead of being thankful to God for his gracious provision, the Hebrew people longed to return to Egypt, to the place where they had suffered so cruelly.

If only Christian and Hopeful had remembered this decisive event in Israel's history, and its tragic consequences! (Numbers 21:6-9; Romans 15:4; 1 Corinthians 10:9-12) What trouble they might have been spared if they realized that unbelief lay at the heart of their present frame of mind, just as with the children of Israel! (Hebrews 3:12-19) Had they recognized and acknowledged their sin, they would have fervently sought the Lord for mercy and guidance instead of looking elsewhere for relief.

The sin of unbelief is an all-too-common failing. When given the opportunity, it will create havoc in our minds by stirring up a tempest of doubt, fear, and confusion. It was unbelief that caused David to say in his heart: *I shall now perish one day by the hand of Saul: there is nothing better for me than that I should speedily escape into the land of the Philistines.* (1 Samuel 27:1) This was the same David who, in his youth, had defied the Philistine army and faced Goliath the giant with exceptional faith and courage. It was the same valiant warrior and man after God's own heart who was chosen by God to be Israel's king. (1 Samuel 13:14; 1 Samuel 16:1-13)

My brother or sister in Christ, the awful sin of unbelief is one to which we are prone as well, is it not? Therefore, we dare not pass judgment upon Christian and Hopeful for their present state of mind. How often have we given in to it as well? In fact, unbelief is probably the single worst enemy with which we must contend. When we listen to its voice, it is a given that our spiritual judgment will be impaired. Another voice, the voice of self-reliance, often asserts itself at the same time, just when we should distrust it the most. If heeded, these enemy voices will determine our decisions and actions. Furthermore, they will convince us that our decisions are right and proper, no matter how rash and imprudent they may actually be. With unbelief and self-reliance at the helm, we may be absolutely sincere in our intentions, and yet be sincerely wrong.

A desire granted

Even though it seems paradoxical, the Lord will sometimes give us the desires that are spawned by our unbelief and fueled by discouragement and discontentment. But in so doing, he in no way rewards us for our sin. When he gives us the desire of our hearts, he does so in order to teach us a valuable lesson that we might not otherwise master. (Psalm 106:10-15)

On a similar note, wrong desires often seem to create their own opportunities. Moreover, these opportunities are frequently ascribed to God's will and leading, even when godly counsel was not sought and the clear teaching of Scripture was generally ignored. In such cases, human reason and self-will deserve full credit for the choices made.

Thus it was with Christian and Hopeful. Since the wish for an easier way was now uppermost in their minds, they were constantly on the lookout for it. When their heart's desire materialized right before them, they may well have presumed that the Lord had granted their request. The provision appeared in the form of an inviting meadow that lay on the left side of the road. A stile (a set of steps for ascending or descending a fence or wall) provided easy access to it. The enticing meadow beyond the stile was known locally as By-Path Meadow, but for reasons best known to the owner of the property, its name was not posted.

Christian was elated! This was just the sort of thing he had in mind! However, since he and Hopeful had no intention of leaving the right path, he took the precaution of climbing the stile in order to better assess the situation. After a quick survey, he was convinced that the going would be much easier on the other side of the fence. Then he spotted a footpath that appeared to follow alongside their designated way. What could be more perfect? Not only could they escape their present difficulty, they would not have to go far out of the way to do so. It seemed a rare opportunity to have their cake and eat it, too. How could they possibly lose their way when the path of life was just beyond the fence?

Humanly speaking, it made perfect sense. By-Path Meadow seemed the ideal solution to their problem while posing minimal risk, and since it was in accordance with Christian's desire, he failed to consider its downside. Moreover, he pressed his brother to agree with his decision saying, "'Tis according to my wish…here is the easiest going; come, good Hopeful, and let us go over."

In the course of his walk with the Lord so far, we have watched Christian struggle with many things, but lack of self-confidence has rarely been one of them. In fact, in this regard we could accurately label him a repeat offender. Remember the day he met Faithful, and the humiliating outcome of their foot race? So even though Hopeful had serious misgivings about taking the alternate route through the meadow, Christian had no such qualms. When Hopeful asked, "But how if this Path should lead us out of the Way?" he posed a highly pertinent question. Christian should have pondered it long and hard, but he laid prudence and caution aside instead and yielded to carnal reason.

In those times when the path of life appears very close to the broad way that leads to destruction, there is very little margin for error. Even a seemingly minor misstep can have dire consequences. Therefore, godly wisdom is imperative if we are to foresee and avoid that misstep. Christian and Hopeful now stood at one of these vital crossroads, but instead of weighing the possible outcome of his decision, Christian did his best to relieve Hopeful's concern. Imagine what his arguments may have been. Perhaps he said something akin to: "Just look at the trail through the meadow and how much easier it will be! Does it not run right beside our designated path, just on the other side of the fence? Even though we will be unable to see it, we will know it is there. How then could we lose our way? I am confident that we really have nothing to fear!" When Hopeful eventually yielded to Christian's arguments, they crossed over the stile into By-Path Meadow.

While our attention naturally centers upon the meadow and its spiritual import, the stile that provided access to it deserves a closer look as well. It was the means by which Christian and Hopeful stepped out of the path of life, although they did not think of it that way. The stile seemed to offer a prime opportunity that was far too promising to pass by. However, all such open doors should be carefully and prayerfully weighed in light of Scripture truth, because many of them are not at all what they appear to be.

Was this provision really of the Lord? How were they to know for sure? It seemed harmless enough and the meadow was certainly easier on their poor, tired feet than the rugged path had been. In essence, the route through the meadow was exactly what they had desired. But as you probably suspect, the stile that provided access to it was one of those false markers of which we have been forewarned. By succumbing to the united voice of unbelief and discontentment, they failed to recognize the stile for what it really was. Moreover, by preferring the path beyond the stile, they sought to escape the difficulty into which God's will and providence had placed them.

As I ponder the reaction of Christian and Hopeful to this latest trial, I am struck anew by the realization of just how closely their experience mirrors my own. Moreover, I am amazed at the extraordinary spiritual insight given to John Bunyan. In his single character named Christian we may trace our own pilgrimage, personality differences and particular circumstances aside. We may fancy that our situation is like no one else's until we remember that there is no new thing under the sun. (Ecclesiastes 1:9) Our struggles are not unique, and neither are our trials. The apostle Peter reminds us: *The same afflictions are accomplished in your brethren that are in the world.* (1 Peter 5:9) This great truth is a challenge to my soul when unbelief and discouragement threaten to overtake my mind, and it is a humbling rebuke in those dark seasons when they do.

None of us is immune to the sin of unbelief and the spiritual declension it triggers. What poor, ungrateful creatures we tend to be! How guilty we are of taking God's blessings for granted! How forgetful we are of his past mercies, and how quick to yield to discouragement and discontentment! But what an affront it is to the goodness and longsuffering of our heavenly Father when we do.

Our struggles in this regard bear witness of just how much we need his correction and discipline. Although we would never deliberately contend against our heavenly Father, we unconsciously resist his will when we murmur and complain rather than humbling our-selves under his mighty hand. (1 Peter 5:6-7) In so doing, we only succeed in troubling our own souls. Moreover, we learn the hard way that nothing robs us of our peace and joy in the Lord faster than the sin of unbelief and its bitter fruit.

True Christian contentment is the secret of spiritual peace and joy, but it is not a thing that is easily acquired. Rather, it is the result of well-tried and highly refined faith, not circumstantial ease or the absence of difficulty. In fact, this godly virtue shines brightest against a backdrop of great conflict and adversity. Hence, it is a relatively rare thing.

We will never know this kind of contentment until we find Christ to be our all in all. (Psalm 34:8-10) But when we do, we will be able to honestly say with the psalmist: *Oh that men would praise the LORD for his goodness, and for his wonderful works to the children of men! For he satisfieth the longing soul, and filleth the hungry soul with goodness.* (Psalm 107:8-9)

It bears repeating that Christian contentment is a thing quite apart from our earthly circumstances. The apostle Paul learned its secret in the midst of terrible suffering, and in so doing, he came to realize the source of his true strength. For him, the Lord Jesus Christ was truly his all in all. Therefore, he could truthfully sum up the creed by which he lived in these few words: *For to me to live is Christ, and to die is gain.* (Philippians 1:21) Moreover he could testify, even while enduring the misery and deprivation of a Roman prison: *Not that I speak in respect of want: for I have learned, in whatsoever state I am, therewith to be content. I know both how to be abased, and I know how to abound: every where and in all things I am instructed both to be full and to be hungry, both to abound and to suffer need. I can do all things through Christ which strengtheneth me.* (Philippians 4:11-13) It was a vital lesson that Christian had yet to learn.

While unbelief is always a bad thing, does the same hold true of self-reliance? In 1 Corinthians 10:12, the apostle Paul warns: *Let him that thinketh he standeth take heed lest he fall.* It is an admonition to keep in mind continually. In the character of Christian, we find both the failure to do so and the folly of undue self-reliance. Up to this point, he has had several notable victories over temptation. Did he not escape from Vanity Fair without being taken in by its alluring, yet empty, promises? Did he not quickly see through the subterfuge of By-ends and stand firm against his humanistic philosophy and religious pretense? Did he not staunchly resist the snare of covetousness when it tempted him in the form of Demas and his silver mine? Yes he did.

In each of these instances, Hopeful had been less discerning than Christian. Therefore, it was reasonable that Hopeful would distrust his own judgment and be more inclined to follow the example of his elder brother. Furthermore, Christian was not above pulling rank. In this instance, however, Hopeful's confidence was sadly misplaced.

Apparently, these recent victories had gone straight to Christian's head, rekindling his tendency to pride and overconfidence. Therefore, he saw little reason to question his judgment in their present situation. Yet now, he who had steadfastly refused to turn aside and view the silver mine on the plain called Ease, fell squarely into the same trap when it tempted him in another form.

There are many ways in which we can be guilty of the sin of covetousness, and some of them are quite subtle and seemingly harmless. To covet is to desire something so fervently that we set our hearts upon it. Being then determined to have it, we do all in our power to obtain it. As for Christian, the difficulty in which he and Hopeful now found themselves tempted him to covet an easier way, and to follow it without question when it appeared before him.

After crossing the stile into By-Path Meadow, the two men gazed down the new path and happened to spy another traveler who had done the same thing. Heartened to know that they were not alone, they called to the man and asked him where the path led. Imagine Christian's smug expression when the man replied that it led to the Celestial City! Up to this point, Christian may have been a little unsure about his decision, but now felt a strong surge of confidence. In fact, he could not help but gloat a little, saying to Hopeful, "Look… did not I tell you so? By this you may see we are right."

O, how he would live to regret those words! The seemingly innocent detour, so close to the right path, was not at all what it appeared to be. Furthermore, Christian had chosen it for all the wrong reasons. Discontentment prompted him to first desire it and then opt for it. Worse still, pride and misplaced confidence bolstered his decision, which would profoundly affect his brother as well. So instead of walking by faith, Christian and Hopeful took the easier route of sight, sense, and human reason. Moreover, even though they could not see it from their current location, the footpath through the lush meadow began to lead them, slowly but surely, away from the King's Highway.

Since they were as yet unaware of this fact, Christian was convinced that they were going to be all right. In due time, the two paths would undoubtedly converge and they would be none the worse for their brief respite in By-Path Meadow. Hopeful was still a little wary, but Christian's confidence was high as they followed the man ahead of them. Presumably, he really did know where he was going and how to get there, but they failed to consider whom it was that they so blindly followed.

Although Christian and Hopeful would not realize it until too late, the man's name was Vain-Confidence, an epithet reserved for those who are wise in their own eyes. (Proverbs 26:12) Could such a fellow really know the way to the Celestial City? Hardly! He could, however, be depended upon to boast of knowledge he did not possess, like Talkative of Prating Row. Moreover, just like Worldly Wiseman, he will lead his followers in the direction of carnal reason and self-determination every time. No good thing has ever come from heeding his advice, for his hope is void of any true substance or foundation. Therefore, in following him, Christian and Hopeful are about to jump from the frying pan into the fire.

We realize, of course, that the character named Vain-Confidence was no literal man. What then may we infer from the fact that Christian and Hopeful were following close behind him? Vain confidence was at work in their hearts, with Christian being the chief offender. Instead of walking by faith, with full confidence in and dependence upon the Lord, he leaned to his own understanding and walked in pride. Yet little did he consider that in doing likewise, many a heedless soul has been led to certain destruction. (Proverbs 16:18)

As night began to fall, the two men could no longer see the man ahead of them, but took comfort in knowing he was there. It never occurred to them that Vain-Confidence could not see any better than they could. Still he strode boldly forward, completely unaware that he was fast approaching a deep pit placed there with the express purpose of catching "vain-glorious fools" who dared to pass that way. So it happened that in seeing neither the path nor the pit, he fell headlong into the latter, and all the confidence he could muster did nothing to deliver him from its depths.

To their utter dismay, Christian and Hopeful heard the poor man's downfall, even though they could not see it, and in hearing, they naturally feared the worst. When the fallen man merely groaned in response to their call, they assumed that he was mortally wounded. We can only imagine their terror at that moment, when they realized they were perhaps just a few steps behind him. Thus they came to an abrupt halt, fearing a plunge into the same pit. Then Hopeful, who had never been fully persuaded that they had done the right thing, turned to Christian and plaintively asked, "Where are we now?" But for once, poor Christian was at a loss for words.

Beyond a doubt, the downfall of Vain-Confidence was a wake-up call for the two brethren. It marked the point at which Christian's bravado and self-assurance took flight. Before, he had relied upon his own judgment and congratulated himself for his superior wisdom. Now he knew that he had made a terrible mistake. Thus he who had all the answers before, now stood mute before his stricken brother, overwhelmed with guilt and shame.

The agony of regret

My friend, have you ever noticed how that in times of great stress, just when you feel sure you can bear no more, things often go from bad to worse? So it happened to poor Christian and Hopeful. As if in direct response to their mental turmoil, ominous clouds gathered overhead as a violent thunderstorm moved into the area. Soon the wind was howling furiously and streaks of lightning cut across the sky, followed quickly by thunder crashing all around them. Caught in the fury of the storm, the two men became so disoriented that they lost all sense of direction. Furthermore, due to the heavy rainfall, local streams and rivers began to rise until they gradually flooded the lower portions of the meadow.

The situation in which Christian and Hopeful now found themselves could hardly have been more desperate. As if the hazards of the storm were not bad enough, an eerie sort of darkness enveloped them, one so impenetrable that they could scarcely see a step ahead of them. The abyss into which Vain-Confidence had fallen waited to swallow them up as well if they ventured too close to its brink. Where was it? They had no idea, but feared there was little hope that they would survive the night.

Christian has experienced this kind of darkness before, when he found himself alone on the summit of the hill Difficulty. At that time, he dropped his precious scroll while slumbering in the arbor when he should have watched and prayed. (Matthew 26:40-41) The ensuing darkness marked the beginning of a great struggle with unbelieving fear and spiritual depression.

In his present situation, the chief culprit was a discontented spirit fueled by mistrust, which is essentially the same thing. Doubt and uncertainty filled the void left by the loss of Christian's vain-confidence, and the sudden storm and impenetrable darkness mirrored his turbulent state of mind. Would he and Hopeful share the same fate as "vain-glorious fools"? Would they be swallowed up by the ramifications of their foolish choice? Would they perish because they left the right path in order to follow an easier way? Or would they be saved from themselves, like Jonah was? As of yet, the outcome was uncertain.

There are few things in life that land us into trouble more quickly than vain confidence, and yet, it is a sin of which we are often guilty. Moreover, it prompts us to actions that are easy enough to justify at the time. Yet like the sin of pride, vain confidence carries its own punishment. While the Lord may allow us to plot our own course for a time, he will not permit us to continue down this path indefinitely.

Thus it was with Christian and Hopeful. They were permitted to cross the stile and follow the easier road through By-Path Meadow for a while. All seemed well until they lost their way in the midst of the raging storm. However, as the gravity of their situation finally dawned upon Christian, he was stunned by the implications of what they had done. Furthermore, he realized that the greater fault lay upon his shoulders. Not only had he sinned personally, he had persuaded his brother in Christ to do the same. Now that they were in grave danger, both men were filled with genuine remorse and regret. To Christian's credit, he showed nobility of character by assuming all the blame for their dire situation. Moreover, he demonstrated true humility by confessing his wrong to Hopeful and begging his forgiveness. In this, we must conclude that his sin was unintentional and due primarily to weakness.

There is a vast difference between inadvertent sin and willful disobedience. Although Christian was very wrong in seeking an escape from the trial into which God's will had placed him, there was no evil intention behind his action. He revealed his heart when he admitted as much to Hopeful. Moreover, he neither defended himself nor made excuses for what he had done.

Hopeful's response to this heartfelt confession also deserves our careful attention, especially in light of the danger in which he now found himself. Instead of blaming Christian and harboring bitterness against him, Hopeful freely forgave him. I cannot help but wonder what I would have done in a similar situation! More noteworthy still, he expressed patient and obedient faith when he said, "I…believe too, that this shall be for our good." Yes!!! Quite an extraordinary response, and one in which we may read much about his character. Like Faithful before him, the young pilgrim was living up to his name.

My brother or sister in Christ, have you ever found yourself in deep trouble of your own making? What thought came first to mind? Was your first reaction to confess your sin, to stand still, and see the salvation of the Lord? Or did you attempt to devise a way out of your situation? Far too often, I fear we are inclined to do the latter, but our effort at self-recovery usually proves to be an exercise in futility, does it not? More humbling still, we will probably come to admit the folly of it in time, and have just cause to thank the Lord for saving us from ourselves.

True to form, self-recovery was Christian's first thought. After all, they could not just stay where they were, could they? They must do something or they would surely perish! The stile!! They must somehow try to find their way back to the stile!!

At this point, it provides a bit of comic relief to learn that while Hopeful was more than willing to retrace their steps, he wanted to lead the way. Who could blame him if he was now a little dubious of his brother's judgment? Christian, however, insisted upon going first. If there was any further danger to be faced, he should bear the brunt of it. So Christian reasoned, but this time from self-recrimination rather than vain confidence. Upon hearing Christian's resolve, Hopeful took a firm stand. He secretly feared Christian's mind had been so adversely affected that he might lead them even further out of the way. Therefore he, Hopeful, would take the lead.

In the midst of their rather heated exchange, both men suddenly fell silent when they heard a voice saying: *Set thine heart toward the highway, even the way which thou wentest, turn again.* Now this was an instructive word that could be safely heeded, for it was the voice of truth taken from Jeremiah 31:21. It perfectly expressed the sentiment of their chastened, contrite hearts; for above all else, they desired to return to the King's Highway. Therefore, they determined to backtrack until they found the right path once again.

While the two men resumed their debate as to which of them should lead the way back to the stile, a situation was quickly developing that would settle the matter for them. The heavy rain from the storm had produced such severe flash flooding that even the smallest streams in the vicinity were now impassable. Gentle brooks that they had waded through earlier with no problem had now become raging rivers, and large portions of the meadow were already under water. Any attempt to cross back over it would be extremely dangerous. However, even though it would be at the hazard of their lives, Christian and Hopeful intended to try. At this point in his narrative, John Bunyan inserts a personal comment saying, "Then I thought that it is easier going out of the way when we are in, than going in when we are out." For sure it is, as Christian and Hopeful are just about to prove!

It is no exaggeration to say that the tendency to vain confidence will come to an ignoble end, sooner or later. Even though Christian and Hopeful did their best to retrace their steps, or rather undo their former mistake, they soon had to concede defeat. After exhausting all of their energy and strength, they finally agreed that they would never make it back to the stile that night, and resigned themselves to wait out the storm. Just as they were about to collapse from stress and fatigue, they happened to come upon a little shed in which to take shelter from the fury of the storm. Then being extremely weary in both body and mind, they fell into a deep sleep almost immediately.

* * * *

Christian and Hopeful's detour through By-Path Meadow did not prove so easy after all, did it? The alluring prospect of sunshine, soft grass, and easy traveling conditions quickly turned to darkness, danger, and unspeakable terror. As of yet, the men still did not realize the full extent of their danger. Neither did they grasp the magnitude of their mistake in crossing the stile into By-Path Meadow. Therefore, while they waited out the storm in their improvised shelter, little did they suspect that their troubles had only begun.

While I would not presume to know exactly what was in their minds right before they fell asleep, perhaps we might speculate as to what their thoughts may have been as they anticipated a new day. They may well have reasoned that eventually the long night of terror would be over and the raging storm would pass by. When the morning came, they would surely be able to find their way back to the stile. As soon as the floodwaters receded sufficiently, all they had to do was retrace their steps through the meadow, cross back over the stile, and re-enter the path exactly where they had left it. In the daylight it should be easy enough, for the treacherous pit would be clearly visible then. They would take care not to go anywhere near it, so perhaps no real harm had been done after all.

It is altogether possible that Christian and Hopeful entertained such thoughts as they laid down to rest. After all, tomorrow was another day. Hopefully it would dawn bright and fair and they would find a way to correct their mistake. Yet little did the sleepers know that due to circumstances beyond their control, it was not to be.

Study Questions

1. Before long, the pleasant river diverted from Christian and Hopeful's path, and the road became increasingly more rugged. What was the underlying meaning behind this sudden reversal of circumstances? In their reaction to it, how were they guilty of the same sins Israel committed when wandering through the wilderness? What primary sin was behind their present frame of mind?

2. Wrong desires often seem to create their own opportunities, and these open doors are frequently and erroneously attributed to God's will and leading. In what way did this very thing happen to Christian and Hopeful? How did Christian try to justify the slight departure from the King's Highway?

3. What did the stile into By-Path Meadow actually represent? Why was Christian so convinced that crossing the stile and following the path through the meadow was the best thing to do, in spite of Hopeful's misgivings?

4. Who were Christian and Hopeful following as they chose the alternate route through the meadow? At what point did they realize they had made a terrible mistake?

5. Quite often, serious missteps have equally serious consequences. How did the providence of God prevent the two men from correcting their mistake and retracing their steps back to the stile?

CHAPTER 41

Prisoners in Doubting Castle!

EACH ERA OF CHURCH HISTORY POSES ITS OWN PARTICULAR CHALLENGES for the people of God. Quite a few of our brethren who lived in times past faced intense persecution for the sake of the Gospel. Many of them took a valiant stand for the truth, and to their uncommon faith and courage we owe a great debt. Some of these choice servants of Christ were willing to pay the ultimate price rather than deny the faith. Yet even though their verbal testimony was silenced long ago by the tyrant's sword, their footsteps still resound along the royal road to Zion.

We who live in the United States of America do not face the same degree of opposition, at least not yet. However, many of our brethren living in other parts of the world are under intense persecution at the present time. Should we be any less valiant for truth than they? Not only should we not be, we must not be. Some call the time in which we live the Post-Christian era. It is an apt description, I fear. The Gospel of Jesus Christ is under severe attack, and not just from the world. Multitudes of churches that were once sound in the faith now proclaim another gospel that is more widely acceptable. As a result, the sword of truth has been largely robbed of its keen edge, and the name Christian has become much more general as to its meaning. (Hebrews 4:12)

One popular watchword of our day declares that there are many paths to God, and each individual is encouraged to find his or her own path. To no surprise, this philosophy has been enthusiastically embraced by those with hearts unbroken by God's Spirit, and stubborn wills that bow to no one. Even though the phrase find your own path is presumed to be modern, enlightened thought, the mindset behind it goes back to the dawn of history. It is the impetus that drives the unsaved person, whether religious or not, and characterizes those who are outwardly moral as well as the openly dissolute. This natural inclination is perfectly summed up in Judges 17:6: *In those days there was no king in Israel, but every man did that which was right in his own eyes.*

Yes, there are many paths from which men may think to choose, but each of them is part and parcel of the broad way that leads to destruction. Our Lord Jesus Christ plainly declared: *I am the way, the truth, and the life: no man cometh unto the Father, but by me.* (John 14:6) There is no viable alternative, no other way to God, except the way of Christ and his cross. Hence, Christians of every age must be valiant for truth and for the ready defense of the Gospel. (Philippians 1:17)

Unlike those who choose their own path, the true followers of Jesus Christ strive daily to do what is right and pleasing in his sight. Even though we stumble and sometimes fall while walking the path of the just, we are not numbered among the willfully disobedient. Yet we are just as capable of inadvertently wandering out of the right way as Christian and Hopeful were. Therefore, it is crucial that we stay in the middle of the path by resting content with God's will and providence. To do otherwise tempts us to seek a greener pasture when the going gets rough.

It is important for us to keep in mind that following the proper path takes place in our inmost being (the inner man). The same holds true for any departure from it. So when Christian and Hopeful left the safety of the King's Highway and crossed the stile into By-Path Meadow, they did so in their hearts. Moreover, it was only after wandering a good distance from the right path that they found out that such steps are not so easy to retrace.

When the sudden thunderstorm forced them to take shelter until the morning, the men made yet another critical mistake. Instead of seeking the Lord diligently in prayer, confessing their sin, and asking for his mercy and guidance, they yielded to the flesh once again. (Mark 14:37-38) Rather than watching and praying throughout the dark, stormy night, they gave in to stress and fatigue. Thus they slumbered and slept, little suspecting that they were about to have a close encounter of the worst sort.

Considering all that happened to Christian and Hopeful during that terrible night, the thought that they had strayed onto private property never entered their minds. Or if it did occur to them, they undoubtedly dismissed it as of little concern. They should not have been so presumptive, however, because By-Path Meadow was within the bounds of a vast estate owned by a giant of infamous repute. The shelter in which they spent the night was actually within earshot of his ancestral mansion.

This particular giant was a fearsome being of a dark and menacing disposition. It was part of his daily routine to rise before dawn and walk about his property, looking for anyone who may have entered his jurisdiction unawares. In this, are we not reminded of our great enemy who *as a roaring lion, walketh about, seeking whom he may devour*? (1 Peter 5:8b) As the creature made his rounds that particular morning, he discovered Christian and Hopeful still asleep in their makeshift shelter. What a terrible shock it must have been to be awakened by the "grim and surly voice" of the giant, whose name was Despair!

After startling the men into full wakefulness, the giant demanded to know why they were trespassing on his property. Although undoubtedly frightened half out of their wits, Christian and Hopeful managed to reply that they were "Pilgrims" who "had lost their Way." While their excuse was plausible enough, and any reasonable landowner would have doubtless let them go their way, not so with Giant Despair. He permitted no one to cross his property with impunity, and showed no mercy to any who dared to try. Like a medieval baron, he was a law unto himself within the boundaries of his domain. Since it was his custom to take all trespassers captive, he seized the poor men violently, and forced them to go with him.

As Christian and Hopeful quickly discovered on that bleak morning, any resistance on their part was futile. Despair was much larger and stronger than they. Furthermore, since they were in the wrong, they were in no position to negotiate with him. There seemed little option but to do as he commanded.

Prisoners of despair

At the very heart of the giant's vast estate was his dark, brooding fortress known as Doubting Castle. Unlike the Palace Beautiful, this castle had nothing to recommend it as a place of refuge. Both its isolated situation and desolate appearance warned of equally austere and inhospitable conditions within. So travelers beware! You will find no warm welcome here! More than anything else, Doubting Castle resembles a prison stronghold offering little hope of escape.

Now that it was too late, Christian and Hopeful realized the fuller implications of choosing the easier way through By-Path Meadow. It was actually a short cut to this terrible place. Therefore, in crossing the stile, they had unknowingly headed directly toward it. What must their thoughts have been as the ruthless owner drove them through the gatehouse of his citadel and cast them down into its lowest dungeon? What sound could be more terrifying than the clang of the massive iron door as it closed behind them?

In common with the typical fortress of the Middle Ages, the lower regions of Doubting Castle were reserved for those prisoners who were, more or less, doomed to be forgotten. Thus they were poor, wretched souls with little hope of ever seeing the light of day again. As with other dungeons of the same period, this one was designed to be a place of misery and torment. Cries for mercy could not be heard beyond its thick stone walls, so as not to disturb the castle residents. So after descending the long, narrow stairway to their underground cell, Christian and Hopeful found themselves in a deplorable condition. Their season of refreshing must have seemed a long, long time ago!

Interestingly, John Bunyan places a precise time frame upon their captivity in Doubting Castle. The two men were captured early on a Wednesday morning and would remain in the giant's power until the pre-dawn hours of the following Sunday. It was just a few days, really, but it undoubtedly seemed a lifetime to the poor prisoners.

Like the writer of Psalm 88, Christian and Hopeful were keenly aware of their helplessness. (Verses 3-4) They had landed in a place that was damp, cold, and unwholesome, a place that savored of death. (Verses 5-6) It was a place in which they were denied the basic necessities of life, but worse still, a place where they felt forsaken by the Lord. (Verses 7, 9-12, 14, 16) No one came to inquire about them, no friend or acquaintance came to comfort them in their affliction. (Verses 8, 18) All things considered, their dungeon seemed likely to become their tomb. (Verse 15)

Of course we understand that Doubting Castle, the seat of the giant's power, was not a literal place at all. It pictured the terrible despondency that now had Christian and Hopeful in its grasp. This is what came of following Vain-Confidence. They escaped the pit into which he fell only to become prisoners of despair. In other words, their spiritual declension had just about reached its lowest point.

Giant Despair was daunting enough, in and of himself, but he was not the only permanent resident of Doubting Castle. He had a wife named Diffidence, whose temperament closely matched his own. Presumably, his inseparable companion was also a giant; but even though the modern definition of her name might suggest it, there was nothing shy about the mistress of Doubting Castle.

In naming her, John Bunyan did so according to the usage of his day. Therefore, in order to accurately sketch her character, we must do so in reference to the archaic definition of her name, which means "mistrust." In understanding that she is the personification of unbelieving fear, we can clearly grasp her significance as the wife of Despair, and her cruel behavior toward their helpless captives.

Since Diffidence preferred to stay within the confines of her home, she was not with her husband on the morning he seized Christian and Hopeful. In fact, she was unaware of their presence until late that evening, after she and her husband had retired for the night. At that time he informed her that he had captured two trespassers, and sought her advice concerning how best to deal with them.

It seems a bit strange to me that this particular giant would seek the advice of anyone, much less his wife. Yet when we ponder the meaning of their respective names, the reason for his action becomes quite clear. Despair may seize and overtake our minds, but unbelieving fear is the impetus behind it. Taken together, despair and mistrust form a powerful alliance that seems impossible to break.

For those who have had the great misfortune to come under the power of Diffidence, her counsel was exactly what you might expect. She advised the giant to beat Christian and Hopeful without mercy, which thing he immediately set out to do the next morning (Thursday). But notice the distinct progression in his assault.

First, Despair attacked the poor men verbally, hurling vicious threats and pessimistic taunts against them. Although he abused them cruelly, they were careful not to respond in such a way that would further enrage him. His bitter recriminations found their mark, however, for hopelessness was quickly gaining control of their minds.

Immediately following his verbal attack, the giant assaulted Christian and Hopeful with a cudgel (a short, heavy club) and beat them until they fell to the floor, nearly senseless. He finally left his two battered prisoners alone in the dungeon, giving them time to reflect upon their misery and speculate as to what lay next in store.

As we think upon the imprisonment of Christian and Hopeful and its spiritual significance, we must keep in mind that Doubting Castle was no literal fortress of stone. Neither was its dungeon a dark, damp underground cell. However, for those who have experienced it, the mental anguish that comes from doubting one's salvation is indeed a kind of prison. Furthermore, mistrust and despair are surely numbered among the cruelest of jailors.

Such was the present case with Christian and Hopeful as they began to reap, in earnest, the consequences of what they had sown. In wandering out of the way, they had unwittingly entered the realm of Doubting Castle, temporarily robbed of their peace and assurance. To be taken captive by this kind of despondency is to be beaten down by fear and unbelief. The agony of soul it produces can be virtually debilitating, tempting the sufferer to abandon hope, yet not quite, for the true child of God. Hope may be hidden by a thick veil of darkness, but it is still his constant companion.

In his well-known poem "To Althea, From Prison," the English poet Richard Lovelace wrote:

> Stone walls do not a prison make,
> Nor iron bars a cage;
> Minds innocent and quiet take
> That for a hermitage.

If I have freedom in my love,
And in my soul am free,
Angels alone that soar above
Enjoy such liberty. [1]

The poet's intention was to show the power of love upon one who is suffering wrongfully. In such a case, love can transcend the most impregnable stone walls and minister comfort to the heart and mind. Therefore, the innocent prisoner may know quietness of heart, peace of mind, and perfect liberty of thought even in his captivity. Neither stone walls nor iron bars can contain the soul thus set free.

However, there is also a prison in the mind that can hold captive those who walk at liberty. The despair that grows out of unbelieving fear and a guilty conscience exerts such a powerful influence upon the mind that it often proves stronger than a fortress of stone. This kind of prison is indeed a dungeon of sorts, in that it virtually banishes light and hope.

John Bunyan knew what it was to experience both kinds of captivity. When he was imprisoned in Bedford jail for preaching the Gospel, he knew the peace that comes from a conscience void of offense. This made his cell a quiet refuge in which he enjoyed the presence and fellowship of his Lord to an extraordinary degree. As a result, his prison became a den of prayer, study, and meditation in God's Word. Moreover, it was a retreat in which his pen did indeed prove a more powerful weapon than the tyrant's sword! Yet his personal testimony reveals that he also knew what it meant to be imprisoned in his mind by doubt and despair. In his spiritual autobiography, *Grace Abounding to the Chief of Sinners*, we read of the spiritual travail he endured as he struggled with doubt and fear concerning his salvation.

So the creator of Doubting Castle knew of what he wrote. Like Christian and Hopeful, he was well acquainted with Giant Despair and his wife Diffidence. He, also, knew what it was to suffer cruelly from despondency and spiritual depression. How else could he have written with such brilliant insight and rare sensitivity? How could he have otherwise had such empathy for his fellow pilgrims who find themselves confined in that same bleak fortress?

It is a particularly difficult thing to suffer when there is no one who really understands our distress, or lends a sympathetic ear, or offers words of comfort and encouragement. Yet even when we are not literally alone, despair tends to isolate us by turning our thoughts inward and keeping them there. Moreover, it stresses the negative aspects of our situation while blinding us to God's mercy and his good purpose in it all. In a word, when despair overtakes our minds, we cannot see beyond our misery. Christian and Hopeful found themselves in just such a condition during the entire day that Giant Despair left them alone in the dungeon.

That night, the giant consulted with his wife once again about their two prisoners. They both marveled that the men were still alive in spite of such harsh treatment. These two pilgrims had proven much more resilient than many others who had been taken captive by this cruel pair. What was to be done with them next? Diffidence instructed her husband to convince them to take their lives. While this was a desperate suggestion, it is not a surprising one, considering its source. Giant Despair may have been the one who seized and imprisoned Christian and Hopeful, but the chatelaine of Doubting Castle was the power behind his actions. My friend in Christ, nothing will rob us of our peace and assurance faster than the sin of unbelieving fear. Moreover, it will tempt us to give up hope and, in some cases, even consider self-destruction. When in this desperate frame of mind, to die might seem an easy solution, perhaps the only way to escape the pain.

So the very next morning (Friday), Christian and Hopeful were assaulted with suicidal thoughts in the person of their cruel warden. He did his utmost to convince them that since they were never likely to escape from his power, they might as well put an end to their suffering. Their wretched condition at the time added significant weight to his argument that things would never be any better for them. The fact that he suggested particular ways in which they might take their lives indicated that they had given the matter some thought, and at least considered doing as he urged.

At this critical point, however, a strange incident occurred in this otherwise bleak melodrama. Christian and Hopeful dared to ask the giant to release them, which seemed an audacious thing to do, under the circumstances. With dark fury evident in every facial feature, he rushed upon them and would doubtless have dispatched them on the spot, had he not fallen into "one of his fits...and lost, for a time, the use of his hand."

This was an unexpected turn of events, to say the least, and the first intimation that the mighty giant had his Achilles heel. John Bunyan elaborates by saying that the giant was prone to these strange seizures whenever the sun was shining. As a result of this sudden onset of weakness, he was forced to leave his prisoners alone for the time being.

Although I will expand upon the giant's sudden weak spell a little later, this strange incident does beg an immediate question or two. Had a slender ray of sunshine managed to break through the gloom of the dungeon? Had a small glimmer of hope arisen in the hearts of the prisoners? Perhaps it had!

That terrible Friday must have seemed endless, as Christian and Hopeful languished in misery. The fearful storm of a few days ago was nothing in comparison to the despondency that now held them in its grasp. Escape from their prison seemed virtually impossible, and they were about as low as they could be. Perhaps they should just give up and die!

To Christian, struggling as he was with an overwhelming sense of guilt, their options seemed limited to but two. They could either live in perpetual misery or die by their own hands, and given their state of mind, to die might have seemed the lesser of two evils. So when he asked Hopeful, "Shall we be ruled by the Giant?" he was not thinking straight. Giant Despair would win the day whether they remained in his power or took their lives.

Fortunately, Hopeful did not share Christian's pessimistic outlook; therefore, he strongly disagreed with his brother. Although he admitted their present circumstances were desperate, and he would welcome death rather than remain as they were, he yet saw reason to hope. Moreover, in my opinion, his words "But yet let us consider..." marked a turning point in their captivity.

The younger pilgrim had apparently done a great deal of thinking during their grueling ordeal, and he had done so to good effect. In weighing the giant's advice in light of Scripture, he wondered aloud how they dared take the giant's counsel that they kill themselves. He also considered the fact that the giant was not in ultimate control, in spite of what he would have them believe. Their fate was not really in his hands. Others had been taken captive by him and managed to escape.

Then he pondered God's providence in their situation, which is a thing that always lifts our spirits upward. Thus he reminded himself, and Christian, that God was in control of it all and he could well give them the opportunity to escape. Perhaps the giant would die, or neglect to lock their cell door. Or perhaps he would have another one of his strange seizures and become temporarily powerless.

For his part, Hopeful was ready to take heart and act upon what he knew deep within his soul to be right. Should the opportunity arise, he would play the man. He chided himself for not making the attempt before, but now proposed that he and Christian be patient and endure their misery a while longer. Under no circumstances should they harm themselves. As Christian listened to his brother's wise counsel, he also began to take heart. Their situation had not improved as yet, but rather than ending their lives, they both determined to wait on the Lord for deliverance.

Dear friend in Christ, did you notice how the firm resolve of one man gave courage to the other, weaker, one? Although we know that Hopeful was a pilgrim in his own right, his presence with Christian in the dungeon of Doubting Castle reminds us of a precious truth. As we walk the path of life, hope is our inseparable traveling companion. It may be battered, badly shaken, and even appear to be on the verge of destruction, but hope cannot be extinguished in the heart of a true Christian. We may certainly find ourselves on the verge of despair, but not as those who have no hope.

Even in our darkest hours, we have the sure promise that God will never abandon us, and because he keeps us by his grace, we will never abandon hope. (Hebrews 13:5-6) Like saving faith, it is a vital principle within, a rare and precious thing of divine origin. Therefore, not only is our hope indestructible, it will eventually prevail.

In spite of their resolution to wait on the Lord, Christian and Hopeful found themselves in a worse condition on their third day of captivity than when first cast into the dungeon. The dank, unwholesome atmosphere was beginning to take its toll, and coupled with the lack of any nourishment, to rob them of needful strength. Moreover, the wounds they had received from the giant's earlier beating were now starting to fester and cause great pain.

The two men were still alive, but just barely. Humanly speaking, they lacked the strength to endure another attack, but Despair has no pity for his victims. So after leaving his prisoners alone all day, he descended into their prison on Friday evening to see how they fared. In particular, he was eager to find out whether they had followed his advice. We can only imagine his fury when he discovered that, even though they were in a sorry state, Christian and Hopeful still lived. They had dared to disobey him in spite of his repeated brutality, and he was so enraged by it that he assured them they would regret ever having been born. However, for all of his show of force and verbal intimidation, he withdrew once again without making good his threat.

Although both men were terrified by the giant's vicious threats, Christian nearly fainted from fear and consternation. Once again, they considered ending their lives, with Christian more inclined to see it as the only way out of their desperate situation. Hopeful countered Christian's depressed mood yet again with words of comfort and encouragement. First, he reminded Christian of how valiantly he had resisted Apollyon's attack in the Valley of Humiliation. Had he not faced that monstrous enemy head on and put him to flight with the sword of the Spirit? (Ephesians 6:17) Then he mentioned Christian's terrible ordeal in the Valley of the Shadow of Death. Had he not passed safely through, even though circumstances made it seem nigh unto impossible?

Thus he challenged Christian to reflect upon his journey so far, especially his former trials and deliverances. He had already passed "through many dangers, toils and snares," [2] as John Newton so fittingly expressed in his hymn "Amazing Grace." In short, Hopeful called to mind that Christian had already come a long way down the path of life. He had come much too far to give up now!

Moreover, he reminded Christian that he was not alone in his prison. Hopeful shared the same dungeon, had been wounded by the same giant, languished in the same darkness and suffered the same deprivation. Christian's faithful companion was right by his side, although Hopeful described himself as being "a far weaker man by nature than thou art." I have my doubts about this, seeing that it was Hopeful who repeatedly advised patient endurance rather than rash action.

In this regard, Hopeful called to mind the courageous stand Christian had taken in Vanity Fair. Although he and Faithful had come under intense persecution there, they faced it without wavering. In the strength of the Lord, Christian had taken a valiant stand for the truth back then. To give in to despair now would be a shameful thing and bring reproach upon the Lord in whom he trusted and whom he served.

As Christian listened to Hopeful's encouraging words and wise counsel, he remembered God's mercy to him in the past. Had he not been in similar straits before, and had not God's faithfulness always seen him through? To be sure, their present circumstances were terrible, yet there was still reason to hope in God's mercy. (Psalm 33:18)

Out of the depths

Late that Friday evening, after the giant and his wife retired for the night, Diffidence asked her husband if the prisoners had done as he told them and ended their lives. To her direct question, Despair was forced to admit that Christian and Hopeful had proven to be uncommonly strong and determined to endure hardship rather than do themselves harm.

When she heard how it was with the two prisoners, Diffidence had another scheme that she felt sure would bring about their downfall. Early the next morning, her husband must take them into the castle courtyard and show them the skeletons of those whom he has already destroyed. Her best advice to him was to "make them believe e're a week comes to an end, thou also wilt tear them in pieces, as thou hast done their fellows before them." It was a last-ditch effort, you might say.

The next morning, Despair did exactly as his wife directed. Dragging Christian and Hopeful outside to the castle grounds, he pointed out the scattered bones of former victims who had also dared to trespass on his property. After taking them prisoner, the fearsome creature cast them into his dungeon, and when it suited his mood, he made a quick end of them.

The giant reinforced this object lesson with the promise that he would do the same thing to them within ten days. Then, with both the gruesome sight and highly credible threat etched upon their minds, the prisoners were driven back to their dungeon to ponder their fate. For the rest of that day, they were filled with despair, even worse than before. Yet this time, they did not so much as mention the possibility of taking their lives.

On Saturday night, when Diffidence and Despair consulted yet again concerning their captives, the giant had to admit that they still lived, in spite of all his threats, intimidation, and abuse. He had done his worst, but they refused to die!

As we reflect upon the giant and his bosom companion, we must admit that they make a formidable team. He supplied the brute strength, but Diffidence apparently did the thinking for both of them. Thus she was quite a power in her own right, and yet, like her husband, she had her weak points as well. This unsuspected weakness came to light that evening when she was suddenly seized with fear. In fact, she was obsessed with the thought that the prisoners might manage to escape, in spite of the castle's extraordinary security. It seemed an unreasonable fear, since every precaution to prevent it had been taken. What then lay behind it?

Her husband's random fits of weakness were undoubtedly her greatest concern. These seizures, which invariably occurred on sunny days, rendered the strong man temporarily helpless. When that happened, his wife could not depend upon him to do her bidding. Perhaps she also feared because she understood her own particular area of vulnerability. Faith and hope were her greatest opponents; so her husband's weakness was, in essence, hers as well. Should faith and hope resurface in the hearts of their prisoners, she would be as powerless as her husband on a bright, sunny day. In that event, the prisoners might very well manage to escape. Therefore, as an added precaution, she ordered her husband to search them in the morning for any evidence that faith and hope had survived their ordeal.

Dear reader, if you are unfamiliar with Doubting Castle and its awful inhabitants, the giant's wife might seem to harbor an irrational fear. However, if you have had the misfortune of being imprisoned there, you understand that her concern had a solid basis in fact. Moreover, it has grown in intensity through the years. She and her husband have taken countless others captive before Christian and Hopeful came their way. While many did perish there, as evidenced by the grisly scene in the castle courtyard, quite a few managed to escape. It was this thought that murdered sleep for Diffidence that Saturday evening.

While sitting in the darkness of their prison cell, Christian and Hopeful had ample opportunity to reflect upon their situation and how they happened to be there. It was a time of deep soul-searching, as they relived all the events leading up to their arrest and imprisonment. God's providence had placed them where human help was of no avail, and this also weighed heavily upon their minds.

For Christian in particular, guilt and remorse were still uppermost in his heart and mind. Perhaps he recalled the man in the iron cage and his hopeless despair. Was he to share the same fate? We may safely presume that Christian wondered how he could really be a child of God and do what he had done. Had he been living a lie all this time? If so, was there any hope for him?

We cannot know for sure the thoughts that may have tormented Christian during this awful time. Yet in spite of his present state of mind, he had something that the man in the iron cage lacked entirely. By the grace of God, something real had taken place in his soul. The gift of saving faith and a living hope had taken deep root there, even though they were not presently in evidence.

What a comfort it is to know that if we belong to the Lord Jesus Christ, there is no depth to which our souls can sink, and no despair quite so all-consuming that God's love cannot reach us there. Moreover, there is no situation so bleak and hopeless that our heavenly Father will not hear our faintest cry for help. This was the psalmist's confident expectation when he wrote: *Out of the depths have I cried unto thee, O LORD. Lord, hear my voice: let thine ears be attentive to the voice of my supplications.* (Psalm 130:1-2)

However, God does permit us to reap the consequences of our sinful actions, as he did with Christian and Hopeful. Their spiritual declension began when they forgot his Word and past mercy to them.

When we find ourselves overtaken by doubt and despair, it is usually because we have done the same thing. Such negligence creates a prime opportunity for unbelieving fear to do its worst. Therefore, we will also tend to lose sight of God's gracious design when he corrects us at such times.

Yet think upon this, my brother or sister in Christ. When our heavenly Father must chasten us, each stroke of his rod is a token of eternal love, a love that will never abandon us to the likes of Giant Despair. It is love that draws us to seek him for mercy, even from the depths of Doubting Castle. (Jeremiah 31:3) It is amazing love that bids us to pray with the psalmist: *If thou, LORD, shouldest mark iniquities, O Lord, who shall stand? But there is forgiveness with thee, that thou mayest be feared.* (Psalm 130:3-4) For many an afflicted soul, this prayer of remembrance has been the turning point in his or her long night of spiritual captivity. (Psalm 130:5-6)

Thus it was with Christian and Hopeful late that Saturday night, when they did what they should have done in the beginning of their ordeal. They had a prayer meeting! Throughout the remainder of the night, they confessed their sins and sought God's mercy and forgiveness. As I think upon their cry from the depths of fear and despair, I am reminded of the prophet Jonah, who found himself in similarly desperate circumstances. When the disobedient prophet finally came to himself, he was in the belly of a great fish, which was a seemingly hopeless situation. However, deliverance was nigh as he prayed: *When my soul fainted within me I remembered the LORD: and my prayer came in unto thee, into thine holy temple. But I will sacrifice unto thee with the voice of thanksgiving; I will pay that that I have vowed. Salvation is of the LORD.* (Jonah 2:7, 9)

I cannot help but believe that the prayers of Christian and Hopeful on that dark Saturday night were closely akin to the cry of the penitent prophet. God alone could save them, and that they knew quite well. Then just before the dawn on Sunday morning, Christian finally remembered something that astounded him and caused him to exclaim: "What a Fool…am I, thus to lie in a stinking dungeon, when I may as well walk at liberty?"

Had poor Christian lost it due to excessive stress and grief? If not, what in the world did he mean by this extraordinary statement? He had a key called Promise safely hidden where Giant Despair, in spite of his diligent search, could neither find nor steal it. This particular key was a thing of incomparable worth, because it alone held the secret that would bring an end to their terrible captivity. Until that moment he had forgotten it, but was now persuaded that it would open every barrier that was between them and sweet freedom.

To young Hopeful, the existence of this priceless key was the best of news. It had been with them all this time, although they had neglected it; but now they put it to good use. As they sought the Lord fervently in prayer, the Word of God came strongly to their hearts and minds once again. With the remembrance of its great and precious promises, rays of light began to infiltrate their prison. Forgetfulness had sparked the great darkness that landed them in the giant's power, but remembrance of God's truth, his faithfulness, and sure mercies would set them free.

With the precious key in hand, Christian inserted it into the lock of the dungeon door by faith. As soon as he turned it, the lock yielded and the door opened with ease. Next, after quietly ascending the stairway and reaching the castle's main floor, the two men came to an exterior door leading directly to the courtyard. Once again, their key opened this door with no problem. But the final barrier, the massive gate that lay between them and the outside world, proved much more difficult. This gate was strategically placed in the perimeter wall surrounding the castle complex. Therefore, it was as strong and well fortified as the giant could make it. Yet even though its mechanism resisted the key at first, the lock finally gave way.

As the outer gate of the prison swung open, it protested with a loud grating noise, signaling to Diffidence that her fears were justified after all. In spite of every precaution she and her husband had taken, their prisoners were getting away! Despair also woke immediately upon hearing the telltale sound and arose with the determination to recapture the two men. As soon as he tried to stand, however, he was stricken with the strange weakness to which he was occasionally subject. So even though he desired nothing more than to arrest the escapees, the thing was beyond his power.

From the unexpected turn of events that morning, we may assume that all vestiges of the storm were now gone. The clouds had cleared and the air was fresh and clean. Once again, the sky was azure blue and the sun was shining brightly. For Christian and Hopeful, the long night of unbelief and despair had finally come to an end. As long as they yielded their minds to doubt and fear, the giant had been too strong for them. With the remembrance of God's Word, however, hope revived and spiritual strength returned. The giant's power over them was broken, for the truth had set them free.

After their escape from Doubting Castle, Christian and Hopeful had no problem finding their way back through the meadow and over the stile to the King's Highway. Yet they did not dare to slacken their pace until they were safely out of the jurisdiction of Giant Despair.

* * * *

Without a doubt, unbelief and despair are formidable enemies when they join forces against us. They may not be able to destroy us, but can certainly shatter our peace and assurance until we are tempted to give up hope. How does this happen? For numerous reasons, the helmet of salvation designed to protect the Christian's mind may slip a bit, creating vulnerability in that vital area. Consequently, many genuine believers have been severely wounded by the enemy.

Dear troubled soul, what about you? What is it that keeps you captive to doubt and fear? When we find ourselves in that terrible condition, we can usually trace it to some sinful attitude or action on our part. Perhaps we have been heedless and negligent in spiritual matters. Or possibly, like Christian and Hopeful, we have grown weary and discouraged due to prolonged trial and difficulty. We are just as capable of yielding to discontentment as they were, and equally prone to vain confidence.

Our heavenly Father, who always has our best interest in mind, will not allow us to walk in a way that dishonors him. Quite often, he uses Doubting Castle as the means of correcting and restoring his erring children. The evil owner of that dark fortress intends to destroy every prisoner he takes, and in the case of those who are Christian in name only, he often succeeds. But he lacks the power to destroy the faith of God's elect. (Titus 1:1) Neither is he able to overthrow the full assurance of hope that indwells and sustains the heirs of salvation. (Hebrews 6:11-12) So even though a child of God may suffer in the giant's dungeon for a season, he holds the key that will secure his release.

As to this, I find it most encouraging to ponder the effect of sunlight upon Giant Despair. It was the only thing stronger than he. When exposed to the sun's brilliant rays, he became helpless to afflict and torment his victims. What an apt illustration this is of the power of God's Word to demolish the stronghold of mistrust and despair! Through the agency of the Holy Spirit, the Word of God effectively penetrates this prison in the mind. It is the only weapon strong enough to deliver those who have been taken captive by unbelieving fear.

What a precious truth is this! There is no lock in Doubting Castle that will not yield to the key called Promise. But O, what forgetful hearers we tend to be! Therefore, we can ill afford to let this valuable key rust from neglect. By keeping it well oiled through constant use, it will serve us well and speed us on our way as we travel the path of life.

Dear brother or sister in Christ, does the account of Giant Despair, Diffidence, and Doubting Castle strike a familiar chord? Even as you read these words, are you are struggling with fear and doubt concerning your salvation? Does it seem that you cannot break free of the mental anguish that has you in its grasp? Ask yourself if you have neglected the key, the gracious provision God has made for your peace and assurance. If so, resolve to use it early and often, while seeking God fervently in prayer.

The sword of the Spirit has the power to put every enemy to flight, but we must make good use of it and be on constant guard against the things that would destroy our peace. Moreover, we must keep the shield of faith carefully in place. Should we happen to lower it, unbelieving fear can gain free access to our hearts. Faith alone can keep this terrible enemy at bay, but it is a constant battle. Keep in mind that even though Giant Despair is disabled by sunlight, he is not destroyed by it. For now he may be sleeping, but he is not dead. So make no mistake! When clouds of fear and doubt begin to gather overhead, and dark, despondent thoughts fill your mind, the terrible giant is about to awaken once again.

Take care then not to stray from the King's Highway and risk wandering into his jurisdiction unawares. Keep to the middle of the path and tread softly while looking ever forward. Above all, watch and pray as you march onward and upward to Zion.

Study Questions

1. While forced to spend the stormy night in a makeshift shelter, Christian and Hopeful made another critical mistake. What was it? What terrible thing happened to them the next morning as a result of their neglect?

2. Since Doubting Castle is not a literal place, of what is it a picture? In what sense was it a prison? What does the giant named Despair represent? How are he and his wife, Diffidence, inseparable companions?

3. Since Giant Despair and Diffidence are allegorical figures rather than literal creatures, how are we to interpret their cruel mistreatment of Christian and Hopeful? What sort of attack did the poor men suffer in the depths of Doubting Castle?

4. How did Hopeful's remembrance of God's Word and contemplation of it mark a turning point in their captivity? In what way was this renewed hope related to Giant Despair's strange fits of weakness?

5. In spite of their ongoing battle between hope and despair, Christian and Hopeful finally escaped out of the depths of their prison. By what means did they make their escape? Why was Giant Despair utterly unable to prevent it?

CHAPTER 42

Warning to Future Travelers

As I think upon all that led up to this latest episode in the lives of Christian and Hopeful, I must admit it strikes me very close to home. What about you, my friend in Christ? How may stiles have you been tempted to cross over when in the midst of great difficulty? Perhaps the Lord spared you even greater trouble by restraining you from actually doing so. Or he may have allowed you to have your own way for a time, until you reaped the consequences of it. If you have known the Lord for very long, you have probably experienced both of these things.

The way in which we respond to adversity is a telling thing, a far better indicator of our spiritual maturity than knowledge alone. It is easy enough to overestimate our growth in grace until unexpected trial exposes the dross that yet remains. Because this dross consists primarily of unbelief and its bitter fruit, it can land us squarely in the depths of Doubting Castle.

Would we be better off if we never had to struggle with fear and mistrust? Human reason would answer loudly in the affirmative, and if we are honest, are we not inclined to second that opinion? No one would willingly become the prisoner of unbelieving fear and despondency, and yet, since this painful struggle is such a common one, we must account it a needful thing.

Another thing that few of us are quick to admit is that we struggle with vain confidence. Some might even deny that a true believer in Christ is capable of such an offense. Is it possible for a child of God to not only be guilty of vain confidence, but also follow it until it leads him out of the right path? Just ask Simon Peter, the Lord's own apostle!

Like the character named Christian, Simon Peter was another who did not suffer from the lack of self-confidence. As we study the Gospel accounts of our Lord's earthly ministry, we notice that Peter figures rather prominently among the twelve disciples. On various occasions, he appears to be their spokesman, and with James and John, was part of the inner circle who were closest to the Lord. (Matthew 17:1-6; Matthew 26:36-38) As to his natural disposition, Simon Peter was bold, outspoken, and more than a little inclined to be rash in both his speech and actions. (Matthew 14:28-31; Matthew 26:31-35; Luke 9:28-35)

However, Peter was a man of genuine faith in spite of his shortcomings, for none of the others gave a more glorious testimony concerning the person of Christ than he. Read Matthew 16:13-18 and mark his response when the Lord asked his disciples: *Whom say ye that I am?* Yet Peter was also known to contradict the Lord upon more than one occasion. (Matthew 16:22-23; John 13:3-9) Even though he always lived to regret it, Peter could not seem to learn from his mistakes. How many of us can identify with that!

Without question, vain confidence did its worst work when it prompted him to think himself the strongest among his brethren. (Matthew 26:31-35) By overestimating his own strength, Peter unwittingly set himself up for a great fall. As the hour of greatest trial drew near, he erred still further by sleeping along with the rest of the disciples in the Garden of Gethsemane while his Lord agonized in prayer. They did so even though the Lord Jesus had expressly warned them: *Watch and pray, that ye enter not into temptation: the spirit indeed is willing, but the flesh is weak.* (Matthew 26:40-41)

Therefore, Simon Peter succumbed to vain confidence, first by trying to defend his Lord when enemies came to arrest him. Although Peter was armed with a sword, one of two that were shared by the twelve, he proved less than proficient in its use. Swinging wildly with the unfamiliar weapon he missed his aim, taking off Malchus' ear rather than his head, which was probably Peter's intention. His action, though misguided, was motivated by the best of intentions; but he still did not understand that his beloved master must die. (John 18:10-11; Matthew 26:49-54)

Once the arrest of the Lord Jesus had taken place, Peter's confidence began to rapidly dwindle. Instead of standing with his Lord as he had staunchly declared he would do, Peter followed him afar off. Next, he entered the enemies' camp and warmed himself by their fire, even though it placed him where he was likely to be recognized. When a young servant girl accused him of being a follower of Jesus, the bold fisherman trembled with fear and denied the allegation. Others who were gathered around the fire then began to eye him with suspicion and question him as to his knowledge of the Lord Jesus. It was the perfect opportunity to make good his boast and take a bold stand with his Lord. Yet in the course of one brief hour, Peter denied him three times. (Luke 22:54-60)

Earlier, when the Lord Jesus Christ foretold his denial, Peter had vehemently protested at the very thought. But after the fact, as he recalled the Lord's words and how quickly they had come to pass, he was stricken with grief and unbearable sorrow. (Luke 22:61-62) Even though Peter's actions might argue to the contrary, he loved the Lord Jesus deeply. His intention to stand firm even if no one else did so had been honorable and sincere. Yet he trusted in his own strength, and therein was his downfall. Therefore, when put to the test, the boasted courage of Peter the strong was quickly reduced to cowardice. Moreover, with the casting down of vain confidence, fear and shame rushed in to take its place. During that dark episode in Peter's life, I strongly suspect that he was taken captive and beaten down by the awful giant named Despair.

Both the incident at By-Path Meadow and Peter's great fall suggest that there is a strong link between vain confidence and the onset of fear, mistrust, and despondency. Moreover, they bear witness of what a dangerous thing vain confidence really is. Even after their deliverance from Doubting Castle, Christian and Hopeful still had no idea of just how narrow their escape had been.

But what about Simon Peter? The Lord Jesus had given him an astounding warning ahead of time that Satan was bent upon his destruction. The evil one was determined to undo the bold, brash fisherman turned follower of Christ. (Luke 22:31-34) Had Peter been left to his own resources, the diabolical plot would undoubtedly have succeeded. Yet it failed utterly because the Lord Jesus prayed for him. In spite of his many faults, Simon Peter was wheat, not chaff. There-fore, by God's grace, his faith was not destroyed but made stronger by the ordeal. Moreover, as the Lord also promised, once Peter was turned again and recovered, he would be used to strengthen his brethren. To this day, he continues to do so.

Ideally speaking, our journey to Zion should be one in which each step we take is both forward and upward. However, we do not travel far down the path of life before discovering it is not quite that simple. So many hindrances lie in our path that we often seem to stumble two steps backward for every step forward. Some might argue that it makes for much wasted effort, but that is not really the case. Even though it may fly in the face of human logic, our greatest spiritual advancement is often made when we feel sure that we have lost ground.

By now, Christian and Hopeful were well acquainted with the frustration that comes from wasted steps. When they finally crossed back over the stile, we might say that they were right back where they started. They were not a step further down the King's Highway, even though they had covered much ground and put forth much effort. Once again, our thoughts return to the time when Christian lost his scroll on the hill Difficulty and had to backtrack in order to recover it. In doing so, he lost a good deal of time and was overtaken by night-fall. Moreover, he discovered that retracing his steps was harder than he could have imagined, much more difficult than passing that way the first time.

However, time lost is not necessarily time wasted. Due to our struggles with sin, none of us will navigate the path of the just without facing similar setbacks, and yet, what valuable learning experiences they prove to be. Some of these lessons are quite painful because they give us deeper knowledge of ourselves and our many frailties. Other lessons are a blessing because they teach us to look away from our-selves and unto the captain of our salvation. Unlike Vain-Confidence, he will never lead us out of the right way.

As Christian and Hopeful stood by the innocent-looking stile, they paused to consider all that had happened since they first crossed over it. Then they thought of those who would pass that way after them. Were they not duty-bound to make the danger known? Should they not warn future travelers that beautiful By-Path Meadow was not an easy short-cut to the Celestial City? After careful deliberation, they decided to mark the spot with a pillar that would capture the attention of all future travelers.

After setting the new marker in place, they engraved it with a warning that Doubting Castle lay beyond the stile, although it was not visible from that point. The enticing meadow was intended to deceive those who pass by, and the path through it led directly to the bleak fortress of Giant Despair. In explicit terms, they described the giant as a vicious, cruel being who was the sworn enemy of the Lord Jesus Christ and his people. Hopefully, a word to the wise would be sufficient!

The concern that Christian and Hopeful felt for their fellow pilgrims was greatly to their credit. Due to their own heedlessness, they had suffered cruelly at the hands of Giant Despair and would spare others the same fate, if possible. But with the erecting of the monument, they had done all they could to help their brethren in the Lord not to make the same mistake. Those who took the time to read the monument and heed its warning would escape grave danger. However, some would undoubtedly ignore the monument and cross the stile into By- Path Meadow in spite of it.

Christian and Hopeful could now continue on their way with a clear conscience, having done what they could to share the valuable lessons they had learned. Furthermore, there was much for which they had cause to be grateful. God had been incredibly merciful to them, in spite of their sin. He had saved them from danger that was far greater than they even now understood. This latest trial had, perhaps, been the worst that either of them had faced thus far. Like the apostle Peter, their faith had come under severe attack and had wavered to an extraordinary degree. Yet by the grace of God, they proved themselves valiant for truth as well.

A personal testimony

Throughout the writing of this book, I have kept any mention of my own experience to a minimum. So even though I have included personal anecdotes here and there, it was with the hope of helping another struggling soul, and never as a basis for comparison. Since each of us has our own race to run, such comparisons can do more harm than good. However, I am equally convinced that the things we learn and experience in the course of our Christian lives are not for our benefit alone. A significant part of our fellowship in the community of saints is to encourage our brethren in the faith and be strengthened by them, in our turn.

During many years as a pastor's wife, it has been my privilege to know quite a few of God's choice servants. Our wide circle of friends in Christ, and their godly example, has proved both a rich blessing and a stirring challenge to my soul. What worth can be placed upon the spiritual insight gained, the godly wisdom shared, and the encouragement derived from our mutual fellowship in the Gospel? The value to my soul has been truly inestimable, more precious than rubies. (Proverbs 3:15)

In pondering this great benefit, I decided to share a little of my history in the hope that it will help a fellow Christian who struggles with the lack of assurance about his or her salvation. How well I understand the painful nature of this terrible trial! There is nothing else quite like it. Even though God has a wise and good purpose for those who pass through this dark valley, it is not his will that his children remain debilitated, imprisoned as it were, by fear and doubt. (2 Timothy 1:7) How can one in such a condition be an effective witness for Christ or a useful servant in his kingdom? More likely, he will be a burden to others as well as to himself.

John Bunyan, creator of the allegorical Doubting Castle, was himself a frequent inmate there, at least in his earlier years as a Christian. Therefore, he had intimate knowledge of what he wrote. This is one reason why I feel such an affinity to him, for I am also well acquainted with Doubting Castle and its fearsome owners.

From earliest childhood I was shy, deeply sensitive, introspective and of a somewhat melancholy disposition. Quite often, I would brood upon the bleaker aspects of life, especially the reality of death and eternity. In general, my thoughts were self-centered and my desire set upon earthly things, for I did not yet know the Lord. However, at various times throughout my growing-up years, I heard the Gospel of Jesus Christ.

When I was nineteen years of age, the Lord saw fit to quicken me to spiritual life and bring me to himself. He delivered me from the path of destruction and set me upon the path of life. Thus my entire outlook upon life was changed, for I was a new creature in Christ. My heart's desire was to follow him and do his will, but another dimension had been added to my introspective tendencies.

At first, I was filled with joy and wonder at the so-great salvation that had come to me. But all too soon, doubts began to creep into my mind. Since my knowledge of Scripture was sketchy at that time, I began to read the Word of God diligently. Yet even though I searched the Scriptures and earnestly believed them, my struggle with doubt and fear only seemed to intensify. Tormenting questions filled my mind and I was unable to lay them to rest because, more than anything else, I feared being deceived. Was my faith real? Was it the right kind of faith? Had I sincerely repented? Did the promises of salvation and eternal life really apply to me, or was I deluded after all?

In all of this, my thoughts were focused inwardly, a place where true assurance is never found. So for the first several years of my Christian life, I was caught in a vicious cycle of unbelieving fear and despondency, a prisoner in Doubting Castle long before reading *The Pilgrim's Progress*!

My ongoing struggle was made far worse because it was such a lonely one. Since at that time I presumed that other Christians did not have the same problem, I was hesitant to share my trouble with anyone. Then one day I was introduced to John Bunyan by way of *Grace Abounding to the Chief of Sinners* and *The Pilgrim's Progress*. What a blessing they have been to me, then and now! I was not alone after all! Hundreds of years ago, John Bunyan had endured a terrible struggle with the same thing; therefore, other believers probably did as well! This stunning realization marked a kind of turning point in my spiritual life.

Many years have passed since that turbulent time. By God's grace, my early struggle with lack of assurance has been laid to rest, for the most part. My hope of eternal life rests entirely in the Lord Jesus Christ and his perfect sacrifice on my behalf, not anything that I have or ever could do. Yet every now and then, dark clouds begin to gather and the sleeping giant named Despair begins to stir once again. Thus

I have learned the hard way that unbelieving fear and doubt are ene-mies that are not to be taken lightly. I must carefully guard against them, for they will seize any opportunity to gain control of my mind, and although I am ashamed to admit it, once in a while they succeed.

While contemplating the subject of unbelieving fear and the bit-ter struggle it entails, I again marvel at the keen insight given to the author of *The Pilgrim's Progress*. In both the Slough of Despond and Doubting Castle he brilliantly depicts this terrible inner conflict, which is much more common that I at first supposed.

Following this same line of thought, one aspect of the character named Diffidence strikes me as worthy of note. There is a sense in which both the archaic and modern usages of her name apply to any pilgrim who struggles with lack of assurance. In such a case, mistrust produces spiritual timidity, which proves a significant hindrance to the full assurance of faith.

In his sequel, *Pilgrim's Progress: the Second Part*, John Bunyan por-trays this kind of believer in the character of Mr. Fearing. Along with Christianna and her children, he was part of Great-heart's congrega-tion, and as his name implies, he was tormented by unbelieving fear to an extraordinary degree. As a result, he was afflicted by an equal measure of spiritual timidity, a thing that must never be mistaken for piety or godly humility.

While godly humility is the fruit of a well-tried and highly refined faith, spiritual timidity is symptomatic of faith that is small and weak. It will cause us to fear venturing all for Christ and cast-ing ourselves completely upon him. Mistrust can be nurtured just as faith can. It will render many a reason to fear, but few to hope. Great-heart understood this truth quite well. Therefore, in his studied opinion, Mr. Fearing was a liability to his own spiritual progress as well as a troublesome soul to pastor. In spite of Great-heart's faithful instruction in God's Word, wise counsel, and pastoral care, nothing seemed to help Mr. Fearing overcome his spiritual timidity.

Although there were others in the little flock who shared the same affliction to some extent, Mr. Fearing's case was an extreme one, a carica-ture, really. Nevertheless, he was a truehearted pilgrim who persevered all the way to the end of his earthly journey. But sad to say, he carried a heavy burden of fear and doubt with him every step of the way.

Need this have been the case? Was poor Mr. Fearing doomed to a life of debilitating fear and doubt, or could it have been avoided? What really lay at the root of the problem? More vital to the issue, what is the remedy?

The antidote for unbelieving fear

In Mark 9, we read the heart-wrenching account of a father who brought his demon-possessed son to the Lord Jesus Christ for healing. In response to the man's desperate plea for help the Lord replied: *If thou canst believe, all things are possible to him that believeth.* (Verse 23) In response, the stricken father cried with tears: *Lord, I believe; help thou mine unbelief.* (Verse 24)

Dear reader, I have often prayed that very same prayer. What about you? Being the recipient of saving faith does not mean that we will never again be vexed by unbelieving fear. Like Jacob and Esau in Rebekah's womb, these two contrary principles dwell together within us, and each will struggle for dominance. Should unbelieving fear gain the mastery, it will prove a cruel overlord that hounds its victims and drives them near the point of despair.

During the course of more than forty years' experience as a pastor's wife, I have met quite a few people who suffered from the lack of assurance of salvation. My heart truly goes out to them. I can testify that fear does indeed bring torment, and what greater fear could there be than this one? What else can so overwhelm the mind that it clouds and distorts rational thought? What other fear can incapacitate to the extent that this one can? There are few, in my opinion.

Due to its highly complex nature, the problem of agonizing fear and doubt is a difficult and frustrating thing with which to deal. Many factors come into play, making it problematic to sort out. While some personalities are more naturally prone to it than others, the lack of assurance about one's salvation is, in its essence, a spiritual problem. Therefore, it has no easy solution. Moreover, great care must be taken when dealing with it, lest we do the sufferer more harm than good.

In attempting to help one who is struggling with fear and doubt about his or her spiritual condition, two extremes must be avoided.

We do not want to break the bruised reed by further discouraging one who is already on the verge of despair. On the other hand, we must take exceptional care not to nurture a false hope by trying to convince the doubting soul that he is saved. In this regard, we must keep in mind that it is not our business to judge whether the afflicted one really knows the Lord or not. To do so is to meddle with things that are too high for us. In either case, the remedy is exactly the same.

When counseling those who are suffering the agony of doubt about their salvation, my first inclination is to empathize with them and try to relieve their misery. After all, I have been where they are and truly know how they feel. Yet I also know that while human help may give temporary relief, it cannot deliver one from the bondage of mistrust and despair. However well intentioned it may be, commiseration alone does no lasting good because it fails to address the underlying cause of the problem. A remedy does indeed exist, but first we must delve into the heart of the matter.

From personal experience I am persuaded that the recurrent problem of unbelieving fear and doubt is not a randomly occurring thing. While it may be partly due to faulty instruction and insufficient understanding of God's Word, it can often be traced to spiritual declension. Such a regression can start gradually and imperceptibly, but like a round object on an inclined plane, it escalates rapidly.

In Song of Solomon 2:15, we are told that it is the little foxes that spoil the vines. Likewise, spiritual regression almost always begins with little neglects and taking the things of God for granted. One may grow lax in his prayer life, that lifeline of communion with the Lord wherein lies the supernatural power to resist temptation, overcome evil, and stay the course set for us. Moreover, neglect in this one area often sets the stage for becoming lukewarm in the matter of reading and meditating in the Word of God. To some, this omission may seem a small matter, but it actually carries great risk. God's Word is spiritual manna, providing nourishment and strength for the inner man; therefore, it is vital to our spiritual growth and well-being. Through the all-sufficient merits of the blood of Christ, his Word cleanses us day by day and arms us for the battle ahead. As the Spirit of God applies its truth to our hearts, the Word becomes a living principle within and the means by which our faith increases and becomes strong. Therefore, diligence in prayer and study of the Scriptures is crucial to our spiritual health and soul prosperity. Nothing can compensate for the lack of it.

When one grows negligent in his personal devotions, he may also become less faithful in attending the assembly of God's people. In so doing, he robs himself of the great benefit to be gained from hearing the Word of God taught and expounded. He also misses the blessing that comes from corporate worship with those of like mind. Moreover, his attitude shows his small regard for both the ministry of the Word and the strength and encouragement that come from fellowship with his brethren in the Lord.

Those who fall into such an extreme pattern of neglecting the means of grace have just cause to question their standing before God. Such behavior is often the fast track to apostasy, so perhaps their fear and doubt is justified after all. At the very least, they have strayed into extremely dangerous territory.

As we saw with Christian and Hopeful, true believers in Christ can also be guilty of neglect in spiritual matters. But when we do, we can expect to feel the sting of divine chastisement. Furthermore, we inadvertently open the door to the malicious taunts of the adversary and expose ourselves to direct attack by Giant Despair. In brief, we find that the sin of unbelief is like a floodgate. When unleashed, it allows fear to rush in and carry us along with its fury. Thus we may find ourselves in the depths of Doubting Castle, while diligence in spiritual matters might have averted it altogether.

Desperate circumstances often tempt us to take equally drastic action; but whatever the problem happens to be, such measures rarely offer the best solution. So it is with those who are plagued with fear and doubt about their salvation. Being desperate to have the full assurance of salvation, they tend to seek a quick fix by looking for it in the wrong places. In particular, they may look inwardly to a past experience or something they have done. They search for some evidence of grace or indication of spiritual growth, some spiritual fruit or personal merit in which to take comfort.

None of this will do!! Cast away all such thinking!! Although there are certain marks that distinguish God's children from all others, they are never to form the basis of our hope of salvation. Assurance will never be ours by looking to self. We will only find more to deplore by doing so. Our heavenly Father will never permit us to trust or rest in anything or anyone other than his beloved Son. To this end, he will cast down every idol in which we trust and knock over every prop upon which we lean until we see Jesus alone.

So the remedy to the vexing problem of doubt and fear is simple, yet deeply profound. Faith is assurance. It lifts our sights heavenward and fixes them upon Christ and his wondrous redemption. If he is not the foundation of all our hope, then we have none. When by faith we look away unto Jesus, we rest in a hope that is both sure and steadfast, one that will never make us ashamed and is as an anchor of the soul. (Romans 5:1-5; Hebrews 6:19) Looking within brings only darkness, confusion, fear and despair, but looking to Jesus brings light, deliverance, hope and peace. Christ within is our hope of glory. (Colossians 1:27) He alone is our hope of eternal life. (Titus 3:7) It is in him alone that we possess a living hope. (1 Peter 1:3)

* * * *

Although the antidote to unbelieving fear is perfectly clear, the full assurance of faith is a fragile thing that must be carefully and diligently maintained. Dereliction of duty in this regard provides an inroad for doubt and fear, as well as many other spiritual ills.

Strange to say, there are some people who seem to glory in their perpetual doubting, as if it made them more spiritual than those who are not similarly afflicted. This attitude reflects spiritual ignorance concerning the nature and root of the problem. True piety is the fruit of faith, humility, and submission to God. It is consistent with a sound spiritual mind, and is never the result of bondage to doubt and fear. (2 Timothy 1:7) Therefore, our struggle with unbelieving fear must never be accounted a noble thing that merits a badge of honor. What are fear and mistrust, if not a united affront to the goodness and mercy of God who gave his only begotten Son for us, and to our Lord Jesus Christ who gave himself for us? Fear and mistrust not only impugn the character of God, but like Despair and Diffidence, they are bent upon our destruction as well. Therefore, we should account them deadly enemies.

Beloved friend in Christ, how is it with you? Are you dwelling in the shadow of Doubting Castle? Have fear and mistrust beaten you down until you are tempted to despair and give up hope? Take heart, for this need not be your case. There is a divine remedy that will lift you above the shadow and enable you to say: *I know whom I have believed, and am persuaded that he is able to keep that which I have committed unto him against that day.* (2 Timothy 1:12b)

Look not to your faith but unto Jesus, who is the object of your faith. The more you look to him and trust in him, the more you will realize how worthy he is of our highest confidence and trust. Assurance is found in a person, not a mere doctrine or creed. It does not lie so much in what we believe as in whom we believe. Where do we see the Lord Jesus Christ? He clearly said: *Search the scriptures; for in them ye think ye have eternal life: and they are they which testify of me.* (John 5:39)

Therefore, make full use of the means that God has ordained for your spiritual growth and well-being. Faithfully attend the Palace Beautiful where the Word of God is central and the Lord Jesus Christ is worshiped in spirit and in truth. Seek the Lord diligently in prayer. Study and meditate in his Word and hide it in your heart. It will prove a priceless reservoir from which you may draw when doubt and fear try to overtake your mind. Its great and precious promises will minister comfort, help, and strength like nothing else, and its truth will shed light upon your darkest night. Abide in Christ and let his Word abide in you, for therein lies the secret to bearing much fruit for the glory of God. (John 15:1-8) Remember that through God's Word, the terrible giant named Despair is rendered helpless. Its truth is the key that sets his prisoners free.

> My hope is built on nothing less than Jesus' blood and righteousness;
> I dare not trust the sweetest frame, but wholly lean on Jesus' name.
>
> When darkness veils his lovely face, I rest upon unchanging grace;
> In every rough and stormy gale my anchor holds within the veil.
>
> His oath, his covenant, his blood support me in the whelming flood;
> When all around my soul gives way, he then is all my Hope and Stay.

When I shall launch in worlds unseen, O may I then be found in him;
Dressed in his righteousness alone, faultless to stand before the throne.
On Christ, the solid Rock, I stand; all other ground is sinking sand. [1]

Study Questions

1. After crossing back over the innocent-looking stile, what did
   Christian and Hopeful do before resuming their journey? Why
   did they feel it was their duty to make the danger known? In
   your opinion, would their warning be heeded by future travelers? Why, or why not?

2. Lack of assurance of salvation is, in its essence, a spiritual problem. In helping those who are struggling with it, what two
   extremes should be avoided?

3. As a general rule, lack of assurance can often be traced to a pattern of spiritual neglect and complacency. What are some areas of
   neglect that can contribute to this terrible problem?

4. In the desperate quest for assurance of salvation, what are some
   things that must be avoided?

5. What is the only true remedy to the problem of doubt and fear?
   Since assurance of salvation is often a fragile thing, by what
   means is it to be maintained?

Part Fifteen

THE HEART OF EMMANUEL'S LAND

Now the God of peace, that brought again from the dead our Lord Jesus, that great shepherd of the sheep, through the blood of the everlasting covenant, make you perfect in every good work to do his will, working in you that which is well-pleasing in his sight, through Jesus Christ; to whom be glory for ever and ever. Amen.
Hebrews 13:20-21

CHAPTER 43

Between Two Vastly Different Worlds

We cannot truly know the heights of spiritual joy until we have first tasted the depths of sorrow. Likewise, we are unfit to dwell on the mountaintop until we have first been made to sojourn in Mesech and dwell in the tents of Kedar. (Psalm 120:5) Our spiritual growth requires both of these things, in such proportions as God in his wisdom deems best. Therefore, when in the depths of sorrow, we may safely trust ourselves to his tender, loving care. In his time, and for our eternal profit, he will unfailingly lead us to higher ground.

Such was the case with Christian and Hopeful after their deliverance from Doubting Castle and Giant Despair. Their pathway now inclined steadily upward, leading them directly to a place called the Delectable Mountains. Deep in the heart of Emmanuel's Land, these high, green hills stand between two vastly different worlds. Like the pilgrims who love to visit there, these mountains are in the world but not of it. From atop their majestic peaks, a remarkable vista opens before our eyes. Looking toward the way we have already come, we can faintly discern the skyline of the City of Destruction. As we trace the pathway we have followed since being delivered from that awful place, we can readily identify many of the places we have already been, and reflect upon the ways the Lord has led us. Then as we gaze forward from the opposite side of the mountains, our sights are fixed upon where we have yet to go, toward the land of Beulah and the Celestial City just beyond it. So the Delectable Mountains afford a prime opportunity to remember our journey as it has been accomplished so far, and anticipate that which is yet to be.

In spite of their imposing height, these mountains are not steep and hard to ascend like the hill Difficulty. Neither are they bleak and menacing like those that form the rocky gorge known as the Valley of the Shadow of Death. The Delectable Mountains were created for another purpose entirely, to provide rest and recovery to weary travelers in need of it.

Even the casual observer will note that someone has given great forethought when designing this place, and spared no expense in providing everything needful for those who visit here. Gardens and orchards flourish in abundance. Vineyards and fountains of pure water abound here as well, and quiet resting places. As you may imagine, Christian and Hopeful beheld all of this with thankful hearts. It was with great relief that they ate and drank freely, and washed themselves clean from the stains accumulated during their lengthy journey.

But what sort of place is this really? What do the Delectable Mountains signify? Like the Palace Beautiful, they denote a banqueting house, a spiritual house of wine, and the same "Lord of the Hill" owns them. (Song of Solomon 2:4) He is the one who has furnished this lavish table in the wilderness.

The Delectable Mountains have several remarkable features that deserve our careful attention. Survey them with me if you will, and observe a scene of exceptional beauty. Take special note of the river below, as it meanders through the gentle rolling hills. Its crystal water flows from a cleft rock high up in the mountains, and irrigates the lush highland meadows for which these mountains are particularly noted.

Now lift your eyes toward the rich pastureland covering the upper regions of the mountains. Do you see the pair of bald eagles soaring high overhead, scanning the landscape below them? Notice how effortlessly they rise upon the currents of wind that generally prevail here. Next, observe the flocks of sheep dotting the meadows and grazing contentedly there. Some of them lie beneath the shade trees, enjoying a cool respite from the heat of the day. Look more closely and you will see newborn lambs resting in the grass near their mothers, while those who are a little older frolic and play with one another.

Viewed from afar, the sheep appear to be alone on the hillsides, but look a little higher up toward the rock formations scattered here and there. Can you see the four men perched high atop the boulders? They are the shepherds of the Delectable Mountains, and the Lord of the Hill has entrusted his sheep into their care. From their elevated position, they have a commanding view of the countryside and are well able to keep a careful watch over the flocks feeding below.

This mountain range is a very special place, a peaceful retreat far from the endless clamor and strife of Vanity Fair. It is a land unsullied by the humanistic philosophy and worldly wisdom so prevalent in the towns of Carnal Policy, Vainglory, and Fair Speech. Altogether, it seems a place set apart as a haven of rest for weary exiles in their journey. And so it is!

To the uninformed, the shepherds of the Delectable Mountains appear to lead an idyllic life and have an occupation that requires little of them. However, those who are of this opinion lack both an understanding of the shepherds' high calling, and the true nature of their service. A solemn charge has been laid upon them that, if faithfully performed, will require the highest and best that they have to give. These humble men serve by royal commission and have the awesome responsibility of caring for sheep that belong to one who knows them all by name and has a vested interest in each one. It is to this great shepherd of the sheep that the four men are directly accountable. (Hebrews 13:17, 20)

Since it is incumbent upon them to constantly monitor the state of their flocks, they must diligently look for any sign of illness, injury, or other kind of trouble. Furthermore, they must make sure that each lamb and sheep is properly nourished with those things that will best promote their healthy growth and vigor. So in addition to the rich pastureland, the shepherds lead their flocks to the banks of the tranquil river where they can drink freely and deeply of its pure water.

In addition to the strenuous labor required to feed and care for the sheep, the shepherds must also be on constant guard against predators that are known to roam these hills. Particular care must be taken of the very young, elderly, sick or injured. If left unattended, these weaker sheep will be an easy prey for enemies that lie in wait. The shepherds are well aware of this danger. Therefore, when need be, they gather up and carry any sheep that is unable to keep pace with the flock.

From this duty alone, we correctly infer that the shepherds' labor is not without personal risk. Yet under his constant watch, the sheep may safely graze and lie down to rest in the green meadows. They can do so without fear because the shepherd has them ever in his sight. Should the need arise, he will place himself in harm's way in order to protect and defend them. Such is the character of the men who labor on the heights of the Delectable Mountains.

Standing at the foot of the high, green hills, Christian and Hopeful looked toward the higher elevations where the shepherds tended their flocks. They must have noticed the striking similarities between this delightful place and the verdant oasis where they had enjoyed such a needful rest. However, after their recent narrow escape, they were determined to exercise caution before lingering here. They had acted in haste before and rushed headlong into big trouble, but neither of them was eager to do it again. So even though they were weary from the strain of travel, they ascended the path in order to talk with the shepherds. In particular, they were curious to know who owned the Delectable Mountains and to whom the sheep belonged. In response to their inquiry, the shepherds informed Christian and Hopeful that the Delectable Mountains were Emmanuel's Land and lay within sight of his city. He was the owner of the sheep who dwelled there because he had laid down his life for them.

Upon hearing this, Christian asked whether they were on the right path to the Celestial City. It was a question of the utmost importance, one that he has asked of strangers before and not always received a truthful answer. However, these shepherds were men who could be trusted when they informed Christian and Hopeful that they were indeed on the right road. The way to the Celestial City led directly over the mountain range.

When Christian then asked how much further they had yet to go, he was told, "Too far for any, but those that shall get thither indeed." He may well have been taken aback by this cryptic reply, for he then inquired whether the way was safe or dangerous. One of the shepherds replied that the way was "Safe for those for whom it is to be safe, but Transgressors shall fall therein."

Once again, this seemed a strange reply to a straightforward question, but the shepherds were not being deliberately ambiguous. Their answers confirm what we already know about the pathway to the city. The two men were indeed on the highway that would eventually take them there. Yet even though they had now entered Emmanuel's Land, they were not yet out of danger. Others had made it this far and yet failed to enter the heavenly Zion. So the message of the shepherds was really unmistakably clear. Christian and Hopeful still had a good distance to go, and the way before them was both dangerous and safe. Therefore, they could not afford to relax their vigilance or lower their guard.

Christian's final question to the shepherds revealed how very needy he and his friend were after their recent ordeal. With a hopeful heart, he asked, "Is there in this place any Relief, for Pilgrims that are weary, and faint in the Way?" Dear friend in Christ, we already have the answer, do we not?

As you undoubtedly know, the shepherds of the Delectable Mountains were not ordinary shepherds. Even though they were kind and gracious toward strangers, experience has taught them to be cautious as well. In the course of their labors, they have acquired an intimate knowledge of both the pathway to Zion and the various kinds of travelers one meets along the way. The Lord of the Delectable Mountains had instructed them to share their bounty with others, and this was the desire of their hearts as well. Yet since they knew that not all comers were genuine pilgrims, the shepherds had some questions of their own. Therefore, they asked Christian and Hopeful, "Whence came you?" "How got you into the Way?" and "By what Means have you so persevered therein?"

In asking these highly pertinent questions, the shepherds did not mean to intimidate strangers or put them on the defensive. Their intent was to determine the true spiritual condition of the inquirers. So they justified their pointed questions by explaining, "Few of them that begin to come hither, do shew their face on these mountains."

However pessimistic an outlook this remark might seem to reflect, it was an honest assessment. Through many years of service, these men have found that not all travelers appreciate what they have to offer. Although the Delectable Mountains provide many wondrous things, each of them is suited to the spiritual mind. There is food and drink in abundance, but nothing to please or appease the flesh. The luxuriant pastures, orchards, vineyards and fountains provide spiritual nourishment for all who hunger and thirst after it. Those who partake of this bounty find it to be of invaluable benefit for the rest of their journey. Yet in their experience, such travelers are relatively few and far between.

Since God's children are the only ones who find the Delectable Mountains really suited to their taste, casual visitors eventually become restive and eager to move on. Through the years, the faithful shepherds have seen quite a few such people come and go. Therefore, it is not surprising that they greet each newcomer with guarded optimism and question them in so direct a manner.

Although we are not told how Christian and Hopeful responded to the shepherds' inquiry, we may safely assume that their answers were the same as those given to others in the past. We may also presume that the shepherds observed them closely as they spoke, and weighed their replies carefully. For after hearing the account of Christian and Hopeful's journey so far, the shepherds received them as true brethren in the Lord and, with open arms, welcomed them to the Delectable Mountains.

* * * *

Scripture often portrays the kingdom of God, the Church of the Lord Jesus Christ, in symbolic language. One prime example is the figure of a great palace or castle. (Psalm 48) John Bunyan drew upon this metaphor when he created the Palace Beautiful. Its very name brings to mind a magnificent structure designed for those of noble descent. Yet even though it is a place of exceptional beauty and grandeur, this palace is a sanctuary for even the humblest of pilgrims. (Isaiah 57:15)

The Lord Jesus Christ is both the owner and builder of this great house and is pleased to make it his royal dwelling place. (Psalm 132:13-14; Ephesians 2:19-22; 1 Peter 2:5-6) All who are the children of God by new birth are part of it, and each of them openly confesses Christ as Lord. In the world's estimation, most of them would be out of place in a splendid palace. Since their royal estate is not an earthly one, men lightly esteem them and their spiritual heritage as the children of God. (Psalm 87:4-6) Therefore, it is no strange thing that the glory of the Palace Beautiful is seen by a relative few. Its beauty is concealed within its walls where the King of Glory dwells with his redeemed people. Thus it has no equal in this present evil world.

Like the Palace Beautiful, the Delectable Mountains are also of heavenly origin. The image they evoke contains a very precious and profound meaning, one that bears vital relevance to the successful completion of our Christian journey. This figurative mountain range is the purchased possession of the Lord Jesus Christ, and it signifies the provisional aspect of his kingdom on earth. (Acts 20:28)

The Word of God frequently depicts kingdoms and empires as mountains, and the kingdom of God is no exception. However, his kingdom is set apart from all the rest and is exalted over them all. In Isaiah 2:2, we learn that *the mountain of the LORD's house shall be established in the top of the mountains, and shall be exalted above the hills.* The prophet Daniel sheds light upon how this establishment and exaltation would take place when he interpreted King Nebuchadnezzar's strange dream. The stone cut out without hands, which struck the feet of the mighty colossus and brought it down, would become a great mountain that would fill the whole earth. (Daniel 2:34-35)

Worldly empires and kingdoms come and go. The strongest and best of them rise and fall in their turn, but God's kingdom is eternal and his sovereignty rules over all. However, it is not through instruments of conventional warfare that he subdues and conquers the nations. (2 Corinthians 10:3-5) He does so through the declaration of the Gospel of peace. (Romans 10:15; Ephesians 6:15) As his truth goes forth into the world, the hearts of men bow to the Lord Jesus Christ and submit to his rule. Thus his kingdom of righteousness and peace increases and is exalted over the whole earth. (Isaiah 2:2-4) Dear friend in Christ, think upon this blessed truth. You and I are part of his glorious kingdom!

In Mount Zion, the beautiful city of God, every inhabitant knows the Lord Jesus Christ and has a heart to serve, honor, and obey him.

(Jeremiah 24:7; Jeremiah 31:33-34) She is a chosen city, greatly beloved of her God. (Psalm 87:2) It is from the heights of Mount Zion that God provides the needs of his sojourning people and renders timely help when they are afflicted and tried. (Psalm 20:1-2; Psalm 46:1-5; Psalm 132:15-16) Moreover, from this shining city on a hill, our heavenly Father pours forth his choice blessings upon his beloved children. (Psalm 103:1-5; Psalm 128:5)

These grand truths come strongly to mind as I think upon the Delectable Mountains and their direct link to the Palace Beautiful, to which the above description also applies. Thus we must consider them together as two figures of the kingdom of God on earth. The Palace Beautiful focuses more upon the internal structure and function of the local church, and the mutual love and fellowship enjoyed by those who are joined together in Christ. The Delectable Mountains depict the pastoral oversight of godly ministers and their spiritual rule in the great house of God. Therefore, a completely different set of metaphors applies.

Rolling hills through which a river of living water flows! Orchards, vineyards, and fountains in abundance! Lush, green pastures as far as the eye can see! Flocks of sheep grazing peacefully on the upper regions of the hills! Shepherds keeping a constant watch upon the sheep! With this vivid description of the Delectable Mountains in mind, let us join Christian and Hopeful on their visit there.

Study Questions

1. For what specific purpose were the Delectable Mountains created? To whom do they belong?

2. List some of the remarkable features of these high, green hills.

3. Who are the shepherds of the Delectable Mountains? Briefly describe the nature of their service and the extent of their responsibility.

4. Eager to learn more about this place, Christian and Hopeful ascended the hills in order to talk with the shepherds. What answers did they receive in response to their questions?

5. Since the shepherds have also learned to be cautiously optimistic concerning strangers who visit these hills, they also had some questions for Christian and Hopeful. What three things did they want to know, and what was their purpose in asking? What kind of provisions do the Delectable Mountains have to offer?

CHAPTER 44

The Shepherds of the Delectable Mountains

SITUATED AS THEY ARE IN THE VERY HEART OF EMMANUEL'S LAND, THE Delectable Mountains stand apart from all the kingdoms of this world, and yet, you will find them wherever God's people gather in his name. From their lofty heights, God's eternal Word is proclaimed as the sole authority of rule and practice, and Christ is head over all. (Ephesians 1:19-23)

The sheep feeding in the high, green meadows portray the children of God, the sheep of his pasture. (Psalm 100:3) What a fitting metaphor this is! The sheep did not place themselves on the heights of these mountains through their own efforts. Once they were lost, scattered, and wandering out of the way. They would have remained so had not Christ, the good shepherd, sought and gathered them into his fold. (Ezekiel 34:11-12; Luke 15:4-6; Luke 19:10; John 10:16) Then having made them partakers of his so great salvation, he placed them under the care of specially appointed watchmen. (Ezekiel 34:12-16)

Thus we have the identity of both the sheep and shepherds of the Delectable Mountains. The Lord Jesus Christ leads his people through under shepherds who have been called to this special service. They are Gospel evangels who declare the Word of God under the authority and power of their risen Lord, and the Delectable Mountains is their field of service. (Matthew 28:18-20; Isaiah 52:7).

So it is from the heights of Mount Zion that these commissioned officers in God's kingdom watch over the souls committed to their charge. God's hand is upon them, as is the power of his Spirit. They may not have attended the world's most prestigious universities, but in God's will and providence, each of them has been prepared and equipped for his great task. (2 Timothy 3:14-17) Moreover, they are placed by God where his sheep are, in the Church of the living God, the pillar and ground of the truth. (1 Timothy 3:15) In the churches, the ministers of Christ fulfill their solemn trust by instructing and exhorting the people from the Word of God. By means of their spiritual oversight, the Lord Jesus Christ feeds and nourishes his redeemed ones and prepares them to be with him forever.

What about the men who serve as shepherds of the Delectable Mountains? They are men who have devoted their lives to the service of Christ and his people, whatever the cost. As such, they bear the same character as the one whose portrait hangs in the antechamber of the Interpreter's House. Therefore, they are men who are worthy of high esteem for their works' sake. (1 Thessalonians 5:12-13)

When John Bunyan assigned specific names to the shepherds watching the sheep on the Delectable Mountains, he called them Knowledge, Experience, Watchful and Sincere. Their names indicate both their character and qualification as the ministers of Christ. As the four virgins of the Palace Beautiful represented the character of the Church, the bride of Christ, so these four shepherds form a composite picture of the true ministers of Christ.

The first shepherd mentioned specifically by name was Knowledge, an order that was undoubtedly of deliberate design by the author. Without question, knowledge is the most fundamental qualification of God's men. When it is lacking, even the most impressive credentials are of little use, for this knowledge is of a highly comprehensive nature and of a very particular sort.

First and foremost, the man of God must know the Lord Jesus Christ in truth and be called by him. This should go without saying, and yet many claim to be ministers of Christ who actually do not know him in a saving relationship. The true servant of Christ may be distinguished from the false in that the Holy Spirit has placed the fear and knowledge of God in his heart. This inward quality of godly wisdom, of which the fear of God is the principal part, will be evident in both his character and manner of life. (Proverbs 1:7; 9:10)

Another essential element to the minister's knowledge is his solid and thorough understanding of the truth as it is in Christ Jesus. Herein is the greater part of his responsibility and labor, for how can he declare and expound what he neither knows nor understands? In order to properly fulfill his sacred trust, he must spend much time in the Interpreter's House. That is, he must labor diligently in the Word of God by studying it, meditating upon it, committing it to memory and seeking God's help for a right understanding of it. Then as he weighs all other knowledge against this infallible standard, he will have the discernment to detect error and protect his flock from its devastating influence. (Titus 1:9)

Yet even this exhaustive labor is not enough. The Word of God must be a living reality in the pastor's heart if he is to effectively minister it to others. His labor to acquire spiritual knowledge is not merely for his own benefit, but for the profit of those under his pastoral care. (1 Timothy 4:13-16; 2 Timothy 3:14-17) Because he possesses truth in the inward parts, he instructs his people through both precept and godly example. (Psalm 51:6)

While a thorough understanding of sound doctrine may make a good preacher, it is not enough to make a good pastor. The shepherd must also know his flock. The man of God must develop and nurture a close relationship with his people. Like Great-heart, he must know them as individuals having unique personalities, strengths, and weaknesses. This knowledge will prove most useful in ministering to the needs of his flock, noting early signs of trouble, and averting it if possible. Moreover, this intimate knowledge of his people will help the pastor to recognize their spiritual gifts and guide them into exercising those gifts for the good of the body. (Ephesians 4:15-16)

Above all, the minister of Christ must have a true heart of love for his people. When this is the case, his chief desire will be that which promotes their highest spiritual good. Self-denying love for his Lord and his people will make of him a faithful servant of Jesus Christ. (1 Corinthians 13:1-3)

Then there is the matter of spiritual oversight, which is also part of the pastor's duty. If he is to properly rule and guide his flock, he has need of exceptional wisdom and knowledge. As a basic principle, he must understand both the nature of this oversight and its scriptural parameters. While God's men are commanded to feed the flock of God and take the oversight thereof, they are expressly forbidden to rule with an iron hand. They are called to be examples to the flock, not lords over God's heritage. (1 Peter 5:2-3) Therefore, their rule is to be administered with godly fear and in a spirit of true humility. Moreover, it is never to be arbitrary in nature, but limited to the sole authority of God's Word. (1 Timothy 5:17) Sola Scriptura, not the commandments and doctrines of men!

Not only does the Word of God set the standard for spiritual oversight in the church, it is also the only proper source of nourishment for God's people. As we hear, receive, and assimilate the Word, we will grow progressively toward spiritual maturity and our Christian character will be more perfectly developed. (1 Peter 2:1-3; 2 Peter 3:18; John 6:35; John 7:37-39)

Occasionally, the idea of spiritual oversight and pastoral authority causes some to bristle with indignation. Such an attitude is most often the result of offended pride and a rebellious, wayward heart. While it is true that some have abused their authority and hurt the sheep of Christ, such men are rare exceptions to the rule in true churches. The minister of Christ has a true shepherd's heart; therefore, he always has the best interest of his people in mind. Even when strong rebuke and correction are necessary, proper spiritual rule is beneficial rather than burdensome. It may be painful in the short term, but will promote the spiritual health and well being of the body. Moreover, the wisest among them will respect and appreciate their pastor for his honesty and love for their souls, even when it hurts.

Pastoral authority has one great governor that tempers any tendency to abuse. The true man of God is constantly aware that he, also, is a man under authority. Those whom he pastors belong to his master, and to this master he will one day give a solemn account of his stewardship. Likewise, those who are blessed to have the benefit of his ministry are responsible to give heed and submit to his spiritual rule. Failure to do so will prove unprofitable to them, in the end. (Hebrews 13:7, 17)

Therefore, comprehensive knowledge is required of God's men in order for them to properly instruct, counsel, guide and feed those who are under their care. Moreover, they have need of greater wisdom and more extensive knowledge than their flock. Like the shepherds high atop the Delectable Mountains keeping watch over their sheep, there is a sense in which the Gospel minister must sit above his people. This is not by reason of a higher standing in Christ, but due to his high calling and solemn responsibility as an officer in God's kingdom. To him much has been given; therefore, of him much will be required.

In the absence of a moderating self-knowledge, all of this could tend to promote pride in the heart of this very special servant of Christ. However, his high position also demands a humble mind, a proper estimate of self, and the awareness of his accountability before the Lord. With this knowledge firmly in place, any tendency toward pride will be kept carefully in check.

If knowledge is the most fundamental qualification required of the ministers of Christ, then Experience, the next shepherd, runs a close second. True wisdom cannot be attained through higher education, natural ability, superior intellect or other such means alone. It is only acquired through the proper application of knowledge. Godly wisdom is the capacity to rightly apply the truth to every aspect of the Christian's life. Therefore, it is an essential quality that the minister of Christ must possess in good measure.

He can hardly be expected to deal prudently with situations in which he has no direct knowledge or experience. At best, his counsel would then consist of general principles and common sense, but would perhaps sound a bit stilted and lacking in conviction. Moreover, his teaching will be theoretical only, if he has not experienced its truth first-hand, and his hearers will be quick to note the difference.

Experience, then, is a beautiful garment that adorns the seasoned pastor, but such men are relatively rare and they do not come ready-made. When God calls a man into the service of his kingdom, he equips that man with all he will need in order to faithfully discharge his duty. However, something else must be added to these ministry gifts. The man himself must be prepared for the great task he has undertaken. Since God alone can perform this work, he trains his servants in the school of experience so that they will have something more substantial to offer than theoretical knowledge and mere rhetoric. A significant part of this training involves spiritual battle in which these men will know both the joy of victory and the sting of defeat. It is through this painful learning process that they become soldiers whose mettle has been thoroughly tested, and veterans who are ready to fulfill the great trust committed to them. Thus the man of God learns to be a spiritual leader of others, but first and foremost, he is a leader led by the Spirit of God.

The congregation who has such a man as their pastor is blessed indeed. He can proclaim the sufficiency of God's grace with firm conviction because he has known its sustaining power in his darkest trials. He can attest that God is faithful, for he has experienced his faithfulness and found his promises true. He can boldly exhort others to pray because he is a man of fervent, prevailing prayer. He can press faith, for he possesses living faith that has been often tried as by fire. He is able to feel with his people when they suffer because he, also, knows what it is to be afflicted.

As the Spirit of God sanctifies the pastor's experience to his heart and life, there will be the added dimension of godly wisdom to his knowledge that nothing else can quite accomplish. It will permeate his entire being, adding depth to his personal life, family relationships, pulpit ministry and interaction with others. Moreover, he can minister to his flock with greater compassion and be a more credible example because he has walked the way before them.

It is important to note, however, that experience is not necessarily synonymous with chronological age. Rather, it is set in contrast to one who is a neophyte as concerns the Gospel ministry. Since pride can be the downfall of an untried man, Scripture commands that a novice not be admitted to the office of bishop ("overseer"), *lest being lifted up with pride he fall into the condemnation of the devil.* (1 Timothy 3:6) On the other hand, the apostle Paul expressed great confidence in Timothy when he exhorted him: *Let no man despise thy youth; but be thou an example of the believers, in word, in conversation, in charity, in spirit, in faith, in purity.* (1 Timothy 4:12) Although Timothy was a young pastor, he was obviously not a novice.

Since the title elder denotes the character of a man rather than his actual age, it is reserved for one who has demonstrated the wisdom and Christ-like character of spiritual maturity. In the exercise of his office, he will often need to draw from the reserve of wisdom and knowledge gained through first-hand experience. While the novice may be knowledgeable concerning sound doctrine, his lack of experience is usually accompanied by a proportionate lack of wisdom. Therefore, pride can be his downfall whatever his chronological age. It is the rare grace of godly humility that sets the veteran pastor apart from the aspiring novice.

With the third shepherd named Watchful, our focus shifts from the qualifications of the minister of Christ to one of his chief duties. Figuratively speaking, he stands as a watchman upon the walls of Jerusalem, the Israel of God, watching over the souls of men. (Isaiah 62:6; Galatians 4:26; 6:16) From this post of duty he keeps a watchful eye on the state of his congregation, looking for any signs of trouble. In so doing, he will be quick to detect the presence of sin in the camp, hopefully in its early stages. Moreover, he must be on constant guard against the seeds of apostasy. Unless he maintains a vigilant watch, false doctrine could gain an inroad among the flock.

In addition to all of this, the man of God must keep a careful eye out for enemies who would attack and scatter the sheep. He knows that his people will be an easy prey unless they are strong in the faith and well-grounded in the truth. When the apostle Paul was about to depart for Jerusalem to face an uncertain future, he warned the Ephesian elders of this ever-present danger saying: *Take heed therefore unto yourselves, and to all the flock, over the which the Holy Ghost hath made you overseers, to feed the church of God, which he hath purchased with his own blood. For I know this, that after my departing shall grievous wolves enter in among you, not sparing the flock. Also of your own selves shall men arise, speaking perverse things, to draw away disciples after them.* (Acts 20:28-30)

Since their commander-in-chief (Satan) never moves his jealous eye away from the sheep of Christ, spiritual predators roam at large just as much today as when the Church was in her infancy. Now, as then, their chief tactic is to corrupt the purity of the Gospel. Therefore, the minister of Christ finds himself on the front line of a mighty conflict in defense of the truth, with the souls of those whom he pastors hanging in the balance.

With so much at stake, it is vitally important that the man of God exercise a highly disciplined self-watch as well as a flock watch. Since our great adversary often attempts to undermine the Gospel by discrediting its ministers, he scores a mighty victory when the minister's life is less than exemplary. This dual watch requires strenuous effort on the minister's part, as the apostle Paul expressed so clearly to pastor Timothy when he said: *Take heed unto thyself, and unto the doctrine; continue in them: for in doing this thou shalt both save thyself, and them that hear thee.* (1 Timothy 4:16)

Since the man of God is not equal to this task in his own strength, he must watch and persevere in prayer both for himself and his people, trusting the Lord for grace to fulfill this all-encompassing duty. Moreover, he must give himself wholly to the ministry of God's Word; for it is primarily through the faithful declaration of the truth that God keeps his people in the path of life.

As to this, it is a sad fact that many who claim to be on the way to Zion eventually fall by the wayside. It is not enough to make a convincing start. We must finish our course if we hope to enter the golden city. Genuine faith will persevere to the end, but we should always keep in mind the instrumental role that watchful pastors have in our final salvation.

Sincere, the fourth shepherd of the Delectable Mountains, is not the least in importance just because he is mentioned last. He expresses a character trait that is absolutely essential in the minister of Christ. One who is entrusted with this high office must be a man of impeccable moral integrity. (1 Timothy 3:7) Such a man will be honest and upright in his dealings and relationships with others. He will be genuine and truehearted, with deeply rooted principles of godliness that are evident in his manner of speech and conduct. Although he is not exempt from the frailties of the flesh, he will strive diligently to be exactly what he appears to be. To this end, he practices a strict self-discipline, both in his pastoral duties and personal life, guarding against hypocrisy by consistently practicing what he preaches. He does all of this for the sake of the Gospel, following the example of the apostle Paul. (1 Corinthians 9:23-27)

The quality of godly sincerity is quite evident in his relationship with his people, for he has a true pastor's heart toward them. Moreover, his love and concern for their spiritual welfare is beyond legitimate question. Even though he runs the risk of incurring their disfavor, he will be honest with their souls and speak the truth to them in love. Therefore, he withholds nothing that is profitable, including rebuke and warning when they are necessary. (2 Corinthians 2:17; Acts 20:26-27)

Thus sincerity often has a high cost attached to it, but the true minister of Christ is ruled by the fear of God rather than the fear of man. As a result, he will be faithful in the execution of his duty and true to the souls of men. Above all, he is faithful to his Lord, and this quality of faithfulness is sufficient in itself to set him apart from the hireling.

A hireling is one who assumes the office of pastor without a commission from the chief shepherd. He claims to be a minister of Christ even though he is not called by God, and entirely lacks the character of one who is. Why then would such a man seek this position when there is nothing of a noble, self-sacrificial spirit about him? He does so because he hopes to gain something from it, like By-ends of Fairspeech. Self-aggrandizement lies at the heart of all he says and does. Whatever he may claim, he has no genuine love for the people of God and is not willing to bear the reproach of the cross. As a general rule, the hireling originates from the land of Vainglory. Therefore, he tells men what they want to hear in order to gain their good opinion.

Although some may find it difficult to tell the true shepherd from the false, the imposter will reveal his true character sooner or later. At the first sign of trouble, he will flee in order to save himself, leaving the sheep to fend for themselves. (John 10:12) Like the wicked kings of Israel and Judah, he will inflict great harm upon the very people he is supposed to lead and protect. (Jeremiah 23:1-2; Matthew 7:15-23) Why? The Lord Jesus answers in John 10:13: *The hireling fleeth, because he is a hireling, and careth not for the sheep.*

On the contrary, the true minister of Jesus Christ will faithfully serve his people as long as he is able, even when it is at great personal cost. Unlike the false pretender, he labors out of self-sacrificial love for his people. Following the character and example of his Lord, he gives his utmost for the spiritual welfare of his beloved flock. As far as this world is concerned, he may labor in obscurity and often have little to show for it. However, *when the chief Shepherd shall appear,* he will receive the recompense of his labor, *a crown of glory that fadeth not away.* (1 Peter 5:4)

The profile of the four shepherds sets a very high standard for the ministers of Christ, but this is right and proper, for Scripture does the very same. However, it is a mistake to think of God's men in overly idealistic terms. They have their struggles just like the rest of us, and certain trials that are unique to their calling. Yet in spite of personal weaknesses and frailties, they are very special men, true-hearted shepherds who faithfully serve their Lord and his sheep, not for worldly glory, but for love.

Dear reader, it has been my privilege to be the wife of such a man for more than forty years now. During that time, I have watched him demonstrate the same godly qualities as the shepherds of the Delectable Mountains in ministering to those under his care. In the process, I have also seen him wounded and brokenhearted, yet remaining faithful through it all, as a good soldier of Jesus Christ. (2 Timothy 2:3) If you are blessed to have this kind of pastor, please do not take him for granted or do anything to cause him grief. Love him, support and pray for him, and thank the Lord for such a rare and precious gift!

* * * *

Now that we have delved into the spiritual significance of the shepherds' names and field of service, it is easy to understand why Christian and Hopeful were content to abide with them on the Delectable Mountains. After their harrowing ordeal in Doubting Castle, the bounty of that special place was exactly what they desired and needed most. However, the abundant provision and help found there was not for them alone. The Delectable Mountains are located wherever God's people gather together under the care of a true minister of Jesus Christ. The very same can be said of the Palace Beautiful. Since they represent two aspects of God's provision for his children, both the Palace Beautiful and the Delectable Mountains figure prominently throughout our entire Christian experience.

In a chronological sense, Christian first united with an assembly of believers in Christ when he visited the Palace Beautiful. At that time, he was very young in the Lord and lacking in both knowledge and experience. By the time he and Hopeful reached the Delectable Mountains, they had gained a great deal of wisdom and spiritual insight. Clearly, although John Bunyan does not actually say so, their spiritual growth indicates that they were active members of a local church in which the Word of God was faithfully taught. Therefore, like Christian's earlier visit to the Palace Beautiful, their respite on the Delectable Mountains was, I am convinced, a regular thing.

The Lord Jesus Christ lives in the hearts of each one of his people by his Spirit, and dwells in them corporately in the midst of his churches. (Revelation 1:12-13, 20) Thus the assemblies where his people meet together are safe havens in the midst of a world filled with spiritual danger. To deliberately neglect this divinely-appointed provision is a very foolish and dangerous thing. (Hebrews 10:23-25) Yet in spite of clear Scripture teaching on the subject, there are some who claim to be followers of Jesus Christ, but prefer to go it alone. They have little desire to join a congregation of God's people, and balk at the idea of being under the authority of an appointed minister of Christ.

In certain cases, there may be no choice in the matter. But as a general rule, our safest course is to unite with an assembly of like-minded believers. The mutual fellowship we enjoy there and the benefits derived from the continual ministry of God's Word are vital to our spiritual health and vitality. So let us take care that we go forth by the footsteps of the flock and feed together beside the shepherd's tents. (Song of Solomon 1:7-8)

What about you, dear reader? Can you honestly say with the pilgrims of old: *I was glad when they said unto me, 'Let us go into the house of the Lord'?* (Psalm 122:1) Does your heart yearn for the Delectable Mountains and the spiritual feast that awaits you there? Are you numbered among those who are marching to Zion? Does your heart cry with the homesick exile: *If I do not remember thee, let my tongue cleave to the roof of my mouth; if I prefer not Jerusalem above my chief joy?* (Psalm 137:6) If not, O seek the Lord Jesus Christ without delay! Come to him as a poor, needy sinner and cast yourself at his feet for mercy. When you do, you will find him a loving Savior and gracious Lord.

If you have already tasted that he is gracious, then you undoubtedly love to partake of the celestial fruits provided for us here below. You love the people of God and prefer their fellowship above all others. Moreover, you treasure the godly pastor who cares for your soul, and you give earnest heed to the truth he declares. In other words, you love to dwell upon the Delectable Mountains and experience a foretaste of the eternal joy that is yet to be. From this bountiful table in the wilderness, you find all that you need in order to live for and serve your Lord until then.

The strength and sustenance derived here will also stand you in good stead when trouble is near. Even then you may confidently say: *Yet I will rejoice in the LORD, I will joy in the God of my salvation. The LORD God is my strength, and he will make my feet like hinds' feet, and he will make me to walk upon mine high places.* (Habakkuk 3:18-19)

Study Questions

1. Identify both the sheep feeding on the hills and the shepherds who care for them. Briefly describe both sheep and shepherds and tell how they happen to be on the Delectable Mountains.

2. The first shepherd, Knowledge, represents what is probably the most fundamental qualification of God's ministers. His name signifies knowledge of a very comprehensive nature and particular sort. Give the various kinds of knowledge a minister of Christ needs in order to pastor the people of God.

3. The shepherd named Experience denotes the preparation of the man himself for the great task to which he has been called. Give some ways in which the Lord trains his men in the school of experience in order to be wise and godly leaders of his sheep.

4. In the third shepherd named Watchful, we find one of the chief duties of the minister of Christ. What are some of the ways in which the godly pastor watches over those who have been entrusted to his care? In what sense is he to also watch over himself?

5. Sincere, the fourth shepherd, expresses a character trait that is absolutely essential in the ministers of Christ. Write a brief character sketch of the man named Sincere, including how he stands in sharp contrast to the hireling.

CHAPTER 45

A Call to Higher Ground

THE DECLARATION OF GOD'S WORD IS THE VERY HEART AND SOUL OF THE church, the Palace Beautiful. It is her spiritual lifeline, vital to her very existence. Figuratively speaking, it is the secret stairs by which we reach the heights of the Delectable Mountains. When the ministry of the Word is diminished and relegated to a place of lesser importance, the church's lifeline is occluded and eventually severed. Therefore, straying in this direction places us at spiritual risk of the highest magnitude. Many a church has done so only to end up with a name that it lives when, in essence, it is dead. (Revelation 3:1)

Above all else, Scripture is to be central in the church and all the counsel of God faithfully proclaimed. (Acts 20:27) It is not enough for God's truth to be prominent. It must be pre-eminent, with everything else in subjection to and ruled by its authority. Through this divinely-appointed means, God regenerates sinners and continues his work of salvation in them. (Romans 10:13-17; 1 Timothy 4:13-16; Hebrews 2:1-3) It is to his chosen servants that he has committed this ministry of reconciliation. (2 Corinthians 5:17-21)

The ministers of Jesus Christ are given to his people in token of his eternal love. As such, they should be highly regarded for their works' sake and given an attentive, respectful hearing. (1 Thessalonians 5:12-13) By means of this gracious provision, God's people become strong in the faith so as to walk as lights in the midst of a perverse and ungodly generation. (Ephesians 4:11-13) However, spiritual growth must be carefully maintained, for like the Hebrew Christians, we also can become dull of hearing and have need of milk instead of strong meat. (Hebrews 5:11-12) The writer of Hebrews tells us further: *Every one that useth milk is unskillful in the word of righteousness: for he is a babe. But strong meat belongeth to them that are of full age, even those who by reason of use have their senses exercised to discern both good and evil.* (Hebrews 5:13-14)

The emphasis here is unmistakable. In the matter of our spiritual progress, it is not possible to maintain the status quo. Either we will continue to grow in the grace and knowledge of the Lord Jesus Christ or we will regress spiritually. Moreover, since regression is the first step toward apostasy, it places us on extremely dangerous ground. So we can never afford to be complacent as to our spiritual condition. It is only by giving diligent heed to the Word of God and putting it into daily practice that we advance toward spiritual maturity.

This principle was one that the shepherds of the Delectable Mountains understood full well. They took delight in teaching the truth, but also knew that not everyone would welcome or receive it. Some would reject them and the truth they declared, thus despising the gifts of God. However, the shepherds took comfort in knowing that the true sheep of Christ would hear and obey his voice as they proclaimed his Word.

As his faithful watchmen, the shepherds were not out to make a name for themselves. They had no higher joy than in seeing their hearers become true disciples of Jesus Christ. Therefore, they invested their lives in service to those who were eager to hear the Word of God and equally zealous to obey it. After their initial conversation with Christian and Hopeful, the shepherds were convinced that the two men were of this kind. Thus they gladly ministered to them of the Bread of Life, making the time spent by the shepherds' tent highly profitable to the weary travelers.

With the dawning of a new day, the shepherds invited Christian and Hopeful to accompany them to the upper regions of the Delectable Mountains. Some might regard an early morning walk around the property as little more than a pleasant form of exercise. But given our prior knowledge of both the shepherds and their field of service, we know that it signified a great deal more than that. It was an opportunity to scale those majestic heights and walk upon the mountaintops. Heeding this call to higher ground will give them an unparalleled view of the surrounding countryside.

Following the shepherds on a trek to the mountaintops will give added depth to the understanding that Christian and Hopeful already possessed. While the view from the lower regions was important, it was also sharply limited in scope. A much more comprehensive outlook lay in store for them once they reached the higher elevations. Spiritually speaking, they would see things in a larger context and a much clearer light. They would acquire deeper insight into truths already known and gain knowledge of things not seen as yet. This deeper knowledge would not come easily, however. It could only be gained as they braved the heights and reached the summit. In order to do so, strenuous effort would be required of them and of the shepherds as well.

The minister of Christ dares not presume to teach others unless he is first taught by the Spirit of God. The labor involved in studying God's Word in order to rightly interpret it demands the very best that he has to give, and something else besides. It requires his continual dependence upon the Spirit of truth. (John 16:13) Therefore, he must constantly abide in the Interpreter's House.

However, we must put forth a cooperative effort as well. In the matter of our spiritual instruction, we must be active participants if we are to achieve a competency in the Scriptures. Furthermore, we must earnestly seek to be taught by the Holy Spirit. If he does not instruct our hearts and enlighten our minds, we will be at a loss to receive and rightly comprehend the clearest, most excellent instruction in the truth.

It is significant that Christian and Hopeful agreed to follow God's men rather than preferring to make the climb alone. Even though they already possessed a fair amount of knowledge, they were keenly aware that the shepherds had far more wisdom and understanding than they. Moreover, their readiness to hear instruction showed a teachable spirit and humbleness of mind that placed them in the way of receiving even more. (Psalm 25:9)

Some professing Christians are content with a very basic level of knowledge. They are not serious students of the Word of God; consequently, they will never attain great heights of spiritual understanding. What about Christian and Hopeful? Were they willing to put forth the necessary effort, or would the shepherds be wasting their valuable time? Since the shepherds had already settled this matter in their minds, the little company headed toward the upper regions of the Delectable Mountains.

A fearful warning

The first hill they climbed was Mount Error. As they neared the top, Christian and Hopeful found it to be a place of deepening shadows with a thick gray mist hovering just above the ground. Those who are unfamiliar with the landscape can become disoriented in the mist, and many a soul has lost his way on this particular mountain. The side by which the men ascended was somewhat deceptive in nature. Its gradual incline gives no hint of the steep, treacherous cliff that forms the opposite face of the hill. So the grave danger just beyond the summit often goes undetected until it is too late.

As the shepherds led Christian and Hopeful close to the precipice, they instructed them to look over the edge and down the steep drop to the base of the mountain. Since there was little trace of fog on this side of Mount Error, Christian and Hopeful had an unobstructed view as they looked over the cliff. Far below, they saw the mangled bodies of several men who had stumbled over the edge and plunged to their death.

The gruesome sight must have shocked and unnerved the two men, for Christian could barely manage to ask, "What meaneth this?" The shepherds replied that the dead bodies lying at the foot of Mount Error were those who had embraced the heresy taught by Hymeneus and Philetus, which was that the resurrection was past. (2 Timothy 2:17-18) However, we understand that this is only one of many deadly errors that can overthrow the faith of those who are Christian in name only. There are as many false voices in the world today as in those early days of church history. Modern men who are reprobate concerning the faith are equally zealous to win others to their opinion. Since they are men of corrupt minds who resist the truth, they lure their unsuspecting followers to certain destruction. (2 Timothy 3:8)

It seems a terrible thing that the broken bodies of those who fell from Mount Error were allowed to remain unburied, but this was also by design. They serve as a grim reminder to others who might be tempted to follow their example. For like the children who ran after the Pied Piper of Hamelin, many are irresistibly drawn too near the brink of this treacherous cliff.

Mount Error is also a powerful lesson for those of us who are in Christ, since we cannot claim immunity to its allure. It reminds us that being well grounded in the truth is not enough. We must also give diligence to walk according to it, and shun those things that are contrary to it; for there is intrinsic danger involved in even giving an ear to that which is false. To do so is to climb too high and venture too close to the dangerous precipice of apostasy.

Therefore, the mount of Error is a thing to be scrupulously avoided, but this poses a significant challenge because we seem to meet it everywhere. Moreover, it beckons to us in a variety of forms, most notably through those who subtly pervert the Gospel until it is more agreeable to the natural mind. These deceivers accomplish this by replacing the offence of the cross with another gospel that has man and his temporal needs at its center. When measured according to the world's standards, their false gospel has been highly successful. Just look at the multitudes that embrace it!

What about those who know and love the truth? In a world in which false voices are heard all around us, how are we to discern truth from error? Solid instruction in the Word of God is the only effective antidote, and this is the Gospel minister's primary duty. However, as he faithfully declares the truth, he will encounter resistance from those who have become weary of sound doctrine. Ironically, many of them make an idol of knowledge, thus joining the ranks of those who are *ever learning, and never able to come to the knowledge of the truth.* (2 Timothy 3:7) In turning away their ears from the truth they will eventually be turned unto fables. (2 Timothy 4:4)

Every true minister of Christ has probably experienced the heartache of dealing with hearers of this sort. Some of them sit in his congregation for years, giving little hint of what lurks in their hearts. When at last their true character is exposed, those who were closest to them are often genuinely shocked. However, the man of God recognized the early signs of apostasy, yet hoped against hope that he was wrong.

This fearful reality brings a searching question to mind. What kind of person is most likely to delve into strange doctrine or give an ear to deadly error? In general, this is a greater temptation to one who is filled with intellectual pride and the desire for vainglory. In such a case, the pride of life prompts him to seek deeper and more extensive knowledge for its own sake. This quest often leads him into the realm of humanistic philosophy and other such things that contradict divinely revealed truth. So the quest for knowledge must be undertaken with an abundance of caution. It can lead the undiscerning soul directly to the summit of Mount Error.

Idle curiosity is another thing that can lure one to the brink of deadly error. Some people are like the Athenians and strangers who gathered to hear Paul speak from Mars' Hill. They did so not because they had a great desire to hear the Gospel, but because they loved to spend *their time in nothing else, but either to tell or to hear some new thing.* (Acts 17:21)

Whatever factors may enter into this equation, the minister of Christ must be on constant guard against the subtle influence of error and warn his flock not to venture too near its perilous brink. Those who have the truth abiding in their hearts will continue in the narrow way. Like the psalmist they can say: *Through thy precepts I get understanding: therefore I hate every false way. Thy word is a lamp unto my feet, and a light unto my path.* (Psalm 119:104-105) These divinely inspired words assure us that the path of the just, upon which the light of truth continually shines, will never lead us in the direction of Mount Error. Such was the experience of Christian and Hopeful. Thanks to the godly instruction of their spiritual leaders, they saw this hill as a thing to be deliberately shunned and avoided.

A shocking revelation

The shepherds knew, far better than the sheep they tended, that many hidden obstacles and enemies lie in wait along the royal road to Zion. Certain of these dangers pose more of a temptation to some than to others, for all travelers are not subject to the same weakness. Many would-be pilgrims find Mount Error to be an irresistible snare, while others have no inclination in that direction. Christian and Hopeful were apparently of the latter sort. Error did not seem to tempt them, and perhaps they congratulated themselves that they had escaped the fate of the poor souls who perished there.

Who can say for sure? Only Christian and Hopeful knew what was in their hearts, but is it not human nature to give ourselves credit when credit is not strictly due? How often have we heard a warning from Scripture and immediately thought of someone else rather than applying the warning to ourselves? How often have we judged another while turning a blind eye to our own failures and shortcomings? Dear reader, must we not be perfectly honest and plead guilty to these things?

Through long years of experience, the shepherds of the Delectable Mountains had become apt students of human nature. Therefore, they were keenly aware of this sinful tendency. In dealing with many difficult situations they learned to be patient teachers of slow learners, instructing in the truth *precept upon precept; line upon line…here a little, and there a little.* (Isaiah 28:10) This they did in order that their people might be established upon the solid rock, upon Christ the precious corner stone and sure foundation of his Church. (Isaiah 28:16)

As to the nature of their instruction, it is important to remember that the range known as the Delectable Mountains consists of numerous peaks, each affording its own unique view. Various lessons are to be learned here, much like those taught in the Interpreter's House. However, I suspect that not all travelers see the same view while there. The Spirit of God deals with us as individuals by rebuking, correcting, and teaching that which is of the greatest spiritual benefit to each of us personally. So it was with Christian and Hopeful. They will be shown several specific views, and each one will bear relevance to their particular situation. But the view from the next mountain will deal them a stunning blow!

On that particular day, the prospect from atop Mount Caution was of a land of darkness and gloom. A storm was brewing in the far distance, for ominous clouds were gathering along the horizon, broken through here and there by intermittent streaks of lightning. The air was warm and sultry, with not the slightest breeze stirring. Except for the occasional rumble of thunder, an uncanny silence filled the region, for even the birds had hushed their singing. It was the calm before the storm.

As the little group stood on the summit of the mountain, the shepherds told Christian and Hopeful to study the view before them. The lay of the land was vaguely familiar, for after all, they had passed that way earlier. But they now saw a thing that had completely escaped their notice before. Although the startled men looked twice in order to assure themselves that their eyes did not deceive them, the gruesome vision was all too real.

Far in the distance they saw an ancient burial ground filled with broken-down tombstones and once-grand monuments, now fallen into varying stages of decay. A rusty iron fence with a huge double gate enclosed the cemetery, and a canopy of gnarled trees draped thickly with Spanish moss completed the gloomy effect. To the vivid imagination it was an eerie place, downright spooky in fact! Still, there is nothing so unusual about that. Many such ancient graveyards are to be found.

Christian and Hopeful were merely curious at first, but their attention was soon riveted upon a sight that completely unnerved them. Several men were stumbling among the tombs, groping blindly and obviously unable to find their way out of the graveyard. Even from such a great distance, they seemed like dead men walking. This unexpected and ghastly sight caused Christian's heart rate to increase significantly. Nevertheless, he managed to ask the shepherds, "What means this?"

Dear reader, I seriously doubt that their explanation caused his pulse and blood pressure to return to normal. Imagine how he felt when the shepherds asked Christian if he and Hopeful had noticed a stile that led into a nearby meadow. We may safely assume that he was stunned by this question, and perhaps even wondered if the shepherds could read his mind. Such is the power of a guilty conscience.

When he and Hopeful answered "Yes," the shepherds explained that there was a path leading directly from the stile to Doubting Castle, owned by one named Giant Despair. (How well Christian and Hopeful remembered the stile, the meadow, the giant and his awful fortress!) Then the shepherds linked this explanation with the men who were wandering among the tombs. Once they had claimed to be pilgrims, but when they reached the rough section of road near the stile, they chose the easier path through its adjacent meadow. In time, each of them had been captured by Despair and cast into his prison fortress. After the giant was finished with them, he blinded them and drove them to the tombs where they now wandered, perpetually lost. (Proverbs 21:16)

As Christian and Hopeful now discovered, the stile into By-Path Meadow appeared in an entirely different light when viewed from the top of Mount Caution. Doubting Castle with its cemetery of lost souls was closer to the King's Highway than they ever imagined. The pitiful, sightless wanderers who were the victims of Giant Despair represented the souls of those whose bones now littered his courtyard. So metaphorically speaking, they really were dead men walking! Once they were professing Christians who made it down the road to the Celestial City as far as the stile into By-Path Meadow. However, when imprisoned in the dungeon of Doubting Castle they eventually yielded to despair, abandoned hope, and renounced their faith. How could that happen? They were never true pilgrims at all, and their ordeal at the hands of Despair made clear the fact. As a result, the light they once claimed to have had been extinguished forever. (Hebrews 6:4-8)

Now they were openly numbered among the spiritually blind, and doomed to wander without hope in the abode of the dead. Saddest of all, this was their true condition all along. However, it was not made known until they crossed the stile into By-Path Meadow.

At last, Christian and Hopeful realized the full extent of their former peril. They now understood clearly that there is no more dangerous misstep than to stray from our designated path. God is in no way obliged to deliver us from such a false step, although he may be merciful and do so. In describing the fate of the blind men, the shepherds expressed exactly what had also happened to Christian and Hopeful, except for the final outcome. How easily they could have been numbered among the living dead! Had they not also wandered out of the way and followed Vain-Confidence? Had they not also been taken captive by the giant and thrown into the depths of despair? Did they not remember seeing the bones scattered in the castle courtyard? Why had they been recovered when so many others have perished there?

What better time for the two brethren to reflect upon the greatness of God's mercy to them! He alone had delivered them from despair that was so complete it had threatened to destroy them. Christian and Hopeful were saved from themselves because they were Christ's own sheep and their names were written in the Lamb's book of life. (Revelation 21:27). The Word of God had taken deep root in their hearts; therefore, faith prevailed in the end. Remembrance brought hope, and hope secured their deliverance. However, they had nothing in themselves of which to boast. The Lord permitted them to be seized and tormented by despair as a result of their sin. Yet he kept them from being consumed by it because his compassions fail not. They are new every morning. (Lamentations 3:21-23) How the realization must have caused their hearts to rejoice and to cry with the weeping prophet: *Great is thy faithfulness*!

It is a fearful thing to know that the light of intellectual knowledge, apart from genuine faith, will eventually be turned to darkness. The terrible fate of the blind men wandering among the tombs was a sight that Christian and Hopeful were not likely to ever forget. Stunned by all they had seen and heard, they looked at one another with tears flowing from their eyes. Feelings of guilt and remorse were mixed with joy and thankfulness to God. The view from Mount Caution spoke loudly to them both of just how narrow their escape had been, and how much they owed to the goodness and mercy of God. The contemplation of it temporarily robbed them of the power of speech. However, I suspect that this was not the only reason they said nothing to the shepherds about their own experience with the stile into By-Path Meadow.

The next stop on their survey of the Delectable Mountains required that Christian and Hopeful descend to the lower regions once again. As they stood near the base of a nameless hill, the shepherds called their attention to a small door in its side. Perhaps Christian and Hopeful recalled the hill named Lucre and wondered if this door was the entrance to another mine of some sort. However, when the shepherds opened the door and told Christian and Hopeful to look inside, what they saw and heard must have made their blood run cold.

A vast chasm lay beyond the door, but because all was dark and smoky within, the two men could actually see very little. Yet they could hear the roaring sound as of a great furnace and the horrid cries of those in torment. Moreover, the air was so filled with sulfurous fumes and the acrid stench of brimstone that the atmosphere beyond the door was stifling. Clearly, no one could enter there and live!

Even though Christian must have had a good idea of the answer he asked: "What means this?" The shepherds replied that the door was "a by-way to Hell, a way that Hypocrites go in at." They further explained that this was the doom of such as Esau, Judas, Alexander the Coppersmith and Ananias and Sapphira. Since Christian and Hopeful had a good foundation of Bible knowledge, they immediately recognized these names and recalled their histories. The remembrance prompted Hopeful to say, "I perceive that these had on them, even every one, a shew of Pilgrimage, as we have now, had they not?" One of the shepherds answered in the affirmative, reinforcing Hopeful's observation that not all who set out for the Celestial City would actually make it there.

How frightening to consider that the gateway to hell lies near the base of the Delectable Mountains! What a tragic thing it is for some to perish right where the truth is faithfully proclaimed! Yet given the spiritual significance of the Delectable Mountains, there is no other way to interpret the meaning of this little door. To be under the sound of the Gospel lays a heavy responsibility upon the hearers. Its truth will either be unto them a savor of life unto life, or death unto death. (2 Corinthians 2:14-17) Eternal destruction is the end of the hypocrite's hope, and the truly wise will lay this to heart.

Christian and Hopeful did just that. Recent experience had shaken their inclination to vain confidence, and that was a very good thing. Moreover, the instruction of the shepherds reinforced the painful lesson by giving them deeper insight into things not fully understood before. So viewing this fearful sight and pondering its meaning had a beneficial effect upon them both. Rather than dismissing it as having no relevance to them, the two men were moved to a healthy self-examination and the resolve to watch their step much more carefully. Just because the Lord had delivered them from a terrible fate, they dared not presume upon his mercy to do so again. Neither could they afford to dwell upon past victories. They were still a good way from the city and had many dangers yet to face.

How the shepherds must have rejoiced in heart when Christian and Hopeful looked at one another and spoke the same thought aloud: "We had need cry to the Strong for strength"! Yes, they had learned a valuable lesson and the shepherds were careful not to say anything that would diminish its effect. They merely replied: "Ay, and you will have need to use it, when you have it, too."

O, dear brother or sister in Christ, so do we! Like Christian and Hopeful, we must take these things to heart and give diligence to make our calling and election sure. Hypocrisy and vain confidence are temptations to us as well. Therefore, like the fourth shepherd, we must continually strive to be sincere and honest in our profession of faith in Christ. Our confidence must ever and always be in him alone.

Undeniably, the view of the side door to hell is deeply troubling, especially since many of those who perished there had the outward appearance of being Christian. Therefore, this thought should trouble us in light of what is at stake. An honest self-examination is crucial lest we be deceived about the foundation of our hope. As an added benefit, we will come to realize all the more, how much we need God's strength to keep us from falling. (Jude 24-25)

A homeward look

At this point in their survey of the Delectable Mountains, Christian and Hopeful felt ready to resume their journey. After all, they could not possibly take in all there was to learn in a single visit. Before they departed, however, the shepherds wished to show them one more thing. So far, each view had contained a warning of grave dangers to be faced as we sojourn through this life. The purpose of such warning is not to terrify or discourage, but to admonish and strengthen us in the faith. All is designed to speed us on our way, fix our sights more closely upon our eternal goal, and increase our longing for our heavenly home. Therefore, the shepherds agreed together that Christian and Hopeful must not leave the Delectable Mountains with only these fearful sights in heart and mind.

The heights of the Delectable Mountains also provide a completely different view, but it can only be seen from Mount Clear, located at the far end of the mountain range. From that distant summit, it is possible to catch a glimpse of the Celestial Gate even though the city is still far away. For this purpose the shepherds have a "Perspective-Glass" designed to enhance one's vision, but only those with adequate skill to use it are able to locate the Celestial Gate.

What a prime illustration of how much we need the continual instruction in God's Word! How limited we are in our capacity to receive and retain its precepts and apply them consistently to everyday life situations. A vital part of the Gospel ministry is to sharpen our focus so that we are able to see and understand spiritual realities more clearly. Each view from the Delectable Mountains requires spiritual vision in order to rightly interpret it, but those who are more mature in the Lord will comprehend it best. It is a sight reserved for those whose treasure is laid up in heaven, and whose minds are not engrossed with the cares and troubles of this life. So this final view from the heights will be most clearly seen by those whose eyes are already steadfastly fixed in that direction.

Dear reader, I am sure you have already surmised that the shepherds' looking glass was not a pair of high-powered binoculars. It was the very Word of God, which is essential in taking this long view. Our Christian experience must always be weighed in the light of God's Word if we are to rightly interpret it, and our spiritual perspective must be firmly rooted in and conformed to the same infallible standard. When this is not the case, we can become easily distracted, even side-tracked. However, with God's Word as our chart and compass, and his Spirit as our helper, guide and teacher, we are not likely to leave the paths of uprightness or walk in the ways of darkness. (Proverbs 2:13)

Figuratively speaking, the shepherds had saved the best wine until last. Perhaps Christian and Hopeful would catch a glimpse of their eternal destination, for conditions were favorable on the day they stood atop Mount Clear and gazed through the looking glass. The air was crisp and clean at that altitude and the sky blue and cloudless. Yet even though Christian and Hopeful tried their best to locate the Celestial City, they faced an impediment that had nothing to do with atmospheric conditions. The remembrance of the door to hell cast such a shadow over their minds that they could not see clearly enough. But for all that, they could faintly perceive the gate of the city and a small measure of its glory.

Like the numerous chambers in the Interpreter's House, the multiple views seen from the Delectable Mountains prompt both hope and fear in the Christian's heart. It is a healthy and profitable balance because each summit teaches a valuable lesson, and all are equally important. Mount Error, Mount Caution, and the by-way to hell were fearful warnings that would be long remembered. Each of them would temper any tendency to carnal security even while nurturing a proper fear. Unbelieving fear is a deadly enemy, as Christian and Hopeful could personally attest; but the fear of God encourages our hearts and keeps our feet in the proper path. (Jeremiah 32:38-40)

The view from Mount Clear is especially designed to strengthen our faith and hasten our steps along the pathway to Zion. From its summit we can catch a glimpse of the glory that lies ahead, if we are skillful enough in the use of God's Word. This fact should be an added incentive for us to be diligent students of the Word. The more clearly we understand the Gospel, the better we will comprehend and the more eagerly we will anticipate the promised joy that awaits us.

Christian and Hopeful had a song in their hearts as they prepared to leave the Delectable Mountains, for such is the beneficial effect of time spent here. Moreover, they now had an even higher regard and appreciation for those who watched for their souls. So even though they were ready to be on their way, Christian and Hopeful gave their full attention to the shepherds' final words of admonition.

By nature of their calling, these special servants of Christ knew what lay ahead of Christian and Hopeful. Therefore, their highest concern was that the two men continue as they had begun and arrive safely at their heavenly destination. In order to do so, they must stay on course for the rest of the way. To this end, each shepherd had a parting word of caution and exhortation, travel instructions if you will. If taken to heart and remembered, their wise counsel would spare Christian and Hopeful many a grief in the days ahead.

The first shepherd gave the two men a "Note of the Way," a map to follow that would keep them in the right path. This note of direction admonished them to keep the Word of God ever in heart and mind, seek its wisdom continually, and walk in its precepts day by day. In brief, they were to remember what they had been taught and make continual use of it. Those who do these things walk in the realm of divine promise, the Lord's own promise given to his obedient children. (Proverbs 4:10-13)

The next shepherd warned Christian and Hopeful to "Beware of the Flatterer," clearly implying that they would encounter such a person somewhere along the way. This rather enigmatic warning is one that none of us can afford to ignore. In conjunction with the view from Mount Error, it places us on notice that as long as we are in the world, we will face things that could lead us astray if we give heed to them. (1 John 5:19-20) Nor are these chance encounters! The Flatterer has one fixed purpose, and that is to lure us out of the path of life. (Proverbs 26:28) However, our note of the way will help us recognize him and resist his evil design. (Psalm 16:11) To the truly wise, to be forewarned is to be forearmed.

The pastoral instruction given by the first two shepherds was very closely connected. Knowledge of the truth, and our continual walking in it, will keep us on course and protect us from the subtle lies of the Flatterer. This is easy enough within the safety of the Delectable Mountains. Outside of this protective fold, however, we venture into the realm and influence of the prince of darkness. Deceivers abound who will attempt to lead us astray and shipwreck our faith, if possible. But through the help of God's Spirit and his infallible Word to lighten our way, we can elude the net of the Flatterer.

The third shepherd added a further word of caution by instructing Christian and Hopeful to take care and not sleep on the Enchanted Ground. They would remember this strange admonition later on in their journey. For now, however, they must have wondered just where the Enchanted Ground was and why it was so dangerous to sleep there.

The parting word from the last shepherd was quite different from that of the other three, just as the final view from Mount Clear differed greatly from all the rest. He spoke but two words, "God Speed." To some, this may have sounded like a mere formality or brief courtesy extended to a departing guest, but it was actually much more than that. This parting benediction was a pastoral blessing upon men who were regarded and loved as true brethren in Christ. Furthermore, it expressed his prayer that God's blessing would be upon Christian and Hopeful, keeping them safe and speeding them on their way.

* * * *

Like the shepherds of the Delectable Mountains, godly pastors love to lead their people to new heights of spiritual understanding, but not simply to make Bible scholars of us. Their chief desire is the same as the apostle John's, who wrote: *I have no greater joy than to hear that my children walk in truth.* (3 John 4) Moreover, they ask no greater reward than to see their people become the humble, obedient servants of Jesus Christ. So it is with our eternal welfare ever in heart and mind that they give their utmost in order to feed our souls and lead us into an ever-increasing knowledge of our Lord and Savior Jesus Christ. (Colossians 1:9-10)

Our ultimate safety lies in making diligent use of God's appointed means for our spiritual growth and maturity. (2 Peter 3:17-18) However, God's people vary widely in their ability to receive and assimilate spiritual instruction. In any given congregation of true believers, you will find those at every level of spiritual understanding. The Word of God is the only proper nourishment for them all, but some will feast on meat while others are only able to digest milk. The wise pastor knows this well, and yet, it makes his task of feeding his flock a challenging one.

If you recall, young lambs grazed in the pastures of the Delectable Mountains along with full-grown sheep. Since these little ones are of particular concern to the shepherds, they watch over them with special care. Likewise, the man of God carefully nurtures the lambs among his congregation. With loving eyes he watches over them and rejoices to see them growing in Christ. Nor does he neglect the rest of his flock. As he declares God's Word to his people, there is bread for all the children of God, whatever their level of spiritual maturity happens to be.

I am so thankful that God has purposed us to grow together in company with those of like precious faith, feeding by the shepherd's tents and following the footsteps of the flock. In so doing we follow Christ, the chief shepherd. Although his church was never intended to be a social organization, we do prefer the fellowship of God's people to any other. After all, as part of the body of Christ, we are members one of another. (1 Corinthians 12:12) We comprise a spiritual organism, a temple composed of living stones, a building fitly framed together forming a holy temple in the Lord. (Ephesians 2:21) We are the household of God growing together into conformity to Christ, each at his own pace. We are a band of brothers, marching onward and upward to Zion under the royal standard of Zion's King!

My brother or sister in Christ, a glorious future is ours. The view from Mount Clear reminds us that our portion is not in this life, and truly, the best is yet to be. If, perhaps, the anticipation of our eternal inheritance is clouded by the remembrance of past failures and shortcomings, it is because our eyes are too focused upon ourselves. Therefore, let us take heart and steadfastly look unto our Lord Jesus Christ, the captain of our salvation. By his good pleasure and in his time, he will bring many sons to glory. (Hebrews 2:10) So even though we now view our glorious destiny through a glass darkly and know but in part, one day soon we will see him face to face. (1 Corinthians 13:12)

Study Questions

1. The declaration of God's Word is the church's spiritual lifeline. It is vital to her very existence. How were the shepherds of the Delectable Mountains faithful to their calling to preach the whole counsel of God? In what sense did they lead Christian and Hopeful to higher ground?

2. A fearful warning lay just beyond the summit of Mount Error. What particular danger did this hill represent? What invaluable lessons are to be learned there?

3. The view from atop Mount Caution dealt Christian and Hopeful a stunning blow. Briefly describe what they saw from there, and why it was such a shocking revelation. How did they react when

they finally realized how narrow their escape from Doubting Castle had been?

4. As Christian and Hopeful stood at the base of a nameless hill, the shepherds pointed out a small door in the hillside. What did this door represent? What fearful possibility does it imply, given its location so near the Delectable Mountains? What effect did the horrific view have upon Christian and Hopeful?

5. Describe the view that could be seen from the summit of Mount Clear. What does the perspective glass represent, and how does looking through it give us clearer vision? What did Christian and Hopeful see when they looked homeward through the looking glass? Why was their vision somewhat cloudy that day?

Part Sixteen

THROUGH MANY A DANGER, TOIL, AND SNARE

No weapon that is formed against thee shall prosper; and every tongue that shall rise against thee in judgment thou shalt condemn. This is the heritage of the servants of the LORD, and their righteousness is of me, saith the LORD.
Isaiah 54:17

CHAPTER 46

Spiritual Ignorance and its Bitter Fruit

How important is the beginning of a thing? It is undoubtedly the most critical part, seeing that a thing is not likely to continue well unless it began well? Nothing can compensate for the lack of a proper foundation, not even a brilliant design and perfect construction. The most substantial of structures will fail to stand the test of time if built upon a faulty or inadequate foundation. Likewise, the most compelling philosophies of the greatest minds will eventually implode without a basis of truth. Therefore, a proper foundation is essential as concerns earthly things. Of how much more importance, then, is it to matters of eternal consequence?

It is certain that no one will persevere in faith unless he first began in faith, but how is this foundation laid? We know that the Spirit of God gives the gift of faith, which has the Lord Jesus Christ as its sole object and foundation. (1 Corinthians 3:11) All true believers have this firm foundation in common. It is, in fact, the bond that joins our hearts to one another. Each of us entered the path of life by the narrow gate at its head, and we all follow the same path afterward, the way of the cross.

However, as we travel along the royal road to Zion, we encounter many who entered the path by another way. These are not true pilgrims, but imposters wearing many disguises and called by many different names. We have met quite a few of them already: Mr. Worldly

Wiseman, Mr. Legality, Civility, Simple, Sloth, Presumption, Formalist, Hypocrisy, Talkative, Demas, and By-ends come quickly to mind.

While these characters differ widely from one another in both situation and temperament, all of them share some notable things in common. Each one claimed to believe, but their so-called faith was based upon a false premise. To a man, they rejected the truth concerning Christ and his salvation, and refused to be shaken from their carnal assurance. Therefore, their expectation of reaching the Celestial City was founded upon a false hope. Some of them turned out of the path of life at some point, but others will maintain their vain hope until the end of their lives.

Thus all who turn from the truth do not lie dead at the foot of Mount Error. Nor do they all wander among the tombs near Doubting Castle. Many such people walk freely among us, even along the King's Highway.

As Christian and Hopeful descended to level ground, they passed close by the country of Conceit located near the base of the rolling hills. A "little crooked lane" from that country merged into the King's Highway at that point, on the left side of the road. But is it not strange that such a place was located so close to the Delectable Mountains?

As Christian and Hopeful approached this intersection, they saw a young man enter the highway via the little crooked lane. This man, whom John Bunyan describes as a "very brisk lad," was a native son of the country of Conceit, and rather proud of it. Like the Wiseman from Carnal Policy, he had a pretty high opinion of himself and was not timid about expressing his views, especially on the subject of religion.

How ironic, considering that his name was Ignorance! In common with his fellow citizens, his name denotes his true character. Although he made a pretense of having great knowledge, he was destitute of the truth, and therefore, lacking in both wisdom and spiritual understanding. Seeing that he lived so near to where the truth was faithfully taught, there was no excuse for his ignorance. But then, his problem was not merely the lack of sufficient instruction, nor did it have anything to do with his intelligence. What he lacked was the fear and knowledge of God.

Since Christian had no idea of the young man's identity at first, he might have wondered if he and Hopeful had met the Flatterer already.

After the shepherds' explicit warning, it would be understandable if they were a bit wary of strangers. In response to Christian's inquiry, Ignorance answered that he was born in the country located just a little to the left of the pathway, but he did not mention its name. Nevertheless, when he added that he was on the way to the Celestial City, Christian immediately saw a difficulty with the young man's being admitted therein.

Why would Christian suspect the lad's spiritual condition from the outset? Was he judging unfairly, or meddling in something that was none of his business by questioning him about it? I don't think so. Christian's suspicion had a solid basis in fact. Therefore, it was out of genuine concern that he challenged Ignorance about his hope of salvation.

The young man's answer was highly illuminating. It revealed that his hope was based entirely upon his own merit, good works, and the fact that he was outwardly moral and dealt honestly with others. In short, he trusted in his own righteousness to get him into heaven. Furthermore, John Bunyan's description of him as "brisk" was quite right, because he was both energetic and conscientious in the performance of good deeds and religious duties. Yet he did so for all the wrong reasons.

While some were undoubtedly impressed by his show of piety, his own words proved that Ignorance nurtured a vain hope. He made no mention of Christ and his redemption, nor did he give evidence of a penitent heart, the consciousness of sin, or his need of cleansing and forgiveness. Although he claimed to believe certain aspects of the Gospel, he rejected those things that he found personally offensive. Therefore, his brand of faith lacked the essential elements of true repentance and obedience to the Gospel. (Mark 1:15; Romans 16:26; 1 Peter 4:17)

In summing up his hope of eternal life, the young man argued that he had left his native country and was now going to the Celestial City. Apparently, nothing could shake his confidence. It was true that he had left the country of Conceit, but it had not left him. He had no new birth, no new heart, and no new name. Yet in spite of all evidence to the contrary, he still fancied himself a pilgrim.

Since Christian was not content to leave matters as they were, he tried a firmer approach in reasoning with the young man. The thing that troubled Christian from the very first was the way in which Ignorance had entered the King's Highway. Rather than entering by way of the Wicket Gate, he did so from the little crooked lane that led from the place of his natural birth. This is an insurmountable obstacle, as Christian knew full well. Seeing as the Wicket Gate is the focal point upon which the destiny of the soul rests, to miss it is to surely miss the Celestial Gate as well. Yet Ignorance was adamant that the little by-path from his hometown served as an entrance to the path of life just as well as the Wicket Gate.

Christian then made so bold as to declare Ignorance a thief and a robber by trying to enter some other way. (John 10:1) By missing the door of the sheepfold, he had no legitimate claim to be one of Christ's sheep. However, he still refused to see that his hope of eternal life was vain.

As Ignorance responded to Christian's arguments, it became clear that his heart was so hardened he was unmoved by what should have alarmed him. Moreover, when he said, "Gentlemen, ye be utter Strangers to me, I know you not," he spoke more truth than he imagined. In a spiritual sense, he did not speak the same language as Christian and Hopeful. He had nothing in common with them, and therefore, no basis for fellowship with them, or they with him.

The best answer he could give was to suggest that Christian and Hopeful "be content to follow the Religion of your country, and I will follow the Religion of mine." It was his considered opinion that any religion would suffice as long as one was sincere. Thus we could summarize his philosophy in a single phrase. To each his own! You do your thing and I will do mine! You serve and worship God as you see fit but grant me the same privilege! There is no need to argue about religion, for are we not all working toward the same place? No, Ignorance, we are not!!

So when Ignorance continued to defend his position by saying, "I hope all will be well," he expressed an extraordinary hope that had no basis whatsoever. (Titus 3:5) But then, no one could ever accuse him of lacking self-assurance. He was truly convinced that his good works were more than enough to gain him an entrance into the Celestial City.

There was also the matter of the Wicket Gate. Since Ignorance felt that he must answer Christian's concerns in that regard, he argued that the Wicket Gate was far away from the country of Conceit. (In this, he certainly spoke truth!) He then told Christian that the men of Conceit did not know the way to the Wicket Gate, nor did they desire to know it. The "little crooked lane," was right at hand, and it was a "fine pleasant green lane."

Here is a telling revelation. The young man's ignorance did not stem from the fact that he had not heard of the Wicket Gate, for clearly he had. His ignorance was rooted in deliberate rejection of the truth that salvation is in Christ Jesus alone. In so saying, he also expressed the mindset of the rest of his countrymen.

Could Christian and Hopeful have met the Flatterer already? Not likely, since they quickly saw through the character of the man Ignorance. Although his name might seem to suggest it, he was by no means mentally deficient. His problem was that pride ruled in his heart. He was wise in his own conceit, which degrades an otherwise rational and intelligent human being to the rank of fool. Worse than a fool, really! (Proverbs 26:12)

While the Lord looks upon a broken, contrite heart with tenderness and great compassion, he deals very differently with the proud in heart. (Psalm 34:18; Isaiah 57:15; Proverbs 6:16-17; Proverbs 16:5; James 4:6) Even when one seems to escape God's anger and righteous indignation for a time, a proud spirit eventually betrays those who are ruled by it. Thus pride is the ultimate folly.

So Christian and Hopeful did Ignorance no injustice when they assessed his character. He may have been quite knowledgeable in other respects, but he was destitute of the knowledge of God. Moreover, his proud spirit rendered him incapable of receiving the truth. Therefore, he was like the fool in Ecclesiastes 10:3 who *walkest by the way*. His boasted wisdom exposed his folly openly, but he could not see it.

At this point, Christian and Hopeful were in conflict about what to do next. Should they attempt to talk further with the young man or leave him alone for the time being? They were not indifferent to him, nor is there any indication that they despised him for his spiritual ignorance. On the contrary, they cared enough for his soul to tell him the truth, even though he refused to believe it. Furthermore, they were unwilling to give up on him. For the present, however, they decided to give him time to reflect upon what he had heard. Perhaps they would have another opportunity to talk with him in the future. So they picked up their pace and hastened down the King's Highway, while he lagged behind.

Since human pride goes hand-in-hand with spiritual ignorance, it is perfectly consistent with being destitute of the truth. (1 Timothy 6:3-5) Moreover, as Christian and Hopeful discovered from this latest encounter, it is virtually impossible to correct those who are wise in their own eyes. Pride creates such a powerful barrier in the heart and mind that it causes one to resist and reject even the most obvious truth.

Speaking through his prophet Jeremiah, God declared: *Is not my word like as a fire? saith the LORD; and like a hammer that breaketh the rock in pieces?* (Jeremiah 23:29) Truly the Word of God is the hammer that brings down the strongholds of the evil one, by which he keeps the hearts and minds of men in bondage to sin. Figuratively speaking, they are altars dedicated to the gods of human reason, worldly philosophy, and false religion, all of which blind men's minds to the truth.

These mighty strongholds must be broken down before the truth can be established. (Jeremiah 1:8-10; 2 Corinthians 10:3-6) It is a daunting task that requires both forceful action and a brave heart, but cannot be accomplished with weapons of conventional warfare. The Gospel of Christ alone has the power to break down the strongholds that resist and war against the truth. His Gospel of peace alone is the power of God unto salvation. (Romans 1:16)

The Holy Spirit makes this mighty weapon effective in the hearts of men. Through the Gospel, he breaks down every barrier when he regenerates the sinner. Thus he who was proud and wise in his own conceit before, willingly bows at the feet of the Lord Jesus Christ and confesses him as Lord. Pride is dethroned in his heart; humility and godly fear take its place. As a result, the child of God will demonstrate a teachable spirit that seeks instruction from those who are wiser than he. (Psalm 25:4-9; Proverbs 1:5-7) But what about the man named Ignorance? Can he yet be convinced of the error of his ways, or is he beyond hope? Only time will tell.

Although it is tempting to dismiss Ignorance as a rather pathetic, harmless character, he and his kind can cause considerable trouble when they join themselves to God's people. Behind a mask of religious hypocrisy, they often cause divisions and offenses contrary to sound doctrine. Moreover, through the use of clever words and fair speech, they can deceive the hearts of the simple. The apostle Paul gave explicit instructions as to how we are to deal with such people when he said to mark them and avoid them. (Romans 16:17-18)

In just a little while, Christian and Hopeful will discover that spiritual ignorance is an ever-present danger, even for those who have taken a bold stand for the truth. Perhaps it is even more so then. We will not be safe from this temptation as long as we are in the world, no matter how far we have advanced in grace. As the apostle Peter made clear in his second epistle, those who are called to glory and virtue must also give diligence to make their calling and election sure. (2 Peter 1:3, 10) Virtue must be added to virtue if we are to be *neither barren nor unfruitful in the knowledge of our Lord Jesus Christ.* (2 Peter 1:5-8) Moreover, truth believed must become truth remembered and put to good use if we would have an abundant entrance into his everlasting kingdom. (2 Peter 1:11)

Shortly after Christian and Hopeful parted company with Ignorance, they entered into what John Bunyan describes as a "very dark lane." It was a sinister-looking place in which they witnessed a sight so ghastly that it held them spellbound. Coming toward them was a man who had been bound with seven ropes and was being carried against his will by seven devils back to the door they had seen in the side of the hill.

How well the two men remembered that door! Therefore, they trembled for the poor man, knowing what his fate was to be. I suspect that they trembled for themselves as well, remembering the other awful sights from the Delectable Mountains. It may also have alarmed them to see that the man was being carried backwards, meaning that he had made it further down the path of life than they had up to that point. The condemned man had once claimed to be a pilgrim on the way to the Celestial City!

As he was forcibly carried past them, Christian thought he recognized the man as one named Turn-away, from the town of Apostasy. Christian was not sure, however, since the wretched man hung his head in shame. Once the man had passed them by, Hopeful took a closer look at him and noticed that he wore a placard on his back, which said: "Wanton Professor, and damnable Apostate." How very like the man in the iron cage! He was facing eternity in the fixed character of an imposter whose disguise had finally been torn away. Now that it was too late, there was nothing left for him but fearful judgment and everlasting shame.

* * * *

In reflecting upon the disturbing nature of this chapter, I cannot help but wonder about the possible connection between the men named Ignorance and Turn-away. Is there any substantial difference between the religious hypocrite and the apostate, or are they essentially the same? I am persuaded that the latter is true since both pretended to be something they were not. If this is correct, the accounts of Ignorance and Turn-away are closely related. Like Formalist and Hypocrisy, each of them portrays an aspect of the nominal Christian. Their histories emphasize the point that while there is only one Wicket Gate, many alternate ways exist by which men hope to reach the Celestial City. But tragically, all of them are little crooked lanes that lead to certain destruction.

Intellectual understanding of the truth is not enough, and neither is a pretense of godliness. Both Ignorance and Turn-away assumed the outward form of a Christian, but never possessed the true character. Under the guise of outward morality and religious talk, they often managed to deceive others, but neither man had experienced a work of divine grace in his soul. Both of them had missed Christ. One of them would carry his false hope until the end of his life, while the other renounced his profession of faith. Both, however, would share the same eternal doom.

The root of this problem lies deep within the human heart. A false professor can no more change his own heart than the medieval alchemist could transmute base metal into gold. (Jeremiah 13:23) The miracle of regeneration is solely the work of God's Spirit, and it never fails to produce spiritual fruit. However, outward profession without the new birth will never go deeper than the superficial. Thus the mask of religious hypocrisy may be likened unto wood veneer covering a piece of furniture. It is beautiful when new, but fragile and easily nicked when subjected to constant use. Once its surface has been broken, the wood veneer can be easily stripped away. The very same thing is true of the religious hypocrite or apostate at heart.

It is interesting that Christian thought he recognized the man named Turn-away. Although this is the first that we have heard of him, Christian must have seen him in the past. Could the two have met earlier, perhaps in the Palace Beautiful? After all, Turn-away once claimed to believe in Christ. This may have been the case, since Christian was obviously acquainted with his history.

How long did he maintain the appearance of following Christ before his true character was made known? How long had he been a church member? How many years had he heard the Word of God proclaimed? Who can say? In all probability he was enlightened to the truth to some extent. Perhaps he had observed the work of God's Spirit in others, a work in which he had no part. Self was central in his life, not the Lord Jesus Christ. Thus he had no vital interest in the things of God.

This being the case, he could easily grow negligent without feeling the pangs of conscience that would torment a true child of God. Moreover, he was the kind of person that was a potential troublemaker. Since pride, bitterness, and discontentment lurked just beneath the surface, he was capable of causing dissension and strife in the body of Christ, with little or no provocation. (Jude 12-13)

For whatever reason, Turn-away eventually had enough. Perhaps someone or something offended him and he used that as an excuse to depart. Yet in reality, he turned from the truth in order to return to that which his heart desired all along. Thus his latter end will be far worse than if he had never professed to be a Christian. (Matthew 12:43-45; Hebrews 6:4-8; 2 Peter 2:20-22)

Why did Christian and Hopeful need to personally witness the awful demise of Turn-away? After all, there is a great contrast between the character of those who truly fear God and those who make a mere pretense of it. However, the difference between the two is not always readily apparent. Perhaps Christian and Hopeful needed to behold the downfall of Turn-away so that they might learn not to judge according to outward appearance.

At times, it seems to us that those who wear a mask of religious hypocrisy get away with it, and this may indeed be the case, as far as we can tell. They walk in pride, boast of their own righteousness, and flaunt their good works while looking down upon others and despising them. Yet for all that, they seem to prosper. (Psalm 73:1-2) Like the writer of Psalm 73, we will find this extremely vexing, especially when we are under affliction. (See verses 13-16) To make matters worse at such times, the religious hypocrite may add insult to injury by assuming the role of Job's comforters when judging us.

But consider their end, dear friend in Christ, and while doing so, consider your end as well! (Psalm 73:16-26) We will be less likely to judge according to outward circumstances if we keep these two things firmly in heart and mind. If you think about it, this latest experience of Christian and Hopeful reinforced what they had already seen from the Delectable Mountains. It serves as a valuable reminder to us as well.

Outright apostasy does not occur overnight. It takes place gradually as the result of small lapses and neglects, very like the aforementioned wood veneer, chipping away a little at a time until a once-beautiful piece of furniture is marred and unsightly. Therefore, the wise in heart will guard against spiritual lethargy by maintaining a careful self-watch. We know that genuine faith will prevail against all that opposes it. However, genuine faith is only known, in finality, in that it does persevere.

Although the danger of apostasy causes us to fear and tremble, just like Christian and Hopeful, it need not shake our assurance of salvation. Genuine faith is assurance. By its very nature, it produces both godly fear and the true assurance of faith in the souls of the redeemed. On the other hand, spiritual ignorance and unbelief bring forth fruit that is bitter indeed. It is a sobering fact that some overcome the world while others are overcome by the world. The grace of God alone makes the difference. By the power of his Holy Spirit within, there is grace to run the race and serve the Lord acceptably with godly fear, until our race is won.

Study Questions

1. Shortly after leaving the Delectable Mountains, Christian and Hopeful saw a young man enter the King's Highway by way of a little crooked lane from the country of Conceit. The young man claimed to be on his way to the Celestial City. Why did Christian suspect the man's spiritual condition before even knowing his name?

2. How did Ignorance respond when Christian asked him about his hope of salvation? What did his answer reveal about his true spiritual condition? What vital things did he lack entirely?

3. What was it about the young man that troubled Christian the most? Was his concern a legitimate one? Why, or why not?

4. In what sense was the young man ignorant? Explain the nature of his particular kind of ignorance. What part does the sin of pride play in this kind of ignorance?

5. Is there a connection between the man named Ignorance and Turn-away the apostate? If so, what is it? Why did Christian and Hopeful need to witness the awful downfall of Turn-away? What warning might it contain for us as well?

CHAPTER 47

The Assault and Robbery of Little-Faith

WHEN WE FIRST COME TO KNOW THE LORD JESUS CHRIST, WE BEGIN A journey that is composed largely of the unknown. How thankful we should be that this is so! If we could see the sum total of our life experience ahead of time, marked with every painful circumstance we must face along the way, would we not be discouraged from the outset? Such knowledge would surely rob us of strength to face each new day and cause us to live under a perpetual cloud of fear and dread. Thus we would have little peace or joy if we knew, in advance, what trials and difficulties are in store for us tomorrow. However, our heavenly Father is very merciful in this regard by unfolding his will and purpose for us gradually, as we are able to bear it.

Of necessity then, the Christian life must be lived by faith one day at a time, and yet for this incredible journey, we have the trustworthiest of guides. As he led the Hebrew people by a pillar of cloud by day and a pillar of fire by night, our Lord also goes before us, causing his light to shine upon our path and make the way plain.

Since as Christians we must live by faith, we cannot glorify our heavenly Father or please him if we fail to trust him as we should. (Hebrews 11:6) Childlike faith trusts him when the way is dark and we cannot see the path before us. It rests confidently in his love when trouble comes unexpectedly, and patiently waits on him instead of rushing headlong before him. Saving faith hopes in his mercy when human reason insists that such hope is vain. (Isaiah 30:18)

On the other hand, unbelief puts up strong resistance to all of these things. By heeding the voice of human reason rather than the Word of God, it demands to see the way clearly and walk by sight and sense. Moreover, when trouble comes, unbelief complains bitterly and calls the love and goodness of God into question.

Mistrust is primarily the sum of all our fears. If not overcome through the strengthening and increase of our faith, it will cause us to stumble over every pebble along the path of life like one who is continually ready to halt. (Psalm 38:17) Small faith produces little joy, and our Lord would not have it so with us. He is the mighty victor who has already secured our safe passage through the merits of his cross. The promise is ours: *Through God we shall do valiantly; for he it is that shall tread down our enemies.* (Psalm 108:13) Therefore, my fellow believer, we need not plod along to Zion with heavy hearts and gloomy countenances, but with songs of gladness and hearts full of joyful anticipation.

As Christian and Hopeful passed through the dark lane where they had witnessed the awful fate of Turn-away, Christian called to mind another incident that took place in the same general vicinity. It concerned the assault and robbery of a man named Little-Faith, who lived in the town of Sincere. Even though his story had a far different outcome, it was still tragic in its own way.

Little-Faith was a truehearted pilgrim on his way to the Celestial City. The name of his hometown speaks for his character, which bore no resemblance to either Ignorance or Turn-away. Then what possible correlation could his story have to theirs? Before we attempt to answer, let us first consider Little-Faith and his history.

Even though Little-Faith was a sincere follower of Jesus Christ, he was known to be weak in faith. On a previous occasion, he had passed through the same dark lane where Christian and Hopeful walked at present. It so happened that a notoriously dangerous intersection was located near this particular stretch of the road, marking the spot where Dead-man's Lane crossed the King's Highway. As its name suggests, this crossroad has been the scene of many a crime against unsuspecting travelers. Robbery! Violence! Even murder! Moreover, it is well documented that many an alleged pilgrimage has come to an abrupt end here. So it is not the sort of place to slacken your pace, much less linger.

Perhaps Little-Faith was unaware of the danger, for he chose that very place to sit down for a while and rest. Surely he did not realize that Dead-man's Lane came directly from Broad-way-gate, and was a thoroughfare for disreputable characters of every sort. Still, by reason of its very name, he should have known better than to tarry there and allow himself to fall asleep.

While he slumbered, three "sturdy rogues" entered the lane from Broad-way-gate and saw him lying there. Seizing what was clearly a prime opportunity, they accosted the poor man just as he was awakening and preparing to resume his journey. But when suddenly faced with their violent intentions, he was too unnerved to make a run for it.

The culprits were actually three brothers closely related in both character and descent. Their names were Faint-heart, Mistrust, and Guilt, and as you might expect, Little-Faith offered little resistance to them. When Faint-heart demanded his purse, however, Little-Faith was hesitant to give it up. Then Mistrust, by far the boldest of the three, snatched the bag right out of the poor man's pocket. So Little-Faith lost most of his traveling money, and when he cried out in protest, Guilt struck him on the head with a large club and knocked him unconscious.

The three evil ones probably intended to finish him off and leave no witness to their crime. However, Little-Faith was not destined to be the latest statistic of that infamous place. As the merciless thugs stood over their helpless victim, they heard the sound of voices nearby and feared that Great-Grace, from the city of Good-Confidence, might be coming down the highway. The mere possibility that he was coming to Little-Faith's rescue was enough to make the thieves flee the scene at once, leaving Little-Faith to fend for himself.

Thus the providence of God spared Little-Faith's life that day, but his reaction to the assault was not what you might expect, considering his name. In spite of the terrible thing that had just happened to him, the little pilgrim was not ready to give up. After the dizziness had passed and his head cleared sufficiently, he set out on his journey once again.

The nature and significance of the robbery

After Christian finished telling of Little-Faith's narrow escape, Hopeful wondered aloud about the extent of his losses. Had the thieves managed to rob him of all he possessed? In fact, they had not. When Mistrust snatched his purse, it is true that he robbed the poor man of most of his spending money. As a result, he was forced to live as a virtual beggar for the remainder of his life. However, since we are dealing in the realm of the allegorical, we must infer that this theft had nothing to do with the loss of literal money. That kind of setback could have been overcome through diligent labor and frugal living. No my friend, it was the sin of unbelief that accosted and robbed poor Little-Faith that day. The result of it was spiritual poverty, which he could ill afford.

Even though the assault resulted in a significant loss for Little-Faith, it was not nearly as bad as it could have been. He had taken a hard hit but not a devastating blow, for he possessed priceless jewels that remained untouched. How could Mistrust have overlooked such valuable treasure? It was hidden in a secret place where no thief could find and snatch it.

What were these priceless jewels that eluded the robber's clever eye? Comprehensively speaking, they represent the unsearchable riches of salvation in Christ, which is spiritual treasure and wealth beyond compare. (Ephesians 3:8) Among these choice jewels was Little-Faith's "certificate of admission" to the Celestial Gate, the loss of which would have been irrevocable. When Hopeful wondered how it was that the robbers did not steal this irreplaceable document, Christian explained that it was due to God's providence rather than Little-Faith's quick thinking. The poor man was so overcome by the stress of the assault that he had "neither power nor skill to hide anything." God's grace alone kept his most valuable possession safely out of the robber's hand.

O, my brother or sister in Christ, consider the implications to your own soul! Has not our heavenly Father done the same for you? Of course we understand that Little-Faith's certificate of admission was not a literal document at all. It denoted his spiritual birthright as a child of God and all the benefits to which it entitled him. Thus it was a rare jewel of the finest sort, an inheritance that is *incorruptible, and undefiled, and that fadeth not away.* (1 Peter 1:4)

The other jewels that remained safely hidden were of the same transcendent quality and worth: genuine faith, eternal life, a living hope and the promise of full salvation. Many years ago, Little-Faith had entrusted his most valuable treasure, his eternal soul, to the Lord Jesus Christ. (2 Timothy 1:12) Although small and weak, his faith rested firmly upon the rock of ages. Therefore, his spiritual treasure was reserved in heaven where enemy hands could not lay hold upon or steal it. (Matthew 6:19-21; 1 Peter 1:4)

What a cause for great rejoicing and giving of thanks! The Lord had delivered Little-Faith from grave danger and kept his most precious treasure secure. Some such thought must have occurred to Hopeful, for he reflected that the poor man should have taken comfort from this fact in spite of his loss. However, as Christian pointed out, Little-Faith seemed unable to do so. For the rest of his journey, he dwelled far more upon his terrible loss than his providential deliverance. On those rare occasions when he was able to find comfort in the things of God, unbelief, discouragement, and guilt would come forward and attack him again. So between the three of them, these robbers managed to keep Little-Faith depressed and defeated most of the time.

What really happened to Little-Faith that day near Dead-man's Lane? Since the three brothers who ambushed him were not ordinary highwaymen, of what did the robbery actually consist? It was a coordinated attack against his heart and mind made by unbelief, discouragement, and debilitating guilt. These three things have the power to inflict untold damage upon their victims, but the loss is always greatest where faith is weakest. Therefore, since Little-Faith was who he was, the three-fold assault resulted in permanent damage, or so it appeared.

The purse containing Little-Faith's spending money denoted the things designed to help him endure the stress and strain of a pilgrim's life. These were spiritual comforts such as peace, assurance, and joy in the Lord. Faith lays hold of these benefits of salvation in Christ and finds comfort in them even in the midst of adversity. Little-Faith possessed these graces in small enough measure as it was. Therefore, he suffered a substantial loss where he could least afford it.

Small wonder then, that he put up so little resistance when attacked by his assailants, or that the experience proved a hindrance for the rest of his life. Perhaps he found some small consolation in telling his story to all who would listen, but this only kept the incident fresh in his mind.

After learning of the deprivation Little-Faith suffered following the robbery, Hopeful was surprised that he did not sell or pawn some of his jewels in order to relieve his poverty. Taken aback by hearing Hopeful say such a thing, Christian exclaimed, "For what should he pawn them? Or to whom should he sell them?" These were good questions. Christian then reminded him that such jewels were of little value to those who lived near to where the robbery took place. Relief was readily available to Little-Faith, if only he had made proper use of it. Furthermore, Christian warned Hopeful that had the man's most precious things been missing when he reached the Celestial Gate, he would have been denied admission there.

Even though his faith was weak, Little-Faith never considered parting with his spiritual treasure in order to obtain more earthly comfort and ease. To do so would be to renounce his faith and turn again to the world, like Demas. Had he done as Hopeful suggested, the three villains might have ceased to trouble him as before, but he would still not be rid of them. Moreover, he would have exchanged priceless treasure for eternal loss.

In spite of Christian's sharp rebuke, Hopeful continued in the same vein, suggesting that Little-Faith might have sold his jewels since Esau sold his birthright when in need. But in so saying, Hopeful exposed some appalling ignorance of his own. Surely he did not realize the full import of what he suggested, or he would certainly have known better than to make such a comparison. Those who know Esau's life story also know that Little-Faith bore no resemblance to him whatsoever.

In the time of the patriarchs, the firstborn son was highly privileged both as to his position in the family and his right to his father's inheritance. In the case of Abraham's descendants, this birthright included spiritual blessings as well. Therefore, the inheritance of Isaac's firstborn son also included the covenant of promise given to Abraham concerning the coming of Christ and the blessings of salvation in him. (Genesis 17:1-8) Likewise, all who possess true saving faith are the spiritual seed of Abraham and heirs to this promise. So even though his faith was small, Little-Faith was a child of Abraham in a truer sense than Esau ever was. (Galatians 3:13-14, 16, 26-29)

According to birth order, Esau's twin brother Jacob was the younger son. Therefore, the birthright legally belonged to Esau. When in circumstances of great hunger, he sold his birthright to Jacob for the price of a single meal, thus exchanging eternal blessings for momentary comfort and satisfaction.

Hopeful should have known better. Esau was a man who was ruled by his flesh, a man devoid of faith. Therefore, he could part with his most valuable possession without a second thought. This was not the case with Little-Faith, however. He treasured his spiritual blessings in Christ above all else.

In trying to convince Hopeful of his erroneous thinking, Christian used some rather blunt language. Even though Hopeful admitted he was in the wrong, he took offense and thought it best to change the subject. Yet he still persisted in his criticism of Little-Faith, this time for not showing more gumption when attacked by the robbers. Hopeful reasoned that they must have been cowards at heart since they fled at the sound of voices on the road. Why did not Little-Faith at least try to take a stand against them? In expressing such thoughts, he clearly implied that Little-Faith was also a coward.

My friend in Christ, before we are too critical of Hopeful for expressing such an opinion, we should ask ourselves if we have not been guilty of pretty much the same thing. How many times have we heard of the troubles of another and said, "If that had been me, I would have…"? Fill in whatever details you will, the implication is clear enough. If we had been in the same situation, we would have handled it far better!

Since Christian was older and wiser in the faith, he spoke from personal experience when he replied, "That they are cowards, many have said, but few have found it so in the time of trial." In so saying, he challenged Hopeful to think the matter through more carefully. It was quite true that Little-Faith was easily discouraged, and concerning spiritual valor, he had none to spare. But would Hopeful really have fared any better in the same situation?

It is easy enough to boast of faith and courage when all is going well with us. Moreover, it is easy to advise another concerning what they should or should not do in a given situation, when we have never faced it. This overconfident spirit is usually displayed by those who have not yet been tried in the crucible of affliction to any extent. The further we go down the path of the just, and the more our faith comes under heavy fire, the less inclined we will be to entertain such thoughts in our hearts, much less give voice to them.

Concerning the three perpetrators of the crime against Little-Faith, their very names identify them as potentially deadly enemies. Anyone who has come under their power will readily concede as much. Faint-heart, Mistrust, and Guilt have the common purpose of destroying faith, and in the case of many a professing Christian, they have won the battle without much of a fight. Yet even when they fail to achieve their primary objective, they are capable of inflicting great spiritual harm.

What about the source of their power? John Bunyan tells us plainly that these enemies serve "under the king of the bottomless pit; who, if need be, will come in to their aid himself, and his voice is as the roaring of a lion." In other words, they are of hellish origin and Apollyon is their master. (Revelation 9:11) In doing his bidding, they have the powers of darkness at their disposal. (Ephesians 6:12) No wonder they cause so much trouble or that Dead-man's Lane is their territory of choice.

This is no strange concept, for is not Satan the ultimate thief and liar? Is he not a destroyer of men's souls? Does Scripture not liken him to a mighty predator who stalks his victims with stealth and supernatural cunning? (1 Peter 5:8-9) Yes, to all three! Beyond a doubt, his most destructive work is done while men sleep, that is, when they have ceased to be alert and watchful. Our Lord said as much when he warned that it was while men slept that the enemy came and sowed tares among the wheat, and went his way. (Matthew 13:25)

In like manner, Satan assaults our minds with the arrows of discouragement, unbelief, and guilt with such cunning that we often do not recognize the true source of the attack. Neither does he give up when he fails to steal our most precious treasure. Our great adversary will rob us whenever and of whatever he can, and the weaker our faith, the more significant our loss is likely to be. So even though he does not succeed in destroying our faith, his ruthless attacks can shatter our peace, assurance, and joy in the Lord. Should that occur, we will be poor examples of God's sustaining grace and our service in God's kingdom will be severely impaired. In other words, we will be just like Little-Faith.

The in-depth understanding of Little-Faith's history, the clarity with which he related it, and the wisdom with which he answered Hopeful's objections, all pointed to Christian's having first-hand knowledge of it. Perhaps Little-Faith was a close acquaintance or a special brother in the Lord. However, I am inclined to think that the brutal assault and robbery of Little-Faith reminded Christian of his own battle with fear and mistrust.

When Little-Faith paused to rest near Dead-man's Lane, he made two potentially fatal mistakes. He rested in the wrong place and slept when he should have been watchful. Clearly he was guilty of placing himself in harm's way, but did not Christian commit a similar offense when he slumbered in the arbor on the hill Difficulty? Did not his sinful sleep give occasion to a similar loss? Perhaps this explains why Christian had compassion upon Little-Faith while Hopeful judged him rather harshly.

According to Christian, the incident on the hill Difficulty was not the only time he had been assaulted by Faint-heart, Mistrust, and Guilt. They overtook him on another occasion and when he endeavored to resist them, in Christian's own words, "in came their master." Although he had been armed for just such an encounter, he was hard pressed that day. Thus he learned by personal experience that discouragement, unbelief, and guilt are hard to withstand, even when one is clothed with the whole armor of God. Therefore, his counsel to Hopeful was, "No man can tell what in that combat attends us, but he that hath been in the battle himself."

To what incident did he allude? He must have been thinking of the assault in the Valley of Humiliation when he was accosted by Apollyon and forced to fight for his life. That experience had left an indelible impression upon him, and now he has given us some deeper insight into his terrible struggle at that time.

This thought convinces me more strongly than ever that our trials are not designed for our exclusive benefit. God has a greater purpose for them than we will probably ever know. As a result of our own trials and afflictions, we will be far less likely to judge others for their weaknesses and struggles. Instead, we will tend to be more loving and compassionate to our brothers and sisters in Christ when they suffer.

The King's champions

Within the realm of God's kingdom, there are some who are mighty men of valor. By the grace of God they are strong in faith and ready to give their utmost in defense of the Gospel of Christ. Such men are soldiers of exceptional courage, noble heroes marching in the vanguard of the battle. These choice men are the King's champions and they serve him by royal commission, under the banner of the cross. Some of them, like Gideon of old, are not bold by nature. Yet in the cause of Christ and his kingdom, they are champions indeed. When facing the wrath of the enemy, they do so as the Lord said to Zerubbabel: *Not by might, nor by power, but by my spirit, saith the LORD of hosts.* (Zechariah 4:6)

God's champions are apt leaders of his people because they are led of his Spirit. He it is who gives them boldness to face the enemy, strength to endure the conflict and wisdom to direct their steps. By his grace and for his glory they lift high the sword of the Spirit, which is the word of God, with courage and effectual power.

David was one such champion. He was little more than a boy when he volunteered to face the Philistines' champion Goliath in mortal combat. The stakes could not have been higher: champion versus champion, winner takes all! To a man, the army of Israel was paralyzed by fear due to the terrible threats of the giant. Not a single one of them was willing to be Israel's champion in what must have seemed a lost cause. None except young David!

After obtaining King Saul's permission to face the giant in battle, David insisted upon being armed with nothing but his staff, his sling, and five smooth stones. (1 Samuel 17:38-40) Wearing the armor of a shepherd, he threw down the gauntlet before the Philistine champion by saying: *Thou comest to me with a sword, and with a spear, and with a shield: but I come to thee in the name of the LORD of hosts, the God of the armies of Israel, whom thou hast defied.* (1 Samuel 17:45)

How could a young shepherd boy face the mighty giant so bravely when Israel's entire army cowered in fear? David had an exceptionally strong faith in God and an uncommon zeal for his glory. Notice that he expressed his complete confidence in God before the battle rather than after the fact, saying: *This day will the LORD deliver thee into mine hand; and I will smite thee, and take thine head from thee; and I will give the carcasses of the host of the Philistines this day unto the fowls of the air, and to the wild beasts of the earth; that all the earth may know that there is a God in Israel. And all this assembly shall know that the LORD saveth not with sword and spear: for the battle is the LORD's, and he will give you into our hands.* (1 Samuel 17:46-47) Thus it was in the strength of the Lord that David faced the giant and won the day.

However, as Christian was quick to point out to Hopeful, "All the King's subjects are not his champions, nor can they, when tried, do such feats of war as he." This is true enough. Some of God's people are strong in faith, while others are weak and easily lose heart. But relatively few can face an enemy such as Goliath with the faith and courage of young David.

Christian identifies Great-Grace for us as one of these relative few, for he was one of the King's champions. As Hopeful listened to Christian talk along these lines, he expressed the wish that the trio of robbers had encountered Great-Grace instead of poor Little-Faith. Was he Little-Faith's pastor? He could well have been.

The character named Great-Grace represents the ministers of Jesus Christ who serve as spiritual leaders in his churches. They are champions in the sense that they defend his cause against those who oppose it. Moreover, since they are officers in his royal army, they find themselves the particular targets of the enemy's malice.

Their daunting task requires an extraordinary degree of spiritual valor, which no man possesses by nature. The courage to fight the good fight while remaining true and faithful must come from the Lord. As his servants require it, he gives sufficient grace to enable them to stand. Thus the name Great-Grace rightly belongs to every true minister of Christ. Still, as Christian also observed, even Great-Grace "might have had his hands full" had Faint-heart, Mistrust, and Guilt managed to "get within him."

That God's choice servants are not exempt from attack by these robbers is evident from the scars on the face of Great-Grace. Yes, dear reader, even he! Likewise the apostle Paul, another mighty champion, was so greatly afflicted at one time that he despaired even of life. (2 Corinthians 1:8) David knew the same desperation later on in his life, as did both Heman and Hezekiah, who according to John Bunyan, were "champions in their day." (See Psalm 38; Psalm 88, which was attributed to Heman in its caption, and Isaiah 36:1–37:7)

What about Peter, who was the only disciple to set himself forth as the Lord's champion? How did he fare when put to the test? Before the fact, he made great boast of his courage and strength. Yet Peter's bravery was short-lived in the hour of trial.

So discouragement, unbelief, and guilt can also get the better of those who are strong in faith. However, remember that even though Great-Grace had done battle with these culprits, they fled at the mere suspicion of his approach. God's men may bear scars from frequent encounters with the enemy, but they have also known many victories. Moreover, they are instrumental in helping countless others who have come under assault from these robbers. No wonder the three villains feared the approach of one of the King's champions. They really were cowards at heart!

Although it is certainly an intimidating thought, we have an adversary who is determined to take us down. He is powerful and tenacious, with many a clever device to use against us. Even those who are strong in faith discover that he is not easily vanquished. All of God's people need to be spiritually valiant in the face of such an enemy. However, the kind of courage that stands fast and trusts in God alone comes only as the result of faith's fiery trial. This is how ordinary men become God's champions.

Having learned better than to think himself an exceptional man of valor, Christian wisely counseled Hopeful, saying, "For such footmen as thee and I are, let us never desire to meet with an enemy, nor vaunt as if we could do better, when we hear of others that they have been foiled, nor be tickled at the thoughts of our own manhood, for such commonly come by the worst when tried." This is sage advice for us as well, dear reader!

Through many years as a pastor's wife, I have known a few people who actually prayed for trouble. More often than not, they were soon granted their request. But in general, they were ill prepared for trial when it came and did not react to it very nobly. We need not pray for trial and affliction out of a misguided notion of piety. It will come soon enough in God's appointed time, and it will work its perfect work. However, it is right and proper to pray for grace and strength to be prepared for battle, and to diligently use the means of grace designed to that end. Countless other robberies have taken place along the King's Highway, like the one committed against Little-Faith. Our conduct when assaulted by the same thieves will largely depend upon our advance preparation.

It takes very little to defeat one whose faith is small and weak, but little faith need not remain so. Through consistent use of God's Word, faith will both increase and become stronger. Then we will be better prepared for battle when it comes. Arrayed with the shield of faith, we will be better able to quench the flaming arrows of the wicked. In conjunction with this defensive armor, we must seek our Lord continually in prayer; for without his constant help, the enemy would make short work of us.

As Christian summed up the account of Little-Faith's assault and robbery, he admitted to Hopeful that he had been engaged in the same battle. However, from his latest dialog with Hopeful, we are struck by the spiritual growth and godly wisdom Christian has attained. He has learned not to boast of his courage or desire to meet the enemy head-on, but he also knew that many additional dangers lay in the path before them.

* * * *

Perhaps you have wondered why Little-Faith sat down and allowed himself to fall asleep in such a notoriously dangerous place. Why did he place himself in harm's way when he should have known better? Given that he did so, how are we to interpret his sleep and its terrible consequences?

Since we are dealing with metaphorical language, we recognize at once that Little-Faith's sleep was far more significant than a mere nap. It denoted both the lowering of his spiritual guard when he needed it the most, and his failure to consider the consequences of his action. What was it that placed him under such extreme duress that he became so heedless? Had he received unexpected news of a devastating nature, such as a serious health diagnosis or the tragic loss of a loved one? Was a family crisis brewing or a major financial setback on the horizon? It could have been anything.

Whatever the exact nature of his trouble, Little-Faith's reaction to it caused an emotional meltdown that left him virtually incapacitated by unbelieving fear. As a result his spiritual judgment, which was not all that sharp at best, became seriously impaired. Thus it was an opportune moment for the enemy to strike where he was weakest.

Like the cruel wife of Giant Despair, unbelieving fear is an enemy that would just as soon take no prisoners. It would destroy us if it could, but failing in that, it will rob us of anything it can. Those who have been caught in its grasp can testify that it opens the door to other spiritual problems, of which discouragement and unreasonable guilt head the list. The only antidote to this enemy is childlike trust in God. Faith alone can banish unbelieving fear and the anxiety it engenders. However, poor Little-Faith had it in short supply; therefore, he had little with which to defend himself against his assailants.

Given the great damage that unbelieving fear can do, we are wise to view it as our mortal enemy. It is interesting that in Revelation 21:8, the fearful and unbelieving head the list of those who will *have their part in the lake which burneth with fire and brimstone, which is the second death.* So at the end of all things, fear and unbelief will return to the place of their origin via the broad way that leads to eternal destruction. Thankfully, this was not to be the destiny of Little-Faith.

Dear brother or sister in Christ, before we judge Little-Faith too critically, perhaps we should take a good look at ourselves. How often do we deserve our Lord's rebuke, *O ye of little faith?* (Matthew 6:30) In my case, far too often! Although it grieves me to admit it, one day I looked into my mirror and saw the image of Little-Faith looking back at me. How well I remember that day in May 2008 when an unexpected diagnosis of Stage 2 colon cancer brought me once again to the border of the Valley of the Shadow of Death. After successful surgery to remove the tumor and six months of oral chemotherapy as a precaution against recurrence, I began a regular schedule of visits with my oncologist for blood work and CT scans. Thus began my own private battle with fear and mental anguish, as I came under repeated attack by the same villains who assaulted Little-Faith.

As I write these words more than nine years later, I must confess that the battle still rages whenever it is time for a scan and lab work. There is always a week to wait before we learn the results. It is an opportunity to patiently wait on the Lord, remember his great mercy to me in the past, and trust myself entirely to him. But as a rule, it is a week in which fear plays havoc with my mind and I find myself praying once again, "Lord I believe. Help thou mine unbelief."

Worldly philosophy has devised its own solution to the universal problem of fear. That solution, which counsels us to bite the bullet and face our fear, is simply a modern adaptation of the ancient philosophy known as Stoicism. However, since it cannot reach the crux of the matter, it offers no true remedy at all.

There is a far more excellent way to deal with the problem of anxious fear. Our loving Lord bids us to bring all our cares and cast them upon him. (1 Peter 5:6-7; Philippians 4:6-7) I am so thankful that we may lean trustingly upon our Savior's breast, like John the beloved, and pour out our hearts to him. Why should we stagger under a heavy burden when he is ready and willing to bear it all? What hinders us from casting upon our Lord those things that torment us the most, and leaving them with him? The awful sin of unbelief!

Denying the problem solves nothing, and neither does attempting to overcome it in our own strength. David knew what it was to wrestle with fear, even though he was one of the King's champions, but he also knew where to take his fear. Therefore, in the hour of crisis and danger he could honestly say: *What time I am afraid I will trust in thee.* (Psalm 56:3)

If only poor Little-Faith had done likewise, he would not have lived under a perpetual cloud of fear, mistrust, and guilt. Had he been less focused upon his own misery, perhaps he would have sought the Lord more diligently through his Word. In doing so, he would have discovered that God's Word is the key that unlocks every door in Doubting Castle. It also forms every stepping stone by which we may cross over the Slough of Despond without falling in. Had he truly sought first the kingdom of God and his righteousness, the little pilgrim would surely have known an increase of his faith.

Even though all believers in Christ are not like Little-Faith, we all must grapple with fear, guilt, and mistrust. However, nothing has the power to rout these enemies like the knowledge of God's great love and tender care for us. Victory over these sinful tendencies can be ours when we bring them to the foot of the cross and trust ourselves completely to our Lord Jesus Christ. Herein lies our peace, when we can honestly say: *Behold, God is my salvation; I will trust, and not be afraid: for the LORD JEHOVAH is my strength and my song; he also is become my salvation.* (Isaiah 12:2)

Faith is not merely an abstract concept, and neither is it a blind leap in the dark. It is a spiritual reality, the substance of things hoped for, the evidence of things not seen. (Hebrews 11:1) Faith has its solid foundation in the Word of God and trusts in him in spite of all that argues against it. Thus it is indeed the victory that overcomes the world, and the shield that protects our inner man from the furious attacks of Satan. (1 John 5:4; Ephesians 6:16)

Since everyone claims to believe in something, "keep the faith" is a popular catchphrase of our day. However, faith must have its proper object. Great trust in the wrong thing will only deceive and condemn one in the end. On the other hand, smallness of faith with the Lord Jesus Christ as its only object will carry one all the way to the Celestial City, although it makes for a particularly difficult journey.

To have little faith is to find ourselves in a constant battle with unbelief and come out on the losing end most of the time. It permits unbelief to rob us of our Lord's promised peace and comfort when we are most in need of them. It will also sap our strength and cloud our spiritual vision. Small faith means little power with God in prayer, and little victory in the hour of trial. Moreover, it gives ground for our assurance of salvation to be easily shaken and the light of our testimony obscured. In short, smallness of faith will prove a significant deterrent that will plague us every day that we live.

Yet for all this, God will never forsake his children because their faith is small and weak. His grace will sustain them as well as his champions because salvation is contingent upon the quality of one's faith, not the quantity of it. Genuine faith, whether small or great, rests entirely upon the Lord Jesus Christ and makes no other plea than his blood and righteousness. In this, we find the vast difference between Little-Faith from the town of Sincere and Turn-away from the town of Apostasy.

However, it is not the will of God that we stumble along the path of life, constantly beaten down by fear and mistrust. When this is our case, we will not only be a burden to ourselves, but a source of discouragement to others as well. The apostle Paul tells us plainly: *God hath not given us the spirit of fear; but of power, and of love, and of a sound mind.* (2 Timothy 1:7) Our Lord desires that we grow strong in faith and bring forth much fruit to his glory. Therefore, pity Little-Faith but do not follow his example! Since he was never able to overcome the effects of the brutal assault and robbery, he was never more than a few steps away from the Slough of Despond or far out of the grasp of Giant Despair.

According to Charles H. Spurgeon, "Little faith will bring your souls to Heaven but great faith will bring Heaven to your souls." [1] May God grant us to be like the pilgrims of old who made the same journey even though it took them through the valley of Baca (the "vale of weeping"). May we not be shaken by every wind of adversity, but be strong in faith and know the blessedness of those whose strength is in the Lord. (Psalm 84:5-7) How do we become strong in the Lord and in the power of his might? (Ephesians 6:10) How do we prevail in spiritual battle? We only do so through quiet submission to God and the patience of faith.

Speaking through Isaiah the prophet, God said: *In quietness and in confidence shall be your strength.* (Isaiah 30:15) Nothing robs us of this needful strength more quickly than fear, mistrust, and guilt. However, in waiting upon the Lord with the patience and obedience of true faith, we will find supernatural strength and abundant grace for the difficult journey ahead.

Study Questions

1. Who was Little-Faith, and what does his hometown say about the kind of man he was? Who were the three thieves who assaulted and robbed him as he slumbered near Dead-man's Lane? What prevented them from murdering Little-Faith as well as robbing him?

2. Since we know that Little-Faith was not physically assaulted and robbed, what kind of attack did he actually suffer? What did his three assailants represent, and what kind of loss did he really suffer? What priceless treasure of his remained safely hidden from the thieves?

3. Christian's detailed account of Little-Faith's assault and robbery suggests first-hand knowledge of it. This would explain why Christian had compassion for Little-Faith while Hopeful thought him a coward. On what occasions had Christian also been attacked by and done battle with Faint-heart, Mistrust, and Guilt?

4. In the story of Little-Faith, we learn that Great-Grace, whom the robbers feared, was one of the King's champions. Who does the character Great-Grace represent? In what sense was he God's champion? Why did the villains fear him even though he bore scars from his own battles with them?

5. Although Little-Faith was a genuine believer in the Lord Jesus Christ, his weak faith proved a life-long hindrance to him. How can we avoid the same thing? What is the scriptural remedy for little faith?

CHAPTER 48

Beware of the Flatterer!

IN PSALM 139:23-24, WE CATCH A RARE GLIMPSE INTO THE HEART OF David, the sweet psalmist of Israel. A veil is lifted, as it were, revealing his inmost thoughts and desires as he prays: *Search me, O God, and know my heart: try me, and know my thoughts: and see if there be any wicked way in me, and lead me in the way everlasting.* David clearly had keen understanding of the sovereignty and omniscience of God, but not merely in the abstract. He comprehended it as it related to him personally, to his entire being. It was in light of this knowledge that he desired God to not only search and try him, but also lead him in the way everlasting. Furthermore, in Psalm 86:11-12, he expressed the heart of one in whom the knowledge of God was pleasant when he prayed: *Teach me thy way, O LORD; I will walk in thy truth: unite my heart to fear thy name. I will praise thee, O Lord my God, with all my heart: and I will glorify thy name for evermore.*

The heart of David finds its counterpart in every true child of God, for they also find their chief delight in God and his ways. Thus we may rightly claim the promises of preservation and deliverance as we journey through this life, of which Psalm 121 is an example. However, these very same promises strongly imply that we have embarked upon a perilous journey.

As we walk the path of the just, we hear and follow the voice of Christ, the voice of wisdom. (Proverbs 8:1-17) We discern his voice through his Word, as his Spirit reveals its truth to our hearts. As we give diligent heed to him, he keeps us from the paths of sin and destruction, directs our steps in the ways of virtue and truth, and arms us against temptation. Thus we are greatly blessed as we walk in wisdom's way. (Proverbs 8:32-35)

Since the royal road to Zion takes us directly through enemy territory, we will also hear the call of other voices that do not speak the truth. Through pleasant-sounding words and subtle persuasion, they attempt to deceive us and subvert our faith. All of these alien voices can be traced to a single source, our great archenemy. He is clever enough to know that when one forsakes the right path he usually does so gradually; therefore, Satan endeavors to lure us away from it a little at a time.

After their recent conversation regarding the assault and robbery of Little-Faith, Christian and Hopeful had good reason to be cautious in general and wary of strangers in particular. Unsavory characters were known to roam the section of highway where they walked at present. Moreover, the shepherds' warning to beware of the Flatterer was still fresh in their minds. They would meet him somewhere in the way ahead, possibly lurking in the shadows beyond the next bend in the road. But after all, they were not like Ignorance, were they? Christian and Hopeful knew the truth, so they may have reasoned that the Flatterer would have a hard time deceiving them. As for Little-Faith, perhaps vain confidence whispered that they were not really like him either. They knew better than to sleep in dangerous places, so the Flatterer would not find it easy to take them by surprise.

Soon afterward, they came to an intersection where another road joined the King's Highway. It was unlike anything they had faced before, because their path now divided into two directions. Which way should they go, and how were they to make the right choice? Either branch of the road could be the right one; but obviously, only one of them led to the heavenly Zion. Which one was it?

While Christian and Hopeful paused to consider which of the two paths to take, they undoubtedly recalled the stile into By-Path Meadow. Neither man was eager to make that mistake again. Like Dead-man's Lane, one of these roads would lead them away from the city, and unless their eyes deceived them, there was no substantial difference between the two. (Proverbs 14:12) Little wonder then, that as they stood gazing at the crossroad, the two men were as confused as they had ever been.

Dear friend in Christ, have you ever been to a place where two ways meet? I suspect you have, since this joining of two paths denotes those critical situations we all must face now and then. They are times when decisions of prime importance must be made and godly wisdom is essential. Our great enemy is near at hand during such times, ready to lead us in the wrong direction. Therefore, the failure to choose the right path could prove both costly and dangerous. Advice comes our way from multiple sources, giving conflicting opinions. What are we to do?

As Christian and Hopeful stood at the crossroad, they were face-to-face with just such a dilemma. While their attention was focused upon the situation at hand, a stranger appeared before them in the road. There was nothing so unusual about that, for they have met many strangers in the way already. Yet even though neither man picked up on it, something was very different about this one.

Underneath a voluminous white robe, the man's flesh was as black as night, but this had nothing whatsoever to do with his race or ethnicity. The color of his skin was figurative only, signifying an evil character within. However, since his true identity was concealed beneath his outer garment, Christian and Hopeful saw no reason to be suspicious. What's more, their minds were so distracted at the moment that they were not as alert as they should have been.

This particular stranger was not the least bit timid. He approached Christian and Hopeful directly and asked why they were just standing there staring at the two roads before them. The men explained their predicament, saying that they were headed to the Celestial City and were now confused as to which path to take. Dear reader, please keep in mind that Christian and Hopeful already had specific directions concerning the right way to go. Had they but consulted the document given them by the shepherds for just such a time as this, they would already have been well on their way.

When the white-robed stranger told them to follow him, for he was also going to the city, Christian and Hopeful should have been immediately on guard. Had not Vain-confidence assured them of the same thing? How quickly they had forgotten where they landed by following him! What about the man named Ignorance? Had he not made the very same claim? Christian and Hopeful had been pilgrims long enough to know that everyone talking about heaven is not going there. They should certainly have known enough to question the stranger thoroughly before taking him at his word. However, his sudden appearance and offer of help came right when they were in desperate need of it.

Although there is no record of any further dialog between Christian and Hopeful and the glib stranger, they decided to follow him. Perhaps they did so because momentary need overcame their better judgment. If so, they could have regarded his offer of help as providential. Yet in following him without question, they acted in haste rather than through godly wisdom and prudence.

As they followed the stranger down one of the paths, which was of course the wrong one, Christian and Hopeful failed to notice a subtle alteration in its course. Since the new path looked very like the old one, and the change of direction occurred so gradually, neither man had the slightest inkling that they were now headed away from the Celestial City.

They had made another terrible mistake, but we need to keep one important factor in mind. While the men did permit themselves to be led out of the right way, they had done so unintentionally. Their hearts' desire had not changed at all; their love for the Lord and resolve to follow him was as firm as ever. As with Little-Faith, this was the material difference between Christian and Hopeful, and Turn-away the apostate. They were surely headed for deep trouble, but not due to willful disobedience.

Caught in a tangled web

Before either man knew what was happening, the stranger led them directly into a net, which he had set in place beforehand. They were now hopelessly entangled and helpless to do a thing about it. Moreover, their worst fears were justified when he laid aside his white robe and revealed his true identity. He was of course the Flatterer against whom they had been explicitly warned. When they had least expected it, they walked squarely into his web of deception.

We might reasonably wonder why Christian and Hopeful became ensnared in spite of prior warning. It is true that the Flatterer's appearance and speech are designed to deceive, but this fact gave all the more reason for them to be watchful. Why were they so easily duped? Distraction and heedlessness blinded them to his true identity until it was too late. As the men quickly discovered, hindsight may be crystal clear, but it serves little purpose after the fact.

This latest mishap in the journey of Christian and Hopeful reminds me of Solomon's words: *Surely in vain the net is spread in the sight of any bird.* (Proverbs 1:17) It is an interesting observation, and a humbling one in its implication. Birds instinctively have enough sense to elude the fowler's net. More sense, it would seem, than many a Christian, for the two men were not the first pilgrims to be caught in the Flatterer's net, nor would they be the last.

The poor men were now in a pathetic condition, lying helpless on the ground and crying for mercy. They feared to think what was going to happen to them next. Perhaps they were to perish here, as others had before them. As they came to grips with the gravity of their situation, Christian was the first to speak. However, instead of complaining about their circumstances, he freely admitted his wrong in not heeding the shepherds' warning. To this confession, Hopeful added that they had also failed to consult the note of direction given to them for just such an emergency. Once again, negligence had cost them dearly; for had they been more circumspect, they would not have been so easily led astray and caught in the net of the Flatterer. (Psalm 17:4; Proverbs 29:5)

It was another valuable lesson learned, but did it come too late? Christian and Hopeful may well have feared that all was over for them. Would the Lord have mercy upon them, or had they erred too far this time? Even though they freely admitted their guilt, the results of heeding the Flatterer can be catastrophic. Through the years, he has led many a would-be pilgrim to his or her destruction. If Christian and Hopeful were to be spared the same fate, it would be by God's mercy alone.

Although the Flatterer had now left the scene, their plight could hardly have been more desperate. So when they saw a Shining One coming toward them with a whip in his hand, they probably feared that the end had come. Was he someone who might help them, or another enemy come to finish them off? In either case, they were completely at his mercy.

As the Shining One stood over the helpless men, he asked where they came from and how they happened to now be in such a condition. Christian and Hopeful answered truthfully that they were on their way to Zion, but had been led out of the right path by a dark stranger dressed in white. They admitted to taking the man at his word and following him without question, because he claimed to be going to the Celestial City.

After this honest confession, the Shining One told the men plainly that the Flatterer was a false apostle posing as an angel of light. Thus he unmasked the great pretender, and having done so, he cut the net and freed Christian and Hopeful. He then asked them where they had rested the night before. Why would he ask such a seemingly irrelevant question? It was certainly not out of idle curiosity or the need for information, for he was well aware of their visit to the Delectable Mountains. Furthermore, he knew of the shepherds' warning and the note of direction they were given. So he asked a leading question designed to cause Christian and Hopeful to examine themselves and consider where their negligence had led them.

Several factors came into play here, the chief one being their failure to consult God's Word when faced with a crucial decision. The shepherds knew well that Christian and Hopeful were to shortly reach the crossroad, and the quandary in which it would place them. They also knew that the Flatterer was known to haunt that area. Therefore, they provided Christian and Hopeful with all the information they would need in order to safely navigate the crossing and escape the enemy's net. The two men were entirely to blame for not making proper use of it.

Getting back to an earlier thought, I cannot help but wonder if they had succumbed to vain confidence once again. Had they been guilty of thinking themselves too knowledgeable to be led astray? It would not be the first time, would it? If so, it is little wonder that they showed such poor discernment. Since they failed to consult the Word of God for direction, they had no basis for making a right judgment. The best excuse they could give was to say they "did not imagine" such a "fine-spoken man" could have been the Flatterer. In other words, they followed him because he was not at all what they expected him to be. Dear reader, he never is!

We rarely judge correctly when we judge according to outward appearance or preconceived notions. Christian and Hopeful violated this important principle even after the express warning to be on the lookout for the Flatterer. Although they did not know him, the men had a mental image of what they thought he would look like. Thus they watched for him at first, but when no such person appeared on the scene, they became distracted and inattentive after a while. When the Flatterer eventually did appear, they were taken completely by surprise.

Beyond a doubt, Christian and Hopeful had taken a false step of such magnitude that the matter had to be addressed. Upon hearing their frank confession and lame excuse, the Shining One ordered them to lie on the ground face down. After they did as commanded, he chastened them severely with the whip. But even though it seemed a drastic measure, it was designed to teach them more perfectly the way in which they were to walk. Moreover, all the while he beat them he said: *As many as I love, I rebuke and chasten: be zealous therefore, and repent.* (Revelation 3:19) In this way, the Shining One ministered both correction and comfort to the penitent men.

Fellow believer, self-examination is always a painful thing, is it not? It reveals such unflattering things by bringing us face to face with what we really are. However, self-examination alone is not enough to keep us walking in the right ways of the Lord. Although our heavenly Father takes no delight in causing us pain, he will not withhold correction when it is due. He loves us far too much to permit us to stray from our designated path without consequence. When we inadvertently do so, his carefully administered chastisement clears our spiritual vision and corrects our course like nothing else can do. (Psalm 119:67)

Christian and Hopeful's reaction to this severe rebuke and chastisement is worthy of our careful attention, for it expresses what our response is to be as well. When the Shining One sent the two men on their way with a reminder to give more heed to what the shepherds had told them, they thanked him for his kindness. We would be quite wrong to think that they were gluttons for punishment. In fact, we know better, do we not? The loving rebuke and correction had worked its intended purpose in their hearts. (Hebrews 12:11) Therefore, in spite of their throbbing wounds, Christian and Hopeful continued on their way singing a song.

Character sketch of the Flatterer

What constitutes a true friend? He or she is one who will always have our best interest at heart, and care enough to tell us what we need to hear rather than what we wish to hear. Such honesty can be quite painful, but a true friend is willing to risk our disfavor, if he must, because he loves us. (Proverbs 17:17; 27:6) Moreover, he is also trustworthy and would never intentionally deceive or mislead us. Such friends are rare, indeed!

Through the character Polonius' counsel to his son Laertes, William Shakespeare gave this advice concerning the nature of true friendship:

> The friends thou hast, and their adoption tried,
> Grapple them to thy soul with hoops of steel
> But do not dull thy palm with entertainment
> Of each new-hatch'd, unfledg'd comrade. [1]

This is wise advice from the bard of Avon, but he spoke of earthly friends, the very best of whom might let us down when we need them the most. The Lord Jesus Christ is our truest, most faithful friend. Unlike the fair-weather sort, he *sticketh closer than a brother,* for he has promised never to leave or forsake us. (Proverbs 18:24; Hebrews 13:5-6) Moreover, his Word is infallibly true and his promises sure. Therefore, he is worthy of our utmost confidence and trust.

Although his ministers have no claim to infallibility, they also are trustworthy and faithful as to their character. Therefore, they do not hesitate in speaking the truth, even though they know well the cost of doing so. Why are they willing to make such a sacrifice? They are true friends who love the souls of men.

Such is not the case with the Flatterer. Although he often poses as a friend, he is a deliberate deceiver who takes great liberties with the truth. So the shepherds spoke no idle words when they warned Christian and Hopeful to beware of him. He will use every means at his disposal to gain the approval of men. One of his most effective tactics is to weigh his words carefully and omit anything that might cause offence. In short, he tells men what they want to hear instead of telling them the truth. Thus through lying words, he gives a false hope and lays a deadly snare for those who believe him.

Since Satan is the ultimate flatterer, he always devises a counterfeit for that which is true. Therefore, he has a false gospel, which is a subtle perversion of the true Gospel of Jesus Christ. Moreover, this chief flatterer has many men who are eager to do his bidding. His ministers, who are flatterers in their own right, zealously declare this other gospel, which is not another. (Galatians 1:6-7) Although they come under the guise of the ministers of Christ and claim to preach his Word, they are hirelings who serve their own interests. As such, they are deceitful workers driven by pride, ambition, or other base motives, and men-pleasers who use fair speech and smooth words in order to gain a following. (2 Corinthians 11:13-15)

The fact that these false teachers are double-tongued makes them all the more dangerous. Blatant error is easy enough to recognize, but these deceivers will say many things that are true while failing to declare the whole truth. To the undiscerning hearer they may sound good; but they are not known so much by what they say as by what they neglect to say. Partial truth is error cleverly disguised, and these flatterers are quite fluent in the use of it. Therefore, they can soothe the consciences of men by telling them what they want to hear, while giving them just enough Scripture to make them think they are hearing the truth.

Since the Flatterer is a master deceiver, how are we to recognize him and guard ourselves against his wiles? How are we to discern truth from subtle error? We do so in much the same way that one becomes skillful in the detection of counterfeit money. Spiritual discernment is not sharpened by the study of that which is false. It is only acquired through a thorough understanding of the truth. This firm foundation, in conjunction with the anointing of God's Spirit, will illuminate our minds and enable us to distinguish truth from error, even when cleverly disguised. (1 John 2:26-27)

Although truth is our shield and buckler, we dare not presume that we cannot be swayed by alien voices. (Psalm 91:4) The powers of darkness are behind them, and so is their prince. Satan uses flattery to lure souls away from the truth and back to the broad way that leads to destruction. To this end, he always appears as an angel of light in order to more effectively carry out his evil design, and so do his servants.

Did not the apostle Paul warn the people of God against such when he said: *Beware lest any man spoil you through philosophy and vain deceit, after the tradition of men, after the rudiments of the world, and not after Christ*? (Colossians 2:8) Moreover, did he not sternly rebuke the Galatians because they were so quick to believe the lies of the flatterers among them? (See Galatians 1:6-9)

Scripture consistently portrays the Flatterer in an evil light and warns us to beware of him. (Proverbs 29:5). With cunning words he casts a net for souls as surely as the fowler lays a snare for birds. (Psalm 5:9; Psalm 12:2) While the true servants of Christ give diligence to declare the whole counsel of God, the Flatterer is deliberately cunning in his speech. (Acts 20:27-30) By means of his smooth manner and fair speech, he charms and beguiles his hearers and easily wins their favor. Yet he is false-hearted and double-tongued, a liar and a deceiver who is guilty of the worst kind of treachery. This is the true character of the Flatterer underneath his clever disguise. (Proverbs 26:28)

The apostle Paul made it clear that although he was zealous to reach the lost with the Gospel, he never resorted to flattery. (1 Thessalonians 2:5) However, many of his contemporaries who claimed to be the servants of Christ were not so committed to the truth. Their top priority was to make a name for themselves by telling men what they wanted to hear.

There is ample evidence in Scripture that such flatterers abounded in the days of the apostles. (Matthew 7:15-20; 2 Peter 2:1-3, 17-18; 1 John 4:1; Jude 16) They flourish in our day as well. I venture to say that every true minister of Christ could name some from among his congregation who eventually became weary of sound doctrine and began to desire something new. In time, these unstable souls were led out of the way of truth by yielding to the voice of the Flatterer. (2 Timothy 4:2-4)

So the warning to beware of the Flatterer is just as relevant to us today as it was when Christian and Hopeful were making their way toward the Celestial City. Gullible souls are still falling prey to his lying words. If we would avoid being caught in his net, we must take heed what we hear and to whom we give a hearing. Moreover, we must judge by something more substantial than an attractive appearance, pleasing personality, and clever speech. As we travel the royal road to Zion, we are sure to encounter the Flatterer sooner or later. May the Word of the living God be the sole standard by which we judge him when we do.

* * * *

Although we are not given the specific nature of Christian and Hopeful's latest transgression, it is sufficient to know that they took the Flatterer at his word and followed him without question. Accordingly, we may draw a spiritual principle from this incident that will prove far more beneficial than dwelling upon minute details.

When the Flatterer makes his appeal to us, he generally does so in one of two ways. The first one appeals to the lust of the flesh and is designed to bring about our moral downfall. In much the same way as the strange woman in Proverbs 7, the Flatterer could try to turn us out of the paths of righteousness. Should he succeed, we would not only bring disgrace upon our own good name, but also bring dishonor and reproach upon the name of our Lord. Such was the case with King David in the matter of Bathsheba. (2 Samuel 12:13-14)

The other approach taken by the Flatterer is not so readily apparent because we can yield to it while remaining outwardly moral and respectable. It is the appeal to intellectual pride, and its purpose is to bring about our spiritual downfall. Employing this tactic, the Flatterer tries to turn our hearts and minds away from the truth by means of deadly error disguised as truth. We dare not presume that we could never be swayed by his voice, because we tend to be more easily influenced than we like to think. Although we do not want to be guilty of judging unfairly, there is a fine line between giving someone the benefit of the doubt and spiritual naïveté. Therefore, it is foolish to indiscriminately yield our minds to every new doctrine that sounds good. Our wisest course is to be extremely careful of what we hear. (Proverbs 4:10-13)

Since this carefulness requires enough spiritual discernment to distinguish every false voice from the true, it is no easy task. What must we do when confronted with diverse opinions and strange doctrines that seem plausible and may confound us? Always defer to the Word of God! No matter how logical or persuasive the argument, or how eloquently presented, we must reject it if it cannot stand up to the test of clear Scripture truth.

Because this particular tactic of the Flatterer has met with uncommon success, it poses a greater risk than we may think. It also underscores our need to be continually under a sound Gospel ministry where we hear the voice of Christ through his faithful servant. Those who abide in the fold are much less likely to be set upon by ravening wolves disguised in sheep's clothing. (Matthew 7:15)

My brother or sister in Christ, perhaps you and I are able to rightly discern the voices of those who would flatter and deceive us by speaking lies. Without question, such a gift is a valuable thing, but does it mean we are out of danger? What about the flatterer that lurks in our own hearts? Are we not still bothered by a sin principle that wars from within and seeks to deceive, dominate, and ensnare us? Does it not often tempt us to commit the respectable sin of being wise in own eyes? Do we not sometimes hear the whisperings of this deceiver within? Heed not when he flatters!

Given the natural inclination of our flesh, the appeal to human pride is perhaps one of the enemy's most successful methods of tactical warfare against us. How easy it is to believe his lies and think more highly of ourselves than we ought to think! It is easy, that is, until we find ourselves caught in his tangled web.

"Flattery makes us stupid"! Brother Conrad Murrell made this statement from the pulpit of Bible Baptist Church at the 2007 Spring Bible Conference in St. Louis, Missouri. It was a stunning declaration intended to do more than merely capture our attention. Although it certainly did that, its chief purpose was to make us think.

How does flattery, or rather giving heed to flattery, make us stupid? It does so by robbing us of objectivity and impeding our better judgment. Flattery spreads a net for our feet by tempting us to believe a lie and accept it as truth. (Proverbs 29:5) It subverts rational thought and sober consideration, thus promoting indiscretion and imprudent action. Perhaps worst of all, it fuels pride and encourages us to follow vain confidence. So flattery not only makes us stupid, it sets us up for divine chastisement.

This thought brings to mind the Shining One with a whip in his hand. Was he an angelic messenger sent to rebuke, correct, and deliver two of Christ's sheep who had inadvertently gone astray? The fact that angels have a part in God's providential care of his people might seem to suggest it. (Hebrews 1:13-14) However, even though they appeared to Old Testament saints now and then, it is unlikely that angels are seen today in visible form, or that we are aware of their intervention on our behalf. They are God's servants, ministering spirits who execute his will behind the scenes.

Although I would not say so dogmatically, I personally believe that the Shining One illustrates the work of the triune God in the souls of his redeemed. The man certainly had an aura of great authority about him, as well as full knowledge of who Christian and Hopeful were and how they happened to be in such a situation. What about his thorough understanding of the one called the Flatterer? Does that not suggest divine omniscience? Moreover, the whip in his hand indicated both the authority to rebuke and chasten the errant men and the power to deliver them from the snare laid for them. These are not minor details, my friend.

Deliverance from the Flatterer is no easy matter. It only comes through the power of God, and often by means of severe correction. Since the whip in the hand of the Shining One was figurative, Christian and Hopeful did not receive a literal beating, but neither should we presume that they got off lightly. Whatever the form of correction may have been, it was severe enough to produce the intended result. As they were led into the right path once again, they resumed their journey with sincerely penitent hearts and a spirit of gratitude for the great mercy shown them.

What a beautiful picture John Bunyan gives us here of the way in which our heavenly Father deals with his children when they go astray! With the appearance of the Shining One upon the scene, can we not perceive his heart of love toward us? His love is so strong and true that nothing can sever our souls from it, and yet, it is perfectly consistent with strong reprimand and correction, when they are warranted. (Romans 8:35-39; Hebrews 12:5-7)

Although we may be tempted to doubt his love when under chastisement, our heavenly Father takes no delight in our suffering. However, it is his good pleasure that we become partakers of Christ's holiness in ever increasing measure. So even though chastening is an exquisitely painful thing, it reinforces both the fear of God and the desire to obey and please him. At the same time, it ministers comfort and assurance to our chastened, contrite hearts.

The writer of Psalm 119 was one who loved the law of God and delighted to walk in its precepts. He was a godly man with the heart of a true pilgrim, but he was also one who was not yet perfect. Therefore, he still had need of divine correction and discipline, and was wise enough to acknowledge both his need of affliction and its benefit to his soul. (Psalm 119:67)

In the duty of child training and discipline, we earthly parents often fall short. We may chasten too severely due to anger, frustration, disappointment or some other selfish motive. Or we may take the other extreme and be negligent and inconsistent in this parental duty. This is never the case with our heavenly Father. His discipline is exactly suited to our particular need, and is always administered out of love for us. (Revelation 3:19) Moreover, its severity is always tempered by his tender mercies. (Psalm 119:77)

Dear friend in Christ, may we always keep these precious truths in heart and mind. Although it seems so hard to bear, God's chastening will produce in us the peaceable fruit of righteousness. Its purpose is never to harm or destroy, but to correct and transform us into the lovely image of his Son. So in the hour of trial, we need to remind ourselves that it is a loving hand that holds the whip. Have we reached the point in our spiritual maturity where we can honestly pray from the heart: *I know, O LORD, that thy judgments are right, and that thou in faithfulness hast afflicted me?* (Psalm 119:75) If so, then perhaps we will be better able to kiss the rod and view it as an evident token of his lovingkindness.

Study Questions

1. What unexpected circumstance brought Christian and Hopeful to a standstill and confused their sense of direction? What did their present situation denote? How important was it that they make the right decision? What had the shepherds given them for such a time as this?

2. Why did Christian and Hopeful fail to recognize the Flatterer when he suddenly appeared before them? Why were they so heedless as to follow a perfect stranger just because he claimed to know the way to the Celestial City? At what point did they realize they had made a terrible mistake?

3. Although Christian and Hopeful were helplessly caught in the Flatterer's net, the Lord was very merciful to them. In the appearance of the Shining One with a whip in his hand, we see the providence of God at work in their behalf. Summarize the instruction and correction that the two men received due to their great error, and the beneficial effect it had upon them.

4. As the ultimate flatterer, Satan has a false gospel and many false teachers to proclaim it. What are some of the ways in which these false teachers ensnare and deceive their hearers? How can we guard ourselves against this web of deception?

5. Even if we are able to discern truth from error when confronted with it, what about the flatterer that lurks in our own hearts? In what way does this flatterer within war against us? How does giving heed to flattery makes us stupid?

CHAPTER 49

Dangerous Trek Across the Enchanted Ground

THE UPPER NIAGARA RIVER IS A TRULY MAGNIFICENT SIGHT, AND THUS A popular spot for recreational boating and fishing. However, this particular river harbors a deadly secret. Once it reaches the border that separates Ontario, Canada from the United States, the Niagara River suddenly plunges over a steep precipice and crashes violently onto huge boulders 300 feet below. Nevertheless, boaters can safely enjoy the placid waters of the upper Niagara, as long as they do not cross its point of no return.

Since the current of the river accelerates gradually at first, an inexperienced boater occasionally drifts into dangerous territory without realizing it. As the river approaches Niagara Falls, it picks up speed at an alarming rate until its waters become raging white rapids. Should one happen to drift across that intangible point of no return, he will find himself trapped in a current so strong that he cannot escape from it. Unless immediate help comes to his rescue, he will be swept over the falls in a terrible tragedy that could have been avoided, if only he had heeded the warning signs.

Likewise, there is a spiritual point of no return that leads to apostasy, and negligence in spiritual matters can draw one perilously close to it. Figuratively speaking, the highway to the Celestial City is littered with the bones of those who once claimed to be pilgrims. To all outward appearance they truly belonged to Christ; but after a time, they turned aside to follow him no more. Witnessing this happen to those we know and love is one of the most painful trials we face as God's people. It is a frightening one as well, for it causes us to wonder if the same thing could happen to us. How can we be certain it will not?

Before we settle this question, we must first remember how apostasy begins. It is the end result of a gradual process, which always begins in the heart. (Psalm 10:4) Eventually, one who has turned from Christ in his heart will begin to demonstrate it by his speech and conduct. Thus he becomes atheistic in both thought and action, saying in essence that there is no God. (Psalm 14:1) Although he may not actually deny the existence of God, his rebel heart feels no accountability and refuses to bow to him.

Christian and Hopeful soon met such a man when they saw a lone traveler far in the distance. He was walking directly toward them "softly," according to John Bunyan, and yet with a decided purpose. After their recent experience with the Flatterer they were much more watchful than before, so they wondered at once why he was going the wrong way. Who could the stranger be? Was he a true pilgrim who had lost his way, or another enemy in disguise? At a distance they could not tell for sure. However, the fact that he was walking away from the Celestial City was enough to place them on high alert, in case he proved to be another flatterer.

They were wise to be cautious, for the stranger's name was Atheist. His bearing was that of a bold, arrogant sort of man, and when he began to speak, there remained no doubt that this was indeed the case. As soon as he came near enough, he asked Christian and Hopeful where they were going, but there was something odd about the way in which he asked it. When the men told him they were headed to Mount Zion, he laughed derisively and said, "I laugh to see what ignorant persons you are, to take upon you so tedious a journey, and yet are like to have nothing but your travel for your pains."

Christian was so taken aback by this response that he completely misinterpreted the man's meaning. When he asked, "Do you think we shall not be received?" Christian was fearful of what the man's answer might be, and greatly relieved when Atheist declared that there was no such place. Why would Christian breathe a sigh of relief upon hearing such a thing? Even though he had no doubt whatsoever about the existence of the city, he was still troubled now and then by the fear that he would not be received there. His faith in Christ was genuine and unshakeable, but the same could not be said concerning his assurance of salvation.

With a patently scornful edge to his voice, Atheist chided Christian and Hopeful for their ignorance. Clearly he was of the opinion that their hope was a flight of fancy and a foolish delusion. Had he tried to convince Christian that he had no hope of being received into the heavenly Zion, Atheist probably would have had some success. However, to his bold assertion that "there is no such place as you dream of in all this world," Christian had the ready answer, "but there is in the world to come." In these few words Christian gave the essence of our hope in Christ. Like Abraham of old, he *looked for a city which hath foundations, whose builder and maker is God.* (Hebrews 11:10)

As Atheist tried his best to convince Christian and Hopeful that their journey was in vain, they made the startling discovery that he once claimed to be a pilgrim. When Christian insisted that the Celestial City was indeed a real place, Atheist admitted that at one time he would have agreed. Long ago, perhaps in his youth, he heard the Gospel and professed to believe in Christ. For twenty years he traveled the King's Highway, going even further than Christian and Hopeful without finding any evidence of the city. When he finally became disillusioned, he gave up the search and headed back to his own country and former life there.

What a tragic story! Could the man Atheist really have searched for the Celestial City for over twenty years, to no avail? Yes, dear reader, such a thing is possible. One of the most heart-breaking aspects of the Gospel ministry is witnessing the gradual apostasy of those for whom we once had great hope. I could name quite a few who showed early promise and seemed quite sincere in their Christian profession, until it finally became apparent that something was terribly wrong. Eventually, they gave up all pretense of following Christ in much the same way as the former pilgrim turned Atheist.

How could he have searched for the Celestial City for so long without finding it? Clearly, he did not seek it by faith. (Hebrews 11:1-6) Although he maintained an outward profession of faith for twenty years, he had never experienced a work of God's grace within. He believed after a fashion, but not to the saving of his soul. (Hebrews 10:38-39) The truth had never taken root in him; therefore, he gave no evidence of spiritual fruit or growth in grace. So Atheist did not lose his salvation; he had no spiritual life to begin with. Like Pliable, he sought those things that would be to his advantage in this life, but the way to Zion does not lie in that direction.

During his conversation with Atheist, Christian might have worried about its effect upon Hopeful. After all, he had shown an appalling lack of discernment in the matter of Little-Faith and his jewels. So Christian put his brother to the test by asking, "Is it true which this man hath said?"

Now it was Hopeful's turn to be shocked. Not understanding the intent behind the question, he responded with incredulity, saying, "Take heed, he is one of the flatterers; remember what it hath cost us once already for our hearkening to such kind of fellows. What! No Mount Zion? Did we not see from the Delectable Mountains, the gate of the city? Also, are we not now to walk by faith? Let us go on…lest the man with the whip overtake us again."

Hopeful continued along this same line, all but certain that Christian was in danger of erring from the truth. (Proverbs 19:27) In so doing, he gave strong evidence of godly fear and showed how effectively God's chastisement had corrected and cleared his spiritual thinking. However, I wonder if perhaps it was with a slight air of superiority that Hopeful said to Christian, "You should have taught me that lesson, which I will round you in the ears withal."

Christian must have smiled to himself upon hearing this indignant reproof. Until that moment, he may still have been a bit unsure of Hopeful because he had criticized Little-Faith for not parting with his precious jewels when in desperate need. Hopeful's thoughts concerning Esau had been a matter of grave concern to Christian at that time, even causing him to fear for the younger man's soul. Therefore, Christian must have been greatly relieved by his reaction.

Dear reader, consider the strong bond of brotherly love that existed between Christian and Hopeful, for it is a rare and precious thing. Each of them cared deeply for the spiritual welfare of the other. Since they were friends in the truest sense, they challenged, encouraged, and even rebuked one another when necessary. (Proverbs 27:6)

I would not venture a guess as to which one of them was stronger in the faith.

For the present they went on their way rejoicing, because they now understood one another and were in perfect agreement concerning the man Atheist. Having recognized him for the flatterer he was, his diabolical words had not shaken them at all. When they turned away from him and made their way onward, faith and hope burned all the brighter in their hearts. As for Atheist, he made his way back toward the broad way that leads to destruction, mocking Christian and Hopeful all the while.

Profile of the Enchanted Ground

The tragic account of Atheist and his aborted pilgrimage reminds us once again that the Christian life is like a race we have entered. Many who begin it will eventually grow weary and drop out of the running. The victor's crown is only promised to those who actually cross the finish line, that is, to those who remain faithful until their journey's end. (Revelation 2:10) To these blood-washed overcomers, and to them alone, will be granted an entrance into the beautiful City of God. (Revelation 7:14; Revelation 22:14) In that day, they will stand without fault before the throne of God, in spite of the struggles and temptations that plagued them throughout their earthly pilgrimage. (Revelation 14:5)

Since Scripture likens the Christian life to a race that must be run to its completion, it is well to observe the seasoned athlete, a marathon runner in particular. In order to go the distance and finish the race, he must prepare himself ahead of time by rigorous training. At the starting line he must set his sights forward and be mentally focused upon the goal. Throughout the 26.2 mile course, he must pace himself and block out anything that would distract his attention. Then he must reserve his last measure of strength for the final sprint across the finish line. By that time his energy will be nearly depleted, but consistent discipline and training will stand him in good stead as he nears the goal.

These same principles hold true concerning our race to eternal glory. The apostle Paul clearly had this analogy in mind when he wrote: *Brethren, I count not myself to have apprehended: but this one thing I do, forgetting those things which are behind, and reaching forth unto those things which are before, I press toward the mark for the prize of the high calling of God in Christ Jesus.* (Philippians 3:13-14) As he penned these words, Paul's earthly race was just about over. Yet even then, he would not claim a premature victory.

It might seem logical to expect our journey to become a little easier the further we go. Faith and hope should gradually become stronger, the world less alluring, and trials a little easier to patiently bear. This should indeed be the case; but presuming victory before the race is won places us at higher risk of succumbing to the age-old enemy, spiritual complacency.

We have seen this play out in Christian's journey repeatedly, often after he has taken a bold stand for truth. Such times call for heightened awareness and watchfulness on our part, not less. So there was a valuable lesson to be learned from the encounter with Atheist. His apostasy reminded Christian and Hopeful that they were not yet out of danger. If our great enemy plots our downfall all along the way, what evil design might he not have in store as we approach our journey's end? We can rest assured that he will never cease to attack us as long as we are on this side of glory.

Chronologically speaking, Christian and Hopeful had now entered this stage of their earthly journey. They still had some distance to go, but not nearly so far as they had already come. At this point, they were seasoned travelers along the path of life, but still well within range of the enemy.

For an indefinite period of time after their encounter with Atheist, they traveled along without significant trial or incident. Eventually, however, they entered the jurisdiction of another country to which they were strangers. It is a peculiar sort of place, with an atmosphere that is almost drug-like. Those who are born and raised there are naturally accustomed to it and go about their daily business unaffected by it. Yet foreigners often find it difficult to resist the strange drowsiness that comes upon them as they pass through this country, known in those parts as the Enchanted Ground.

Before long, Hopeful began to feel the effects of the noxious air around them. As his faculties became increasingly more impaired, he felt that he could go no further without taking a nap. Although he was not conscious of it, the toxic atmosphere had begun to affect his mind. Had it not been for his brother's greater discernment, Hopeful might have fallen into deep trouble here. Thankfully, Christian recognized the danger at once and warned him against yielding to it. But Hopeful tried his best to convince Christian that it was all right, saying, "Sleep is sweet to the laboring man; we may be refreshed if we take a nap." It seems a logical argument, does it not? In fact, Hopeful drew from Scripture in so saying, but did he make proper application of it, or misuse it to suit his own desire? (Ecclesiastes 5:12) The latter, I fear!

How was it that Christian clearly saw the danger to which Hopeful was oblivious? He remembered the shepherds' warning to "Beware of the Enchanted Ground." Moreover, Christian realized that they must now have come to that place, and understood the warning to mean that they should resist the urge to sleep there.

Although the Word of God never mentions the Enchanted Ground by name, it often refers to the world as a place of spiritual danger for the Christian. Like the City of Destruction and Vanity Fair, the Enchanted Ground is synonymous with this present evil world under the rule of Satan, the god of this world. No boundaries exist to separate the three. They are differing aspects of the same thing, and as such, they pose an ever-present danger to the people of God.

Since the Enchanted Ground is the sphere of their operation, flatterers and false teachers are found there in abundance. Therefore, spiritual chaos is the accepted norm in a world turned upside down, a world in which men call good evil and evil good. Truth and right are viewed in relative terms, and tolerance is the rule of the day for just about anything except Christ and his truth.

In particular, the Enchanted Ground depicts the intoxicating effect of the world and the things that are in the world. Like the merchandise sold in Vanity Fair, everything about it appeals to man's fallen nature, but is directly opposed to our new life in Christ. Unsaved men live under its influence and desire nothing else, but the Enchanted Ground is also designed to charm and entice the hearts of those who are in Christ. Its intent is to wear down our resistance and fill our hearts with vain things until we become spiritually insensible. Its ultimate goal is to allure and reclaim God's people for the kingdom of darkness, if possible. Therefore, sleeping on the Enchanted Ground can have dire consequences.

My brother or sister in Christ, to sleep on the Enchanted Ground is to yield to its hypnotic effect and become too comfortable and settled there. A little neglect is all that is necessary for one to unknowingly sink into this condition. Moreover, it is easier to fall under the spell of the world's enchantment than we might think. As a rule, our greatest danger is not that we will commit some great moral transgression. The greater likelihood is that our hearts will be drawn away from the pursuit of God and the priority of seeking first his kingdom and righteousness.

It is not sinful to enjoy the material blessings God has given to us. (1 Timothy 6:17-19) However, we tread upon extremely dangerous ground when our eyes are moved from eternal realities and fixed upon temporal blessings. God gives these things to us in trust, and only for a little while. Therefore, we must keep them in their proper place and hold onto them lightly, lest they become idols in our hearts. (1 John 5:21)

Given the fact that the Enchanted Ground is everywhere, Christian and Hopeful could not avoid passing over it, but they must resist the urge to settle there. Many have lain down intending to nap there for a brief time, but never woke again. If Christian and Hopeful are to avoid the same end, they must remain awake and watchful during the entire passage. (Revelation 16:15)

What a good thing for Hopeful that he was not alone at this time! Had that been the case, who knows what might have happened to him? His humble attitude is also worthy of special note. He could have become angry and defensive when Christian reminded him that Scripture said: *Let us not sleep, as do others; but let us watch and be sober.* (1 Thessalonians 5:6) Instead, he was quick to acknowledge his wrong and quote Solomon's words: *Two are better than one; because they have a good reward for their labor, for if they fall, the one will lift up his fellow: but woe to him that is alone when he falleth; for he hath not another to help him up.* (Ecclesiastes 4:9-10) In so saying, Hopeful expressed deep gratitude for his brother's help.

Naturally speaking, sleep is sweet to the laboring man. It refreshes him in both body and mind, and gives renewed strength for the day ahead. However, physical sleep is not the issue here. It is but a figure portraying the complacency of heart and mind that, if allowed to go unchecked, can lead to spiritual darkness and insensibility. That spiritual lethargy can indeed be a serious problem for us is clear from Paul's admonition to believers in Romans 13:11-12: *And that, knowing the time, that now it is high time to awake out of sleep: for now is our salvation nearer than when we believed. The night is far spent, the day is at hand: let us therefore cast off the works of darkness, and let us put on the armour of light.*

How does spiritual lethargy overtake us? It does so much like carbon monoxide in a poorly-ventilated space, little by little so that we never suspect what is happening. For whatever reasons, we become weary in well-doing, which soon progresses to neglect of spiritual duties. Neglect leads to a divided heart, a distracted mind, and forgetfulness of God's Word. Before we know it, we are sleeping on enchanted ground!

At the very least, should this happen to us, we could suffer the loss of those things that sweeten our earthly journey and help us along the way. Little-Faith is a prime example of this kind of loss. But if taken to the extreme, and here Atheist comes to mind, spiritual negligence can progress to outright apostasy. How do we guard ourselves against this terrible danger? How do we maintain the spiritual alertness needed to safely complete our journey? First, by heeding the apostle Peter's exhortation when he says: *Gird up the loins of your mind, be sober, and hope to the end for the grace that is to be brought unto you at the revelation of Jesus Christ.* (1 Peter 1:13)

Peter's words remind me of Proverbs 4:23: *Keep thy heart with all diligence; for out of it are the issues of life.* The heart (the mind; the inner man) is where this battle is either won or lost. In order to keep our hearts with all diligence, we must never forget the diligence with which our adversary plots our downfall. Like a ravenous beast, he is constantly on the prowl. So in order to resist him steadfastly in the faith, we must maintain a sober, vigilant watch over our own souls. (1 Peter 5:8-9) At no time can we afford to slumber and sleep, that is, become lethargic and careless in our Christian walk. On the contrary, we must be on constant alert to the danger around us by maintaining a sound spiritual mind. (1 Corinthians 15:33-34; 1 Corinthians 16:13; Ephesians 5:14-16)

This self watch is to characterize our entire manner of life as we anticipate our Lord's imminent return. (Matthew 24:42-43; Matthew 25:13; Mark 13:34-37; Luke 12 37-40; Revelation 3:2-3) However, we must never presume that we can accomplish it in our own strength. Fervent prayer and dependence upon our Lord must always go hand-in-hand with diligent watchfulness. Without his constant guidance and help, our best efforts are doomed to failure. (Luke 21:34-36; Ephesians 6:18; Colossians 4:2; 1 Peter 4:7) Truly, we *can do all things through Christ which strengtheneth* us, but it is equally certain that without him we can do nothing. (Philippians 4:13; John 15:5)

How does this watchfulness become a practical reality in our lives? By what means can we counter the intoxicating effects of the Enchanted Ground? Just how do we obey the command to keep our hearts with all diligence? The apostle Paul gives the key in Philippians 4:8: *Finally, brethren, whatsoever things are true, whatsoever things are honest, whatsoever things are just, whatsoever things are pure, whatsoever things are lovely, whatsoever things are of good report; if there be any virtue, and if there be any praise, think on these things.* When our hearts and minds are fixed upon the Lord Jesus Christ and his Word, we will be much less inclined to succumb to the evil influences around us. (Psalm 119:97-104) Moreover, we will be far more likely to remain alert and watchful of the dangers that lie in our path. (Colossians 3:1-3; Hebrews 12:1-3)

Another invaluable means of help comes from fellowship with our brethren in Christ. Who can measure the benefit gained from speaking often to one another concerning our mutual faith and Christian walk? (Malachi 3:16) As long-term fellow travelers, Christian and Hopeful have learned this well. Moreover, they had experienced first-hand the truth: *Iron sharpeneth iron; so a man sharpeneth the countenance of his friend.* (Proverbs 27:17) So in order to remain alert as they passed over the dangerous Enchanted Ground, they agreed to talk of things that would be spiritually profitable. Then, as if in anticipation of the benefit they would receive, Christian sang this pilgrim song:

> When saints do sleepy grow, let them come hither,
> And hear how these two pilgrims talk together,
> Yea, let them learn of them in any wise

Thus to keep ope' their drowzy slumb'ring eyes;
Saints fellowship if it be manag'd well,
Keeps them awake, and that in spite of hell."

While working on this particular chapter and pondering the meaning of the Enchanted Ground, I had an unnerving experience that served as an illustration of its danger. My husband and I were traveling home after attending a Bible conference in the Midwest. Feeling the need to stretch our legs, we stopped at a rest area with a grassy field nearby. Since it was early spring, the grass was thick and green, and had been recently mowed.

As we walked along, I happened to glance down and see what appeared to be a small section of garden hose right at my feet. Giving little heed to its strange markings, I stepped over it, but as I did so a thought occurred to me, prompting me to stop and take a closer look. Then I saw the small rounded head and beady eyes that had escaped my notice before. It was a snake in the grass and I had nearly stepped on him! Had I done so, he would certainly have struck, but thankfully, the snake was not aggressive. He undoubtedly saw me before I saw him, yet laid still while I stepped directly over him.

Perhaps it was a mere coincidence, but I believe that everything in nature contains a spiritual lesson for us if we have eyes to see it. What could I learn from stepping across a snake lying still and watchful in the grass? It reminded me that our adversary, the old serpent himself, does the very same thing. Whether lurking furtively in the shadows or taking a more direct approach, he waits until we are distracted and strikes when we least expect it. Therefore, we should take care and watch our step.

The sin of worry and its antidote

As I think of the Enchanted Ground and the terrible danger it poses, I find a striking similarity between one who has fallen asleep there and the thorny ground hearer in our Lord's Parable of the Sower. In both cases, the cares and riches and pleasures of this life were given precedence until they finally choked out the good seed of the Word of God so that it brought forth no fruit to perfection. (Luke 8:14)

By contrast, the heart of a true Christian is good ground that has been prepared by God to receive the seed of his Word. Having heard and received it in an honest and good heart, he keeps it and brings forth fruit with patience. (Luke 8:15) The implications of the parable are clear that those who savingly believe in Christ will bring forth spiritual fruit. However, we must still contend with the same things that clutter and overtake the heart of the thorny ground hearer.

Notice the two broad categories into which these things fall: the cares of this life, and the riches and pleasures of this life. (Luke 8:14) They are seemingly opposite problems, but both are equally dangerous because they focus the attention upon things pertaining to this life only.

Dear friend in Christ, since we are not exempt from these temptations, I dare say that you and I could chronicle our own struggles with the affairs of this life. Something as simple as the evening news can provide a means of direct assault against our hearts and minds. How easy it is to become distracted and filled with anxiety when each day's breaking news seems more scandalous and shocking than yesterday's headlines. How our hearts can be carried away if we fail to view these things from the perspective of God's absolute sovereignty.

Without question, we live in fearfully uncertain times. What about the threats to our rapidly diminishing freedom, our very way of life as we know it? How will we survive if our nation is truly headed for economic collapse and we lose everything for which we have labored so hard? What about the ruinous decisions being made by our nation's leaders that threaten to destroy the cornerstone upon which our Republic was founded? Many seek to overthrow the principles for which our Founding Fathers were willing to pledge their lives, their fortunes, and their sacred honor in order to establish. Even more worrisome, how can we protect our families and ourselves from the rampant ungodliness and moral corruption of the society in which we live? Before we know it, we are reeling from the toxic effects of the Enchanted Ground and our hearts threaten to fail us for fear.

As you have probably surmised, this particular temptation has vexed me greatly, as of late. Perhaps it is a problem for you as well. As I write these words, I am keenly aware of the Enchanted Ground all around me, as well as its power to influence my mind. It is so, even though I firmly believe that the Lord Jesus Christ is the absolute ruler over the affairs of men, and the hearts of our leaders are in his omnipotent hands. (Psalm 103:19; Proverbs 21: 1, 31)

My husband was quick to recognize my problem and warn me of it, in much the same way Christian did with Hopeful. He also reminded me of how spiritually detrimental it is to become consumed with worry, and also of our Lord's prohibition against it. (Matthew 6:24-34) He was right, as usual. Our main business is to serve the Lord faithfully by trusting him and doing what he has given us to do. My husband's wise counsel reminded me of the motto by which Oswald Chambers lived: "Trust God, and do the next thing." [1]

To trust and obey is pretty much the sum of our duty as God's children, but it can seem more difficult in light of the evening news. After all, everything about the Enchanted Ground is directly opposed to our life of faith and unswerving obedience to our Lord. Moreover, since our pathway goes right through it, we cannot escape its influence entirely. Yet we can and must arm ourselves against it. So take courage, fellow pilgrim, as we march across the Enchanted Ground. Each step forward may meet with fierce resistance, but mark well the footprints along the path. They belong to our brethren in Christ who have passed this way before and made it safely over.

The temptation to be caught up with earthly worries and cares is a life-long struggle for most of us, but this is probably not the most dangerous aspect of the Enchanted Ground. It seems to hold a special kind of trial in reserve for those who have been in Christ for many years. John Bunyan must have had some such thought in mind when he placed the Enchanted Ground near the end of Christian and Hopeful's journey.

At the outset, when one is newly born again, his heart burns with love for his Lord and the fervent desire to serve and honor him. During the early years of his journey and well into the prime of life, he labors diligently in the service of God's kingdom. However, as he approaches his golden years, he faces a trial of another sort, one that he may not even perceive as a trial.

For perhaps the first time in his life, a measure of prosperity takes the place of earlier financial struggles. Simultaneously, he may enjoy a season of relative freedom from stress when all seems to be going well, for a change. At the same time, he may also be tempted to let down his guard a bit in spiritual matters. After all, he has been in the battle for a long time now. Has he not earned a rest? Is it not time to retire from active duty and enjoy his blessings?

Many sincere Christians are tempted to think such thoughts as they anticipate the autumn season of life. After decades of active employment with its constant pressures and vexations, they look forward to retirement as an opportunity to take it easy, pursue other interests, and enjoy the fruits of their labor. However, they place themselves in grave danger if they retire from active spiritual duty as well.

Our great adversary understands this natural desire quite well. So it is not by chance that the Enchanted Ground extends all the way to the end of our earthly sojourn. As God's people, we are expressly warned against seeking our rest and comfort in this world. (Micah 2:10; Luke 8:14) Even the most worthwhile of earthly pursuits will prove a dangerous stumbling block if allowed to capture our hearts. Therefore, we dare not let down our spiritual guard or presume upon the grace of God just because we have followed the Lord for many years. Our lion-like adversary crouches nearest when we are least aware of it. He can, and does, devour the heedless. Therefore, it is more important than ever that our hearts remain fixed on things above and our minds finely-tuned to the things of God. In Matthew 24:12 the Lord Jesus warned of what would happen to many of his professed disciples when he said: *Because iniquity shall abound, the love of many shall wax cold.* Dear Christian friend, let us take care not to be numbered among them.

* * * *

At the beginning of our journey, how can we know for sure that we will be able to complete it? Perhaps we cannot. Whether faith is genuine or not is only known for sure in that it endures. If we would be followers of them who through faith and patience inherit the promises, we must show the same diligence to the full assurance of hope unto the end. (Hebrews 6:11-12) Then by his grace and power, we will overcome and be victorious. (Revelation 3:12)

We should not expect the journey to become easier with the passing of time, nor suppose that our adversary will cease to war against us as we grow older and weaker in body. However, such is the nature of God's faithfulness that he will be with us and keep us through every season and circumstance of life. He whose wisdom planned it all and ordered each step will guide us safely home. Far from his tender care diminishing as we grow more fragile with age, we have his precious promise: *Even to your old age I am he; and even to hoar hairs will I carry you: I have made, and I will bear; even I will carry, and will deliver you.* (Isaiah 46:4)

Although we live in a culture that worships before the shrines of youth and beauty, let us not be tempted to adopt the same mindset. There is nothing quite as lovely as the Christ-like countenance of those who are advanced in grace as well as age. For these godly brothers and sisters, white hair is indeed a crown of glory that adorns them as they near the end of their earthly lives. (Proverbs 16:31)

Concerning those who have been in Christ for many years, the psalmist gives great encouragement, saying: *The righteous shall flourish like the palm tree: he shall grow like a cedar in Lebanon. Those that be planted in the house of the LORD shall flourish in the courts of our God. They shall still bring forth fruit in old age; they shall be fat and flourishing; to shew that the LORD is upright: he is my rock, and there is no unrighteousness in him."* (Psalm 92:12-15) If we truly belong to Christ, our fruitfulness in his kingdom will not diminish with the passing of time.

Therefore, dear friend in Christ, let us resolve to make our golden years spiritually profitable ones. Let us redeem the time and seize the opportunity to be as active in the service of our Lord as our physical health permits. Moreover, let us be diligent and watchful in our personal walk with him, as we pass over the Enchanted Ground. (Ephesians 5:15-17) The longer we walk with the Lord, the more clearly we understand that every season of life has its unique struggles and trials. Do not be tempted to give up the battle, whatever form it may take. One day, perhaps sooner than you think, faith's fiery trial will end in faith's final triumph!

On Him Almighty vengeance fell, that must have sunk a world to hell;
　　He bore it for a chosen race, and thus became their hiding place.
A few more rolling suns at most, shall land me safe on Canaan's coast;
There I shall sing the song of grace, to Jesus Christ my hiding place. [2]

Study Questions

1. How did a former professing Christian become the man named Atheist? What compelling evidence was there that he was never truly born again? What effect did the encounter with him have upon Christian and Hopeful?

2. When Hopeful was on the verge of succumbing to the toxic atmosphere of the Enchanted Ground, why did Christian recognize the danger to which his brother was oblivious? What is the figurative meaning of the Enchanted Ground?

3. What does it mean to sleep on the Enchanted Ground? What particular danger does it pose for the Christian?

4. Since spiritual lethargy is an ever-present danger that often has dire consequences, how are we to guard ourselves against it? How do we maintain the spiritual alertness needed in order to complete our journey? By what means can we counter the intoxicating effect of the Enchanted Ground?

5. Although the sin of worry is a spiritually detrimental thing, it is not the most dangerous aspect of the Enchanted Ground. What particular kind of trial does it hold in reserve for those who have been in Christ for many years?

CHAPTER 50

A Tribute to God's Amazing Grace

As we endeavor to live for our Lord and share his Gospel with others, our efforts can seem futile when met with scoffing and rejection. Yet we never know what may result from our testimony. It is our duty to faithfully sow the seed of God's Word and leave the results to the Lord of the harvest. (Luke 10:2) Even though we may not witness the outcome, we have his assurance that our labor is not in vain. (1 Corinthians 15:58) Therefore, our greatest encouragement must come, not from seeing results, but from our Lord's own promise: *For as the rain cometh down, and the snow from heaven, and returneth not thither, but watereth the earth, and maketh it bring forth and bud, that it may give seed to the sower, and bread to the eater: so shall my word be that goeth forth out of my mouth: it shall not return unto me void, but it shall accomplish that which I please, and it shall prosper in the thing whereto I sent it.* (Isaiah 55:10-11)

Through the faithful witness of others, Christian and Hopeful heard the joyful sound of the Gospel, and for quite some time now, they have been fellow travelers along the King's Highway. Since the day God's providence caused their paths to cross, they have shared many things in common, both trials and blessings. As a result, a strong bond of brotherly love existed between them.

Now that they had reached the Enchanted Ground, they both understood the importance of remaining alert and watchful. So in anticipation of a dangerous passage of indefinite length, the two men agreed to spend the time in profitable conversation. What better way to ensure their time was well spent than to talk of spiritual things? Since they both thought it best to start at the beginning, Christian asked Hopeful about the way in which God first began to work in his soul. It seems a bit strange that the subject had not come up before, but for whatever reason, the time was now right.

You may recall that when Christian escaped from Vanity Fair, Hopeful followed him afterward and eventually joined him. Until that time, the young man was just another anonymous resident of that awful place. But through God's amazing grace, a lad who had no hope became the pilgrim named Hopeful. The following is his story, a first-hand account of how God used the example and testimony of two of his servants to deliver a soul from destruction and set him on the path of life.

As a native son of Vanity Township, Hopeful's former life consisted of the pursuit of happiness and personal fulfillment. He sought these things by partaking freely of the worldly pleasures for which the town's fair is noted. Thus he lived from day to day, an empty life in spite of his expectations to the contrary, until Christian and Faithful came to town.

If you remember, the two pilgrims caused a near riot among the residents of Vanity just by being noticeably different. Many accused them of being disturbers of the peace because their godly conduct and speech made others uncomfortable. Yet in spite of threats from the local authorities, they declared the Gospel openly to the people, and Hopeful just happened to be one of those who heard them.

This was apparently the first time he had heard the Gospel, and at first, Hopeful was seemingly unmoved by it. Like many a convicted sinner when confronted with the truth, he fled from the light before fleeing to it. So he closed his mind to the truth when it first began to disturb him, and refused to consider his sin and the judgment to come. Yet for all of his efforts to deny it, something had happened to him. The Spirit of God was working in his heart, although he had no idea of it at the time.

Why did he resist the light of the Gospel and the outcries of his own conscience? Sin was still sweet to him and he was not yet willing to forsake it. Neither was he willing to part with his old friends. However, a greater power was at work within him, and Hopeful could not get away from it. He had no peace; try as he might, he could not break free of the distress that had seized hold of him. When denial was no longer possible, he did his best to stifle the conflict within. But even though there were brief periods when he was able to suppress the fear of conviction, it always returned in full force.

Thus began a period of deep turmoil and misery for the young man. His sinful condition was now uppermost in his heart and mind; moreover, the remembrance of past sins came back to haunt him. (Romans 7:8-13) In fact, they taunted him every time he heard the Word of God or witnessed the godly example of those who knew the Lord. Then recalling the Scripture truth that the wages of sin is death, he began to be tormented by a new dread, the fear of death. He could hardly bear to hear that someone was ill or had died because it reminded him of his own mortality. In spite of all attempts to suppress such thoughts, Hopeful knew that he was not ready to die and face God in judgment. The knowledge weighed heavily upon him, like the burden that almost sank Christian in the Slough of Despond.

The time finally came when he was so afflicted by his guilty conscience that he began to loathe his life of sin. Furthermore, he resolved to forsake and return to it no more, by which means he hoped to rid himself of the terrible guilt and gain peace of mind. Hopeful now undertook to clean up his life, as suppression gave way to self-reformation.

To all outward appearance, he was a new man. He no longer indulged in sinful practices as before, and shunned the company of his former friends. In addition, he became religious and began to pray, read God's Word, and weep over his sins. He even went so far as to speak the truth to his friends and neighbors. In short, Hopeful did everything he could to make himself righteous, and for a while it seemed to work. Reformation brought a measure of relief, but not for long.

Although he had cleaned up his act it was not enough, and deep down, Hopeful knew it. Since he had heard the Word of God concerning the only way of salvation, certain passages of Scripture now came to his mind, killing any notion that good works could make him righteous before God. One such passage was Isaiah 64:6: *But we are all as an unclean thing, and all our righteousnesses are as filthy rags; and*

we all do fade as a leaf; and our iniquities, like the wind, have taken us away.
Another is found in Galatians 2:16: *Knowing that a man is not justified by
the works of the law, but by the faith of Jesus Christ, even we have believed in
Jesus Christ, that we might be justified by the faith of Christ, and not by the
works of the law: for by the works of the law shall no flesh be justified.*

Once these great truths began to dawn upon him, Hopeful found
himself in a terrible quandary. Even supposing he could live the rest
of his life without sinning again, what about his former sins? He
already owed a great debt to divine justice, which he was powerless
to repay. So as he reflected upon his recent efforts to reform himself,
Hopeful realized how utterly futile they were. Even the very best he
could do was tainted with sin. In spite of his best efforts, he was still
an unprofitable servant. (Luke 17:10) Now convinced that he could
never produce a righteousness that would be acceptable to God, he
was at the point of near despair. In anguish of soul he cried, "I have
committed sin enough in one duty to send me to hell, tho' my former
life had been faultless."

The poor soul was desperate, and did not know what to do about
it. Finally, and here is an unexpected twist, he took Faithful into his
confidence, for they were close acquaintances. As Hopeful opened
his heart to his godly friend, Faithful shared the Gospel with him.
Earlier, he had undoubtedly been part of the crowd who mocked
Christian and Faithful, but God had prepared his heart to receive the
truth, and that made all the difference. (Luke 8:15)

When Faithful told him that he must "obtain the righteousness of
a man that never had sinned," for no other righteousness would do,
Hopeful agreed. But where was such a man to be found? Certainly
not in Vanity Fair! Then Faithful told him of the Lord Jesus Christ, the
Lamb of God, which taketh away the sin of the world. (John 1:29) Moreover,
Faithful explained that he is the spotless, sinless Son of God who died
for the sins of others, and that righteousness could only be found
in him. Without the Lord Jesus Christ, Hopeful had no hope! But in
Christ, he could be reconciled to God and justified freely by his grace.
(2 Corinthians 5:20-21; Romans 3:19-26) Herein is God's way of peace.
(Romans 5:1) The sinner has no works to bring and no merit to claim.
Christ is his only hope, his only plea. Hopeful must come to him by
faith and receive all from him.

Like many quickened sinners, Hopeful was brought up short at this point. He understood the Gospel in part, but barriers still existed in his mind. They must all be removed in order for him to come to Christ and trust him alone. One difficulty was the fear that God would not accept him, and therefore, it would be presumptuous of him to come to Christ for salvation.

Such fears can only be laid to rest by clear and thorough instruction in God's Word, so Faithful took care to do just that. The notion that God is somehow reluctant to save sinners is not to be found in Scripture. Did he not give his only begotten Son to save sinners? (John 3:16; Romans 5:8) Did not the Lord Jesus Christ state plainly that he came to seek and to save that which was lost? (Luke 19:10)

The Gospel invitation to burdened sinners is given throughout Scripture in the most gracious of terms. Needy sinners can freely come to Christ, believe on him, eat and drink of him and rest in him. (Isaiah 55:1-3; John 6:47-51; John 7:37-38; Matthew 11:28-30) The Gospel feast has been spread and those who hunger and thirst after righteousness are bidden to come and partake freely. They may look unto the Lord Jesus Christ and be saved. (Isaiah 45:22)

As if the Gospel invitation found throughout Scripture was not enough, its gracious call is reiterated in its conclusion in Revelation 22:17: *And the Spirit and the bride say, 'Come.' And let him that heareth say, 'Come.' And let him that is athirst come. And whosoever will, let him take the water of life freely.* Therefore, any barrier exists solely in the mind of the sinner, making him without excuse. Neither is it enough to merely hear the Gospel and comprehend it intellectually. One must come to Christ and trust in him. The sinner must actually enter in through the Wicket Gate, for only then will he find true peace and rest.

Dear reader, I feel sure the striking similarities between the experience of Hopeful and that of Christian did not escape your notice. As Christian listened to his brother tell of his deliverance from Vanity Fair, he must have relived his own flight from the City of Destruction. Moreover, while Hopeful related his spiritual struggles prior to conversion, Christian would certainly have remembered the awful time when fear and doubt cast him headlong into the Slough of Despond. Although the slough was a barrier that existed solely in his mind, Christian was nonetheless unable to break free of it until Help came along and extended a hand. By instructing Christian more clearly in the Gospel of God's grace, Help threw him a spiritual lifeline, just as his friend Evangelist had done. It was through the power of the Gospel that the barrier created by fear and despondency was finally broken down.

Faithful ministered to Hopeful in exactly the same way, first by refuting every notion that salvation could be obtained through self-reformation or the performance of good works and religious duties. Then, through diligent instruction in the Gospel, Faithful stressed the vital truth that salvation is in Christ alone. Justification, being declared righteous before God, comes by faith in him alone. Moreover, Faithful assured him that the Lord Jesus invited him to come as a needy sinner. He could come as he was and be made whole! He could repent, confess his sins, and plead for mercy and forgiveness! He was bidden to believe the Scriptures with all of his heart and trust his soul to Christ alone! There is a fountain opened for sin and uncleanness. (Zechariah 13:1) When plunged beneath its cleansing flow his sins, though…as scarlet, would be as white as snow. (Isaiah 1:18)

Following Faithful's instruction, Hopeful began to earnestly seek the Lord in prayer, but his struggle with doubt and fear was not yet over. It seemed that God would not answer his prayers; therefore, Hopeful thought to give up, but not for long. Truth had taken deep root in his soul and he must have Christ or else perish. So he resolved to "die at the throne of grace," if perish he must.

Why did God not immediately relieve Hopeful's anguish? Perhaps he did so in order to show him even greater mercy. Quite often, the Lord will wait, that he may be gracious to us. (Isaiah 30:18) The greater our struggles, the more we become aware of our helplessness before God. The greater the travail of conviction for sin, the deeper our gratitude to God for his abundant mercy and grace. Thus in waiting to be gracious, God's free grace in Christ is magnified all the more.

The promise is unmistakably clear. Those who seek the Lord with all their hearts will surely find him. (Jeremiah 29:11-13) His Word has the power to break down every stronghold that hinders the seeking soul. Thus it was with Hopeful. As the eyes of his understanding were opened, and he believed the record that God gave of his Son, he beheld the glory of Christ and assurance began to flood his soul. It was not an assurance based upon feelings or emotional response, but founded solidly upon the Word of God. (Romans 10:13-17)

Now as he prayed, the promises of Scripture came immediately to mind, laying every troubling question to rest. He finally understood that believing in Christ and coming to him are one and the same, and that all who come to Christ by faith are welcomed and received with open arms. (John 6:37; Luke 15:17-24) At last his doubts were over and the stronghold of unbelieving fear was broken down. Hopeful rejoiced in the words of the apostle Paul who declared: *This is a faithful saying, and worthy of all acceptation, that Christ Jesus came into the world to save sinners; of whom I am chief.* (1 Timothy 1:15) Should unbelieving fear ever rear its ugly head in the future, Hopeful had the promise: *He is able also to save them to the uttermost that come unto God by him, seeing he ever liveth to make intercession for them.* (Hebrews 7:25) Hopeful now trusted a living Savior and bowed to a reigning Lord.

* * * *

As Hopeful neared the end of his testimony, Christian had no doubt but that Christ had been revealed to him in truth. However, he was curious to know what effect the knowledge of salvation had upon Hopeful. Dear reader, as we well know, this is indeed the crux of the matter.

After the Lord saved him, Hopeful saw things in a completely different light. He understood that the world, and its brand of righteousness, was under condemnation. It offered no true hope for mankind, only the false promise of it. Through the redemption of Christ, however, God the Father was both just and the justifier of all who believe in Christ. This knowledge of God's free grace had a sanctifying effect upon Hopeful. For him, Vanity Fair had lost its charm and appeal. He was greatly ashamed of his former life there, and of the spiritual ignorance that had blinded him for so long.

By faith, he beheld the Lord Jesus Christ in his glory, and above all, Hopeful desired to live a holy life in which his Lord would be honored and glorified. If need be, he was willing to give his life for the one who had died to save him, and given what had just happened to his friend Faithful, I doubt that he expressed this sentiment lightly.

Thus the good shepherd sought and found one of his lost sheep from among the multitudes in Vanity Fair. Up to that time, he was just another nameless man who lived without hope. But from that day forward, all who knew him called him Hopeful.

This is a true account of Hopeful's conviction and conversion, told in my own words from his conversation with his companion as they traveled across the Enchanted Ground. It may have contained a surprise or two for Christian, especially when he learned how God used his and Faithful's testimony to save one of the native sons of Vanity. It was not mere coincidence that placed Hopeful in the disorderly crowd that day. He was there by divine appointment, just like Saul of Tarsus at the stoning of Stephen.

More often than not, we remain unaware of the reasons why we must suffer particular trials and difficulties. Yet once in a while, the Lord gives us a retrospective glimpse into his purpose for them. Christian experienced one of these rare moments as he listened to Hopeful's testimony. The loss of his brother Faithful was still a painful memory. However, at last he better understood the reason why he and Faithful had suffered so much at the Fair in the town of Vanity.

Study Questions

1. As Christian and Hopeful began their long journey across the Enchanted Ground, Hopeful shared his testimony with Christian for the first time. When did Hopeful first hear the Gospel? What was his initial reaction to it? Why did he resist the light of the Gospel at first?

2. As his conviction of sin deepened, Hopeful became tormented by the fear of death. Eventually, his guilty conscience drove him to try to rid himself of sin through reformation. In what ways did he attempt to clean up his life and reform himself? What did these efforts finally cause him to realize?

3. When Hopeful reached the point of desperation, he turned to Faithful for help. In what way did Faithful help him? How did Faithful minister to Hopeful in much the same way as Help and Evangelist ministered to Christian?

4. As he sought to follow Faithful's instructions, Hopeful continued to struggle with doubt and fear. What happened when the eyes of his understanding were finally opened? Upon what was his assurance of salvation based?

5. After hearing Hopeful's testimony, Christian wanted to know what effect the knowledge of salvation had upon him. What did Hopeful say in response to this most vital question?

CHAPTER 51

The Never-Ending Battle for the Christian's Mind

HOW IMPORTANT ARE OUR THOUGHTS? DO THEY REALLY MATTER ALL that much, or should we not be overly concerned about them? Since the Word of God says that as a man thinks in his heart, so is he, our thoughts must be of utmost importance. They reflect the inner workings of our hearts and define who and what we really are. According to the Lord Jesus Christ, the heart of an unregenerate person is a fountain of evil and the source of his defilement. (Mark 7:21-23) Concerning his thought processes, the unsaved man is vain in his imaginations and his foolish heart is darkened. (Romans 1:21) As for his conduct, he follows the dictates of his sinful heart and mind.

However, it is quite different with the child of God, for he has been born again and given a new heart. Old things have passed away and all things have become new. (2 Corinthians 5:17) Yet even though we have forsaken our former sinful life, we find ourselves fully engaged in a battle for our hearts and minds. Our adversary will try his utmost to subvert our faith and lure our hearts away from Christ. Thus we have the divine imperative: *Keep thy heart with all diligence; for out of it are the issues of life.* (Proverbs 4:23)

The apostle Peter gave a timely warning when he wrote: *Gird up the loins of your mind, be sober, and hope to the end for the grace that is to be brought unto you at the revelation of Jesus Christ; as obedient children, not fashioning yourselves according to the former lusts in your ignorance.* (1 Peter 1:13-14) In this, we find that there is a relationship between persevering hope and a carefully guarded mind. The promise of God is the basis of all our hope and it will be fully realized at the appearing of Christ. Until then, we need to engage in watchful preparation, lest coming suddenly, he finds us sleeping.

A prepared mind is one that has been transformed by the power of the Holy Spirit and is yielded in prayerful submission to the Lord Jesus Christ. (Ephesians 4:17-24; Colossians 4:2) It is both watchful and disciplined. (Matthew 25:1-13; 2 Corinthians 10:3-5) Above all, a prepared mind is one that follows the example of the Lord Jesus Christ. (Philippians 2:5-8)

Seeing that our faith is sure to come under heavy fire, truth and righteousness must be our first line of defense. (Ephesians 6:10-14) How else will we be able to stand our ground? Since truth is the strength of righteousness, we must have truth within in order to endure the conflict. (John 17:17; Psalm 119:11) We must have Christ within, for he is the truth. Moreover, he is the source and standard of our righteousness, the sum total of our armor in the face of the enemy. (Romans 13:11-14)

If righteousness must be upheld by truth in this battle for the Christian's mind, it is crucial that we know the truth as revealed in God's Word. Yet due to a strange quirk of human nature, many blunders are made in this regard. As a rule, the greater one's knowledge, the more conscious he is that there is much yet to learn. But the more ignorant one is, the more he tends to overestimate his wisdom and understanding. Such errors in judgment cause enough trouble when applied to knowledge in general, but how much more problematic are they in the realm of spiritual truth?

It has now been quite some time since Christian and Hopeful had their run-in with the man Ignorance from the town of Conceit. Much has happened to them since then. They passed through the dark lane where the assault and robbery of Little-Faith took place, and discussed it at some length. At that time, Hopeful showed some shocking ignorance of his own. They both fell into the net of the Flatterer, and most recently they came upon a man named Atheist who once claimed to be a Christian. It was perhaps as a result of this disturbing incident that Hopeful opened his heart to Christian and shared how the Lord had saved him by his grace.

All this time Ignorance had been lagging behind Christian and Hopeful, but now he rejoined them. Hoping that the man had used his solitude to consider the things they had discussed before, Christian came right to the point and asked: "Come how do you? How stands it between God and your soul now?" As soon as the young man spoke, it was obvious that he was of the same mind still. He trusted in his own righteousness and was convinced that he had forsaken his former life and was now following the Lord. When Christian pressed him further as to his assurance of heaven, Ignorance confirmed his suspicions by saying: "My heart tells me so."

How very sad that he trusted his own heart in so vital a matter! (Jeremiah 17:9) There was a great discrepancy between who Ignorance really was and who he thought himself to be; therefore, his hope of salvation rested upon a false premise. When Christian pointed this out to him, Ignorance would have none of it. He knew what he knew!

The only way for us to avoid the same mistake is by looking into the mirror of God's Word with an honest heart. We cannot judge ourselves rightly unless we do so according to its infallible standard. The apostle Paul gives an excellent definition of spiritual ignorance and its bitter fruit in Ephesians 4:17-19. However, as he makes clear in verse 20, these things in no way characterize a true child of God.

Since Ignorance had no real understanding of God's Word, he saw a distorted image of himself whenever he looked therein, an image composed of what he fancied himself to be. So in spite of his assertion to the contrary, his thoughts on the subject were not good thoughts at all because they were not according to truth.

For all this, Christian was unwilling to give up on the young man, perhaps because he remembered having once been in the same condition. Rather, he patiently tried to correct his thoughts concerning the human heart and its sinful condition. Scripture makes it clear that unsaved men are under the dominion of sin and the divine verdict has been given. (Ephesians 2:1-3 Romans 3:19-20). Unless one is truly born again, he cannot please God in either his thoughts or his deeds, yet Ignorance still insisted that he could. In his mind, the performance of good deeds and religious duties was enough to earn favor with God. Thus he presumed that he was as good a Christian as anyone else.

My brother or sister in Christ, what about our thoughts? How do they measure up? Good thoughts are right thoughts, thoughts that square with truth. Are we willing to agree with them, even when we must take sides against ourselves to do so? The Word of God is indeed a mirror in which we see many things. Looking therein, we learn what we are by nature and what we have become by God's grace. Moreover, as we behold the lovely image of our Lord, we see what we are destined to be. (2 Corinthians 3:18) In him, we find the perfect pattern of what we should be, and are brought low in realizing how far we fall short of it.

Ignorance saw none of these things, however. Christian argued that in order for our thoughts concerning God and his salvation to be right, they must be in full accord with his Word. God sees us as we really are, not as we like to imagine. Nothing is hidden from his all-discerning eye, not even the inmost thoughts and intents of our hearts. (Psalm 139:1-4) Thus gazing into the mirror of his Word, there is no room at all for self-righteousness or vain confidence. Yet once again, Ignorance bristled with offended pride.

Did Christian take him for a fool? Of course he knew he must "believe in Christ for justification" rather than coming to God through his own best efforts! If taken at face value, this sounded pretty good, but Christian intended to find out what he really meant by it. He quickly discovered that while Ignorance claimed to know that he must believe in Christ, he had no proper understanding of his sinful condition before God. He deemed his own good works to be quite enough; therefore, in what sense did he believe in Christ?

In his own words Ignorance said, "I believe that Christ died for sinners, and that I shall be justified before God from the curse, through his gracious acceptance of my obedience to his law. Or thus, Christ makes my duties, that are religious, acceptable to his Father by virtue of his merits, and so shall I be justified."

Those who know no better might possibly be taken in by his pious talk and assume that Ignorance was indeed a good Christian. However, his idea of justification was a dangerous hybrid of truth and error. He believed after a fashion, but not according to true knowledge. (Romans 10:1-4) Of evangelical repentance, he knew nothing, and of saving faith in Christ, he had none. He was completely deceived and Christian knew it. Even though Christian explained that human merit and good works have no part in justification, Ignorance refused to relinquish the notion that he must contribute something. (Romans 3:21-28; Romans 4:1-8; Romans 5:1) Then thinking to give added weight to his argument, he stated that if justification were as Christian really said, it would give believers a license to sin.

In Romans 6, the apostle Paul laid this argument to rest once for all by elaborating upon the sanctifying effects of justification by faith alone. Saving faith produces the fruit of righteousness in the hearts and lives of the redeemed. Good works have no part whatsoever in our justification before God, but they are the certain result of it. (Ephesians 2:8-10)

However, Ignorance was content with a form of godliness. In common with Formalist and Hypocrisy, he had a high view of himself, and consequently, a low view of God. (Psalm 50:21; Isaiah 55:7-9) Since he was able to put on a rather convincing performance, there were some who shared his good opinion of himself, but he did not pass muster with Christian and Hopeful.

After observing quietly all this time, Hopeful finally broke his silence and said to Christian, "Ask him if ever he had Christ revealed to him from heaven?" Hopeful knew from first-hand experience that salvation is the revelation of Christ to the soul by the Holy Spirit. However, Ignorance had no knowledge of the new birth; therefore, he derided Hopeful and dismissed his concern as the mere fancy of a deranged mind. To his way of thinking, his faith was every bit as good as Christian and Hopeful's.

His case reminds me of the apostle Paul's words in 1 Corinthians 14:37-38: *If any man think himself to be a prophet, or spiritual, let him acknowledge that the things that I write unto you are the commandments of the Lord. But if any man be ignorant, let him be ignorant.* Once again the young man heard the truth and rejected it, and in this, he played a more dangerous game than he supposed. Time was running out for him. In just a little while now he will face the consequences of his willful ignorance.

My friend in Christ, must we not be honest and admit to at least a casual acquaintance with the man named Ignorance? In the never-ending battle for our hearts and minds, do we not quickly find that spiritual ignorance is never far away? Assuming a variety of forms, it will invade our thoughts when we least expect it, and attempt to lead us astray. Under the guise of human reason, it puts up resistance to a life of walking by faith and living in obedience to Christ. When we are faced with crucial decisions, it tempts us to resort to worldly wisdom rather than acting in accordance with the Word of God. In either case, pride will back it up and reinforce the notion that we are using spiritual discernment, when in fact we are guilty of being wise in our own conceit. It is little wonder, then, if we fail to recognize spiritual ignorance for what it really is. Therefore, let us take care and be watchful, for spiritual ignorance is no fit traveling companion. Its presence will do us no good at all, and if heeded, it can do a great deal of harm.

Christian and Hopeful were now alone again, and with this welcome solitude came the realization that each step was taking them closer to their journey's end. The day was fast approaching when friends and loved ones, many of them still unsaved, must be left behind. So this was a time of bittersweet reflection for the two men as well. As for Ignorance, they pitied him even though they found his company irksome. Now that he had separated himself from them, Christian and Hopeful were free to discuss him further. In particular, they wondered to what extent he may have been enlightened by the Word of God and convicted of sin.

Christian was persuaded that one could experience conviction that falls short of actual conversion, and in this belief he had scriptural support. The writer of Hebrews warned of some who were enlightened to the truth to a point, but later turned from it. (Hebrews 6:4-6) Under the preaching of the Gospel, they were convicted of sin, professed faith in Christ, and gave all the appearance of being genuinely born again. However, time proved them otherwise, and for such persons the writer of Hebrews held out little hope. Should not this frightening possibility cause us to search ourselves and see if it is truly well with our souls?

It is the fear of the Lord within that distinguishes the true Christian from every sort of false pretender. (Proverbs 1:7; Proverbs 9:10) Moreover, it is God's grace alone that produces this godly fear. Unbelieving fear is a clever counterfeit that can prompt one to stifle his guilty conscience through self-reformation and a form of godliness. Thus it has laid the foundation for many a false profession. In the early days of enlightenment and conviction, it is not always easy to tell whether godly fear or unbelieving fear is at work.

Remember that this had been the case with Hopeful when God first began to deal with him. So he now said to Christian, "I know something of this myself; before I knew myself, it was so with me." At first, he tried to flee from the light of truth and stifle the conviction for sin that weighed so heavily upon him, but to no avail. The fear of God convinced him of sin, and moved him to flee to Christ and trust him alone for salvation. Afterward, that same fear became an inward principle of godliness that was transforming his character and conduct into the likeness of his Lord. So Hopeful could truly say with John Newton: "Twas grace that taught my heart to fear, and grace my fears relieved. How precious did that grace appear the hour I first believed!" [1]

* * * *

Their lengthy trek across the Enchanted Ground had been an arduous one for Christian and Hopeful, but it was just about over. By keeping their hearts and minds engaged upon the things of God, they managed to stay alert during the entire passage. But as to what lay beyond the Enchanted Ground, they had yet to see.

It may seem strange that the subject of apostasy and related topics dominated their conversation for much of this time. Did they overdo it by dwelling upon negative themes rather than things that were more uplifting in nature? Or did they show an abundance of caution that was well in order, given the perilous nature of their journey? The latter, I think.

Their very last dialog before leaving the Enchanted Ground concerned a mutual acquaintance, a notorious reprobate named Temporary from the town of Graceless. He was another who had once been disturbed over his sins and professed to believe in Christ. Hopeful had personally witnessed his distress and could vouch that his conviction and conversion seemed real at the time. However, his true character came to light when he was confronted with the high cost of following Christ. As a result, early resolve quickly gave way to self-interest, and like Pliable, he joined the ranks of those who had once called themselves pilgrims.

It could have been this sad remembrance that now prompted Christian and Hopeful to discuss the reasons for apostasy. Then again, they may have connected recent events with the Lord's solemn warning: *Strait is the gate, and narrow is the way, which leadeth unto life, and few there be that find it.* (Matthew 7:14) Whatever the particular reason, they began to share their thoughts concerning why some professing Christians depart from the faith, and the manner in which they do so. The following are my thoughts on the subject, based loosely upon their conversation.

In my opinion, the wrong kind of fear lies at the heart of the problem, the fear of death and hell, for example. Since this kind of fear naturally pricks the conscience and causes great distress, it can result in an apparent conversion even though the heart is unchanged. Such conviction is bound to be temporary, however; once it subsides, so does the desire to follow Christ.

Then there is the fear of man, which always brings a snare. If we would know the favor of God, we cannot live to please men. Conflicts will inevitably arise, forcing us to choose a side. If we take a bold stand for the Lord and his Word, we will experience the disapproval, and often the malice, of the world. In some cases, it will entail loss of an exquisitely painful sort. (Matthew 10:34-38) Those who do not know Christ in truth will be unwilling to bear the cost of doing so.

Closely akin to the fear of man is the fear of shame. Open identification with the Lord Jesus Christ will expose us to the ridicule of ungodly men, sooner or later. This reproach is not an easy thing to bear, even for the genuine believer. But the nominal professor has a particular dread of the shame that comes by faithfully following Christ. Therefore, he holds to the same philosophy as By-ends.

Unbelieving fear, which includes but is not limited to all of the above, can actually hinder the convicted sinner from coming to Christ. It may also drive him to make a false profession in order to ease his guilty conscience. Any conviction driven solely by craven fear will eventually subside, leaving the sinner's heart harder than it was before. Should unbelieving fear motivate one to maintain his false profession long term, it fosters a vain hope that can scarcely be shaken. Of this, the residents of Morality are an excellent case in point.

When the Holy Spirit convicts a sinner and moves him to flee to Christ by faith, it is a work of a much finer sort that will prove its worth by enduring the test of time. Since our high calling in Christ Jesus is a call to glory and virtue, to know him in truth is to become increasingly more like him in character and conduct. However, when one first makes a profession of faith in Christ, only time will tell whether he possesses genuine saving faith or not.

Apostasy is like a terrible lodestone drawing men to destruction by imperceptible degrees. One who once was zealous for the Lord begins to grow indifferent and negligent in spiritual matters, and his heart begins to seek other things. Eventually, he turns from Christ openly and follows a way of his own choosing. It is far too easy to take a step in that direction, and once caught in its downward spiral, the backslider in heart will perish, without divine intervention.

My brother or sister in Christ, we have an adversary who is determined to take us down. To this end, he has conceived a clever battle plan aimed squarely at our hearts and minds. Therefore, we must be watchful of his subtle devices and covered with the whole armor of God, for this is a battle like none other.

Speaking to the church in Smyrna, the Lord Jesus said: *Be thou faithful unto death, and I will give thee a crown of life.* (Revelation 2:10b) His command is given to all of his people without exception, not just those who die as martyrs. We are charged to continue steadfast in the faith and be his faithful witnesses wherever his will and providence should lead us. The hallmark of patient and obedient faith distinguishes the true pilgrim from every kind of imitator.

As we run the race set before us, we quickly discover how much we need one another. How often when in deep distress have we found comfort and encouragement from a fellow believer? How many times have we been spared from making a grave mistake because we heeded the wise counsel of our brethren? How often has a friend in Christ spoken a word of compassionate understanding just when we needed it the most? How many times have we been challenged and strengthened in our walk with the Lord by the example of godly brethren?

William Jay wisely said: "A God of knowledge and truth has said, 'It is not good for man to be alone.' If it was so with regard to a paradise, how much more with regard to a wilderness?" [2] The mutual benefit that Christian and Hopeful gained from their constant association proved the truth of our dear brother's observation. None of us is so spiritual that we do not need the help and encouragement of our brethren in Christ. None of us is so strong that we dare try to go it alone.

Study Questions

1. Since the Christian is fully engaged in a battle for his heart and mind, he must also engage in watchful preparation. Of what does a prepared mind consist? (Give Scripture references) Since his faith is sure to come under heavy fire, what is his first line of defense? How important is it for him to know the truth as it is revealed in the Word of God?

2. The man named Ignorance had a distorted view of himself, and therefore, his hope of salvation was a false one. He trusted in his own heart regarding this vital matter, and his heart had utterly deceived him. What is the only way that we can avoid the same mistake? What are some of the things that Christians see when we look into the mirror of God's Word?

3. In the never-ending battle for the Christian's mind, spiritual ignorance is never far away. When we least expect it, this enemy will invade our thoughts and seek to lead us astray. What are some of the ways in which it does this?

4. The man Ignorance is a prime example of one who is Christian in name only. He may have been convicted of sin to a certain extent, but not to the point of regeneration. Therefore, he was quite content with a form of godliness. What is one vital thing that separates him from a genuine Christian?

Part Seventeen

IN THE PRESENCE OF THE KING!

Thine eyes shall see the king in his beauty:
they shall behold the land that is very far off.
Isaiah 33:17

CHAPTER 52

Almost Home! The Delights of Beulah Land

THIS BEAUTIFUL EARTH UPON WHICH WE LIVE IS A PLACE SUBJECT TO continual change. Like the rest of the creation, it is growing old and will one day pass out of existence. As I write these words, the days are unseasonably mild even though the year is well into autumn. For now, the trees are ablaze with vibrant color, but soon they will shed their leaves and remain bare until spring.

The inevitable approach of winter is a poignant reminder that we, too, are changing. Our earthly lives are fragile and swiftly passing, like a vapor that appears for a brief time and then vanishes away. (James 4:14) Each day brings us a step closer to eternity, but if we are in Christ, this thought should not cause us to fear and dread.

As we observe the changes taking place all around us, what a comfort it is to know the one who changes not. (Hebrews 1:10-12) Of him Walter Chalmers Smith wrote: "To all life thou givest, to both great and small; in all life thou livest, the true life of all; we blossom and flourish like leaves on the tree, and wither and perish; but naught changeth thee." [1] Our Lord Jesus Christ is ever faithful and true. (Revelation 19:11) In him is no variableness, neither shadow of turning. (James 1:17) Moreover, his mercies to us are new every morning. (Lamentations 3:21-23) What a blessed hope we have in him!

Wakening very early this morning, I stepped out onto our deck to look for the morning star. There it was shining brightly through the trees, the promise of a new day even though the sky was still quite dark. As the most brilliant of the stars, it silently rules the pre-dawn hours; but with the first blush of sunrise, the morning star gradually fades from sight

What a lesson for us, my dear brother or sister in Christ, and a comfort as well if we can truly lay it to heart. Christ is the day star of whom Peter wrote in 2 Peter 1:19-21. (Also see Numbers 24:14; Revelation 2:28; and Revelation 22:16). When he came into the world as the Word made flesh, he was the true light shining in the darkness; but he also came as the Sun of righteousness, with healing in his wings. (John 1:1-14; Malachi 4:2) The brightness of his glory transcends the sun in its full strength.

These two metaphors remind me of our Lord's tender care for us as we stumble along the path of life, and O, how often we do stumble! As he led the children of Israel by a pillar of fire by night and a pillar of cloud by day, he watches over and guides us all through our earthly journey. (Exodus 13:20-22) He is near at hand in seasons of darkness when we would lose our way without the light of his very present help. (Psalm 46:1) He is just as near in seasons of light, when we are tempted to walk by sight and undue self-reliance. Whatever our circumstances, we may confidently say with David: *The LORD is my rock, and my fortress, and my deliverer; my God, my strength, in whom I will trust; my buckler, and the horn of my salvation, and my high tower.* (Psalm 18:2)

To David's words, Christian and Hopeful could add their hearty "Amen," for such had been their experience as well. Their long and arduous journey across the Enchanted Ground was finally over, and a goodly land now stretched before them. They had reached the beautiful land of Beulah.

Shortly after entering its border, the two weary travelers noticed a dramatic change of atmosphere. Unlike the toxic fumes they had tried so hard to resist, the air here was wholesome and sweet. What a welcome relief to be able to breathe freely and deeply without fear of harmful side effects! Moreover, while crossing over the Enchanted Ground they had not dared to slacken their pace, much less stop for a while. But here, Christian and Hopeful could safely pause for a time of much needed rest.

As their lungs expanded with the fresh, clean air, it was as if their senses awakened to the great beauty all around them. This was not a figment of their imagination. Rather than making one lethargic and sleepy, the air in Beulah Land is invigorating and favorable to the keen enjoyment of its many delights. At last, the deepening shadows through which they had passed seemed almost forgotten.

Since this pleasant country is filled throughout with light and life, spring-like conditions prevail there all year long. Many say that it savors of Eden before man's fall, with flowers of every imaginable color and variety blooming throughout the countryside. Their sweet fragrance drifts across the land on gentle breezes, as does the joyful sound of birdsong. These feathered choristers herald a long-awaited promise fulfilled. At last, *the winter is past, the rain is over and gone; the flowers appear on the earth; the time of the singing of birds is come, and the voice of the turtle* [dove] *is heard in the land.* (Song of Solomon 2:10-12)

To new arrivals, the incomparable beauty of the land is an earnest that their long winter of trial and affliction is just about over, as is their journey through a desolate wilderness. Situated as it is on the very border of heaven, Beulah is a land of pure delight that is quite unlike anything of earth. Once safely within its boundaries, pilgrims are well beyond the Valley of the Shadow of Death, and out of sight of Doubting Castle and its terrible proprietor. Perhaps this explains why former cares and troubles do not seem to weigh as heavily upon them here as before.

According to John Bunyan's vivid description, Beulah Land is a place where heaven and earth almost touch one another. It is a blessed country where mortal men dwell and commune with angelic beings and glorified saints. However, since Beulah is a heavenly figure, he must have had something else in mind.

A royal wedding

In describing the land of Beulah, John Bunyan drew from three metaphors commonly found in Scripture in order to better illustrate one grand truth. Each of these figures depicts an important aspect of our union with the Lord Jesus Christ. By considering all three together, we should be better able to grasp a fuller measure of our standing in him.

The first metaphor is that of a bride and bridegroom, and the loving union that binds their hearts to one another exclusively. In this case the betrothal is a royal one; it is the marriage contract between the King of Glory and his chosen bride. Therefore, it is a high and holy union of incomparable love, tracing its roots to the meaning of the name Beulah.

The word Beulah occurs only once in Scripture, in Isaiah 62:4. Used in reference to the nation Israel, it is a symbolic name meaning "married." Thus it depicts Israel as the bride of Jehovah, but she was an unfaithful wife who repeatedly violated her marriage covenant. So it was against a backdrop of national apostasy that the prophet Isaiah told of coming judgment upon Judah and Jerusalem, and the desolation of the land. He also spoke of future blessing to come upon Jerusalem, her children, and her land. However, it would not come in the form of national favor and privilege as before.

In spite of the great light that Israel knew under the rule of God and his law, she had a long history of flagrant rebellion and idolatry. So great was her sin of spiritual adultery that God dealt with her like a man would his unfaithful wife. (Hosea 1:2-4, 2:2-5) Because she had continually broken covenant with her divine husband, who had been ever good and faithful to her, he finally divorced her.

As a result, Israel was cast off and forsaken, yet not altogether. Hosea also spoke of another betrothal of an entirely different sort when he prophesied: *I will betroth thee unto me for ever; yea, I will betroth thee unto me in righteousness, and in judgment, and in lovingkindness, and in mercies. I will even betroth thee unto me in faithfulness: and thou shalt know the LORD.* (Hosea 3:19-20) In so saying, the prophet entered New Testament ground and the spirituality of the New Covenant. (Jeremiah 31:31-34; Romans 9:22-26; 1 Peter 2:9-10)

In spite of Israel's apostasy as a nation, there was always a remnant of truehearted and faithful souls. (Romans 9:27-29) Like Simeon and Anna, who rejoiced to see the infant Jesus, this small remnant waited for the consolation of Israel and looked for redemption in Jerusalem. (Luke 2:25-30; Luke 2:36-38) Israel's only hope lay in the promised redeemer, the suffering servant of Jehovah, but few recognized him when he came. For the high crime of rejecting their Messiah, the house of national Israel was left desolate, and yet, something wonderful arose from the ashes of her ruin. (Matthew 23:37-39; Amos 9:11-15) It did not come in the form of national restoration, however, but with the establishment of the kingdom of God upon the earth. (John 18:36; Acts 2:29-36; Romans 14:17)

The relative few who received the Lord Jesus Christ as their promised Messiah also bowed to him as the true King of Israel. (Isaiah 9:6-7) They formed the nucleus of a kingdom that was small in its inception, but would eventually grow until it overspread the earth. (Matthew 13:31-32) Gentiles would also be part of this glorious kingdom, for the hope of Israel is also the desire of all nations. (Haggai 2:7) Unlike an earthly political kingdom, this one is spiritual in nature, consisting of the saved from among every nation and people of earth. It is also called a strong city into which only the *righteous nation which keepeth the truth may enter in.* (Isaiah 26:1-2)

This righteous nation forms the true Israel of God spoken of by the apostle Paul. (Galatians 6:16) She is the virgin bride of Christ betrothed unto him forever, clothed with the garments of salvation, and covered with the robe of his righteousness. (Isaiah 61:10) The name Beulah properly applies to these redeemed ones alone, for they are the rightful heirs to all the promises made to Israel. (Galatians 3:16, 29) They alone enjoy the blessings and privileges that belong to the betrothed bride of Jesus Christ, his beloved Hephzibah in whom his soul takes delight. (Isaiah 62:4)

Is it any wonder that the land of Beulah rings with the sound of joyful celebration? In this most pleasant place, the Lord Jesus calls his people away from earthly vanities and unto him in the springtime of a love that is ever fresh and new. (Song of Solomon 2:10-13) Here we may commune with him and know the light of his presence. Here, through the riches of his grace, we may know true peace, rest, and fullness of joy. (Psalm 16:11) As weary and battered as Christian and Hopeful were from their rigorous journey, they stood greatly in need of all of these things.

Before reaching the land of Beulah, the ways of God's providence can tend to perplex and trouble us. At times we may even be tempted to question his will and purpose for us, especially when in the crucible of affliction. But conditions in Beulah Land are highly favorable for clearer understanding of his ways. Furthermore, dwelling there gives us ample time to think upon his eternal, unchangeable love, which has planned all that concerns us. (1 Peter 1:18-19) As a result, we experience anew the reaffirmation of his love and the quietness and assurance of heart it brings.

With this fuller realization of our loving union with the Lord Jesus Christ, we will find Beulah to be a fruitful place. It is truly a land of goodness and plenty, of which ancient Canaan was but a faint shadow. Sweet Beulah Land flows with blessings long desired and hoped for. How she alters our perspective from the earthly and fixes it upon our rich heritage in Christ! Such is her beneficial effect that the pilgrim heart cries with David: *The LORD is the portion of mine inheritance and of my cup: thou maintainest my lot. The lines are fallen unto me in pleasant places; yea, I have a goodly heritage.* (Psalm 16:5-6)

Yet travelers take note, for the delights of Beulah are entirely spiritual in nature. Those who are worldly minded will find them distasteful and want no part of them. But O, how the children of God love to dwell here and enjoy the bounty of the land! Here we may feast upon celestial fruits, which are sweeter by far than the clusters of grapes discovered in historic Canaan. (Numbers 13:23-27)

The delights of Beulah, and the rich heritage in Christ they represent, belong to all of God's people without exception. However, they are savored best and appreciated most by those who are nearing the end of their earthly journey. This beautiful country is a foretaste of heaven for those who are at the border of the Celestial City. Time spent here denotes a special season of communion with the Lord for those who are shortly to see him face to face.

What a wondrous thing to know that the joy is not all on our side, for the Lord Jesus Christ actually rejoices over his people with singing. Even as he spoke of devastating judgment to come upon Judah, the prophet Zephaniah gave this astounding promise to the daughter of Zion: *The LORD thy God in the midst of thee is mighty; he will save, he will rejoice over thee with joy; he will rest in his love, he will joy over thee with singing.* (Zephaniah 3:14, 17) Since our Lord rejoices over each sinner he rescues and saves, how much more will his heart sing when he is about to receive them into his presence?

Beulah Land is probably life's best opportunity to think upon these blessed truths, and such is the consistent testimony of all who reach that beautiful place. What better time to reflect upon past mercies and contemplate the best things that are soon to be? How joyful the anticipation of the great marriage supper of the Lamb, when all our hope in Christ will be fully realized! (Revelation 19:7-9)

Come, we that love the Lord, and let our joys be known;
Join in a song with sweet accord, and thus surround the throne.

Let those refuse to sing who never knew our God;
But children of the heav'nly King may speak their joys abroad.

The men of grace have found glory begun below;
Celestial fruit on earthly ground from faith and hope may grow.

The hill of Zion yields a thousand sacred sweets
Before we reach the heav'nly fields, or walk the golden streets.

Then let our songs abound, and every tear be dry;
We're marching thro' Emmanuel's ground to fairer worlds on high. [2]

A royal city

The next metaphor concerns the Celestial City itself – Zion, city of the living God and royal dwelling place of the great King. (Psalm 48:1-2) Christian and Hopeful last saw it from the summit of Mount Clear. At that distance, their vision was considerably limited even though they stood on high ground. However, in the upward march to Zion, Beulah Land is higher still, so high that some say it touches the very border of the city.

From such close range, Christian and Hopeful could see the New Jerusalem with greater clarity than ever before. (Revelation 21:2) As they gazed upon her splendor, certain architectural features that had escaped their notice before now came into sharp focus. For example, they could see that the city was constructed from materials of the highest quality and value, such as flawless pearls, pure gold, and precious gemstones. (Ephesians 2:19-22)

High atop the hill of Zion, the golden city was resplendent with the glory of God, for the Lamb is the light thereof. (Revelation 21:23) He was the light that guided her steps safely through her wilderness journey, and he will be her eternal light in that land of cloudless day. According to Ezekiel the prophet, the name of this city is *The LORD is there.* (Ezekiel 48:35) John the apostle fully agreed. While beholding the holy city in vision, John *heard a great voice out of heaven saying, Behold, the tabernacle of God is with men, and he will dwell with them, and they shall be his people, and God himself shall be with them, and be their God.* (Revelation 21:3)

Thus dear reader, we find the meaning of this metaphor within the identification of the shining city. The city is also the bride! Her marriage union with the Lord Jesus Christ is an eternal union. Moreover, she is the joyful mother of innumerable children. The spiritual birthright and citizenship of every true son and daughter of Zion is recorded within her walls. (Psalm 113:9; Isaiah 54:1; Galatians 4:26-28)

When John saw her in Revelation 21:1-10, the city that is also the Lamb's wife, every stain and imperfection had been purged away and she was adorned for her royal wedding. At last, she was holy and without blemish, a glorious church, not having spot, or wrinkle, or any such thing. (Ephesians 5:27) She is truly a rare jewel whose price is far above rubies. (Proverbs 31:10) By reason of her virtue and nobility she is set apart from all the daughters of men, whatever their earthly station. (Proverbs 31:29; Psalm 45:13)

This golden city pictures the Church in her perfected state. Unlike the ancient stronghold of Zion, she has no actual geographical location; for she is a city which hath foundations, whose builder and maker is God. (Hebrews 11:10) Her glory is his glory, and her light that which is reflected from him.

We know quite well that the Lord Jesus Christ is not married to brick and mortar, or to literal pearls, precious gemstones, and fine gold. These building materials represent his people, the living stones of which his temple is being built. (1 Peter 2:5; Ephesians 2:19-22) It is a spiritual temple of which Christ is both the builder and chief corner stone. (1 Peter 2:6) The gemstones, each one of which he has carefully laid in place, show forth the beauty of his bride and her preciousness in his sight. We are his jewels, crown jewels for his royal diadem. (Malachi 3:17; Isaiah 62:3) As for the fine gold that is so abundant throughout the city, it is not the metallic element that men prize so highly. It is that which is of incomparable worth before God, the faith of his people after it has been tried until it glistens like pure gold, clear as crystal. (Job 23:10; Zechariah 13:7-9; 1 Peter 1:6-7; Revelation 21:18)

When at last her lengthy preparation is over, and the Church stands prepared as a bride adorned for her husband, he will look upon her and say: *Thou art all fair, my love; there is no spot in thee.* (Revelation 21:2; Revelation 21:9-21; Song of Solomon 4:7) In that day when every vestige of sin has been purged away, he will look into her face and behold his own lovely image reflected there. (Romans 8:29) Until then, however, she is painfully aware of her many blemishes.

Dear friend in Christ, this explains why Christian and Hopeful could still not bear to look upon the city's full radiance. They had to view it through a special instrument designed just for that purpose, as they had previously done from the Delectable Mountains. As they looked toward the golden city, they were stricken with homesickness like never before. (Song of Solomon 5:8) The Lord Jesus was more real and precious to them than ever, and so was the prospect of finally seeing him.

Whatever physical infirmities they must struggle with during their final days on earth, all would soon be over and they would join the spirits of just men made perfect. (Hebrews 12:23) Shortly, they will see their Lord face to face and fully know what they now knew only in part. (1 John 3:2) With these thoughts uppermost in heart and mind, they were better able to bear the overwhelming weariness and longing that came upon them since arriving in Beulah Land. Each step forward was one step nearer home, and in that certain knowledge, they found strength to press forward.

A royal garden

As Christian and Hopeful followed the pathway through Beulah, they discovered it to be a land of plentiful orchards, vineyards, and gardens. Each of these carefully tended places had its own gate, which opened directly to the King's Highway. Since these gardens were specially set in place for the comfort and help of pilgrims in their journey, the gardeners invited Christian and Hopeful to come inside and refresh themselves. They could do so without fear because, unlike the arbor on the hill Difficulty, it was perfectly safe to rest and take nourishment there. By this time, the two men were nearly overcome with exhaustion, so they were thankful to do just that.

The individual gardens growing throughout the land of Beulah are really integral parts of a single, royal garden belonging to the Lord Jesus Christ. It is a place that is very dear to his heart, one that he purchased for himself and securely enclosed with walls of salvation. (Song of Solomon 4:12; Jeremiah 31:3; 1 Peter 1:18-19 Isaiah 26:1) In many respects it is a secret garden because its beauty and inherent worth are largely unseen and unknown by outsiders. Yet this magnificent royal garden, planted and fenced by grace, is the third great metaphor of Beulah Land. It portrays the living union between the Lord Jesus Christ and his Church, his chosen bride. She is a garden of redeemed souls and her Beloved delights to dwell in her midst. (Matthew 28:18-20; Hebrews 13:5-6; Revelation 1:12-13, 20)

Within this lovely garden many kinds of plants, flowers, vines and trees are found growing together and bearing fruit under his watchful eye. (Revelation 7:9-10) As to its specific arrangement, all was done by divine design; each individual plant was selected and set in place as it pleased the royal master. (1 Corinthians 12:13-20; Ephesians 1:5; Ephesians 2:19-22; Ephesians 4:15-16) In order to keep his garden healthy and thriving, he has appointed special gardeners to oversee the task and answer directly to him. Like their fellow laborers, the shepherds of the Delectable Mountains, these men watch over, care for, and nurture the fragile plants growing in their master's garden.

As a result, the land of Beulah is filled with pleasant fruits and fragrant spices, and is a beautiful respite of green in the midst of a desolate wilderness. (Song of Solomon 4:13-14) However, the most diligent labor on the part of God's faithful servants is not enough to accomplish all of this. The garden of Christ thrives due to its own dedicated water source: *a well of living water, and streams from Lebanon.* (Song of Solomon 4:15) A land where living water flows! Dear reader, we have seen this before, have we not?

The Spirit of Christ is the living water by which he sustains the life that he gives. (John 4:10-14; John 7:38-39) He alone can cause the tender plants to grow strong and bear fruit. Situated as she is in a hostile world, the garden of Christ is often blasted by the winds of adversity and bitter trial. Like a searing desert wind, the dreaded sirocco, these things would destroy the garden if not for the constant help of the Holy Spirit. (Psalm 125:1-2; Isaiah 33:20-21; Matthew 16:18) When he breathes upon his garden he does so like a gentle southerly breeze, a zephyr, stirring up the wounded plants so that they emit the aroma of fragrant spices. (Song of Solomon 4:16)

This explains the sweet fragrance drifting throughout the land of Beulah. The garden of Christ was never meant to be merely ornamental. Above all, she is designed to be a fruitful place, but her fruitfulness depends solely upon her living union with the Lord Jesus Christ. (John 15:5) Therefore, the fruit she brings forth is indeed celestial fruit. (Galatians 5:22-23)

As Christian and Hopeful tarried and slept in the gardens of Beulah, they dreamed and talked in their sleep, which was not a usual thing with either man. According to the gardeners, "It is the nature of the fruit of the grapes of these vineyards to go down so sweetly, as to cause the lips of them that are asleep to speak."

This is a strange phenomenon, to say the least. Could it be the effect of wine, perhaps? Yes it was, but not as you might suppose. The vineyards of Beulah produce grapes that are far superior to those found growing by the brook of Eschol. (Numbers 13:23-27) These grapes bring forth new wine, of which Christian and Hopeful drank deeply, but they were not intoxicated as if from too much alcohol. This wine was of another kind altogether. Like the living water mentioned above, it is symbolic of the indwelling Holy Spirit. (Acts 2:13-18) So to partake of it is to be under the control of God's Spirit, which is to have our hearts filled with the knowledge of Christ and things that are altogether lovely. (Ephesians 5:18-21) The effect of his control is striking, for it causes us to rejoice in the Lord with a grateful heart, to have our speech seasoned with grace, and to demonstrate humility and godly fear in our dealings with others.

This new wine is the symbol of the New Covenant, ratified by the blood of Christ. (Matthew 26:27-29) Therefore, it speaks to our hearts of his wondrous love, the greatness of his redemption, and pardon for sin. Figuratively speaking, it is new wine that has been placed into new wineskins for safekeeping. (Matthew 9:15-17)

The Word of God condemns drunkenness in no uncertain terms and explicitly warns of the consequences of too much wine. Intemperance is linked with loss of sensibility and self-control, contention and physical injury, lewd speech and shameful conduct. (Proverbs 23:29-35) However, this new wine contains great blessing in it. (Isaiah 65:8-9) When consumed, it produces spiritual joy and purity of heart, self-control, soundness of mind and every other godly virtue.

When Christian and Hopeful awoke from their refreshing sleep, it was time to be on their way. Very soon now, they will enter the golden city and their hearts glowed with anticipation at the thought of finally seeing their Lord. Yet even though they were so close, they still viewed him through a glass darkly. (1 Corinthians 13:12) It would not be until the veil of their flesh was taken away that they could gaze upon the glory that excelleth. (2 Corinthians 3:10) Only then could they look fully upon the Lamb of God, who is the everlasting light of his people. (Revelation 21:23)

As the two men pressed wearily onward, they met "two men in raiment that shone like gold," and whose "faces shone as the light." These unidentified men were eager to hear all the details of their journey and Christian and Hopeful were happy to oblige them. Thus they gave one final account of their pilgrimage, and there was much more to tell this time. In the telling, they called to remembrance all the ways that God had led them, including each trial and blessing, sorrow and joy, and failure and victory. With grateful hearts they reflected upon his providential care and unfailing mercy through it all.

Who were these two beings that showed such a keen interest in Christian and Hopeful? Could they be part of the great cloud of witnesses spoken of in Hebrews 12:1? Were they angelic beings, which were known to frequent the King's Highway? Or were they merely a figment of John Bunyan's imagination, added for further dramatic effect?

There is no scriptural warrant to believe they were redeemed souls who actually returned to earth from heaven in order to accompany Christian and Hopeful. Even though they could have been the result of poetic license on the author's part, John Bunyan clearly identifies them a little later as angelic beings, Shining Ones seen occasionally throughout *The Pilgrim's Progress*.

Although angels have no part in Christ's redemption, they have a marked interest in those who do. (1 Peter 1:10-12). As ministering spirits to those who are the heirs of salvation, they have a vested interest in our spiritual welfare. Although we are not conscious of it, they are present with us throughout our lives, before and after conversion. So presumably, they will be with us when our time comes to depart this life.

When the brothers asked if the men would accompany them, they agreed; but they also warned Christian and Hopeful of two more difficulties they must yet face. There was one final barrier to cross and one final battle to win. Like every former trial, Christian and Hopeful must overcome them by faith. With this final exhortation in mind, they pressed onward until the Celestial gate was in full sight.

* * * *

My friend in Christ, one day you and I will enter the final season of our earthly lives. Perhaps your journey to Zion began in your youth, which was my case. Or perhaps you came to Christ when older, as have many others. But whether we travel the path of the just for many years or for relatively few, all true pilgrims eventually arrive in Beulah Land.

Many people look forward to their golden years as a season of well deserved rest and indulgence, a time to lay aside pressing obligations and think of self for a change. Retirement from active employment is anticipated as the opportunity to enjoy life, or what is left of it, to the fullest. To those who do not know the Lord, this attitude makes perfect sense, but it also places them in wretched company. (Luke 12:16-21)

As God's people, we must soundly reject this self-centered mentality. Our sunset years should be as fruitful in the service of our Lord, and perhaps even more so, as the days of our youth. Even if we must struggle with physical afflictions and limitations, this is no time to become spiritually negligent. Rather than shifting our focus toward a life of leisure and earthly pleasure, this is the time to cherish the things of Christ more than ever, and seek his kingdom and righteousness even more fervently.

No one should be more fruitful in the kingdom of God than those dear saints who have been long planted by the river of life. (Psalm 92:12-14) These veteran soldiers of the cross usually prove to be the strongest in the Lord, and their long experience in battle gives them an invaluable place in the Palace Beautiful. Even though they often suffer from the infirmities of advancing age, their wisdom and godly example will be of great benefit to their younger brethren.

The beautiful land of Beulah is perfectly suited to one who has attained not merely old age, but advanced spiritual maturity. It appeals most to one in whom the grace of God is so evident that there is an almost ethereal quality about him. Earthly cares and pleasures do not have the same hold as in the past, for he has heard the call of his Beloved saying, *Rise up, my love, my fair one, and come away.* At the sound of his voice, his pilgrim heart burns with joyous expectation. (Song of Solomon 2:10-13) Looking homeward, he seems to hear the voices of his brethren who have gone before. How he longs to join them, but his work on earth is not yet done. He must be content to abide here for a little while longer.

Since the metaphorical land of Beulah corresponds to the Christian's final season of life, its rich spiritual imagery reflects his heart as it should be. Time spent here, whether lengthy or brief, signifies his final preparation for departure. As he nears the shore and gazes toward the shining city, he would not go back again even if he could do so in the full strength of his youth. So my fellow pilgrim, it is not so much that we dwell in Beulah Land as that Beulah Land dwells in us.

As I write these words and as you read them, the sands of time are sinking for us both. Before we know it, we will reach the great divide and the Golden Strand beyond. Therefore, let us not waste the time given us in spiritual idleness and vain pursuits. On the contrary, let us regard each day as a precious gift, and seize the opportunity to be useful servants of Jesus Christ. Until our heavenly Bridegroom calls us home, let us strive to be faithful and diligent in the work he has given us to do.

Moreover, as we look forward to the land of perfect day, let us faithfully abide in the Palace Beautiful. In that special place where God's providence has put us, we will hear the voice of our Beloved and feed upon his Word. (Deuteronomy 8:3; John 6:48-51) Within her beautiful gates we will enjoy sweet fellowship with those of like precious faith.

I often think that our meeting together as a body here on earth is like a foretaste of heaven. Surely it prefigures that great homecoming when the entire family of God will be gathered together forever before the throne of God and of the Lamb.

> Until the day of life dawns above,
> let there be unrestrained fellowship with Jesus;
> Until fruition comes, may I enjoy the earnest
> of my inheritance and the firstfruits of the Spirit;
> Until I finish my course with joy may I pursue
> it with diligence, in every part display the resources of
> the Christian, and adorn the doctrine of thee my God in all things. [3]

Study Questions

1. Briefly describe the beautiful land of Beulah. What does this allegorical country signify to new arrivals there?

2. John Bunyan uses three scriptural metaphors to describe the nature of the Christian's union with Christ. What is the first metaphor he uses, and what does it depict? Although the nation Israel apostatized from God, a believing remnant remained true, and formed the nucleus of a righteous nation (Isaiah 26:1-2). Who is this righteous nation? What is her relationship to the Lord Jesus Christ? To whom alone does the name Beulah rightly belong?

3. What is the second metaphor used to describe Beulah Land? Briefly explain its spiritual significance. What links this metaphor with the first one? What does the golden city represent? Of what sort of building materials is it constructed?

4. The third metaphor is that of a royal garden. What sort of garden is it, and to whom does it belong? What does this very special garden portray? What kinds of provision has the owner made in order to insure that the plants in his garden grow strong and bear fruit?

5. To what does the metaphorical land of Beulah correspond? To whom does it appeal the most?

CHAPTER 53

Nearing the Shore! The Passing of a Pilgrim

IN THE BOOK OF ECCLESIASTES WE FIND THE UNIVERSAL TRUTH: *To every thing there is a season, and a time to every purpose under the heaven.* (Chapter 3:1) Heading the list of divine appointments is the inescapable fact that there is a time to be born, and a time to die. Humanistic philosophy would have us believe that death is merely another part of life. Through the clever substitution of euphemisms, it attempts to soften the blow of what men know intuitively: *It is appointed unto men once to die, but after this the judgment.* (Hebrews 9:27) Of all the trials and uncertainties of life, death is feared and dreaded above them all.

As Christians, we view the end of mortal life from an entirely different perspective. While death is truly an inevitable part of our journey, it is but the final barrier before reaching our eternal destination. As such, it is the last trial we shall face, the last enemy to be vanquished, the finish line at the end of our race to eternal glory. (Revelation 2:10) Nevertheless, the death of the body is a mysterious and fearful thing, taking us into unknown regions where none have returned to give report. Therefore, even the most devout Christian is likely to be apprehensive when his time comes to depart this life.

Although we naturally dread it, this passage will release us from every hindrance and earthly limitation and bring us into the actual presence of our Lord. (2 Corinthians 5:8) By means of death, we will enter into the full realization of eternal life because our Lord Jesus

Christ *abolished death, and hath brought life and immortality to light through the gospel.* (2 Timothy 1:10) So even though we must experience the death of the body, its sting has been forever removed. Its victory over us has been vanquished by the blood of Christ and its power broken through his glorious resurrection.

No wonder the apostle Paul could taunt death with such confidence and boldness! (1 Corinthians 15:55-57) Take heart then, dear reader. If you are truly in Christ, there is no just cause to fear. He in whom you have trusted throughout your earthly pilgrimage will be with you at your journey's end.

Christian and Hopeful believed these things with all their hearts. Therefore, in spite of the great weariness that has slowed them down considerably of late, they now quickened their pace. Their long exile was just about over and the gate of the city now in full view. Very shortly they will reach the Father's house toward which they have been traveling for so many years. But what is this that has suddenly appeared before them and blocked their way? The two men came to a complete halt, flabbergasted to find that their path ended abruptly at the edge of a dark river. The very sight of it was enough to fill them with fear and consternation. As far as they could tell, the river was a hopeless impediment, for it seemed both broad and deep. Moreover, they looked in vain for any sort of bridge by which to cross over to the other side.

What were they to do now? Their two escorts confirmed what they already suspected. If Christian and Hopeful were to enter the Celestial City, they must pass through this seemingly impassable river. Although there was one other way, only two souls have been permitted to take it. Among the people of God throughout the ages, only Enoch and Elijah entered God's presence without having to pass through this dreaded river. (Genesis 5:21-24; 2 Kings 2:1-12) When the Lord Jesus Christ returns, an untold number of his people will be changed and put on incorruption and immortality without having to experience death. (1 Corinthians 15:51-57) Until that day, however, we all must face this dark river sooner or later.

At the unexpected shock of seeing the deep, dark water, Christian sank into despondency while his companion managed to avoid it. If we think about it, this comes as no surprise. Throughout his entire pilgrimage, Christian has been subject to occasional bouts of unbelieving fear. One might expect that he had conquered it by now, but from out of the blue, his old enemy had him in its terrible grasp as strongly as it ever had. But Hopeful lived up to his name even though faced with the same obstacle. As we consider the different ways in which the two men reacted to the same thing, we conclude that just as every Christian's earthly pilgrimage is unique, so is each one's experience at the end of it.

As to this, the waters of this dark river have a peculiar characteristic that cannot be known by simply looking at it. Its depth is subject to sudden fluctuation according to the measure of one's faith. Consequently, some of God's people have an easy crossing while others endure a terrible struggle here. Since it is hard to predict ahead of time how any individual believer will react, many surprises lie in store at the edge of the river. Some who seemed confident and self-assured will panic at the mere sight of it. Others whom we might expect to recoil with horror, such as Mr. Despondency[1] and Much-afraid,[2] cross over with great peace and joy. Even Mr. Fearing,[3] an extreme case of unbelieving fear if there ever was one, found the water shallow once he actually stepped into it.

When no possible alternative could be found, Christian and Hopeful stepped bravely into the chilly water. Although Hopeful could feel the river's bottom firmly under his feet, Christian began to go under almost at once. Due to his agitated state of mind, he fancied the water to be deeper than it actually was; therefore, he felt as if he was drowning. Although Hopeful did his best to assure his poor brother, Christian despaired of ever seeing the goodly land beyond the river.

Dear reader, imagine his horror to think that having almost reached the end, he was not going to make it after all! The very thought caused an awful darkness to seize control of his mind, overshadowing the remembrance of God's Word with its precious promises and comfort. Such was the power of unbelieving fear when it made its final assault against him. He was going to perish, he just knew it! Had he not always feared that he might never make it to the Celestial Gate? Surely, that which he feared had now come upon him! What's worse, the sins he had committed both before and after his conversion came strongly to mind, tormenting him to the point of near despair.

Altogether, he was in a desperate condition as he floundered in the cold, dark water. Hopeful did his best to help, but it was all he could do to keep poor Christian's head above the water. More than once Christian slipped from his grasp and nearly drowned, but each time he somehow managed to break the surface.

Since Hopeful could clearly see the Celestial gate and men waiting to receive them, he did his best to allay his brother's fear. But it was as if Christian refused to be comforted, for he insisted: " 'Tis you, 'tis you they wait for; you have been Hopeful ever since I knew you." Then Hopeful, who knew his brother better than Christian knew himself, must have smiled inwardly as he replied, "And so have you."

As he clung tightly to poor Christian, Hopeful spoke to him of Asaph's terrible dilemma recorded in Psalm 73. His experience reminds us that things are not always as they appear. Godly Asaph judged according to outward circumstances; therefore, he completely misjudged his situation at first. During that dark time Asaph complained bitterly of the wicked, saying: *For there are no bands in their death: but their strength is firm. They are not in trouble as other men; neither are they plagued like other men.* (Psalm 73:4-5) However, when he went into the sanctuary of God and sought God's help in order to understand aright, his eyes were opened to see the truth of the matter. (Psalm 73:17-28)

God did not reject Asaph just because he grappled unwisely with a most difficult and perplexing situation. Neither had he forsaken Christian just because the poor man was momentarily overcome by fear and doubt. The dark river served as a final opportunity to remember God's former mercy and goodness. It was one last time to reflect upon his great love and trust in him.

By reminding Christian of these things, Hopeful gave him some excellent food for thought. He seized upon it at once, laying the words to heart and pondering them for a while. Unbelieving fear still made the river seem an impassable barrier. However, even though Christian's hope seemed to be all but gone, he possessed what Charles H. Spurgeon called "the true Jerusalem blade of childlike faith" [4] in Christ. So in the end, faith and hope conquered doubt and fear.

As Christian began to recall Scripture and the many dangers from which God had delivered him in the past, he knew that the

Lord was still with him. Moreover, concerning the remembrance of his sins, Hopeful whispered: *Be of good cheer, Jesus Christ maketh thee whole.* (From Acts 9:34)

These few words brought renewed assurance of sins forgiven through Christ and his perfect redemption. By faith, Christian heard his Lord on the cross crying *It is finished* as he *bowed his head and gave up the ghost.* (John 19:30) He also remembered how the veil of the temple was rent in two from top to bottom when the Savior spoke his final words, showing that the way to the Most Holy Place had been opened. (Matthew 27:50-51) The wrath-averting sacrifice had been offered to God and fully accepted. With the eyes of faith, Christian saw the Ark of the Covenant with free access to the Mercy Seat. (Hebrews 7:24-27; Hebrews 13:20-21)

Suddenly the darkness lifted and Christian cried aloud: "Oh, I see him again! And he tells me: *When thou passest through the waters, I will be with thee; and through the rivers, they shall not overflow thee.*" (Isaiah 43:2) With this precious promise in heart and mind, Christian could now feel the ground solidly under his feet. In fact, the river actually seemed shallow as both men moved together toward the Celestial shore. Their great enemy had done his utmost to prevent them from reaching it, but from this time forth he would trouble them no more.

Likewise, my brother or sister in Christ, eternal joy awaits us at the end of our journey; but in order to reach it, we must face the same dark river. As the Jordan lay between the Israelites and their promised inheritance, so the river of death stands between the Christian and the heavenly Canaan. We must cross it in order to enter that blessed country of which Beulah Land is but a preview. Yet he who carries us as lambs in his bosom throughout our earthly sojourn will undoubtedly do so in the hour of our departure. (Isaiah 40:11)

In Israel's crossing of the Jordan, we have a beautiful picture of how it will be when the time comes for us to make our passage. Before the people entered the chilly water, priests bearing the Ark of the Covenant went before them. (Joshua 3:3-4) With the waters parted and standing in a heap, the priests stood on dry ground in the midst of the river while all the people crossed over. The Israelites may have been terrified by the sight of a wall of water on either side of them, but every single one of them made the passage safely. (Joshua 3:14-17)

In like manner, our Lord Jesus Christ has divided the waters for us. As our great high priest, he opened the way to the Father through the sacrifice of himself. Thus he provided safe passage through the dreaded river of death for all who trust in him.

Take heart then, fellow pilgrim. When he calls us home, we will not have to cross Jordan alone. The sight of its murky water may well fill us with fear and dread, for it will separate us from all that is familiar to us now. However, what a blessing to know that *Precious in the sight of the LORD is the death of his saints.* (Psalm 116:15)

The Word of God likens the death of the Christian's body to the dissolution of a house in exchange for *a building of God, a house not made with hands, eternal in the heavens.* (2 Corinthians 5:1) In this mysterious exchange, we who *have borne the image of the earthy…shall also bear the image of the heavenly.* (1 Corinthians 15:49) Furthermore, Scripture describes the Christian's body after death as being asleep and awaiting the sure and certain hope of the resurrection. (1 Corinthians 15:51-54; 1Thessalonians 4:13-18) So of all men, Christians alone have a living hope that looks beyond the grave for its full realization. O, for grace to look across that great divide by faith and gaze upon our heavenly possession lying just beyond the river!

Christian's encounter with the dark river and passage through it reminds us one final time that his life story is allegorical. There is no literal river at the end of our earthly journey, but rather that which the river depicts, the death of our mortal bodies. Still it is a crossing of sorts, for it will carry us from the earthly realm into the heavenly. Moreover, this passage from mortality to immortality is a highly significant event in the believer's life for another reason. It is his final testimony to those whom he must leave behind.

Although little mention has been made of Christian's family since the day he left the City of Destruction, his entire pilgrimage took place in their presence and under their close scrutiny. Thus they were witnesses to his everyday life as a believer in Christ. It is unlikely that he shared much of his spiritual struggles with them, such as his battle with doubt and fear, for they would never have understood. Yet they certainly observed his reaction to trials and affliction. Perhaps they chided him for his weakness and occasional inconsistency, but must also have noted the progressive development of his Christ-like character. Admittedly, his example before them was not a perfect one, but he had remained steadfast in the faith and true to his Lord. Moreover, it is certain that he continued to pray for them and tell them of God's saving grace in Christ.

When time came for him to cross the dark river, Christian was undoubtedly lying in his own bed surrounded by his weeping family. Perhaps his pastor and Christian friends had also been called to his side. What were their inmost thoughts as they watched him slip away? What were his final words to his beloved family in that hour? Since he had been unable to convince them to come to Christ, he may have felt like a failure in that respect. Yet he never gave up hope. Therefore, we can safely assume that he expressed his undying love to his family, and his dearest hope that they would yet trust in the Lord Jesus Christ.

Although John Bunyan gives no indication of Christian's socio-economic status, he was probably just an ordinary man. It is highly unlikely that he left his family a legacy of houses, lands, and great wealth. However, he bequeathed to them an inheritance of a far superior kind, the legacy of a life lived to the glory of God. For many years they had observed his life, and now they marked his death. (Psalm 37:37) Who can tell what indelible impression it left upon hearts long hardened toward Christ and his Gospel?

Kim's story

Most of God's people spend a number of years in the land of Beulah. They enter the autumn season of life and continue to be spiritually fruitful even while their health and strength begin to diminish. In the normal scheme of things, their approach to the dark river is gradual and the crossing of it deferred until they have reached an advanced age.

Due to circumstances beyond their control, others are drawn toward the river suddenly and with little advance warning. Such was the case with Kim Sweeney, one of our beloved sisters in Christ at New Hope Baptist Church. When Kim was just in her early forties, she was diagnosed with an aggressive form of ovarian cancer. In spite of surgery to remove the tumor and months of chemotherapy thereafter, the Lord saw fit to take her home when she was only forty-four years old.

"Cut off in the prime of life," most would say. I must admit that we felt pretty much the same. After all, she left behind her loving husband Jim, and her teenage daughter Natalie. It was hard not to question why the Lord allowed it to happen. Why would he take one who was loved and needed so very much? Although it was beyond our capacity to understand the reason why, we were comforted to know that God's will is perfect. He makes no mistakes. He took her to be with him forever, but it was extremely painful to witness her rapid physical decline beforehand.

Humanly speaking, Kim's arrival in Beulah Land was premature and her time there was brief. However, the rapid transformation we witnessed in her during those last weeks as the Lord prepared her to enter his presence was a wondrous thing indeed. Near the end she was ready to depart, even though her heart was broken for those whom she must leave behind. But as she stood on the shore of the great river, it was clear to us that her sights were fixed upon the Celestial City beyond.

In the providence of God, Kim's final struggle with cancer coincided with my initial study of the last portion of *The Pilgrim's Progress*. Lying helpless in her hospital bed, she never knew how much she helped me understand what John Bunyan was trying to convey. Until the time that Christian and Hopeful arrived in Beulah Land, I could relate to every aspect of their journey. After that, they entered territory where I have not yet been. However, Kim had reached the edge of the mysterious dark river, and I was privileged to be a witness. It was not by anything she said, but by her patient faith and submission to the will of God that she demonstrated how it is to be with us in our final hour. At the time, I had no idea that my early study would one day result in this book. But as the manuscript gradually took form, I knew in my heart that it must include Kim's story.

Her courageous battle with cancer lasted for about eighteen months, the last several weeks of which she spent in the hospital. Near the end, she was not always conscious when my husband Ron and I visited her, but an extraordinary thing happened upon one such occasion. Several of our church family, including her husband Jim, had gathered in Kim's room at the same time. On that particular day, she did not appear to be fully conscious. Nevertheless, as we quoted Psalm 23 together, she spoke up clearly and distinctly, saying every word of it with us. How our hearts rejoiced to witness the faith and hope that were sustaining her at such a time!

Another notable thing occurred during my husband's final visit with Kim early one Wednesday evening. Jim was there and so was George Gumbleton, one of our dear brothers from New Hope. At that point, Kim was in a coma. No one knew whether she heard what was said or not. Ron told me later that as they prayed together, something highly unusual happened. As a rule, he gives little credence to mystical experiences; in fact, he is highly skeptical of them. So he admitted that what he sensed in Kim's room that evening could have been due to the emotionally-charged atmosphere. But whether it was my husband's imagination or something much more real, he said it seemed to him that while he prayed, every evil presence was banished and a supernatural peace filled the room.

A few hours later the call came, and our dear sister quietly slipped away. Her soul left her body and was set free. Did an angelic escort stand nearby, silent and unseen, waiting to usher her into the presence of the Lord Jesus Christ? Yes, I think they did.

Kim's funeral service was no ordinary one, for it was a home going celebration. (1 Thessalonians 4:13-18) She was a rather quiet, unassuming lady and never one to draw attention to herself. Yet the large chapel was filled to overflowing that day in tribute to one who was greatly loved by all who knew her.

The text from which my husband spoke was Deuteronomy 33:27: *The eternal God is thy refuge, and underneath are the everlasting arms: and he shall thrust out the enemy from before thee; and shall say, Destroy them.* How fitting it was for our dear sister, with her gentle spirit and childlike faith! In the hour of crisis, she overcame the last enemy (death) with uncommon courage and passed over the dark river with dignity and grace.

Throughout her ordeal, Kim embraced her Lord's promise *I will never leave thee, nor forsake thee* as her very own. (Hebrews 13:5) In our assembly this great and precious promise came to be known as "Kim's Promise." Her picture, along with this verse and what it meant to her, hangs near the entrance to our fellowship hall. Thus our dear sister lives on in the hearts of all who knew and loved her.

Study Questions

1. With the shining city now in full view, Christian and Hopeful hastened toward it until they reached a seemingly hopeless impediment. What was it? What did they realize that they must do? What very different reactions did Christian and Hopeful have to this unexpected barrier? Why?

2. What happened to Christian almost as soon as he and Hopeful stepped into the chilly water? Why did Christian react as he did? What old enemy attacked him here, causing darkness to overtake take him for the last time?

3. In what way did Hopeful help Christian as the poor man struggled to keep from drowning? How did Christian respond to Hopeful's words of comfort and exhortation? By what means was his darkness finally lifted, bringing renewed assurance of salvation to Christian's heart and mind?

4. What does the dark river represent? What precious assurance does the Christian have when his time comes to cross it?

CHAPTER 54

Jerusalem the Golden!

DEAR READER, OUR CONTEMPLATION OF JOHN BUNYAN'S TALE OF TWO spiritual cities is just about over, and what an incredible journey it has been! Through his brilliant use of word pictures, we have followed Christian from the time that he fled from the City of Destruction and been eye witnesses to all that happened to him thereafter. We have watched him press onward in spite of all that came against him, and now we are about to experience, by proxy, his royal welcome into the Celestial City.

Since the Word of God does not reveal exactly what will take place when our souls leave our mortal bodies, John Bunyan takes us to realms he had not seen. Yet in so doing, he draws from sound scriptural truth concerning the eternal estate of God's people, even though he expresses it in figurative terms. For instance, when he places an interval of time between Christian's death and his entrance into the Celestial gate, he in no way contradicts the apostle Paul's clear teaching that to be absent from the body is to be present with the Lord. (2 Corinthians 5:8) Seeing that John Bunyan has spoken in metaphors throughout his great allegory, we freely acknowledge his right to continue in the same vein as he concludes it. So come with me and let us explore his final thoughts together, and seek the precious gems of truth that are contained therein.

When Christian and Hopeful reached the Celestial shore, the two Shining Ones that accompanied them to the river's edge were waiting for them. Looking upward they could see the city gate high upon a hill. John Bunyan describes their ascent toward it as rising through the air quickly and easily. The physical limitations that bound them to earth, that is, their mortal bodies, had been left behind in the dark waters. Thus like ships loosed from their mooring, they left the realm of the earthly and rose toward the heavenly region, in company with their angelic escort.

As they ascended toward the towering city, they talked with the Shining Ones of things revealed in Scripture. Concerning beautiful Zion and the glory that awaited them there, Christian and Hopeful had already enjoyed a preview, first in the Palace Beautiful, and later from the heights of the Delectable Mountains. In God's wise design, our gathering together in his name here below is a token of the fellowship and communion we will enjoy forever in heaven.

Moreover, through our oneness in Christ we have communion with our brethren who are already there, those whose race is already won. The writer of Hebrews spoke in the present tense when he wrote: *But ye are come unto mount Zion, and unto the city of the living God, the heavenly Jerusalem, and to an innumerable company of angels, to the general assembly and church of the firstborn, which are written in heaven, and to God the Judge of all, and to the spirits of just men made perfect.* (Hebrews 12:22-24)

This is our standing in Christ and we may experience a measure of it even now. However, even in the best of churches where Christ is supreme and the people truly love him and one another, issues and conflicts can arise and disturb the peace. Strong wills clash, pride rears its ugly head, and the fight is on! Therefore, we must continually strive to keep the unity among those with whom we are in union. It is a difficult task requiring us to deal with one another *with all lowliness and meekness, with long-suffering, forbearing one another in love; endeavoring to keep the unity of the Spirit in the bond of peace.* (Ephesians 4:2-3)

It is hard to imagine a time when these things will vex us no more because every point of strife and division has been removed. In that day, every selfish thought, misunderstanding, ungracious feeling and prideful reaction will have been banished. For now, we still struggle with all of these sinful tendencies, but what will it be when every stain of sin and human weakness has been purged away? All will be perfect harmony and unbroken fellowship, for in that day, our focus will no longer center upon self or even one another. Our full attention will be fixed upon the Lamb who sits upon his throne.

In her great hymn, "The Sands of Time Are Sinking," Anne R. Cousin wrote: "The bride eyes not her garment, but her dear bridegroom's face; I will not gaze at glory, but on my King of grace; not at the crown he gifteth, but on his pierced hand: the Lamb is all the glory of Emmanuel's land." [1] How perfectly she expressed the heart of God's children when at last we see the Lord Jesus Christ face to face. Christian and Hopeful are just about to discover the joy of dwelling in his presence and partaking of the fruit of the *tree of life which is in the midst of the paradise of God*. (Revelation 2:7)

Their long night of exile is finally over and eternal day has dawned in their souls. In beautiful Zion, city of the great King, the former things of earth are known no more at all. There will be no more tears or sorrow and no more pain or suffering, for death, the last enemy, is vanquished forever. (Revelation 21:4) The two happy pilgrims are just about to join the great congregation of all the saved who have gone before. Shortly now, they will meet those brethren of whom they have heard but never seen, including the champions of Jesus Christ, the great heroes of the faith. What's more, they will soon be reunited with friends and loved ones who died in the Lord.

John Bunyan speaks of a heavenly host that came to meet Christian and Hopeful with trumpet fanfares and shouts of joy. Although we can only imagine how it will be, we may be certain that a royal welcome awaits us. As children of the King, and part of his beloved bride, we will need no introduction, for he knows each of us by name. Those who are called unto the marriage supper of the Lamb need never fear that they will not be recognized and received. (Revelation 19:9)

What a day it will be when we join the vast multitude of spirits of just men made perfect, and the church of the firstborn receives one of her own! Moreover, one glorious day the entire family of God will be gathered together before his throne. While the Word of God does speak of crowns to be given and received, they will not be such as adorn the heads of earthly monarchs. Whatever their exact nature, we will cast our crowns at the feet of our Savior and King in grateful tribute crying, *Thou are worthy, O Lord*. (Revelation 4:10-11). He alone is worthy of our highest worship and praise. All glory, honor, and blessing belong to him alone. When we see the King in his beauty, we will worship and serve him as we long to do now, perfectly and without restraint.

When Christian and Hopeful arrived at the city gate, they read the golden inscription written upon it: *Blessed are they that do his commandments, that they may have right to the tree of life, and may enter in through the gates into the city*. (Revelation 22:14) At the bidding of the angels, they called at the gate and Enoch, Moses, and Elijah looked over. Christian and Hopeful were identified as pilgrims who had fled from the City of Destruction out of love for the Lord Jesus Christ. After this they turned in their certificates, which were carried to the King. Upon hearing that two of his children were outside the gate, he commanded that it be opened and the men admitted.

John Bunyan's description of the scene at the gate of the city begs a couple of questions. Do the saints who have gone before know us and observe our earthly pilgrimage? Are they even now cheering us on as we struggle to run the race here below? Are they part of the great cloud of witnesses spoken of in Hebrews 12:1? Although we cannot say for sure, perhaps they are.

Then there is the matter of the certificates that were turned in and taken to the King before Christian and Hopeful could enter the gate. We must remember that these certificates were not actual paper documents that were passports to the city. They represented heaven-born faith in Christ, which is itself the gift of God. They received it when they were born again; it had sustained them throughout their journey, and they still had it in their possession.

Once again, John Bunyan uses poetic liberty in order to convey revealed truth. There was no question about whether Christian and Hopeful would be admitted to the city or not, for they bore the marks of Zion's true children. They were sincere followers of the Lamb of God, whose names were written in his Book of Life. (Revelation 20:12, 15) Without hesitation, the King acknowledged them as his very own, and gave the royal command to open the gates so that they could enter in.

After the two happy brethren entered the city, they were given spotless garments of glistening white. At last, every travel stain accumulated during their long journey was gone and their glorious transformation was complete. It is little wonder that Christian and Hopeful joined their voices with the vast multitude of the redeemed crying: *Blessing, and honor, and glory, and power, be unto him that sitteth upon the throne, and unto the Lamb forever and ever.* (Revelation 5:13b) Immediately afterward, the gate of the city was closed once more.

* * * *

Dear brother or sister in Christ, although we still dwell on this side of the dark river, we may catch a glimpse of Jerusalem the Golden even now. Through the mirror of God's Word we may look within its gate and see a measure of the glory that awaits us there, all of which will center upon the Lamb of God on his eternal throne.

As to the glory that dwells in Emmanuel's Land, nothing of man's devising will have a part in it, not even the best works of the godliest men and women. All such things must be left behind in the cold waters of the dark river. Nothing will be found in the eternal City of God except those things that he has wrought. The redeemed who walk the golden streets are dressed in royal apparel of spotless white, which the King himself has provided. No other covering will do, only the fine linen of Christ's perfect righteousness. Moreover, no one will wear this royal wedding apparel in the New Jerusalem except those who are clothed with the garments of salvation and covered with the robe of righteousness while still on earth.

On this same note, do you think it strange that there is a nightmarish ending to the dream that inspired *The Pilgrim's Progress*? At first, some such thought occurred to me. However, what could be a more fitting conclusion to John Bunyan's soul-searching work? Surely it was a stroke of genius to leave his readers with the final impression that the path of life is never far away from the path that leads to destruction.

A great many people leave the City of Destruction but never make it to the City of God. We met quite a few of them in the course of Christian's journey. When they started out for the Celestial City, they did so via the broad way of humanistic religion and self-righteousness rather than the Wicket Gate. Yet little did they suspect that in having done so, they also missed the only path that leads to the golden city.

How long can a deluded soul maintain a false profession of faith in Christ? How far can he seemingly follow the path of life? Tragically, a great many make it to the end, clinging to their false hope until it is forever too late. Such was the case with the young man named Ignorance.

As you remember, he had followed close behind Christian and Hopeful on the King's Highway for much of the latter part of their journey. On at least two occasions, they confronted him and tried to convince him of the error of his ways, but all to no avail. When he reached the edge of the dark river, he was of the same mind still.

Unlike Christian and Hopeful, Ignorance was not at all alarmed by the sight of the deep, dark river because he found a ferryman who was willing to take him across. Once he reached the opposite shore, he began to ascend the hill of Zion. Even though he had no angelic escort, he approached the gate with confidence and knocked boldly, fully expecting to be welcomed.

However, Vain-Hope was the boatman who took him across the river, and as Christian and Hopeful feared, Ignorance was unknown in the city. (Matthew 7:21-23) He lacked the royal wedding garment worn by all the inhabitants of the land. (Matthew 22:11-13) Those who looked over the gate did not recognize him because his name was not inscribed in the family register. It was still recorded in the archives of the City of Destruction.

Accordingly, he was unable to give an acceptable account of himself. Ignorance had many good works of which he boasted but no certificate, no spiritual birthright to show. Thus he who had never been at a loss for words was struck speechless. Vain-Hope had carried him this far but could take him no further, and now that it was too late, it abandoned him altogether.

The King's verdict was not long in coming. He commanded the imposter to be bound hand and foot and cast through the "door" in the "side of the hill," which Christian and Hopeful had seen from the Delectable Mountains. Therefore, the young man named Ignorance suffered the same fate as the religious hypocrite and apostate. So just before the dreamer awoke, he made this chilling observation: "Then

I saw that there was a way to hell, even from the gates of heaven, as well as from the City of Destruction."

Hopefully, the awful fate of Ignorance will awaken some other deceived soul before it is too late. Yet it contains a needful warning to those of us who are true believers as well. If we are to avoid spiritual complacence and its inherent dangers, we must give diligence to make our calling and election sure. (2 Peter 1:10) Only then will our faith be shown to be of that enduring sort, which is the living faith of God's elect. (Titus 1:1)

Like Christian and Hopeful, one day we will leave all of our earthly attainments behind us and cross the dark river. When we enter the City of God we will take only three things with us: faith, hope, and love, all of which were wrought in us by the Spirit of God. Saving faith, the heart companion of every heaven-born soul, will sustain and keep us until it becomes sight in the presence of the Lord. Hope, signified by Christian's inseparable friend, will uphold us with confident expectation through good times and bad until it becomes a living reality. Love for our Lord, and the knowledge of his great love for us, will attain its highest perfection when we see him face to face.

Jerusalem the Golden! How we long for the eternal joys that await us there! Shame on us if we seek happiness and contentment in the things of earth! Dear friend in Christ, may we never forget that our birthright, our citizenship, is in heaven. May we never lose sight of the fact that we are pilgrims and exiles from our true fatherland, passing through this world but not belonging to it.

As we march along the royal road to Zion, may our constant watchword be "Excelsior!" With our eternal goal always in view, may each step we take lead us ever onward and always upward until we reach the land of perfect day.

> Jerusalem the golden, with milk and honey blest,
> Beneath thy contemplation sink heart and voice oppressed.
> I know not, O I know not, what joys await us there;
> What radiancy of glory, what bliss beyond compare.

> They stand, those halls of Zion, all jubilant with song,
> And bright with many an angel, and all the martyr throng.

The Prince is ever in them, the daylight is serene;
The pastures of the blessed are decked in glorious sheen.

There is the throne of David; and there, from care released,
The song of them that triumph, the shout of them that feast;
And they who with their Leader have conquered in the fight,
Forever and forever are clad in robes of white.

O sweet and blessed country, the home of God's elect!
O sweet and blessed country that eager hearts expect!
Jesus, in mercy bring us to that dear land of rest;
Who art, with God the Father and Spirit, ever blest. [2]

Study Questions

1. John Bunyan uses figurative language in describing Christian and Hopeful's ascent to the city. What is implied by their free and rapid rise upward? What had they left behind in the dark river?

2. When Christian and Hopeful reached the Celestial gate, they turned in their certificates. These were then taken to the King before the two men were admitted to the city. What did their certificates represent? Was there a question about whether they would be received or not? What truth was John Bunyan conveying here, using poetic language?

3. As Christians, how can we catch a glimpse of Jerusalem the Golden even now? What is the glory of Emmanuel's Land?

4. How did Ignorance react when he reached the dark river? Who was the ferryman who took him across, and what did he represent? What happened to Ignorance when he boldly knocked at the Celestial gate? What was the verdict that the King issued against him?

5. Why do you think John Bunyan concluded *The Pilgrim's Progress* with a nightmarish ending?

EPILOGUE

High atop the hill overlooking the field where their historic flight took place, there stands a large stone monument honoring Orville and Wilbur Wright. The inscription upon this memorial to their vision and perseverance concludes with the words: "Achieved by Dauntless Resolution and Unconquerable Faith." It is a most fitting tribute to two remarkable men for their momentous contribution to modern aviation.

During a recent trip to the Outer Banks of North Carolina, my husband and I visited the Wright Brothers' Memorial again. As I stood at its base and pondered the inscription, the thought occurred to me that the very same thing is true of the Christian life. How do we run the race that is set before us and finish it in spite of all the obstacles and difficulties that lie in our path? Must it not be through dauntless resolution and unconquerable faith? Yes, O yes it must!

Here is the key to the successful completion of our race to eternal glory, but it will require more of us than is within our human ability to do. In order to go the distance and finish the course, we must do so through the power of our Lord Jesus Christ. He is the source of our dauntless resolution and unconquerable faith. He alone is able to keep us from falling, and to present us faultless before the presence of his glory with exceeding joy. (Jude 24)

For now, as we walk the path of the just, it often seems that our pilgrim songs are songs in the night. Yet one day the darkness that so often plagues us now will be banished forever. The Lamb of God, who is our light throughout our earthly journey, will be our everlasting light in the New Jerusalem. (Revelation 21:23) In that day we will lift our voices in praise to his glorious grace saying: *Blessing, and honor, and glory, and power, be unto him that sitteth upon the throne, and unto the Lamb forever and ever.* (Revelation 5:13b)

Therefore take heart, dear brother or sister in Christ, as you ponder the path before you. Each day we live is bringing us a day's march nearer home. One glorious day we will enter the regal halls of Zion where we will join the company of the redeemed with everlasting joy and gladness.

> For ever with the Lord!
> Amen, so let it be:
> Life from the dead is in that word,
> 'Tis immortality.
> Here in the body pent,
> Absent from Him I roam,
> Yet nightly pitch my moving tent
> A day's march nearer home. [1]

Ω
By God's Grace and for His Glory

Carolyn Staley

INDEX OF NOTES

Chapter 1. The City of Destruction: Its Description, Nature and Citizens
1. William Ernest Henley, "Invictus."
2. Henry David Thoreau, *Walden.*

Chapter 2. Escape from the City!
1. Jehoida Brewer, "Hail Sovereign Love," verses 1 and 2.

Chapter 3. Trouble at the Outset
1. William Shakespeare, *The Complete Works of William Shakespeare,* "Romeo and Juliet," Act II, Scene II (New York: Crown Publishers, Inc. 1975)

Chapter 7. The Secret Place of Thunder
1. Katharina von Schlegel, "Be Still My Soul."
2. Charles H. Spurgeon, *Morning by Morning,* "July 14" (Pennsylvania: Whitaker House, 1984)
3. Jehoida Brewer, "Hail Sovereign Love," verse 3.

Chapter 9. Beatitude of Sovereign Grace
1. Joseph Hart, "Come Ye Sinners, Poor and Needy."
2. Ibid.
3. Charles H. Spurgeon, *Faith's Check Book,* "Perfect Willingness" (Pennsylvania: Whitaker House, 1992)

Chapter 11. Our Race to Eternal Glory
1. Isaac Watts, "Am I a Soldier of the Cross?"
2. John S. B. Monsell, "Fight the Good Fight."

Chapter 12.   Onward to Zion by the Road Less Traveled
1. Robert Frost, "The Road Not Taken."
2. Isaac Watts, "Am I a Soldier of the Cross?"

Chapter 14.   Invaluable Instruction by the Master Teacher
1. Dante Alighieri, *The Inferno.*
2. John Newton, "Amazing Grace."

Chapter 15.   Gateway to the City
1. Isaac Watts, "When I Survey the Wondrous Cross."
2. Horatius Bonar, "By the Cross of Jesus Standing."

Chapter 16.   A Troubling Question
1. Charles Wesley, "Arise, My Soul, Arise."

Chapter 19.   An Unexpected Impediment!
1. Fanny Crosby, "All the Way My Savior Leads Me."

Chapter 21.   Alone in the Dark!
1. Johann B. Freystein, "Rise My Soul, to Watch and Pray."

Chapter 22.   Haven by the Wayside
1. Charles H. Spurgeon, *Pictures from Pilgrim's Progress* (Texas: Pilgrim Publications, 1992)

Chapter 23.   Family Life in the Palace Beautiful
1. William Jay, *The Christian Contemplated* (Virginia: Sprinkle Publications, 2003)
2. Isaac Watts, "How Sweet and Awful is the Place."
3. Ibid.

Chapter 24.   The Palace Framework and Remarkable History
1. Charles Wesley, "Soldiers of Christ, Arise."

Chapter 25.   Descent into the Valley of Humiliation
1. Thomas Boston, *The Crook in the Lot* (London: Silver Trumpet Publications Limited, 1989)

Chapter 26. The Valley of Humiliation Contemplated

1. John Milton, *Paradise Lost*, Book I, lines 251-263 (New York: The Ronald Press Company, 1953)
2. Martin Luther, "A Mighty Fortress."
3. Charles H. Spurgeon, *Faith's Check Book*, "The Magnitude of Grace" (Pennsylvania: Whitaker House, 1992)
4. Oswald Chambers, *My Utmost for His Highest* (Ohio: Barbour Publishing, Inc.)
5. Thomas Boston, *The Crook in the Lot* (London: Silver Trumpet Publications Limited, 1989)

Chapter 28. Journey out of Darkness

1. William Jay, *The Christian Contemplated* (Virginia: Sprinkle Publications, 2003)
2. Oswald Chambers, *My Utmost for His Highest* (Ohio: Barbour Publishing, Inc.)
3. John Bunyan, *Complete Works of John Bunyan*.
4. Ray Palmer, "Lord, My Weak Thought."

Chapter 29. The Cave of the Giants

1. William Jay, *The Christian Contemplated* (Virginia: Sprinkle Publications, 2003)

Chapter 30. One Brother Meets Another

1. George Whitefield, "The Lord Our Righteousness."
2. John Flavel, "Free Grace Broadcaster," Issue 193, p. 13.
3. William Jay, *Morning Exercises* (Virginia: Sprinkle Publications, 1998)

Chapter 31. Anatomy of a Hypocrite

1. Thomas Adams, "Puritan Nuggets of Gold" # 45, Wednesday, March 4, 2015
2. Ibid.

Chapter 33. Incident in the Town of Vanity

1. Charles Spurgeon, *Flowers from a Puritan's Garden* (Virginia: Sprinkle Publications, 1997)

Chapter 34. Tried in the Court of Vanity Fair!
1. Webster's New Collegiate Dictionary (Massachusetts: G. & C. Merriam Co., 1959)

Chapter 35. Beauty for Ashes
1. Hugh Latimer, spoken to Nicolas Ridley
2. John Donne, "Meditation XVII"

Chapter 36. The Subtle Snare of Covetousness: By-ends of Fair Speech
1. Charles H. Spurgeon, *Flowers from a Puritan's Garden* (Virginia: Sprinkle Publications, 1997)
2. Ibid.

Chapter 38. A Season of Refreshing
1. John Newton, "Glorious Things of Thee Are Spoken."

Chapter 41. Prisoners in Doubting Castle!
1. Richard Lovelace, "To Althea, from Prison."
2. John Newton, "Amazing Grace."

Chapter 42. Warning to Future Travelers
1. Edward Mote, "The Solid Rock"

Chapter 47. The Assault and Robbery of Little-Faith
1. Mrs. Charles E. Cowman, *Streams in the Desert*, Vol. 1 (Michigan: Zondervan Publishing House)

Chapter 48. Beware of the Flatterer!
1. William Shakespeare, *The Complete Works of William Shakespeare*, "Hamlet, Prince of Denmark," Act I, Scene III (New York: Crown Publishers, Inc., 1975)

Chapter 49. Dangerous Trek across the Enchanted Ground
1. Oswald Chambers
2. Jehoida Brewer, "Hail Sovereign Love," verse 4.

Chapter 51.   The Never-Ending Battle for the Christian's Mind
1. John Newton, "Amazing Grace."
2. William Jay, *Morning Exercises* (Virginia: Sprinkle Publications, 1998)

Chapter 52.   Almost Home! The Delights of Beulah Land
1. Walter Chalmers Smith, "Immortal, Invisible."
2. Isaac Watts, "Come, We That Love the Lord."
3. *The Valley of Vision*, "God Honoured" (Edinburgh: The Banner of Truth Trust)

Chapter 53.   Nearing the Shore! The Passing of a Pilgrim
1. John Bunyan, *The Pilgrim's Progress: the Second Part.*
2. Ibid.
3. Ibid.
4. Charles H. Spurgeon, *Flowers from a Puritan's Garden* (Virginia: Sprinkle Publications, 1997)

Chapter 54.   Jerusalem the Golden!
1. Anne R. Cousin, "The Sands of Time Are Sinking."
2. Bernard of Cluny, "Jerusalem the Golden."

Epilogue
1. James Montgomery, "Forever with the Lord."

CPSIA information can be obtained
at www.ICGtesting.com
Printed in the USA
FFHW020647250419
51993482-57405FF

9 781599 253992